Winter Blockbuster 2022

Michelle Smart · Cat Schield
Amy Ruttan · Cassie Miles

MILLS & BOON

CONTENTS

Buying His Bride
Of Convenience

Michelle Smart

MODERN

Power and passion

Michelle Smart's love affair with books started when she was a baby, when she would cuddle them in her cot. A voracious reader of all genres, she found her love of romance established when she stumbled across her first Harlequin book at the age of twelve. She's been reading—and writing—them ever since. Michelle lives in Northamptonshire, England, with her husband and two young Smarties.

To the always amazing Nic Caws, thanks for everything you do—your encouragement and enthusiasm never fail to lift my spirits xxx

CHAPTER ONE

'WILL YOU KEEP STILL?' Eva Bergen told the man sitting on the stool before her. She'd staunched the bleeding from the wound on the bridge of his nose and had the tiny sterilised strips ready to close it up. What should be a relatively simple procedure was being hampered by his right foot tapping away and jerking the rest of his body.

He glared at her through narrowed eyes, the right one of which was swollen and turning purple. 'Just get it done.'

'Do you want me to close this up or not? I'm not a nurse and I need to concentrate, so keep still.'

He took a long breath, clenched his jaw together and fixed his gaze at the distance over her shoulder. She guessed he must have clenched all the muscles in his legs too as his foot finally stopped tapping.

Taking her own deep breath, Eva leaned forward on her stool, which she'd had to raise so she could match his height, then hesitated. 'Are you sure you don't want one of the medics to look at it? I'm sure it's broken.'

'Just get it done,' he repeated tersely.

Breathing through her mouth so she didn't inhale his scent and taking great care not to touch him anywhere apart from his nose, she put the first strip on the wound.

It was amazing that even with a busted nose Daniele Pellegrini still managed to look impeccably suave. The quiff of his thick, dark brown hair was still perfectly placed, his hand-tailored suit perfectly pressed. He could still look in a mirror and wink at his reflection.

He was a handsome man. She didn't think there was a female aid worker at the refugee camp who hadn't done a double-take when he'd made his first appearance there a month ago. This was only his second visit. He'd called her thirty minutes ago asking, without a word of greeting, if she was still at the camp. If he'd bothered to know anything about her he would've known she, like all the other staff based there, had their own quarters at the camp. He'd then said he was on his way and to meet him in the medical tent. He'd disconnected the call before she could ask what he wanted. She'd learned the answer to that herself when she'd made the short walk from the ramshackle administrative building she worked from to the main medical facility.

When Hurricane Ivor had first hit the Caribbean island of Caballeros, the Blue Train Aid Agency, which already had a large presence in the crime-ridden country, had been the first aid charity to set up a proper camp there. Now, two months after the biggest natural disaster the country had ever known and the loss of twenty thousand of its people, the camp had become home to an estimated thirty thousand people, with canvas tents, modular plastic shelters and makeshift shacks all tightly knit together. Other aid agencies had since set up at different sites and had similar numbers of displaced people living in their camps. It was a disaster on every level imaginable.

Daniele was the brother of the great philanthropist and humanitarian, Pieta Pellegrini. Pieta had seen the news about the hurricane and how the devastation had been amplified by the destruction of a large number of the island's hospitals. He'd immediately decided that his foundation would build a new, disaster-proof, multi-functional hospital in the island's capital, San Pedro. A week later he'd been killed in a helicopter crash.

Eva had been saddened by this loss. She'd only met Pieta a few times but he'd been greatly respected by everyone in the aid community.

She and the other staff at the Blue Train Aid Agency had been overjoyed to learn his family wished to proceed with the hospital. The people of the island badly needed more medical facilities. They and the other charities and agencies did the best they could but it wasn't enough. It could never be enough.

Pieta's sister, Francesca, had become the new driving force for the project. Eva had liked her very much and admired the younger woman's determination and focus. She'd expected to like and admire his brother too. Like Pieta, Daniele was a world-famous name, but his reputation had been built through his architecture and construction company, which had won more design awards than any other in the past five years.

She'd found nothing to like or admire about him. Although famed for his good humour and searing intellect, she'd found him arrogant and entitled. She'd seen the wrinkle of distaste on his strong—now busted—nose when he'd come to the camp to collect her for their one evening out together, a date she'd only agreed to because he'd assured her it *wasn't* a date and that he'd just wanted to get her input on the kind of hospital he should be building as she was something of an expert on the country and its people. He'd flown her to his exclusive seven-star hotel on the neighbouring paradise island of Aguadilla, spent five minutes asking her pertinent questions, then the rest of the evening drinking heavily, asking impertinent questions and shamelessly flirting with her.

She would go as far as to say his only redeeming features were his looks and physique and the size of his bank account. Seeing as she was immune to men and cared nothing for money, those redeeming features were wasted on her.

The look on his face when she'd coldly turned down his offer of a trip to his suite for a 'nightcap' had been priceless. She had a feeling Daniele Pellegrini was not used to the word 'no' being uttered to him by members of the opposite sex.

He'd had his driver take her back to the airfield without a word of goodbye. That was the last she'd seen of him until she'd walked into the medical tent ten minutes ago and found him already there, waiting for her. It was immediately obvious that someone had punched him in the face. She wondered who it was and if it was possible to track them down and buy them a drink.

'I'm not a nurse,' she'd said when he'd told her he needed her to fix it.

He'd shrugged his broad shoulders but without the ready smile she remembered from their 'date'. 'I only need you to stop the bleeding. I'm sure you've seen it done enough times that you have a basic idea of what needs to be done.'

She had more than a basic idea. Principally employed as a co-ordinator and translator, she, like most of the other non-medical staff, had often stepped in to help the medical team when needed. That didn't mean she felt confident in patching up a broken nose, especially when the nose belonged to an arrogant billionaire whose suit likely cost more than the average annual salary of the Caballerons lucky enough to have a job.

'I'll get one of the nurses or—'

'No, they're busy,' he'd cut in. 'Stem the bleeding and I'll be out of here.'

She'd been about to argue that she was busy too but there had been something in his demeanour that had made her pause. Now, as she gently placed the second strip on his nose, she thought him like a tightly coiled spring. She pitied whoever would be on the receiving end of the explosion that was sure to come when the coil sprang free.

Taking the third and last strip, she couldn't help but notice how glossy his dark hair was. If she didn't know it was a genetic blessing, having the same shine as the rest of the family members she'd met, she'd think he took a personal hairdresser with him everywhere he travelled. And a personal dresser.

If she was feeling charitable she could understand his distaste for the camp. Daniele lived in luxury. Here there was only dirt and squalor that everyone's best efforts at cleaning barely made a dent in. Being in front of him like this made her acutely aware of the grubbiness of her jeans and T-shirt and the messy ponytail she'd thrown her hair back into.

Who cared about her appearance? she asked herself grimly. This was a refugee camp. All the staff were prepared to turn their hand to anything that needed doing. Dressing for a fashion shoot was not only wholly inappropriate but wholly impractical.

It was only this hateful man who made her feel grubby and inferior.

'Keep still,' she reminded him when his foot started its agitated tapping again. 'Almost done. I'm just going to clean you up and you can go. You'll need to keep the strips on for around a week and remember to keep them dry.'

Reaching for the antiseptic wipes, she gently dabbed at the tiny drops of blood that had leaked out since she'd first cleaned his nose and cheeks.

Suddenly a wave of his scent enveloped her. She'd forgotten to hold her breath.

It was perhaps the most mouthwatering scent she'd ever known, making her think of thick forests and hanging fruit, a reaction and thoughts she would have laughed at if anyone had suggested such romantic notions to her.

How could such a hateful, arrogant man be so blessed? He had more talent in his little finger than she could spend a lifetime hoping for.

And he had the most beautiful eyes, an indecipherable browny-green, his surroundings dominating the colour of them at any particular moment. Eyes that were suddenly focussed on her. Staring intently into hers.

She stared back, trapped in his stare before she forced herself to blink, push her stool back and jump down.

'I'll get an ice pack for your eye,' she murmured, flustered but determined not to show it.

'No need,' he dismissed. 'Don't waste your resources on me.' He dug into his inside suit jacket pocket and pulled out his wallet. From it he took some notes and thrust them into her hand. 'That's to replace the medical supplies you used.'

Then he strolled out of the medical tent without a word of thanks or goodbye.

Only when Eva opened the hand that tingled where his skin had brushed it did she see he'd given her ten one-hundred-dollar bills.

'There has got to be an alternative,' Daniele said firmly, pouring himself another glass of red wine, his grip on the bottle tight enough to whiten his knuckles. '*You* can have the estate.'

His sister Francesca, who he'd directed this at, shook her head. 'I can't. You know that. I'm the wrong gender.'

'And I can't marry.' Marriage was anathema to him. He didn't want it. He didn't need it. He'd spent his adult life avoiding it, avoiding any form of commitment.

'Either you marry and take control of the estate or Matteo gets it.'

At the mention of his traitorous cousin's name, the last of his control deserted him and he flung his glass at the wall.

Francesca held out a hand to stop Felipe, her fiancé, an ex-Special Forces hard man, who'd braced himself to step in. Her voice remained steady as she said to Daniele, 'He's the next male heir after you. You know that's a fact. If you don't marry and accept the inheritance, then Matteo gets it.'

He breathed deeply, trying to regain control of his temper. The red liquid trickled down the white wall. Looking at it from the right angle, it was as dark as the blood that had poured from his nose when anger had taken possession of him and he'd flown at Matteo, the pair exchanging blows that would have been a lot worse if Felipe hadn't stepped in and put a halt to it. Since that exchange he'd felt the anger inside him like a living being, a snake coiled in his guts ready to spring at the slightest provocation.

Matteo had betrayed them all.

'There has got to be a legal avenue we can take to override the trust,' he said as the wine, splattered over the wall, obeyed the laws of gravity and trickled to the floor. He'd have to get it repainted before he got new tenants in, he thought absently. He owned the apartment in Pisa but his sister had lived in it for six years. Now she was marrying Felipe and moving to Rome, and unless he thought of an alternative he would be forced to marry too. 'It's archaic.'

'Yes,' she agreed. 'We all know that. Pieta was working with the trustees to get it overturned but it isn't as easy as we hoped it would be. The trust is cast-iron. It'll take months, maybe years, to get that clause overturned and while we're waiting, Matteo can marry Natasha and take the inheritance.'

The bloody inheritance. The family estate, which included a six-hundred-year-old *castello* and thousands of acres of vineyards, had belonged to the Pellegrini family and its descendants since the first stone had been laid by Principe Charles Philibert I, the original bad-boy Prince of the family. The family had renounced their titles decades ago but the *castello* remained their shining jewel. To keep the estate intact, primogeniture ruled and thus the eldest male descendant always inherited. This ruling hadn't been enough to satisfy Principe Emmanuel II, a particularly cruel and mad prince from the nineteenth century, who had suspected his eldest son of being a homosexual and so had drawn up a ruling, still enforced to this day, that the eldest male descendant could only inherit if he was married. Principe Emmanuel must have had some insight to how social mores would evolve in the future because the marriage clause had specifically stated the spouse had to be female.

This archaic marriage clause had never been an issue. After all, *everyone* married eventually. It was what people did, especially those of the aristocracy. But times, along with social mores, changed.

Daniele had been a toddler when his grandfather had died and his own father had inherited the estate. Being the second son, Daniele had always known Pieta would inherit when their father died. He was comfortable with that. He didn't want it. He hated the draughty old *castello* that leaked money as quickly as it leaked water, and he especially hated the idea of marriage. It had given him perverse satisfaction throughout his adult life to remain single, to be the antithesis of the dutiful, serious Pieta.

But now Pieta was dead.

For two months Daniele had clung to the hope that Pieta's wife Natasha might be pregnant—if she was and the child was a boy, the child would inherit the estate and Daniele would be free to continue living his life as he'd always enjoyed.

It transpired that Natasha was indeed pregnant. Unfortunately, Pieta wasn't the father. Before her husband was even cold in the ground, she had embarked on an affair with their cousin Matteo, the cousin who had lived with them as a sibling from the age of thirteen. The disloyal bastard himself had told Daniele that she was pregnant with his child.

Now there were two routes that could be taken. Daniele either found himself a wife and gave up all his cherished freedoms to inherit an estate he didn't want, or their disloyal cousin inherited everything his father and brother had held dear.

He clenched his jaw and rolled his neck, thinking of his mother and her own love and pride in the family and the estate she had married into as a nineteen-year-old girl.

When it came down to it, there was only one route.

'I have to marry.'

'Yes.'

'And soon.'

'Yes. Do you have anyone in mind?' Francesca asked quietly. She knew how much he loathed the idea of marriage. She had an even sharper legal mind than Pieta had done. If she couldn't think of a way to overturn the clause without Matteo taking everything, then it couldn't be done.

One day it would, he vowed. The next generation of Pellegrinis would never be forced into a deed they didn't want, a deed that came with such a heavy price.

Daniele's mind flickered through all the women he'd dated throughout the years. He estimated that of those who were still unmarried, approximately one hundred per cent of them would high-tail it to a wedding dress shop before he'd even finished proposing.

And then he thought of his last date. The only date he'd been on that hadn't ended in the bedroom.

Unthinkingly, he touched his bruised nose. The steri-strips Eva had so carefully put on him were still there, the wound healing nicely. He remembered the distaste that flashed in her crystal-clear blue eyes whenever she looked at him.

She'd acted as a translator for him on his first trip to Caballeros a month ago. On an island surrounded by so much destruction, the prevalent colour brown with all the churned-up mud, she'd shone like a beacon in the gloom. Or her scarlet hair had, which she wore in a girlish ponytail. It was a shade of red that could only have come from a bottle and contrasted with her alabaster skin—she must lather herself in factor fifty sun cream on an hourly basis to keep it so colour free—so beautifully he couldn't see how any other colour, not even that which nature had given her, could suit her so well.

Despite dressing only in scruffy jeans and an official Blue Train Aid Agency T-shirt, Eva Bergen was possibly the most beautiful and definitely the sexiest woman he'd met in his entire thirty-three years. And she hated his guts.

Daniele looked at his sister's worried face and gave a half-smile. 'Yes,' he said with a nod. 'I know the perfect woman to marry.'

When he left the apartment an hour later, he reflected that

whatever else happened, at least his mother would finally be happy with a choice he'd made.

Eva queued patiently at the staff shower block, playing a game on her phone to pass the time. There was limited fresh water at the camp and the staff rationed their own use zealously. She'd become an expert at showering in sixty seconds of tepid water every three days. Like the rest of the staff, she experienced both guilt and relief when she took her leave, which was every third weekend, and she had the luxury of flying over to Aguadilla and checking into a basic hotel. There, at her own expense, she would laze for hours in sweet-smelling, bubbly, limitless water, dye her hair, do her nails and cleanse her skin, all the while trying to smother the guilt at all the displaced people at the camp who couldn't take a few days off to pamper themselves.

One thing that wasn't in short supply at the camp was mobile phones. It seemed that everyone had one, even the tiny kids who barely had a change of clothes to their name. The current craze was for a free game that involved blasting multiplying colourful balls. A technology whizz had linked all the camp players together, refugees and staff alike, to compete against each other directly. Eva had become as addicted to it as everyone else and right then was on track to beat her high score and crack the top one hundred players. At that moment, playing as she waited for her turn in the skinny showers, she had three teenagers at her side, pretending to be cool while they watched her avidly.

When her phone vibrated in her hand she ignored it.

'You should answer that,' Odney, the oldest of the teenagers, said with a wicked grin. Odney was currently ranked ninety-ninth in the camp league for the game.

'They'll call back,' Eva dismissed, mock-scowling at him.

With an even wickeder grin, Odney snatched the phone from her hand, pressed the answer button and put it to his ear. 'This is Eva's phone,' he said. 'How may I direct your call?'

His friends cackled loudly, Eva found herself smothering her own laughter.

'English?' Odney suggested to the caller, who clearly didn't speak Spanish. 'I speak little. You want Eva?'

Eva held her hand out and fixed him with a stare.

Glee alight on his face, Odney gave her the phone back. 'Your game didn't save,' he said smugly to more cackles of laughter.

Merriment in her voice—how she adored the camp's children, toddlers and teenagers alike—Eva finally spoke to her caller. 'Hello?'

'Eva? Is that you?'

All the jollity of the moment dived out of her.

'Yes. Who is this?'

She knew who it was. The deep, rich tones and heavy accent of Daniele Pellegrini were unmistakable.

'It's Daniele Pellegrini. I need to see you.'

'Speak to my secretary and arrange an appointment.' She didn't have a secretary and he knew it.

'It's important.'

'I don't care. I don't want to see you.'

'You will when you know *why* I need to see you.'

'No, I won't. You're a—'

'A man with a proposal that will benefit your refugee camp,' he cut in.

'What do you mean?' she asked suspiciously.

'Meet me and find out for yourself. I promise it will be worth your and your camp's while.'

'My next weekend off is—'

'I'm on my way to Aguadilla. I'll have you brought to me.'

'When?'

'Tonight. I'll have someone with you in two hours.'

And then he hung up.

CHAPTER TWO

EVA'S HEART SANK at the sight of the plush hotel at the end of the long driveway Daniele's driver was taking her down. It was the same hotel Daniele had tricked her into dining with him in at on their 'date'. She supposed anywhere else would be beneath him. The Eden Hotel was the most luxurious hotel in Aguadilla and catered to the filthy rich. She was wearing her only pair of clean jeans and a black shirt she'd been unable to iron thanks to a power cut at the camp. She couldn't justify using the power that came from the emergency generators to iron clothing when it was needed to feed thousands of people.

When Daniele had driven her—he'd actually deigned to get behind the wheel himself then—into the hotel's grounds the first time her hackles had immediately risen. She'd turned sharply to him. 'You said this was an informal discussion about the hospital.' She'd thought they would dine in one of the numerous beachside restaurants Aguadilla was famed for that served cheap, excellent food, upbeat music and had an atmosphere where anyone and everyone was welcomed.

'And so it is,' he'd replied smoothly, which had only served to raise her hackles further. They'd walked past guests dressed to the nines in their finest, most expensive wear. She'd been as out of place as a lemming in a pigpen.

Dining in the restaurant had been a humiliating experience the first time around but this time she at least had that experience to fall back on, and it served to steel her spine as she walked into the hotel's atrium with her head held high. She wouldn't allow herself to feel inferior even if she did look like a ragamuffin, despite her sixty-second shower.

A hotel employee headed straight for her. At close sight she saw the title of 'General Manager' under his name on the gold pin worn on his lapel.

'Ms Bergen?' he enquired politely, too well trained to even wrinkle his nose at her.

She nodded. She guessed she'd been easy to describe. Just look for the scarlet-haired woman who doesn't fit in.

'Come with me, please.'

Like a docile sheep, she followed him past an enormous waterfall, past the restaurant she'd dined in a month ago, past boutiques and further restaurants and into an elevator that came complete with its own bellboy. It was only when the manager pressed the button for the top floor that warning bells sounded.

'Where are you taking me?'

'To Mr Pellegrini's suite.'

They'd arrived at the designated floor before he finished answering. The bellboy opened the door.

Eva hesitated.

Dining in a private hotel suite had very different connotations to dining in public. Under no sane marker could it be considered sensible to go into a rich man's suite alone.

The manager looked at her, waiting for her to leave the safety of the elevator and be led into the lion's den.

All she had to do was say no. That would be the sensible thing. Say no. If Daniele Pellegrini needed to see her so badly that he'd flown to the Caribbean for the sole purpose of talking to her, then he could dine with her in public. She could demand that and he would have no choice but to comply.

But, for all his numerous faults, including being a sex-mad

scoundrel with no scruples over who he bedded, her gut told her Daniele was not the sort of man to force a woman into anything she didn't want. She wasn't being led into the lion's den to be served as dinner.

She stepped out of the elevator and followed the manager up the wide corridor to a door on which he rapped sharply.

It was opened immediately by a neat, dapper man dressed in the formal wear of a butler.

'Good evening, Ms Bergen,' he said in precise English. 'Mr Pellegrini is waiting for you on the balcony. Can I get you a drink?'

'A glass of water, please,' she said, trying very hard not to be overawed by the splendour of the suite, which was the size of a large apartment.

Having a butler there relieved her a little. It was good to know she would have a chaperone, although she couldn't fathom why she felt she needed one.

The manager bade her a good evening and left, and Eva was taken through a door into a light and airy room, then led out onto a huge balcony that had the most spectacular view of the Caribbean Sea, dark now, the stars twinkling down and illuminating it. To the left was a private oval swimming pool, to the right a table that could comfortably seat a dozen people but was currently set for two. One of those seats was taken by the tall, dynamic figure of Daniele Pellegrini.

He got to his feet and strolled to her, his hand outstretched.

'Eva, it is great to see you,' he said, a wide grin on his face that was in complete contrast to the set fury that had been on it three days ago when he'd demanded she fix his nose.

Not having much choice, she reached her own hand out to accept his. Rather than the brisk handshake she expected, he wrapped his fingers around hers and pulled her to him, then kissed her on both cheeks.

Her belly did a little swoop at the sensation of his lips on her skin, diving again to inhale his fresh scent, which her senses so absurdly danced to.

As much as she hated herself for the vanity of it, she was thankful she'd so recently showered. Daniele looked and smelled too good, his easy, stomach-melting smile back in its place. And he was clean, his dark grey trousers and white shirt immaculately pressed. Everything here in this hotel, including the guests, was spotless. Standing before this beautifully smelling, impossibly handsome man made her feel, again, like a ragged urchin. No matter how hard she tried to keep herself presentable, living in a refugee camp where dust and mud were prevalent made it an impossible task.

She was even more thankful when he let her go, and had to stop herself wiping her hand on her jeans in an attempt to banish the tingles from where his fingers had wrapped around hers.

'Your nose looks like it's healing well,' she said, for want of something to say to break the fluttering beneath her ribs. The swelling had gone down substantially and her vanity flickered again to see the butterfly stitches she'd applied were still perfectly in place. There was slight bruising around his left eye but that was the only other indication he'd been in a fight. Her curiosity still itched to know who his opponent had been. One of Caballeros's corrupt officials? A jealous boyfriend?

'You did a good job.'

She managed the smallest of smiles. 'Did you see a doctor?'

He made a dismissive noise in his throat. 'No need.'

The butler, who she hadn't noticed leave the terrace, returned with a tray containing two tall glasses and two bottles of water.

'I didn't know if you'd prefer still or sparkling so I brought you both,' he said, laying them on the table. 'Can I get you anything else before I serve dinner?'

'Not for me, thank you,' she said.

'Another Scotch for me,' Daniele requested. 'Bring the bottle in.'

'As you wish.'

Alone again, Daniele indicated the table. 'Take a seat. To save time, I've ordered for both of us. If you don't like it, the chef will cook you something else.'

Eva bristled. She wasn't a fussy eater—with her job she couldn't be—but his presumption was another black mark against him. 'What have you ordered?'

'Broccoli and Stilton soup, followed by beef Wellington.' He flashed his smile again as he took his seat. 'I thought you'd be homesick for English food.'

Bemused, she took the place laid out opposite him. 'Homesick for English food? But I'm from the Netherlands.'

'You're *Dutch*?'

His surprise almost made her smile with the whole of her mouth but not out of humour, out of irony. They'd spent a whole evening together in which he'd flirted shamelessly with her but not once had he cared to ask anything of substance about her. She'd just been a woman he was attracted to, whom he'd been determined to bed. He'd assumed she'd be so honoured to be singled out by him that she would accompany him to his suite—this suite?—like some kind of fawning groupie and climb into bed with him. 'Born and raised in Rotterdam.'

A groove appeared in his forehead. 'I thought you were English.'

'Many people do.'

'You have no accent.'

'English people notice it but you're Italian so it's not obvious to your ear.'

The butler brought Daniele's bottle of Scotch and asked if Eva wanted anything stronger to go with her meal.

She shook her head and fixed her eyes on Daniele. 'I think it's best I keep a clear head this evening.'

Daniele smiled grudgingly. He should keep a clear head himself but after the last few days he liked the idea of numbing everything inside him. The Scotch would also help him get through the forthcoming conversation.

'What other languages do you speak?' Eva spoke English so precisely and fluently it hadn't occurred to him that she was any nationality but that. When he'd first met her she'd acted as a translator for him and his now despised cousin Matteo. He had only a rudimentary comprehension of Spanish but her translations between them and the Caballeron officials had sounded faultless.

'I speak English, Spanish and French with full fluency and passable Italian.'

'Prove it,' he said, switching to his own language.

'Why?' she retorted, also in Italian. 'Are you trying to catch me out?'

He shook his head and laughed. 'You call that passable?' It had been rapid and delivered with near-perfect inflection.

'Until I can watch a movie in the host's tongue without missing any cadence, I don't consider myself fully fluent,' she said, switching back to English. 'I have a long way to go before I reach that with Italian.'

'Then let us speak Italian now,' he said. 'It will help you.'

Her ponytail swished as she shook her head. 'You said you had important things to discuss with me. Your English is as good as mine and I would prefer to understand everything and not have anything lost in translation that will give you the advantage.'

'You don't trust me?'

'Not in the slightest.'

'I admire your honesty.' It was a rare thing in his world. His family were faultlessly honest with him but since he'd really stamped his authority in the architecture world and made his first billion—canny investments alongside his day job had helped with that—he hadn't met a single outside person who openly disagreed with a word he said or ever said no to him.

The butler returned to the terrace with their first course. He set the bowls out on their placemats and placed a basket of bread rolls between them.

Eva dipped her head to inhale the aroma and nodded approvingly. 'It smells delicious.'

The butler beamed. 'The rolls are freshly baked but we have some gluten-free ones if you would prefer.'

'I'm not gluten-intolerant,' she said with a smile. 'But I thank you for the offer.'

Eva was the only woman Daniele had been on a date with in at least three years who hadn't been gluten-intolerant or on a particular fad diet. It had been refreshing, yet another difference between herself and the other women he'd dated. It showed on her physically. She had curves for a start and heavy breasts that just begged to have a head rested upon them. Eva Bergen was one sexy lady and he couldn't wait to see what she looked like when wearing feminine clothes. No clothes at all would be even better.

When they were alone again, she helped herself to a bread roll and broke it open with her fingers. 'What is it you wished to discuss?'

'Let's eat first and then talk.'

She put the roll down. 'No, let's talk while we eat or I'll think you've brought me here under false pretences again.'

'There were no false pretences on our last date,' he countered smoothly.

'I was very specific that it wasn't to be a date. You made it one. The questions you asked me about the hospital could have been dealt with over a five-minute coffee.'

'Where would the fun have been with that?'

'My work isn't fun, Mr Pellegrini—'

'Daniele.' He must have told her a dozen times not to address him so formally during their date that, according to Eva, wasn't a date. It hadn't occurred to him that she would be anything but delighted with his attention. His family name and looks had always been a magnet for the ladies. Once the architectural accolades and money had started rolling in he couldn't think of a single woman who hadn't looked at him with fluttering eyelashes, not until he'd met Eva. There had been a spark of interest there, though, a moment when their eyes had locked together for the first time and a zing of electricity had passed between them.

It had been the first real hit of desire he'd experienced since his brother had died. In the two months since Pieta's death, Daniele had lost all interest in women. The opposite sex had flown so far off his radar that the electricity between him and Eva had been a welcome reminder that he was alive.

After that initial zing her manner had been nothing but calm and professional towards him, which he'd assumed had been a product of the environment they'd been in. He'd also assumed that getting her out of the pit of hell that was Caballeros and into the more picturesque setting of Aguadilla would remove the straitjacket she'd put around herself. He'd certainly got that wrong.

Despite the zings of electricity that had flown between them that evening, she'd remained cool and poker-faced, his usually winning attempts at flattery being met with stony silence. She'd outright rejected his offer of a nightcap. Not only that, but there had been contempt in her rejection too.

There had been no denying it—Eva Bergen had been looking down her pretty little nose at him. At *him*.

No one had ever looked at him like that before. It had felt bitter and ugly in his guts and he'd dismissed her without a second thought. Rejection he could deal with but contempt?

It had been too much like the expression he'd seen on his father's face when the media reported on one or another of Daniele's dalliances with the opposite sex. His parents had been desperate for him to marry. Pieta had found a woman to settle down with—even though it had taken him six years to actually exchange vows with her—which meant it had been time for Daniele to settle down too.

Daniele had had no intention of ever settling down. His life was fun. He pleased himself, not answerable to anyone. If he wanted a weekend in Vegas, all he had to do was jump on his jet and off he would go, collecting some friends on the way to share the fun with. His perfect brother had never behaved anything but...perfectly, and he'd been held up as the shining beacon for Daniele to emulate. He'd been held up as the shining beacon before Daniele had even been out of nappies.

Well, Daniele had had the last laugh. He'd earned himself a fortune worth more than Pieta's personal wealth and the estate Pieta would inherit combined.

And then the last laugh had stopped being funny. Pieta had died in a helicopter crash and the man he'd loved and loathed in equal measure, his brother, his rival, was no longer there. He was dead. Gone. Passed. All the terms used to convey a person's death but none with the true weight of how the loss felt in Daniele's heart.

'I take my job very seriously, *Mr Pellegrini*. I'm not here to have fun.' Eva said it as if it were a dirty concept. 'Your flirting was inappropriate and your offer of a nightcap doubly so.'

No doubt his sister would call him a masochist for choosing to marry a woman who openly despised him. Francesca wouldn't understand how refreshing it was to be with a woman without artifice. She wouldn't understand the challenge Eva posed, like an experienced mountaineer peering up from the base of Everest, the peak so high it was hidden in the clouds. To reach the top would be dangerous but the thrills would make every minute of danger worthwhile.

The only danger Eva posed was to his ego and he would be the first to admit that his ego could use some knocks. He despised thin-skinned men and looking back to his reaction when Eva had rejected his offer of a nightcap, he could see he'd been as thin-skinned as the worst of them.

'I would have thought an intimate meal for two in a Michelin-starred restaurant was the most appropriate place to flirt with a beautiful woman.'

The faintest trace of colour appeared on her cheeks. 'If you flirt with me again I'll leave.'

'Without hearing what I wish to discuss first?'

'That's up to you. If you can control your natural tendency to flirt and actually get to the point, it won't be an issue.' She put a spoonful of soup into her wide, full-lipped mouth.

Daniele took hold of his spoon. 'In that case I shall get straight to the point. I need a wife and want you to take the role.'

A groove appeared in her forehead, crystal-clear blue eyes flashing at him. 'That is not funny. What do you really want?'

He sipped at his soup. Eva was right. It was delicious. 'What I *want* is to get on my jet and fly away from here, but what I *need* is a wife, and you, *tesoro*, are the perfect woman for the job.'

There was a moment of stunned silence before she pushed her chair back and rose to her feet. 'You are despicable, do you know that? You can keep your mind games to yourself. I don't want to play. And for the record, I am *not* your darling.'

Snatching her canvas bag from the foot of her chair, Eva turned to stalk away from the terrace, out of the suite, and far away from this arrogant man who she had no intention of ever seeing again.

She hadn't taken two paces when the sound of clicking echoed in the air and Daniele said, 'Before you leave, I have something to show you.'

'You have nothing I want to see.'

'Not even a million dollars in cash?'

Against her better judgement—again—Eva turned her head.

There on the table, beside his bowl of soup, lay an open briefcase.

She blinked. How had he moved so fast? What was he? Some kind of magician?

The briefcase was neatly crammed with wads of money.

She blinked again and met his eyes.

'Do I have your attention now?' he asked. All his previous good humour, which she had already suspected of being a façade, had been stripped away.

She nodded. Yes. He had her attention, but there was a part

of her that thought she had to be dreaming. A briefcase stuffed with cash only existed in dreams or the movies. Not in real life.

Daniele Pellegrini didn't exist in real life either. He was a billionaire from an old and noble family. His life couldn't be more different from her reality than if he'd been beamed in from the moon.

'If you agree to marry me, this money, all one million dollars of it, will be handed to the Blue Train Aid Agency tomorrow morning. And this is only the start.'

'The start?' she asked faintly, looking back at all that lovely money.

'If you sit back down I will explain everything.'

Eva inched her way back to her seat, resting her bottom carefully while she kept her gaze fixed on Daniele so he couldn't pull another rabbit out of a hat that wasn't even there.

He downed his Scotch, poured another three fingers into the glass and pushed it to her.

She didn't hesitate, tipping the amber liquid down her throat in one swallow, not caring that his lips had pressed against the same surface just moments before. It was the smoothest Scotch she'd ever tasted and she had no doubt the bottle cost more than her weekly salary.

'Agree to marry me and this money goes directly to your charity. On the day of our marriage I will transfer another two million into their account and a further three million dollars for every year of our marriage. I will give you a personal allowance of a quarter of a million dollars a month to spend on whatever you wish—you can donate the whole lot for all I care, it won't matter as I will also give you an unlimited credit card to spend on travel and clothing and whatever else you require for the duration of our marriage.'

Eva's head spun. Had she slipped into some kind of vortex that distorted reality?

'Can I have some more of that Scotch?' she mumbled.

He took a drink himself then passed the glass back.

Drinking it didn't make his words any more comprehensible.

She shook her head and took a breath. 'You want to pay me to be your wife?'

'Yes.'

'Why would you want to marry me?'

'It's nothing to do with want. It's to do with need. I need a wife.'

'You've already said that, but why would you choose *me* for the role when there are hundreds of women out there who would take the job without having to be bribed into it? Why marry someone who doesn't even like you?' There was no point in pretending. She didn't like him and he damn well knew it.

'That is the exact reason why I want you to take the role.'

'You've lost me.'

A tight smile played on his lips. 'I don't want to marry someone who's going to fall in love with me.'

CHAPTER THREE

HE WAS MAD. He had to be. No sane person could make such a suggestion.

And then she looked into those green-brown eyes and thought them the eyes of a man who was perfectly sane and knew exactly what he was doing. Far from reassuring her, the expression in them frightened her, and Eva was not a woman who scared easily. She'd learned to hide it. She hid it now.

'There's no chance of *that*,' she said, hoping Daniele couldn't hear the beats of her hammering heart in her words.

He shrugged and took the glass back, pouring himself another hefty measure. 'Good. I don't want a wife with romantic dreams. I'm not marrying for love. I'm marrying to inherit my family estate.' He must have read her blank expression for he added, 'My brother died without children. I'm the spare son. I can only inherit if I'm married.'

'What do you need the estate for? You're worth a fortune as you are.'

'To keep it in the family.' He swirled his Scotch in his glass before drinking it. 'Duty has finally come calling for me.'

'You need a wife to inherit?'

'*Si*. The estate is...' She could see him struggle to find the correct English. 'It is bound by an old trust that states only a married heir can inherit.'

'Is that legal?'

He nodded grimly. 'To unravel the trust and make it fit for the modern age will take years. I don't have years. I need to act now.'

'Then find someone else.'

'I don't want anyone else. Everyone else is too needy. You're tough.'

'You don't even know me,' she protested darkly. 'Twenty minutes ago you thought I was English.'

If she was tough it was because she'd had to be. To turn her back on her family when it had made her heart bleed, then to lose Johann and find that same heart torn apart had put a shell around her. It had been an organic process, not something she had consciously built, a shell she'd only become aware of four years ago, back when she'd been living and working in The Hague and a drunk colleague had accused her of being an unfeeling, ball-breaking bitch. She'd returned home to the small apartment she'd once shared with Johann and looked in the mirror and realised there was truth in what her colleague had said. Not the part about being a ball-breaking bitch. She wasn't those things, she knew that. But unfeeling…? Yes. That, she had been forced to accept when she'd looked in that mirror and realised she no longer felt anything at all. She was empty inside.

'I know all I need to know, *tesoro*,' he countered. 'I don't need to know anything else. I have no interest in your past. I don't want to exchange pillow talk and hear about your dreams. This will be a partnership, not a romance. I want someone practical and cool under pressure.'

And he thought that person was her?

She didn't know whether to laugh or cry. Had she become so cold that someone could think she would be agreeable to such an emotionless proposition?

Once she had been warm. She had felt the sun in her heart as well as on her skin.

And what did his proposal say about him? What had made him this way? she wondered. How could someone be so cynical about marriage?

'Marriage is not a game,' she said slowly, thinking hard, her eyes continually drawn between the wads of cash and Daniele's smouldering gaze. That money would make an incredible difference at the camp. The Blue Train Aid Agency was fully dependent on donations and there never seemed to be enough of it to go around all its different projects.

Those eyes…

She pulled her gaze away and stared into the distance at the sea, unable to believe she was even entertaining this ludicrous proposal.

'I'm not playing games,' he said, his words soaking through her. 'Marry me and we all win. Your charity gets a guaranteed income to spend as it sees fit, you get unlimited funds to spend on yourself, my family get the knowledge the family estate is secure for another generation and I get my inheritance. You're a practical person, Eva. You know what I'm suggesting makes excellent sense.'

She hadn't always been a practical person. She'd been a dreamer once. She'd had so many hopes but they'd all been flattened into the dust.

'I don't know…' She tightened her ponytail. 'You say it isn't a game but then you say everyone's going to be a winner out of it. Marriage is a commitment by two people who love each other, not two people who don't even like each other.'

He raised his hefty shoulders and leaned forward. 'My family's ancestry goes back as far as there are written records. The most successful marriages were arranged for practical reasons; to build alliances, not for love. I've never wished to commit my life to one particular person but I am prepared to commit myself to you. It won't be a marriage built on love and romance, but I can promise you a marriage built on respect.'

'How can you respect me if you're trying to buy me?'

'I won't be buying you, *tesoro*. Consider the cash an inducement.'

'I won't be your property.' She'd never be someone's property again. She'd run away from her family the moment she'd turned eighteen, the day she'd stopped belonging to her parents, no longer subject to their stringently enforced rules. She flexed her left hand and felt the phantom ache in the tendons of her fingers. The fingers had long since healed but the ache in them remained, a ghost of the past, a reminder of everything she had run from.

'If I wanted a woman I could own, I wouldn't choose you.'

Before she could think of a response to this, the butler came in to clear away their soup. Eva was surprised to find her bowl empty. She couldn't remember eating it.

She waited until their next course was brought in, a beef Wellington that was sliced and plated before them, before asking her next question.

'If I say yes, what's to stop me taking the cash you give me and running off with it?'

'You won't receive any money for yourself until we're legally married. Under Italian law, you won't be allowed to divorce me for three years but that wouldn't stop you leaving me. I have to trust that you wouldn't leave without discussing it with me first.'

He would have to trust her. But the question, she supposed, was whether she could trust him.

The beef Wellington really was superb. Having never eaten it before, Eva had always assumed it consisted of an old boot baked to within an inch of its life. Instead she cut into the pinkest beef wrapped in a mushroom pâté, parsley pancakes and delicate layers of puff pastry.

'If you don't want a traditional marriage, what kind of marriage do you have in mind for us?' she asked after she'd taken her second mouth-watering bite. She couldn't entertain a traditional marriage either, not with Daniele or anyone. But a marriage of convenience where pots of cash were given to the charity she held so close to her heart…that, she found to her surprise, she *could* entertain.

Daniele Pellegrini was an exceptionally handsome man. He had an innate sex appeal that poor Johann would have given both his skinny arms for. But that was all on the surface. Her body might respond to him but her heart would be safe. *She* would be safe. Daniele didn't want romance or pillow talk, the things that drew a couple together and forged intimacy and left a person vulnerable to heartbreak.

She would never put herself in a vulnerable position again. She couldn't. Her heart had been fractured so many times that the next blow to it could be permanent.

'The outside world will see us as a couple,' he replied. A slight breeze had lifted a lock of his thick dark hair on the top of his head so it stuck up and swayed. 'We will live together. We will visit family and friends as a couple and entertain as a couple.'

'We will be each other's primary escorts?'

He nodded. 'That's an excellent way of putting it. And one day we may be parents…'

Immediately her food stuck in her throat. Pounding on her chest, Eva coughed loudly then took a long drink straight from the bottle of water.

'Are you okay?' Daniele asked. He'd half risen from his seat, ready to go to her aid.

'No.' She laughed weakly and coughed again. 'I thought you said something about us being parents.'

'I did. If we're going to marry, then we're going to share a bed.'

'You didn't think to mention that?'

'I didn't think it needed spelling out. Married couples sleep together, *tesoro*, and I will sleep with you.' His eyes gleamed. 'Sharing a bed with you is the one plus point to us marrying.'

'I don't want to have sex with you.'

Instead of offending him, he laughed. 'That, I think, is the first lie you have told me. You cannot deny your attraction to me.'

'If I was attracted to you, I wouldn't have turned your offer of a nightcap down.'

'If you weren't attracted to me, you wouldn't have hesitated before turning it down. You think I don't know when a woman desires me? I can read body language well and you, my light, show all the signs of a woman fighting her desire. I understand why—it can't be an easy thing to admit that you desire a man you dislike so much.'

'Have you always been this egotistical?'

'It's taken years of practice but I got there in the end. And you still haven't denied that you're attracted to me.'

'I'm not attracted to you.'

'Two lies in two minutes? That's bad form for a woman who's going to be my wife.'

'I haven't agreed to anything.'

'Not yet. But you will. We both know you will.'

'Let me make this clear, if I agree to marry you, I will not have sex with you.'

'And let me make this clear, when we marry, we will share a room and a bed. Whether we have sex in that bed will be up to you.'

'You won't insist on your conjugal rights?'

'I won't need to insist. Deny it until your face goes blue but there is a chemistry between us and lying under the same bed sheets will only deepen it.'

'But will you try to force me?'

Distaste flickered over his handsome face. 'Never. I can't promise that I won't try and seduce you—*Dio, tesoro*, you're a sexy woman... I'd have to be a saint not to try—but I respect the word no. The moment you say no, I will roll over and go to sleep.'

It was on the tip of her tongue to ask if he planned to take a mistress. It stood to reason that if she wouldn't have sex with him he would get it from someone else.

But that was a whole new quagmire that instinct told her

to leave alone. She'd been celibate for six years and had never missed sex. She had missed the cuddles but never the sex, which deep in the heart of her she had always found underwhelming. Why people made such a big deal out of it she would never understand, but they did and to expect Daniele to be celibate was like expecting a lion not to eat the lame deer that limped in front of it.

'If I agree I will want to continue working.' If he could list his requirements, then she should too.

'You won't need to work.'

'Are you going to quit *your* job?'

He raised his eyebrows. They were very nice eyebrows, she noted absently.

'You don't need to work,' she pointed out. 'You could retire right now and never want for anything for the rest of your life.'

'You *want* to work?'

'I love my job.'

Now his brows knitted together in thought before he said slowly, 'You won't be able to work at the camp any more.'

Her heart sank. She loved working at the camp. Her job might be listed as administrative but it was so much more than that. She was useful there. She'd learned skills she would never have picked up anywhere else. In her own way, she'd made a difference to many of the people who'd lost so much.

'I can't just leave,' she whispered.

'Why not? The charity will be losing one employee but gaining three million dollars a year from it. Any loss of salary for you will be more than replaced by the allowance you'll get from me.'

'It's not about the money.'

'Then what is it about?'

She inhaled deeply. How could she explain that her job in the camp had given her a purpose? In the midst of all the deprivation she'd found hope when she'd been so sure there was no hope left inside her. And even if she could find the words to explain it, what would Daniele care? For him, money ruled everything. Marrying her meant he stood to inherit even more filthy lucre.

That made her mind up for her.

Fixing her eyes on him, she said, 'Five million a year. That's what you'll have to pay the charity for me to marry you. And I'll want it in writing. A legal document.'

His eyes didn't flicker. 'It will form part of our prenuptial agreement.'

'I will have my own lawyer approve it.'

'Naturally.'

'I need to give a month's notice and—'

'No.' His refutation was sharp. 'That is too long. There are many things that need to be arranged and it can't wait. I want us to be married in Italy as soon as possible and there is much to organise. You will hand your notice in tomorrow and tell your bosses you'll be leaving with immediate effect or this suitcase of cash stays with me and I find another wife.'

He must have noticed her mutinous expression at his non-subtle warning that he could easily find another woman to be his wife, and likely one who was a hundred times more malleable, for he added, 'I will arrange for someone suitable to take your place until the charity can find a permanent replacement for you.'

'And if you can't find a suitable replacement?'

'I will.' He looked so smugly confident in his assertion that she longed to smack him. 'But the second I hand over the cash tomorrow you are committed to marrying me. There will be no going back on your word.'

'Providing my lawyer agrees that the prenuptial agreement is unbreakable, I will not go back on my word.'

'Then do we have a deal? You will marry me? You will quit your job and come to Italy with me tomorrow?'

'Only if the agency agrees that your "suitable replacement" is suitable.'

'They will,' he said in that same smugly confident tone.

'I'll need to go home before I go to Italy.'

Now he drummed his fingers on the table with his impatience. 'What's your excuse for that?'

'You're an Italian national but I'll be considered an alien. I used to work at the Ministry of Foreign Affairs so I know what I'm talking about. I need to go to my home in The Hague to collect the papers your officials will require from me.'

'I'll send someone to get them.'

'I'm not having a stranger go through my possessions.'

He studied her for a moment before giving a sharp nod. 'Okay, I will take you to the Netherlands first. But that is it. I will agree to no further delays. Does this mean we have a deal? Do I instruct my lawyers to draft the prenuptial agreement?'

Her throat suddenly running dry, Eva cleared it, trying to ignore the chorus of rebuttals ringing in her head.

What did it matter if she was agreeing to a cold, emotionless marriage when her life had been cold and emotionless for six years? Marrying Daniele meant the Blue Train Aid Agency would have the wonderful benefit of his money, which would be of far more value to it than she was as a lowly employee.

As Daniele himself had said only minutes ago, marrying him meant everyone was a winner.

But still the chorus in her head warned that for there to be a winner someone had to be the loser.

How could *she* be the loser in the deal? She wasn't giving Daniele her heart, only her physical presence. She wasn't giving him *anything* of herself so how could she be the loser?

So she ignored the chorus and met his gaze, her cold heart battering her ribs. 'Yes. We have a deal.'

'You will marry me?'

Closing her mind to the image of Johann that had fluttered to its forefront, she nodded.

'Say it,' Daniele commanded.

'Yes. I will marry you.'

His firm lips turned at the corners, more grimace than smile. 'Then I suggest we have a drink to drown our sorrows in.'

Daniele, looked at his watch and sighed. The money had been handed over to the astounded Blue Train Aid Agency bosses, his temporary replacement for Eva approved with only the most cursory of glances at the replacement's CV, and the prenuptial agreement was in the hands of his lawyers and expected to be completed by the time they landed in Europe. Her canvas back-pack had been put in the boot of his car by his driver, all the paperwork for the termination of her employment done. They should be long gone from this godforsaken camp by now but Eva had disappeared, muttering something about needing to say some goodbyes. He'd imagined it would take only a few min-utes but she'd been gone for almost an hour.

He accepted another sludge-like coffee from a female em-ployee who turned the colour of beetroot every time he looked at her and forced a smile. All he wanted was to be gone and away from this place that made him hate himself for the privileges he'd been born to. Although he would never admit this to Eva, he would have donated the million dollars cash to the charity that morning even if she'd turned his proposal down.

Just as he drained the last of the disgusting liquid—he'd have to add a lifetime supply of decent coffee for all staff and refu-gees to his donation, he decided—Eva appeared in the dilapi-dated building he'd been hiding in.

'Ready to go?' he asked in a tone that left no room for doubt that she'd better be ready to go or he'd chuck her over his shoul-der and carry her out.

She nodded. She'd hardly exchanged a word with him since his arrival at the camp mid-morning and hadn't met his eyes once.

'Come on then.'

It was only a short walk to his car. His driver spotted their approach and opened the passenger door.

'Eva!'

They both turned their heads to the sound and saw three teenage boys come flying over to them, jabbering and calling out in Spanish.

Eva's face lit up to see them.

She embraced them all tightly in turn and, much to their pretend disgust, kissed their cheeks and ruffled their hair. Only after she'd embraced them all for a second time did she get in the car.

Daniele hurried in behind her so she couldn't use another excuse to delay, and tapped the partition screen so his driver knew to get going.

The boys ran alongside the car as they left the camp, waving, hollering, blowing kisses, which were all returned by Eva.

Only when they were on the open road with the camp far behind them did Daniele see the solitary tear trickle down her face.

CHAPTER FOUR

EVA STEPPED INTO the small one-bedroom apartment she'd shared with Johann with a weight sitting heavily in her chest.

As she walked slowly through the living room, dust dislodged and filtered through the air. She hadn't set foot in it for over a year. She hadn't lived in it properly in four years. Intellectually she knew she should sell it or at the very least rent it out, but she couldn't bring herself to.

All the old photos were where she'd left them. She picked up one on the windowsill, dislodging more dust. The picture was of her and Johann in the snow. Not even the thick winter clothing he'd been bundled up in could disguise Johann's skinny frame. They both looked so young. They'd *been* so young, only nine-teen when the picture had been taken.

She kissed the cold glass and put the frame back where it had been, pushing the old memories clamouring in her head aside and ignoring the urge to get the duster and vacuum cleaner out. She'd promised Daniele she would only be ten minutes.

He hadn't been happy at her insistence he wait in the car. She didn't want him in her apartment. This was the place she and Johann had made into a home when they'd been little more than children playacting at being grown-ups, neither having any real idea of what it entailed, learning as they went along, right down to when she'd put a nail in the kitchen wall to hang a picture, not having any idea that electric cables were nestled behind it and that she'd drilled right into them until they started receiving electric shocks every time they touched the tap or fridge. The electrician they'd had to scrape all their loose change together to afford had sternly told them they'd had a lucky escape—if either of them had touched the nail they would have been electrocuted. Even today, she couldn't believe she'd been so lucky. What had been the odds that she could hang the picture without touching that live nail? At the time she'd considered it as evidence of their good luck; vindication that running away with him had been right.

But their luck had run out.

With a sigh, she pulled the suitcase down from the top of the wardrobe and quickly filled it with her meagre number of warm clothes. Snow was settling on the streets outside, the weather a complete contrast to the glorious sunshine she'd left in Caballeros.

She didn't take anything else. She'd known when she'd accepted Daniele's proposal that what she was agreeing to would not be permanent. But she could manage a few years, of that she was certain.

Daniele's *castello* was almost identical to how Eva had imagined it, sitting high in the rolling Tuscan hills. Evening was falling and the few lights on gave it an ethereal, gothic quality. Thinking of how it would look with all the lights blazing in the total darkness, she could easily see where it got its name. Castello Miniato, the illuminated castle, would have shone for miles in medieval times.

What had once been a castle of majesty and splendour in a bright salmon pink was now on the verge of being a crumbling relic.

'Are you renovating it?' she asked as she got out of the car, which the driver had brought to a stop in an enormous court-yard. She could just make out scaffolding poles along a far wall.

'My brother started on a renovation programme. He finished the south wing and now I need to think about what I want to do with the rest of it.' There was a distinct lack of enthusiasm in his voice.

'You don't like it here?'

He shrugged. 'I prefer modern architecture. If I could get away with it, I would pull it down and start again.'

She followed him through a wide solid oak door and found herself standing in a high-ceilinged room that, despite its size and grandeur, had a dank, cold feel to it.

The temperature change from what she'd been used to in the Caribbean hadn't bothered her until that point. The cold weather front had engulfed the whole of Europe, with Tuscany expecting its own share of the white stuff over the coming days, but it wasn't until she stepped into the *castello*'s reception room that Eva felt the cold in her bones.

'The chef has prepared a meal for us,' Daniele said, rubbing his hands briskly together. 'I'll show you to our living quarters.'

She trailed him for a good few minutes before he opened a door into a wide corridor lined with high, wide windows.

'This is the family quarters,' he said, then pointed to a door. 'That is my room, which will be our room once we're married.' He threw the glimmer of a smile. 'Of course, if you wish for it to be our room before then, you're welcome to join me in it.'

She threw back a smile that quite clearly showed hell would freeze over first. 'Which is my room?'

'Take your pick. Serena, who runs the place, got the staff to put fresh bedding in all the rooms. The only one off limits is Francesca's.' He indicated another door, this time his smile indulgent. 'If you want to make yourself a widow, just tell my sister I let you sleep in her room. She would kill me.'

'Does Francesca live here?' She'd assumed not but only now she was here did she realise she knew next to nothing about

Daniele or his family, not on a personal, familiar level. All her dealings with them had been in Caballeros where medieval *castellos* and family trees had never cropped up in conversation.

'No, but she visits a lot. We all have our own keys and there's been a long-standing agreement that any family member can stay here whenever they like and for however long they like. Francesca spends more time here than any of us... I suppose that will change now she's getting married and moving to Rome.'

'Her fiancé seems nice.' Actually, Eva had found Francesca's fiancé, a security expert who was in charge of all the security for the hospital site in Caballeros, rather terrifying.

Daniele snorted. 'I don't think *nice* is the word you're looking for, but he'll look after her and that's all I care about.'

'You and your sister are close?'

He considered this and nodded. 'You've met her, haven't you?'

'Yes. I liked her.'

'Good, because you're going shopping with her tomorrow.'

'What for?'

He cast a critical eye over the outfit she was wearing, her usual uniform of old jeans this time topped with a thick jumper. 'Clothes. Francesca loves spending my money and is happy to help you spend it too.'

'Your money? We're not married yet.'

His smile was faint. 'You're here. You've resigned from your job. Judging by everything I've seen you wear, you need new clothes. Your allowance will kick in from the day we marry but I'm happy to give you a credit card now. We've got a meeting first thing at your consulate for the *nulla osta*.'

The *nulla osta* was the legal document she'd need to prove there was no impediment to them marrying.

'Then we have an appointment at the registry office to give notice of the wedding. Francesca will meet us there and take you shopping when we're done. She knows all the best shops in Florence.'

Eva thought better of warning Daniele that there was no

chance of her being given the *nulla osta* straight away. He'd learn for himself that willing their marriage to take place immediately did not mean it could happen. Then she thought of her pitiful wardrobe, which hadn't even nearly filled her suitcase, and tried to remember the last time she'd gone clothes shopping. It had been before she'd joined the Blue Train Aid Agency. Working for them had required practical clothing. The only new stuff she'd brought for herself in the past four years had been direct replacements for items that had worn out. She couldn't remember the last time she'd worn something that hadn't been jeans or shorts.

'Choose the room you want,' he said when she made no verbal response. 'That door at the other end of the corridor takes you through to a living area where we'll have our dinner tonight.'

'Are there any other rooms off limits?'

'No. Francesca's the only one who kept her childhood room as her own personal territory. My mother has informed me she won't be sleeping here again. If she visits she'll return to her villa in Pisa. Pieta last slept here on the day he got married.' Daniele's nose wrinkled as if he'd detected a foul smell.

'Are we going to live here?' She knew he had a number of other homes. If they were staying here she definitely needed that shopping trip. The warm clothes she'd packed wouldn't be warm enough unless she wore them all at the same time.

'Only until all the paperwork is sorted out and I'm declared the legal owner. Choose a room and make yourself at home. I'll join you for dinner in half an hour.' And with that, he opened his bedroom door and disappeared inside.

Alone, she gazed at the doors along the right side of the corridor and opted for the one furthest from Daniele's. It was a relatively small room, with thick lined faded wallpaper and wood panelled ceiling. It had a four-poster bed, a wardrobe, a chest of drawers, heavy curtains for the windows and a cosy-looking fireplace. The door also had a lock with a key in it.

Yes. This would do her perfectly for the next three or four weeks.

She would worry about sharing a bed with Daniele when the time came.

They left early the next morning for the consulate in Florence. To Eva's utter astonishment, the *nulla osta* was produced immediately, and an Italian-speaking consular official was there on hand to translate copies of her other documents so there would be no unnecessary delays. Daniele's smug grin as they left the building made her shake her head, that feeling of not knowing whether to laugh or cry going through her again.

'Who did you have to bribe to get it done there and then?' she asked when they were back in the car and heading to the registry office.

'No one. I simply made a few calls before we left.' He flashed a grin at her. 'When I want something, I never take no for an answer.'

'So I've noticed,' she murmured.

His efficiency at getting things done was astounding. She'd discovered that last night when she'd joined him for dinner and found the draft prenuptial agreement printed off for her to read. He'd stuck to his word on every aspect. Once they'd finished eating, he'd then produced a map of the *castello* for her, which he'd drawn himself, with every wing clearly marked and little comments like, 'Don't go in this wing unless you like getting rained on.' This random act of thoughtfulness had astounded her more than anything else.

It was such a short ride to the registry office that by the time they'd parked, she thought it would have been quicker to walk.

The registrar greeted them and took them straight to his office, where a pot of coffee sat on a sideboard, the fresh aroma filling the room.

For perhaps the tenth time since she'd joined Daniele on the terrace of his hotel suite, Eva wondered if she'd slipped into some kind of vortex. Here she was, sitting down to arrange a wedding with a man she barely knew and intensely disliked but it didn't feel real, felt like she'd slipped out of her body and was watching it all happen to someone else.

Daniele was keen to get on and forced a smile as the registrar, a plodding, laborious man, asked in hesitant English if Eva needed a translator.

'Italian will be fine, if you don't mind going slowly,' she said, speaking his language faultlessly.

The registrar beamed his approval and inspected the *nulla osta* she'd passed to him carefully. 'This seems to be in order. You both have your passports?'

They handed them over, Eva passing her translated documents with hers. They were all inspected with the same careful consideration.

Only when copies had been made were they handed back in a pile together.

Daniele took them and opened the top passport to check whose it was, saw it was Eva's and passed it to her. About to pass her the other documents, which he'd not even glanced at until that point, his attention was caught by the top one.

In silence he scanned it, the beats of his heart turning to thumps that hammered loudly throughout the rest of their meeting, through the vibration of his phone alerting him to a message from his sister who'd arrived at the building, and through all the other formalities that would allow him to marry Eva Bergen, formerly Eva van Basten.

By the time Francesca and Felipe joined them in the room, his heart was like a crescendo in his ears.

He'd not had the faintest idea that the ice-cool, beautiful woman he'd chosen to marry was a widow.

'What do you think?' Eva asked the woman who was going to be her sister-in-law in five days.

Five days.

The registrar had agreed to reduce the banns notice to just five days.

She could hardly believe it would happen so quickly. She'd expected to wait for weeks. Had *hoped* to wait for weeks, figuring it might give her the time to get used to the idea.

She really needed to keep herself on high alert around Daniele. The man was more than just a magician. He could make anything happen.

As soon as their appointment had ended, Daniele had given Eva his credit card and a key to the *castello*, said something about needing to get on with his work and then disappeared in his car.

Confused at his abruptness, she'd watched him be driven away with a certainty that something had angered him. Then Francesca had whisked her away shopping and she'd pushed Daniele from her mind.

Or tried to. In five days he would be her husband. For better or worse, they were going to be legally tied together. Suddenly it all felt very real.

Now she stood in the changing room of an extremely expensive boutique surrounded by a pile of vibrantly colourful clothes in all shapes, sizes and materials, Francesca and her keen sense of style a welcome presence.

'When do you move to Rome?' Eva asked as she unbuttoned the silk electric-blue shirt she'd just tried on and adored. She'd balked when she'd first seen the price tag but Francesca had been insistent, pointing out that the money that would pay for these purchases had been legally earned. But, still, twenty-eight years of frugality would not be overcome by one shopping trip.

'We were going to move this weekend but are going to wait until after your wedding.' Francesca took Eva's hands to stop her undoing any more buttons. 'Keep this on. You look fabulous in it.'

'Will I be allowed to?'

'You've got Daniele's credit card in your pocket. You can do whatever you like.'

Eva laughed. She really did like Francesca. 'I'll be cold.'

'Then we'll get you a coat to go with it. Wear it with the black jeans and black boots.'

The black jeans were nothing like the jeans she usually wore. These were a real skinny fit and had little diamond studs ringing the pockets. The boots were like nothing she'd ever worn either, reaching her knees and with four-inch heels. Slut shoes, her mother would have called them. Her mother would turn puce if she could see them, then have a heart attack when she saw the price.

How would Daniele react to see her in such different clothing...?

'Have you thought of the type of wedding dress you want?' Francesca asked, cutting through Eva's veering thoughts of Daniele.

Who cared what he thought of the clothes she bought and how she looked in them? Not her.

Yet those were her flushed cheeks reflecting back at her...

'I'm sure I'll find something,' she murmured, dragging her attention back to Francesca's question. As she didn't want to think of the actual ceremony, she hadn't allowed herself to consider what she would exchange her vows in.

'There's a lovely bridal shop in Pisa I can take you to. I found my wedding dress in it. Can I be your bridesmaid?'

'I don't think it's going to be that kind of wedding.'

'Don't be silly. A wedding's a wedding. And who knows—maybe you and Daniele will fall in love with each other! That would be brilliant.'

Eva was so shocked at this that for a moment she could only gape at the younger woman. 'You know?'

'That Daniele's paying you to marry him? Yes, I know. So does Felipe. And our *mamma*,' she added as an afterthought.

'It doesn't bother you?'

'We need to keep the *castello* in the family. That's more important than ever after what Matteo and Natasha have done.'

'Matteo? Your cousin? The one who's a doctor?'

Francesca nodded, her face darkening in exactly the same way her brother's did when he thought of something unpleasant. 'Did Daniele not tell you about it?'

'Tell me what?'

'Matteo's been having an affair with Pieta's wife, Natasha. She's pregnant with his child.'

Eva's jaw dropped. 'For real?'

Francesca nodded grimly. 'We found out last week. It was in all the papers.'

'I don't follow the news,' Eva said absently as the pieces suddenly clicked together. Daniele and Matteo in Caballeros together… Daniele's busted nose… His grim mood… 'Last week? Did Daniele and Matteo get in a fight about it?'

'Yes. It's such a betrayal. I don't dare see him. I think I would be sick before I could punch him. He was like a brother to us. Natasha…we all loved her. We thought she loved us too. They betrayed us.' She took a deep breath, blinked a number of times then brightened. 'I'm very glad you've agreed to marry Daniele. I know he can be a pig but he's not all bad. And by marrying you the *castello* stays with our side of the family, otherwise if Matteo marries Natasha then he will be next in line to inherit.'

Eva swallowed, remembering Francesca's visit to Caballeros to purchase the land to build the hospital on. Eva had met her there, happy to impart as much of her local knowledge as she could to assist her. It was through that meeting she'd learned Daniele would be building the hospital and Matteo supplying all the medical equipment and overseeing the employment of the doctors and nurses who would work there. She'd seen the two men together, witnessed the good-natured ribbing and the easy familiarity. The family had put aside their grief over Pieta's death to pull together to make the hospital happen, and now they had been torn apart.

For the first time she felt a pang of sympathy for Daniele. He was human. He felt pain.

His brother had died and now he'd lost the cousin who'd been as close as a brother too.

CHAPTER FIVE

DANIELE WAS STILL very much on Eva's mind when Francesca and Felipe, who'd waited in a café while they'd shopped, dropped her back at the *castello* late that afternoon. He'd been in her thoughts all day, a shadow in her mind she couldn't rid herself of.

Felipe insisted on carrying her bags in but they both shook their heads when Eva asked if they would be staying for a drink.

'Thanks but we've got somewhere to be,' Francesca said, her eyes darting to her fiancé.

Eva suspected their 'somewhere to be' meant a bed. Their obvious love and desire for each other sent another little pang through her, this one of envy. She'd been in love once, with Johann, and it had been as sweet as a bag of sugar-coated doughnuts, but the desire had never been there.

She bit her lip. There was no point in wishing for something she had never felt and that she suspected she wasn't built to feel.

But then she thought of the man she'd be marrying and that little fluttery feeling set off in her stomach. He truly was the most attractive man she'd ever met. He had the looks of someone who, when she'd been a younger teenager, she would have wanted to pin posters of to her walls so she could gaze at him to her heart's content.

Her sister Tessel had once put a poster up on the bedroom

wall they'd shared. Eva remembered begging her to take it down before their mother saw it but Tessel had been stubbornly brave and refused. She had paid for that stubborn bravery, and Eva had never been tempted to follow suit. She'd always learned from her sister's mistakes. Well, mostly. There had been so many rules that sometimes breaking the odd one had been inevitable.

Shaking the thoughts away, she pulled out the map Daniele had drawn for her from the bottom of the new handbag Francesca had insisted she buy. He wrote in precise block capitals, she noted, unsure why seeing his penmanship set the flutters in her belly off again.

It took her three trips to her new bedroom before she had all her new bags and boxes in there and strewn over the bed. The *castello* was shrouded in such silence she felt certain she was alone.

Thirsty, she studied the map again and saw the quickest way to the kitchen was through the huge family living area. Maybe she would find someone there, the chef who'd cooked their evening meal and provided them with fresh pastries before they'd left for Florence that morning.

The fluttery feeling turned into a buzz when she found Daniele at the large dining table they'd eaten at the night before. He was wearing a thick navy sweater and had his head bent over a large scroll of paper, a range of pens and pencils spread out before him.

She hovered in the doorway, a sudden shyness preventing her from stepping over the threshold. Whatever he was working on had his complete attention. She'd never imagined he could be so still.

Just as she thought she should cough or something, he turned his head.

She saw something pulse in his eyes as he stared at her before he straightened and put his hands to his ears to tug out a pair of earphones he had connected to his phone. 'My apologies. I didn't hear you. I always listen to music when I work but haven't got round to setting up a music system here yet. Have you been back long?'

'Twenty minutes. Am I disturbing you?'

'Not at all.' He pulled his sleeve up to look at his watch, revealing an intensely masculine forearm covered in fine dark hair. 'I didn't realise how late it was. How was your shopping trip?'

'It was okay.' She pulled her gaze away from his arm and saw his own gaze sweeping over her with an intensity that sent a burst of unexpected heat surging through her veins.

Utterly flustered but determined not to show it, she raised her chin. 'I'm sorry. I spent a lot more than I meant to.' She hadn't realised when she'd set out on her shopping trip that Francesca would only take her to designer boutiques. At the time, with Francesca enthusiastically encouraging her to spend as if there were no tomorrow, she'd allowed herself to get caught in the moment but was now dealing with a serious case of buyer's remorse.

Daniele shrugged then rolled his shoulders. He'd been hunched over the table for four hours and his back ached, but Eva's return had perked him up. Her new clothes looked amazing on her. She'd look even better if she let her hair down, something he looked forward to in both a literal and metaphorical sense. 'It's part of our deal—you get an unlimited credit card to spend on whatever you like.'

'Your sister's taking me to Pisa tomorrow to buy a wedding dress. I won't need to buy anything after that, not for a long time.'

'Need is not that same as want.'

Had she worn a wedding dress for Johann? he wondered moodily. He'd brooded over that man for hours, finally drowning the name by plugging his earphones in and cranking up the sound to lose himself in the plans for the refurbishment of the theatre that homed the Orchestre National de Paris. 'I'm one of the richest men in Europe. Buy whatever your heart desires. It's part of our deal.'

'Being rich doesn't mean it's right to be wasteful.'

Was that a deliberate dig at him? He worked hard for his money. Why should he not enjoy the fruits of his labour? 'You sound like a puritan.'

Her pretty face tightened, fresh colour heightening her cheeks. 'You don't need to be a puritan to think being wasteful is wrong.'

'Maybe not,' he conceded. 'But if you have money then spending it is good for everyone. It boosts the economy for a start and filters down.'

She tilted her head as if considering his words then scrunched her nose and raised her shoulders, and stepped properly into the room.

He scanned her from head to foot all over again. *Dio*, her new skin-tight sexy jeans emphasised her curves beautifully; a Bernini sculpture come to life. If not for the flashes of colour on her face he could believe she was made of marble. His loins tightening to imagine the real texture of her naked form. When he got her naked he would discover the texture for himself and learn her natural colouring...

'I'm not an economist, only a woman who's lived and worked with some of the poorest people on our planet.'

He forced his mind away from the delights of imagining her naked. Soon enough he wouldn't have to imagine it...

'Marrying me means those people get the benefit of my money.'

'That's why I agreed to it.'

'Has your lawyer got back to you on the prenuptial agreement?'

She nodded. 'He's advised me to sign.'

'I'm not surprised.' Daniele had given his own lawyer instructions to make the agreement as simple and unambiguous as it could be. He had a loathing of complicated clauses allegedly there for protection but which were, to his eyes, a showcase of the drafter's self-perceived legal brilliance. The prenuptial agreement was three clauses long and didn't deviate from what they'd privately agreed on in Aguadilla.

'There was one thing...'

'What?' he asked when her voice trailed off and she gazed down at the floor.

'There was nothing in it about us sharing a bed.'

'You want me to put that in?' he asked, bemused.

'No,' she said quickly, shaking her head vigorously, her pony-tail whipping through the air.

'Are you sure? We can have it spelt out that you and I are to share a bed every night of our married life if you want to hold me to it.'

She crossed her arms, pulling the new chunky cardigan she was wearing across her chest and covering the new silk shirt that was *extremely* flattering on her. He wondered if she was aware how the cut and the material clung to the fullness of her breasts. Crossing her arms hid the effect but, *Dio*, she was one sexy lady and knowing his reward for marrying her meant he got to share a bed with her every night meant there was heady anticipation mingling with his dread at the forthcoming loss of his freedom.

'I just assumed you would put it in the document,' she murmured.

'It's a private agreement between us. *I* assumed I could trust you to stick to your side of it. Are you telling me I can't?'

For the first time since he'd met her she seemed genuinely flustered but that didn't stop her raising her eyes to meet his with defiance. 'I will stick to my side of our agreement.'

'Then there is nothing else to say on the matter. I'll tell my lawyer to come here first thing so we can get it signed.'

She jerked a nod and, keeping her arms tightly crossed around her midriff, walked past him towards the door that led to the *castello* kitchens.

'When were you going to tell me you'd been married before?' he asked to her retreating back.

She stopped in her tracks and slowly turned to face him. Her face was an emotionless mask. 'You said you didn't want to know about my past.'

He kept his response emotionless too, although he acknowledged to himself the truth in her rejoinder. It was something he'd brooded on during her shopping spree. Eva was so cold towards him that he'd allowed himself to believe she was that way with everyone, even when he'd seen the evidence with his own eyes that with people she liked, she had the ability to be warm, like with those kids who'd come running to wave her off in Caballeros. To discover she'd been close enough to someone that she'd actually married them had been disconcerting, although he couldn't put a finger on why. 'That you've been married is something I should have known.'

'I am not a psychic. I cannot be expected to know what you think you should know when, as I just said, you expressly told me you have no wish to know anything about me.'

And he thought his sister was quick off the mark. The difference between them was that Francesca would fire her retorts back where Eva kept a veneer of icy calm around her that was both a thing of beauty and disturbingly infuriating. She really could be made of marble.

Realising his jaw was clenched so tight his teeth could grind wheat into flour, he concentrated on relaxing it to say as politely as he could, to let her know two could play at the icy calm veneer, 'Is there anything else important about you that I should know?'

Now her eyebrow rose a touch but she kept her defensive stance. 'How am I supposed to know what you think is important?'

Did you marry Johann for love?

He kept that question to himself. It wasn't important. So unimportant was it that he couldn't fathom why he would even have thought of it.

Instead, he lightened his tone, taking them away from this dangerous territory. 'Do you have a criminal record?'

Instead of the instant rebuttal he'd expected, she hesitated before shaking her head.

'You don't seem very sure about that,' he said.

'No criminal record,' she said with more decisiveness, then indicated to the door she'd been heading towards. 'I'm going to get a coffee. Can I get you anything?'

'I'll call a member of staff to get it for us.'

'I didn't think there was anyone here.'

'There's kitchen staff in.'

'Then I should go and meet them.' She raised her shoulders. 'If I'm going to live here for the foreseeable future I need to get to know them and learn my way around this place.'

'Follow the corridor to the second set of stairs then take your first left at the bottom. I'm afraid the service elevator's out of use. We need to get it repaired, like everything else in this bloody place.'

She gave a noncommittal shrug. As she reached the door he couldn't hold back the other question clamouring inside of him.

'What happened to your husband?'

'How did he die?'

He nodded. If he hadn't been so shocked to have the man's death certificate in his hands he would have read it more carefully.

'A brain tumour.'

'I'm sorry.'

Her chest rose as her lips pulled in together and she gave a sharp nod. 'Thank you.'

He paused before asking, 'How long were you married?'

'Four years.'

'You must have been young when you married.'

'We were both eighteen.'

He winced. Eva was a modern, independent woman. Why would a woman like her marry so young?

If he asked her she would tell him. The way she stood by the door, her blue stare not flinching from his, he knew she would tell him anything he wished to know. If he asked why she'd hesitated about having a criminal record she would tell him that too. She would answer any question he wished to ask.

But he didn't wish to ask. He didn't need to know anything more than had already been revealed.

He especially didn't need to know if she'd married Johann for love.

To Eva's consternation, the next four days flew by. Every time she looked at the clock, expecting to see ten or twenty minutes had passed since her last look, she would find another hour gone. She didn't see much of Daniele. He had a host of work to get finished before they exchanged their vows, leaving her to her own devices while he flew to Paris and then Hamburg and then on to somewhere else she didn't catch the name of. She knew that would all change when they married.

Francesca took her to the wedding dress shop in Pisa as she'd promised, then surprised her by taking her to lunch where Vanessa Pellegrini, the woman who in a few short days would be her mother-in-law, joined them. Much to Eva's relief, the elder Pellegrini woman was as warm and hospitable as her daughter and clearly thrilled her remaining son was going to marry. If it concerned Vanessa that her son was paying Eva to be his wife, she kept it to herself.

Eva spent the rest of her days exploring the *castello* and the estate grounds. The vineyards in the winter cold were barren and lifeless but she could imagine them packed full of fat, juicy grapes in the hot summer months. At least that was something to look forward to.

She also visited the *castello*'s private chapel in which they would marry. She had misgivings about marrying in a religious house, something she had shared with Daniele after they'd signed the prenuptial agreement. His response had been a nonchalant, 'If we're both committing to this marriage then there's no hypocrisy or sacrilege.'

'But we don't mean it.'

He'd fixed those green-brown eyes on her. 'My ancestor, Emmanuelle the third, married his wife Josephine of Breton in the chapel with her father holding her arms behind her back to stop her running away. What we're doing is tame compared to that and they were married for twenty years.'

'Were they happy for twenty years?' she'd asked cynically, while her heart twisted for the agony the long-dead Josephine must have lived through. She doubted she would cope with marriage to Daniele for twenty weeks never mind twenty years.

His laughter had been short but full-throttled. 'Unlikely. But you don't have to stay married to me for that long. You are free to leave whenever you like.'

'Which proves my point that we don't mean it. Why can't we marry in a registry office?'

'Because I *do* mean it. You will be my only wife. If you leave then you leave, but it won't be something I do again. It will make my mother happy to see me married here.' He'd run his fingers through his hair and stared at the frescoed ceiling. 'God knows, she could do with some joy in her life right now.'

And that had been the end of that conversation. After meeting Vanessa, Eva had found herself coming to Daniele's way of thinking. As warm and amiable as she was, Vanessa Pellegrini had a sadness to her that Eva saw in Francesca's eyes too. They put their brave faces on but she could see that inside their hearts had been torn over the loss they'd suffered with Pieta's death. If Daniele felt the loss of his brother as acutely as they did he kept it well hidden but he had to feel it too, didn't he? She'd seen his anger over Matteo and Natasha's betrayal of Pieta. She'd seen *him*, she'd patched him up. She hadn't witnessed it since though; on the contrary, his mood was generally flirty and affable but that darkness... Yes, there were times when she looked at him and glimpsed it hidden deep inside him.

* * *

Midnight struck. Eva saw her bedside clock mark the hour with a constricted chest.

This was it. She was officially getting married again, that very day. In twelve hours she would forsake Johann's name and become Mrs Pellegrini.

The fire in the room burned sporadically and mostly ineffectually. She'd snuggled down deep under the heavy bedsheets and was as warm as she could get in this freezing *castello* but, try as she might, sleep wouldn't come.

The floor was cold under her bedsocked feet as she slipped on her new dressing gown and left her room, intending to get a hot drink. Immediately she was struck with the scene from the condensation-covered windows that lined the corridor and which her heavy drawn bedroom curtains had hidden from her. She wiped a pane to see more clearly. It was snowing.

In wonder, she perched on the cold windowsill, wiped more condensation with her sleeve and pressed her face to the lead-lined window to stare out at the Pellegrini vineyards and surrounding rolling hills encased in shining white, a magical scene that made her heart ache at the beauty of it all.

The living-room door opened and Daniele appeared, his dark hair dishevelled, a roll of architectural drawings under his arm.

Exhaustion lined his face and thick stubble covered his jaw but still her senses leapt with awareness at the sight of him.

'I thought you were in bed,' he said when he neared her.

Her heart suddenly battering her ribs, she tightened the sash of her dressing gown. 'I couldn't sleep.'

'Excitement about tomorrow?' he asked drolly.

'The excitement is killing me,' she replied, matching the drollness by the skin of her teeth.

Their eyes met. That pulse of electricity she was becoming far too familiar with flashed between them, a hung silence developing, only broken when he said with a glimmer of amusement, 'You'll catch a cold if you sit there too long.'

'It's snowing.'

He sat on the sill beside her and wiped condensation from a pane of glass. 'So it is. I can't remember when we last had snow here.' He swore as the pane misted up again. 'These windows are a disgrace.'

Twisting round so his back was to the window, he stretched his neck. 'I need an office. I can't keep working at the dining table.'

'There's enough rooms to choose from.' Her words were automatic, spoken without any input from her brain, which was as fixated as her eyes were on the muscular thighs wrapped in heavy denim only inches from her own thighs.

They were as physically close to each other as they'd ever been, close enough for her to smell the last vestiges of his cologne.

'They're all full of damp and cold. The living room's warm.'

She was no longer cold, she realised. Whether it was his physical proximity or some strange alchemy happening inside her, her body no longer felt the *castello*'s chill.

A burst of heat throbbed deep inside her to think that tomorrow night she would lie beside him and benefit from his body heat all night long...

'Why didn't your brother renovate the family wing first?' she asked with abrupt desperation.

Daniele was too attractive, too masculine. He smelled too good. No matter how hard she tried to keep it switched off, there was something about him the base part of her responded to and she *had* to get a handle on it.

She needed to keep a distance from this man as much as she could but how could she manage that when she had to share his bed and wake to his handsome face every morning?

His smile was tight as he answered, 'He saw it as the *castello* needing to pay for itself. Pieta renovated the south wing first because the largest state rooms are there and they bring the money in. Corporations hire them out. The bedrooms on that wing are hired out too. People come for romantic week-ends and ghost hunts.'

She shivered but not with cold. 'Is it haunted?'

'If you believe in that stuff. Do you?'

'No.' She believed in what she could see and feel before her. But that didn't stop the gothic atmosphere of the castle from evoking her imagination in a way it hadn't for a long, long time.

'Good. It's rubbish. The *castello* has a bloody history so play-ing up to that is a good money spinner. I give Pieta credit there. He saw a market for murder mystery weekends and luxury ghost hunts and ran with it.'

'But...?'

'He didn't think of the family. Being the owner of the *cas-tello* is like being a guardian. It's never yours. It's just in your keeping. My mother won't stay here any more because it's too cold for her. Not that she complained to Pieta about it,' he said with a faint hint of bitterness that he quickly shrugged off. 'I offered him the money to renovate the family quarters but he turned it down.'

'Why was that?'

His nostrils flared. 'He didn't want my money or my input. The *castello* was his and he was going to run it how he wanted.'

Daniele, feeling the old bitterness curdle in his guts, inhaled through his nose to drive the bad feelings out. His brother was dead and their fraternal rivalry dead with him. What did any of it matter any more? He should be above feeling slighted that all the accolades that had rained down on him and all the ar-chitectural awards he'd won had been received by Pieta with a patronising smile. Sure, Pieta would often open a bottle of the *castello*'s finest wine to celebrate Daniele's success but that had been the actions of a man behaving properly, in the manner ex-pected of him, rather than anything heartfelt. Daniele had cele-brated every one of his brother's successes as if it were his own, even if he always did secretly determine to smash it with his own success. When he'd made the Rich List for the first time,

Pieta had murmured that a man should never measure his success in monetary terms but in the good they did in the world.

That was one area Daniele hadn't bothered trying to compete with his brother in. Pieta's philanthropy had been all his, and their family had thought him like a deity for it.

How could he compete with a deity? It was impossible. And he didn't want to. In every other aspect of life he used his brother as his benchmark but when it came to charity, Daniele preferred his involvement to entail nothing more than writing out discreet large cheques.

'You can run it how you want to now,' Eva said softly, cutting through his cynical reminiscences.

He shouldn't be thinking like this. For everything that had wound him up about him, Pieta had been a good brother, even if that goodness had always felt as if it were for show, a display of his humility rather than sincere.

Dio, he was doing it again. He had to stop this.

'Yes, I can. And my priority will be to make our living quarters fit to live in.' He'd never wanted the responsibility of the *castello* and the rest of the estate but fate, along with Eva's consent to marry him, had put it in his hands...

He looked at the woman he would be marrying in a few short hours, her head resting on the window pane, intense blue eyes fixed on his. The velvet robe she hugged around herself was a deep indigo blue, setting off the redness of her plaited hair perfectly. She looked ethereal yet substantial. In the dark moonlight he could believe she'd been made to live in this gothic *castello*. If he were a sculptor, he would strip her naked but keep her in that pose and carve her likeness in marble. And then he would make love to her. He would kiss every part of that creamy skin and bring the marble to life until she was liquid in his arms.

His loins tightened and burned at his vivid imaginings.

'Just think,' he murmured, leaning his face close to hers. He could smell her skin, a delicate fragrance that made his blood thicken and his pulse surge. Her pink, sensual lips had parted a fraction, almost begging to be kissed. She really was incredibly beautiful. 'Tomorrow night you get to share my bed.'

Her eyes held his starkly, a glimpse of the fire he was experiencing sparking from them before they narrowed, her lips closed into a tight line and she pulled her robe tighter around her.

He laughed and reluctantly got to his feet. *Dio*, his groin *ached*. 'With that happy thought I bid you goodnight. See you at the chapel, *tesoro*.'

He felt her eyes follow him all the way to the bedroom that in one short night she would share with him.

It was the only bright thought for a day that filled him with dread.

CHAPTER SIX

FEELING LIKE THE biggest fraud in the world, Eva took a deep breath and opened her mouth to recite her vows to the kindly priest who was making short work of the ceremony.

She wondered if they were setting a record, not only for the quickest wedding ceremony in Italian history but for the lowest number of guests.

There were six of them in the pretty chapel, not including the priest. Her, Daniele, his mother, his aunt, Francesca and Felipe. He'd asked her if she wanted to invite anyone. True to form, he hadn't questioned her response to the negative.

She hadn't invited anyone to her first wedding either. She would have asked Tessel to that one but hadn't dared to in case her parents had found out. Now, marrying for a second time a decade later, her terror of her parents long done with, she couldn't ask Tessel for the simple reason that her sister no longer wanted to be contacted.

Those that were there today were all dressed in traditional wedding attire. At Daniele's request, she wore a traditional wedding dress, in which she felt ridiculous. It was beautiful but she was very much aware that white was not a colour that flattered her and she itched to get out of it and into something she felt comfortable in. She hadn't worn a traditional dress for Johann and she had meant her vows to him.

Would Johann understand what she was doing, marrying Daniele? She liked to think he would. He'd been the sweetest, sunniest person she'd ever known, an anomaly not just of men but people in general. He'd married her to protect her and keep her safe.

Daniele, wearing a black tuxedo, was marrying her for an inheritance he didn't want. He wasn't marrying her for his own sake. He was marrying her for the older woman sitting watching them with tears rolling down a face that teetered between joy and grief. He was marrying her to keep the estate that had belonged to his family for six hundred years intact. For all his many selfish faults she had to respect that in this instance he was behaving selflessly.

In truth, she hadn't seen any evidence of his selfishness since they'd landed in Italy. In marrying her he was behaving as selflessly as Johann had, albeit for completely different reasons.

The other difference was that she'd married Johann with relief flooding her veins and hope in her heart. For all Daniele's insistence that everyone would be a winner from their marriage, she recited her vows without a shred of hope for them. Neither of them meant them for what they should mean, even if her heart did thud heavily as she spoke the words that would bind them together.

Then it was Daniele's turn. He stared right at her as he said his vows but for once there was no humour in his stare. He spoke them like a condemned man with no hope of clemency. Yet something sparked between them as they went through the motions of marrying that Eva hadn't expected, like a bond was snaring itself around them, pulling them together as conspirators, uniting them in their mutual loathing of what they were doing. And something else was there too, something deeper that tugged at her stomach and made the thuds of her heart turn into a skip and her chest tighten.

We're together now, his look said. *This is it. You and I.*

Only when he took her hand in his and slid the gold band on her wedding finger and she felt the weight of it on her skin did the bond fall apart and Eva come to her senses.

She'd worn a ring on that finger before. It had been the cheapest they could afford but had meant so much more. It had been given and received with faith and love. All that had been missing was desire. She hadn't known that. She doubted Johann had either.

When they were done and officially declared husband and wife, they left the chapel side by side but not hand in hand. There had been no kiss for the bride and that she would count as a blessing. If she ever had to kiss him she didn't want an audience for it.

A fresh smattering of light snow had fallen during the ceremony but the estate's groundsmen had been busy scattering salt to melt a pathway for them. Now the sun was out in the cold blue sky, the air crisp. Eva was thankful Francesca had insisted she buy a cream faux fur wrap to put over her shoulders. It staved off a little of the December chill.

'Let's get the picture taken here,' Daniele said.

'In front of the chapel?' she asked. This would be the picture they would send to the media. She still didn't know how she felt about having her photo given to the press but accepted that she was marrying—*had* married—a famous man and that their marriage would be deemed news. The odds of any of her family seeing it were slim and even if they did...what did it matter? They couldn't touch her or hurt her now.

He nodded. 'Let's keep it simple. One picture. A brief announcement of us having married and leave it at that. We only need to feed the wolves, not give them a banquet. Felipe, can you take it for us?'

'*I'll* take it,' Francesca said, beaming at them. 'The camera on my new phone is amazing.'

Eva noticed the indulgent eye roll Felipe gave his fiancée and felt another of those envious pangs in her stomach.

'Right, you two, stand in front of the door—Mamma, can you close it for them, please? Perfect. Daniele, put your arm around your bride.'

Eva met Daniele's eye and the pang turned into a flutter.

Amusement quirked on his lips at his sister's bossiness but there was something quite different in his eyes, a challenge to her.

Touch me and look adoringly at me, they said. *I dare you.*

And then he slid an arm around her waist and pulled her to him.

His physique had been a good indication that he was strong but she would never have guessed the solidity behind it, or the warmth that radiated from him, which seeped into her skin at the first touch.

'Get closer,' Francesca ordered. 'You've just married. The whole of Italy and much of the rest of the world is going to be looking at this picture.'

Eva inched a little closer so that her breast pressed lightly against his torso.

She blinked, shocked at the instant flash of sensation that pulsed through her.

'Now put your hand with the flowers to his chest.'

Breathing heavily, her heart hammering louder and more painfully than it had ever done in her life, Eva did as ordered, resting her hand as lightly against him as she could.

'Daniele, take her hand so you're both holding the flowers.'

A warm hand enveloped hers, the movement pressing her closer so she found herself flush against him. She could hear the heavy beats of his heart. The scent of his cologne was no longer a trace that she caught but right there, firing into her senses, setting them alight. The hand around her waist slid over to cup her hip, his fingers digging painlessly into her.

Lifting her eyes, Eva gazed up at him.

The returning green-brown stare swirled and pulsed, boring into her, explicit confirmation that his desire for her was more than just words, that when he got her into his bed he had every intention of seducing her and that it would be down to her own resolve to stop herself from succumbing.

An ache spread out low inside her as her gaze drifted to his lips. There was such sensuality in that mouth...

'Perfecto!'

Francesca's shout of approval brought Eva back to her senses and she pushed against Daniele's chest and stepped back.

'You're done?'

'Yes. Do you want to see it?'

'Can we wait until we get back inside? I'm freezing.'

But she wasn't cold. Being held by Daniele had warmed her so thoroughly she needed to lie on the white ground and make snow angels to cool down.

Daniele finished the last of his wine and grimaced.

So, it had been done. He was now a married man.

They'd returned to the *castello* for a short celebratory meal with his family that, for Daniele, had felt like a wake. Not only had he done the one thing he'd sworn he'd never do but as the day had gone on a Pieta-shaped absence had emerged. This was the first family event without him. He'd missed him and he knew his mother and sister had too. The two women had smiled and laughed and celebrated his marriage but neither had been able to hide the sadness in their eyes.

And now it was time for them to leave, his mother and aunt back to their villa in Pisa, his sister and Felipe flying on to their new home in Rome.

As they left, his mother cupped his cheeks and said, 'Thank you for doing this, Daniele. I know marriage is not what you wanted but I think, with Eva, you've found someone you can be happy with.'

He wanted to laugh at the irony of it. Since when had his

happiness been a factor in his mother's thoughts towards him? Even the success he'd made in his professional life, which had far exceeded his brother's, had come second place in their minds to his absolute refusal to settle down and marry. But he'd always known his own mind and followed his own path and every nudge by his parents to 'be more like your brother' had only driven him further up that path, and driven him in a number of extremely fast and extremely expensive sports cars that should, according to his parents, have been replaced by luxury cars like the Bentley his brother had driven. At the time of his father's death just over a year ago he'd barely been on speaking terms with him, his father's fury at a kiss and tell by another of Daniele's girlfriends driving the semi-estrangement.

Why can't you be like Pieta? He would never bring such shame on our family.

It had been a constant refrain throughout his life. Be like Pieta. Be sensible. Make the right choices. Think of the family name. Be like Pieta.

He'd never wanted to be like Pieta. The only person he had ever wanted to be was himself, but in his family's eyes he hadn't been good enough as himself.

But the estrangement was something Daniele deeply regretted. He couldn't lay all the blame for it at his parents' door. He was an adult. He had to take responsibility for his own part in it. His mother was grieving for her firstborn and in emotional disarray at the betrayal of the nephew she'd raised as her own from his teenage years and the daughter-in-law she'd so wholeheartedly welcomed into the family.

So instead of laughing or making a sarcastic retort, he kissed his mother and embraced her tightly.

Marrying Eva had kept the *castello* and the rest of the estate in their branch of the family and eased a little of his mother's pain. He didn't deny that it made his chest swell to know he'd done something that brought her comfort and happiness. Pieta, and to a lesser degree Matteo, had always been the one to do that before.

Eva hung back while he made his goodbyes. He caught the startled pleasure in her face when his mother moved from him and took her new daughter-in-law in her arms.

The day had been as difficult for her as it had been for him but she'd coped stoically. He had no doubts that he'd made the best choice of wife that he could. She hadn't put a foot wrong, had made a concerted effort to smile and at least pretend that marrying him wasn't her idea of purgatory, even if it had been for his family's sake and not his.

That look in her eye, though, when they'd pressed themselves together for the photograph... He'd seen those ice-blue eyes darken and the tinge of colour spread over her cheeks. He'd felt her curvy body quiver against his.

Once his family had gone and they were alone in the armoury where they'd had their meal, she sighed heavily and said, 'Is there any wine left?'

'I'll get another bottle brought in.'

'Don't worry about it. I'm going to get changed.' There was a slight wrinkle in her nose as she looked down at the wedding dress she'd been in for hours.

He let his gaze drift over her. The dress she'd married him in was long and white with a high lacy neck and long lacy sleeves. Her long scarlet hair was wound in a coil at her nape and she'd applied minimal make-up. While she looked beautiful he thought Eva was made for dark, bold colours, not something as insipid as white.

'Let's go out,' he said impulsively.

'Now?'

'We'll change out of these monkey suits first.'

Their eyes met, understanding flowing between them. A glimmer of amusement played on her lips. It didn't need saying. The charade they'd been acting was over.

'Where do you want to go?'

'Club Giroud will do. We can dress up in clothes that don't look as if we've just got married, have a drink, and pretend for a few hours that we haven't thrown our lives away.'

'Your whole attitude to marriage stinks, did you know that?'

'Do you feel any different?'

She shrugged. 'I didn't have a life to throw away. But, yes, let's go out. See if you can convince me over the next few hours that you're worth the commitment I've just made to you.'

'I thought it was my money you'd committed to.'

Now she bestowed him with one of her rare smiles. It was like being shone on with starlight. 'It was. Unfortunately getting that money means I'm now tied to you.'

'Then let us hope the ties don't cut either of us.'

An hour later Daniele was showered and changed into a suit of a very different hue that made him feel like himself and not a man playing dress-up. He normally liked wearing a tuxedo but marrying in one had made it feel like he was wearing a straitjacket.

Now he waited in the large reception room for Eva to join him. He'd tapped on her bedroom door—it would be the last time she used it as a bedroom—and she'd called out that she would be ready in ten minutes.

While he waited, he fiddled with his phone. After a few minutes swiping through the news outlets, and coming across an article about Matteo and Natasha, he chucked it to one side and sighed.

The torrid affair his cousin and sister-in-law had begun before his brother was even cold in his grave was a matter of greedy public consumption.

His anger for what they'd done was still as fresh as it had been when he'd first learned about it, but a little time and distance had given him time to think. That time and distance had only increased his anger towards them. The rumours his sister had whispered to him earlier that they'd broken up did nothing to quell it. They were having a baby together. They'd spent the two months since his brother's death secretly screwing each other while pretending that Natasha had travelled to Miami for a break. He would never have believed his cousin could behave so dishonourably or tell such bold-faced lies.

Had Pieta meant so little to them that they could betray his memory and everything he'd been to them? He'd never believed in his brother's saint-like persona but that didn't mean his brother hadn't been a good person. He hadn't deserved that from his wife and the man who'd been closer than he, his own brother, had been to him.

Then he forgot all about his brother and the rest of his family for the clacking of Eva's heels introduced her appearance.

And what heels they were too, black stilettoes that supported legs he could have been forgiven for thinking didn't exist as she always kept them covered up. Her long black winter coat was buttoned up and covered whatever else she was wearing but her smooth, shapely calves were on show and he had an almost irresistible urge to get on his knees and kiss the arch where they met her pretty ankles.

He let his gaze drift up to her face. The collar of her coat was up and around her ears to protect her from the chill but it looked to him as if she'd left her hair loose.

He'd never seen it loose before.

Her usually bare lashes were thickened with dark mascara, a sheen of glittery eyeshadow on the lids, her lips...

Her lips were painted a deep, utterly kissable red.

He couldn't wait to see what lay beneath the coat. And then he couldn't wait to see what lay beneath that.

Eva was his wife now. Which meant she was fair game for him to seduce. And from the challenge firing from her eyes, she remembered that part of their deal as well as he did.

Try it, those ice-blue eyes said. *Try it and see what happens. Try it but remember that I have the right to say no.*

His loins tightened and heated to think of all fun he was

MICHELLE SMART   77

going to have in making those eyes fire at him with a desire that screamed *yes*.

He had no doubt at all that he would succeed.

Sooner or later his wife would be putty in his hands.

CHAPTER SEVEN

THE EXTERIOR OF Florence's Club Giroud looked a typical Renaissance masterpiece, a beautiful piece of architecture as beautiful as the rest of the city. But inside…

Once they were admitted by the bouncers who guarded it like a pair of Rottweilers, scanning Daniele's card and returning it with a nod of respect, the inner sanctum was like stepping inside a classy, sensual courtesan's boudoir.

In the entrance room Eva gazed at deep mahogany stained walls and the fleshy nude Renaissance paintings that lined them. Florence was a stunning city rich in history and heritage and this one room encapsulated its earthier history while retaining its expensive class.

The concierge greeted them with a wide smile. 'Good evening, Mr Pellegrini,' she said in Italian, before nodding politely at Eva. 'May I take your coats?'

When Daniele had suggested going out her instinct had been to tell him to go without her. The day had been long and far more emotional than she'd anticipated. In truth, she'd felt dead inside for so long that she hadn't expected to feel any emotion other than maybe some guilt, even though she knew Johann wouldn't want her guilt. He'd been gone so long that if she were ever to allow herself to be vulnerable again, which she never would, it wouldn't be a betrayal to him. She'd mourned him. She'd picked up her life and carried on without him, slowly becoming anaesthetised until she felt nothing at all.

Perhaps she'd been naïve thinking she could get through this day with her emotions buried. Emotions had been flickering inside her since her arrival in Italy, heightening whenever she was with Daniele. But even so...

She hadn't expected to feel like she was choking. She hadn't expected her lungs to cramp so tightly that breathing had taken effort.

She hadn't expected that she would feel differently to have his ring on her finger or that she would look at his bare finger with resentment. Whether Daniele wore a ring or not shouldn't matter to her. She hadn't asked him to.

But they were married now. They needed to get to know each other. They didn't have to know each other's deepest secrets but if their marriage was to be painless, they deserved to at least see if there was a chance they could live in harmony, if not friendship.

Escaping the *castello* for a few hours to let their hair down together had sounded like the ideal way to start.

She'd opened her wardrobe and fingered the deep red dress that had caught her eye the moment she'd walked into the second boutique with Francesca. Slipping it on in her bedroom she'd sent a mental word of thanks to Francesca for insisting she disregard the price tag and buy it.

It was like nothing she'd ever worn before.

Strapless and sleeveless, it showed only the tiniest amount of cleavage and hugged her curves to fall just below her knees. Unlike the wedding dress that had made her feel like a washed-up china doll, this dress made her feel elegant, something she hadn't had the opportunity to feel for more years than she could remember.

It made her feel like a woman.

By the time she'd finished getting ready and met up with

Daniele in the cold *castello* entrance room, tendrils of excitement had curled in her stomach. The look in his eyes when she'd walked in had reinforced that new feminine feeling inside her.

She'd never suffered from vanity before but with Daniele...

For reasons she couldn't begin to understand, being with him made her want to check her appearance every five minutes. She brushed her hair with extra care then became irritated with herself for it and pulled it back into a ponytail or a bun. She kept her make-up minimal. She didn't want him to think she was making an effort for him. She would deny her attraction to him until she was, as he'd once suggested, blue in the face.

But she couldn't deny it to herself. All she could do was contain it.

A night out, though, was a different kettle of fish from being alone in the *castello* with him. She remembered all too vividly her humiliation during their 'date' in Aguadilla when she'd been in her work clothes and everyone else had been dressed in their finest.

She'd chosen this dress because she liked it. She'd put the red lipstick on because it complemented the dress, *not* for him.

Now she carefully removed her coat and handed it to the concierge, doing her best to appear confident and not betray her nerves.

Then she met Daniele's eye.

Her feminine vanity bloomed to see the unadorned appreciation in his stare.

He'd removed his own coat, revealing a sharp light grey pinstriped suit and navy tie. His hair was mussed in the way she liked and...

Mussed in the way she *liked*?

Since when had she liked anything about him other than the money he would give to her charity?

But, gazing into those hypnotising green-brown eyes, she had to admit that she didn't dislike him any more.

His eyes glimmering, he held his arm out for her. 'Ready to go in, Mrs Pellegrini?'

She couldn't fight the smile that spread over her face at his insouciance.

Slipping her arm through his, she said, 'I thought this evening was all about trying to forget we were married.'

He walked her to the elevator, his voice dropping into a caress. 'With you looking like that? I've changed my mind. Tonight I want everyone to know you're mine.'

Her jaw dropped open at his arrogance while a pulse of heat melted her core in a way that flustered her as much as his words infuriated her. 'Just as I was starting to like you, you say something like that?'

'You're starting to like me?' he asked with interest, tightening his elbow so she couldn't remove her arm from the crook of his. The elevator door pinged open.

'I *was*, but then you went and ruined it by saying I'm yours. I'm not *yours*. I belong only to myself.'

He steered her inside and pressed the button for the third floor.

It was an old, creaking elevator and took a few moments to get going, time enough for Daniele to release his hold on her arm and somehow pin her in the corner, his hand resting on the wall by her head, not quite touching her but close enough for the scent of his earthy cologne to play havoc with her senses.

A smile played on his lips, amusement and something in his eyes that made her belly squelch. 'You know that every man who sees you tonight is going to want you.'

She had to swallow to get her throat working. Her words were hardly above a whisper. 'I know no such thing.'

'They will,' he said with authority. 'They will *all* want you, but I can guarantee that none of them will want you more than me.'

She felt colour crawl over her face that deepened when he traced a thumb over her cheek.

Her throat moved but she couldn't find the words she wanted to say; couldn't say them or think them. Her brain had turned to mush.

'And you want me too.' He brought his mouth close to her ear. 'You cannot tell me you didn't choose that dress and imagine what it would feel like for me to strip it off you.'

She wanted to deny it and throw his arrogant assertion back in his face with a cutting retort that would wipe the conceit off it.

'Stop it,' was all she could whisper.

'We are married now, which means that you, *tesoro*, are fair game for me to seduce. But I am a man of my word and I gave you my word that whenever you told me to stop, I would.' He took a step back and raised the palms of his hands. 'And now I stop.'

The elevator doors pinged and began their slow slide open.

The amusement that had been on his face lessened, a serious expression forming on his chiselled features. 'When I said they would know you are mine it's because that's the assumption people make about couples who are married. We will never belong to each other but we *are* married now and you are an incredibly beautiful woman. There isn't a man alive who wouldn't walk with a swagger with you on his arm.'

Fresh colour suffusing her, Eva had to fight to keep her stare level with his and not let it drop.

No one had ever spoken to her like that before. No one had ever looked at her the way he did.

No one had made her stomach melt with a look before either.

The door now fully open, Daniele took her hand in his. 'Come on, Mrs Pellegrini. Let's have some fun.'

The floor they walked out onto in Florence's Club Giroud was like stepping into an idealised magazine spread of what a billionaire's playhouse should look like. Trying to ignore the tingling sensation that having her fingers laced so tightly in Daniele's as they walked the narrow, higgledy-piggledy corridors evoked, Eva didn't doubt for a minute that the people spread out in the vast array of rooms were from the ranks of the filthy rich. It wasn't just the expensive cut of their clothes or the diamonds that sparkled from every woman's fingers, earlobes and neck but the confidence they carried. It was a confidence she'd seen before, from the guests that had made her feel so inferior at the Eden Hotel in Aguadilla.

Tonight, dressed as she was, she could hold her head high and meet the curious yet surprisingly friendly eyes that caught hers.

All the rooms seemed to serve a specific purpose whether as restaurants or gambling rooms or bars. Some had only a handful of people in them, others were packed. Some were quiet, others filled with raucous laughter.

Daniele led her into a bar that had a pianist in a lounge suit playing contemporary music in a jazz style in a corner and an abundance of dark leather sofas and low round tables.

As they took their seats on a sofa that managed to be supportive and also incredibly soft and luxurious, a hostess in a surprisingly smart uniform approached them with a welcoming smile on her face. Eva had formed the wrong impression that the hosts would all be squeezed into gold leather or something equally vulgar.

'It's a delight to have you here again, Mr Pellegrini,' she said. 'What will be your pleasure this evening? There's a poker tournament starting in an hour.'

'Just drinks for us tonight, Anita,' he answered smoothly, then said to Eva, 'Champagne?'

'I'd prefer a gin and tonic,' she admitted.

'Two gin and tonics,' he said to the hostess.

'I had no idea a place like this even existed,' Eva murmured as the hostess bustled away, a little overawed but very much intrigued.

'It's a private members' club and the best-kept secret in Italy. There's quite a few Clubs Giroud around the continent. My personal favourite is the Vienna one.'

She cast her eyes around the walls, tastefully covered in framed photos of famous musicians.

'If you don't like this room we can move somewhere else.'

'No, this is fine,' she said, then almost felt her eyes pop out of her head to see a famous movie star sitting on a sofa across the room from them.

Daniele, seated beside her but with his head to the back of the far end of the sofa, followed her starstruck gaze. 'I heard she was filming in Florence,' he mused. 'Now stop staring.'

Eva cringed at her own gaucheness. 'Sorry.'

'The members come to relax and enjoy themselves away from the spotlight.'

'Message understood.'

He grinned. 'I brought Francesca here once and she nearly fainted when she spotted her favourite singer in the champagne bar.'

'It's good to know I'm not the only one.'

'You'll get used to it. Many of the Club Giroud members are well-known faces. Just remind yourself they're human and all have the same basic needs as every other human and you'll be fine. Either that or work on your poker face.'

As he said that, Daniele thought that on the whole Eva had an excellent poker face. It was very hard to read what was going on in her head or guess what her thoughts were. He'd learned the best way to read her was through her eyes. They never lied.

Their hostess returned with their drinks, their tall glasses filled with ice and a slice of lemon. Eva took hers and sipped at it then nodded her appreciation.

'It's good?' he asked.

She nodded and settled back in the sofa, carefully crossed her legs then looked around the room again. 'When I woke up this morning I didn't think I'd be finishing the day somewhere like this.'

'It's not finished yet,' he said, loading his contradiction with meaning.

'Did you have to remind me?'

'Why not? It's all I can think about. Is it not the same for you? Have you not spent the day thinking that tonight is the first night we spend together in my bed?'

'Actually, I've been trying very hard to forget.'

'You're a terrible liar.'

'And you're a terrible egotist.'

'And you're reduced to insulting me because it's easier than admitting the truth that you want me.'

The tiniest flash of colour seeped across her cheekbones. 'Oh, suck on your lemon.'

'My point is proved.'

'Your point is invalid.'

He shifted to settle against the back of the sofa so he could face her properly. 'There is no shame in desiring your husband.'

'You're not...' Then she checked herself and shook her head. Her loose hair, which was far longer and thicker than he'd imagined, swished with the motion. The scarlet colour suited the dress she wore and her lipstick so well they could all have been made for each other. He could spend the evening doing nothing more than stare at her and not feel any boredom.

'I was going to say that you're not my husband. But you are.' And then she laughed and drank half her gin and tonic in one go. 'You're my husband. God help me.' She said the latter with a sigh and a roll of her eyes but with a definite trace of resigned amusement.

'God help us both,' he said drily before raising his glass. 'To us and a marriage of the absurd.'

She chinked her glass to his and in unison they drank.

They had hardly placed their empty glasses on the table when their hostess returned with fresh drinks for them, placing them on the table before disappearing as unobtrusively as she'd arrived.

'Excellent service,' Eva commented idly. 'I can see that being rich has it perks.'

'And you will come to love those perks.'

She pulled a wry face.

'What would you rather be? Rich and miserable or poor and miserable?' he asked.

'Rich. But anyone would answer the same. Being poor is a horrible state to be in.'

'Have you ever been poor?'

'Not in the way the people of Caballeros and certain other countries are, but Johann and I struggled for years. I know what it's like to wonder if there's enough money to feed you until payday.'

'I'm surprised an intelligent woman like you didn't go to university.'

She glowed at the compliment in a way she never glowed when he complimented her on her looks.

'I *did* go to university. I did a degree in International Business and Languages in Amsterdam.'

'I thought you said you got married at eighteen?'

'I did. Being married and going into higher education aren't mutually exclusive.'

'How could you fund and support yourself doing a degree?'

'Johann worked.' She shrugged. 'I worked weekends and holidays. It wasn't easy but we managed. When I graduated I got a job as a translator at the Ministry of Foreign Affairs in The Hague and we stopped having to struggle so much. We could even afford to buy our own little apartment.'

'What did Johann do?'

'He worked in a bicycle shop.'

'He didn't have ambition for himself?'

'He had lots of ambition,' she said with a trace of sadness. 'He wanted to be an engineer but we couldn't afford for us both to study and support ourselves. He had so many dreams but he put them on the backburner so I could pursue mine and never got the chance to realise his own.'

Daniele's heart gave an unexpected lurch at the melancholy in her voice for her dead husband.

Did she still miss him? Was it because of her great love for him that she'd vowed never to remarry?

Why did that thought make him feel so inadequate? He'd worked hard for his money. He'd been fortunate to have wealthy parents who could afford to put him through university but he hadn't taken a cent from them since he'd graduated. He'd made a great success of his life and had the satisfaction of knowing everything he had he'd earned for himself.

But deep down he knew that whatever he did, he would never inspire anything like the loyalty and affection Eva held for Johann. She would always compare him to her first husband and find him wanting, just as his mother would always compare him to her first son and find him wanting.

It didn't matter. He would demand Eva's loyalty as his wife but he didn't need her approval. He didn't want her affection in any place other than the bedroom.

Just as he was telling himself he didn't care, that Eva's past meant nothing to him and was irrelevant to their own marriage, he heard himself say, 'You know what I don't understand?'

She shook her head and reached for her drink.

'Why you married so young.'

She contemplated him as she drank, this time through the straw, her eyes clearly saying, *I thought my past was irrelevant to you.*

'I'm curious,' he said with an affected nonchalance to overshadow the heavy thuds of his heart. 'Most intelligent modern women like yourself choose to marry later in their lives—my sister is an example of that.' At least she had been until she'd met Felipe and fallen madly in love. 'But you bucked that trend.'

She drank a little more, then cradled her glass in both hands.

He prepared himself for tales of teenage hormones and rebellion.

'We married to protect me.'

'What did you need protection from?' he asked with astonishment.

She contemplated him some more but now he couldn't read the meaning in her piercing eyes. A shutter had come down on them.

Then her chest rose and she gave the slightest nod before saying, 'Not what. Who. My parents.'

His astonishment doubled. 'You needed protection from your *parents*?'

Her lips pulled in before she gave another nod. 'I would say I left home on my eighteenth birthday but I didn't—I ran. Turning eighteen meant their authority over me ended but I wanted the protection marriage would give me. I didn't know what they would do to find me or the lengths they would go. Johann and I knew that if we married and I took his name it would make it harder for them, whatever they did. I was scared that if they found me they would go to the courts to try and force me back.'

Scared? Eva? He hadn't thought anything frightened her. 'Would they have been able to do that?'

'Legally no, but I know my parents. They would have tried anything they could. They would have had me declared incompetent or...anything, really.'

'But why?'

'Because I *belonged* to them. We all did. They gave us life and therefore they owned us. It was for them to choose what we wore and where we went and who we saw. They knew best about everything and their rules were rigid. If we didn't obey it was because there was something wrong with us and we needed to be punished.' She took another sip of her drink. Somehow she'd kept her composure throughout this brief retelling of her childhood that he knew hadn't even scratched the surface, seemingly relaxed into the sofa, her legs curled beneath her bottom, her eyes on his. She'd managed to keep her dress from riding any higher than her knees.

This composure was all surface, he was sure of it. There

were little signs to confirm it, the way her throat now moved of its own accord, the way her back teeth seemed to be grinding together.

Eva's family...

He'd wondered briefly why she hadn't invited them to the wedding but, assuming it was down to her not wanting to put her family through what they both considered to be a charade, hadn't questioned her about it.

A loud, booming voice suddenly chimed in his ear. 'Daniele Pellegrini! It's good to see you, man.'

Standing above them was the mountainous form of Talos Kalliakis.

Delighted to see him—and, he had to acknowledge, more delighted at the interruption of a conversation that had veered dangerously close to too personal and which he had been on the verge of taking further—Daniele got to his feet and embraced his old friend.

'What are you doing here? I didn't know you were planning a trip to Italy.'

'Amalie's playing at the Opera di Firenzi this week,' Talos replied, referring to Florence's new opera house, designed by an architect Daniele had long admired. He wasn't interested in the arts and culture itself but the buildings that housed them had sparked his imagination from a very young age. He remembered being dragged every few months to some production or other at the *Teatro di Pisa* as a child and spending all his time gawping at the brilliant interior rather than paying attention to the onstage production.

Talos's wife, Amalie, was a violinist who played so movingly that even Daniele could appreciate its beauty.

'You're on your own? Come, join us.' Then, turning to Eva, he made the introductions. 'Eva, this is my old friend, Talos Kalliakis. Talos, this is Eva...my...wife.'

'Your *wife*?' Talos didn't bother hiding his shock. 'You dark horse. I didn't know you'd got married.'

'That's because we only married today,' Eva piped up, getting to her feet and sticking her hand out to him. She'd had a few breathless moments there when she'd wondered exactly how Daniele was going to introduce her. 'Nice to meet you.'

It was *very* nice. The interruption was exactly what they'd needed.

Despite her best efforts over the years to move on and forget her torrid childhood, discussing her family and her past still had the power to hurt her. She could lay the facts out in simple, unambiguous language but the memories that lay behind them...

That was an area she would prefer not to delve into, especially with the man who'd explicitly told her that he had no interest in her past, hence no interest in *her*. Daniele desired only her body. She was a means to an end for him and she would do well to remember that, just as she had to remember that he was nothing but a means to an end for her too.

Ignoring her hand, the giant planted an enormous kiss on both her cheeks and embraced her tightly. 'Congratulations to you both. Are you sure it's okay to join you? I won't be offended if you'd rather be alone.' He looked quizzically at Daniele as he said this, clearly wondering why a married couple would spend their wedding night anywhere other than in bed.

'Not at all,' Daniele insisted in that relaxed, good-natured manner he had that Eva knew she would never be able to emulate. He took her hand and brought it to his lips. 'Eva and I have the rest of our lives to be alone.'

Talos called for champagne to be brought over and, before she knew it, the three of them had formed their own little group that slowly expanded as more people drifted over to join them, including the movie star Eva had been enraptured by earlier, more bottles of champagne were ordered as word got out that the notorious bachelor Daniele Pellegrini had finally settled down.

CHAPTER EIGHT

EVA STARED AT the eclectic mix in which they were the star attraction with that old feeling of falling into a vortex engulfing her again. It didn't help that Daniele kept her so close to him for the rest of the evening that she ended up squished against him on the sofa with his arm around her and his large warm hand resting possessively on her thigh. He made sure she was included in all the conversations and, to the natural question asked *ad infinitum* of how they'd met, he proudly told them all about her work in Caballeros. He even sounded genuine about it, which thrilled her more than she cared to admit.

These were some of the richest and most famous people in the world and they were treating her as their equal. She almost choked on her champagne when she realised Talos was, in fact, a prince and that his wife was the violinist whose latest album Eva had downloaded. When they finally left it was with a dozen invitations to parties and dinner ringing in her ears.

'What did you think?' Daniele asked when they were in the back of the car, his driver taking them back to the *castello*. 'Did you enjoy yourself?'

'It was surreal but, yes, I did.' She'd surprised herself by how much she'd enjoyed it. She'd felt like a fish out of water but his friends had been so hospitable and welcoming—even if some of the women had looked at her a little bit too pityingly for her liking—that she'd almost relaxed.

'I thought you did amazingly.' His admiration sounded as genuine as his pride when discussing her work. She hadn't expected that, not for a minute.

But Daniele was proving to be nowhere near as shallow as she'd thought when she'd first met him. She'd formed preconceptions about him, which his behaviour on their 'date' had confirmed for her. She hadn't given him any credit for what he was doing in Caballeros; a project that his brother had set in motion. The brother who had died just a month before their date.

Other than the flirting, she hadn't seen any sign of that selfish, shallow behaviour since. Quite the opposite if she was being honest. On the whole, he was a perfect gentleman.

'Thank you,' she said softly.

'For what?'

'For including me. For not ignoring me.'

'Why would I do that?' he asked, seemingly bemused.

Suddenly she realised they were still holding hands.

She carefully disentangled her fingers from his and put her hands together on her lap. Her fingers tingled their disappointed resentment.

'I don't know.' She took a long breath. 'I hadn't thought about what would happen when we met your friends. It just surprised me that you included me in the conversations. I guess I had an image in my head that when rich men get together the cigars come out and the little women are banished to another room.'

'If that still happens it's not in the circles I mix in.' He didn't sound put out by her less than charitable pre-assessment.

'Have you taken many women there before?' She couldn't summon the courage to ask if any of the women with the pitying stares had been ex-girlfriends of his.

Had they pitied her because of their own pasts with him or were those looks based solely on his reputation?

Why did it even matter? It shouldn't. His past held no more interest to her than hers did to him...

She felt his hand cover hers and had to close her eyes and will herself not to take hold of it again.

'*Tesoro*, would you do me a favour?'

'If I can.'

'Stop assuming the worst of me. I'm not an angel. I know my reputation with women isn't good—and deservedly, I admit—but I'm not the pig you think. I meant what I said when we first discussed marriage, about it being based on respect. I would never be so disrespectful as to take you somewhere I've taken other women.'

She opened her eyes and turned her head to face his intent stare. 'I'm starting to believe that,' she murmured.

'Good.' Then he ruined it all by grinning lasciviously at her and kissing her knuckles. 'And I also meant what I said when I promised to try and seduce you at every given opportunity.'

She glared at him but couldn't quite summon her usual force, not when her whole body now ached to be kissed in places far more intimate than her hands.

'You can let go of my hand now,' she said, hating that her voice pitched itself so low.

He laughed in as low a pitch but did as she said. 'I'm starting to think that marriage to you is going to be fun.'

She flexed her fingers. 'I'm a laugh a minute.'

'You're a lot more fun than I thought you would be,' he admitted, twisting so he faced her with his whole body.

'I've never had much time to explore my fun side,' she said drily. 'I've always been too busy studying and working.' She didn't add that the concept of fun had been banned in her household when growing up. Fun was something other families had, not the van Bastens.

'I've always studied and worked hard too,' he pointed out. 'It never stopped me having fun.'

'I don't imagine there's anything that would stop you in your pursuit of pleasure.'

'*You're* stopping me,' he said, dropping his head a touch to look woebegone, but then his eyes sparkled and he inched closer to her. 'But not for much longer, and I can promise you the pleasure will belong to us both.'

'Do you only think of sex?' She shouldn't be encouraging this conversation but sense seemed to have gone out of the window. And she shouldn't be leaning closer to him...

'Have you not looked in a mirror? What man wouldn't look at you and think of sex?'

'I am more than just my body.'

'And I am more than just my sex drive. I'm learning to appreciate all your other qualities too.'

'If you're more than just your sex drive, why do you hate marriage so much?'

'I don't hate marriage. It's just an institution I never wanted to join. But now that I have joined it, I mean to make the most of its positive aspects, which involves sleeping beside your warm, delicious body every night.'

With her body leaning ever closer to his, Daniele's gorgeous mouth near enough that one quick push forward would link their lips together, it was with great relief that Eva saw the lights of the *castello* glowing brightly in the night sky.

She snatched a breath and forced herself away from him.

They were home. It was time to go to bed.

Daniele stoked the fire before getting into the four-poster bed that had been a feature of the *castello* for so many years it was considered an antique. He'd already replaced the curtains on the high window with the thickest available, and made a mental note to call his head contractor in the morning. He wasn't prepared to wait a day longer. The renovation of this wing would start immediately.

His thoughts puffed away when Eva emerged from the bathroom with her thick robe wrapped around her.

Her composure, as had become her trademark, was exactly as it always was. It had been the same when she'd first stepped into his room and looked around it coolly before giving a little nod that he took to be approval.

He'd arranged for the staff to move her stuff over to his bedroom while they were out, and she'd opened the doors to her new dressing room, which had been used by his ancestors as a prayer room, as if she'd opened them a hundred times before. She'd selected her nightwear then gone into the bathroom as if it were something she'd been doing for years.

It was only as she walked barefoot to their bed that he saw a faltering in her step.

She slid under the sheets and gave a little gasp. 'You don't use any kind of bed warmer?'

Not tonight he didn't. Tonight he'd left deliberate instructions to the staff not to warm the bed for them. Underhanded but necessary. 'If you're cold I'm very happy to warm you.'

'I'll get warm without your help soon enough.' She flashed a knowing smile at him. 'Especially if I keep my robe on over my pyjamas.'

'Are they sexy pyjamas?'

Settling onto her side and burrowing under the covers so only the top of her vibrant red hair peeked through, she said, 'If you won't use a bed warmer you'll never find out. Goodnight, Daniele.'

'No goodnight kiss for your new husband?'

'No.'

'It *is* our wedding night.'

'Happy wedding night.'

Laughing softly, Daniele switched the bedside light off, pitching the room into black. Done, he settled himself down as close to the middle of the bed as he could without encroaching on her space in a way she could complain about, facing towards her.

Well, facing towards her back, which his eyes took a while to adjust to the darkness to see with any form of clarity.

He could smell the faint trace of her shampoo. And the mint of her toothpaste. And the remnants of the perfume she wore, which he was coming to adore.

She shifted a little, her movements those of someone trying to get warm.

'Still cold?'

'I'm warming.'

They fell into silence, the only sound the rustling of the sheets where Eva had entangled herself.

'Are you always such a fidget?' he teased.

'Do you always talk so much?'

'I can get you warm.'

'I'm fine.'

'Prove it and stop fidgeting.'

'I don't have to prove anything.' But she stopped moving. For almost a whole minute before the rustling started again.

Grinning to himself, Daniele inched closer and lifted the sheets where they were tight across her back.

'What are you doing?' she asked sharply.

'Using my body heat to warm you. Don't worry, you're perfectly safe.'

'Touch me inappropriately and *you* won't be.'

Taking full advantage of her tacit, if reluctant agreement, Daniele hooked an arm across her belly, taking great care not to touch her anywhere she could deem inappropriate, and pulled her so she was spooned against him.

'Better?' he asked into the top of her head. The strands of her hair brushing the underside of his chin had the texture of silk.

She gave a noncommittal mumble. She was hardly melting into him but neither was she attempting to escape.

It surprised him how good this felt, just holding her. He wasn't going to try anything else—though he wouldn't mind in the least if she turned over and jumped on him—and found himself content to simply lie there with her voluptuous curves nestled against him, all the scents that combined to make *her* filling his senses.

It was too much to expect his loins to behave with the same decorum as the rest of him. He'd fantasised about getting Eva into his bed for weeks and having her in his arms, even as chastely as this, was playing havoc with his reactions to her.

He heard an intake of breath and knew she could feel his lack of decorum for herself.

'Relax,' he murmured. 'You're safe.'

She must have believed him for she sighed but stayed exactly where she was. When he moved his hand over her belly and the tie of her robe knotted around it, and found her hand, she didn't resist when he covered it with his own. When he laced his fingers through hers he felt the lightest of pressure in return.

Her fingers were cold.

A smattering of guilt settled in him. Eva had lived in the Caribbean for...how long, he didn't know. He hadn't asked. But he knew it had been a long time. The only thing Caballeros had going for it was its year-round sunny climate. She must have adjusted to that and now she was living here in this draught-ridden ancient castle in a winter far colder than was the norm for this region, she was having to adjust again.

She hadn't complained. She'd simply got on and coped with the cold draughts and mostly ineffective log fires. If he'd known how much she felt the cold he would have got his tradesmen in immediately to sort their living quarters out, not decide to concentrate on getting as up to date with his work as he could before their wedding.

And he would have got the bed warmed up for them too. Wanting her to be a little bit cold so he could take advantage of it was a different matter from making her body temperature plunge to that akin to a fridge.

But she *was* warming up now. And relaxing.

His heart beating harder with every passing second, Daniele willed himself to relax too.

It was a long struggle, one he knew he'd brought on himself by holding her so close, even with that thick robe separating their bodies. The only parts of their flesh that touched were their hands, which neither of them seemed to be in any hurry to part.

'Can I ask you something?' she whispered just as his brain was starting to switch off.

'Sure.'

'You've had so many lovers…didn't you have feelings for *any* of them?'

So she was thinking of him with lovers…

He didn't know if that was a good thing or a bad thing. Probably the latter, which he couldn't blame her for.

'There were some I liked more than others,' he answered honestly, his mind flickering to a few years back when he'd been dating a French model who'd been capable of holding a decent conversation. Not a decent conversation like he could have with Eva but compared to his other girlfriends she'd been an Einstein. He hadn't bored of her as quickly as he usually did. A few weeks into their relationship—a record for him—he'd taken her to a party at an embassy in Paris that his brother had also attended. She'd spent the entire night flirting with Pieta, who'd made no effort to discourage her even though he'd been engaged to Natasha, who in turn had been absent from the event. Daniele had dumped her without a backward glance. Whenever he thought of that night it wasn't her he thought of but his brother.

Daniele had been the one with the reputation of a Lothario but he would never have flirted with Natasha or any of Pieta's girlfriends that had come before her. He would never flirt with any woman who had a partner. His sense of honour might be warped in some people's view but his loyalty was absolute. It had angered and astounded him that Perfect Pieta's honour and loyalty could be so fickle and that he could have been so blind to it.

'But none you would have considered marrying instead of me?' she asked in the same soft whisper.

'No.' His fingers tightened against hers reflexively. He didn't want to think of his brother and his less than perfect behaviour. He needed to remember the good, not the bad, and there had been far more of the former. 'You are the only woman I could have taken this step with.'

He knew with a certainty that he couldn't explain that Eva would never demean herself or be so insensitive as to flirt with a man when she belonged to someone else.

Not that she belonged to him, he quickly reminded himself. Of course not. And if she could read that thought he was quite sure she'd kick him.

But none of this did anything to alter the proprietorial feeling in his chest as he held her so tight against him.

Eva awoke feeling as snug as she'd ever felt in her life, so warm and dreamy that she was reluctant to open her eyes and break the spell.

Daniele's large warm body was still pressed against hers, keeping her warm as if he were her own life-sized hot-water bottle. At some point in the night their fingers had unlocked and his hand had burrowed under the knotted tie of her dressing gown and through its gap to rest over her pyjama top on her belly.

She hadn't thought she'd be able to sleep in the same bed as him but she'd slept as deeply and sweetly as a baby. She'd felt his erection pressing against her. The heat it had conjured... It had been enough for her to move away from him with the truth that she was no longer cold.

But she'd stayed exactly where she was. She hadn't wanted to move. She'd ached to press back against him and tempt him into acting on his desire and kiss the word 'no' away from her lips...

That same feeling was in her now. An ache that had spread into every part of her, heat pooled so low and so deep inside that she had to fight to remember all the very good reasons why she was determined to keep their marriage platonic.

She inhaled deeply through her nose then opened her eyes. The darkness that had cloaked them throughout the night had turned into a grey haze, the morning sun struggling to filter through the room's thick heavy curtains as much as she was struggling to understand the depth of her craving for the man she'd married.

Pushing the covers off her in one decisive movement, Eva climbed out of bed and hurried to the bathroom.

Once safely locked inside her temporary sanctuary, she stepped into the shower and prayed for the steaming water to rinse her of these feelings that had broken through the shell she'd erected around herself.

'Did you sleep well, *tesoro*?'

Eva looked up from the cup of coffee she'd just put to her lips and felt her heart lurch dangerously. After finishing in the bathroom she'd slipped into her dressing room. As she'd been deciding what to wear she'd heard the shower start and known Daniele was up and about.

Suddenly feeling shy for reasons she couldn't comprehend, she'd dressed quickly and shoved her damp hair back in a ponytail, wincing to see her dark roots poking through on her hairline. In a couple of days it would be noticeable.

She'd then hurried through the bedroom before he could appear from the bathroom and had taken herself to the dining area. A member of staff had arrived with a tray of coffee and a selection of fruit, cold meats, cheeses and fresh pastries for breakfast, looking disappointed when Eva had turned down the offer of something cooked.

This was the first she'd seen of Daniele since she'd hightailed it from his bed.

Was she imagining it or did he get even more handsome every time she looked at him?

Today he'd dressed casually in black chinos and a round-necked chunky grey flecked sweater. His mussed hair was still damp and he carried the strong scent of shower gel and fresh cologne.

His eyes sparkled as they met hers.

She cleared her throat discreetly and stopped her hand from pressing against her racing heart. 'Well enough, thank you. And you?'

'Well enough for a man who feared his balls turning blue,' he said with a grin that could only be described as sinful.

She cleared her throat again. 'Perhaps you wouldn't have that problem if you slept on your own.'

He shook his head with mock regret. 'I have been suffering from chronic unfulfilled desire since you moved in with me. Just thinking of you in a bed is enough.' He tilted his head as if considering this assertion. 'Actually, just thinking of *you* is enough.'

'Coffee?' she suggested pointedly.

'I don't think that works as a cure for Chronic Unfulfilled Desire syndrome but, yes, please.'

Trying to disguise the tremors in her hands, she poured him a cup and pushed it across the table to where he'd just sat down and helped himself to a Danish pastry.

'Thank you,' he said with a grin. 'Now eat up and pack a bag.'

'Are we going away?'

'Only to my house in Siena for a couple of days. The weather's not any better but the house has proper insulation. I've got my men coming in to make some changes here so you don't feel like you're sleeping in an igloo.'

But that was the problem, she mused a short while later while selecting some clothes to take with her. She'd liked sleeping in an igloo. She'd liked that it had meant she could accept the warmth of Daniele's body insulating her.

CHAPTER NINE

DANIELE'S HOME ON the outskirts of Siena turned out to be a sprawling villa of his own design, sympathetic to the city's heritage yet undeniably modern. It was so well insulated Eva could have walked around naked without feeling a chill.

They took a leisurely drive there, stopping at a traditional Italian restaurant in a hillside town for some lunch, spent the afternoon touring around the cathedral; the evening in yet another restaurant where they dined on *ribolitta* soup and *pappardelle* pasta and a Chianti so smooth Eva had to resist drinking more than two glasses.

As the climate in his home was so constant, she got into the bed without her dressing gown on but with her pyjamas fully done up. Refusing, again, Daniele's seductive request for a good-night kiss, she'd again slept with her back to him.

In the morning, though, she'd awoken to find herself spooned against him, his hand holding her belly and a heavy thigh draped over hers, and the warm sensation of desire curling through her veins.

Not until she'd slipped out of the bed without waking him did she notice where on the bed they'd slept curled together. She must have inched her way back to meet him in the middle.

The same thing happened the next night too, but this time Eva woke to find herself curled in his arms with her face pressed against his bare chest, breathing in his warm, musky scent. She'd gone from feeling like she was in some kind of drugged state to being wide awake in an instant and shot out of the bed quicker than a rocket. When her pulses had finally calmed enough for her to leave the sanctuary of the bathroom she'd pretended not to see the knowing gleam in his eyes.

She would deny this attraction for ever if she could. She would ignore her surging heart rate evoked by a simple look and her raging pulses whenever his hand brushed against her.

After two nights and a lazy morning spent wandering around a museum, they made the drive back to the cold *castello* so they could get ready for a night out with Francesca and Felipe, who were in Pisa for the day.

As soon as they drove into the courtyard Eva could see something major had happened in their absence.

Scaffolding had been erected around their wing, an army of men working against the cold December air repointing the stonework.

The first thing she noticed when they reached their quarters was the lack of draught.

'New windows,' Daniele explained with a grin. 'Wait until you see our bedroom.'

She took one step inside and came to an abrupt halt.

Daniele watched her reaction closely. 'What do you think?'

'I had no idea you were doing this,' she said a little breathlessly, turning to him with a look of wonder.

In the short time they'd been gone his team of contractors had redecorated, replacing the old wallpaper with a gold-leaf pattern that remained sympathetic to the *castello*'s heritage but with a much more modern twist, and new, thicker carpet put on the floor. The hearth had been cleaned out and heavy curtains that matched the ones he'd had put up on the window were tied back on the posts of the bed.

'I think you'll find the insulation in here much more effective now,' he said, breaking the silence. 'I figured I had to do something to warm the *castello* just in case the cold spurred you into running away with all the money I give you.'

'We've only been married for three days. Give me time.' But the softness in her eyes suggested that any thoughts of ending their marriage quickly had been put aside.

She was softening towards him like a snowman melting in the thaw.

'Do I get a thank-you kiss for doing all this?' he asked.

Expecting her to pull a face or make a sarcastic retort, he was taken aback when she closed the space between them, rested her hands lightly on his shoulders and pressed her lips on his cheek.

Her lips were as soft as he'd imagined but she pulled away too quickly from him.

'You call that a kiss?' he demanded, snatching at her wrists and holding them with enough strength that she couldn't wriggle out.

Colour slashed her face and the blue of her eyes darkened. 'What kind of a kiss were you thinking of?'

Never one to look a gift horse in the mouth if there was the chance delay or further conversation might make it bolt, he tugged her so she was pressed flush against him, close enough for him to feel the little quivers of excitement racing through her.

'One like this,' he whispered, releasing her hands and sliding his fingers up her arms and over her shoulders to cradle her face and fuse his mouth to hers.

There was only the slightest resistance from her, a quick inhaled gasp of shock that turned as quickly into a sigh before she almost seemed to sink into his kiss.

Desire, never far from the surface these days, bloomed through his veins, the heat of her mouth and the heat of her response stoking it. Her tongue darted into his mouth, all the encouragement he needed to deepen the kiss and move his hands from her face to tug out the band holding her ponytail in place and spear her silky hair and cradle her head tightly.

But then, all too soon, Eva broke it, turning her face so his lips lingered on her cheek.

'You can stop now,' she said in a voice that seemed to be searching for air and not at all as confident as she usually sounded.

His groin aching, Daniele closed his eyes and breathed in deeply, which only made things worse as he inhaled her wonderful unique scent.

'You're killing me,' he groaned.

She gave a short laugh. 'I think I might be killing us both.'

'Then what's stopping you?'

Backing away from him and gathering her hair at the back of her head, ready to tie it back but either forgetting or not realising he had it in his hand, she bit into her lip.

'Daniele,' she began, her voice still not quite working properly. She took another breath then said, 'I've only been with one man. I've been celibate for six years. I'm...' She blinked, clearly struggling to find the word to explain what she was feeling. 'I'm scared, okay?'

'Of me?'

She shook her head and looked away from him. 'Of how I feel.'

His stomach lurched. 'And how do you feel?'

'Confused.' She dropped her hold on her hair and it fell softly over her shoulders and down her back. 'I've never experienced desire before. I didn't know it could make a sensible head want irrational things.'

His brain pulsed at the admission she'd never felt desire before him and with it came the instinct to put a stop to this conversation. He didn't need to know any more details.

He already knew she'd been married for four years and that she'd married Johann to escape from her parents. That was more than enough. He didn't want to complicate their marriage with feelings. Especially not his own.

But to hear that she'd never felt desire for the man whose memory he'd been fighting against thinking of as a rival...

To hear *he* was the first man she'd ever experienced desire for...

'There is nothing irrational about wanting someone,' he said carefully, knowing he was avoiding asking the question of what irrational things her head wanted and knowing it had to be this way. 'Desire is what makes the world turn, whether it's the desire for money or power or for another person; it's what drives us. I want you. You want me. We're married. What's irrational about any of that?'

She looked back at him with what looked like a touch of sadness. 'You make it sound so simple.'

'It's only complicated if you make it so.'

After holding his gaze a moment longer, her shoulders dropped and she gave a short laugh. 'Yes, you're right. I do have a tendency to overthink things.'

He held his arms out wide. 'Then stop overthinking and come here.'

But she stayed where she was, a smile playing on her lips. 'I'll think about it.'

Strolling to her, he took her face in his hands and planted a firm kiss on her mouth. 'There,' he whispered in her ear. 'That will help you think.'

Then he let her go and strode to the bathroom. 'And when we go to bed tonight... I promise to help you think some more.'

Francesca and Felipe were in excellent spirits at the exclusive but friendly restaurant they met up at in Pisa. Exclusive but friendly, Eva was coming to think, perfectly summed up the Pellegrinis.

Listening to Francesca speak nineteen to the dozen about their new home and all their wedding plans almost took Eva's mind off the kiss she and Daniele had shared...

She shivered just thinking of it.

She mustn't think of it. Not here. Not now. Not in a restaurant where people would notice the heat she still felt from it spreading over her neck and face.

So she made a concerted effort to forget all about it and forget about what the night would bring, and relaxed into the warmth and camaraderie, heightened at the waves and hails from other diners recognising them, some stopping to exchange a few words. Daniele knew so many people; had so many friends.

It felt that she'd spent her entire life keeping people at arm's length. Most people learned to make friends in childhood but Eva had never acquired the skill. Friendships had been discouraged. Inviting a fellow child over for a playdate had been a non-starter. It had taken her a year to pluck up the courage to return one of Johann's shy, sweet smiles. After they'd married and with his help, she'd become better at socialising but he'd remained the only real friend she'd ever had. Until now. Daniele had a wide circle of friends all eager to welcome her into it.

A couple with a sleeping baby heading for the exit spotted them and came over to say hello, the father introduced as an old friend of Daniele's. The baby, on the verge of becoming a toddler, shifted in his arms, yawned widely then opened her eyes and fixed them on Eva.

Eva smiled automatically and found herself on the receiving end of a smile so wide and adorable that she couldn't resist reaching out to stroke the little girl's chubby cheek.

'She likes you,' the mother observed with an indulgent smile at her daughter.

'She's beautiful,' she said simply, her eyes soaking in the plump wrists now waving at her and the small tuft of blonde hair, and felt something move in her heart strong enough to steal her breath.

Such a beautiful, beautiful child...

She'd never thought of having children before. When she'd been married to Johann it had been hard enough scraping the money together to feed themselves, never mind bringing a child into their world. Since he'd died, she'd been on her own, closed off from everyone, so shut off from her own emotions that the thought of children hadn't even entered her head. She loved the children at the camp in Caballeros but in the detached way infant teachers loved their little charges.

Since Daniele had steamrollered her into his life all those shut-off emotions had started seeping out, a gentle trickle that she could feel building momentum inside her.

For the first time she allowed herself to imagine what it would be like to have a child of her own. Someone to love. Someone to love her.

Then she looked at Daniele and saw his gaze was fixed firmly on her, just as it always seemed to be, and her heart moved again.

They could have a baby together.

As quickly as the thought came, she pushed it away.

They'd only been married for five minutes, far too soon to be thinking of having a child together. A child meant a lifetime commitment and that was one thing she hadn't promised him. She could walk away whenever she wanted.

Her eyes flickered to his again. He was grinning at something Francesca had said. He must have run his hands through his hair since she'd last looked for the top was sticking up. She longed to reach out and smooth it down, then let her hand move down to the nape of his neck.

Another delicious anticipatory shiver raced up her spine.

Their marriage would last as long as she wanted and right then she knew she had no intention of walking away from it.

Daniele held Eva's hand in the back of the car as they were driven back to the *castello*. Rather than delight that she seemed content to let him hold it, he found his mind going over everything he'd discovered about her that evening courtesy of his nosy sister's incessant questioning.

He'd learned Eva had spent her first three years with the Blue Train Aid Agency working in the poorest countries in Africa, co-ordinating food aid and medicine and making sure it got to the people who'd needed it. As she'd put it, 'Lots of paperwork.' She'd been transferred to Caballeros a year ago on the basis that she spoke Spanish, again co-ordinating food aid and medicine to those in need, which in that country was a significant percentage of its people. When the hurricane hit, she'd been fortunate to take shelter with her colleagues in the concrete building they'd been using as an office. That Eva and her colleagues had been right there, ready to swing into action and get working on the refugee camp, had been sheer luck.

That's what she'd called it—luck. Luck that she'd been stuck in the middle of one of the most powerful hurricanes on record. She'd related it so matter-of-factly that he could believe she hadn't experienced any fear during it. Eva had said as much when questioned about it by an agog Francesca.

'There was nothing for me to be scared of,' she'd said with a small shrug. 'If it was my time then it was my time.'

That she could be so blasé about her own safety, her own *life*, had sent chills up his spine and through his bloodstream. Those chills were still there in his veins.

What kind of life had she lived where she could see no value to it?

He released her hand and ran his fingers through his hair.

'I've been thinking, you could start your own consultancy business advising the rich and famous how best to help those in need.'

She blinked at him in surprise. 'Really?'

'Why not? You didn't want to give up your job and I know you were bored in the days running up to our wedding. It can be as formal or as informal as you like. People like to be philanthropic but it's not always easy knowing where to start or knowing that the money they give is going where they think it's going. You must have lots of contacts in the charity world.' He raised his palms. 'It's something to think about.'

She nodded slowly. 'You continually surprise me.'

'In what way?'

'When we met I thought you were nothing but a selfish play-boy but you're not, are you? Beneath your don't-care exterior I see a man who does care and does want to help. You've donated money to good causes before, haven't you.'

It wasn't phrased as a question.

'Guilt money. I leave the true philanthropy to others.' Like his brother.

She twisted a little in the seat, her eyes holding his and study-ing him as if she was trying to read him. 'At least you're hon-est about your motives and don't use it to further an agenda or because you crave adulation.'

'You know people who do that?'

She nodded. 'For some, I get the impression that their phi-lanthropy is an act.'

'An act? In what way?'

She grimaced. 'Please, don't think I'm speaking badly of them. What they do is wonderful, whatever their motives. It's just that there's some I never think mean it on an emotional level. You understand what I mean? That it's all for show? That it's the adulation and plaudits they crave, not a genuine, emotional de-sire to help or make things better. Only some of them, I should add. I met many you could see genuinely cared.'

'What about my brother? What category did you put him in?'

Expecting the usual waffle of what an amazing man Pieta was, he was slightly thrown when she hesitated and bit into her lip.

'You put my brother in the category of doing his great acts of philanthropy for the adulation?' he asked slowly, a prickle of anger setting loose inside him.

'I didn't say that.'

'You don't deny it.'

'I only met him a couple of times and never on a one-to-one basis. I hardly knew him.'

Her evasive non-answer made the prickles deepen. 'You thought you knew him well enough to judge him.'

'I didn't judge him,' she protested. 'He was an amazing person—what he did to help those in need was incredible...'

'But you still felt he did it for show.' His heart battering against his ribs, Daniele leaned forward. 'My brother did more than anyone I know to help others. He spent so much time fundraising and organising projects for his foundation and going into dangerous situations with little thought to his own safety because he wanted to help and he knew he was in a position to help, and he never took a cent for himself, unlike charity employees such as yourself who are paid a salary for your good works. And you have the nerve to criticise him?'

Eva remained incredibly still during his tirade. He didn't know where that had come from, spoken even as the rational part of his brain knew he was being unfair to her but unable to stop.

In his entire life he had never heard a word of criticism towards his brother. Not one word.

'I didn't criticise him,' she refuted steadily but with a tremor in her voice. 'You asked for my thoughts and I gave them. Your brother did incredible things, and nothing can or should change that, certainly not my private opinion, which isn't worth anything.'

Daniele breathed deeply and dug his fingers into the car seat.

Painful as it was to acknowledge, Eva's opinion matched precisely his own. He'd always thought Pieta's good deeds were for show, a way to display to the world what a magnificent man he was. He'd never believed it had come from the heart.

But his private thoughts towards his brother were one thing. He was his brother, it was his job to pick faults and criticise. No one else's.

'You have a right to your opinion,' he said, doing his best to modulate his tone. 'But you should remember that he was my brother and I will always defend him.'

'I understand,' she said quietly. 'Families are complicated but the bonds can be very powerful. Even when they're the worst kind of human, the instinct to protect them is strong.'

He didn't have to ask to know she spoke from experience and that fired the stabbing prickles in his blood off again.

He wouldn't ask for details. He didn't want to know any more about her. Their marriage was supposed to be a long-term parlour game where emotions were placed in the box labelled 'no', a marriage that was a means to an end for them both.

Their vows were supposed to tie them together in a figurative sense.

He wasn't supposed to feel anything for her but desire.

CHAPTER TEN

EVA COULDN'T UNDERSTAND why she felt so wretched. She hadn't said anything derogatory about Daniele's brother but she knew she'd angered him.

She wished she'd kept her mouth shut. She hadn't been thinking of his brother when she'd mentioned the philanthropists who did their good deeds for the adulation. She'd been thinking of Daniele and how beneath the seemingly egotistical, selfish outer layer lived a good, thoughtful man who had no need for adulation. She was coming to think adulation was something he actively worked against receiving.

The last ten minutes of the drive back to the *castello* had been conducted in silence. When they'd pulled up in the courtyard, he'd got out first and offered his hand to help her, but instead of taking the opportunity to keep hold of it as he usually did, he'd dropped it as soon as she was on her feet.

The silence had continued all the way to the now warm bedroom. He'd offered her the use of the en suite, muttering something about using the bathroom next door before walking back out again.

So she'd taken a shower, wishing she knew the words to say to make things right between them again.

After drying herself, she stared at the clean pyjamas she'd brought in to change into and swallowed, indecision racking her.

It amazed and scared her how quickly her feelings towards Daniele had changed. Her relationship with Johann had developed over many years, sweetly and shyly. In his own way, Johann had been as sheltered as she had, a small-town boy with big dreams and an even bigger heart. Love and friendship had been their driving force, not, she was sad to acknowledge, passion. When she'd looked at him she would feel content and safe. When she'd kissed him she'd felt comfort.

When she looked at Daniele she felt as if she had two hearts beating in her chest. When he'd kissed her she'd felt her desire for him like it had a heart and life of its own, a blazing force of nature she'd only just managed to tame.

Not tame. No, that was the wrong word. How could you tame a force of nature? All you could do was run away and hope you ran fast enough to beat it, or hide somewhere and hope your hiding place was good enough to save you. All she had done to escape the feelings that had roared through her with their kiss had been to run, but she knew she could never run fast enough to escape it. For as long as she was with Daniele, it would be there, glowing red-hot between them, provoking and tempting her to fight her fears and confront it.

But what was she even frightened *of*? It was only sex.

She was overthinking things again.

Sex had always meant so little to her before so why blow it up out of all proportion now? She'd told Daniele right from the beginning that she would never have sex with him because she'd needed to keep some power in her own hands and because their marriage was a contract based on money and she could never countenance having her body used as a form of return payment. To her, it would have been nothing short of prostitution.

Her feelings had changed. *They'd* changed. Making love with him... It wouldn't be prostitution. What power would making love give him over her? She was free to leave whenever she wished.

Suddenly she snatched at her robe hanging on the door and, still naked, slipped it on, tying it securely around her waist.

No more thinking. No more worrying. No more complicating things in her own mind when the facts of the matter were simple.

She wanted Daniele and he wanted her. What was there to fear about that? What was there to fear about acting on it?

Not prepared to hang around in the bathroom a moment longer and give her imagination the time to answer, she opened the door and stepped into the bedroom.

Daniele was already in bed, lying on his side under the covers, facing the wall. He'd turned the main light off, leaving her bedside one on.

There was no movement from him, no acknowledgement of her presence.

Softly she stepped over to her side of the bed. Instead of climbing in, she untied the curtain tied to the post and pulled it to the centre of the bar connecting the posts together.

He turned over slowly onto his back.

With Daniele watching her wordlessly, she made her way around the bed, untying the curtains and drawing them shut until the entire bed was surrounded by the heavy maroon drapes. Then she slipped between the two that had come together on Daniele's side. They fell back into place with a swoosh, enclosing them in.

It was like stepping into the past. She could imagine his ancestors doing the very same thing centuries ago, closing off the world along with the chill of the night air. The utmost in privacy. The only illumination came from the soft glow of tiny lights running atop the wooden headboard, which he must have switched on while she'd been closing the drapes, bathing them in a flickering red glow.

Daniele now had a hand behind his head and was staring at her with an incomprehensible expression in his eyes.

Eva stood beside him and placed her hand on the bedspread that covered the rest of the sheets on the bed, all resting on his chest. Working from his stomach, she smoothed her hand up the sheets until she reached the top and then, not giving doubt or fear any space in her head, pulled them down to his feet.

Then she just stood there and drank him in.

In all the time they'd been living together she'd only seen him fully clothed, never bare, not even those nights they'd slept together and he'd slept nude beside her.

He was naked now and he was glorious.

Muscular legs and thighs led up to snake hips between which jutted an erection so huge she almost blinked to make sure it wasn't a trick of the flickering light, reaching up to his flat navel. His chest was muscular and defined with a light smattering of dark hair in the space between his brown nipples.

Deep inside her something throbbed and pulsed, the force of nature she'd been running from awakening and curling its tendrils through her veins. She welcomed its hold, her resistance a thing of the past.

This was now. This was what she wanted; what they both wanted.

Her gaze drifted back down to his large and surprisingly handsome feet. She'd never known feet could be handsome. She reached out and placed her hand flat on the right one. His toes made a little wiggling motion. Slowly and gently she traced her fingers over his ankle and up the leg and thigh, over the washboard stomach covered in fine dark hair that pulled in at her touch, past the straining erection, up over his rapidly rising and falling chest and collarbone, up the side of his neck to his jawline, coming to a stop when she reached his mouth.

His lips parted and he strained towards her. Pressing her forefinger down on his lips in lieu of a kiss, she then, finally, sat on the edge of the bed beside him.

Keeping her gaze on his now darkly hooded eyes, she unknotted the sash around her waist.

Her robe fell open, exposing her to him as he was exposed to her. The widening of his eyes and the movement of his throat drove away any shyness she might have felt.

She took the hand resting by his side and held it between hers. He made no movement, letting her run her fingers over the length of his, so much longer and thicker than hers, and stroke the smooth palm before brushing her lips over it and tracing the lifeline scored on it with her tongue.

His breathing had deepened, become ragged.

Then she placed his hand on her aching breast.

The sensation it evoked was like heated darts firing through her skin and her head rocked back with the force of it.

Daniele felt as if he'd fallen asleep and woken to the most erotic dream he could have wished for.

All the tormented emotions he'd carried up to the bedroom were forgotten.

With the bed curtains drawn around them it could be only the two of them in this world.

Eva was seducing *him*.

He could hardly believe it was real.

The heavy weight of her breast in his hand felt real. The breathless sigh that escaped her mouth when he gently squeezed it sounded real. It sounded like his dreams come to life.

He'd never seen such concentrated desire as he did then from the ice-blue eyes that had become so heated they could be molten.

He'd never felt such desire within himself.

Such beautiful breasts, he thought dimly. He'd imagined them more times than he could ever count but they surpassed everything his feeble brain could conjure, as white as snow with nipples as pink as pale raspberries, and the texture...the texture of satin.

All of her was beautiful. Exquisite.

He stared again into her eyes and felt the connection between them flow like a running tide.

Raising himself up, he put a hand to her slender waist and took her breast in his mouth.

Her head rocked back again, a mew escaping from the lips he suddenly hungered to kiss.

He caught hold of the robe hanging open on her and tugged it off so she was as naked as him and then turned his attention to her other breast, kissing and licking it, his desire heightening when her hands cradled his head, her fingers digging into his skull, and she arched into him, silently asking for more.

He needed to kiss her.

But first he wanted to look at her again.

Taking hold of her hips, he used his strength to lift her so she straddled him, then lay back down.

One small adjustment and he could be inside her.

His erection gave a powerful throb at the thought and he concentrated his mind away from the ultimate pleasure that would come soon enough.

Eva's long red hair had spilled over her shoulders and over the heavy yet pert breasts that tasted like nectar. Her stomach had a rounded womanly softness to it...*she* was soft. All of her, a complete contrast to the hardness of his own body. The perfect complement to him.

How could he have imagined her like marble?

He reached out to palm her stomach then walked the tips of his fingers lower to touch the dark downy hair between her legs...his instinct that she was a natural brunette had been proven right. She quivered and closed her eyes.

Then she leaned down and her hair spilled over him as her mouth found his and he was pulled into a kiss so deep and full of meaning he could drown in it. Her tongue swept into his mouth and he caught that taste again, one he could never describe but that was as uniquely Eva as her scent was and had played on his tongue like a remembrance since their earlier kiss. As their fused lips and tongues devoured each other, he wrapped an arm around her neck and swept a hand over her back and then down to her bottom, which was as ripe as the most succulent of peaches.

He tightened his hold and rolled her over so she was the one flat on her back and he on top. The feel of her breasts close against his chest was simply incredible.

Pulling his lips from hers, he stared in wonder into eyes that returned everything he was feeling.

It was as if his entire life had been a dress rehearsal for this moment.

He ached to be inside her but he wasn't ready, not yet. First he needed to discover Eva's final flavour, the only one he had yet to experience.

With one last passionate kiss, he began his exploration of the woman who had driven him mad for so long, using his tongue and his fingers to touch and feel and taste, her moans and writhing body urging him on. When he reached her most intimate, feminine part and gently parted her thighs, she gave a shudder before he'd even put his lips to the beautiful folds.

This taste… This was Eva. This was her muskiness, her desire. And it belonged to *him*.

At the first press of Daniele's lips to the part of her that had never been kissed before, Eva thought she was going to lose her mind and clenched her hands into fists to stop herself from jerking away.

She hadn't been prepared for any of this. She could never have been. It would have been impossible.

Intimacy such as this couldn't be real.

But it was very real.

Shivers and sensation had bloomed into every part of her, burning her with such a craven need for everything Daniele was doing to her and for…

His tongue found her most sensitive part.

Lieve God…

It felt as if the pleasure surging through her had been gifted by a benevolent creator.

She could feel the sensations massing together into a heavy tightening cluster that throbbed and burned. A moan echoed softly in the den they'd created...that wanton sound had come from *her*.

Just as the cluster reached a point that had her breaths shorten in anticipation of something, she didn't know what, Daniele shifted and kissed her inner thigh. Her cry of disappointment was muffled when fresh sensations started over her skin and he dragged his lips back up over her belly and breasts...she had never known her breasts could ache so much...and up the sensitive skin of her neck, his body moving with the motion until he was positioned between her legs, his erection prodding between her thighs, staring down at her.

The heady desire she read in his eyes made her throat close and her chest expand.

When his lips came back on hers for a kiss that was almost restrained, she tasted something new and realised with a jolt that the taste belonged to her.

Sliding a hand around his neck, she dragged her fingers through his hair and deepened the kiss and as his tongue swept into her mouth his buttocks moved and he slowly inched his way inside her.

Lieve God...

He made love to her slowly, groaning into her mouth, bodies entwined, their chests crushed together, as close as two people could ever be. She wrapped her legs tightly around him, all the sensation flowing through her thickening and gathering into a mass again, but this time he didn't pull away, driving slowly and languidly inside her. Her cries became louder yet somehow muffled to her ears, the mass tightened and tightened until, without any hint of what was going to happen, it exploded and the purest, headiest form of pleasure imaginable burst through her.

As if he recognised what was happening to her, Daniele stilled, breathing heavily into her ear, allowing her to cling to him and ride the waves until they lessened, and then, with a groan, he started again, this time harder, as if he'd been waiting for her release of pleasure before taking his own.

His thrusts became more frenzied, his groans deeper and then, with one last long, forceful drive, he shuddered wildly and then collapsed on top of her.

With the echoes of her own climax still pulsing through her, Eva held him tightly in her arms, welcoming his weight and his hot breath dancing on the skin of her neck.

Drums beat loudly through her, in her head, in her ears, so loudly he must be able to feel it too.

It seemed to take for ever for all the sensations to evaporate but even when the throbs in her core had stopped she could still feel the remnants of what they'd just shared, a newness in her veins that she'd never known before.

Brushing her lips against his damp cheek, a feeling of blissful contentment settled in her chest and she took a long breath.

'Am I hurting you?' he asked hoarsely, his voice muffled against her neck.

'No.' She stroked her fingers over his back and breathed again. Her throat was closing and her lungs tightening but it wasn't Daniele's weight causing it. She swallowed and felt her chest hitch, felt hot tears burn in her eyes that she blinked back frantically.

She was going to cry.

She *mustn't* cry.

But as soon as she thought it, a tear leaked out and landed with a soft plop on the pillow.

There was a delicious languidness in Daniele's limbs. Sleep was snaking its way in his brain but he resisted the need to switch off, certain he must be crushing Eva with his weight. Reluctantly, he moved off her and rested his head on the pillow beside hers, and hooked an arm around her waist.

He'd never experienced before in his life anything like what they'd just shared.

It had been more than just sex, although he couldn't have said why, just knew that it had been incredible. He felt different...

As he was trying to pinpoint what felt so different inside him he saw with a start that Eva's eyes were shining with tears.

'What's wrong, *tesoro*?' Instinctively he gathered her to him so she was draped against him with her face resting on his chest.

He felt her swallow and heard the choke of held-back tears.

'Was my lovemaking so bad it's made you want to cry?' He strove for a lightness in tone but the fresh thuds of his heart made him fail.

It worked, though. She gave a tiny, shuddering laugh and groped for his hand. Entwining their fingers together, she squeezed.

'I didn't know it could be like that,' she whispered.

Making circular motions over her back with his free hand, he rested his cheek on the top of her head. 'Are you saying it like a good thing or a bad thing?'

'Both.'

'How can it be both?'

'It just is.' She was silent for a moment before saying, 'I wasn't taught anything about sex when I was growing up. Johann and I were both virgins when we married. Neither of us really knew what we were doing. Johann knew the basics but I was clueless.' Her voice dropped even lower. 'I didn't know it could feel so good.'

She didn't have to say anything more. She'd already confessed that she'd never felt desire for the boy she'd married when she'd been only eighteen, a marriage he'd now formed a solid impression of that had been more of a friendly affection than that of true lovers.

He knew without her having to say that what they'd just shared had conjured up a wealth of mixed emotions in her. He guessed guilt played a part in it that she had found something with him that had been missing from the boy she'd had a genuine, if friendly, love for. It should make him preen but it didn't.

All it did was make him feel sad for the young life that had been taken away too soon, which was actually quite disconcerting. Empathy had never been one of his traits.

'Eva...' He hesitated. He no longer felt sleepy. 'Eva, you're Dutch. Your country is famous for its adult approach to sex education. How could you have not been taught about it?'

'The word was forbidden in my house,' she said softly. 'I knew it was how babies were made but not how or why.'

'But what about school? Did you not learn it there?'

'My sisters and I were all withdrawn from those lessons.'

He hadn't heard her mention sisters before.

'Did your friends not tell you about it?' He thought of his own school friends. As soon as any of them had discovered something to do with women and sex they would immediately relate it to the others like the revealing of some grand secret.

It was a long time before she answered. 'I didn't have any friends.'

His mind reeled. No friends?

All children had friends. They would roam in groups, like attracting like, the popular kids together, the trendy kids together, the cool kids together, the geeks together, the misfits who didn't fit into any particular group coming together like stray cats to form their own pack.

'The other children avoided us.'

'Children can be cruel.'

She nuzzled into his chest and squeezed harder on his hands. 'I look back and I understand why. Compared to them we were strange.'

'How?'

'Well... We had no television for a start, which immediately made us freaks. Our mother cut our hair, always in the same pudding basin style; she made our uniforms and our other clothes too and they were always plain and ugly clothes, which made *us* plain and ugly. I didn't know how to speak to people. I didn't know how to make friends. I had nothing to share or give to make the other children like me and could never have invited them home if I had made friends. Strangers were not welcome in our home. We lived a very controlled, very sparse life.'

Hearing her speak now, Daniele wondered how he could have thought her English. There was a true musical lilt to her voice that he would have heard before if he'd only opened his ears to listen. It was the most beautiful and seductive of voices.

'Did Johann go to your school?'

'We went to an all-girls school. He lived on the same road as us. I thought he was strange because he always smiled at me.'

'How did you become friends?'

She was silent as she thought about it. 'I don't remember. It evolved over many years. Just secret smiles, you know? We didn't actually talk to each other until we went to high school. His finished before mine and he'd wait for me at my school gate and walk me home. Tessel covered for me so Angela and Kika didn't see. They would have told our parents and I would have been punished.'

'They're your sisters?' he asked, his brain hurting to hear the word 'punished' and not yet ready to ask what she meant by it, his heart thumping as if beating down the heavy hands of impending doom.

What had been the most fulfilling and, yes, he could admit it, emotional experience was turning on its head and dragging him to a place he didn't want to go.

No pillow talk. No confidences exchanged. That's what they'd agreed on.

'Yes. Angela was the oldest, then Kika, then Tessel, then me.'

'Was?' he queried, picking up on the past tense she'd used, his burning curiosity to uncover her secrets overriding the clanging sirens in his head to stop this conversation and go to sleep.

'Are. Is. I haven't seen them in ten years.'

'Since you ran away?'

'Yes. I reached out to Tessel a year after I left and she told me our parents had disowned me. They'd forced the truth out of her and then confronted Johann's parents—they knew my home situation and had given us a little money to help us—and learned we'd got married. Tessel said they burned all the pictures of me and cut me out of all family group photos.'

'So you're still in contact with her? With Tessel?'

'Not any more. I haven't spoken to her since before Johann died.' She raised her head and rested her chin on his chest. 'The last time we spoke she told me about this group she'd joined. When my emails to her started bouncing back I looked into it. It's a cult, a harmless one, I think, if there can be such a thing as a harmless cult, but one that insists on no contact with outsiders. So she ran away too. It just took her longer that me.'

Resting her cheek back on his chest, she sighed. 'It's strange how life turns out, isn't it? Tessel was always the rebellious one. Angela and Kika were very subservient and always obeyed our parents' rules. And there were a *lot* of rules. So damn many of them. It was so easy to break one and not know you were doing it, and Tessel seemed to break them all. You would think she'd have been the one to run away as soon as she could but she didn't, and when she finally did it was escaping one form of imprisonment for another.'

'You think of your parents as jailers?'

'We were their property. You have to understand, we were indoctrinated from birth to obey them. We were terrified of them and for good reason. We knew the consequences for disobedience.'

He swallowed and closed his eyes before asking, 'What were they?'

'It depended on the offence and their mood. If they were in a good mood you might just be forced to sleep in the garden shed for the night. If they were in a bad mood...well.'

'Well?'

'Tessel was once whipped across her back with a belt for bringing mud into the house.' Her fingers tightened on his. 'My mother once stamped on my fingers when I couldn't finish a meal and tried to sneak the scraps into a bin.'

Daniele swore quietly. His stomach was churning so violently he feared he would be sick. 'How did people not know? Your neighbours?'

'My father was the local doctor. He fixed our injuries when they went too far. Adults thought him eccentric but they respected him. And I think adults tend to be blind. It was the children who knew something was wrong but they didn't know what they were seeing. They just saw a family of freaks.'

Nothing more was said for a long time. Daniele's mind was in a whirl.

He fingered the long strands of her hair. The vibrant colour that he'd always admired suddenly gained in significance. 'When did you start colouring your hair?'

'It was the first thing I did when we got to Amsterdam.' She gave the lightest of laughs but it warmed his blood that had slowly chilled to thick ice while he'd listened to her. 'You should have seen the bathroom when I'd finished. It looked like there'd been a murder.'

And then, before he could react to the quip that had lightened the heavy atmosphere that had enveloped them, she suddenly moved so her thighs straddled him and her face hovered above his.

Her nipples brushed against his chest and, despite everything she'd just revealed and despite having been replete such a short time before, his loins flickered back to life.

She stared intently into his eyes, loaded meaning firing from hers. 'Do you understand why I could never have agreed to this marriage if it had meant I was to be your possession? Us making love doesn't change anything, okay?'

His blood warmed a little more, relief pushing through his veins, yet, strangely, his heart tightened.

The rules they'd established from the outset were still in place.

Their pillow talk hadn't altered that.

But as her mouth closed around his, his last coherent thought before the desire reignited between them was to wonder if the colour she'd chosen to dye her hair had been a deliberate imitation of the colour of deadly creatures warning others that to come too close meant danger.

He wondered if it had been a subconscious signal to the world to keep its distance from her.

CHAPTER ELEVEN

THE NEXT WEEK passed in a flash. With all the work being done in their wing of the *castello*, they spent much of their time together exploring Florence and Pisa, visiting museums and eating long lunches, the nights spent making love with abandon.

They got to know more about each other, practical things, Daniele's architecture, his quest to create homes and buildings that were works of art, sympathetic to the location's heritage yet modern, the perfect blend of old and new. They discussed how Eva could start a not-for-profit consultancy business advising the rich and famous how best to help those in need. It was something they both agreed should be put on the back burner until the *castello* had been transferred into Daniele's name and they knew where they'd make their main home. They talked about so many things but never anything that could be construed as intimate.

It was safer that way.

Eva hadn't planned to tell him about her childhood but now it was done she didn't regret it. It wasn't something she had spoken about since Johann had died and in many ways it had been cathartic. Daniele was her husband. He *should* know about her past even if it was something he'd prefer not to know. It had also been a reminder to herself of her need to keep possession of herself. She would never belong to Daniele or anyone. She would not give him the tools to hurt her.

She was not a fool. Things were great between them at the moment but it was early days. Sooner or later Daniele would get bored and seek new adventures. She would learn when it happened if she was capable of turning a blind eye. If she couldn't she would pack her bags and leave.

She hoped he didn't stray too soon. She hoped he was capable of being faithful until their first anniversary so the charity could get its next huge injection of cash from him.

That's what she told herself. Only in the early hours when she'd wake in the safety of his arms did she hear the voice in her head telling her she was fooling herself if she believed any of that.

None of this stopped her wishing this wonderful honeymoon-like phase didn't have to end, but nothing lasted for ever and six days after they'd become lovers they returned from a matinee performance at the Teatro di Pisa to find Daniele's new office, created by knocking two bedrooms into one, finished.

'It's incredible they did it so quickly and so well,' Eva observed, staring at the teal-painted walls and rows of beautifully carved walnut cabinets and shelves. All that needed to be done was for it to be filled with his stuff.

'That's what you get when you pay your workforce triple time,' he said with the grin she'd come to adore. 'Most of them worked on the hospital in Caballeros and got used to the long hours and the extra cash at the end of the month.'

'It should be completed soon, shouldn't it?'

'The grand opening is in a month.' He pulled a face as he said this, making her laugh.

'Are we going?'

'If we don't, my sister will kill us.'

'What about your mother?'

'Nothing would keep her away from her favourite son's memorial.'

He spoke lightly but something made her think he wasn't jesting.

A swelling in Eva's chest erupted, propelling her to reach out a hand to gently stroke his face. 'I wouldn't know if he was her favourite or not, but I know she adores you.'

His jaw tightened but the smile stayed intact. 'I've never doubted my mother's love.'

Then he took the hand still resting on his cheek and kissed the palm. 'I need to check back into the real world. I need to check with my PA that my business is still in one piece, call my lawyer for progress on the deeds being transferred into my name, and call my accountant to make sure my fortune's still intact.'

'Anything I can do?'

He scrutinised her for a moment, a musing look crossing his face. 'Do you realise it's going to be Christmas in eight days?'

'That hadn't even occurred to me.' Christmas was something she'd only celebrated with Johann. It had been considered a worthless pagan festival by her parents, who had refused to even celebrate their children's birthdays. She and Johann had tried to create their own Christmases on their limited budget and she remembered how childlike their attitude had been towards it. Since he'd died there had been no one to celebrate it with so she'd learned to blank out the month of December, had perfected the art of walking without seeing, so the houses aglow with fairy lights and the stores gleaming with decorations didn't register in her consciousness. She'd even learned to tune out the Christmas songs that belted out of all the stores.

'I'm putting you in charge of decorating our quarters. We'll need a tree—something at least twelve feet tall—and whatever else you think is needed to make the place look festive.'

'I've not had much experience at that,' she warned, although Daniele detected a flash of excitement in the blue eyes he couldn't believe he'd once imagined were cold. Eva's eyes were as warm as her curvy body and her musical voice when she looked at him now.

'Serena can help if you need her.'

'Okay. That could be fun.' Then she asked in a more hesitant voice, 'What do you normally do on Christmas Day?'

'It's the one day of the year I'm nagged to spend with my family,' he said ruefully.

'Will I be coming this year?' There was the same hesitancy in her question.

Daniele look at her closely. He thought back to their talk the first night they'd made love. He would bet the *castello* that Eva had never celebrated Christmas in her childhood.

Who would she have celebrated it with since her first husband had died? He'd been forced to the conclusion that it hadn't been shame at their reasons for marrying that had stopped Eva from inviting anyone to it, but that there had been no one she'd felt close enough with to invite.

She'd had no friends growing up. There were no signs she'd had any since. Not real friends.

Enveloping her into his arms, he held her tightly. 'You're my wife. My mother and sister both adore you and would lynch me if you didn't join us. I'll make some calls and find out what's happening.'

There was more hesitancy in her voice as she asked, 'Do you want me to get presents for them?'

'Would you mind?'

'Not at all. It will be nice to buy them things. They've been very welcoming to me.'

Making a mental note to call his sister and tell her she didn't need to bother buying the family presents on his behalf this year—something she'd been doing for him since she was about thirteen—he wondered what he should buy his wife.

He'd pick Francesca's brain about it. But what he wouldn't do was allow his sister to buy it for him.

Eva deserved something special and she deserved to have her husband choose it for her.

He might not be able to eradicate her childhood memories but he could start creating new ones for her.

There was nothing sophisticated or muted in the way Eva had decorated their living quarters, Daniele mused a couple of days later. She'd taken him at his word and made the place look festive. So festive he could be forgiven for thinking he'd stepped into Santa's Grotto. The Christmas tree reached the high ceiling but he could see hardly any of the fragrant pine because she'd covered practically every inch of it with tinsel and shining baubles. Decorations hung everywhere, fake snow and stars sprayed artistically over all the windows, Christmas-themed throws and cushions on the sofas and their bed, Christmas ornaments filling every other available space. There was no great theme or underlying colour as his mother always ensured in her home, and nothing matched.

It was the gaudiest display ever and the complete opposite of what he'd imagined the usually serious and practical Eva would come up with. It was like someone had let a class of hyperactive toddlers loose on the place.

And he'd never seen a better display. He'd never walked into the *castello*'s living area before and instantly smiled with pleasure.

He'd never made love to a woman under a Christmas tree before either, but he had with Eva.

He kept waiting for her allure to fade but it wasn't happening. Not even walking into the bathroom to find her dyeing her hair had broken the spell she'd woven around him. He'd sat on the bathroom chair and watched, then, when the dye had been in for the allotted time, had rinsed it off for her. When he'd questioned why she didn't go to a hairdresser to do it and had been given the answer that she didn't trust them to get the colour right, he'd got on the phone to a contact to have a salon created for her in one of the spare rooms. When it was done in the New Year she could bring a hairdresser to the *castello* and give them the bottle of colourant.

Two days before Christmas and with Eva having disappeared in one of his cars on another shopping trip, Daniele took the opportunity to go through the brief of an underground house in the Swiss Alps he'd been recently commissioned to produce and construct. It would involve excavating tonnes of earth and...

His phone rang.

He picked it up, saw it was his PA, and turned down the music he had blaring.

'You're supposed to be on leave,' he scolded when he'd put it to his ear.

'Daniele... Have you seen the news?'

Something in her tone immediately put him on the alert. 'What news?'

'An exposé...'

He groaned. This was the last thing he needed, another of his ex-girlfriends cashing in on their brief time together, and immediately thought of Eva. He didn't want to think of her reaction if she should read it.

'Who's sold me out this time?'

His PA cleared her throat. 'It's not an exposé on you. It's your brother.'

'*Pieta?*' That was most unlikely. She must mean Matteo. His cousin had lived with them as a sibling for many years and people often mistook him for one of them.

'Yes. I'm sorry.'

'Sorry for what?' So his brother had been human after all? Well, so what? Who was he to judge? Who was anyone to judge? His brother was dead. He had no right to reply.

Just thinking that made his brain start to burn.

Who the hell did this woman think she was, selling out a dead man?

'Daniele... Please, just have a look.'

'Which paper's it in?'

'By now it's in all of them. It's everywhere.'

Disconnecting his phone, he reached for his tablet and turned it on.

Thirty seconds later he stared at it, numb with disbelief.

Eva got back to the *castello* much later than she'd anticipated. She'd gone to a specialist music shop in Florence and had ended up spending hours there.

Now all she had to do was hide her gifts with the rest of Daniele's presents in Francesca's room. It was the one room he wouldn't go into on his eternal *castello* modernisation quest. He seemed to earmark one room or another for a new purpose on a daily basis.

Once put away, she closed the door behind her then went to find him.

Their bedroom and his office were empty so she went to the living area.

The moment she stepped over the threshold she came to an abrupt stop.

All the happiness that had been glowing inside her drained away in an instant as she took in the devastation that had taken place.

The Christmas decorations had been ripped down, every single one of them, and all the ornaments smashed. Shards and chunks of porcelain lay strewn across the carpet. A chair lay on its side, two of its legs broken and splintered as if they'd been bashed against something, the bureau upended too, the drawers fallen open and the contents spilled out.

Her immediate thought was that there had been burglars, but then she saw the Christmas tree was still intact and the presents she'd spent so many hours wrapping were all whole under it.

'Daniele?' she whispered into the empty room, suddenly terrified.

As if he'd heard her call, the door that led to the *castello*'s kitchens burst open and Daniele came flying into the room, a quarter-full bottle of something that looked like Scotch in his hand. Or should that be three-quarters empty? For when he noticed her standing there and his eyes met hers, the wildness in them had her convinced that he was steaming drunk.

Staggering barefoot into the room, he said in Italian, 'Good trip?'

Did he not see the mess?

'Daniele, what's happened?'

'What?' He twisted round to inspect the room. 'Oh. Yes. This. Sorry. I lost my head a little. I'll get new decorations tomorrow. I didn't touch the tree,' he added, as if that was a good thing.

Eva couldn't have cared less about the tree. Right then she couldn't care about anything other than her husband who was clearly in some kind of shock. Since she'd left that morning he looked like he'd aged a decade.

'You did this?' she asked, making sure to keep her voice calm and non-threatening. 'Why? Has something happened?'

He nodded vigorously. 'You could say that. Yes. You could. Something. Has. Happened.'

'Do you want to tell me?'

'No.' He took a drink from the bottle and wiped his mouth with his sleeve. 'But you're going to hear about it anyway. You must be the only person in the world who doesn't know.'

'Know what?'

His face contorted into something ugly as he lurched towards her. 'That my perfect brother with the perfect life and perfect wife was gay. My perfect brother was a cheating *liar*.'

Utterly dumbstruck, Eva didn't know what to say or how to react.

That he was being deadly serious was not in doubt.

'Did you hear what I said?' he asked, taking another swig.

'I heard you,' she whispered.

'Do you know what it means?'

She shook her head, although she had a good idea.

'It *means*,' he stressed with venom, 'that my brother was a liar. Mr Perfect who everyone always said I should live up to, who everyone always said was better than me and could do no wrong, was a cheating *liar*.' And with that he swore violently and raised the bottle in the air as if preparing himself to throw it at something.

'Daniele, please, no.' Terrified he was going to hurt himself, Eva rushed to him and grabbed his arm. The muscles were all bunched as he prepared himself to release the bottle.

'Let me go,' he snarled.

'No. If you let go of that bottle now it will fall on me and hurt me. Is that what you want?'

His bloodshot eyes filled with confusion. 'I would never hurt you.'

'Then please, my love, put it down. Don't do any more damage.'

Whether it was her slip-of-the-tongue endearment or the pleading he must have read in her eyes, he relaxed his arm and allowed her to take the bottle from him.

As soon as she had hold of it she threw it onto the sofa, where it immediately spilled its little remaining contents onto the expensive fabric.

Then she took his hands and brought them together and waited until she had his wandering, drunken attention again. He swayed.

'Daniele, will you do me a favour?'

His brow furrowed in a question but he nodded.

'Come to the bedroom with me. I'm worried you're going to fall onto this mess and hurt yourself.'

'Oh.'

'You'll come with me?'

She caught a sudden flash of sobriety. 'Yes.'

He let her lead him out of the living area where she tried to create a pathway where the least amount of debris lay.

Her hopes that she could get him to the bedroom proved

forlorn when halfway down the corridor he suddenly slumped against the wall and slid down to the floor.

He raised his knees and put his head in his hands, swearing out loud.

She lowered herself down on the floor to face him.

After a long pause he rested his head against the wall, stretched his legs out so his feet lay on her lap and gave a rueful smile. 'I'm drunk.'

'I know.'

'I'm sorry.'

'Don't be.'

She wrapped her hands around the handsome feet on her lap and gently rubbed them with her thumbs. It amazed her that he hadn't damaged them walking over all that debris.

He sighed and closed his eyes.

They sat like that for an age, pained silence enveloping them, Eva doing nothing more than massaging his feet in the hope it would calm some of the demons plaguing him. Her heart wanted to cry for him.

'Why did he lie?' he asked suddenly, opening his eyes and staring at her as if she could provide the answers he craved.

'Why does anyone lie?' she answered steadily. 'Normally it's because the liar thinks the consequences of the truth are too great.'

'What consequence would there have been for Pieta to tell the truth about who he was?'

'I don't know. The *castello*?'

'If he wanted it that much he could have still married.'

'He did marry,' she pointed out.

'He could have married honestly.' His face contorted again and his hands clenched into fists. 'He was in love with Alberto. They were together for over ten years.'

'Alberto? The man who ran his foundation with him?'

He nodded grimly. 'He's come out to the press. He's told them everything. He has handwritten letters and photos.'

'Why did he come out now?'

'To stop the media hounding Natasha.'

'Pieta's wife? The one who is having your cousin's baby?'

Daniele blinked. Even in the thudding fog of his drunk head it occurred to him that he had never discussed Matteo and Natasha with Eva.

Eva cast him that same gentle look again. 'Francesca told me about them when we went shopping together the first time.'

'You never said.'

She shrugged, her eyes full of compassion. 'I didn't think you wanted to talk about it.'

'I didn't.'

'There you are, then.'

'I called him.'

'Alberto?'

'He told me Natasha only found out about them after she married. She'd been protecting his secret for his family's sake. For our sake. Do you think that's true?'

'How would I know? I've never met her.'

'Guess.'

'I can't. You know her. You tell me.'

He swallowed and tried to picture his sister-in-law. He'd known her all his life. Pieta had homed in on her the moment she'd turned eighteen then kept her waiting for six years before marrying her. He'd let it be known he'd put off the marriage so she could enjoy her young adulthood before taking the final step when all along it had been so he could continue his affair without the added danger of a nosy wife to catch him out. He'd only married in the weeks before their father died so he could then inherit the *castello* and the rest of the Pellegrini estate.

He took a deep breath in an attempt to quell the nausea roiling violently within him.

'She was protecting us. Not him. She'd waited for him to marry her for six years.'

And Eva, with her gentle touch on his feet, was protecting

him now, using nothing more than her fingers and an understanding, non-judgmental calmness of voice.

It came to him that if she'd been there when he'd first discovered the truth he would never have gone on his furious rampage.

'I'm so sorry,' he said, guilt hitting him with force. 'All your decorations.'

She smiled. 'They're only decorations. We can get more.'

He gave a short nod. 'Yes. We can replace them. I can't replace my brother. I can't ask him why he lied.' He took a long breath. 'You know, all my life I've been compared to him. My father would always tell me to be like him. Nothing I did was ever good enough on its own, it always had to be compared to him and his achievements, even when my achievements were better.'

'You were rivals?'

'He was my rival.' He felt the bitterness well up in him. 'But I wasn't his. He had this way of speaking to me like I wasn't a worthy competitor. Without saying a word, he let me know that he could have much more than me if only his time and energy wasn't put into his oh-so-worthy foundation. I hated him.'

It was the first time he'd ever admitted that, not just to another person but to himself.

It felt good to admit the truth.

'I hated him. I hated his patronising attitude. I hated that my family thought the sun shone out of his arse.' Suddenly he looked at the calm face of his wife with fresh eyes. 'But not you. You saw through him.'

She didn't shy away from his stare. 'I thought he was a great man. I still do. But I think you're worth a hundred of him. A thousand of him.'

Her words were as soothing as the feel of her thumbs on his feet.

And just as suddenly as the bitterness had bitten him, a fresh wave of nausea sloshed into its place.

He gazed again at the only person in the world who he could

ever talk so freely and openly to as he was at that moment. 'Tell me this, wife, if I hated him so much then why aren't I rejoicing that he's dead? Why do I feel so...bad?'

Her lips pulled together, a bleakness filling her eyes. She opened her mouth then closed it, then carefully moved his feet off her lap and shuffled forward to kneel at his side.

Putting her hands on his cheeks, she stared intently into his eyes and said, 'The reason you feel so bad is because you loved him. I'm afraid you have no choice over that. It's hardwired into you, the same as my love for my parents is hardwired into me. I hate them. I hate what they did to me and to my sisters, but if someone had asked me when I was a child if I wanted them reported to the police or social services I would have said no. I would have been terrified of being taken away from them. I have been free of them for ten years and have never reported their abuses and why? Because for all the damage they did to me I still love them.'

He wanted to laugh at her and tell her she was a fool to love people who had treated her worse than an animal. They didn't deserve her love.

But he thought there was something in what she said. He'd had no choice about loving his brother. Pieta being gone was a pain he had never imagined he could feel.

'I'm sorry for how I treated you that night when I tricked you into a date. I was in a bad place then.' This time he did laugh. 'I didn't know what a bad place I was in. No wonder you told me to get lost.'

She placed the lightest of kisses on his lips. 'Apology accepted. Now, shall we get you to bed before you fall asleep here?'

CHAPTER TWELVE

THREE HOURS LATER, Eva got into bed. She hadn't drawn the curtains around it. Daniele, who was fast asleep beside her, needed air. He'd thrown his clothes onto the floor, taken the painkillers with the glass of water she'd given him then fallen onto his back and gone straight to sleep. He hadn't moved a muscle since. She'd put a fresh glass of water on the bedside table for when he woke in the middle of the night with a raging thirst. Which he would. She had no doubt about that.

Facing him, she stared at his sleeping face and felt another wave of empathy. Those waves just kept coming.

She knew it wasn't the revelation about Pieta's sexuality that had been so hard for him to learn but all the lies his brother had taken to conceal it, all the deception. She could have understood it if the Pellegrinis were old-fashioned in their view of the world but she hadn't seen any evidence of that. Daniele had gay friends—one of them had joined them in Club Giroud and chatted happily about his own wedding plans. Francesca, who had called an hour ago to see how Daniele was and been unsurprised to hear he was passed out on the bed, had sounded completely bewildered by the revelations. Her primary emotion had been hurt that her eldest brother had felt unable to confide in her.

Stroking Daniele's stubbly jaw, Eva closed her eyes to another wave of emotion for her husband.

He hadn't wanted any of this. He'd never wanted to inherit the *castello* and the accompanying estate and had never wanted to marry. He'd done it for his family's sake and had never lied about it. The people he loved knew the truth. He'd never hidden anything from them. He'd never lied to her either. He hadn't fed her a pile of baloney to get her to marry him; he'd been completely open about his reasons. Even the priest who'd married them had known the truth but had been happy to officiate because he'd been content with their promises that they would take the vows they were making seriously.

Daniele had kept all his promises. He hadn't broken a single one.

Another huge pang hit her as she recalled his promise to never love her and she squeezed her eyes even tighter as the pang hit her heart and set it into a pounding boom.

She'd sworn to him she would never fall in love with him. It had been a promise made in the heat of anger when she had looked at him and wanted nothing more than to punch his arrogant, supercilious face. She'd hated him then. Everything about him. But she'd feared her sensory awareness of him, and she had been right to fear it. Making love to him had opened a whole new part of her that had been hidden away from her all her life, an earthy, pleasure-seeking side that was entirely centred round *him*.

She had to remind herself that overwhelming tenderness for the man she had amazing sex with did not mean she was falling in love. Daniele had chosen her specifically for her level head and her ability to contain her emotions and now she needed to use that level head and see things from a logical point of view rather than from an aching romantic viewpoint he would laugh at scornfully if he were to know of it.

The record Daniele was listening to came to a stop. He got up from his office chair and stood at the old-fashioned record player he had on display on a low cabinet, lifted the stylus and carefully placed the record that had been playing in its sleeve, then flipped through the dozens of twelve-inch vinyl albums stacked beside it. Eva had got it all for him. It had been his main Christmas present from her.

On a monetary level it was a drop in the ocean but the thought that had gone into it, and the time and effort she had taken getting it all together made his heart hurt to think about it. He remembered one very brief conversation where he'd told her how much better music sounded on vinyl records and she hadn't just committed it to memory but hunted one down for him *and* all his favourite albums to play on it. It had made his gift of a sports car that was all her own seem trifling in comparison.

Strange, he thought, how the simplest things could make a man feel so damned awful.

Christmas had come and gone with the joyousness of a wake. All the planning and preparation Eva had done for it had come to nothing. Daniele wished she had complained but, in her usual calm way, she had displayed only compassion and understanding, which made him feel even worse.

His mother had confined herself to her bedroom. Losing her beloved husband and favourite beloved son in a year of each other had knocked her badly but she'd forced herself to carry on in the way the Pellegrinis always carried on. Learning her favourite son had been a closet homosexual who had kept the love of his life a secret from her had knocked the last of her stuffing out. She couldn't stop crying.

Eva had said to him privately, gently, that she thought it was the grief of Pieta's death finally hitting her that had her acting like this because this was the first time his mother—all of them—had desperately needed to talk to him and confront him since his death but he wasn't there to either defend himself or ask for their forgiveness. He was dead.

Daniele had given a noncommittal grunt in answer and bitten back from shouting at her that she didn't know what she was talking about. He'd been on edge around her since he'd woken on Christmas Eve with a thumping hangover and a throat as dry as the Gobi Desert. The glass of water on his bedside table had glimmered at him like a mirage, but it had been no illusion. Eva had thought to put it there for him. Of course she had.

At first memories of his drunken rampage had been hazy, little flickers that had taken their time to come together to create a whole scene. The drink had loosened his tongue. He'd revealed things to Eva that he'd never even admitted to himself and now there was a crater in his guts and a tightness in his chest that wouldn't ease. He'd revealed too much. That's if his memories could be relied upon. He could swear he remembered her addressing him as, 'my love'.

Neither of them had mentioned their talk. She'd enquired about his head and offered to get more painkillers for him but had said nothing about his confession.

His office door opened and the woman he'd been thinking of stepped hesitantly inside.

'Can I speak to you?' she asked, a hint of caution in her musical voice.

The easy closeness that had developed between them in the first three weeks of their marriage had gone. They were unfailingly polite to each other but now it was like they walked on invisible eggshells. He didn't know if this was Eva feeding off his own distance or if she too had realised at the same time as he that they had become too intimate too quickly and that it was time to take a step back and put their marriage on the footing that had originally been intended.

Or maybe his drunken rampage and cruel words about his brother had been the reminder she'd needed that despite the great sex between them and for all her words that he was worth a thousand of his brother, she saw much to dislike in him.

Whatever it was, the distance between them was good.

'Sure. Come in.' He went back to his desk and sat down.

She closed the door then stood with her back to it.

Tucking her hair behind her ear, she looked at him as if weighing up his mood—which she probably was—and said, 'Your sister just called me.'

He shrugged. Francesca and Eva had developed a close friendship. As far as he knew, they spoke every few days.

'She said you're refusing to go to the hospital opening next week.'

Eva saw his jaw clench and her heart sank.

'My sister knows my feelings about it.'

And so did she, although he hadn't said anything about it to her. Daniele no longer spoke to her, not about anything important.

Since he'd woken on Christmas Eve, he'd been a changed man. A distant man. The easy, sexy smile was gone. The witty quips and innuendoes were a thing of the past. Now he just got on with his work and spent hours with his lawyers, trying to get the transferral of the *castello* into his name speeded up. He'd mentioned over dinner the other night that it should be done within days. That had been right before he'd informed her he was going out. He hadn't said where he was going or asked her to join him.

Her pride had refused to let her question him and her pride had made her feign sleep when he'd got into bed hours past midnight.

The only thing they still did together was have sex and even that had taken a different hue. Only when they woke in the middle of the night already in each other's arms did the barriers they'd silently erected between themselves come down and they could make love with the emotional abandon she'd become dangerously used to.

It was as well Daniele had distanced himself from her, she thought, although it made her lungs cramp and her brain burn to think it. It made it easier for her to put her level head on and remind herself of what their marriage agreement was all about, which absolutely was not about emotions or feelings.

Instinct told her Daniele hadn't found another lover yet but she knew it wouldn't be long. A man like him thrilled in the chase. She'd been his prey, he'd caught her, and sooner or later he'd seek his next target.

And when he did...?

The cramp in her lungs extended to her stomach, twisting it with such violence it felt as if someone had put a vice in it.

'I understand why you don't want to go,' she said, choosing her words carefully. 'But you have to.'

This was something she couldn't keep her distance from any longer, not after Francesca had begged her to help. She seemed to be under the impression that Daniele listened to her and had been as cloth-eared as her brother when Eva had tried to correct this impression.

But she wasn't having this conversation for Francesca's sake. She was having it for Daniele's. If he didn't go to the opening he would regret it for the rest of his life. She knew better than to phrase it like that, though. These were waters she'd have to navigate cautiously.

His eyes narrowed dangerously. 'I don't have to do anything.'

'In this case you do. Do you want the world to think you're ashamed of your brother's sexuality?'

'That is *not* what this is about,' he said, a snarl forming on his lips and his hands curling into tight fists.

'I know that.' She refused to drop her stare from his. These were words he needed to hear. 'But that is how it will look.'

'I. Don't. Care. How. It. Looks.'

'This isn't about you.' Although it was to her. 'This is about your family. They need you—your mother needs you. If she's going to put on a brave face to the world's media, she needs your support.'

'She has never needed my support before,' he dismissed tightly.

'How do you know? Have you ever asked her?'

'What?'

'Have you ever asked her if she needs your support, or have you always assumed that because she had your brother and sister to hold her up that she didn't need you too? Because if that was what you thought, you were wrong.'

He half hovered off his chair and leaned forward, speaking as if she were an impertinent child. 'You don't know anything about it.'

'I know she loves you and I know she needs you. Did you know Matteo and Natasha are going?'

'They wouldn't dare.'

Eva breathed in deeply. 'They love each other. They never went behind Pieta's back, although in light of what's come out about your brother, I think they could have been forgiven for it. Your mother is desperate to make amends with them. She's desperate to bring her family back together. She loves you all. She wants to honour Pieta by attending the hospital opening but she needs you at her side.'

'If my mother wants all this then why hasn't she spoken to me about it?'

'Because you refuse to talk about it. Daniele… Your brother deserves this memorial. Whatever he did wrong it doesn't take away the good he did. If his own wife can forgive him and show that forgiveness publicly, then you can too.'

It was as if all the fight went out of him.

He closed his eyes and sank back down on his seat, then bowed his head and dug his fingers into his hair.

Unable to witness his pain—and she knew in her heart that Daniele was in terrible torment—Eva stepped over to him and placed a hand lightly on his shoulder. Swallowing to get moisture into her dry throat, she said, 'I told you when you were drunk that you're worth a thousand of your brother. Prove me right. Be the man I think you are, not the man I thought you were when I first met you.'

Silence filled the room before he answered with a coldness that chilled her. 'I haven't changed, Eva. Whatever you thought or think you know about me, I will never change.' Then he covered her hand resting on his shoulder and pushed it gently away. 'Please excuse me. I have work to do.'

Fighting with all her might to hide her hurt, she managed the smallest of smiles. 'Will you at least think about coming to the opening?'

He jerked a nod and opened a desk drawer. 'I will think about it.'

'Thank you.'

As she walked out of his office, she couldn't help but note that he'd only addressed her by her given name since the day the truth about his brother had come out.

Daniele was as good as his word. Two days later he told her over breakfast that he'd thought about it and would attend the opening of the hospital in Caballeros, which would be the permanent memorial to his brother.

And now here they were, five days after that decision, in a convoy of cars with the tightest of security driving over the potholed narrow Caballeron roads to the hospital itself.

It felt like a lifetime ago since Eva had been in this country but it had hardly been two months. She didn't see any material changes, not until their driver slowed for a security cordon and showed their pass, and they were directed to the hospital car park where she saw what Daniele and his family had created.

In the middle of a city where the electricity failed on a daily basis stood a huge gleaming white building that was obviously a hospital but which had been constructed with a sympathy to the country's Spanish-Caribbean heritage. Hundreds of people stood inside the cordon, the vast majority of them from the press. A little apart from them, heavily guarded by Felipe's men, were Daniele's mother, sister, aunt, cousin and sister-in-law, along with dozens of other faces she didn't recognise but guessed were friends or colleagues of Pieta Pellegrini. She saw the Governor of the city and his entourage too. They were all keeping a wary eye on Felipe, who hadn't let go of his fiancée's hand since their arrival.

On the other side of the cordon stood, literally, thousands of Caballerons, there to witness the opening of a hospital in their desolate country, a place they could give birth in, take their injured children to and be treated for all manner of diseases and ailments.

Daniele held her hand tightly as they joined his family. He embraced his mother and sister then looked at Matteo.

Eva held her breath. She thought she heard everyone else hold theirs too.

Matteo held his hand out to him.

The last time Daniele and Matteo had seen each other had been the fight that had brought Daniele to her refugee camp so she could patch him up.

Then, the flashlight of cameras going off all around them, Daniele ignored his cousin's hand and pulled him into a bear hug that made Eva's belly turn to mush. After this wonderful display of Italian affection, Daniele then stood before his sister-in-law and kissed and embraced her too.

With the Pellegrinis all back together, they stood by the main hospital entrance, beneath the plaque that bore Pieta's name.

A small podium with a microphone had been set up for the speeches that would follow.

To Eva's shock, Daniele stepped onto it first.

Silence fell.

He cleared his throat and darted a glance at her. Her hand at her throat, she gave the briefest of nods.

He spoke in English. 'Ladies and gentlemen, I thank you all for coming here today for the opening of the hospital my brother, Pieta, had planned to build before he was so cruelly taken away from us. My brother was a good, inspirational man who always used the privilege he was born with to help others.'

A murmur rippled through the crowd. Eva didn't need to guess what it was for.

'I'm sure many of you have read the stories about him in recent weeks. They are all true.'

Now the murmurs turned into muffled gasps. No one had expected him to tackle the issue head on.

'He made mistakes. He was human. He lied and he cheated and like every one of us here his blood ran red.'

Now hushed silence fell again.

'I wish—we, his family, we all wish—that he'd had the courage to be open with us about his sexuality. Nothing would have changed. We would have still loved him. We *do* still love him and we want nothing to detract from the good work my brother did or detract from the immense courage he showed in the rest of his life. Without him, without his vision, without his refusal to simply accept that some things could never be done, none of us would be here today and this ground we stand on would be the wasteland it once was. This hospital was Pieta's response to the hurricane that devastated this country and I know that if there's a heaven he'll be the happiest soul in it to see what's been accomplished in his memory.'

Then he nodded his thanks to his captive audience and stepped off the podium and went straight back to Eva's side, taking her hand and holding it tightly.

'That was amazing,' she whispered, so full of pride she struggled to get the words out.

He squeezed a response and then they both watched as the self-important corrupt Governor took his place on the podium.

Her heart was beating too loudly to hear anything else that was said.

It wasn't just Daniele's acceptance of his brother and the past that had her so choked, it was the way he held her hand.

Other than in the bedroom, there had been no affection between them since Christmas and only now that he was showing it again did she realise how badly his withdrawal had hurt her. She'd carried on as best she could, pretending to herself that it didn't matter, that this was the marriage she'd signed up to, but now, his fingers locked through hers, her pride for him as real and as filling as anything she'd ever known, the truth hit her like a cold slap.

She didn't want the marriage she'd signed up for. She wanted the real thing. She wanted to have a dozen of his babies and raise them with him. She wanted to watch his hair turn from dark to grey. She wanted to see the lines that had begun to etch his face deepen into grooves. She wanted to hold his hand for ever.

'Are you okay?'

She blinked out of the trance she'd fallen into.

The speeches were over and Daniele was staring at her with the creased brow that would one day turn into the groove she wanted to be there to see.

She needed to smile some reassurance at him but the muscles in her face didn't want to work.

'I'm fine. Just a little overwhelmed.' No, not a little over-whelmed. *Completely* overwhelmed, by her feelings and by the sheer terror making her skin chill and her blood feel like ice.

She'd been frightened before, many times, but never had she felt fear like this.

She'd done the worst thing she could have possibly done and fallen in love with him.

How could she be so *stupid* and make herself so vulnerable as to love someone who could never love her back?

And then she looked at the worry in his eyes. Even if he didn't love her, he did feel something for her. Didn't he…?

He cupped her cheek. 'Do you still want to go to the camp?'

She'd mentioned that she'd like to visit the children there and see how everyone was getting on. He'd suggested she go after the memorial as they'd be flying back to Italy in the morning. He'd then surprised her by asking if she wanted him to go with her. Thinking he should spend the time with his family, she'd reluctantly said no. The Pelligrinis would fly to the neighbour-ing island of Aguadilla and she would join them in a few hours. It was all arranged. Felipe had arranged for three of his men to go with her. She'd laughed at the idea of having bodyguards until Daniele had reminded her, with more force than he usually spoke with, that she would only go to the camp with armed protection at her side, that she needed to remember she was a wealthy woman married into a famous family and so would have a price on her head.

Remembering that insistence made her wonder again if it was possible his feelings for her had developed as hers had for him. Now that all the stress that had been hanging over him had gone, could they look at creating a proper future together, as a real husband and wife? Was there a chance for her, for them, to be happy?

Eva raised herself onto her toes and kissed him lightly on the mouth. 'I'm sure. Go be with your family. I'll only be a few hours behind you.'

His eyes bored intently into hers. 'Promise me you'll be careful.'

'I promise.'

Then he kissed her, his first real kiss in so long that she felt she could cry from the joy of it.

Tonight, she promised herself as she got into the waiting car that would take her to the camp. Tonight she would talk properly with him. She would tell him her feelings and see if they had a true future together.

CHAPTER THIRTEEN

'WHAT ARE YOU so worried about?'

Daniele turned his head to find his sister standing by his side.

'Eva's still not here.'

He was sitting at a table near the entrance in one of the Eden Hotel's bars, a huge glittering room with an open wall that led out to the moonlit beach.

Francesca took the seat beside him. He could sense her rolling her eyes. 'She messaged you an hour ago to say she would be late. A delay at the airport, wasn't it?'

He nodded. When they'd made their plans to leave Caballeros for Aguadilla, they hadn't factored in that scores of press would also be fleeing the country en masse. No one with any sense would stay in Caballeros any longer than necessary, not unless they were compassionate people like his wife, who would still be working in the refugee camp there if he hadn't paid her to marry him. The airport was backlogged with aeroplanes trying to take off.

'She'll be here soon enough.'

'Her phone's battery was going flat.' If Eva needed him she wouldn't be able to get in touch. Anything could happen to her and wouldn't know until it was too late.

He should have insisted on going to the camp with her but

at the time it hadn't sounded at all unreasonable for her to go without him so long as she had adequate protection.

'So? Seb and a couple of his men are with her. Nothing's going to happen to her so stop worrying.' Seb was Felipe's right-hand man and ex-British Special Forces.

Francesca pointed at their mother, who was having a tearful but animated conversation with a noticeably pregnant Natasha. Their aunt Rachele was chatting with Matteo, who was staring at her with barely concealed bemusement. From her wildly gesticulating arms and the frizzing of her hair, Aunt Rachele was already two sheets to the wind. 'I'm so glad we've all made amends. I still feel guilty about cutting them off.'

'Don't. You didn't know.'

She sighed. 'No. I didn't. I should have known, though.'

'What? That Pieta was gay?'

'No, silly. I meant that Matteo wouldn't have touched Natasha if he hadn't had such strong feelings for her, and Natasha would never have started an affair with Matteo if she were grieving for Pieta like a real wife.'

'What's a real wife supposed to mean?'

'One who loves her husband and is loved in return. The way Felipe and I feel for each other and the way you and Eva feel for each other.'

'Eva and I don't feel anything for each other, not in the way you mean.'

'Don't pretend, Daniele. I've seen the way you look at her. You can't tell me you're not developing feelings for her.'

His heart made a sudden thump against his ribs. 'We get along well,' he said stiffly. 'But that's the extent of it. We were very firm about what we wanted our marriage to be and it's not one like you're suggesting and nor will it ever be.'

'What's that smell?'

'What smell?' he asked, perplexed.

'Oh. I know what it is. It's bull.'

'Francesca…'

She ignored the warning tone in his voice. 'You're falling in love with her.'

'How much have you drunk? Love and romance are for fools. I know that and Eva knows that. We agreed on the rules when we agreed to marry.'

'Rules are made to be broken.'

'Not in this instance. I'm not in love with her and I never will be.'

'If you say so.'

'I do.'

'Shall I tell Felipe you think he's a fool? He's romantic. And he loves me.'

'Either we talk about something else or you can find someone else to annoy.'

'Am I getting under your skin?'

'Yes.'

She laughed. 'How's Eva getting on with the Maserati you got her for Christmas?'

'Francesca...'

'Drop the threatening tone, you big bully. I've changed the subject.'

He had to laugh. His sister was incorrigible. He had no idea how Felipe put up with her. Eva adored her too.

He sucked in a breath.

He didn't know how he would have got through that speech without Eva standing there with her silent but heartfelt support. Just that one small nod of her head and the glistening in her eyes had been enough for the words to pour out.

But for his sister to suggest he was falling in love with her was ridiculous.

There was a light tap on his shoulder.

Daniele whipped his head round and found Eva standing behind him. She must have come in through the side door.

She gave a smile that didn't meet her eyes. 'Sorry I'm late. The airport was in chaos.'

He got to his feet and looked closely at her. She was as white as a sheet, the starkness of her pallor contrasting strongly with the red of her hair and the black trouser suit she wore. 'Are you okay? You look like you've seen a ghost. Did Seb and his men look after you?'

'They were great, thank you, but I've got a really bad headache. Have you got our room key? I hope you don't mind but I'm going to go to bed.'

'I'll come with you.'

'*No.*' Her sharpness took him aback. She gave another smile and said in a softer tone, 'Sorry. Please, stay with your family. I just need some sleep. I'll be fine.'

With great reluctance he gave her the spare key. 'We're in the same suite as last time.'

'The suite you bribed me into marrying you in?' There was no malice in her tone but still he looked closely again at her. She really did look ill.

'I'll be up soon.'

'Okay.' Then she leaned over to Francesca and kissed her cheek. 'I'm sure I'll see you at breakfast.'

She walked away without giving Daniele a kiss.

He met Francesca's worried stare.

'She's had a long day,' he said, unsure if his explanation was for his sister's benefit or his own.

For once Francesca kept her mouth shut. 'I'll get us some more drinks.'

When Daniele made it to the suite only his bedside light was on. Eva was curled up under the covers on her side of the bed, her eyes closed, her breathing deep and even.

He made as little noise as he could so as not to disturb her but even as he climbed under the sheets with great care, he couldn't help but feel certain that she was wide awake.

Eva opened her eyes and stared at the dark wall before her. From the sound of his breathing, Daniele had fallen asleep. One of his hands rested on her hip and it was taking everything she had not to shove it away. It had taken everything she had not to flinch when he'd first put it there.

He didn't love her and he never would.

She'd heard it from his own mouth.

I'm not in love with her and I never will be.

You didn't get clearer than that.

How could she have been so careless? Daniele had chosen her because he'd believed she would never fall in love with him. He'd been so abundantly clear about his feelings he might as well have etched it in wood.

Staying with him was out of the question. Now that she knew the truth about her feelings, how could she sleep with him every night and listen to his intimate caresses that would always fall short of the words she burned to hear? Without love, there was nothing to glue them together. There would be nothing to stop his eye from wandering and nothing to stop her heart smashing into pieces to witness it.

She couldn't do it. She couldn't take the pain.

As soon as they got back to the *castello* she would pack her things and leave.

The flight back to Pisa airport felt like the longest flight Daniele had ever taken. His mother and aunt travelled with them in his jet but not even their presence could push out the feeling of impending doom that had lodged in his gut.

Eva had woken with the same headache that had seen her take herself to bed so early the night before. An hour into the flight she'd excused herself to get some more sleep in their bedroom.

She insisted it was only a headache but he was certain she was lying. He would have to wait until they got home and had some privacy before shaking whatever was troubling her out of her. Whatever it was, it spelt trouble. He could feel it in his marrow.

So while she slept, he passed the time playing cards with his mother and aunt. He only learned the two sprightly women were keen poker fiends after they'd cleared him out of all his cash.

He was coming to realise there was lots about his mother he didn't know and, despite his worry about Eva, he found himself enjoying this time with her.

He didn't know if Eva was right that his mother had always needed him but he knew that right then they were enjoying each other's company even while the guilt at all the neglect he'd shown her throughout his adult life pecked at him like an angry woodpecker.

So many thoughts were crowding in his head he was in danger of getting a headache of his own. About to make his excuses and crawl into bed with Eva, his mother dug into the giant handbag she carried everywhere and pulled out a travel-sized game of backgammon.

'Do you want to see if you can beat me at this?' she asked, her eyes gleaming with challenge.

His aunt Rachele cackled wickedly.

Never one to resist a challenge, even if it came from the sixty-six-year-old woman who'd given birth to him and her younger sister, Daniele cleared the table of the cards. And soon found himself thrashed at the game by both of them.

It was mid-afternoon when they landed back in Pisa. His driver was there to collect them. They dropped his mother and aunt home first and then, finally, he was alone with Eva.

'How are you feeling?' he asked her.

'I'm getting there.'

Before he could question her further, she suddenly asked, 'Has the *castello* been transferred into your name yet?'

'All done. I received official confirmation yesterday when you were at the camp.' His lawyer had emailed him. 'I've got a number of calls to make when we get in and then I'm going to take you out.'

She shrugged her shoulders.

'And while we're out you're going to tell me exactly what's wrong with you. And no more lies about a headache.'

'I haven't lied about a headache,' she answered listlessly.

'But there is something troubling you.'

She didn't answer but as they'd arrived home, he told himself it could wait for half an hour while he got his affairs in order. He could then give her his undivided attention without fear of interruption. He would take her out somewhere private and neutral, switch his phone off, insist she turn hers off too, and get her to open up.

It would also give him time to prepare himself...

Suddenly it occurred to him that she could be pregnant. They hadn't discussed having children since that meeting in his suite in Aguadilla when he'd bribed her into marrying him. She'd scorned at the idea of having his children then but everything had changed since then and they'd never used contraception...

He was no pregnancy expert but was sure, having heard from friends with offspring, that tiredness was a big thing in the early stages. It wasn't beyond the realms of possibility for loss of skin colour and headaches to also be factors, was it?

If she was pregnant, he'd have to learn fast.

Holed up in his office while Eva disappeared to their bedroom to shower and change, Daniele called his lawyer and then checked in with Talos Kalliakis to firm up the dates for the renovation of the concert hall Talos owned in Paris.

Him, a father. With Eva's brains and looks their child could be anything in the world. An astronaut. A brain surgeon. A Michelin-starred chef. Anything.

'Daniele, did you hear what I said?' came Talos's gruff tones down the line.

'Sorry. I was miles away. What did you say?'

'Amalie's next to me and is insisting I arrange a date for us to get together. She wants to meet Eva.'

'That sounds great. Let me get my diary.' He refused to trust modern technology when it came to his diary and put all his appointments and meetings in a thick leather-bound tome.

Now, where had he put it?

Spotting it on the sideboard by his record player, he got up from his seat. Just as he stretched his fingers out to grab it, something caught his eye from outside.

Abandoning the diary, he walked to the window, which overlooked the courtyard, and looked out.

Eva was putting a suitcase in the boot of the car he'd brought her.

All thoughts of his conversation forgotten, he dropped his phone and banged on the window.

'Eva!'

She looked around, clearly trying to see where the noise had come from.

He banged on it again. If he used any more force the glass would shatter.

Now she saw him.

Even with the distance between them he saw the panic in her eyes.

Never in his life had his fingers been as useless as they were right then as he tried to open the latch of the window. She'd closed the boot shut and was rushing to the driver's side when he finally threw the window open and hollered out, 'Don't you dare go anywhere. Do you hear me? Stay right where you are.'

Then he ran, through the corridors, down the stairs, through more corridors, every step he took the certainty growing that by the time he reached the courtyard she'd be gone.

She wasn't gone. And neither had she moved.

'Where are you going?' he demanded, racing over to her and snatching the car keys from her hand.

But he already knew the answer.

The answer had been with him since she'd arrived at the hotel last night as white as a sheet and throughout the long night when she had slept like a statue beside him. He'd just refused to see it.

'Away.'

'Away where? For how long?'

He knew the answer to the latter question too.

She closed her eyes and rubbed a knuckle on her forehead. 'Daniele, I can't do this any more. The *castello*'s in your name. It can't be taken away from you. It's safe with your family. You don't need me any more. I'm free to leave.'

'Without saying goodbye? Without even a word of explanation? You were just going to leave?'

'I've left a note for you in our bedroom.'

His hand clenched around the keys, fury shooting through him and overriding the dread that had clutched at his throat when he'd looked out of his window and known exactly what she was doing. 'Well, that makes everything fine. You left me a note'

'Please, Daniele, don't make this any harder for me than it already is. Give me the keys and go back inside.'

'You want the keys? Come and get them. But you're not going anywhere until you tell me why you're prepared to up and leave without a word to me, and don't you dare mention that bloody note. I've never thought you a coward before. Tell me to my face why you would treat me with such contempt.'

'Me treat *you* with contempt?' She rubbed her forehead again then raised her eyes to the sky. When she lowered them and fixed them on his, the panic and fear he'd seen in them had gone. Now they blazed. '*Me?* How you have the nerve to say that after the way you spoke about me to your sister...'

'What are you talking about?'

'I heard you,' she snarled. 'I heard everything you said. *Love and romance are for fools. I'm not in love with her and I never will be.* You said it. You said that about *me*.'

'So what? That's what we agreed on when we—'

'To hell with what we agreed!' she screamed, charging forward to thump his chest. 'This is why I wanted to escape without seeing you. I knew you'd be blasé about it, just as I knew I wouldn't be able to bear to hear you dismiss what we have to some stupid agreement we made.' She thumped at his chest again. 'You thought you'd married some emotionless bitch who would never be so stupid as to fall in love with you. *Love and romance are for fools. I know that and Eva knows that. We agreed on the rules when we agreed to marry.*'

Her mimicry over, she stepped back, visibly shaking, her face twisted with a strange combination of grief and fury that it hurt him to see. 'I've broken the rules. I've screwed up. I've fallen in love with you and I do not want to pretend happy marriages any more. I want a real happy marriage. I want you to love me. Can you love me? Can you?'

She threw her words at him as a challenge.

'Eva…'

'Of course you can't. I heard you say it. You're emotionally spineless.'

Her insult stoked his anger at what she was doing and his incomprehension. 'You call me emotionally spineless when you're the one running away?'

'I'm not running, I'm leaving.'

Like that made any difference whatsoever.

'You *always* run away. You ran away from your parents and then when you lost Johann you ran away from your life, and now you're running away from me, and you know why? Because you're too much of a coward to stay and fight.'

'How was I supposed to fight my parents? I was a *child*!'

'Running from them taught you the only way to cope is by running away.'

'Well, seeing as you're now a self-appointed shrink, maybe you could tell me what kind of life I was supposed to fight for after Johann. What life did I have? Who did I have? I'd cut myself off from my family. Johann's family had emigrated to Australia. I had no real friends. So you tell me what life it was I was fighting for.'

'*Your* life! Not a life hiding away in a Third World country shunning friendships and relationships.'

'Oh, so now you're an expert on relationships as well as a shrink? You're the one who's spent their entire life shunning relationships, not me, too busy trying to best your brother in everything you did and prove your worth to the family that has always loved you, living the playboy life, showing off in your fast cars and your jets and your yachts and hand-stitched clothes to want anything deeper or meaningful. Everything's disposable for you, including me!'

His fury coiled into such rage he shook with the violence of it. 'You've gone too far.'

'The truth hurts, doesn't it?' she spat. 'A nice, simple marriage with a woman with the emotional capacity of a goldfish, that's all you can cope with, isn't it? Well, sorry to disappoint you but it turns out I'm a lot more emotional than you thought. Sorry I'm not level-headed, sensible Eva. Turns out I actually do have feelings and unless you can return them then there is nothing for me to fight for so I suggest you give me those car keys and let me *go.*'

'Eva...' He took what felt like the longest, deepest breath of his life. If he didn't get hold of his anger right now there was every chance he would throw her over his shoulder and march her back inside and lock her in the cellar.

'Unless you can tell me that you love me or that there's a chance you could one day love me, I don't want to hear another word.'

The pounding in his chest vibrated through every part of him, from the soles of his feet to the hair on his head, the noise so loud he could hardly think straight. 'How can I make a promise like that? I want you. I like and respect you. Isn't that enough?'

'Not for me it isn't. I want everything. I want your babies. I want to grow old with you.'

'I want, I want, I want,' he mimicked. 'Everything's about what you want, isn't it? Where does what *I* want come into it?'

'Well what *do* you want?'

'The marriage we agreed on!'

'Then that's too bad because that's not what I want. And seeing as you don't want to hear what I do want, I'll tell you what I *don't* want. I don't want to waste the best years of my life pining for you and wishing like a lovesick fool for you to feel things you're not capable of feeling. I might not have much but I do have my self-respect. Now, for the last time, *give me the keys*.'

'Fine.' He threw them as hard and as far as he could, at the other side of the car from where she stood. 'You want the keys, then you go and get them. You want to leave then be my guest. I never wanted a needy wife in the first place.'

CHAPTER FOURTEEN

HATE AND FURY filling her so much she could vomit, Eva scrambled on the cold ground for the keys to her escape while Daniele shoved his hands in his pockets and strolled back into the *castello* without a backward glance. All that was missing was a cheery whistle.

Hands shaking so much she had to put one on top of the other to insert the key into the ignition, it took three attempts to turn the engine on.

The sound of the wheels screeching as she sped out of the courtyard was extremely satisfying.

She must have been mad to think she loved him. Must have been. How could anyone love a bastard like Daniele Pellegrini? He was cruel beyond belief.

Why couldn't he have just let her go without making a fuss? He was the one who wanted to stick to their original deal, and their original deal had been that she could leave without any issue, any time she wanted. Sure, he'd asked her to explain her decision if she ever did decide to leave, and she'd done that. She'd left him a letter.

How dared he accuse her of cowardice and of running away? He was the coward, not her, the selfish, egotistical...

Almost too late, she saw the tight hairpin bend mere yards

ahead and slammed her foot on the brake. The car skidded and there was one long moment that seemed to last for ever, when she was certain the car was going to fly off the road with such force that not even the metal barrier would stop her hurtling down the steep olive grove on the other side of it.

The barrier did its job.

When she finally had the car under control and had brought it to a stop, both her knees were jerking manically. She caught a glimpse of her reflection in the rear-view mirror and saw her face was as white as her knuckles holding onto the steering wheel for dear life.

A little ahead of her was a passing place and somehow she managed to steer the car to it, crawling at a snail's pace in fits and spurts.

Then she turned the engine off and rested her head back, taking deep shuddering breaths into her petrified body.

The passenger door had buckled under the impact of the collision with the barrier.

But no matter how many breaths she took it wasn't enough for her to keep it together a minute longer. The first tear spilled out and landed on her jumper with a splash, the second and third falling in quick succession until she was crying so hard her eyes were blinded and her heart felt like it was ripping out of her.

Eva had left her note on the dressing table.

Daniele snatched it up, scrunched it into a tight ball, and threw it into the fire.

He didn't care what she'd written. She'd said everything she wanted to say. They'd both said everything that needed saying.

Good riddance to her.

It was just a shame she'd only had the time to pack one suitcase before running away like the yellow-bellied coward he'd never thought she could be. Her dressing room was still filled with the clothes he'd paid for.

He stared at them for a long time then slowly backed out of

the dressing room, his hands clenched in fists to stop himself from grabbing it all and shredding it into rags.

It felt like he had a living being inside him, twisting and biting into his guts, and it needed purging and killing *now*.

He'd hardly drunk a drop of alcohol since his drunken exploits when he'd learned the truth about his brother; even yesterday in the hotel after the memorial he'd limited himself to only a couple. Now seemed the perfect time to remedy that, and while he was remedying it, he could celebrate having his freedom back.

Yes, that's what he would do. He would celebrate his regained freedom. He'd get changed and go to Club Giroud...

Before he could take more than two paces back to his bedroom, his phone rang in his pocket.

He pulled it out and was disconcerted to find his hands were shaking.

His heart sank to his feet to see it wasn't Eva's name that flashed up.

Why would he want her to call? he asked himself bitterly. For someone who professed to be in love with him, she clearly didn't think he was worth enough to stay and fight for. She didn't think what they had was worth fighting for.

If it had been anyone but his mother, he would have ignored the call but he couldn't ignore her. He'd spent enough of his adult life avoiding her calls.

She wanted to know if Eva was feeling any better.

Opening his mouth to say, 'I don't know and I don't care. Eva's gone and she's never coming back,' he instead found himself saying, 'Yes, she's much better.'

Eva was so much better that she'd driven away with a parting screech of tyre for good measure.

'Good,' his mother said. 'I was worried about her.'

'You have nothing to worry about.' He quickly changed the subject, swallowing back the monster in his guts that had reared up again.

The chatted for a couple more minutes before he said, 'I need to go now, Mamma.'

He couldn't remember the last time he'd addressed her so informally.

'Okay, my son. I'll see you soon. I love you.'

'I love you too,' he whispered.

Disconnecting the call, he closed his eyes.

When had he and his mother last verbalised their love for each other? He honestly could not remember.

For so many years he'd practically demonised her in his own head, just as he'd demonised his father.

He'd let his semi-estrangement from his father prevent him from being there for him when he'd died and it was something he regretted more and more as time passed. All those years when his father had been ill and still Daniele had kept his distance.

He slumped onto the floor, dimly aware this was almost the same spot he'd slumped down at before when he'd been drunk and Eva had been so compassionate and attentive in her care of him.

Eva was right. He *was* selfish.

The only member of his family he'd ever been close to was his sister and that was because she was impossible not to love and, he had to admit, a bit of a wayward rebel just as he'd been but with different things to rebel against.

What had his parents ever done for him to create such distance from them? Comparisons to his brother? Encouragement for him to be more like his brother? Chastisement for the times his exploits had brought shame on them?

The feeling that nothing he did would ever be good enough for them?

What about all the good times, and there had been many of those. His mother's face lighting up when he'd walked into her private hospital room as an eleven-year-old meeting his brand-new baby sister for the first time. His mother had made room on her bed for him to sit beside her so she could cuddle him tightly to her.

And what about the time his father had taken a teenage Daniele, and only Daniele, to the Monza track for a day driving at high speed, the pair of them racing each other like lunatics.

It had been too easy to push aside the good memories and embrace only the bad.

His father was dead. It was too late to make his peace, but it wasn't too late for him and his mother. She was a loving woman. She had her flaws but who didn't? Daniele had so many that Eva had spat them all at him just a short while ago.

He'd married Eva for the sake of his family's happiness and peace of mind. He'd never cared for the *castello* and would have been happy for it to be sold off.

Through Eva he'd learned to love the cold castle where they'd made their home and now he found himself wanting to be embraced back into the bosom of the family he'd neglected for so long.

Had the distance between him and his parents been a creation of his own making, driven by his jealousy and single-minded rivalry with his brother? Because surely it was his relationship with Pieta that had clouded every other relationship he'd ever had; that feeling of always being second best.

Eva never made him feel second best. When she looked at him she saw him whole. She knew him better and more intimately than anyone else had ever done and still she loved him.

Eva loved him.

Eva had driven out of the courtyard like a woman possessed...

A sudden image of her car lying in a crumpled heap struck pure terror into his veins, followed by an eruption of emotion so big the waves rippled out of him; the truth he'd refused to see flashing in colours so bright he could no longer deny them.

Eva loved him.

And he loved her.

Snatching his phone, he dialled her number—he'd learned it by heart—but found it went straight to voicemail. She'd either turned it off or hadn't bothered to recharge the battery.

He scrambled to his feet and raced around, looking for a set of car keys.

The first ones he located were for the Ferrari, and he ran to it with lungs fit to burst.

He had to find her. He couldn't let her go. He couldn't.

His clever, serious, compassionate, passionate, beautiful wife *loved* him.

What they hell had he been thinking, letting her drive away?

Which way had she gone? Left to Pisa or right to Florence?

Instinct told him she would have gone left to Pisa. She was familiar with its airport.

Yes, that's where she'd gone.

He blinked the image of her crumpled in her car from his mind. If he let it take that route he would go mad long before he found her.

Fighting the need to thrash the hell out of his Ferrari, he nevertheless raced through the winding roads, leaving a trail of dust behind him.

Ten minutes into his drive and he only just remembered to brake in time to steer round the tight hairpin bend everyone familiar with this stretch of road knew as the Death Bend, for obvious reasons.

Fresh tyre tracks lay on it, evidence that someone had had a near-miss here very recently…

His heart lodged fully in his throat, he steered round the straight and slowed even more.

Then his heart just stopped.

The barrier that was there to stop cars hurtling down the steep olive grove had a contortion in it that hadn't been there when they'd driven back from the airport earlier.

Someone had recently—very recently—crashed into it.

But where was the car?

* * *

Eva had run out of tissues with which to blow her nose.

She couldn't stop crying. Every time she thought she was all cried out and capable of driving, fresh tears would fall. All she had left to cry into was a napkin she'd scavenged from the bottom of her handbag.

But she couldn't stay here. The sun was starting to set and she needed to find her way to the airport on roads she still wasn't completely familiar with in a car she loved but still hadn't quite got to grips with.

She had the rest of her life to mourn.

Taking one more deep inhalation, she turned the engine back on and gritted her teeth.

Her heart might feel it had been ripped out of her but that didn't mean she was suicidal. On the contrary.

She wanted to live. And that meant driving without tears blinding her.

Her feelings for Daniele had crystallised during her few hours back at the camp in Caballeros. So many of the children and teenagers had come over to say hello and embrace her, Odney hunting her down specifically to show off his number three ranking in the colourful ball phone game. The few senior members of staff at the camp at the time had been thrilled to see her—a rich husband who'd donated three million dollars in recent months was bound to make her popular with *them*. But none of her regular colleagues, who knew nothing about Daniele's donation, had gone out of their way to say hello.

She'd never realised the distance she'd created between her colleagues and herself. She'd always thought they got along well, and they *had* but only in a professional sense. She'd turned down their social offers so many times that they'd stopped asking her. Her weekends off had always been spent alone in a cheap hotel room.

Daniele had brought the sunshine into her life without her even realising.

How had she lived without that sunshine? But, then, she hadn't been living, had she? Ever since Johann had died she'd been alone in the world and simply functioning.

Daniele had made her feel again, all the things she'd been so frightened of because having real emotions and feelings for people meant you could get hurt.

She was hurting now, hurting more than she'd ever hurt before in her life, yet, somehow, the sunshine he'd blessed her with felt like a gift and she knew if she drove the sunshine out of her again and slipped back into the darkness she would stay in that black hole for ever...

Slamming her foot on the brake, she brought her car back to a stop.

What did she mean, *if* she drove the sunshine out again?

She was driving this car. She was driving it away from Daniele and away from the sunshine. The sun would still beat down on her but it wouldn't beat as strongly. She would never feel it soak into her skin and into the very heart of her without him.

And she wasn't driving away, was she?

She was running away.

Daniele was right. She was a coward. She'd thrown her feelings at him and then thrown a tantrum because he hadn't returned them. She'd already told herself what response to expect from him, had overheard his talk with his sister and convinced herself that what he'd said was the truth and he would never love her.

But what about the truth in the loving, possessive way he made love to her? Or the truth in the way he looked at her and valued her as a person as well as his lover? Or the truth that he had kept every promise he'd ever made to her?

Wasn't all that worth fighting for?

A car hooted loudly as it swerved past her, jolting her out of her trance.

She needed to go back.

Spinning the car round, she sped back along the road she'd just travelled, having to control herself to keep only just above the legal limit.

Please be there, Daniele, she prayed. *Please be at home…*

She screeched the brakes again as she flew past the passing place she'd only recently steered the car away from.

She recognised the car that was parked exactly where she had so recently parked.

She recognised the man looking over the barrier, a distance ahead of the car.

Only just remembering to use her mirrors to make sure no one was approaching her from behind, she reversed sharply and slid her car into the tight space in front of his.

Throwing herself out, she saw his long legs were already marching towards her.

And then her own legs, which so desperately wanted to run to him, turned to jelly.

She couldn't take a step. She couldn't work her vocal cords to make a sound.

It didn't matter.

Daniele was before her in moments, his face grim and twisted. He didn't hesitate, simply grabbed hold of her and pulled her to him to crush her against his chest, holding her so tightly that she couldn't breathe.

'Don't you ever do that to me again,' he said into her hair, speaking in a voice she'd never heard before. 'Do you hear me? Don't you *ever* leave me.'

Managing to dislodge herself enough to look up at him, she realised with complete shock why his voice sounded so different.

Daniele was crying.

He took her face roughly in his hands and brought his down to hers, his salty tears falling onto her cheeks.

'I thought you were *dead*.' His voice broke completely. 'I saw the damage to the barrier and thought you'd gone over.'

And then he was kissing her, her mouth, her cheeks, her nose, her eyes; smothering her, the kisses born of desperation and relief. Then with an oath he crushed her to him again, one hand tight around her waist, the other wrapping itself in her hair.

'I have never been so scared in my life. I thought I'd lost you.'

'Never,' she whispered, her words muffled against his sweater. 'I'm sorry for—'

'Don't,' he cut her off. '*Dio*, Eva...'

For a long time, they just stood there clinging to each other, Daniele's heart thudding heavily against her ear, her heart thudding heavily against his abdomen, his mouth pressing into the top of her head.

'You're mine, Eva Pellegrini,' he whispered. 'You belong to me and I will never let you go again.'

She'd never thought she would want to hear those words but hearing them from Daniele's lips made her heart swell with such joy the tears started falling again.

'And I belong to you,' he continued in the same low voice. 'My heart is yours to do with as you will. You're my wife and I love you. I would do anything for you. Anything. I want you to have my babies and I want to wake up beside you every day and know you are mine and that we belong together. I want to wear your ring on my finger as you wear mine. I'm sorry for the cruel things—'

'Don't,' she said, this time the one to cut *him* off. No explanations were needed. They knew each other too well for that. 'We both said cruel things.' She raised herself to breathe into his neck. 'I love you.'

'Not as much as I love you.'

'More.'

'Not possible.'

He took her face in his hands again and their tears mingled as his lips found hers and he kissed her with such tender passion that it was as if the fading sun had given one last burst of energy to shine a spotlight on them.

When a car drove past them and honked loudly at their entwined figures, Daniele broke the kiss with a laugh.

'Let's go home, wife.'

'As long as I'm with you, I don't care where we go, husband.'

EPILOGUE

THE FAMILY WING of the *castello* was completely overrun with children. Everywhere Daniele went he seemed to tread on some toy or other and had grinned wickedly when he'd seen his cousin Matteo walk barefoot onto a tiny building block.

Daniele's three children were playing hide-and-seek with their cousins. After the game of War Against the Girls, this seemed safer. His sister's son Sergio, a sturdy six-year-old with his mother's bossy nature, had teamed up with Daniele's middle child, Pieta. The two imps had stalked then cornered the two older girls, Matteo and Natasha's shy daughter Lauren, and his and Eva's oldest daughter Tessel, and fired a round of rubber bullets at them. There had been lots of screams and name calling after that.

Those damn rubber bullets got everywhere. He wondered if his mother knew she had one stuck in her hair.

He dreaded to think what kind of state the place would be in tomorrow when all the Christmas presents had been opened.

Sneaking out of the living room, he dodged small children and threw himself into his bedroom with mock relief.

Eva was on the bed, reading, the look on her face serene.

'Escaping again?' she queried with a raised brow.

'It's all right for you,' he grumbled, getting onto the bed and snuggling up next to her. 'You've got a perfect excuse to escape the carnage.'

His beautiful wife was two weeks away from giving birth to their fourth child. This meant she could legitimately hide herself away when the noise rose to the level of a rock concert on the pretext that she needed to rest.

'You can carry the next one if you want,' she teased.

'The next one? You want *five* children?'

'No.' She grinned. 'I was thinking of six.'

Completely unable to resist, he kissed her. 'I'm happy to keep going until you say stop.'

She hooked an arm around his neck. 'You might live to regret that.'

It amazed him that even now, after six years together and with Eva huge with child, he still desired her as much as he ever had.

But there was no chance to act on it when their bedroom door flew open and Pieta and Sergio charged in.

'Mamma, Papa, Father Christmas is here!' Pieta shouted, his little face alight with glee.

'Really? Are you sure?'

'He's really here,' Sergio confirmed, nodding his head vigorously. 'Mamma says you've got to stop playing alone with Aunty Eva and come!'

Exchanging a secret smile with his wife, Daniele helped her off the bed and they all went back into the living room, where Father Christmas was making bellows of 'Ho-ho-ho!' whilst drinking a large glass of red wine.

If any of the children cared to look beneath the bushy white beard they would see the less bushy black beard of his macho brother-in-law Felipe who, much to his disgust, had been coerced into playing Father Christmas a number of years ago, and now found himself stuck with the role every year. And every year Daniele's evil sister would cackle like a loon to watch him do it.

'Your sister is evil,' Eva whispered into his ear, her thoughts, as was so often the case, concurring perfectly with his.

'She certainly is,' he agreed, kissing her temple.

From the corner of his eye he saw Matteo and Natasha whispering together with giggles and felt quite sure they were saying the same thing. Or maybe they were laughing at Aunt Rachele, who'd fallen asleep with a glass of sherry still in her hand.

All his family. All here together. Just how he liked it.

And, best of all, his Eva was holding his hand and tonight he would go to bed and make very gentle love to her.

She was definitely his happy Eva after.

* * * * *

Two-Week Texas Seduction

Cat Schield

DESIRE

Scandalous world of the elite.

Cat Schield has been reading and writing romance since high school. Although she graduated from college with a BA in business, her idea of a perfect career was writing books for Harlequin. And now, after winning the Romance Writers of America 2010 Golden Heart® Award for Best Contemporary Series Romance, that dream has come true. Cat lives in Minnesota with her daughter, Emily, and their Burmese cat. When she's not writing sexy, romantic stories for Harlequin Desire, she can be found sailing with friends on the St. Croix River, or in more exotic locales, like the Caribbean and Europe. She loves to hear from readers. Find her at catschield.com and follow her on Twitter, @catschield.

Books by Cat Schield

Harlequin Desire

The Black Sheep's Secret Child
Nanny Makes Three

The Sherdana Royals

Royal Heirs Required
A Royal Baby Surprise
Secret Child, Royal Scandal

Las Vegas Nights

At Odds with the Heiress
A Merger by Marriage
A Taste of Temptation

Texas Cattleman's Club: Blackmail

Two-Week Texas Seduction

Visit her Author Profile page at
millsandboon.com.au,
or catschield.com, for more titles!

Dear Readers,

I'm excited to be participating in my third Texas Cattleman's Club series with *Two-Week Texas Seduction*. Almost from the start I knew Brandee and Shane were going to be a blast to write. From their sexy banter to the slow disintegration of their guards, every moment I spent with them was a joy. This blackmail series is going to be such fun to read. I hope you enjoy Brandee and Shane's story.

All the best,

Cat Schield

For everyone trying to make ends
meet while keeping your dreams alive.
Never give up, never surrender.

CHAPTER ONE

BEFORE SHE'D MOVED to Royal, Texas, few people had ever done Brandee Lawless any favors. If this had left her with an attitude of "you're damned right I can," she wasn't going to apologize. She spoke her mind and sometimes that ruffled feathers. Lately those feathers belonged to a trio of women new to the Texas Cattleman's Club. Cecelia Morgan, Simone Parker and Naomi Price had begun making waves as soon as they'd been accepted as members and Brandee had opposed them at every turn.

Her long legs made short work of the clubhouse foyer and the hallway leading to the high-ceilinged dining room where she and her best friend, Chelsea Hunt, were having lunch. At five feet five inches, she wasn't exactly an imposing figure, but she knew how to make an entrance.

Instead of her usual denim, boots, work shirt and cowboy hat, Brandee wore a gray fit-and-flare sweater dress with lace inset cuffs over a layered tulle slip, also in gray. She'd braided sections of her long blond hair and fastened them with rhinestone-encrusted bobby pins. She noted three pair of eyes watching her progress across the room and imagined the women assessing her outfit. To let them know she wasn't the least bit bothered, Brandee made sure she took her time winding through the diners on her way to the table by the window.

Chelsea looked up from the menu as she neared. Her green eyes widened. "Wow, you look great."

Delighted by her friend's approval, Brandee smiled. "Part of the new collection." In addition to running one of the most profitable ranches in Royal, Texas, Brandee still designed a few pieces of clothing and accessories for the fashion company she'd started twelve years earlier. "What do you think of the boots?"

"I'm sick with jealousy." Chelsea eyed the bright purple Tres Outlaws and grinned. "You are going to let me borrow them, I hope."

"Of course."

Brandee sat down, basking in feminine satisfaction. With all the hours she put in working her ranch, most saw her as a tomboy. Despite a closet full of frivolous, girlie clothes, getting dressed up for the sole purpose of coming into town for a leisurely lunch was a rare occurrence. But this was a celebration. Her first monthlong teenage outreach session was booked solid. This summer Hope Springs Camp was going to make a difference in those kids' lives.

"You made quite an impression on the terrible trio." Chelsea tipped her head to indicate the three newly minted members of the Texas Cattleman's Club. "They're staring at us and whispering."

"No doubt hating on what I'm wearing. I don't know why they think I care what they say about me."

It was a bit like being in high school, where the pretty, popular girls ganged up on anyone they viewed as easy prey. Not that Brandee was weak. In fact, her standing in the club and in the community was strong.

"It's pack mentality," Brandee continued. "On their own they feel powerless, but put them in a group and they'll tear you apart."

"I suppose it doesn't help that you're more successful than they are."

"Or that I've been blocking their attempts to run this club like their personal playground. All this politicking is such a distraction. I'd much rather spend my time holed up at Hope Springs, working the ranch."

"I'm sure they'd prefer that, as well. Especially when you show up looking like this." Chelsea gestured to Brandee's outfit. "You look like a million bucks. They must hate it."

"Except I'm wearing a very affordable line of clothing. I started the company with the idea that I wanted the price points to be within reach of teenagers and women who couldn't afford to pay the designer prices."

"I think it's more the way you wear your success. You are confident without ever having to build yourself up or tear someone else down."

"It comes from accepting my flaws."

"You have flaws?"

Brandee felt a rush of affection for her best friend. An ex-hacker and present CTO of the Hunt & Co. chain of steak houses, Chelsea was the complete package of brains and beauty. From the moment they'd met, Brandee had loved her friend's kick-ass attitude.

"Everyone has things about themselves they don't like," Brandee said. "My lips are too thin and my ears stick out. My dad used to say they were good for keeping my hat from going too low and covering my eyes."

As always, bringing up her father gave Brandee a bittersweet pang. Until she'd lost him to a freak accident when she was twelve, he'd been her world. From him she'd learned how to run a ranch, and the joys of hard work and a job well done. Without his voice in her head, she never would've had the courage to run from the bad situation with her mother at seventeen and to become a successful rancher.

"But you modeled your own designs for your online store," Chelsea exclaimed. "How did you do that if you were so uncomfortable about how you looked?"

"I think what makes us stand out is what makes us interesting. And memorable. Think of all those gorgeous beauty queens competing in pageants. The ones you remember are those who do something wrong and get called out or who overcome disabilities to compete."

"So the three over there are forgettable?" With a minute twitch of her head, Chelsea indicated the trio of mean girls.

"As far as I'm concerned." Brandee smiled. "And I think they know it. Which is why they work so hard to be noticed."

She'd barely finished speaking when a stir in the air raised her hackles. A second later a tall, athletically built man appeared beside their table, blocking their view of the three women. Shane Delgado. Brandee had detected his ruggedly masculine aftershave a second before she saw him.

"Hey, Shane." Chelsea's earlier tension melted away beneath the mega wattage of Shane's charismatic white grin. Brandee resisted the urge to roll her eyes. Shane would love seeing proof that he'd gotten to her.

"Good to see you, Chelsea." His smooth Texas drawl had a trace of New England in it. "Hello, Brandee."

She greeted him without looking in his direction. "Delgado." She kept her tone neutral and disinterested, masking the way her body went on full alert in his presence.

"You're looking particularly gorgeous today."

Across from her, Chelsea glanced with eyebrows raised from Shane to Brandee and back.

"You're not so bad yourself." She didn't need to check out his long legs in immaculate denim jeans or the crisp tan shirt that emphasized his broad shoulders to know the man looked like a million bucks. "Something I can do for you, Delgado?" She hated that she was playing into his hands by asking, but he wouldn't move on until he'd had his say.

"Do?" He caressed the word with his silver tongue and almost made Brandee shiver.

She recognized her mistake, but the damage was done. Her

tone grew impatient as she clarified, "Did you just stop by to say hello or is there something else on your mind?"

"You know what's on my mind." With another man this might have been a horrible pickup line, but Shane had elevated flirting to an art form.

Brandee glanced up and rammed her gaze into his. "My ranch?" For years he'd been pestering her to sell her land so he could ruin the gorgeous vistas with a bunch of luxury homes.

To his credit, the look in his hazel eyes remained friendly and compelling despite her antagonism. "Among other things."

"You're wasting your time," she told him yet again. "I'm not selling."

"I never consider the time I spend with you as wasted." Honey dripped from every vowel as he flashed his perfect white teeth in a sexy grin.

Brandee's nerve endings sizzled in response. Several times in the last few years she'd considered hooking up with the cocky charmer. He possessed a body to die for and offered the perfect balance of risk and fun. Sex with him would be explosive and memorable. Too memorable. No doubt she'd spend the rest of her days wanting more. Except as far as she could tell, Shane wasn't the type to stick around for long. Not that she was looking for anything long-term, but a girl could get addicted to things that weren't necessarily good for her.

"In fact," he continued, sex appeal rolling off him in waves, "I enjoy our little chats."

"Our chats end up with me turning you down." She gave him her best smirk. "Are you saying you enjoy that?"

"Honey, you know I never back down from a challenge."

At long last he broke eye contact and let his gaze roam over her mouth and breasts. His open appreciation electrified Brandee, leaving her tongue-tied and breathless.

"Good seeing you both." With a nod at Chelsea, Shane ambled away.

"Damn," Chelsea muttered, her tone reverent.

"What?" The question came out a little sharper than Brandee intended. She noticed her hands were clenched and relaxed her fingers. It did no good. Her blood continued to boil, but whether with lust or outrage Brandee couldn't determine.

"You two have some serious chemistry going on. How did I not know this?"

"It's not chemistry," Brandee corrected. "It's antagonism."

"Po-tay-to. Po-tah-to. It's hot." Either Chelsea missed Brandee's warning scowl or she chose to ignore it as she continued, "How come you've never taken him for a test drive?"

"Are you crazy? Did you miss the part where he's been trying to buy Hope Springs Ranch for the last three years?"

"Maybe it's because it gives him an excuse to stop by and see you? Remember how he came by the day after the tornado and stayed to help?" Two and a half years earlier an F4 tornado had swept through Royal. The biggest to hit in almost eighty years, it had taken out a chunk of the west side of town including the town hall and a wing of Royal Memorial Hospital before raging on to cause various degrees of damage to several surrounding ranches.

"He wasn't being altruistic. He was sniffing around, checking to see if because of the hit the ranch took whether I was in a position where I had to sell."

"That's not why he spent the next few days cleaning up the storm damage."

Brandee shook her head. Chelsea didn't understand how well Shane hid his true motives for being nice to her. He lived by the motto "You catch more flies with honey than vinegar." The smooth-talking son of a bitch wanted Hope Springs Ranch. If Brandee agreed to sell, she'd never hear from Shane again.

"Where Shane Delgado is concerned, let's agree to disagree," Brandee suggested, not wanting to spoil her lunch with further talk of Shane.

"Okay." Chelsea clasped her hands together on the table and leaned forward. "So, tell me your good news. What's going on?"

"I found out this morning that Hope Springs' first summer session is completely booked."

"Brandee, that's fantastic."

Since purchasing the land that had become Hope Springs Ranch, Brandee had been working to create programs for at-risk teens that helped address destructive behaviors and promote self-esteem. Inspired by her own difficult teen years after losing her dad, Brandee wanted to provide a structured, supportive environment for young adults to learn goal-setting, communication and productive life skills.

"I can't believe how well everything is coming together. And how much work I have to do before the bunkhouses and camp facilities are going to be ready."

"You'll get it all done. You're one of the most driven, organized people I know."

"Thanks for the vote of confidence."

It had taken years of hard work and relentless optimism, but she'd done her dad proud with the success she'd made of Hope Springs Ranch. And now she stood on the threshold of realizing her dream of the camp. Her life was perfect and Brandee couldn't imagine anything better than how she felt at this moment.

Shane strode away from his latest encounter with Brandee feeling like he'd been zapped with a cattle prod. Over the years, he'd engaged in many sizzling exchanges with the spitfire rancher. After each one, he'd conned himself into believing he'd emerged unscathed, while in reality he rarely escaped without several holes poked in his ego.

She was never happy to see him. It didn't seem fair when everything about her brightened his day. Usually he stopped by her ranch and caught her laboring beside her ranch hands, moving cattle, tending to the horses or helping to build the structures for her camp. Clad in worn jeans, faded plaid work shirts and dusty boots, her gray-blue eyes blazing in a face streaked with sweat and dirt, she smelled like horses, hay and hard work. All tomboy. All woman. And he lusted after every lean inch of her.

She, however, was completely immune to him. Given her impenetrable defenses, he should have moved on. There were too many receptive women who appreciated that he was easy and fun, while in Brandee's cool gaze, he glimpsed an ocean of distrust.

But it was the challenge of bringing her around. Of knowing that once he drew her beneath his spell, he would satisfy himself with her complete surrender and emerge triumphant. This didn't mean he was a bad guy. He just wasn't built to be tied down. And from what he'd noticed of Brandee's social life, she wasn't much into long-term relationships, either.

And so he kept going back for more despite knowing each time they tangled she would introduce him to some fresh hell. Today it had been the scent of her perfume. A light floral scent that made him long to gather handfuls of her hair and bury his face in the lustrous gold waves.

"Shane."

His mental meanderings came to a screeching halt. He nodded in acknowledgment toward a trio of women, unsure which one had hailed him. These three were trouble. Cecelia, Simone and Naomi. A blonde, brunette and a redhead. All three women were gorgeous, entitled and dangerous if crossed.

They'd recently been admitted to the Texas Cattleman's Club and were making waves with their demands that the clubhouse needed a feminine face-lift. They wanted to get rid of the old boys' club style and weren't being subtle about manipulating votes in their favor.

Brandee had been one of their most obstinate adversaries, working tirelessly to gather the votes needed to defeat them. She'd infiltrated the ranks of the oldest and most established members in order to preach against every suggestion these three women made. The whole thing was amusing to watch.

Shane responded to Naomi's wave by strolling to their table. "Ladies."

"Join us," Cecelia insisted. She was a striking platinum blonde with an ice queen's sharp eyes. As president of To The Moon, a company specializing in high-end children's furniture, Cecelia was obviously accustomed to being obeyed.

Putting on his best easy grin, Shane shook his head. "Now, you know I'd love nothing more, but I'm sorry to say I'm already running late." He glanced to where his best friend, Gabriel Walsh, sat talking on his cell phone, a half-empty tumbler of scotch on the table before him. "Is there something I can do for you ladies?"

"We noticed you were talking with Brandee Lawless," Simone said, leaning forward in a way that offered a sensational glimpse of her ample cleavage. With lush curves, arresting blue eyes and long black hair, she, too, was a striking blend of beauty and brains. "And we wanted to give you some friendly advice about her."

Had the women picked up on his attraction to Brandee? If so, Shane was losing his touch. He set his hands on the back of the empty fourth chair and leaned in with a conspiratorial wink.

"I'm always happy to listen to advice from beautiful women."

Cecelia nodded as if approving his wisdom. "She's only acting interested in you because she wants you to vote against the clubhouse redesign."

Shane blinked. Brandee was acting interested in him? What had these three women seen that he'd missed?

"Once the vote is done," Simone continued, "she will dismiss you like that." She snapped her fingers and settled her full lips into a determined pout.

"Brandee has been acting as if she's interested in me?" Shane put on a show of surprise and hoped this would entice the women to expound on their theories. "I thought she was just being nice."

The women exchanged glances and silently selected Naomi to speak next. "She's not nice. She's manipulating you. Haven't you noticed the way she flirts with you? She knows how well liked you are and plans to use your popularity to manipulate the vote."

Shane considered this. Was Brandee flirting with him? For a second he let himself bask in the pleasure of that idea. Did she fight the same intoxicating attraction that gripped him every time they met? Then he rejected the notion. No. The way she communicated with him was more like a series of verbal jousts all determined to knock him off his white charger and land him ass-first in the dirt.

"Thank you for the warning, ladies." Unnecessary as it had been. "I'll make sure I keep my wits about me where Brandee is concerned."

"Anytime," Naomi murmured. Her brown eyes, framed by long, lush lashes, had a sharp look of satisfaction.

"We will always have your back," Cecelia added, and glanced at the other two, garnering agreeing head bobs.

"I'll remember that." With a friendly smile and a nod, Shane left the trio and headed to where Gabe waited.

The former Texas Ranger watched him approach, a smirk kicking up one corner of his lips. "What the hell was that about? Were you feeding them canaries?"

"Canaries?" Shane dropped into his seat and gestured to a nearby waiter. He needed a stiff drink after negotiating the gauntlet of strong-willed women.

"That was a trio of very satisfied pussycats."

Shane resisted the urge to rub at the spot between his shoulder blades that burned from several sets of female eyes boring into him. "I gave them what they wanted."

"Don't you always?"

"It's what I do."

Shane flashed a cocky grin, but he didn't feel any satisfaction.

"So what did they want?" Gabe asked.

"To warn me about Brandee Lawless."

Gabe's gaze flickered past Shane. Whatever he saw made his eyes narrow. "Do you need to be warned?"

"Oh hell no." The waiter set a scotch before him and Shane swallowed a healthy dose of the fiery liquid before continuing. "You know how she and I are. If we were kids she'd knock me down and sit on me."

"And you'd let her because then she'd be close enough to tickle."

"Tickle?" Shane stared at his best friend in mock outrage. "Do you not know me at all?"

"We're talking about you and Brandee as little kids. It was the least offensive thing I could think of that you'd do to her."

Shane snorted in amusement. "You could have said *spank*."

Gabe closed his eyes as if in pain. "Can we get back to Cecelia, Simone and Naomi?"

"They're just frustrated that Brandee has sided against them and has more influence at the club than they do. They want to rule the world. Or at least our little corner of it."

On the table, Gabe's phone chimed, signaling a text. "Damn," he murmured after reading the screen.

"Bad news?"

"My uncle's tumor isn't operable."

Several weeks ago Gabe's uncle Dusty had been diagnosed with stage-four brain cancer.

"Aw, Gabe, I'm sorry. That really sucks."

Dale "Dusty" Walsh was a dynamic bear of a man. Like Gabe he was a few inches over six feet and built to intimidate. Founder of Royal's most private security firm, The Walsh Group, he'd brought Gabe into the fold after he'd left the Texas Rangers.

"Yeah, my dad's pretty shook up. That was him sending the text."

Gabe's close relationship with his father was something Shane had always envied. His dad had died when Shane was in his early twenties, but even before the heart attack took him, there hadn't been much good about their connection.

"Hopefully, the doctors have a good alternative program to get Dusty through this."

"Let's hope."

The two men shifted gears and talked about the progress on Shane's latest project, a luxury resort development in the vein of George Vanderbilt's iconic French Renaissance château in North Carolina, but brimming with cutting-edge technology. As he was expounding on the challenges of introducing the concept of small plates to a state whose motto was "everything's bigger in Texas," a hand settled on Shane's shoulder. The all-too-familiar zap of awareness told him who stood beside him before she spoke.

"Hello, Gabe. How are things at The Walsh Group?"

"Fine." Gabe's hazel eyes took on a devilish gleam as he noticed Shane's gritted teeth. "And how are you doing at Hope Springs?"

"Busy. We've got ninety-two calves on the ground and another hundred and ninety-seven to go before April." Brandee's hand didn't move from Shane's shoulder as she spoke. "Thanks for helping out with the background checks for the latest group of volunteers."

"Anytime."

Shane drank in the soft lilt in Brandee's voice as he endured the warm press of her hand. He shouldn't be so aware of her, but the rustle of her tulle skirt and the shapely bare legs below the modest hem had his senses all revved up with nowhere to go.

"See you later, boys." Brandee gave Shane's shoulder a little squeeze before letting go.

"Bye, Brandee," Gabe replied, shifting his gaze to Shane as she headed off.

All too aware of Gabe's smirk, Shane summoned his willpower to not turn around and watch her go, but he couldn't resist a quick peek over his shoulder. He immediately wished he'd fought harder. Brandee floated past the tables like a delicate gray cloud. A cloud with badass boots the color of Texas bluebonnets on her feet. He felt the kick to his gut and almost groaned.

"You know she only did that to piss off those three," Gabe

said when Shane had turned back around. "They think she's plotting against them, so she added fuel to the fire."

"I know." He couldn't help but admire her clever machinations even though it had come with a hit to his libido. "She's a woman after my own heart."

Gabe laughed. "Good thing you don't have one to give her."

Shane lifted his drink and saluted his friend. "You've got that right."

CHAPTER TWO

AFTERNOON SUNLIGHT LANCED through the mini blinds covering the broad west-facing window in Brandee's home office, striping the computer keyboard and her fingers as they flew across the keys. She'd been working on the budget for her summer camp, trying to determine where she could siphon off a few extra dollars to buy three more well-trained, kid-friendly horses.

She'd already invested far more in the buildings and infrastructure than she'd initially intended. And because she needed to get the first of three projected bunkhouses built in time for her summer session, she'd been forced to rely on outside labor to get the job done.

Brandee spun her chair and stared out the window that overlooked the large covered patio, with its outdoor kitchen and fieldstone fireplace. She loved spending time outside, even in the winter, and had created a cozy outdoor living room.

Buying this five-thousand-acre parcel outside Royal four years ago had been Brandee's chance to fulfill her father's dream. She hadn't minded having to build a ranch from the ground up after the tornado had nearly wiped her out. In fact, she'd appreciated the clean slate and relished the idea of putting her stamp on the land. She'd set the L-shaped one-story ranch house half a mile off the highway and a quarter mile from the buildings that housed her ranch hands and the outbuildings central to her cow-calving operation.

The original house, built by the previous owner, had been much bigger than this one and poorly designed. Beaux Cook had been a Hollywood actor with grand ideas of becoming a real cowboy. The man had preferred flash over substance, and never bothered to learn anything about the ranching. Within eighteen months, he'd failed so completely as a rancher that Brandee had bought the property for several million less than it was worth.

Brandee was the third owner of the land since it had been lifted from unclaimed status ten years earlier. Emmitt Shaw had been the one who'd secured the parcel adjacent to his ranch by filing a claim and paying the back taxes for the five thousand acres of abandoned land after a trust put into place a century earlier to pay the taxes had run out of money. Health issues had later compelled him to sell off the land to Beaux to pay his medical bills and keep his original ranch running.

However, in the days following the massive storm, while Brandee was preoccupied with her own devastated property, Shane Delgado had taken advantage of the old rancher's bad health and losses from the tornado to gobble up his ranch to develop luxury homes. If she'd known how bad Beaux's situation had become, she would've offered to buy his land for a fair price.

Instead, she was stuck sharing her property line with his housing development. Brandee liked the raw, untamed beauty of the Texas countryside, and resented Delgado's determination to civilize the landscape with his luxury homes and fancy resort development. Her father had been an old-school cowboy, fond of endless vistas of Texas landscape populated by cattle, rabbits, birds and the occasional mountain lion. He wouldn't be a fan of Shane Delgado's vision for his daughter's property.

Her smartphone chimed, indicating she'd received a text message. There was a phone number, but no name. She read the text and her heart received a potent shock.

Hope Springs Ranch rightfully belongs to Shane Delgado.
–Maverick

Too outraged to consider the wisdom of engaging with the mysterious sender, she picked up the phone and texted back.

Who is this and what are you talking about?

Her computer immediately pinged, indicating she'd received an email. She clicked to open the message. It was from Maverick.

Give up your Texas Cattleman's Club membership and wire fifty thousand dollars to the account below or I'll be forced to share this proof of ownership with Delgado. You have two weeks to comply.

Ignoring the bank routing information, Brandee double-clicked on the attachment. It was a scan of a faded, handwritten document, a letter dated March 21, 1899, written by someone named Jasper Crowley. He offered a five-thousand-acre parcel as a dowry to the man who married his daughter, Amelia. From the description of the land, it was the five thousand acres Hope Springs Ranch occupied.

Brandee's outrage dissipated, but uneasiness remained.

This had to be a joke. Nothing about the documentation pointed to Shane. She was ready to dismiss the whole thing when the name Maverick tickled her awareness. Where had she heard it mentioned before? Cecelia Morgan had spoken the name before one of the contentious meetings at the TCC clubhouse. Was Cecelia behind this? Given the demands, it made sense.

Brandee had been doing her best to thwart every power play Cecelia, Simone and Naomi had attempted. There was no way she was going to let the terrible trio bully their way into leadership positions with the Texas Cattleman's Club. Was this their way of getting her to shut up?

She responded to the email.

This doesn't prove anything.

This isn't an empty threat, was the immediate response. Shaw didn't search for Crowley's descendants. I did.

That seemed to indicate that Maverick had proof that Crowley and Shane were related. Okay, so maybe she shouldn't ignore this. Brandee set her hands on the edge of the desk and shoved backward, muttering curses. The office wasn't big enough for her to escape the vile words glowing on the screen, so she got up and left the room to clear her head.

How dare they? She stalked down the hall to the living area, taking in the perfection of her home along the way.

Everything she had was tied up in Hope Springs Ranch. If she wasn't legally entitled to the land, she'd be ruined. Selling the cattle wouldn't provide enough capital for her to start again. And what would become of her camp?

Sweat broke out on Brandee's forehead. Throwing open her front door, she lifted her face to the cool breeze and stepped onto the porch, which ran the full length of her home. Despite the chilly February weather, she settled in a rocker and drew her knees to her chest. Usually contemplating the vista brought her peace. Not today.

What if that document was real and it could be connected to Shane? She dropped her forehead to her knees and groaned. This was a nightmare. Or maybe it was just a cruel trick. The ranch could not belong to Shane Delgado. Whoever Maverick was, and she suspected it was the unholy trio of Cecelia, Simone and Naomi, there was no way this person could be right.

The land had been abandoned. The taxes had ceased being paid. Didn't that mean the acres reverted back to the government? There had to be a process that went into securing unclaimed land. Something that went beyond simply paying the back taxes. Surely Emmitt had followed every rule and procedure. But what if he hadn't? What was she going to do? She couldn't lose Hope Springs Ranch. And especially not to the likes of Shane Delgado.

It took a long time for Brandee's panic to recede. Half-frozen, she retreated inside and began to plan. First on the agenda was to determine if the document was legitimate. Second, she needed to trace Shane back to Jasper Crowley. Third, she needed to do some research on the process for purchasing land that had returned to the government because of unpaid back taxes.

The blackmailer had given her two weeks. It wasn't a lot of time, but she was motivated. And if she proved Shane was the owner of her land? She could comply with Maverick's demands. Fifty thousand wasn't peanuts, but she had way more than that sitting in her contingency fund. She'd pay three times that to keep Shane Delgado from getting his greedy hands on her land.

And if she absolutely had to, she could resign from the Texas Cattleman's Club. She'd earned her membership the same way club members of old had: by making Hope Springs a successful ranch and proving herself a true cattleman. It would eat at her to let Cecelia, Simone and Naomi bully her into giving up the club she deserved to be a part of, but she could yield the high ground if it meant her programs for at-risk teenagers would be able to continue.

Bile rose as she imagined herself facing the trio's triumphant smirks. How many times in school had she stood against the mean girls and kept her pride intact? They'd ridiculed her bohemian style and tormented anyone brave enough to be friends with her. In turn, she'd manipulated their boyfriends into dumping them and exposed their villainous backstabbing to the whole school.

It wasn't something Brandee was proud of, but to be fair, she'd been dealing with some pretty major ugliness at home and hadn't been in the best frame of mind to take the high road.

When it came to taking care of herself, Brandee had learned how to fight dirty from her father's ranch hands. They'd treated her like a little sister and given her tips on how to get the upper hand in any situation. Brandee had found their advice useful after she'd moved in with her mother and had to cope with whatever flavor of the month she'd shacked up with.

Not all her mother's boyfriends had been creeps, but enough of them had turned their greedy gaze Brandee's way to give her a crash course in manipulation as a method of self-preservation.

And now those skills were going to pay off in spades. Because she intended to do whatever it took to save her ranch, and heaven help anyone who got in her way.

Standing in what would eventually become the grotto at Pure, the spa in his luxury resort project, The Bellamy, Shane was in an unhappy frame of mind. He surveyed the half-finished stacked stone pillars and the coffered ceiling above the narrow hot tub. In several months, Pure would be the most amazing spa Royal had ever seen, offering a modern take on a traditional Roman bath with a series of soothing, luxurious chambers in which guests could relax and revive.

Right now, the place was a disaster.

"I'm offering people the experience of recharging in an expensive, perfectly designed space," Shane reminded his project manager. "What about this particular stone says expensive or perfect?" He held up a sample of the stacked stone. "This is not what I ordered."

"Let me check on it."

"And then there's that." Shane pointed to the coffered ceiling above the hot tub. "That is not the design I approved."

"Let me check on that, as well."

Shane's phone buzzed, reminding him of his next appointment.

"We'll have to pick this up first thing tomorrow." Even though he was reluctant to stop when he had about fifty more details that needed to be discussed, Shane only had fifteen minutes until he was supposed to be at his mother's home for their weekly dinner, and it was a twenty-minute drive to her house.

Shane wound his way through The Bellamy's construction site, seeing something that needed his attention at every turn. He'd teamed with hotelier Deacon Chase to create the architectural masterpiece, and the scope of the project—and the investment—was enormous.

Sitting on fifty-plus acres of lavish gardens, the resort consisted of two hundred and fifty luxury suites, tricked out with cutting-edge technology. The complex also contained fine farm-to-table dining and other amenities. Every single detail had to be perfect.

He texted his mother before he started his truck, letting her know he was going to be delayed, and her snarky response made him smile. Born Elyse Flynn, Shane's mother had left her hometown of Boston at twenty-two with a degree in geoscience, contracted to do a field study of the area near Royal. There, she'd met Shane's father, Landon, and after a whirlwind six-month romance, married him and settled in at Bullseye, the Delgado family ranch.

After Landon died and Shane took over the ranch, Elyse had moved to a home in Pine Valley, the upscale gated community with a clubhouse, pool and eighteen-hole golf course. Although she seemed content in her six-thousand-square-foot house, when Shane began his housing development near Royal, she'd purchased one of the five-acre lots and begun the process of planning her dream home.

Each week when he visited, she had another architectural design for him to look over. In the last year she'd met with no fewer than a dozen designers. Her wish list grew with each new innovation she saw. There were days when Shane wondered if she'd ever settle on a plan. And part of him dreaded that day because he had a feeling she would then become his worst client ever.

When he entered the house, she was standing in the doorway leading to the library, a glass of red wine in her hand.

"There you are at last," she said, waving him over for a kiss. "Come see how brilliant Thomas is. His latest plan is fantastic."

Thomas Kitt was the architect Elyse was currently leaning toward. She hadn't quite committed to his design, but she'd been speaking of him in glowing terms for the last month.

"He's bumped out the kitchen wall six inches and that gives me the extra room I need so I can go for the thirty-inch built-in wine storage. Now I just need to decide if I want to do the one with the drawers so I can store cheese and other snacks or go with the full storage unit."

She handed Shane the glass of wine she'd readied for him and gestured to the plate of appetizers that sat on samples of granite and quartz piled on the coffee table.

Shane crossed to where she'd pinned the latest drawings to a magnetic whiteboard. "I'd go with the full storage. That'll give you room for an extra sixty bottles."

"You're right." Elyse grinned at her son. "Sounds like a trip to Napa is in my future."

"Why don't you wait until we break ground?" At the rate his mother was changing her mind, he couldn't imagine the project getting started before fall.

"Your father was always the practical one in our family." Elyse's smile faded at the memory of her deceased husband. "But you've really taken over that role. He'd be very proud of you."

Landon Delgado had never been proud of his son.

You've got nothing going for you but a slick tongue and a cocky attitude, his father had always said.

Elyse didn't seem to notice the dip in her son's mood as she continued, "Is it crazy that I like the industrial feel to this unit?" She indicated the brochure on high-end appliances.

Shane appreciated how much fun his mother was having with the project. He wrapped his arm around her and dropped a kiss on her head. "Whatever you decide is going to be a show-stopper."

"I hope so. Suzanne has been going on and on about the new house she's building in your development to the point where I want to throw her and that pretentious designer she hired right through a plate-glass window."

Growing up with four older brothers gave Elyse a competitive spirit in constant need of a creative outlet. Her husband hadn't shared her interests. Landon Delgado had liked ranching and believed in hard work over fancy innovation. He'd often spent long hours in the saddle moving cattle or checking fences. His days began before sunup and rarely ended until long after dinner. When he wasn't out and about on the ranch, he could be found in his office tending to the business side.

To Landon's dismay, Shane hadn't inherited his father's love of all things ranching. Maybe that was because as soon as Shane could sit up by himself, his father had put him on a horse, expecting Shane to embrace the ranching life. But he'd come to hate the way his every spare moment was taken up by ranch duties assigned to him by his father.

You aren't going to amount to anything if you can't handle a little hard work.

About the time he'd hit puberty, Shane's behavior around the ranch had bloomed into full-on rebellion, and when Shane turned fifteen, the real battles began. He started hanging out with older friends who had their own cars. Most days he didn't come home right after school and dodged all his chores. His buddies liked to party. He'd been forced to toil alongside his father since he was three years old. Didn't he deserve to have a little fun?

According to his father, the answer was no.

You're wrong if you think that grin of yours is all you need to make it in this world.

"So what have you cooked up for us tonight?" Shane asked

as he escorted his mother to the enormous kitchen at the back of the house.

"Apricot-and-Dijon-glazed salmon." Although Elyse employed a full-time housekeeper, she enjoyed spending time whipping up gourmet masterpieces. "I got the recipe from the man who catered Janice Hunt's dinner party. I think I'm going to hire him to cater the Bullseye's centennial party," Elyse continued, arching an eyebrow at her son's blank expression.

Shane's thoughts were so consumed with The Bellamy project these days, he'd forgotten all about the event. "The centennial party. When is that again?"

"March twenty-first. I've arranged a tasting with Vincent on the twenty-fourth of this month so we can decide what we're going to have."

"We?" He barely restrained a groan. "Don't you have one of your friends who could help with this?"

"I do, but this is *your* ranch we're celebrating and *your* legacy."

"Sure. Of course." Shane had no interest in throwing a big party for the ranch, but gave his mother his best smile. "A hundred years is a huge milestone and we will celebrate big."

This seemed to satisfy his mother. Elyse was very social. She loved to plan parties and when Shane was growing up there had often been dinners with friends and barbecues out by the pool. Often Shane had wondered how a vibrant, beautiful urbanite like his mother had found happiness with an overly serious, rough-around-the-edges Texas rancher. But there was no question that in spite of their differences, his parents had adored each other, and the way Landon had doted on his wife was the one area where Shane had seen eye to eye with his father.

At that moment Brandee Lawless popped into his mind. There was a woman he wanted to sweep into his arms and never let go. He imagined sending her hat spinning away and tunneling his fingers through her long golden hair as he pulled her toward him for a hot, sexy kiss.

But he'd noticed her regarding him with the same skepticism he used to glimpse in his father's eyes. She always seemed to be peering beyond his charm and wit to see what he was made of. He'd never been able to fool her with the mask he showed to the world. It was unsettling. When she looked at him, she seemed to expect…more.

Someday people are going to figure out that you're all show and no substance.

So far he'd been lucky and that hadn't happened. But where Brandee was concerned, it sure seemed like his luck was running out.

CHAPTER THREE

AFTER SNATCHING TOO few hours of sleep, Brandee rushed through her morning chores and headed to Royal's history museum. She hadn't taken time for breakfast and now the coffee she'd consumed on the drive into town was eating away at her stomach lining. Bile rose in her throat as she parked in the museum lot and contemplated her upside-down world.

It seemed impossible that her life could implode so easily. That the discovery of a single piece of paper meant she could lose everything. In the wee hours of the morning as she stared at the ceiling, she'd almost convinced herself to pay Maverick the money and resign from the TCC. Saving her ranch was more important than besting the terrible trio. But she'd never been a quitter and backing down when bullied had never been her style. Besides, as authentic as the document had looked, there was no reason to believe it was real or that it was in the museum where anyone could stumble on it.

Thirty minutes later, she sat at a table in the small reference room and had her worst fears realized. Before her, encased in clear plastic, was the document she'd been sent a photo of. She tore her gaze from the damning slip of paper and looked up at the very helpful curator. From Rueben Walker's surprise when she'd been waiting on the doorstep for the museum to open,

Brandee gathered he wasn't used to having company first thing in the morning.

"You say this is part of a collection donated to the museum after Jasper Crowley's death?" Brandee wondered what other bombshells were to be found in the archives.

"Yes, Jasper Crowley was one of the founding members of the Texas Cattleman's Club. Unfortunately he didn't live to see the grand opening of the clubhouse in 1910."

"What other sorts of things are in the collection?"

"The usual. His marriage license to Sarah McKellan. The birth certificate for their daughter, Amelia. Sarah's death certificate. She predeceased Jasper by almost thirty years and he never remarried. Let's see, there were bills of sale for various things. Letters between Sarah and her sister, Lucy, who lived in Austin."

Brandee was most interested in Jasper's daughter. The land had been her dowry. Why hadn't she claimed it?

"Is there anything about what happened to Amelia? Did she ever get married?"

Walker regarded Brandee, his rheumy blue eyes going suddenly keen. "I don't recall there being anything about a wedding. You could go through the newspaper archives. With someone of Jasper's importance, his daughter's wedding would have been prominently featured."

Brandee had neither the time nor the patience for a random search through what could potentially be years' worth of newspapers. "I don't suppose you know of anyone who would be interested in helping me with the research? I'd be happy to compensate them."

"I have a part-time assistant that comes in a few times a week. He might be able to assist you as soon as he gets back from helping his sister move to Utah."

"When will that be?"

"Middle of next week, I think."

Unfortunately, Maverick had only given her two weeks to

meet the demands, and if the claims were true, she needed to find out as soon as possible. Brandee ground her teeth and weighed her options.

"Are the newspaper archives here?"

The curator shook his head. "They're over at the library on microfiche."

"Thanks for your help." Brandee gave Reuben a quick nod before exiting the building and crossing the street.

The library was a couple blocks down and it didn't make sense for her to move her truck. She neared Royal Diner and her stomach growled, reminding her she hadn't eaten breakfast. As impatient as she was to get to the bottom of Maverick's claim, she would function better without hunger pangs.

Stepping into Royal Diner was like journeying back in time to the 1950s. Booths lined one wall, their red faux leather standing out against the black-and-white-checkerboard tile floor. On the opposite side of the long aisle stretched the counter with seats that matched the booths.

Not unexpectedly, the place was packed. Brandee spotted local rancher and town pariah, Adam Haskell, leaving the counter toward the back and headed that way, intending to grab his seat. As she drew closer, Brandee noticed a faint scent of stale alcohol surrounded Haskell. She offered him the briefest of nods, which he didn't see because his blue bug-eyes dropped to her chest as they passed each other in the narrow space.

Once clear of Haskell, Brandee saw that the spot she'd been aiming for was sandwiched between an unfamiliar fortysomething cowboy and Shane Delgado. Of all the bad luck. Brandee almost turned tail and ran, but knew she'd look silly doing so after coming all this way. Bracing herself, she slid onto the seat.

Shane glanced up from his smartphone and grinned as he spotted her. "Well, hello. Look who showed up to make my morning."

His deep voice made her nerve endings shiver, and when she bumped her shoulder against his while sliding her purse onto the conveniently placed hook beneath the counter, the hairs on her arms stood up. Hating how her body reacted to him, Brandee shot Shane a sharp glance.

"I'm not in the mood to argue with you." She spoke with a little more bluntness than usual and his eyes widened slightly. "Can we just have a casual conversation about the weather or the price of oil?"

"I heard it's going to be in the midfifties all week," he said, with one of his knockout grins that indicated he liked that he got under her skin. "With a thirty percent chance of rain."

"We could use some rain."

Heidi dropped off Shane's breakfast and took Brandee's order of scrambled eggs, country potatoes and bacon. A second later the waitress popped back with a cup of coffee.

"Everything tasting okay?" Heidi asked Shane, her eyes bright and flirty.

"Perfect as always."

"That's what I like to hear."

When she walked off, Brandee commented, "You haven't taken a single bite. How do you know it's perfect?"

"Because I eat breakfast here twice a week and it's always the same great food." Shane slid his fork into his sunny-side up eggs and the bright yellow yolk ran all over the hash on his plate.

Brandee sipped her coffee and shuddered.

"What's the matter?" Shane's even white teeth bit into a piece of toast. He hadn't looked at her, yet he seemed to know she was bothered.

"Nothing." Brandee tried to keep her voice neutral. "Why?"

"You are looking more disgusted with me than usual." His crooked smile made her pulse hiccup.

"It's the eggs. I can't stand them runny like that." The same flaw in human nature that made people gawk at car accidents was drawing Brandee's gaze back to Shane's plate. She shuddered again.

"Really?" He pushed the yolk around as if to torment her

with the sight. "But this is the only way to eat them with corn-beef hash."

"Why corn-beef hash and not biscuits and gravy?"

"It's a nod to my Irish roots."

"You're Irish?"

"On my mother's side. She's from Boston."

"Oh." She drew out her reply as understanding dawned.

"Oh, what?"

"I always wondered about your accent."

"You thought about me?" He looked delighted.

Brandee hid her irritation. Give the man any toehold and he would storm her battlements in a single bound.

"I thought about your accent," she corrected him. "It has a trace of East Coast in it."

Shane nodded. "It's my mom's fault. Even after living in Texas for nearly forty years, she still drops her *r*'s most of the time."

"How'd your mom come to live in Texas?"

Even as Brandee asked the question, it occurred to her that this was the most normal conversation she and Shane had ever had. Usually they engaged in some sort of verbal sparring or just outright arguing and rarely traded any useful information.

"She came here after college to study oil reserves and met my dad. They were married within six months and she's been here ever since." Shane used his toast to clean up the last of the egg. "She went back to Boston after my dad died and stayed for almost a year, but found she missed Royal."

"I'm sure it was you that she missed."

Shane nodded. "I am the apple of her eye."

"Of course." Brandee thanked Heidi as the waitress set a plate down on the counter. With the arrival of her breakfast, Brandee had intended to let her side of the conversation lapse, but something prompted her to ask, "She didn't remarry?"

Never in a million years would Brandee admit it, but Shane's story about his mother was interesting. Shane's father had died over a decade earlier, but Elyse Delgado had accompanied her son to several events at the TCC clubhouse since Brandee had bought Hope Springs Ranch. Her contentious relationship with Shane caused Brandee to avoid him in social situations and she'd never actually spoken to his mother except to say hello in passing. Yet, Brandee knew Elyse Delgado by reputation and thought she would've enjoyed getting to know the woman better if not for her son.

"There've been a couple men she's dated, but nothing serious has come out of it. Although she was completely devoted to my father, I think she's enjoyed her independence."

"I get that," Brandee murmured. "I like the freedom to run my ranch the way I want and not having to worry about taking anyone's opinions into account."

"You make it sound as if you never plan to get married." Shane sounded surprised and looked a little dismayed. "That would certainly be a shame."

Brandee's hackles rose. He probably hadn't intended to strike a nerve, but in the male-dominated world of Texas cattle ranching, she'd faced down a lot of chauvinism.

"I don't need a man to help me or complete me."

At her hot tone, Shane threw up his hands. "That's not what I meant."

"No?" She snorted. "Tell me you don't look at me and wonder how I handle Hope Springs Ranch without a man around." She saw confirmation in his body language before he opened his mouth to argue. "Thanks to my dad, I know more about what it takes to run a successful ranch than half the men around here."

"I don't doubt that."

"But you still think I need someone."

"Yes." Shane's lips curved in a sexy grin. "If only to kiss you senseless and take the edge off that temper of yours."

The second Brandee's eyes cooled, Shane knew he should've kept his opinion to himself. They'd been having a perfectly nice conversation and he'd had to go and ruin it. But all her talk of not needing a man around had gotten under his skin. He wasn't sure why.

"I have neither a temper nor an edge." Brandee's conversational tone wasn't fooling Shane. "Ask anyone in town and they'll tell you I'm determined, but polite."

"Except when I'm around."

Her expression relaxed. "You do bring out the worst in me."

And for some reason she brought out the worst in him. "I'd like to change that." But first he had to learn to hold his tongue around her.

"Why?"

"Because you interest me."

"As someone who sees through your glib ways?"

"I'll admit you've presented a challenge." Too many things in his life came easily. He didn't have to exert himself chasing the unachievable. But in Brandee's case, he thought the prize might be worth the extra effort.

"I've begun to wonder if convincing me to sell Hope Springs had become a game to you."

"I can't deny that I'd like your land to expand my development, but that's not the only reason I'm interested in you."

"Is it because I won't sleep with you?"

He pretended to be surprised. "That never even occurred to me. I'm still in the early stages of wooing you."

"Wooing?" Her lips twitched as if she were fighting a smile. "You do have a way with words, Shane Delgado."

"Several times you've accused me of having a silver tongue. I might have a knack for smooth talking, but that doesn't mean I'm insincere."

Brandee pushed her unfinished breakfast away and gave him her full attention. "Let me get this straight. You want us to date?" She laughed before he could answer.

He'd thought about it many times, but never with serious intent. Their chemistry was a little too combustible, more like a

flash bang than a slow burn, and he'd reached a point in his life
where he liked to take his time with a woman.

"Whoa," he said, combating her skepticism with lighthearted
banter. "Let's not get crazy. How about we try a one-week cease-
fire and see how things go?"

Her features relaxed into a genuine smile and Shane realized
she was relieved. His ego took a hit. Had she been dismayed
that he'd viewed her in a romantic light? Most women would be
thrilled. Once again he reminded himself that she was unique
and he couldn't approach her the same way he did every other
female on the planet.

"Does that mean you're not going to try to buy Hope Springs
for a week?" Despite her smile, her eyes were somber as she
waited for his answer.

"Sure."

"Let's make it two weeks, then."

To his surprise, she held out her hand like it was some sort
of legal agreement. Shane realized that for all their interaction,
they'd never actually touched skin to skin. The contact didn't
disappoint.

Pleasure zipped up his arm and lanced straight through his
chest. If he hadn't been braced against the shock, he might have
let slip a grunt of surprise. Her grip was strong. Her slender fingers bit into his hand without much effort on her part. He felt
the work-roughened calluses on her palm and the silky-smooth
skin on the back of her hand. It was a study in contrasts, like
everything else about her.

Desire ignited even as she let go and snatched up her bill.
With an agile shift of her slim body, she was sliding into the
narrow space between his chair and hers. Her chest brushed his
upper arm and he felt the curve of her breasts even through the
layers of her sweater and his jacket.

"See you, Delgado."

Before he got his tongue working again, she'd scooped her
coat and purse off the back of the chair and was headed for the

front cash register. Helpless with fascination, he watched her go, enjoying the unconscious sashay of her firm, round butt encased in worn denim. The woman knew how to make an exit.

"Damn," he murmured, signaling to the waitress that he wanted his coffee topped off. He had a meeting in half an hour, but needed to calm down before he headed out.

A cup of coffee later, he'd recovered enough to leave. As he looked for his bill, he realized it was missing. He'd distinctly recalled Heidi sliding it onto the counter, but now it was gone. He caught her eye and she came over with the coffeepot.

"More coffee, Shane?"

"No, I've got to get going, but I don't see my bill and wondered if it ended up on the floor over there." He indicated her side of the counter.

"All taken care of."

"I don't understand."

"Brandee got it."

Had that been the reason for her brush by? In the moment, he'd been so preoccupied by her proximity that he hadn't been aware of anything else. And he understood why she'd paid for his meal. She was announcing that she was independent and his equal. It also gave her a one-up on him.

"Thanks, Heidi." In a pointless assertion of his masculinity, he slid a ten-dollar tip under the sugar dispenser before heading out the door.

As he headed to his SUV, he considered his action. Would he have been compelled to leave a large tip if Gabe or Deacon had picked up his tab? Probably not. Obviously it bothered him to have a woman pay for his meal. Or maybe it wasn't just any woman, but a particular woman who slipped beneath his skin at every turn.

Why had he rejected the idea of dating her so fast? In all likelihood they'd drive each other crazy in bed. And when it was over, things between them would be no worse. Seemed he had nothing to lose and a couple months of great sex to gain.

As he headed to The Bellamy site to see how the project was going, Shane pondered how best to approach Brandee. She wasn't the sort to be wowed with the things he normally tried and she'd already declared herself disinterested in romantic entanglements. Or had she?

Shane found himself back at square one, and realized just how difficult the task before him was. Yet he didn't shy from the challenge. In fact, the more he thought about dating Brandee, the more determined he became to convince her to give them a shot.

But how did a man declare his intentions when the woman was skeptical of every overture?

The answer appeared like the sun breaking through the clouds. It involved the project nearest and dearest to her heart: Hope Springs Camp for at-risk and troubled teenagers. He would somehow figure out what she needed most and make sure she got it. By the time he was done, she would be eating out of his hands.

Brandee left the Royal Diner after paying for Shane's breakfast, amusing herself by pondering how much it would annoy him when he found out what she'd done. She nodded a greeting to several people as she headed to the library. Once there, however, all her good humor fled as she focused on finding out whether there was any truth to Maverick's assertion that Shane was a direct descendant of Amelia Crowley.

It took her almost five hours and she came close to giving up three separate times, but at long last she traced his family back to Jasper Crowley. Starting with newspapers from the day Jasper had penned the dowry document, she'd scrolled through a mile of microfiche until she'd found a brief mention of Amelia, stating that she'd run off with a man named Tobias Stone.

Using the Stone family name, Brandee then tracked down a birth certificate for their daughter Beverly. The Stones hadn't settled near Royal but had ended up two counties over. But the state of Texas had a good database of births and deaths, and the town where they'd ended up had all their newspapers' back issues online.

Jumping forward seventeen years, she began reading newspapers again for some notice of Beverly Stone's marriage. She'd been debating giving up on the newspapers and driving to the courthouse when her gaze fell on the marriage announcement. Beverly had married Charles Delgado and after that Brandee's search became a whole lot easier.

At last she was done. Spread across the table, in unforgiving black and white, was the undeniable proof that Shane Delgado was legally entitled to the land where Hope Springs Ranch stood. A lesser woman would have thrown herself a fine pity party. Brandee sat dry-eyed and stared at Shane's birth certificate. It was the last piece of the puzzle.

In a far more solemn mood than when she'd arrived, Brandee exited the library. The setting sun cast a golden glow over the street. Her research had eaten up the entire day, and she felt more exhausted than if she'd rounded up and tagged a hundred cattle all on her own. She needed a hot bath to ease the tension in her shoulders and a large glass of wine to numb her emotions.

But most of all she wanted to stop thinking about Shane Delgado and his claim to her land for a short time. Unfortunately, once she'd settled into her bath, and as the wine started a warm buzz through her veins, that proved impossible. Dwelling on the man while lying naked in a tub full of bubbles was counterproductive. So was mulling over their breakfast conversation at the Royal Diner, but she couldn't seem to shake the look in his eye as he'd talked about kissing her senseless.

She snorted. As if her current problems could be forgotten beneath the man's chiseled lips and strong hands. She closed her eyes and relived the handshake. The contact had left her palm tingling for nearly a minute. As delightful as the sensation had been, what had disturbed her was how much she'd liked touching him. How she wouldn't mind letting her hands wander all over his broad shoulders and tight abs.

With a groan Brandee opened her eyes and shook off her sensual daydreams. Even if Shane wasn't at the center of her biggest nightmare, she couldn't imagine either one of them letting go and connecting in any meaningful way.

But maybe she didn't need meaningful. Maybe what she needed was to get swept up in desire and revel in being female. She'd deny it until she was hoarse, but it might be nice to let someone be in charge for a little while. And if that someone was Shane Delgado? At least she'd be in for an exhilarating ride.

The bathwater had cooled considerably while Brandee's mind had wandered all over Shane's impressive body. She came out of her musings to discover she'd lost an hour and emerged from her soaking tub with pruney fingers and toes.

While she was toweling off, her office phone began to ring. It was unusual to have anyone calling the ranch in the evening, but not unheard-of. After she'd dressed in an eyelet-trimmed camisole and shorts sleepwear set she'd designed, Brandee padded down the hall to her office, curled up in her desk chair and dialed into voice mail.

"I heard you're looking for a couple horses for your summer camp." The voice coming from the phone's speaker belonged to Shane Delgado. "I found one that might work for you. Liam Wade has a champion reining horse that he had to retire from showing because of his bad hocks. He wants the horse to go to a good home and is interested in donating him to your cause."

Brandee had a tight budget to complete all her projects and was doing a pretty good job sticking to it. When she'd first decided to start a camp, she'd done a few mini-events to see how things went. That was how she'd funded the meeting hall where she served meals and held classes during the day and where the kids could socialize in the evenings. Thanks to her successes, she'd forged ahead with her summer-camp idea. But that required building a bunkhouse that could sleep twelve.

With several minor issues leading to overages she'd hadn't planned for, getting a high-quality, well-trained horse for free from Liam Wade would be awesome. She already had three other horses slated for the camp and hoped to have six altogether to start.

Brandee picked up the phone and dialed Shane back. Knees drawn up to her chest, she waited for him to answer and wondered what he'd expect in return for this favor.

After three rings Shane picked up. "I take it you're interested in the horse."

"Very." Her toes curled over the edge of the leather cushion of her desk chair as his deep, rich voice filled her ear. "Thank you for putting this together."

"My pleasure."

"It was really nice of you." Remembering that he had the power to destroy all she'd built didn't stop her from feeling grateful. "I guess I owe you…" She grasped at the least problematic way she could pay him back.

"You don't owe me a thing."

Immediately Brandee went on alert. He hadn't demanded dinner or sexual favors in exchange for his help. What was this new game he was playing? Her thoughts turned to the blackmailer Maverick. Once again she wondered whether Shane was involved, but quickly rejected the idea. If he had any clue she was squatting on land that belonged to his family, he would be up front about his intentions.

"Well, then," she muttered awkwardly. "Thank you."

"Happy to help."

After hanging up, she spent a good ten minutes staring at the phone. Happy to help? That rang as false as his "you don't owe me a thing." What was he up to? With no answers appearing on the horizon, Brandee returned to her bedroom and settled in to watch some TV, but nothing held her attention.

She headed into the kitchen for a cup of Sleepytime herbal tea, but after consuming it, she was more wide-awake than ever. So she started a load of laundry and killed another hour with some light housekeeping. As the sole occupant of the ranch house, Brandee only had her cook and cleaning woman, May, come in a couple times a week.

Standing in the middle of her living room, Brandee surveyed her home with a sense of near despair and cursed Maverick. If she found out who was behind the blackmail, she'd make sure they paid. In the meantime, she had to decide what to do. She sank down onto her couch and pulled a cotton throw around her shoulders.

Her choice was clear. She had to pay the fifty thousand dollars and resign from the Texas Cattleman's Club. As much as it galled her to give in, she couldn't risk losing her home. She pictured the smug satisfaction on the faces of the terrible trio and ground her teeth together.

And if Maverick wasn't one or all of them?

What if she'd read the situation wrong and someone else was behind the extortion? She had no guarantee that if she met the demands that Maverick wouldn't return to the well over and over. The idea of spending the rest of her life looking over her shoulder or paying one blackmail demand after another appalled Brandee. But what could she do?

Her thoughts turned to Shane once more. What if she could get him to give up his claim to the land? She considered what her father would think of the idea and shied away from the guilt that aroused. Buck Lawless had never cheated or scammed anyone and would be ashamed of his daughter for even considering it.

But then, Buck had never had to endure the sort of environment Brandee had been thrust into after his death. In her mother's house, Brandee had received a quick and unpleasant education in self-preservation. Her father's position as ranch foreman had meant that Brandee could live and work among the ranch hands and never worry that they'd harm her. That hadn't been the case with her mother's various boyfriends.

She wasn't proud that she'd learned how to manipulate others' emotions and desires, but she was happy to have survived that dark time and become the successful rancher her father had always hoped she'd be. As for what she was going to do about Shane? What he didn't know about his claim on Hope Springs Ranch wouldn't hurt him. She just needed to make sure he stayed in the dark until she could figure out a way to keep her land free and clear.

CHAPTER FOUR

AT BULLSEYE RANCH'S main house, Shane sat on the leather sofa in the den, boots propped on the reclaimed wood coffee table, an untouched tumbler of scotch dangling from the fingers of his left hand. Almost twenty-four hours had gone by since Brandee had called to thank him for finding her a horse and he'd been thinking about her almost nonstop. She'd sounded wary on the phone, as if expecting him to demand something in return for his help. It wasn't the response he'd been hoping for, but it was pure Brandee.

What the hell was wrong with the woman that she couldn't accept a kind gesture? Well, to be fair, he hadn't acted with pure altruism. He did want something from her, but it wasn't what she feared. His motive was personal not business. Would she ever believe that?

His doorbell rang. Shane set aside his drink and went to answer the door. He wasn't expecting visitors.

It was Brandee standing on his front porch. The petite blonde was wearing her customary denim and carrying a bottle wrapped in festive tissue. She smiled at his shocked look, obviously pleased to have seized the upper hand for the moment.

"Brought you a little thank-you gift," she explained, extending the bottle. "I know you like scotch and thought you might appreciate this."

"Thanks." He gestured her inside and was more than a little bewildered when she strolled past him.

"Nice place you have here." Brandee shoved her hands into the back pockets of her jeans as she made her way into the middle of the living room.

"I can't take the credit. My mom did all the remodeling and design."

"She should have been an interior designer."

"I've told her that several times." Shane peeled the paper off the bottle and whistled when he saw the label. "This is a great bottle of scotch."

"Glad you like it. I asked the bartender at the TCC clubhouse what he'd recommend and this is what he suggested."

"Great choice." The brand was far more expensive than anything Shane had in his house and he was dying to try it. "Will you join me in a drink?"

"Just a short one. I have to drive home."

Shane crossed to the cabinet where he kept his liquor and barware. He poured shots into two tulip-shaped glasses with short, stout bases and handed her one.

Brandee considered it with interest. "I thought you drank scotch from tumblers."

"Usually, but you brought me a special scotch," he said, lifting his glass to the light and assessing the color. "And it deserves a whiskey glass."

"What should we drink to?" she asked, snagging his gaze with hers.

Mesmerized by the shifting light in her blue-gray eyes, he said the first bit of nonsense that popped into his head. "World peace?"

"To world peace." With a nod she tapped her glass lightly against his.

Before Shane drank, he gave the scotch a good swirl to

awaken the flavors. He then lifted the glass to his nose and sniffed. A quality scotch like this was worth taking the time to appreciate. He took a healthy sip and rolled it around his tongue. At last he swallowed it, breathed deeply and waited. At around the six-second mark, the richness of the scotch rose up and blessed him with all its amazing flavors—citrus, pears, apples and plums from the sherry barrels it was aged in, along with an undertone of chocolate and a hint of licorice at the very end.

"Fantastic," he breathed.

Brandee watched him with open curiosity, then held up her glass. "I've never been much of a scotch drinker, but watching you just now makes me think I've been missing out. Teach me to enjoy it."

She couldn't have said anything that pleased him more.

"I'd be happy to. First of all you want to swirl the scotch in the glass and then sniff it. Unlike wine, what you smell is what you'll taste."

She did as he instructed, taking her time about it. "Now what?"

"Now you're going to take a big mouthful." He paused while she did as instructed. "That's it. Get it onto the middle of your tongue. You'll begin to tease out the spice and the richness." He let her experience the scotch for a few more seconds and then said, "Take a big breath, swallow and open your mouth. Now wait for it."

She hadn't blinked, which was good. If she had, it would mean the scotch flavor was too strong. Her expression grew thoughtful and then her eyes flared with understanding.

"I get it. Tangerine and plum."

"The second sip is even better."

Together they took their second taste. The pleasure Shane received was doubled because he was able to share the experience with Brandee. She didn't roll her eyes or make faces like many women of his acquaintance would have. Instead, she let him lead her through an exploration of all the wonderful subtleties of the scotch.

Fifteen minutes later, they had reached a level of connection unprecedented in their prior four years of knowing each other. He was seeing a new side of Brandee. A delightful, sociable side that had him patting himself on the back for putting her in touch with Liam. Convincing her they should give dating a try was going to be way easier than he'd originally thought.

Brandee finished her last sip of scotch and set the glass aside. "I had another reason for dropping by tonight other than to say thank-you."

Shane waited in silence for her to continue, wondering if the other shoe was about to drop.

"I thought about what you said in the diner yesterday." She spoke slowly as if she'd put a lot of thought into what she was saying.

Shane decided to help her along. "About you needing to be kissed senseless?" He grinned when he saw the gap between her eyebrows narrow.

"About us calling a truce for two weeks," she countered, her tone repressive. "I know how you are and I realized that after those two weeks, you'd be back to pestering me to sell the ranch."

Right now, he didn't really give a damn about buying her ranch, but he sensed if he stopped pestering her about it she would forget all about him. "You have a solution for that?"

"I do. I was thinking about a wager."

Now she was speaking his language. "What sort of wager?"

"If I win you agree to give up all current and future attempts to claim Hope Springs Ranch and its land."

"And if I win?"

"I'll sell you my ranch."

A silence settled between them so loud Shane could no longer hear the television in the den. Unless she was convinced she had this wager all sewn up, this was a preposterous offer for her to make. What was she up to?

"Let me get this straight," he began, wanting to make sure he'd heard her clearly. "After years of refusing to sell me your land, you're suddenly ready to put it on the table and risk losing it?" He shook his head. "I don't believe it. You love that ranch too much to part with it so easily."

"First of all, what makes you think you're going to win? You haven't even heard the terms."

He arched one eyebrow. "And the second thing?"

"I said I'd sell the land. I didn't say how much I wanted for it."

He'd known all along that she was clever and relished the challenge of pitting his wits against hers. "Ten million. That's more than fair market value."

Her blue-gray eyes narrowed. She'd never get that much from anyone else and they both knew it.

"Fine. Ten million."

The speed with which she agreed made Shane wonder what he'd gotten himself into. "And the terms of our wager?"

"Simple." A sly smile bloomed. "For two weeks you move in and help me out at the ranch. Between calving time and the construction project going on at my camp, I'm stretched thin."

Shane almost laughed in relief. This was not at all what he'd thought she'd propose. Did she think he'd shy away from a couple weeks of manual labor? Granted, he rarely came home with dirt beneath his fingernails, but that didn't mean he was lazy or incompetent. He knew which end of the hammer to use.

"You need someone who knows his way around a power tool." He shot her a lecherous grin. "I'm your man."

"And I need you to help with the minicamp I have going next weekend."

Now he grasped her logic. She intended to appeal to his altruistic side. She probably figured if he got a close look at her troubled-teen program that he would give up trying to buy the land. This was a bet she was going to lose. He didn't give a

damn about a camp for a bunch of screwed-up kids who probably didn't need anything more than parents who knew how to
set boundaries.

"That's it?" He was missing something, but he wasn't sure
what. "I move in and help you out?" Living with Brandee was
like a dream come true. He could survive a few backbreaking
days of hard work if it meant plenty of time to convince her they
could be good together for a while.

"I can see where your mind has gone and yes..." She paused
for effect. "You'll have ample opportunity to convince me to
sleep with you."

A shock as potent as if he'd grabbed a live wire with both
hands blasted through him. His nerve endings tingled in the
aftermath. He struggled to keep his breathing even as he considered the enormity of what she'd just offered.

"You call that a wager?" He had no idea where he found the
strength to joke. "I call it shooting ducks in a barrel."

"Don't you mean fish?" Her dry smile warned him winning
wasn't going to be easy. "Getting me to sleep with you isn't the
wager. You were right when you said I was lacking male companionship."

Well, smack my ass and call me a newborn. The phrase, often
repeated by Shane's grandma Bee, popped into his head unbid-
den. He coughed to clear his throat.

"I said you needed to be kissed senseless."

She rolled her eyes at him. "Yes. Yes. It's been a while since
I dated anyone. And I'll admit the thought of you and I has
crossed my mind once or twice."

"Damn, woman. You sure do know how to stroke a man's
ego."

"Oh please," she said. "You love playing games. I thought
this would appeal to everything you stand for."

"And what is that exactly?"

"You get me to say I love you and I sell you the ranch for
ten million."

He hadn't prepared himself properly for the devastation of that other shoe. It was a doozy. "And what needs to happen for you to win?"

"Simple." Her smile was pure evil. "I get you to say 'I love you' to me."

Brandee stood on her front porch, heart beating double-time, and watched Shane pull a duffel out of his SUV. In his other hand he held a laptop case. It was late afternoon the day after Brandee had pitched her ridiculous wager to Shane and he was moving in.

This was without a doubt the stupidest idea she'd ever had. Paying Maverick the blackmail money and quitting the TCC was looking better and better. But how would she explain her abrupt change of heart to Shane? No doubt he would consider her back-pedaling proof that she was afraid of losing her heart to him.

At least she didn't have to worry about that happening. There was only room in her life for her ranch and her camp. Maybe in a couple years when things settled down she could start social-izing. She'd discovered that as soon as she'd started thinking about seducing Shane, a floodgate to something uncomfortably close to loneliness had opened wide.

"Hey, roomie," he called, taking her porch steps in one easy bound.

Involuntarily she stepped back as he came within a foot of her. His wolfish grin was an acknowledgment of her flinch.

"Welcome to Hope Springs Ranch."

"Glad to be here."

"Let me show you to your room. Dinner's at seven. Break-fast is at six. I don't know what you're used to, but we get up early around here."

"Early to bed. Early to rise. I can get on board with the first part. The second may take some getting used to."

Brandee let out a quiet sigh. Shane's not-so-subtle sexual innuendo was going to get old really fast. It might be worth sleeping with him right away to get that to stop.

"I'm sure you'll manage." She led the way into the ranch house and played tour guide. "Kitchen. Dining room. Living room."

"Nice." Shane took his time gazing around the uncluttered open-plan space.

"Your room is this way." She led him into a hallway and indicated a door on the left. "Guest bedrooms one and two share that bathroom. I put you in the guest suite. It has its own bathroom and opens to the patio."

Shane entered the room she indicated and set his duffel on the king-size bed. "Nice."

The suite was decorated in the same neutral tones found throughout the rest of the house. It was smaller than her master bedroom, but she'd lavished the same high-end materials on it.

"You'll be comfortable, then?" She imagined his master suite at Bullseye was pretty spectacular given what she'd seen of his living room.

"Very comfortable." He circled the bed and stared out the French doors. "So where do you sleep?"

He asked the question with no particular inflection, but her body reacted as if he'd swept her into his arms. She shoved her hands into her back pockets to conceal their trembling and put on her game face. She'd get nowhere with him if he noticed how easily he could provoke her.

"I'll show you."

Cringing at the thought of inviting him into her personal space, Brandee nevertheless led the way back down the hall and past the kitchen. When she'd worked with the architect, she insisted the master suite be isolated from the guest rooms. Passing her home office, Brandee gestured at it as she went by and then strode into her private sanctuary. It wasn't until Shane stood in the middle of her space, keen eyes taking in every detail, that she realized the magnitude of her mistake.

It wasn't that giving him a glimpse of her bedroom might clue him in to what made her tick. Or even that she'd imagined him making love to her here. It was far worse than that. She discovered that she liked having him in her space. She wanted to urge him into one of the chairs that faced her cozy fireplace and stretch out in its twin with her bare feet on his lap, letting him massage the aches from her soles with his strong fingers.

"Nice."

Apparently this was his go-to word for all things related to decorating. She chuckled, amusement helping to ease her anxiety.

Shane shot her a questioning look. "Did I miss something?"

"You must drive your mother crazy."

"How so?"

"She loves to decorate. I imagine she's asked your opinion a time or two. Tonight, your reaction to every room we've been in has been—" she summoned up her best Shane imitation "—nice." Her laughter swelled. "I'm imagining you doing that to your mother. It's funny."

"Obviously." He stared at her as if he didn't recognize her. But after a moment, his lips relaxed into a smile. "I'll make an effort to be more specific from now on."

"I'm sure your mother will appreciate that."

Deciding they'd spent more than enough time in her bedroom, Brandee headed toward the door. As she passed Shane, he surprised her by catching her arm and using her momentum to swing her up against his body.

"Hey!" she protested even as her traitorous spine softened beneath his palm and her hips relaxed into his.

"Hey, what?" He lowered his lips to her temple and murmured, "I've been waiting too many years to kiss you. Don't you think it's time you put me out of my misery?"

She should've expected he'd make his move as soon as possible, and should've been prepared to deflect his attempt to seduce her. Instead, here she was, up on her toes, flattening her breasts against the hard planes of his chest and aching for that kiss he so obviously intended to take.

"I'm going to need a couple glasses of wine to get me in the mood," she told him, stroking her fingers over his beefy shoulders and into the soft brown waves that spilled over his collar.

"You don't need wine. You have me." His fingers skimmed the sensitive line where her back met her butt, sending lightning skittering along her nerve endings.

She trembled with the effort of keeping still. Seizing her lower lip between her teeth, she contained a groan, but the urge to rub herself all over him was gaining momentum. She needed to decide the smart move here, but couldn't think straight.

Summoning all her willpower, she set her hands on his chest and pushed herself away. "It's not going to happen, Delgado."

Shane raked both hands through his hair, but his grin was unabashed and cocky. "Tonight or ever?"

"Tonight." Lying to him served no purpose.

Given the seesaw of antagonism and attraction, she couldn't imagine them lasting two weeks without tearing each other's clothes off, but she refused to tumble into bed with him right off the bat.

"Fair enough."

Brandee led the way back into the main part of the house and toward the kitchen. When she'd made this wager, she hadn't thought through what sharing her home with Shane would entail. She hadn't lived with anyone since she'd run away from her mother's house twelve years earlier. Realizing she would have to interact with him in such close quarters threw her confidence a curve ball.

"I'm going to open a bottle of wine. Do you want to join me or can I get you something else?" She opened the refrigerator. "I have beer. Or there's whiskey."

"I'll have wine. It wasn't an I-could-use-a-beer sort of day."

Brandee popped the cork on her favorite Shiraz and poured out two glasses. "What sort of day is that?"

"One where I spend it in the saddle or out surveying the pastures." His usually expressive features lost all emotion. And then he gave her a meaningless smile. "You know, ranch work."

"You don't sound as if you're all that keen on ranching."

Because he seemed so much more focused on his real-estate developments, she'd never considered him to be much of a rancher. He gave every appearance of avoiding hard work, so she assumed that he was lazy or entitled.

"Some aspects of it are more interesting than others."

With an hour and a half to kill before dinner, she decided to build a fire in the big stone fireplace out on her covered patio. The cooler weather gave her a great excuse to bundle up and enjoy the outdoor space. She carried the bottle of wine and her glass through the French doors off the dining room.

The days were getting longer, so she didn't have to turn on the overhead lights to find the lighter. The logs were already stacked and waiting for the touch of flame. In a short time a yellow glow spilled over the hearth and illuminated the seating area.

Choosing a seat opposite Shane, Brandee tucked her feet beneath her and sipped her wine. "You do mostly backgrounding at Bullseye, right?"

Backgrounding was the growing of heifers and steers from weanlings to a size where they could enter feedlots for finishing. With nearly fourteen thousand acres, Shane had the space to graze cattle and the skills to buy and sell at the opportune times. He had a far more flexible cattle business than Brandee's, which involved keeping a permanent stock of cows to produce calves that she later sold either to someone like Shane or to other ranches as breeding stock.

"I like the flexibility that approach offers me."

"I can see that."

She'd suffered massive losses after the tornado swept through her property and demolished her operations. She hadn't lost much of her herd, but the damage to her infrastructure had set her way back. And loss of time as she rebuilt wasn't the sort of thing covered by insurance.

Shane continued, "I don't want to give everything to the ranch like my father did and end up in an early grave." Once again, Shane's easy charm vanished beneath a stony expression. But in the instant before that happened, something like resentment sparked in his eyes.

This glimpse behind Shane's mask gave Brandee a flash of insight. For the first time she realized there might be more to the arrogant Shane Delgado than he wanted the world to see. And that intrigued her more than she wanted it to.

She couldn't actually fall for Shane. Her ranch was at stake. But what if he fell in love with her? Until that second, Brandee hadn't actually considered the consequences if she won this desperate wager. And then she shook her head. The thought of Shane falling for her in two weeks was crazy and irrational. But wasn't that the way love made a person feel?

Brandee shook her head. She wasn't in danger of losing her heart to Shane Delgado, only her ranch.

CHAPTER FIVE

TOSSING AND TURNING, his thoughts filled with a woman, wasn't Shane's style, but taking Brandee in his arms for the first time had electrified him. After a nearly sleepless night, he rolled out of bed at five o'clock, heeding her warning that breakfast was at six. The smell of coffee and bacon drew him from the guest suite after a quick shower.

He'd dressed in worn jeans, a long-sleeved shirt and his favorite boots. He intended to show Brandee that while he preferred to run his ranch from his office, he was perfectly capable of putting in a hard day's work.

Shane emerged from the hallway and into the living room. Brandee was working in the kitchen, her blond hair haloed by overhead recessed lighting. With a spatula in one hand and a cup of coffee in the other, she danced and sang to the country song playing softly from her smartphone.

If seeing Brandee relaxed and having fun while she flipped pancakes wasn't enough to short-circuit his equilibrium, the fact that she was wearing a revealing white cotton nightgown beneath a short royal blue silk kimono hit him like a two-by-four to the gut.

Since she hadn't yet noticed him, he had plenty of freedom to gawk at her. Either she'd forgotten he was staying in her guest room or she'd assumed he wasn't going to get up in time for breakfast. Because there was no way she'd let loose like this if she thought he'd catch her.

The soft sway of her breasts beneath the thin cotton mesmerized him, as did the realization that she was a lot more fun than he gave her credit for being. Man, he was in big trouble. If this was a true glimpse of what she could be like off-hours, there was a damn good chance that he'd do exactly what he swore he wouldn't and fall hard. He had to reclaim the upper hand. But at the moment he had no idea how to go about doing that.

"You're into Florida Georgia Line," he said as he approached the large kitchen island and slid onto a barstool. "I would've pegged you as a Faith Hill or Miranda Lambert fan."

"Why, because I'm blond or because I'm a woman?"

He had no good answer. "I guess."

She cocked her head and regarded him with a pitying expression. "The way you think, I'm not surprised you have trouble keeping a woman."

He shrugged. "You got any coffee?"

"Sure." She reached into her cupboard and fetched a mug.

The action caused her nightgown to ride up. Presented with another three inches of smooth skin covering muscular thigh, Shane was having trouble keeping track of the conversation.

"What makes you think I want to keep a woman?"

"Don't you get tired of playing the field?"

"The right woman hasn't come along to make me want to stop."

Brandee bent forward and slid his mug across the concrete counter toward him, offering a scenic view of the sweet curves of her cleavage. In his day he'd seen bigger and better. So why was he dry-mouthed and tongue-tied watching Brandee fixing breakfast?

"What's your definition of the right woman?" She slid the plate of pancakes into the oven to keep them warm.

"She can cook." He really didn't care if she did or not; he just wanted to see Brandee's eyes flash with temper.

She fetched a carton of eggs out of the fridge and held them out to him. "I don't know how to make those disgusting things you eat. So either you eat your eggs scrambled or you make them yourself."

This felt like a challenge. His housekeeper didn't work seven days a week and he knew how to fix eggs. "And she's gotta be great in bed."

"Naturally."

He came around the island as she settled another pan on her six-burner stove and got a flame started under it.

"So as long as she satisfies what lies below your belt, you're happy?" She cracked two eggs into a bowl and beat them with a whisk.

"Pretty much." Too late Shane remembered that their wager involved her falling in love with him. "And she needs to have a big heart, want kids. She'll be beautiful in a wholesome way, passionate about what she does and, of course, she's gotta be a spitfire."

"That's a big list."

"I guess." And it described Brandee to a tee, except for the part about the kids. He had no idea whether or not she wanted to have children.

"You want kids?"

"Sure." He'd never really thought much about it. "I was an only child. It would've been nice to have a bunch of brothers to get into trouble with."

Her silk kimono dipped off her shoulder as she worked, baring her delicate skin. With her dressed like this and her fine, gold hair tucked behind her ears to reveal tiny silver earrings shaped like flowers, he was having a hard time keeping his mind on the eggs he was supposed to be cracking. His lips would fit perfectly into the hollow of her collarbone. Would she quiver as she'd done the evening before?

Silence reigned in the kitchen until Shane broke it.

"Do you do this every day?" He dropped a bit of butter into his skillet.

"I do this most mornings. Breakfast is the most important meal of the day and trust me, you'll burn this off way before lunch."

Based on the mischief glinting in her eyes, Shane didn't doubt that. What sort of plan had she devised to torment him today? It was probably a morning spent in the saddle cutting out heavies, the cows closest to their due date, and bringing them into the pasture closest to the calving building.

It turned out he was right. Brandee put him up on a stocky buckskin with lightning reflexes. He hadn't cut cows in years and worried that he wouldn't be up to the task, but old skills came back to him readily and he found himself grinning as he worked each calf-heavy cow toward the opening into the next pasture.

"You're not too bad," Brandee said, closing the gate behind the pregnant cow he'd just corralled.

She sat her lean chestnut as if she'd been born in the saddle. Her straw cowboy hat had seen better days. So had her brown chaps and boots. The day had warmed from the lower forties to the midsixties and Brandee had peeled off a flannel-lined denim jacket to reveal a pale blue button-down shirt.

"Thanks." He pulled off his hat and wiped sweat from his brow. "I forgot how much fun that can be."

"A good horse makes all the difference," she said. "Buzz there has been working cows for three years. He likes it. Not all the ones we start take to cutting as well as he has."

Shane patted the buckskin's neck and resettled his hat. "How many more do you have for today?" They'd worked their way through the herd of fifty cows and moved ten of them closer to the calving building.

"I think that's going to be it for now." Brandee guided her horse alongside Shane's.

"How many more are set to go soon?"

"About thirty head in the next week to ten days, I think. Probably another fifteen that are two weeks out."

"And it's not yet peak birthing season. What kind of numbers are you looking at in March?"

With her nearly five thousand Texas acres, Shane guessed she was running around seven hundred cows. That translated to seven hundred births a year. A lot could go wrong.

"It's not as bad as it seems. We split the herd into spring and fall calving. So we're only dropping three to four hundred calves at any one time. This cuts down on the number of short-term ranch hands I need to hire during calving and keeps me from losing a year if a breeding doesn't take."

"It's still a lot of work."

Brandee shrugged. "We do like to keep a pretty close eye on them because if anything can go wrong, chances are it will."

"What are your survival rates?"

"Maybe a little better than average. In the last three years I've only lost four percent of our calves." She looked pretty pleased by that number. "And last fall we only had two that were born dead and only one lost through complications." Her eyes blazed with triumph.

"I imagine it can be hard to lose even one."

"We spend so much time taking care of them every day between feeding, doctoring and pulling calves. It breaks my heart every time something goes wrong. Especially when it's because we didn't get to a cow in time. Or if it's a heifer who doesn't realize she's given birth and doesn't clean up the calf or, worse, wanders off while her wet baby goes hypothermic."

Over the years he'd become so acclimated to Brandee's coolness that he barely recognized the vibrant, intense woman beside him. He was sucker punched by her emotional attachment to the hundreds of babies that got born on her ranch every year.

This really was her passion. And every time he approached

her about selling, he'd threatened not just her livelihood but her joy.

"My dad used to go ballistic if that happened," she continued. "I pitied the hand that nodded off during watch and let something go wrong."

"Where's your dad now?"

Her hat dipped, hiding her expression. "He died when I was twelve."

Finding that they had this in common was a surprise. "We both lost our dads too early." Although Shane suspected from Brandee's somber tone that her loss was far keener than his had been. "So, your dad was a rancher, too?"

She shook her head. "A foreman at the Lazy J. But it was his dream to own his own ranch." Her gaze fixed on the horizon. "And for us to run it together."

Shane heard the conviction in her voice and wondered if he should just give up and concede the wager right now. She wasn't going to sell her ranch to him or anyone else. Then he remembered that even if he was faced with a fight he could never win, there was still a good chance she'd sleep with him before the two weeks were up. And wasn't that why he'd accepted the wager in the first place?

At around two o'clock in the afternoon, Brandee knocked off work so she could grab a nap. It made the long hours to come a little easier if she wasn't dead tired before she got on the horse. Normally during the ninety-day calving season Brandee took one overnight watch per week. She saw no reason to change this routine with Shane staying at her house.

Brandee let herself in the back door and kicked off her boots in the mudroom. Barefoot, she headed into the kitchen for a cheese stick and an apple. Munching contentedly, she savored the house's tranquillity. Sharing her space with Shane was less troublesome than she'd expected, but she'd lived alone a long time and relished the quiet. Shane had a knack for making the air around him crackle with energy.

It didn't help that he smelled like sin and had an adorable yawn, something she'd seen a great deal of him doing these last three days because she'd worked him so hard. In the evenings he had a hard time focusing on his laptop as he answered emails and followed up with issues on The Bellamy job site.

Today, she'd given him the day off to head to the construction site so he could handle whatever problems required him to be there in person. She didn't expect him back until after dinner and decided to indulge in a hot bath before hitting her mattress for a couple hours of shut-eye. It always felt decadent to nap in the afternoon, but she functioned better when rested and reminded herself that she'd hired experienced hands so she didn't have to do everything herself.

Since receiving Maverick's blackmail notice, she hadn't slept well, and though her body was tired, her mind buzzed with frenetic energy. Disrupting her routine further was the amount of time she was spending with Shane. Despite questioning the wisdom of their wager, she realized that having him in her house was a nice change.

Four hours later, Brandee was fixing a quiet dinner for herself of baked chicken and Caesar salad. Shane had a late business meeting and was planning on having dinner in town. He'd only been helping her for three days, but already she could see the impact he was having on her building project at the camp.

He'd gone down to the site and assessed the situation. Last night he'd studied her plans and budget, promising to get her back on track. As much as she hated to admit it, it was good to have someone to partner with. Even if that someone was Shane Delgado and he was only doing it to make her fall in love with him.

There'd been no repeat of him making a play for her despite the way she fixed breakfast every morning in her nightgown. Standing beside him in the kitchen and suffering the bite of sexual attraction, she'd expected something to happen. When nothing had, she'd felt wrung out and cranky. Not that she let him see that. It wouldn't do to let him know that she'd crossed the bridge from it's never going to happen to if it didn't happen soon she'd go mad.

Shane returned to the ranch house as Brandee was getting ready to leave. Her shift wouldn't begin for an hour, but she wanted to get a report on what had happened during the afternoon. As he came in the back door and met up with her in the mudroom, he looked surprised to see her dressed in her work clothes and a warm jacket.

His movements lacked their usual energy as he set his briefcase on the bench. "Are you just getting in?"

"Nope, heading out." She snagged her hat from one of the hooks and set it on her head. "It's my night to watch the cows that are close to calving."

"You're going out by yourself?"

She started to bristle at his question, then decided he wasn't being patronizing, just voicing concern. "I've been doing it for three years by myself. I'll be fine."

"Give me a second to change and I'll come with you."

His offer stunned her. "You must be exhausted." The words slipped out before she considered them.

He turned in the doorway that led to the kitchen and glared at her. "So?"

"I just mean it's a long shift. I spend between four to six hours in the saddle depending on how things go."

"You don't think I'm capable of doing that?"

"I didn't say that." Dealing with his ego was like getting into a ring with a peevish bull. "But you have worked all day and I didn't figure you'd be up for pulling an all-nighter."

"You think I'm soft."

"Not at all." She knew he could handle the work, but was a little surprised he wanted to.

"Then what is it?"

"I just reasoned that you don't…that maybe you aren't as used to the actual work that goes into ranching."

"That's the same thing."

Brandee regretted stirring the pot. She should have just invited him along and laughed when he fell off his horse at 2:00 a.m. because he couldn't keep his eyes open any longer.

"I don't want to make a big deal about this," she said. "I just thought you might want to get a good night's sleep and start fresh in the morning."

"While you spend the night checking on your herd."

"I took a three-hour nap." His outrage was starting to amuse her. "Okay. You can come with me. I won't say another word."

He growled at her in frustration before striding off. Brandee grabbed a second thermos from her cabinet. Coffee would help keep them warm and awake. To her surprise, Brandee caught herself smiling at the thought of Shane's company tonight. Working together had proven more enjoyable than she'd imagined. She didn't have to keep things professional with Shane the way she did when working with her ranch hands. She'd enjoyed talking strategy and ranch economics with him.

As if he feared she'd head out without him, Shane returned in record time. She handed him a scarf and watched in silence as he stepped into his work boots.

"Ready?" she prompted as he stood.

"Yes."

"Do you want to take separate vehicles? That way if you get…" She trailed off as his scowl returned. "Fine."

Irritation radiated from him the whole drive down to the ranch buildings. In the barn, she chatted with her foreman, Jimmy, to see how the afternoon had gone. H545 had dropped her calf without any problems.

"A steer," he said, sipping at the coffee Brandee had just made.

"That makes it fifty-five steers and fifty-two heifers." While the ratio of boys to girls was usually fifty-fifty, it was always nice when more steers were born because they grew faster and weighed more than the girls. "Anyone we need to keep an eye on tonight?"

"H729 was moving around like her labor was starting. She's a week late and if you remember she had some problems last year, so you might want to make sure things are going smoothly with her."

"Will do. Thanks, Jimmy."

The moon was up, casting silvery light across the grass when Shane and Brandee rode into the pasture. The pregnant cows stood or lay in clusters. A couple moved about in a lazy manner. H729 was easy to spot. She was huge and had isolated herself. Brandee pointed her out.

"She's doing some tail wringing, which means she's feeling contractions. I don't think she'll go tonight, but you can never tell."

"How often do they surprise you?"

"More often than I'd like to admit. And that drives me crazy because there's nothing wrong with nearly eighty percent of the calves we lose at birth. Most of the time they suffocate because they're breeched or because it's a first-calf heifer and she gets too tired to finish pushing out the calf."

"How often do you have to assist?"

"On nights like this it's pretty rare." The temperature was hovering in the low forties; compared to a couple weeks earlier, it almost felt balmy. "It's when we get storms and freezing rain that we have our hands full with the newborns."

Shane yawned and rubbed his eyes. Brandee glanced his way to assess his fatigue and lingered to admire his great bone structure and sexy mouth. It was an interesting face, one she never grew tired of staring at. Not a perfect face—she wasn't into that, too boring—but one with character.

"What?" he snapped, never taking his focus off the cows. Despite the shadow cast by the brim of his hat, Brandee could see that Shane's jaw was set.

"I was just thinking it was nice to have your company tonight."

For the briefest of moments his lips relaxed. "I'm glad to be here."

She knew that showing she felt sorry for him would only heighten his annoyance. Big strong men like Shane did not admit to weakness of any kind. And she rather liked him the better for gritting his teeth and sticking with it.

"That being said, you can take my truck and head back if you want. I don't think much of anything is going to happen tonight."

"I don't like the idea of you being alone out here."

"I've been doing this since I was ten years old."

"Not alone."

"No. With my dad. On the weekends, he used to let me ride the late-night watch with him."

"What did your mom say about that?"

"Nothing. She didn't live with us."

Shane took a second to digest that. "They divorced?"

"Never married."

"How come you lived with your dad and not your mom?"

Insulated by her father's unconditional love, Brandee had never noticed her mother's absence. "She didn't want me."

It wasn't a plea for sympathy, but a statement of fact. Most people would have said her mother was a bad parent or uttered some banality about how they were sure that wasn't true.

Shane shrugged. "You are kind of a pain."

He would never know how much she appreciated this tactic. Shane might come off as a glib charmer, but the way he watched her now showed he had a keen instinct for people.

"Yes," Brandee drawled. "She mentioned that often after my dad died and I had to go live with her."

Judging from his narrowed eyes, he wasn't buying her casual posture and nonchalant manner. "Obviously she wasn't interested in being a parent," he said.

Brandee loosed a huge sigh and an even bigger confession. "I was the biggest mistake she ever made."

CHAPTER SIX

SHANE'S EXHAUSTION DWINDLED as Brandee spoke of her mother. Although he'd grown up with both parents, his father's endless disappointment made Shane sympathetic of Brandee for the resentment her mother had displayed.

"Why do you say that?"

"She gave birth to me and handed me over to my dad, then walked out of the hospital and never looked back. After my dad died and the social worker contacted my mom, I was really surprised when she took me in. I think she wanted to get her hands on the money that my dad left me. He'd saved about fifty thousand toward the down payment on his own ranch. She went through it in six months."

"And you got nothing?"

"Not a penny."

"So your father died when you were twelve and your mother spent your inheritance."

"That about sums it up." Brandee spoke matter-of-factly, but Shane couldn't imagine her taking it all in stride. No child grew up thinking it was okay when a parent abandoned them. This must have been what led to Brandee erecting her impenetrable walls. And now Shane was faced with an impossible task. The terms of her wager made much more sense. There was no way he was going to get her to fall for him.

After a slow circle of the pasture, Brandee declared it was quiet enough that they could return to the barn. Leaving the horses saddled and tied up, they grabbed some coffee and settled in the ranch office. While Brandee looked over her herd data, updated her birth statistics and considered her spring-breeding program, Shane used the time to research her.

"You started a fashion line?" He turned his phone so the screen faced her.

She regarded the image of herself modeling a crocheted halter, lace-edged scarf and headband. "A girl's got to pay the bills."

"When you were eighteen?"

"Actually, I was seventeen. I fudged my age. You have to be eighteen to open a business account at the bank and sell online."

"From these news articles, it looks like you did extremely well."

"Who knew there was such a huge hole in the market for bohemian-style fashion and accessories." Her wry smile hid a wealth of pride in her accomplishment.

"You built up the business and sold it for a huge profit."

"So that I could buy Hope Springs Ranch."

He regarded her with interest. "Obviously the fashion line was a moneymaker. Why not do both?"

"Because my dream was this ranch. And the company was more than a full-time job. I couldn't possibly keep up with both." She picked up her hat and stood. "We should do another sweep."

Back in the saddle, facing an icy wind blowing across the flat pasture, Shane considered the woman riding beside him. The photos of her modeling her clothing line had shown someone much more carefree and happy than she'd ever appeared to him. Why, if there'd been such good money to be made running a fashion company, had she chosen the backbreaking work of running a ranch?

Was it because she'd been trying to continue her father's

legacy, molded by him to wake up early, put in a long day and take satisfaction in each calf that survived? From the way she talked about her dad, Shane bet there'd been laughter at the end of each day and a love as wide as the Texas sky.

He envied her.

"Is that the cow you were watching earlier?" He pointed out an animal in the distance that had just lain down.

"Maybe. Let's double-check."

When they arrived, they left their horses and approached the cow on foot. Judging from the way her sides were straining, she was deep in labor.

It struck Shane that despite spending his entire life on a ranch, he'd only witnessed a few births, and those had been horses not cows. He took his cue from Brandee. She stood with her weight evenly placed, her gloved hands bracketing her hips. Although her eyes were intent, her manner displayed no concern.

"Look," she said as they circled around to the cow's rear end. "You can see the water sack."

Sure enough, with the moon high in the sky there was enough light for Shane to pick out the opaque sack that contained the calf. He hadn't come out tonight expecting excitement of this sort.

"What did you expect?" It was as if she'd read his mind.

"Frankly I was thinking we'd be riding around out here while you kept me at arm's length with tales of your brokenhearted ex-lovers."

With her arms crossed over her chest, she pivoted around to face him, laboring cow forgotten.

"My brokenhearted what?"

"I don't know," he replied somewhat shortly. "I'm tired and just saying whatever pops into my mind."

"Why would you be thinking about my brokenhearted ex-lovers?"

"Are you sure she's doing okay?" He indicated the straining cow, hoping to distract Brandee with something important.

Unfortunately it seemed as if both females were happy letting nature take its course. Brandee continued to regard him like a detective interviewing a prime suspect she knew was lying.

"What makes you think that any of my lovers are broken-hearted?"

"I don't. Not really." In truth he hadn't given much thought to her dating anyone.

Well, that wasn't exactly true. To the best of his knowledge she hadn't dated anyone since moving to Royal. And despite the womanly curves that filled out her snug denim, she always struck him as a tomboy. Somehow he'd gotten it into his head that he was the only one who might've been attracted to her.

"So which is it?"

"Is that a hoof?"

His attempt to distract her lasted as long as it took for her to glance over at the cow and notice that a pair of hooves had emerged.

"Yes." And just like that she was back staring at him again. "Do I strike you as the sort of woman who uses men and casts them aside?"

"No."

"So why would you think I would end my relationships in such a way that I would hurt someone?"

Shane recognized that he'd tapped into something complicated with his offhand remark and sought to defuse her irritation with a charming smile. "You should be flattered that I thought you would be so desirable that no one would ever want to break up with you."

"So you think I'm susceptible to flattery?"

He was in so deep he would need a hundred feet of rope to climb out of the hole he'd dug. What had happened to the silver-tongued glibness she liked to accuse him of having?

"Is she supposed to stand up like that?"

"Sometimes they need to walk around a bit." This time Brandee didn't spare the cow even a fraction of her attention. "She may be up and down several times."

"I think our arguing is upsetting her," he said, hoping concern for the cow would convince Brandee to give up the conversation.

"We're not arguing," she corrected him, her voice light and unconcerned. "We're discussing your opinion of me. And you're explaining why you assume I'd be the one to end a relationship. Instead of the other way around."

At first he grappled with why he'd said what he had. But beneath her steady gaze, he found his answer. "I think you have a hard time finding anyone who can match up to your father."

She obviously hadn't expected him to deliver such a blunt, to-the-point answer. Her eyes fell away and she stared at the ground. In the silence that followed, Shane worried that he'd struck too close to home.

Brandee turned so she was once again facing the cow. The brim of her hat cast a shadow over her features, making her expression unreadable. Despite her silence, Shane didn't sense she was angry. Her mood was more contemplative than irritated.

"I never set out to hurt anyone," she said, her voice so soft he almost missed the words. "I'm just not good girlfriend material."

Was that her way of warning him off? If so, she'd have to work a lot harder. "That's something else we have in common. I've been told I'm not good boyfriend material, either."

Now both of them were staring at the cow. She took several steps before coming to a halt as another spasm swept over her. It seemed as if this would expel the calf, but no more of the baby appeared.

"Is this normal?" Shane asked. "It seems like she can't get it out."

"We should see good progress in the next thirty minutes or so. If we don't see the nose and face by then, there might be something wrong."

Shane was surprised at the way his stomach knotted with

anxiety. Only by glancing at Brandee's calm posture did he keep from voicing his concern again.

"How do you do this?"

"I have around seven hundred cows being bred over two seasons. While I never take anything for granted, watching that many births gives you a pretty good feel for how things are going."

"Your business is a lot more complicated than mine." And offered a lot more potential for heartbreak.

He certainly wasn't standing in his field at three o'clock in the morning waiting for new calves to be brought into the world. He bought eight-month-old, newly weaned steers and heifers and sent them out into his pastures to grow up. Unless he was judging the market for the best time to sell, he rarely thought about his livestock.

"Not necessarily more complicated," Brandee said. "You have to consider the market when you buy and sell and the best way to manage your pastures to optimize grazing. There are so many variables that depend on how much rain we get and the price of feed if the pastures aren't flourishing."

"But you have all that to worry about and you have to manage when you're breeding and optimize your crosses to get the strongest calves possible. And then there's the problem of losing livestock to accidents and predators."

While he'd been speaking, the cow had once again lain down. The calf's nose appeared, followed by a face. Shane stared as she began to push in earnest.

"She's really straining," he said. "This is all still normal?"

"She needs to push out the shoulders and this is really hard. But she's doing fine."

Shane had the urge to lean his body into Brandee's and absorb some of her tranquillity. Something about the quiet night and the miracle playing out before them made him want to connect with her. But he kept his distance, not wanting to disturb the fragile camaraderie between them.

Just when Shane thought the whole thing was over, the cow got to her feet again and he groaned. Brandee shot him an amused grin.

"It's okay. Sometimes they like finishing the birthing process standing up."

He watched as the cow got to her feet, her baby dangling halfway out of her. This time Shane didn't resist the urge for contact. He reached out and grabbed Brandee's hand. He'd left his gloves behind on this second sweep and wished Brandee had done the same. But despite the worn leather barrier between them, he reveled in the way her fingers curved against his.

After a few deep, fortifying breaths, the cow gave one last mighty push and the calf fell to the grass with a thud. Shane winced and Brandee laughed.

"See, I told you it was going to be okay," Brandee said as the cow turned around and began nudging the calf while making soft, encouraging grunts.

A moment later she swept her long tongue over her sodden baby, clearing fluid from the calf's coat. The calf began to breathe and the cow kept up her zealous cleaning. Brandee leaned a little of her weight against Shane's arm.

That was when Shane realized they were still holding hands. "Damn," he muttered, unsure which had a bigger impact, the calf being born or the simple pleasure of Brandee's hand in his.

He hadn't answered the question before she lifted up on tiptoes and kissed him.

Being bathed in moonlight and surrounded by the sleepy cows seemed like an ideal moment to surrender to the emotions running deep and untamed through Brandee's body. At first Shane's lips were stiff with surprise and Brandee cursed. What had she been thinking? There was no romance to be found in a cold, windswept pasture. But as she began her retreat, Shane threw an arm around her waist and yanked her hard against his body. His lips softened and coaxed a sigh of relief from her lungs.

She wrapped her arms around his neck and let him sweep her into a rushing stream of longing. The mouth that devoured her with such abandon lacked the persuasive touch she'd expected a charmer like Shane to wield. It almost seemed as if he was as surprised as she.

Of course, there was no way that could be the case. His reasons for being at her ranch were as self-serving as hers had been for inviting him. Each of them wanted to win their wager. She'd intended to do whatever it took to get Shane to fall in love with her. Her dire situation made that a necessity. But he'd been pestering her for years to sell and she was sure he'd pull out every weapon in his arsenal to get her to fall for him.

This last thought dumped cold water on her libido. She broke off the kiss and through the blood roaring in her ears heard the measured impact of approaching hooves all around them. It wasn't unusual for the most dominant cows in the herd to visit the newborn. Half a dozen cows had approached.

"He's looking around," she said, indicating the new calf. "Soon he'll be trying to get up."

Usually a calf was on its feet and nursing within the first hour of being born. Brandee would have to make sure her ranch hands kept an eye on him for the next twelve hours to make sure he got a good suckle. And they would need to get him ear-tagged and weighed first thing. The calves were docile and trusting the first day. After that they grew much more difficult to catch.

Brandee stepped away from Shane and immediately missed their combined body heat. "I think it's okay to head back."

"I'm glad I came out tonight," Shane said as they rode back toward the horse barn. A quick sweep of the pasture had shown nothing else of interest.

"You're welcome to participate in night duty anytime."

"How often do you pull a shift?"

"Once a week."

"You don't have to."

"No." But how did she explain that sitting on a horse in the middle of the night, surrounded by her pregnant cows, she felt as if everything was perfect in her world? "But when I'm out here I think about my dad smiling down and I know he'd be happy with me."

She didn't talk about her dad all that much to anyone. But because of Shane's awestruck reaction to tonight's calving, she was feeling sentimental.

"Happy because you're doing what he wanted?"

"Yes."

"How about what you want?"

"It's the same thing." Brandee's buoyant mood suddenly drooped like a thirsty flower. "Being a rancher is all I ever wanted to do."

"And yet you started a fashion business instead of coming back to find work as a ranch hand. You couldn't know that what you were doing with your clothing line would make you rich."

"No." She'd never really thought about why she'd chosen waitressing and creating clothing and accessories after running away from her mother's house over getting work on a ranch. "I guess I wasn't sure anyone would take me serious as a ranch hand." And it was a job dominated by men.

"You might be right."

When they arrived at the barn, this time Brandee insisted Shane take her truck back to the ranch house. She wasn't going to finish up work until much later. He seemed reluctant, but in the end he agreed.

The instant the truck's taillights disappeared down the driveway, Brandee was struck by a ridiculous feeling of loneliness. She turned on the computer and recorded the ranch's newest addition. Then, hiding a yawn behind her hand, she made her way to the barn where they housed cows and calves that needed more attention.

Cayenne was a week old. A couple days ago a ranch hand had noticed her hanging out on her own by the hay, abandoned by her mother. At this age it didn't take long for a calf to slide downhill, so it paid to be vigilant. Jimmy had brought her in and the guys had tended to a cut on her hind left hoof.

They'd given her a bottle with some electrolytes and a painkiller and the calf had turned around in two days. She was a feisty thing and it made Brandee glad to see the way she charged toward the half wall as if she intended to smash through it. At the very last second she wheeled away, bucking and kicking her way around the edge of the enclosure.

Brandee leaned her arms on the wood and spent a few minutes watching the calf, wondering if the mother would take back her daughter when they were reunited. Sometimes a cow just wasn't much of a mother and when that happened they'd load her up and take her to the sales barn. No reason to feed an unproductive cow.

Talking about being abandoned by her own mother wasn't something Brandee normally did, but it had proven easy to tell Shane. So easy that she'd also divulged the theft of her inheritance, something she'd only ever told to one other person, her best friend, Chelsea.

In the aftermath of the conversation, she'd felt exposed and edgy. It was partially why she'd picked a fight with him about his "brokenhearted ex-lovers" comment. She'd wanted to bring antagonism back into their interaction. Fighting with him put her back on solid ground, kept her from worrying that he'd see her as weak and her past hurts as exploitable.

At the same time his offhand comment had unknowingly touched a nerve. She'd asked if he saw her as the sort of woman who'd use a man and cast him aside. Yet she'd done it before and had barely hesitated before deciding to do so with Shane. She was going to make him fall for her and trick him into giving up his legal claim to Hope Springs Ranch. What sort of a terrible person did that make her?

Reminding herself that he intended to take the ranch didn't make her feel better about what she was doing. He had no clue about the enormity of their wager. Keeping him in the dark wasn't fair or right. Yet, if he discovered the truth, she stood to lose everything.

As during her teen years living with her mother, she was in pure survival mode. It was the only thing that kept her conscience from hamstringing her. She didn't enjoy what she was doing. It was necessary to protect what belonged to her and keep herself safe. Like a cat cornered by a big dog, she would play as dirty as it took to win free and clear.

Several hours later, after one final sweep of the pasture, she turned the watch over to her ranch hands and had one of them drop her off at home. She probably could've walked the quarter-mile-long driveway to her house, but the emotional night had taken a toll on her body as well as her spirit.

The smell of bacon hit her as she entered the back door and her stomach groaned in delight. With loud country music spilling from the recessed speakers above her kitchen and living room, she was able to drop her boots in the mudroom and hang up her coat and hat, then sneak through the doorway to catch a glimpse of Shane without him being aware.

Her heart did a strange sort of hiccup in her chest at the sight of him clad in baggy pajama bottoms, a pale blue T-shirt riding his chest and abs like a second skin. She gulped at the thought of running her hands beneath the cotton and finding the silky, warm texture beneath. While the man might be a piece of work, his body was a work of art.

"Hey." She spoke the word softly, but he heard.

His gaze shifted toward her and the slow smile that curved his lips gave her nerve endings a delicious jolt. She had to hold on to the door frame while her knees returned to a solid state capable of supporting her. He was definitely working the sexy-roommate angle for all it was worth. She'd better up her game.

"I'm making breakfast just the way you like it." He held up the skillet and showed her the eggs he'd scrambled. "And there's French toast, bacon and coffee."

Damn. And he could cook, too. Conscious of her disheveled

hair and the distinctive fragrance of horse and barn that clung to her clothes, Brandee debated slinking off to grab a quick shower or just owning these badges of hard work.

"It all sounds great." Her stomach growled loudly enough to be heard and Shane's eyebrows went up.

"Let me make you a plate," he said, laughter dancing at the edges of his voice. "Here's a cup of coffee. Go sit down before you fall over."

That he'd misinterpreted why she was leaning against the doorway was just fine with Brandee. She accepted the coffee and made her way toward the bar stools that lined her kitchen island. Unconcerned about whether the caffeine zap would keep her awake, she gladly sipped the dark, rich brew.

"It's decaf," he remarked, sliding a plate toward her and then turning back to the stove to fill one for himself. "I figured you'd grab a couple hours before heading out again."

"Thanks," she mumbled around a mouthful of French toast. "And thanks for breakfast. You didn't have to."

His broad shoulders lifted in a lazy shrug. "I slept a few hours and thought you'd be hungry. How's the new calf?"

"On my last circuit he was enjoying his first meal."

"Great to hear." Shane slid into the seat beside her and set his plate down. His bare feet found the rungs of her chair, casually invading her space. "Thanks for letting me tag along last night." He peered at her for a long moment before picking up his fork and turning his attention to breakfast.

"Sure."

As they ate in companionable silence, Brandee found her concern growing by the minute. The night's shared experience and his thoughtfulness in having breakfast ready for her were causing a shift in her impression of him. For years she'd thought of Shane as an egomaniac focused solely on making money. Tonight she'd seen his softer side, and the hint of vulnerability made him attractive to her in a different way.

A more dangerous way.

She had to stay focused on her objective and not give in to the emotions tugging at her. Letting him capture her heart was a mistake. One that meant she would lose everything. Her home. Her livelihood. And worst of all, her self-respect. Because falling for a man who wouldn't return her love was really stupid and she'd been many things, but never that.

CHAPTER SEVEN

IT WAS ALMOST six o'clock in the evening when Shane returned from checking on the building site at Brandee's teen camp. As he entered the house through the back door, the most delicious scents stopped him dead in his tracks. He breathed in the rich scent of beef and red wine as he stripped off his coat and muddy boots. In stockinged feet, he entered the kitchen, where Brandee's housekeeper stood at the stove, stirring something in a saucepan.

"What smells so amazing?"

"Dinner," May responded with a cheeky grin and a twinkle in her bright blue eyes.

The fiftysomething woman had rosy cheeks even when she wasn't standing over the stove. She fussed over Brandee like a fond aunt rather than a housekeeper and treated Shane as if he was the best thing that had ever happened to her employer.

"What are we having?"

"Beef Wellington with red potatoes and asparagus."

Shane's mouth began to water. "What's the occasion?"

"Valentine's Day." May pointed toward the dining table, where china and silverware had been laid. There were white tapers in crystal holders and faceted goblets awaiting wine. "You forgot?"

Eyeing the romantic scene, Shane's heart thumped erratically. What special hell was he in for tonight?

"I've been a little preoccupied," he muttered.

Between helping out at Hope Springs, keeping an eye on the construction at The Bellamy and popping in at Bullseye to make sure all was running smoothly, he hadn't had five minutes to spare. Now he was kicking himself for missing this opportunity to capitalize on the most romantic day of the year to sweep Brandee off her feet.

Obviously she hadn't made the same mistake.

May shook her head as if Shane had just proven what was wrong with the entire male sex. "Well, it's too late to do anything about it now. Dinner's in half an hour." She arched her eyebrows at his mud-splattered jeans.

Catching her meaning, Shane headed for his shower. Fifteen minutes later, he'd washed off the day's exertions and dressed in clean clothes. He emerged from his bedroom, tugging up the sleeves of his gray sweater. Black jeans and a pair of flip-flops completed his casual look.

Brandee was peering into her wine fridge as he approached. She turned at his greeting and smiled in genuine pleasure. "How was your day?"

"Good. Productive." It was a casual exchange, lacking the push and pull of sexual attraction that typified their usual interaction. Time to step up his game. "Did May head home?"

"Yes. She and Tim were going out for a romantic dinner."

"Because it's Valentine's Day. I forgot all about it."

"So did I." Brandee selected a bottle and set it on the counter. With her long golden hair cascading over the shoulders of her filmy top, she looked like a cross between a sexy angel and the girl next door. White cotton shorts edged in peekaboo lace rode low on her hips and bared her sensational, well-toned thighs. "Can you open this while I fetch the glasses? The corkscrew is in the drawer to your right."

"I guess neither one of us buys into all the romantic mumbo jumbo," he muttered.

He should've been relieved that the fancy dinner and beautifully set dining table hadn't been Brandee's idea. It meant that she hadn't set out to prey on his libido. But that didn't mean the danger had passed.

"Or we're just cynical about love." She gazed at him from beneath her long eyelashes.

Shane finished opening the bottle and set it aside to breathe. He worked the cork off the corkscrew, letting the task absorb his full attention. "Do you ever wonder if you're built for a long-term relationship?" He recognized it was a strange question to ask a woman, but he suspected Brandee wouldn't be insulted.

"All the time." She moved past him as the timer on the stove sounded. Apparently this was her signal to remove the beef Wellington from the oven. "I don't make my personal life a priority. Chelsea's on me all the time about it."

"My mom gives me the same sort of lectures. I think she wants grandchildren." And he was getting to an age where he needed to decide kids or no kids. At thirty-five he wasn't over the hill by any means, but he didn't want to be in his forties and starting a family.

"I imagine she's feeling pretty hopeless about the possibility."

"Because I haven't met anyone that makes me want to settle down?"

Brandee shook her head. "I can't imagine any woman being more important to you than your freedom."

And she was right. His bachelor status suited him. Having fun. Keeping things casual. Bolting at the first sign of commitment. He liked keeping his options open. And what was wrong with that?

"And what about you, Miss Independent? Are you trying to tell me you're any more eager to share your life with someone? You use your commitment to this ranch and your teen camp to keep everyone at bay. What are you afraid of?"

"Who says I'm afraid?"

Bold words, but he'd seen the shadows that lingered in her eyes when she talked about her mother's abandonment. She might deny it, but there was no question in Shane's mind that Brandee's psyche had taken a hit.

"It's none of my business. Forget I said anything." Shane sensed that if he pursued the issue he would only end up annoying her and that was not how he wanted the evening to go.

"Why don't you pour the wine while I get food on the plates." From her tone, she was obviously content to drop the topic.

Ten minutes later they sat down to the meal May had prepared. Shane kept the conversation fixed on the progress she was making at her teen camp. It was a subject near and dear to her heart, and helping her with the project was sure to endear him to her. Was it manipulative? Sure. But he wanted to buy her property. That's why he'd accepted the bet and moved in.

Shane ignored a tug at his conscience and reminded himself that Brandee was working just as hard as he was to make him fall for her. He grinned. She just didn't realize that she'd lost before she even started.

"This weekend I'm hosting a teen experience with some of the high school kids," Brandee said. "Megan Maguire from Royal Safe Haven is bringing several of her rescue dogs to the ranch for the teens to work with. Chelsea is coming to help out. I could use a couple more adult volunteers." She regarded him pointedly.

The last thing he wanted to do was spend a day chaperoning a bunch of hormonally charged kids, but he had a wager to win and since he'd dropped the ball for Valentine's Day, he could probably pick up some bonus points by helping her out with this.

"Sure, why not." It wasn't the most enthusiastic response, but he hoped she'd be pleased he'd agreed so readily.

"And maybe you could see if Gabe is interested, as well?"

If it made Brandee go all lovey-dovey for him, Shane would do as much arm-twisting as it took to get his best friend on board. "I'll check with him. I'm sure it won't be a problem."

After putting away the leftovers and settling the dirty dishes in the dishwasher, Brandee suggested they move out to the patio to enjoy an after-dinner scotch. This time, instead of taking the sofa opposite him, she settled onto the cushion right beside him and tucked her feet beneath her.

While the fire crackled and flickered, Shane sipped his drink and, warmed by alcohol, flame and desire, listened while Brandee told him about the struggling calf they'd saved and reunited with her mother today. He told himself that when Brandee leaned into him as she shared her tale she was only acting. Still, it was all Shane could do to keep from pulling her onto his lap and stealing a kiss or two.

"You know, it is Valentine's Day," she murmured, tilting her head to an adorable angle and regarding him from beneath her long lashes.

With her gaze fixed on his lips, Shane quelled the impulses turning his insides into raw need. She was playing him. He knew it and she knew he knew it. For the moment he was willing to concede she had the upper hand. What man presented with an enticing package of sweet and spicy femininity would be capable of resisting?

"Yes, it is," he replied, not daring to sip from the tumbler of scotch lest she see the slight tremble in his hand.

"A day devoted to lovers."

Shane decided to follow her lead and see where it took him. "And romance."

"I think both of us know what's inevitable."

"That you and I get together?" To his credit he didn't sound as hopeful as he felt.

"Exactly." She leaned forward to kiss him. Her lips, whether by design or intent, grazed his cheek instead. Her breath smelled of chocolate and scotch, sending blood scorching through his veins. "I've been thinking about you a lot."

Her husky murmur made his nerve endings shiver. He gripped the glass tumbler hard enough to shatter it. "Me, too. I lay in bed at night and imagine you're with me. Your long hair splayed on my pillow." Thighs parted in welcome. Skin flushed with desire. "You're smiling up at me. Excited by all the incredible things I'm doing to you."

From deep in her throat came a sexy hum. "Funny." Her fingertips traced circles on the back of his neck before soothing their way into his hair. "I always picture myself on top. Your hands on my breasts as I ride you."

Shane winced as his erection suddenly pressed hard against his zipper. "You drive me crazy," he murmured. "You know that, right?"

He set down his drink with a deliberate movement before cupping her head. She didn't resist as he pulled her close enough to kiss. Her lashes fluttered downward, lips arching into a dreamy smile.

Their breath mingled. Shane drew out the moment. Her soft breasts settled against his chest and he half closed his eyes to better savor the sensation. This wouldn't be their first kiss, but that didn't make it any less momentous. Tonight they weren't in the middle of a pasture surrounded by cows. This time, the only thing standing in the way of seeing this kiss through to the end was if she actually felt something for him.

Was that what made him hesitate? Worry over her emotional state? Or was he more concerned about his own?

"Let's go inside," she suggested, shifting her legs off the couch and taking his hand. Her expression was unreadable as she got to her feet and tugged at him. "I have a wonderful idea about how we can spend the rest of the evening."

The instant they stepped away from the raging fire, Brandee shivered as the cool February air struck her bare skin. She'd dressed to show off a ridiculous amount of flesh in an effort to throw Shane off his game. Naturally her ploy had worked, but as they crossed the brick patio, she wished she hadn't left the throw behind. Despite how readily Shane had taken her up on her offer, she was feeling incredibly uncertain and exposed.

In slow stages during their romantic dinner, her plan to methodically seduce him had gone awry. She blamed it on the man's irresistible charm and the way he'd listened to her talk about the calf and her camp. He hadn't waited in polite silence for her to conclude her explanation about the program she and Megan Maguire had devised to teach the teenagers about patience and responsibility. No, he'd asked great questions and seemed genuinely impressed by the scope of her project.

But the pivotal moment had come when she saw a flash of sympathy in his eyes. She'd been talking about one particular boy whose dad had bullied him into joining the football team when all the kid wanted to do was play guitar and write music. Something about the story had struck home with Shane and for several seconds he'd withdrawn like a hermit crab confronted by something unpleasant. She realized they were alike in so many ways, each burying past hurts beneath a veneer of confidence, keeping the world at bay to keep their sadness hidden.

As they neared the house, a brief skirmish ensued. Shane seemed to expect that Brandee would want their first encounter to be in her bedroom. That was not going to happen. She'd invited him into the space once and it had been a huge mistake. Her bedroom was her sanctuary, the place she could be herself and drop her guard. She didn't want to be vulnerable in front of Shane. Seeing her true self would give him an edge that she couldn't afford.

"Let's try out the shower in your suite," she suggested, taking his hand in both of hers and drawing him toward the sliding glass door that led to his bedroom. "I had such fun designing the space and haven't ever tried it out."

"The rain shower system is pretty fantastic."

The four recessed showerheads in the ceiling and integrated chromotherapy with mood-enhancing colored lighting sequences were ridiculous indulgences, but Brandee had thought her grandmother would get a kick out of it and had been right.

Shane guided her through the bedroom. His hand on the small of her back was hot through the semisheer material of her blouse and Brandee burned. How was it possible that the man who stood poised to take everything from her could be the one who whipped her passions into such a frenzy? They hadn't even kissed and her loins ached for his possession. She shuddered at the image of what was to come, a little frightened by how badly she wanted it.

While Shane used the keypad to start the shower, Brandee gulped in a huge breath and fought panic. How was she supposed to pretend like this was just a simple sexual encounter when each heartbeat made her chest hurt? Every inch of her body hummed with longing. She was so wound up that she was ready to go off the instant he put his hands on her.

Shane picked that second to turn around. Whatever he saw in her expression caused his nostrils to flare and his eyes to narrow. Her nerve collapsed. Brandee backed up a step, moving fully clothed into the shower spray. She blinked in surprise as the warm water raced down her face. Shane didn't hesitate before joining her.

As he circled her waist, drawing her against his hard planes, Brandee slammed the door on her emotions and surrendered to the pleasure of Shane's touch. She quested her fingers beneath his sweater, stripping the sodden cotton over his head. The skin she revealed stretched over taut muscle and sculpted bone, making her groan in appreciation.

Almost tentatively she reached out to run her palm across one broad shoulder. His biceps flexed as he slid his hands over her rib cage, thumbs whisking along the outer curves of her breasts. She shuddered at the glancing contact and trembled as he licked water from her throat. Hunger built inside her while her breath came in ragged pants.

The water rendered her clothes nearly transparent, but Shane's gaze remained locked on her face. He appeared more interested in discovering her by touch. His fingertips skimmed her arms, shoulders and back with tantalizing curiosity. If she could catch her breath, she might have protested that she needed his hands on her bare skin. An insistent pressure bloomed between her thighs. She felt Shane's own arousal pressing hard against her belly. Why was he making her wait?

In the end she took matters into her own hands and stripped off her blouse. It clung to her skin, resisting all effort to bare herself to his touch. Above the sound of the rain shower, she heard a seam give, but she didn't care. She flung the garment aside. It landed in the corner with a plop. At last she stood before him, clad only in her white lace shorts and bra. And waited.

Shane's breath was as unsteady as hers as he slipped his fingers beneath her narrow bra straps and eased them off her shoulders. Holding her gaze with his, he trailed the tips of his fingers along the lace edge where it met her skin. Brandee's trembling grew worse. She reached behind her and unfastened the hooks. The bra slid to the floor and she seized Shane's hands, moving his palms over her breasts.

Together they shifted until Brandee felt smooth tile against her back. Trapped between the wall and Shane's strong body, hunger exploded in her loins. She wrapped one leg around Shane's hip and draped her arms over his shoulders. At long last he took the kiss she so desperately wanted to give and his tongue plunged into her mouth in feverish demand.

Brandee thrilled to his passion and gave back in equal measures. The kiss seemed to go on forever while water poured over his shoulders and ran between their bodies. Shane's hands were everywhere, cupping her breasts, roaming over her butt, slipping over her abdomen to the waistband of her shorts.

Unlike his jeans with their button and zipper, her lacy cotton shorts were held in place by a satin ribbon. He had the bow loosened and the material riding down her legs in seconds. A murmur of pleasure slipped from his lips when he discovered her satin thong, but it was soon following her shorts to the shower floor.

Naked before him, Brandee quaked. In the early years of her fashion line, she'd modeled all the clothes up for sale at her on-line store, even the lingerie. She'd lost all modesty about her body. Or so she'd thought.

Shane stepped back and took his time staring at her. She pressed her palms against the tile wall to keep from covering herself, but it wasn't her lack of clothing that left her feeling exposed. Rather, it was the need for him to find her desirable.

"You are so damned beautiful," he said, sweeping water from his face and hair. His lips moved into a predatory smile. "And all mine."

She hadn't expected such a provocative claim and hid her delight behind flirtation. Setting her hands on her hips, she shot him a saucy grin. "Why don't you slip out of those wet jeans and come get me?"

Without releasing her from the grip of his intense gaze, he popped the button on his jeans and unzipped the zipper. He peeled off black denim and underwear. Brandee's breath lodged in her throat at what was revealed.

The man was more gorgeous than she'd imagined. Broad shoulders tapered into washboard abs. His thighs were corded with muscle. The jut of his erection made her glad she still had the wall at her back because her muscles weakened at the sight of so much raw masculinity.

"Come here." She had no idea how her voice could sound so sexy and calm when her entire being was crazy out of control.

He returned to her without hesitation and captured both her hands, pinning them against the wall on either side of her head. His erection pressing against her belly, he lowered his head and kissed her, deep and demanding. Brandee yielded her mouth and surrendered all control.

This was what she needed. A chance to let go and trust. He was in charge, and in this moment, she was okay with that.

When he freed her hands, she put her arms around his neck, needing the support as he stepped between her feet, widening her stance. His teeth grazed her throat while his hand slid between their bodies and found her more than ready for his possession.

She moaned feverishly as he slid a finger inside her, the heel of his palm grazing the over-stimulated knot of nerves. Gasping, she writhed against his hand while hunger built. She needed him inside her, pumping hard, driving her relentlessly into a massive orgasm.

It was hard to concentrate as he masterfully drove her forward into her climax, but Brandee retained enough of her faculties to offer him a small taste of the torment he was inflicting upon her. She cupped her palm over the head of his erection and felt him shudder.

"Jeez" was all he could manage between clenched teeth.

"We need a condom." She rode his length up and down with her hand, learning the texture and shape of him. "Now."

"Yes."

"Where?"

"Jeans."

"You're prepared." A bubble of amusement gave her enough breathing room to stave off the encroaching orgasm.

"Since I arrived."

She bit her lip as his hand fell away from her body, but kept the dissatisfied groan from escaping while he took a few seconds to reach into his jeans pocket and pull out a foil-wrapped pack.

"Let me." She plucked it from his fingers and deftly ripped it open.

He winced as she rolled the condom down his length. Another time, she might have made more of a production of it to torment him, but her body needed to join with his, so she skipped the foreplay.

Almost as soon as she was done, he was lifting her off the floor and settling her back against the wall once more. Brandee stared out the shower door at the mirror that hung over the double vanity. She could just make out the back of Shane's head and her fingers laced in his hair. Every muscle in her body was tensed. Waiting.

"Look at me."

She resisted his demand. She needed him inside her, but she couldn't let him see what it would do to her. This wasn't just sex. Something was happening to her. In the same way she'd liked having him in her bedroom and found comfort riding beside him out in the pasture, she craved intimacy that went beyond the merely physical.

"Look at me." His rough voice shredded her willpower. "You're going to watch what you do to me."

That did it. She could no longer resist him. Her eyes locked with his. A second later he began to slide inside her, and Brandee began to shatter.

CHAPTER EIGHT

SHANE WASN'T SURE what he'd said to make Brandee meet his gaze, but from the way her big blue-gray eyes locked on him, he was certain he'd regret it later. The ache she'd aroused needed release, but he took his time sliding into Brandee this first time. He wanted to remember every second, memorize every ragged inhalation of her breath and quiver of her body.

The first flutters of her internal muscles began before he'd settled his hips fully against hers. Her eyes widened to a nearly impossible size and she clutched his shoulders, her fingernails biting into him. As the first shudder wracked her, it was all he could do to keep from driving into her hard and fast and taking his own pleasure. Instead, he withdrew smoothly and pressed forward again. He watched in utter fascination as a massive orgasm swept over her, nearly taking him with it.

"Damn, woman." He thought he'd known lust and desire before, but something about what had just happened with Brandee told him he was diving straight off a cliff with nothing at the bottom to keep him from crashing and burning. "That was fast."

She gave him a dreamy smile as her head dropped back against the wall. Her lashes appeared too heavy to lift. "It's been a while," she said weakly. At long last her gaze found his and a mischievous glint lurked in the depths of her eyes. "And you're pretty good at this."

"You haven't seen anything."

She slid her fingers up his shoulders and into his hair, pressing the back of his head to urge his mouth toward hers. "Then let's get this party started."

"I thought we already had."

Before she could come up with another sassy retort, he claimed her mouth. Apparently the orgasm hadn't dampened her fire because Brandee kissed him back with ardent intensity.

Shane began to move inside her once more, determined to take his time and make her climax again. Had he ever been with a woman as wildly sensitive and willing to give herself wholeheartedly to pleasure as Brandee? Her whispered words of encouragement accompanied his every thrust and drove his willpower beyond its limits. But he held on until he felt the tension build in her body again. At last he let himself go in a rush of pleasure as her body bucked and she began to climax again. Sparks exploded behind Shane's eyes as they went over together.

In the aftermath, there was only the hiss of water pouring from the showerheads and ragged gasps as they strained to recover. But these were distant noises, barely discernible over the stunned, jubilant voice in Shane's head. He'd known making love to Brandee would be a singularly amazing experience, but he'd underestimated the power claiming her would have on his psyche.

"You should put me down," she said, her low, neutral tone giving nothing away. "Before something happens."

Something had already happened. Something immense and unforgettable. Powerful and scary. He was both eager and terrified to repeat the experience. But not yet. First he needed a few seconds to recover. And not just physically.

As soon as she was standing on her own, he reached to turn off the water, and the instant he took his eyes off her, she scooted out of the shower. He started to follow, but was slowed when a towel shot toward his face. The emotions that had been gathering in him, unsettling yet undeniable, retreated as he snatched the thick terry from the air.

Brandee had used his momentary distraction to slip a robe off the back of the door and wrap it around herself. Water dripped from the ends of her blond hair as she whirled to confront him, chuckling as she caught up another towel and knotted it around her head. Cocooned in plush white cotton, she watched him wrap the towel around his waist.

"Wow," she said with a bright laugh. "I knew that was going to be fantastic, but you exceeded my expectations."

Her delight found no matching gladness inside him. From her nonchalant cheerfulness, the experience hadn't been as transformative for her as it had been for him.

"That's me," he said, straining for a light tone. "Satisfaction guaranteed."

"I'll make sure I rate you five stars online." She yawned. "Well, it's been quite a day. And I still need to get a little work done. See you tomorrow, Delgado."

Shane had assumed there'd be a round two and now watched in stunned silence as Brandee blew him a kiss and disappeared out the bathroom door. Shane retreated to his room, shadowed by an uneasiness he couldn't shake. Chasing after her would only give her the upper hand in this wager.

Few knew his inner landscape didn't match the witty, life-of-the-party exterior people gravitated to. If he went after Brandee right now, he honestly didn't think he could pull off the cocky, charming version of himself that was his trademark.

She'd blown his mind and then walked away, leaving him hungry for more. But it wasn't so much his body that was in turmoil, but his emotions. And not because he was worried she might not be as into him as he'd thought.

He'd intended to make love to her again and then spend the night snuggling with her.

Snuggling.

With a groan, Shane flipped open his laptop and stared at the screen, unable to comprehend anything on it. Brandee had definitely won this round. Now it was up to him to make sure that didn't happen again.

The following day, Shane agreed to meet Gabe for a drink at the TCC clubhouse bar before dinner. While he waited on his friend, he followed up on a text he'd received a few minutes earlier. The call wasn't going well.

"I thought I told you last week that I needed that changed," Shane snarled into his cell phone. "Get it done."

"Sheesh," Gabe commented as he slid into the empty seat beside Shane. "Did you wake up on the wrong side of the bed, or what?"

The question hit a little too close to home. In fact, he hadn't woken up at all. He'd never fallen asleep. After Brandee's abrupt departure the night before, he'd busied himself until two o'clock and then laid awake thinking about her and replaying what had happened between them in the shower. And afterward.

Never before had a woman bolted so soon after making love. If anyone put on their clothes and got out, it was him.

"Sorry," Shane muttered. "Things are way behind at The Bellamy and we're due to open in a couple months."

"Things are always running behind. You usually don't take it out on your contractors."

Shane wasn't about to get into why he was so cranky. Not even with his best friend. So he shrugged his shoulders, releasing a little of the tension, and sipped his scotch.

"I'm feeling stretched a bit thin at the moment," he said. "I told you that I'm helping Brandee with her ranch. It's made me lose sight of some of the details at The Bellamy and I'm annoyed at myself."

"Oh."

Just that. Nothing more.

"Oh, what?" Shane demanded, not sure he wanted to hear what his friend had to say.

"It's just this wager of yours..." Gabe looked deep into the tumbler before him as if he could find the answer to life's mysteries at the bottom.

"Yes?" Shane knew he should just let it drop, but whatever was or wasn't happening between him and Brandee was like an itch he couldn't quite reach. And if Gabe had some insight, Shane wanted to hear it.

"It's just that I know you, Shane. I've seen you around a lot of women. You like this one. I mean really like her."

His first impulse was to deny it, but instead, he said, "Your point?"

"Let's say you somehow win the bet and she falls madly in love with you. Then what?"

"I guess we keep dating."

"You guess?" Gabe shook his head. "Do you really think she's gonna want to have anything to do with the guy who made her fall in love with him so he could take away the ranch she loves?"

"I don't have to buy the ranch." In fact, after spending time on it, he didn't really want the ranch to become home to hundreds of luxury estates. "I could just tell her I changed my mind."

"Have you?"

"Maybe."

"Does anyone ever get a straight answer out of you?"

"It depends."

"And what happens if Brandee wins?"

"That's not going to happen. I might really like this woman, but that's as far as it goes. She and I are too much alike. Neither one of us is interested in a relationship. We talked about it and we agree. Sex is great. Romance is..."

He'd been about to say *tiresome*, but he had to admit that over the course of several dinners and long talks by the fireplace on the patio, he was enjoying himself a great deal.

"Romance is...?" Gabe prodded.

"Too complicated, and you know I like things casual and easy."

With a nod, Gabe finished the last of his drink. "As long as you realize what you're doing can have repercussions and you're okay with whatever happens, my job as your conscience is done."

"I absolve you of all responsibility for any missteps I make with Brandee."

Gabe didn't look relieved as he nodded.

"One last thing before we get off the topic of Brandee," Shane said, remembering his promise to her the night before. "She asked me if you'd be willing to help tomorrow with her teen group. Apparently Megan Maguire from Safe Haven is bringing by some of her rescue dogs for the kids to work with."

"Sure. Let me know what time I need to be there."

Brandee surveyed the camp meeting hall for any details left undone. It was nearly ten o'clock in the morning and she was expecting a busload of teenagers to arrive at any moment. Megan had brought fifteen dogs, one for each teenager. Currently the rescues were running around in the paddock, burning off energy.

"Thank you for helping me out today," Brandee said to Gabe.

"My pleasure."

He and Chelsea had moved tables and organized the kitchen, while Brandee had helped Megan with the dogs and set up the obstacle course they would use later in the afternoon.

The plan for the day was for Megan to talk about the benefits of dog training for both the owner and pet and demonstrate her preferred method of clicker training. Then they would turn the kids loose in the paddock with the dogs so everyone could get to know each other.

After lunch, the teenagers would be issued clickers and dog treats. Megan was in charge of pairing up child with dog. Some of the kids had been through this before, so they would be given less experienced dogs. And the dogs that were familiar with clicker training would be matched with newcomers.

"Have you heard from Shane?" Gabe asked. "I thought he was going to be here today."

"He promised he would be, but he had something to check on at his hotel project."

"Well, hopefully that won't take him all day."

Brandee heard something in Gabe's tone, but before she could ask him about it, the camp bus appeared around a curve in the driveway. She pushed all thought of Shane's absence to the back of her mind. They'd completed the preliminary work without him, and there wouldn't be much to do while Megan spoke. Hopefully, Shane would arrive in time to help with lunch.

"Here we go." Megan Maguire came to stand beside Brandee. The redhead's green eyes reflected optimism. With her kind heart and patient manner, Megan was one of the most likable people Brandee had ever met. "I hope this group is as good as the last one."

"Me, too. We had such a great time."

"Of the ten dogs I brought that day, three of them were adopted almost immediately. The little bit of training they get here really helps."

"I know most of the kids enjoy it. Some act as if they are just too good for this. But it's funny, a couple of those girls that gave us such a hard time last month are back to do it again."

Brandee wasn't sure if it was because their parents were forcing them or if deep down inside they'd actually had fun. And what wasn't fun about hanging out with dogs all day?

The bus came to a halt and the door opened. The first teenager who emerged was Nikki Strait. She was one of the girls who'd been so bored and put out the prior month. She looked no better today. Neither did her best friend, Samantha, who followed her down the bus steps. Brandee sighed. Perhaps she'd been a little too optimistic about those two.

"Welcome to Hope Springs Camp," she said as soon as all the

teenagers were off the bus and gathered in an ungainly clump. "On behalf of Megan Maguire of Royal Safe Haven and myself, we appreciate you giving up your Saturday to help with the dogs."

There were a couple smiles. A lot of looking around. Some jostling between the boys. All normal teenage behavior.

"We'll start our day in the camp meeting hall, where Megan will demonstrate what you'll be doing today. If you'll follow me, we can get started."

The teenagers settled into the folding chairs Chelsea had set up and more or less gave Megan their attention as she began speaking about Royal Safe Haven and the number of dogs that people abandoned each year in Royal.

"Dogs are pack animals," Megan explained. "They need a pack leader. Today it will be your job to assert yourself and take on that role. This doesn't mean you will mistreat the dogs or get angry with them. Most dogs perform better with positive reinforcement. That's why we use this clicker and these treats to get them to perform basic tasks such as recognizing their name, and commands such as *sit* and *down*. We'll also work with them on recalls and a simple but potentially life-saving maneuver I like to call 'what's this.'"

Megan set about demonstrating with her dog how effective the method was. She then switched to a nine-month-old Lab mix that had come to the shelter only the day before and was full-on crazy rambunctious.

Brandee surveyed the teens, noting which ones seemed engaged in the process and which couldn't be bothered. To her surprise Nikki was one of the former. The same could be said for Samantha.

Next, Megan brought the kids to the paddock so they could meet the dogs. Brandee turned her attention to lunch preparations. May had helped with the food. She'd fixed her famous lasagna and they would be serving it with salad, warm garlic bread and brownies for dessert. Last month they'd done chili and corn bread. As for next month…who knew if she'd even be around. With Maverick causing trouble, and Shane acting distant one minute and amorous the next, there were too many variables to predict.

A much more animated group of teenagers returned to the meeting hall. Playing with a group of dogs would do that.

Shane still hadn't arrived by the time the tables were cleared and the teenagers got down to the serious business of clicker training. Brandee shooed Gabe and Chelsea out of the kitchen with plates filled with lasagna and began the tedious job of cleaning up. She wrapped up what was left of the main meal and put the pans into the sink to soak while she nibbled at some leftover salad and scarfed down two pieces of May's delicious garlic bread.

It was almost one o'clock when Shane strolled into the meeting hall. Brandee had finished washing the plates and the silverware. All that was left was to scrub the pans.

"How's it going?" he asked, snagging a brownie. Leaning his hip against the counter, he peered at her over the dessert before taking a bite. "This is delicious."

"It's going fine," Brandee said, more than a little perturbed that after promising to help, he hadn't. "I didn't realize your business was going to take you all morning. You missed lunch."

"That's okay, I grabbed something in town."

"I thought you had a meeting at The Bellamy."

"I did, then David and I needed to chat, so we headed over to Royal Diner." He was gazing out the pass-through toward the gathered teenagers. "I'm here now. What can I do?"

She was tempted to tell him everything was done, but then she remembered the lasagna pans and grinned. "You can finish the dishes." She flung a drying towel over his shoulder and pointed at the sink. "I always leave the worst for last and now they're all yours."

As she went to join the others, her last glimpse of Shane was of him rolling up his sleeves and approaching the sink as if it contained a live cobra. She doubted the man had ever done a dish in his life and reminded herself to double-check the pans later to make sure they were clean to her standards.

Banishing Shane from her thoughts, Brandee circled the room to check on everyone's progress. To her surprise, Megan had paired Nikki with the hyper Lab mix. Nikki had seemed so disinterested the previous month, but with the puppy, she was completely focused and engaged. Already the teenager had the puppy sitting and lying down on command.

Brandee sidled up to Megan. "After how she was last month, what made you think to put Nikki and the Lab mix together?"

Megan grinned. "She and her mom have come by the shelter a couple times to help with the dogs and she has a real knack with them. I think last month she was bored with Mellie. This puppy is smart, but challenging. You can see how well it's going."

Next, Brandee turned her attention toward Justin Barnes. He'd isolated himself in a corner and was spending more time petting the dog than training her. It had been like this last month, too. The high school sophomore was disengaged from what was going on around him. She glanced in Gabe's direction, thinking he might be able to engage Justin, but Gabe was helping Jenny Prichard work with an adorable but very confused shih tzu/poodle mix.

Shane's voice came from right behind her. "Who's the kid over there?"

"Justin. He's the one I told you about whose dad wants him to play football rather than the guitar."

"Sounds like he and I might have a few things in common."

Brandee wasn't sure what Shane could say that might help Justin, but she'd asked for Shane to come today. It seemed wrong not to give him a chance to pitch in. "Maybe you could talk to him about it?"

"It's been a long time since I was a teenager, but I can give it a try."

"Thanks." Any animosity Brandee might have felt for his tardiness vanished. "I'll finish up the pans."

"No need. They're done."

"Already?"

"Just needed a little elbow grease." He arched an eyebrow at her. "It's not good for my ego that you look so surprised."

"I'm sure your ego is just fine." It was familiar banter between them, yet for one disconcerting moment, Brandee craved a more substantive connection. She dismissed the feeling immediately. What was she thinking? That she was interested in a *relationship* with Shane Delgado? Her stomach twisted at the thought, but the sensation wasn't unpleasant. Just troubling.

"You're right." He smirked at her. "It's great being me."

She watched him walk away and laughed at her foolishness. Even if she'd never made the bet with Shane, falling in love with him would be a disaster. They were too much alike in all the bad ways and complete opposites in the good ones. Nope, better to just keep things casual and breezy between them. Fabulous, flirty, sexy fun. That was all either of them wanted and all she could handle.

As he ambled toward Justin, Shane passed Gabe and raised his hand in greeting. Gabe acknowledged him with a broad grin and Shane wondered if he saw a touch of relief in his friend's eyes. No doubt Gabe appreciated that he was no longer the only guy.

Snagging a spare chair, Shane carried it to Justin's corner and set it down beside the kid, facing the dog.

"Hey," he said as he dropped a hand on the dog's caramel-colored head. "How's it going?"

"Fine." Justin mumbled the word and punched down on the clicker. The dog's ears lifted and he focused his full attention on the treat in Justin's hand.

"What's his name?" Shane indicated the dog.

"*Her* name is Ruby."

"Hey, Ruby." He fussed over the dog for a bit and then slouched back in his chair. "I'm Shane."

"Justin."

With niceties exchanged, the two guys settled down to stare at the dog, who looked from one to the other as if wondering where her next treat was coming from.

After a bit, Shane ventured into the silence. "What are you supposed to be doing?"

"Clicker training."

"How does that work?"

"Ruby."

The dog met Justin's glance. He clicked and gave her a treat.

"That's great."

Justin nodded.

So, obviously this whole connecting-with-kids thing wasn't easy. Shane's respect for Brandee's dedication grew. He shifted forward in the chair, propped his forearms on his thighs and mashed his palms together.

"She made me do dishes," he murmured. "Can you believe that?"

"Who did?"

"Brandee. She's always making me do stuff I don't want to."

"That sucks." Justin cast a sidelong glance his way. "Why do you do it?"

"Because she's pretty and I really like her. I'm not sure she likes me, though. Sometimes I feel like no matter what I do, it's not good enough, ya know?"

"Yeah." More silence, and then, "It's like that with my dad. He makes me play football, but I hate it."

"My dad was the same way." After all these years, Shane couldn't believe he still resented his father, but the emotion churned in him. And really, it was all about not being good enough in Landon Delgado's eyes. "He expected me to follow in his footsteps and take over the family ranch, but I hated it."

And in a community dominated by ranching, it felt like treason to criticize your bread and butter.

"What did you want to do instead?" Justin was showing more interest than he had a few seconds ago.

"I dunno. Anything but ranching." Shane thought back to when he'd been Justin's age. There wasn't much he'd been interested in besides hooking up with the prettiest girls in school and hanging out with his friends. He could see where his dad might've found that frustrating.

"So what do you do now?"

"Still have the ranch. And I develop properties. Heritage Estates is mine. And right now I'm working on a luxury hotel outside town called The Bellamy."

Justin's eyes had dimmed when Shane admitted he still had the ranch. "So you did what your father wanted you to do after all."

"The ranch has been in my family for almost a hundred years," Shane explained, deciding he better make his point awfully fast or he'd lose Justin altogether. "It wasn't as if I could walk away or sell it after my dad died. But I found a way to make it work so that I can do what I want and also respect my father's wishes."

"It isn't that easy for me."

"What do you want to do instead of playing football?" Shane asked, even though he already knew the answer."

"Play guitar and write music."

"Sounds pretty cool. How long have you been into that?"

"My dad gave me the guitar for my birthday a couple years ago."

"If your dad didn't want you to play the guitar, why did he buy you one?"

"He'd rather I play football," Justin said, his tone defensive and stubborn.

"Do you know why?"

"Because he did in high school and he got a scholarship to go to college." Justin gave a big sigh. "But I'm not that good. No college is going to want to put me on their team."

"Maybe your dad is worried about paying for your college?"

"I guess." Justin shrugged. "But I'm not really sure I want to go to college. I want to write songs and have a music career."

"You're way ahead of where I was at your age in terms of knowing what you want. That's pretty great." Shane had used money he'd inherited from his grandmother to start his real-estate development company shortly after graduating from college. When his dad found out what he'd done, he hadn't talked to him for a month. "I didn't know what I was going to do when I graduated high school, so I got a degree in business."

"College is expensive and I don't know if it would help me get what I want."

Shane wanted to argue that Justin would have something to fall back on if the music didn't work out, but he could see from the determined set of the boy's features that he would have a career in music or nothing else. Shane hoped the kid had some talent to back up his ambition.

"I'm sure this thing with your dad and football is because he's worried about your future. Maybe you could agree to try football in exchange for him agreeing to helping you with your music."

"Is that what you did with your dad?"

Not even close. "Absolutely. We came to an understanding and I figured out a way to keep ranching and at the same time pursue my interest in real estate."

"Was he proud of you?"

The question tore into Shane's gut like a chain saw. "My dad died before my business really got going, but I think he saw the potential in what I was doing and was impressed."

Shane didn't feel one bit bad about lying to the boy. Just because Shane hadn't been able to communicate with his father didn't mean Justin would have the same problem. And maybe if someone had offered him the advice he'd just given to the teenager, things with his dad might've gone better.

"I'll give it a try," Justin said.

"And if you want to talk or if you want me to have a heart-to-heart with your dad, here's my card. Call me anytime."

"Thanks." Justin slid the business card into his back pocket and seemed a little less glum. Or at least he showed more interest in the dog training.

Shane stuck around to watch him for a little while longer and then excused himself to go help a girl who seemed to be struggling with a brown-and-white mop of a dog.

Over the next thirty minutes, he worked his way around the room chatting with each kid in turn. By the time Megan called for everyone to take the dogs outside to the obstacle course, Shane had gotten everyone's story.

"How do you do that?" Brandee joined him near the back of the crowd. "Everyone you talk to was smiling by the time you walked away. Even Justin."

"How do you not realize what a great guy I am?" He grinned broadly and bumped his shoulder into hers. "I would think after living with me this past week you'd have caught the fever."

"The fever?" she repeated in a dubious tone.

"The Shane fever." He snared her gaze and gave her his best smoldering look. "Guaranteed to make your heart race, give you sweaty palms and a craving for hot, passionate kisses."

Her lips twitched. "I'm pretty sure I'm immune." But she didn't sound as confident as she once had.

"That sounds like a challenge."

"It's a statement of fact."

"It's your opinion. And if I'm good at anything, I'm good at getting people to see my point of view. And from my point of view, you're already symptomatic."

"How do you figure?"

With everyone's attention fixed on Megan, Shane was able to lean down and graze his lips across Brandee's ear. He'd noticed she was particularly sensitive there. At the same time, he'd cupped his hand over her hip and pulled her up against his side. The two-pronged attack wrenched a soft exclamation from her lips.

A second later he let her go and greeted her glare with a smirk. "Tell me your heart isn't racing."

"You aren't as charming as you think you are," she said, turning her attention to what was going on among the poles, small jumps and traffic cones set up near the meeting hall.

He let her get the last word in because he'd already annoyed her once that day and that wasn't the way to this woman's heart.

"Do you think there's something going on between Gabe and Chelsea?" Brandee asked after a couple more kids had taken their dogs through the obstacle course.

Shane followed the direction of her gaze and noticed the couple standing together on the outskirts of the crowd. "Going on how?"

"Like maybe they could be interested in each other?"

"Maybe." Shane paid better attention to the body language between the two and decided there might be an attraction, but he was pretty sure neither one had noticed it yet.

For a second Shane envied the easy camaraderie between Gabe and Chelsea. With the bet hanging over their heads, he and Brandee couldn't afford to let down their guards. And maybe that was okay. Sparring with Brandee was exciting. So was making love to her. He liked the way she challenged him, and figuring out how to best her kept him on his toes.

Besides, he wasn't in this for the long haul. This was his chance to have some fun and try to win a bet. Eventually he would move out of Brandee's house and life would return to normal. But what if it didn't? What if he wanted to keep seeing Brandee? He snuck a peek at her profile. Would she be open to continuing to see where things went? Or was this just about the wager for her?

Shane didn't like where his thoughts had taken him. He liked even less the ache in his chest. Gabe's words from several days earlier came back to haunt him.

As long as you realize what you're doing can have repercussions and you're okay with whatever happens...

It was looking more and more like he had no idea what he was doing and the repercussions were going to be a lot more complicated than he'd counted on.

CHAPTER NINE

To THANK CHELSEA, Gabe and Shane for their help at Hope Springs Camp's mini-event, Brandee treated them to dinner at the Texas Cattleman's Club. Their efforts were the reason the day had gone so smoothly and Brandee was able to relax at the end of the successful event.

As soon as they finished dinner and returned to the ranch house, she and Shane headed out to the patio to sit by the fire.

Brandee tucked her bare feet beneath her and sipped at her mug of hot, honey-laced herbal tea. "Despite your very late start," she said to Shane, keeping her tone light, "you were a huge help today. I think it was good to have both you and Gabe there. Usually we have trouble keeping the boys on task."

"A couple of them were a little rowdy while they were waiting for their turn at the obstacle course, but once they got working with the dogs it was better."

"The clicker training keeps both handler and dog engaged. Megan was very satisfied how the day went."

"She said she might even get some adoptions out of it."

"I wish Seth Houser could be one of them. He's been working with Sunny for almost three months. And making great strides." The Wheaton terrier was a great dog, but way too hyper. He'd been adopted twice and returned both times. A talented escape artist with abandonment issues, he needed to go to someone as active as he was.

"I was really amazed by how well Seth handled him." Shane puffed out a laugh. "I think Tinkerbell and Jenny were my favorite pair."

The adorable shih tzu/poodle mix with the bad underbite had been recently turned in by a woman who had to go into a nursing home. Jenny was a goth girl of fifteen who'd shuffled through the day with stooped shoulders and downcast eyes. But she'd bonded with her short-legged black-and-white dog and together they'd won the obstacle course.

"Megan has a knack for matching the right dog to the perfect handler."

They lapsed into silence for a time while the fire popped and crackled. The longer they went without speaking, the more Brandee could feel the tension building between them. The last time they'd sat together out here, she'd ended up dragging Shane into the shower.

The day after, she'd been busy with her cattle herd and hadn't gotten home until late every night. Part of her wondered if she'd been avoiding Shane. The way she'd felt as he'd slid inside her for the first time had shocked her. She'd expected to enjoy making love with Shane, but couldn't have predicted to what extent. It was like all the best sex she'd ever had rolled into one perfect act of passion.

And ever since, all she wanted to do was climb into the memory and relive it over and over. But not the aftermath when she'd bolted for the safety of her room before Shane could notice that her defenses were down. Standing naked in the bathroom, she'd been terrified that, with his appetite satisfied, he wouldn't want her to stick around. So, she'd fled.

Now, however, after a couple days to regain her confidence, she was ready to try again. Anticipation formed a ball of need below her belly button. The slow burn made her smile. She was opening her mouth to suggest they retire to his bedroom when he spoke.

"I see why you find it so rewarding."

Brandee sat in confused silence for several seconds. "What exactly?"

"Working with teenagers."

With a resigned sigh, Brandee turned down the volume on her libido. "I wish I could say it was all success and no failure, but these kids don't have nearly the sorts of issues of some I've worked with."

"You do a good job relating to them."

He hadn't done so bad himself. Watching him with Justin, Brandee had been impressed with the way he'd gotten the kid to stop looking so morose.

"I remember all too well what it was like to have troubles at home," she said.

"Your mom?" Shane asked gently.

For a second Brandee was tempted to give a short answer and turn the topic aside, but part of her wanted to share what her childhood had been like after losing her dad. "It wasn't easy living with someone who only wants you around so she can steal your money."

"I can't imagine." Shane shifted his upper body in her direction until his shoulder came into companionable contact with hers.

Brandee welcomed the connection that made her feel both safe and supported. "It didn't make me the ideal daughter."

"You fought?"

"Not exactly." Brandee let her head fall back. Her eyes closed and images of the cramped, cluttered house filled her mind. A trace of anxiety welled as memories of those five suffocating years rushed at her. "She yelled at me, while I said nothing because I'd tried arguing with her and she'd just freak out. So I learned to keep quiet and let her have her say. And then I'd rebel."

"By doing what?"

"The usual. Partying with my friends. Drinking. Drugs. For a while my grades slipped, then I realized she didn't give a damn about any of it and I was only hurting myself."

"So, what happened?"

"I cleaned up my act. Not that she noticed anything going on with me." Or cared. "But I continued to avoid the house as much as possible."

"That sounds a lot like how I spent my teen years. I made sure I was gone as much as possible. That way I wasn't around when it came time to help out on the ranch. It drove my dad crazy." Shane fixed his gaze on the hypnotic dance of the flames, but didn't seem to be seeing the fire. "He was a firm believer in hard work, a lot like your dad. He was fond of telling me I wasn't going to make anything of myself if I wasn't willing to work for it. I didn't believe him. I was pretty happy with what I had going. I had a lot of friends and decent grades. I was having a good time. And all he cared about was that I wasn't in love with ranching like he was."

Brandee didn't know how to react to the bitter edge in Shane's voice. She loved her ranch and couldn't imagine giving it up. That ranching was something Shane only did out of obligation was a disconnect between them that reinforced why she shouldn't let herself get too emotionally attached.

"What was it about the ranching you didn't like?" she asked, shifting to face him and putting a little distance between them.

"I don't honestly know. One thing for sure, I didn't see the point in working as hard as my dad did when there were more efficient ways to do things. But he wouldn't listen to anything I had to say. He expected me to follow exactly in his footsteps. I wasn't going to do that."

"What did you want to do?"

"Justin asked me that today, too. I guess I just wanted to have fun." He grinned, but the smile lacked his typical cocky self-assurance. "Still do."

She let that go without comment even as she was mentally shaking her head at him. "So, how'd you get into real-estate developing?"

"A buddy of mine in college got me into flipping houses. I liked the challenge." Satisfaction reverberated in Shane's voice. He obviously took great pride in his past accomplishments. And present ones, too. From everything she'd heard, The Bellamy was going to be quite a resort.

"I got my first job when I turned sixteen," Brandee said. "Stocking shelves at a grocery store after school and on weekends. It gave me enough money to buy a used junker with no AC and busted shocks. I didn't care. It was freedom. I used to park it around the corner from the house because I didn't want my mom knowing about it."

"What would've happened if she'd known about it?"

"She would've given it to Turtlehead or Squash Brain." Those days were blurry in her memory. "Mom always had some loser boyfriend hanging around."

"She lived with them?"

Brandee heard the concern in his voice and appreciated it more than she should. "They lived with her. She rented a crummy two-bedroom house right on the edge of a decent neighborhood because she thought it was great to be so close to people with money. I don't know what she was like when my dad met her, but by the time I went to live with her, she wasn't what anyone would call a class act."

"What did she do?"

"She actually had a halfway-decent job. She cut hair at one of those chain salons. I think if she had better taste in boyfriends she might have been more successful. But all she attracted were harmless jerks." She thought back to one in particular. "And then Nazi boy showed up."

"Nazi boy?"

"A skinhead with the Nazi tattoos on his arms and all over

his chest. For a while I just hung in there figuring he'd soon be gone like all the rest."

"But he wasn't?"

"No. This one had money. Not because he worked. I think he and his white-supremacist buddies jacked cars or ran drugs or something. He always had money for blow and booze." She grimaced. "My mom took a bad path with that one."

"How old were you?"

"I'd just turned seventeen."

"Did he bother you?"

"Not at first. He was more into my mom than a dopey-looking kid with bad hair and ill-fitting clothes. But his friends were something else. I think initially they started to bug me out of sheer boredom. I was used to having my ass grabbed or being shoved around by some of the other guys my mom hooked up with. Nazi boy's friends were different, though."

As she described her encounters, Shane's muscles tensed. "Did they hurt you?"

She knew what he was asking. "If you're trying to be delicate and ask if I got raped, the answer is no."

Shane relaxed a little. "So what happened?"

"For a while it was okay. I was hiding behind bad hygiene and a dim-witted personality. Then one day I was taking a shower and thought I was alone in the house."

"You weren't?"

"Nazi boy had taken off with his buddies to go do something and I wasn't expecting them back. I never showered when he was home. Most days I either took clothes to school and cleaned up there or did the same thing at a friend's house."

"That's pretty extreme."

The unfinished mug of tea had gone cold in Brandee's hands, so she set it on the coffee table. "I'd seen how he could be around my mom and it made me feel way too vulnerable to be naked in the house."

"So he came home unexpectedly and caught you in the shower?"

Those days with her mom weren't something she liked talking about and part of her couldn't believe she was sharing this story with Shane. The only other person she'd told was Chelsea.

"I was coming out of the bathroom wearing nothing but a towel. The second I saw him, I jumped back into the bathroom and locked the door. He banged on the door, badgering me to open it for twenty minutes until my mom came home."

"Did you tell her what happened?"

"No. Why bother? She'd just accuse me of enticing him. Either she was scared of him or she liked the partying too much. This one wasn't going away anytime soon."

"Did he come after you again?"

"For a while I tried to stay away as much as possible, but sometimes I had to go home. When I did, I was careful to do so when my mom was home. He left me alone while she was around."

"I don't suppose you had a teacher or adult that could help you out."

"That might have been smart. But I felt like all the adults I'd reached out to had failed me. Instead, I found the biggest, meanest football player in our school and made him the most devoted boyfriend ever." She batted her eyelashes and simpered. "Oh, Cal, you're just so big and strong." Her voice dripped with honey. "Do you think you could get that terrible man who lives with my mother to stop trying to put his hands all over me?"

"Did that work?"

"Like a charm. Nazi boy was all talk and glass jaw. He knew it and I knew it. At five-ten and 170, he might have scared me, but he was no match for a six-five, 280-pound linebacker."

Shane regarded her with admiration and respect. "So your linebacker kept you safe until you finished high school?"

Brandee shifted her gaze out toward the darkness beyond

the patio and debated lying to him. "I didn't actually finish high school."

"How come?"

"Because two months before graduation my mom finally figured out that her boyfriend was coming on to me and rather than kicking him to the curb, she blamed me. That's when I ran away for good."

Shane's first instinct was to curse out her mother, but the way Brandee was braced for his reaction, he knew he had to take a gentler approach or risk her fleeing back behind her defenses.

"Wow, that sucks."

This part of her story was different than the last. As she'd spoken of her difficulties with Nazi boy, she'd sounded strong and resilient. Now, however, she was once again that abandoned child, learning that she was the biggest mistake her mother had ever made. Her loneliness was palpable and Shane simply couldn't stand to be physically separated from her. He reached for her hand and laced their fingers together, offering her this little comfort.

"What did you do?" he asked.

"I should've gone to live with my grandmother in Montana."

"Why didn't you?"

Her fingers flexed against his as she tightened her grip on him. A second later she relaxed. "Because I was angry with her for not taking me in after my dad died."

"So what did you do instead?"

"I stayed with my best friend for a couple days until I found a room and a waitressing job that paid better."

"When did you start your business?"

"I'd learned how to crochet and knit from one of my friends' moms and had been making headbands and adding lace embellishments to stuff I found at the thrift store. I bought a used sewing machine and started doing even more stuff. It was amazing how well things sold online. All I did was waitress, sew and market my stuff."

"The rest is history?"

"Not quite. Nazi boy and his friends tracked me down. Fortunately I wasn't home. But the homeowner was. They shoved her around and scared her pretty good. After that they went into my room and took everything, including the five hundred dollars I'd saved."

"What happened then?"

"The homeowner pressed charges and they all got picked up by the cops. But she kicked me out. Once again I had nowhere to go and nothing to show for all my hard work."

"Did you stay in Houston?"

"Nope. I moved to Waco and lived out of my car for two weeks."

"At seventeen?"

"Haven't you figured out I'm tougher than I look?" She gave a rueful laugh. "And I'd turned eighteen by then. In fact, I'd been out celebrating my birthday with friends when Nazi boy robbed me."

"What happened after that?"

"That's when things get boring. I found another waitressing job and another place to live. Took a second job at a tailoring shop. The owner let me use the machines after hours so I could create my designs. In four months I was making enough by selling my clothes and accessories online to quit my waitressing job. In a year I moved into a studio apartment and was bringing in nearly ten thousand a month."

Shane had a hard time believing her numbers could be real. "That's a lot for a solo operation."

"I didn't sleep, was barely eating and the only time I left my apartment was to get supplies or ship product."

"How long before it got too big for you to handle?"

"By the time I turned twenty, I had four seamstresses working for me and I was in over my head. I was paying everyone in cash and eventually that was going to catch up to me. So I talked to a woman at the bank I really liked and Pamela hooked me up with a website designer, lawyer and an accountant. But between the designing and running things, there was still too much for me to do, so I hired Pamela to manage the business side. And then things really took off."

"And now here you are running a ranch." He smiled ruefully. "It's not an ordinary sort of career move."

"Probably not, but it's a lot better for me. While I loved designing and promoting my fashion lines, I'm not cut out to sit in an office all day looking at reports and handling the myriad of practical decisions a multimillion-dollar business requires."

"You'd rather ride around in a pasture all night, keeping an eye on your pregnant cows."

She nodded. "Exactly."

"So, you sold the business."

"A woman in California bought it and has plans to take it global." Brandee shook her head. "It's still a little surreal how much the company has grown from those first few crocheted headbands."

"I can't help but think it was a lot to give up."

"It wasn't my dream. Hope Springs Ranch is. And I still design a few pieces each year. So, I get to be creative. It's enough. And now I expect to be busier than ever with Hope Springs Camp starting to ramp up."

His gaze fastened on her softly parted lips and a moment later, he'd slid his hand beneath the weight of her long hair and pulled her toward him. After the first glancing slide of his mouth over hers, they came together in a hungry crush.

Tongues danced and breath mingled. Shane lifted her onto his lap, the better to feel her soft breasts press against him through her cotton shirt. With her fingers raking through his hair, Shane groaned her name against the silky skin of her long neck. Despite the longing clawing at him these past few days, he'd underestimated his need for her.

"I can't wait to be inside you again," he muttered, sliding his tongue into the hollow of her throat while his fingers worked her shirt buttons free. "You are like no woman I've known."

Brandee stripped off her shirt and cast it aside. "You're pretty awesome yourself, Delgado." Her fingers framed his face, holding him still while she captured his gaze. "You've made me feel things I've never known before."

Her mouth found his in a sweet, sexy kiss that stole his breath. He fanned his fingers over her back, reveling in her satiny warmth, the delicate bumps of her spine and the sexy dimples just above her perfect ass. This time around, Shane was determined to take his time learning everything about what turned her on.

He shifted so that her back was against his chest and his erection nestled between her firm butt cheeks. This gave him full access to her breasts, stomach and thighs, while she could rock her hips and drive him to new levels of arousal. As trade-offs went, it wasn't a bad one.

Shane unfastened her bra and set it aside. As the cool night air hit her nipples, they hardened. He teased his fingertips across their sensitive surface and Brandee jerked in reaction. Her head fell back against his shoulder as a soft *yes* hissed past her teeth.

"Do that again," she murmured, her eyelids half-lowered, a lazy smile on her lips. "I love the feel of your hands on me."

"My pleasure."

He cupped her breasts and kneaded gently, discovering exactly what she liked. Each breathy moan urged his passion higher. His fingers trembled as they trailed over her soft, fragrant skin. Her flat stomach bucked beneath his palm as he slipped his fingers beneath the waistband of her leggings and grazed the edge of her panties.

"Let's get these off." His voice was whisky-rough and unsteady.

"Sure."

She helped him shimmy the clingy black cotton material over

her hips and down her legs. He enjoyed sliding his hands back up over her calves and knees, thumbs trailing along the sensitive inner thigh. Catching sight of her lacy white bikini panties, Shane forgot his early determination to make her wait.

He dipped his fingertips beneath the elastic and over her sex. She spread her legs wider. Her breath was coming in jagged gasps and her body was frozen with anticipation as he delved into her welcoming warmth.

They sighed together as he circled her clit twice before gliding lower. He found a rhythm she liked, taking his cues from the way her hips rocked and the trembling increased in her thighs. She gave herself over to him. She was half-naked on his lap, thighs splayed, her head resting on his shoulder, eyes half-closed. She sighed in approval as he slid first one, then two fingers inside her.

The tension in her muscles increased as he slowly thrust in and out of her. He noted how her eyebrows came together in increased concentration, saw the slow build of heat flush her skin until all too soon, her lips parted on a wordless cry. And then her back arched. She clamped her hand over his and aided his movements as her climax washed over her in a slow, unrelenting wave. He cupped her, keeping up a firm, steady pressure, and watched the last of her release die away.

"We need to take this indoors," he murmured against her cheek, shuddering as she shifted on his lap, increasing the pressure of her backside against his erection. The sensation made him groan.

"Give me a second," she replied. "I'm pretty sure I can't walk at the moment."

Wait? Like hell.

"Let me help you with that." He lifted her into his arms and stood.

"Your room," she exclaimed before he'd taken more than two steps. "Please. I've been imagining you all alone in that big bed and thinking about all the things I'd like to do to you in it."

He liked the way her mind worked. "I've been picturing you there, as well." He slipped through the French doors and approached his bed. "We'll take turns telling each other all about it and then acting every scenario out."

"Sounds like we're going to have a busy night."

"I'm counting on it."

Tonight, he'd make sure she didn't have the strength to leave until he was good and ready to let her go.

CHAPTER TEN

THE ROYAL DINER was packed at nine o'clock on Sunday morning, but Brandee had gotten there at eight and grabbed a table up front. As Chelsea slid into the red vinyl booth across from her, Brandee set aside the newspaper she'd been reading.

"Thanks for meeting me," Brandee said. "I needed to get out of the house. This thing with Shane is not going as I'd hoped."

"I told you it was a bad idea."

Brandee winced. "Let's put it down to me being in a desperate situation and not thinking straight."

"So, have you finally given in to that wild animal magnetism of his?"

"I haven't *given in* to anything," Brandee retorted. "However, we have been having fun." A lot of fun.

"You are such a fake." Chelsea laughed. "You act all cool chick about him, but I watched you yesterday. When he was talking to the kids, you were all moony. You've got it bad."

Brandee wasn't ready to admit this in the relative safety of her mind much less out loud to her best friend in a public restaurant. "It's just sex. I've been out of circulation for a long time and he's very capable."

Chelsea shook her head in disgust and picked up her menu. "Is that why you look so tired out this morning?"

"No. I actually got a good night's sleep."

That was true. After they'd worn each other out, Brandee had fallen into the deepest slumber she'd had since Maverick had sent that vile demand. Snuggling in Shane's arms, his breath soft and warm against her brow as she'd drifted off, she'd gained a new perspective on the amount of time she spent alone. Where she'd thought she was being smart to direct her energy and focus toward the ranch, what she'd actually done was maintain a frantic pace in order to avoid acknowledging how lonely she was.

"Thanks again for your help yesterday," Brandee said once they'd put in their breakfast orders and the waitress had walked away. "I couldn't have managed without you and Gabe and, once he showed up, Shane. I hope this wasn't my last mini-event."

"Anything new from Maverick?"

"No, but my resignation from the TCC and the money are due in two days. And I don't know if Shane's going to sign away his claim to Hope Springs Ranch before the deadline."

"You don't think Shane is falling in love with you?"

Brandee's heart compressed almost painfully at Chelsea's question. "I don't know. Do you think he is? Even a little?" She sounded very insecure as she asked the question.

"It's hard to tell with Shane. He hides how he feels nearly as well as you do." Chelsea eyed her friend over the rim of her coffee cup. "But given the way he looked at you during dinner last night, I'd say that he's more than a little interested."

Brandee still felt an uncomfortable pang of uncertainty. "That's something, I guess."

"Which makes the whole wager thing a bummer because it's going to get in the way of you guys being real with each other."

Thinking over the prior evening's conversation and the lovemaking that followed, Brandee wasn't completely sure she agreed. She'd felt a connection with Shane unlike anything she'd ever known before. Maybe sharing their struggles with their parents had opened a gap in both their defenses.

"I'd like to call off my wager with Shane," Brandee admitted. "What started out as a good idea has gotten really complicated."

"So do it."

"How am I supposed to explain my change of heart to Shane?"

"You could tell him that you really like him and want to start with a clean slate."

Brandee threw up her hands, her entire body lighting up with alarm. "No. I can't do that. He'll think he's won and I'll have to sell him Hope Springs."

Besides, leaving herself open to be taken advantage of—or worse, rejected—went against all the instincts that had helped her to survive since she was twelve years old. She didn't want to be that girl anymore, but she was terrified to take a leap of faith.

Chelsea blew out her breath in frustration. "This is what I'm talking about. You have to stop working the angles and just trust that he feels the same way."

"But what if he doesn't?" Already Brandee had talked herself out of canceling the wager. "What if it's just that he's done a better job of playing the game than me?"

"And what if he's really fallen for you and is afraid to show it because that means you'll win the wager? Shane loves a challenge. You two have squared off against each other almost from the day you met. Frankly, I'm a little glad this Maverick thing came along to bring you two together."

Chelsea's frustrated outburst left Brandee regarding her friend in stunned silence. She'd never considered that being blackmailed could have an upside. Yet she couldn't deny that her life was a little bit better for having gotten to spend time with Shane.

The sound of angry voices came from a table twenty feet away.

Chelsea, whose back was to the drama, leaned forward. "Who is it?"

"Looks like Adam Haskell and Dusty Walsh are at it again."

The two men hated each other and tempers often raged when they occupied the same space. "I can't quite tell what it's about."

"You're nothing but an ignorant drunk." Walsh's raised voice had the effect of silencing all conversation around him. "You have no idea what you're talking about."

"Well, he's not wrong," Chelsea muttered, not bothering to glance over her shoulder.

Brandee's gaze flickered back to her best friend. "He needs to learn to mind his own damn business." She remembered how when she first bought Hope Springs Ranch, Adam had stopped by to inform her that ranching wasn't women's work.

"You're gonna get what's coming to you." Haskell's threat rang in the awkward silence that had fallen.

"You two take it outside." Amanda Battle stepped from behind the counter and waded into the confrontation. "I'll not have either of you making a ruckus in my diner."

Most people probably wouldn't have tangled with either Haskell or Walsh on a normal day, much less when they were going at each other, but Amanda was married to Sheriff Nathan Battle and no one was crazy enough to mess with her.

"He started it," Walsh grumbled, sounding more like a petulant five-year-old than a man in his sixties. It was hard to believe that someone like Dusty could be related to Gabe. "And I'm not done with my breakfast."

"Looks like you're done, Adam." Amanda glanced pointedly at the check in his hand. "Why don't you head on over to the register and let Karen get your bill settled."

And just like that it was over. Brandee and Chelsea's waitress appeared with plates of eggs, biscuits and gravy, and a waffle for them to share. She returned a second later to top off their coffee and the two women dug in.

After a while Brandee returned to their earlier conversation. "I've been thinking more and more about what Maverick brought to light."

"That it's not really fair to keep Shane from knowing that his family is the rightful owners of the land Hope Springs sits on?"

"Yes. I can't exactly afford to walk away from ten million dollars, but I can make sure that after I'm gone the land will revert back to his family."

Chelsea was silent for a long time. "This really sucks."

"Yes, it does." Brandee was starting to think that no matter what she did, her time with Shane was drawing to a close. "Whoever Maverick is, the person has a twisted, cruel personality."

"Still think it's one or all of the terrible trio?"

"I can't imagine who else." Brandee hadn't given up on her suspicions about Cecelia, Simone and Naomi. "Although it seems a little extreme even for them."

"But you've really been a burr in their blankets and I could see them siding with Shane."

"And considering what Maverick wants..."

"Money?"

"Fifty grand isn't all that much. I think Maverick asked for money more to disguise the real purpose of the blackmail, which was getting me out of the Texas Cattleman's Club." Something she could see the terrible trio plotting to do. "Regardless of what I do or don't know, the fact is that I can't afford for Shane to find out the truth."

"But if you don't win the wager, what are you going to do?"

"As much as I hate the idea, I think I'm going to do as Maverick demands."

"So, what does that mean for you and Shane?"

"I think from the beginning we were both pretty sure this thing was going to end up in a stalemate."

"So neither of you is going to admit that you've fallen for the other."

"Nope."

"And yet I'm pretty sure you've fallen for him."

"I can't let myself go there, Chels." Brandee rubbed her

burning eyes and let her pent-up breath go in a ragged exhale. "There's too much at stake."

"And if the fate of your ranch didn't hinge on you admitting that you had it bad for him?"

"The problem is that it does." As much as Brandee wished she was brave enough to risk her heart, she could point to too many times when trusting in things beyond her control hadn't worked in her favor. "So, I guess that's something we'll never know."

The rain began shortly after three o'clock that afternoon. Brandee fell asleep listening to it tap on the French doors in the guest suite, a rapid counterpoint to the steady beat of Shane's heart beneath her ear. It was still coming down when she woke several hours later.

They hadn't moved during their nap and his strong arms around her roused a contentment she couldn't ignore. For as long as she could remember, she'd bubbled with energy, always in motion, often doing several things at once and adding dozens of tasks to the bottom of her to-do list as she knocked off the ones at the top.

Around Shane she stepped back from the frenetic need for activity. He had a way of keeping her in the moment. Whether it was a deep, drugging kiss or the glide of his hands over her skin, when she was with him the rest of the world and all its problems slipped away.

"Ten more minutes," he murmured, his arms around her tensing.

"I'm not going anywhere."

His breath puffed against her skin as his lips moved across her cheek and down her neck. "I can feel you starting to think about everything that needs to get done in the next twelve hours."

"I'm only thinking about the next twelve minutes." She arched her back as his tongue circled her nipple. A long sigh escaped her as he settled his mouth over her breast and sucked.

In the end it was twenty minutes before she escaped his clever hands and imaginative mouth and made her way on shaking legs to her shower. As tempted as she'd been by his invitation to stay and let him wash her back, they'd already lingered too long.

They grabbed a quick dinner of May's chili to fortify them for the long, cold night, before heading out. With the number of cows showing signs of delivering over the next twenty-four hours, it was all hands on deck.

Icy rain pelted Shane and Brandee as they maneuvered the cows. By three o'clock in the morning, Hope Springs Ranch had seen the addition of two heifers and three steers. On a normal night, emotions would be running high at all the successful births, but a sharp wind blew rain into every gap in their rain gear, leaving the group soaked, freezing and exhausted.

Brandee cast a glance around. Although most of the newborns were up on their feet and doing well, a couple still were being tended to by their moms. That left only one cow left to go. The one Brandee was most worried about: a first-time heifer who looked like she was going to be trouble.

"We might want to take this one back to the shed," Brandee shouted above the rain, moving her horse forward to turn the heifer they'd been keeping tabs on in the direction of the ranch buildings.

Her water had broken at the start of the evening and now she'd advanced to the stage where she was contracting. They'd been watching her for the last twenty minutes and things didn't seem to be progressing.

Shane shifted his horse so that the cow was between them and they could keep her heading where they wanted. It seemed to take forever and Brandee's nerves stretched tighter with each minute that passed. As many times as she'd seen calves drop, each birth held a place of importance in her heart.

They got the heifer into the barn and directed her into a chute. At the far end was a head gate that opened to the side and then closed after the cow stuck her head through. Once the heifer was secure, Brandee put on a long glove and moved to her back end.

"I've got to see what's going on up there," she explained to Shane, who watched her with interest.

"What can I do?"

"There's an obstetric chain, hooks and a calf puller over there." She indicated a spot on the wall where the equipment was kept. "Can you also grab the wood box propped up against the wall, as well?" Two feet square and four inches high, the box was used to brace against the heifer when she started pulling the calf out.

"Got it."

Now that they had the cow inside where it was dry and light, Brandee needed to examine the birth canal to determine the size and position of the calf. She was dreading that the calf was breeched. Most calves were born headfirst, but sometimes they were turned around, and if the legs were tucked up, it would mean she'd have to go rooting around an arm's-length distance to see if she could find a hoof and wrap the chain around it.

Brandee knew she was in trouble almost immediately. Chilled to the bone, exhausted and anticipating a hundred things that could possibly go wrong with this birth, she cursed.

"Problem?" Shane stood beside her with the equipment.

"Calf's breeched." She took the chain from Shane and indicated the puller. "You can put that aside. We're not going to need it yet."

She hoped not at all. If she could get the calf straightened out, the cow's contractions might be able to help her. Brandee just hoped the heifer wasn't worn-out from pushing the breeched baby.

"What do you do with that?" Shane indicated the chain. It was several feet in length with circles on each end, reminiscent of a dog's choke collar.

"I need to get this around the calf's legs so I can get them straightened out. Right now its hind end is toward the birth canal and its legs are beneath it."

"Isn't this something a vet should handle?"

"Only if things get complicated." And she hoped that wouldn't happen. "I've done this before. It's just tricky and time-consuming, but doable."

"What can I do to help?"

Her heart gave a silly little flutter at his earnest question. Usually she had one of the guys helping her with this, but they were all out, tending to little miracles of their own. She could handle this.

She eyed Shane's beefy shoulders with a weary but heartfelt grin. "I'm going to let you show off your manly side."

"Meaning?" He cocked an eyebrow at her.

"You get to do all the pulling."

Her last glimpse of Shane before she focused all her attention on the cow was of his sure nod. He had his game face on. This aspect of ranching was one he'd never known, but he'd stepped up and she respected him for that.

Brandee made a loop with one end of the chain and reached in until she located the calf's legs. The snug fit and the way he was positioned meant that getting the chain over the hoof required dexterity and patience. To block out all distractions, Brandee closed her eyes and "saw" with her fingers. Before she could get the loop over the hoof, she lost the opening and the chain straightened out.

Frustration surged. The miserable night had worn her down. Feeling raw and unfocused, she pulled her arm out and re-created the loop before trying once more. It took her three attempts and ten agonizing minutes before she'd captured both hooves. She was breathing hard past the tightness in her throat as she turned to Shane.

"Okay, now it's your turn." Her voice was thick with weariness and she struggled not to let her anxiety show. "We'll do this slow. I need you to pull one side and then the other to get his hooves pointed outward. I'll let you know which to pull and when."

Working together in slow stages, they got the calf's back legs straightened so that both were heading down the birth canal. Both Brandee and Shane were sweating in the cool barn air by the time stage one was complete.

"What now?" Shane asked, stepping back to give Brandee room to move around the heifer.

"We need to get her down on her right side. It's the natural position for birthing. I want as little stress on her as possible."

Brandee slipped a rope around the cow right in front of her hip bones and tightened it while rocking her gently to get her to lie down. Once the heifer was on her side, Brandee made sure the chains were still properly positioned around the calf's cannon bones.

"Good," she said, noting that the cow was starting to contract once more. "Let's get this done."

She sat down on the ground and grabbed the first hook. When the cow contracted, Brandee pulled. Nothing happened. She set her foot against the cow for leverage and switched to the second hook. With the next contraction, she pulled again without success. This breeched baby was good and stuck.

"Let me help." Shane nudged her over and sat beside her.

After alternating back and forth between the two chains a few times, Brandee dropped her head onto her arms as frustration swallowed her whole.

"Damn it, I don't want to use the calf puller." But it was very much appearing like she'd have to.

An uncharacteristic urge to cry rose in her. She wanted to throw herself against Shane's chest and sob. Brandee gritted her teeth. She never got emotional like this.

"Come on," Shane said, bumping her shoulder with his in encouragement. "We can do this."

His focus was complete as he timed his exertions with the cow's contractions. Following his example, Brandee put her energy into willing the damned calf to move. The heifer groaned, Shane grunted and Brandee's muscles strained.

After four more contractions, they were able to get more of

the legs out and Brandee felt some of the tension ease from her chest. There was still no guarantee that the calf would be alive when they were done, but at least they were making progress.

"Here," she said, shifting the wood platform and sliding it against the cow's backside between the calf's legs and the floor. Now she and Shane had a better brace for their feet. "He's starting to loosen. A few more contractions and we'll have him."

Then like a cork coming loose from a champagne bottle, the rear half of the calf was suddenly out. They scooted back to make way and then scrambled to their feet. With one final contraction and two mighty pulls from Brandee and Shane, the calf slipped free in a disgusting expulsion of amniotic fluid and blood.

Shane gave a soft whoop as he and a very relieved Brandee dragged the limp calf ten feet away from the cow.

"Is it alive?" Shane bent down and peered at the unmoving calf while Brandee peeled the sack from its face and cleared fluid from its nostrils.

"It sure is." She exuberantly roughed up its coat in a simulation of its mother's rough licking and watched it begin to draw breath into its lungs.

Shane peeled off the rubber gloves he'd donned and turned them inside out to avoid transferring the gore to his skin. "What a rush."

"It can be." Brandee released the head gate and walked out of the birthing area. "Let's get out of here so she can get up and smell her baby."

The calf still hadn't moved, but now the cow got to her feet and managed a lumbering turn. She seemed a little disengaged from what had just happened.

"She doesn't seem too interested in her baby," Shane commented, his voice low and mellow.

"Give her a minute."

And sure enough the cow ambled over to the baby and gave him a good long sniff. This seemed to stimulate the calf and he gave a little jerk, which startled the cow for a second. Then Mama gave her baby another couple sniffs and began licking.

"What do you know." Shane gently bumped against Brandee. "Looks like we did okay."

She leaned her head on his shoulder. "We sure did."

Within an hour the calf was on its feet and Brandee wanted very badly to get off hers. Several hands had swung by to check in and thumped Shane on the back when they found out he'd participated in his first calf pulling.

"I think we can leave these two for now," Brandee said, pushing away from the railing. "I really want a shower and some breakfast."

"Both sound great."

Twenty minutes later, clean and dressed in leggings and an oversize sweater, Brandee pulled her damp hair into a topknot and padded into the kitchen, where Shane had already put on a pot of coffee and was staring into the refrigerator. He hadn't noticed her arrival and she had an unguarded few seconds to stare at him.

He'd been a huge help tonight. She wondered if he still disliked ranching as much as he had when he'd first arrived. Seeing his face light up as they'd pulled the calf free had given her such joy. She was starting to get how being partners with someone could be pretty great. Too bad there was a sinkhole the size of Hope Springs Ranch standing between them.

He must have heard her sigh because he asked, "What are you hungry for?"

He turned to look at her and she realized he was the manifestation of every longing, hope and fantasy she'd ever had. She had closed the distance and was sinking her fingers into his hair before the refrigerator door closed.

"You."

CHAPTER ELEVEN

SHANE'S ARMS LOCKED around her as their mouths fused in a hot, frantic kiss. She was everything sweet and delicious. And sexy. He loved the way her hips moved against him as if driven by some all-consuming hunger. He sank his fingers into them and backed her against the counter.

If he'd thought she made him burn before, the soft moans that slipped out when he palmed her breast awakened a wildness he could barely contain. The big island in the kitchen had enough room for them both, but before he could lift her onto it, she shook her head.

"My room."

For an instant he froze. Over the last week, she'd made it pretty clear that her bedroom was off-limits. What had changed? He framed her face with his hands and peered into her eyes. She met his gaze with openness and trust. His heart wrenched and something broke loose inside him.

"You're the most amazing woman I've ever known," he murmured, dipping his head to capture her lips in a reverent kiss.

She melted into his body and he savored the plush give of her soft curves. Before the kiss could turn sizzling once more, Shane scooped Brandee off her feet and headed to her bedroom.

She'd left the nightstand lamps burning and he had no trouble finding his way to her bed. Setting her on her feet, he ripped off his T-shirt and tossed it aside. She managed to unfasten the button on his jeans before he pushed her hands aside and finished the job himself. Once he stood naked before her, he wasted little time stripping off her clothes.

Together they tumbled onto the mattress and rolled. Breathless, Shane found himself flat on his back with a smiling Brandee straddling him. Gloriously confident in her power, she cupped her breasts in her hands and lifted them in offering to him.

Shane's erection bobbed against her backside as he skimmed his palms up her rib cage and lightly pinched her tight nipples. He wanted what happened between them tonight to be something neither one would ever forget and tangled one hand in her hair to draw her mouth down to his.

Again they kissed with more tenderness than passion. The heat that had driven them earlier had given way to a curious intimacy. Shane kissed his way down her throat and sucked gently at the spot where her shoulder and neck came together. Her fingers bit into his shoulder as she shivered.

"You like that," he said, teasing the spot with his tongue and smiling at her shaky laugh.

"I like a lot of things that you do to me."

"Like this?" He brushed his hand over her abdomen. Her thighs parted in anticipation of his touch, but he went no lower.

"Not like that," she murmured, pushing his fingers lower. "Like this." Her back arched as he slid a finger along the folds that concealed her intimate warmth. "Almost, but not quite... there."

Her shudder drove his willpower to the brink. Sensing she'd rush him if he let her, Shane eased down her body, gliding his mouth over the swell of one breast, and then the other. Brandee's fingers sifted through his hair as she sighed in pleasure.

But when his tongue drew damp patterns on her belly, she tensed, guessing his destination. His mouth found her without the preliminaries he usually observed. This time he wasn't here to seduce, only to push her over the edge hard.

Her body bowed as he lapped at her. A moan of intense pleasure ripped from her throat. The sound pierced him and drove his own passion higher. In the last week he'd learned what she liked and leveraged every bit of knowledge to wring his name from her lips over and over.

With her body still shaking in the aftermath of her climax, she directed him to her nightstand and an unopened box of condoms. The sight of it made him smile. She'd been planning to invite him to her room. This meant that her walls were crumbling, if only a little. Was he close to winning their bet?

The thought chilled him. If she fell in love with him and he took away the ranch that meant so much to her, would she ever be able to forgive him?

He slid on the condom and kissed his way up her body. She clung to him as he settled between her thighs and brought his lips to hers for a deep, hot kiss. Her foot skimmed up the back of his leg as she met his gaze. Then she opened herself for his possession. He thrust into her, his heart expanding at the vulnerability in her expression.

She pumped her hips, taking him all the way in, and he hissed through his teeth as her muscles contracted around him. For a long second he held still, breathing raggedly. Then he began to move, sliding out of her slowly, savoring every bit of friction.

"Let's go, Delgado," she urged, her nails digging into his back. She wrapped her leg around his hip, making his penetration a little deeper, and rocked to urge him on.

"You feel amazing." At the end of another slow thrust, he lightly bit her shoulder and she moaned. "I could go like this all night." He was lying.

Already he could feel pleasure tightening in his groin. He was climbing too fast toward orgasm. He surged into her, his strokes steady and deep, then quickening as he felt her body tighten around him. She was gasping for air, hands clamped down hard on his biceps as they began to climax nearly at the same moment. He'd discovered timing his orgasm to hers required very little attention on his part. It was as if some instinct allowed their bodies to sync.

But tonight Shane grit his teeth and held off so he could watch Brandee come. It was a perfect moment, and in a lightning flash of clarity, he realized that he'd gone and done it. He'd fallen for her. Hard. Caught off guard by the shock of it, Shane's orgasm overcame him, and as his whole body clenched with it, pleasure bursting inside him, a shift occurred in his perception.

This was no longer a woman climaxing beneath him, but his woman. He couldn't imagine his life without her in it. He wanted her in his bed. Riding beside him on a horse. Laughing, teasing, working. Yes, even working. He wanted to be with her all the time.

Stunned by what he'd just admitted to himself, Shane lay on his back and stared at the ceiling while Brandee settled against his side, her arm draped over his chest, her breath puffing against his neck. Contentment saturated bone, muscle and sinew, rendering him incapable of movement, but his brain continued to whirl.

Brandee was already asleep, her deep, regular breathing dragging him toward slumber. Yet, despite his exhaustion, something nagged at him. As perfect as their lovemaking had been, there was a final piece of unfinished business that lay between them.

Leaving Brandee slumbering, Shane eased out of bed. He needed to do this while his thoughts were clear. He suspected doubts would muddy his motivation all too soon.

The first night he'd arrived, she'd shown him the two contracts. He'd taken both copies to his lawyer to make sure there was nothing tricky buried in the language. Turned out, it had been straightforward. If he signed the paperwork, he agreed to give up all claim to the land. If she signed, she agreed to sell him the land for ten million.

Several times in the last two weeks, she'd reminded him that his contract awaited his signature in her office. He headed there now. Turning on the desk light, he found a pen and set his signature to the document with a flourish.

As he added the date, it occurred to him he was declaring that he'd fallen for her. Opening himself up to rejection like this wasn't something he did. Usually he was the one making a break for it as soon as the woman he was dating started getting ideas.

Except Brandee wasn't like the women he usually went for. She was more like him. Fiercely independent. Relentlessly self-protective. And stubborn as all get-out.

Shane reached across the desk and turned off the lamp. A second after Brandee's office plunged back into darkness, her cell phone lit up. The text message caught his eye.

Pay up tomorrow or Delgado gets your land back.

Shane stared at the message in confusion. "Your land back"? Those three words made no sense. And what was this about "pay up tomorrow"? As far as Shane knew, Brandee owned the land outright. Could there be a lien on the property he didn't know about? Shane was still puzzling about the text as he sat down in Brandee's chair, once again turned on the lamp and pulled open her file drawer.

Her organizational skills betrayed her. A hanging file bearing his name hung in alphabetical order among files for property taxes, credit card and bank statements, as well as sketches for her upcoming clothing line. Shane pulled out his file and spread the pages across the desk.

His heart stopped when he saw the birth certificates going back several generations. He reviewed the copy of Jasper Crowley's legal document that made the Hope Springs Ranch land his daughter's dowry. After reading through the newspaper clippings and retracing his ancestry, Shane understood. Brandee intended to cheat him out of the land that should belong to his family.

Leaving everything behind, he returned to the bedroom to wake Brandee and demand answers. But when he got to the room, he stopped dead and stared at her sleeping form. He loved her. That was why he'd signed the document.

Not one thing his father had ever said to him had hurt as much as finding out he'd fallen in love with a woman who was using him.

Torn between confronting her and getting the hell away before he did something else he'd regret, Shane snatched his clothes off the floor and headed for the back door. He slid his feet into his boots, grabbed his coat with his truck keys and went out into the night.

Brandee woke to a sense of well-being and the pleasant ache of worn muscles. She lay on her side, tucked into a warm cocoon of sheets and quilts. Her bedroom was still dark. The time on her alarm clock was 5:43 a.m.

The room's emptiness struck her. There was no warm, rugged male snoring softly beside her. She didn't need to reach out her hand to know Shane's side of the bed was cool and unoccupied. After the night they'd shared, she didn't blame him for bolting before sunrise. The sex had been amazing. They'd dropped their guards after the difficult calf birthing, permitting a deeper connection than they'd yet experienced.

Part of her wanted to jump out of bed and run to find him. She longed to see the same soul-stirring emotion she'd glimpsed in his eyes last night. But would it be there? In her gut, she knew he felt something for her. No doubt he was as uncomfortable at being momentarily exposed as she'd been.

As much as she'd grown accustomed to having him around and had put aside her fierce independence to let him help, she was terrified to admit, even to herself, that she craved his companionship as much as his passionate lovemaking. But was it worth losing her ranch?

Brandee threw off the covers and went to shower. Fifteen

minutes later, dressed in jeans and a loose-fitting sweater, she headed for the kitchen, hoping the lure of freshly made coffee would entice Shane.

And she'd decided to come clean about Maverick, Hope Springs Ranch and the blackmail.

Over a hearty breakfast, she would explain her fear of losing the ranch and see if he would agree to letting her keep it for now as long as she agreed to leave it to him in her will.

While she waited for the coffee to brew, Brandee headed to her office to get the document Maverick had sent to her as well as the ones she'd found during her research. Dawn was breaking and Brandee could see her desk well enough to spy the papers strewn across it. She approached and her heart jerked painfully as she realized what she was staring at.

With her stomach twisted into knots, Brandee raced from the room and headed straight for her guest suite. The room was empty. Next she dashed to the back door. Shane's coat and boots were gone. So was his truck. Her knees were shaking so badly she had to sit down on the bench in the mudroom to catch her breath.

No wonder he'd left so abruptly during the night. He knew. Everything. She'd failed to save her ranch. She'd hurt the man she loved.

It took almost ten minutes for Brandee to recover sufficiently to return to her office and confront the damning documents. How had he known to go into her filing cabinet and look for the file she'd made on him? Had he suspected something was wrong? Or had Maverick tipped him off early?

The answer was on her phone. A text message from Maverick warning her time was almost up. But how had Shane seen it? She gathered the research materials together and returned them to the file. It was then that she noticed Shane's signature on the document revoking his claim to her land.

She'd won.

It didn't matter if Shane knew. Legally he couldn't take her ranch away from her.

But morally, he had every right to it.

Brandee picked up the document. While the disclosure she'd been about to make was no longer necessary, the solution she'd intended to propose was still a valid one.

Brandee grabbed the document and her coat and headed for her truck. As she drove to Bullseye, the clawing anxiety of her upcoming confrontation warred with her determination to fix the situation. It might be more difficult now that he'd discovered she'd been lying to him all along before she had a chance to confess, but Shane was a businessman. He'd understand the value of her compromise and weigh it against an expensive court battle.

Yet, as she stood in the chilly morning air on his front steps, her optimism took a nosedive. Shane left her waiting so long before answering his doorbell that she wondered if he was going to refuse to see her. When he opened the door, he was showered and dressed in a tailored business suit, a stony expression on his face.

She held up the document he'd signed and ignored the anxious twisting of her stomach. "We need to talk about this."

"There's nothing to talk about. You won. I signed. You get to keep the ranch."

Brandee floundered. On the way over, she hadn't dwelled on how Shane might be hurt by her actions. She'd been thinking about how to convince him of her plan so they both got what they wanted.

"I didn't win. And there's plenty more to talk about. I know what you must think of me—"

He interrupted, "I highly doubt that."

"You think I tricked you. You'd be right. But if I lose the ranch, I lose everything." Immediately she saw this tack wasn't going to be effective. So, maybe she could give him some idea of what she was up against. "Look, I was being blackmailed, okay? Somebody named Maverick sent me the Jasper Crowley document."

"That's your story?" Shane obviously didn't believe her. "You're being blackmailed?"

"Maverick wanted fifty thousand dollars and for me to resign from the Texas Cattleman's Club." To Brandee's ears the whole thing sounded ridiculous. She couldn't imagine what would convince Shane she was telling the truth. "I should've done as I was asked, but I really thought it was..."

Telling him that she suspected Cecelia, Simone and Naomi wasn't going to make her story sound any more sympathetic. Shane liked those women. Brandee would only come off as petty and insecure if she accused them of blackmail without a shred of proof.

"Look," she continued, "I should've come clean in the beginning. Maybe we could've worked something out." She took a step closer, willing him to understand how afraid she'd been. "But when I proposed the wager, I didn't know anything about you except that for years you've been after me to sell. I didn't think I could trust you."

"Were you ever going to tell me the truth?"

The fear of opening herself up to rejection and ridicule once again clamped its ruthless fingers around her throat. "Last night..." She needed to say more, but the words wouldn't come.

"What about last night?"

"It was great," she said in a small voice, barely able to gather enough breath to make herself heard.

"You say that after I signed away my rights to *my family's* land."

Why had he? He could have torn up the agreement after finding out he owned the land, but he hadn't. He'd left it for her to find. Why would he do that?

"Not because of that," she said, reaching deep for the strength to say what was in her heart. "I say it because I think I might have fallen in love with you."

His face remained impassive, except at the corner of his eyes where the muscles twitched. "Is this the part where I say I'm not going to pursue legal action against you?"

She floundered, wondering if that was what he intended. "No, this is me talking to you without this between us." She tore the document he'd signed down the middle, lined the pieces back up and tore them again.

"Is that supposed to impress me? Do you think that document would've stood up in court?"

Brandee hung her head. "It was never supposed to get that far."

"I imagine you were pretty confident you could get away with cheating me," Shane said, the icy bite of his voice making her flinch.

"I wasn't confident at all. And I wasn't happy about it. But the ranch is everything to me. Not just financially, but also it's my father's legacy. And the camp could have done so much good." Brandee ached with all she'd lost. "But I am truly sorry about the way I handled things. I didn't do it to hurt you."

He stared at her in silence for several heartbeats before stepping back.

"You didn't."

And then the door swung shut in her face.

CHAPTER TWELVE

FIVE DAYS AND FOUR LONG, empty, aching nights after Shane slammed the door in Brandee's face, he slid onto the open bar stool beside Gabe at the Texas Cattleman's Club and ordered a cup of coffee.

Ignoring the bartender's surprise, he growled at his friend, "Okay, you got me here. What's so damned important?"

Gabe nodded toward a table in the corner. A familiar blonde sat by herself, hunched over an empty glass. Brandee's long hair fell loosely about her face, hiding her expression, but there was no misreading her body language. She was as blue as a girl could be.

"Yeah, so?" Shane wasn't feeling particularly charitable at the moment and didn't have time to be dragged away from The Bellamy. He had his own problems to contend with.

"You don't think there's something wrong with that picture?" Gabe nodded his head in Brandee's direction.

There was a lot of something wrong, but it wasn't Shane's problem.

"Tell me that's not why you dragged me here. Because if it is, you've just wasted an hour of my time."

Gabe's eyes widened at Shane's tone. "I think you should talk to her."

"As I explained yesterday and the day before and the day before that, I'm done talking about what happened. She screwed me over."

"In order to keep her ranch," Gabe replied, his quiet, calm voice in marked contrast to Shane's sharp tone. "She stood to lose everything. How would you have behaved if the situation was reversed and you were about to lose Bullseye?"

It wasn't a fair comparison.

"I'd say good riddance." Shane sipped his coffee and stared at the bottles arranged behind the bar. "I would've sold it years ago if I thought it wouldn't upset my mom."

"You don't mean that."

"I do."

Or he mostly did. Ranching had been in his father's blood and Shane associated Bullseye with being bullied and criticized. Every memory of his father came with an accompanying ache. He'd never be the rancher his father wanted. In some ways it had been a relief when Landon had died. There, he'd admitted it. But by admitting it, he'd lived up to his father's poor opinion of him. He was a bad son. Guilt sharpened the pain until it felt like spikes were being driven into his head.

"I've never seen you like this." Gabe leaned back in his seat as if he needed to take a better look at his friend. "You're really upset."

"You're damned right," Shane said. "She intended to cheat me out of what belongs to my family."

"But you said the land was unclaimed..."

"And what really gets me—" Shane was a boulder rolling down a steep grade "—is the way she went about it."

She'd made him fall in love with her. There. He'd admitted that, too. He was in love with Brandee Lawless, the liar and cheat.

Shane signaled the bartender. Maybe something strong was in order. "Give me a shot of Patrón Silver."

She'd ruined scotch for him. He couldn't even smell the stuff without remembering the way she'd tasted of it the first night they'd made love. Or her delight when he'd introduced her to the proper way to drink it. And his surprise when she'd poured a shot of it over him and lapped up every drop.

Shane downed the tequila shot and signaled for another.

"Are you planning on going head down on the table, too?" Gabe's tone had a mild bite.

"Maybe." But instead of drinking the second shot, Shane stared at it. "You gonna sit around and watch me do it, or are you going to make sure she gets home safe?"

"I've already taken care of Brandee." Gabe nodded his head toward the entrance, where Chelsea had appeared. "If you feel like drowning your sorrows, I'll stick around to drive you home."

Shane rotated the glass and contemplated it. He'd spent the last four nights soaking his hurt feelings in alcohol and after waking up that morning with a whopping hangover had decided he was done moping. He pushed the shot away.

"No need. I'm getting out of here."

But before he could leave, Chelsea had gotten Brandee to her feet and the two women were heading toward the door. Despite how Brandee had looked staring morosely into the bottom of her glass, she wasn't at all unsteady on her feet.

Not wanting to risk bumping into her, Shane stayed where he was and turned his back to the departing women. He couldn't risk her or anyone else noticing the way his hungry gaze followed her. She'd ditched her jeans and was wearing another of those gauzy, romantic numbers that blew his mind. This one was pale pink and made her look as if a strong wind could carry her all the way to Austin. Gut-kicked and frustrated that she still got to him, he reminded himself that she was strong, independent and could take care of herself.

"Look at you three sitting here all smug and self-important." Brandee's voice rang out and conversations hushed. "Well, congratulations, you got your way."

Gabe caught Shane's eye and gave him a quizzical look. "Any idea why she's going after Cecilia, Simone and Naomi?"

With an abrupt shake of his head, Shane returned to staring at his untouched drink, but he was far less interested in it than he was the scene playing out behind him.

"I'm not going to be around to oppose you any longer. I've resigned from the Texas Cattleman's Club. It's all yours." Brandee didn't sound intoxicated exactly. More hysterical and overwrought than anything.

"We don't know what you're—" Cecelia Morgan began, only to be interrupted.

"Where do you three get off ruining other people's lives?"

The entire room was quiet and Brandee's voice bounced off the walls. None of the women answered and Brandee rambled on.

"You must have thought it would be great fun, but blackmail is an ugly business. And it will come back to bite you in the ass."

At the mention of blackmail, Shane turned around in time to see Brandee push herself back from the table where she'd been looming over the three women. They were all staring at Brandee in openmouthed shock and fear.

Brandee punched the air with her finger. "Mark my words."

As Chelsea tugged Brandee toward the exit, the trio of women erupted in nervous laughter.

"I don't know what that was about," Simone said, her voice pitched to carry around the room. "Obviously she's finally snapped."

"It was only a matter of time," Naomi agreed, tossing her head before sipping her fruity drink.

Only Cecelia refrained from commenting. She stared after Brandee and Chelsea, her eyes narrowed and a pensive expression on her beautiful face. Moments later, however, she joined her friends in a loud replay of the clash. Around them, side conversations buzzed. News of Brandee's behavior and her wild accusations would spread through the TCC community before morning.

"She thinks those three blackmailed her?" Gabe glanced at Shane. "Did you know she was planning to resign from the TCC?"

"I don't know why she needed to. I signed her damned document giving up my right to the ranch." Yet, when Brandee had come to his house to apologize, he had refused her attempt to make amends.

"You said she tore it up."

"Well, yeah." Guilt flared. But Shane refused to accept blame for Brandee's overwrought state. "None of that had anything to do with me."

"That—" Gabe gestured at the departing women "—has everything to do with you." His features settled into grim lines. "Of all the times you should have come through and helped someone."

"What's that supposed to mean?"

Gabe looked unfazed by Shane's belligerent tone. "Everybody thinks you're a great guy. You make sure of that. You've always been the life of the party. But when it comes to helping out…" The former Texas Ranger shook his head.

Shane heard the echoes of his father's criticism in Gabe's words and bristled. "Why don't you come right out and say it? No one can count on me when it comes to things that need doing."

"Mostly you're good at getting other people to do stuff."

Shane recalled the expression on Megan Maguire's face when she'd spotted him helping out with Brandee's teen day. She'd been surprised.

And if he was honest with himself, Brandee's tactics to hold on to her land weren't all that different from his own way of doing things. He'd held back important information a time or two. And what Gabe had said about his getting other people to volunteer when there was work to be done…

Growing up, his father had accused him of being lazy and Shane had resented it, despite knowing there was a bit of truth to it. So, what was he supposed to do? Change who he was? He was thirty-five years old and far too accustomed to doing things his way.

"How is it I'm the bad guy all of a sudden?" Shane demanded. "And where do you get off making judgments about me?"

"I just want to point out that while Brandee may have manipulated you, it's not like you haven't done the same to others. She's not perfect. You're not perfect. But from watching you both, you might be perfect together."

And with that, Gabe pushed away from the bar and headed out, abandoning Shane to a head filled with recriminations and a hollow feeling in his gut.

It took until Brandee was seated in Chelsea's car before the full import of what she'd just done hit her. By the time Chelsea slid behind the wheel, Brandee had planted her face in her hands and was muttering incoherent curses.

As she felt the car begin to move forward, Brandee lifted her head and glared at her best friend. "Why didn't you stop me?"

"Are you kidding?" Chelsea smirked. "You said what half the membership has been dying to. Did you see the look on their faces?"

The brisk walk across the chilly parking lot had done much to clear Brandee's head, but she was still pretty foggy. When was the last time she'd had this much to drink? She didn't even know how many she'd had.

"All I saw was red." Brandee groaned and set her head against the cool window. "Take me to the airport. I'm going to get on a plane and fly to someplace no one has ever heard of."

Chelsea chuckled. "Are you kidding? You're going to be a hero."

"No, I'm not. No one deserves to be talked to like that. I run..." She gulped. Hope Springs Camp was an impossibility now that Shane knew he owned her ranch. "I had hoped to run a camp that gave teenagers the skills to cope with their problems in a sensible, positive way. And what do I do? I stand in the middle of the Texas Cattleman's Club and shriek at those three like a drunken fishwife." The sounds coming from the seat beside her did not improve Brandee's mood. "Stop laughing."

"I'm sorry, but they deserved it. Especially if any one or all three is Maverick."

"Do you really think it's possible they're behind the blackmail?"

"I think someone needs to look into it."

"Well, it isn't going to be me. I'm going to be sitting on a beach, sipping something fruity and strong."

"You'll get a new guy? He'll have it going on?"

Despite her calamitous exit from the TCC clubhouse, Brandee gave a snort of amusement as Chelsea twisted the Dierks Bentley song lyrics from "Somewhere on a Beach" to suit the conversation. Then, despite her dire circumstances and the fact that she'd just humiliated herself, Brandee picked up the next line and in moments the two girls were singing at the top of their lungs.

They kept it up all the way to Chelsea's house, where Brandee had agreed to spend the night. She couldn't bear to be alone in her beautiful custom-tailored ranch home that she would soon have to pack up and move out of.

Tucked into a corner of Chelsea's couch, wrapped in a blanket with a mug of hot chocolate cradled in her hands, Brandee stared at the melting mini marshmallows and turned the corner on her situation. It wasn't as if it was the first time she'd lost everything. And in the scheme of things, she was a lot better off than she'd been at eighteen, broke and living out of her car.

"I guess I get to re-create myself again," she said, noticing the first hint of determination she'd felt in days.

"I think you should fight for your ranch. Take Shane to court and make him prove the land belongs to him."

Brandee didn't think she had the strength to take Shane on in a legal battle. She was still too raw from the way he'd slammed the door in her face.

"I'll think about it."

Chelsea regarded her in concern. "It isn't like you to give up like this."

"I know, but I'm not sure."

"Brandee, you can't just walk away from a ten-million-dollar property."

"It sounds crazy when you say it, but that's what I intend to do. Legally I might be able to get a court to determine the land is mine, but I think morally it belongs to Shane's family."

"What are you going to do?"

"Sell everything and start over?" The thought pained her more than she wanted to admit, but in the last five days she'd come to terms with her loss. "I wasn't kidding about finding a beach somewhere and getting lost."

"You can't seriously be thinking of leaving Royal?"

The pang in Chelsea's voice made Brandee wince. "I don't know that I want to stay here after everything that's happened." Just the thought of running into Shane and seeing his coldness toward her made her blood freeze. "Look, it's not like I have to do anything today. It's going to take me a while to sell my herd and settle things on the ranch. With The Bellamy still under construction and taking up all his energy, Shane isn't going to have time to start developing the ranch right away."

"And maybe you and Shane can work out an arrangement that will benefit you both."

"Did you see the way he acted as if I didn't exist?" Brandee shook her head, fighting back the misery that was her constant companion these days. "No, he hates me for what I tried to do to him and there's no going back from that."

"Now, aren't you glad we warned you off of Brandee Lawless?"

"Did you see how she spoke to us?"

"I think she had too much to drink. And happy hour's barely started."

"I've said from the beginning that she has no class."

"She must've had a reason for going after you," Shane said. He recalled what had happened to Wesley Jackson, and thought there'd been some buzz around the clubhouse that Cecelia had been behind it. An anonymous hacker had exposed Wes as a deadbeat dad on social media and it had blown a major business deal for him. What had happened to Brandee was in the same vein.

"She's been out to get us from the moment we joined the Texas Cattleman's Club."

"That's not true," Shane said, a hint of warning in his tone. "She just hasn't bought into what you want to do with the place. A lot of people haven't."

"But she's been actively working to drum up resistance," Naomi said.

"That doesn't make her your enemy." Shane shook his head. "Not everyone wants the clubhouse to undergo any more changes, especially not the kind you're interested in making."

"Well, it doesn't matter anymore. She resigned her membership."

"And with her gone, the others will come around," Cecelia said. "You'll see."

"Sounds like everything is going your way." Shane set his hands on their table the way Brandee had and leaned forward to eye each woman in turn. "If I find out any of you three were behind what happened to Brandee, you'll have to answer to me."

He loomed menacingly for several heartbeats, taking in each startled expression in turn. Instinctively, they'd leaned back in their chairs as if gaining even a small amount of distance would keep them safe. At long last, satisfied they'd received his message, he pushed upright, jostling the table just enough to set their cutlery tingling and their drinks sloshing.

"Ladies." With a nod, he headed for the exit.

Icy gusts blew across the parking lot as Shane emerged from the clubhouse. He faced the north wind and lifted his hat, not realizing how angry he'd been until he dashed sweat from his brow. Damn Brandee for making him rush to defend her. He should've left well enough alone.

The cold reduced his body temperature to normal as he headed toward his truck. A row back and a few spaces over, he caught sight of her vehicle.

"Great."

Now he'd have to make sure she wasn't driving in her condition. But the truck was empty. Brandee was long gone. Shane headed to his own truck.

As he drove the familiar roads on his way to The Bellamy, he tried to put Brandee out of his thoughts, but couldn't shake the image of her going after Cecelia, Simone and Naomi. The outburst had shocked more than a few people.

Brandee's public face was vastly different from the one she showed in private. Not once in all the years that he'd pursued her to sell the ranch had she ever cracked and lost her temper with him. Because of her cool, composed manner, he'd worked extra hard to get beneath her skin. From getting to know her these last two weeks, he recognized that she put a lot of energy into maintaining a professional image. It was why she was so well respected at the male-dominated Texas Cattleman's Club.

Today, she'd blown that. Her words came back to him. Why had she quit the TCC? Did she really think he had any intention of taking her ranch? Then he thought about how she'd torn up the document he'd signed, relinquishing his claim. The damned woman was so stubborn she probably figured she'd turn the place over to him regardless of what he wanted.

And if she did? What would she do? Where would she go? The ranch was everything to her. With her capital tied up in her land and her cows, she probably figured she'd have to downsize her herd in order to start over.

After checking to make sure everything was on track at The

Bellamy, he headed home and was surprised to see his mother's car as well as a catering van in the driveway. Shane parked his truck, drawing a blank. He was pretty sure he'd remember if there was a party scheduled.

When it hit him, he cursed, belatedly remembering he'd promised his mother to help her make catering decisions this afternoon for the party being held in four weeks to celebrate Bullseye's hundred-year anniversary. He'd neglected to add the appointment to his calendar any of the four times she'd reminded him of the event.

He rushed into the house and found everything set up in the dining room. "Hello, Mother." He circled the table to kiss the cheek she offered him.

"You're late," she scolded, more annoyed than she sounded.

The way she looked, he was going to need a drink. "I'm sorry."

"Well, at least you're here now, so we can begin."

Until that second, Shane had been hoping that his mother had already sampled everything and made her decisions. Now he regarded the food spread over every available inch of table and groaned. The appetizers ran the gamut from individual ribs glazed in sweet-smelling barbecue sauce to ornate pastries begging to be tasted. Three champagne flutes sat before Elyse. She gestured toward the dining chair nearest her with a fourth glass.

"Vincent, please pour my son some champagne so he can give his opinion on the two I'm deciding between."

"I'm sure whatever you decide is fine," Shane said, edging backward. He was in no mood to sit through an elaborate tasting.

"You will sit down and you will help me decide what we are going to serve at your party."

If her tone hadn't been so severe, he might have protested that the party hadn't been his idea and he couldn't care less what they served. But since he'd already alienated Gabe today and ruined any hope of future happiness with the woman he loved several days earlier, Shane decided he needed at least one person in his corner.

It took a half an hour to taste everything and another fifteen minutes for them to narrow it down to ten items. Elyse generously included several selections Shane preferred that she'd described as too basic. He wondered if she gave him his way in appreciation of his help tonight or if it was a ploy to make him more pliable the next time she asked for his assistance.

And then he wondered why he was questioning his mother's motives. Was this what playing games had turned him into? Had he become suspicious of his own mother?

And what about Brandee? Was she solely to blame for the way she'd tried to trick him? If he'd been more like Gabe, honest and aboveboard, might she have come to him and negotiated a settlement that would have benefited both of them? Instead, because he liked to play games, she'd played one on him.

"I'm sorry I forgot about today," he told his mother as Vincent packed up his edibles and returned the kitchen to its usual pristine state.

She sipped champagne and sighed. "I should be used to it by now."

Shane winced. With Gabe's lecture foremost in his thoughts, he asked, "Am I really that bad when it comes to getting out of doing things?"

"You're my son. And I love you." She reached out and patted his hand. "But when it comes to doing something you'd rather avoid, you're not very reliable."

It hurt more than he imagined it would to hear his mother say those words. Realizing he wasn't his mother's golden child humbled Shane. "Dad yelled at me about that all the time, but you never said a word."

"Your father was very hard on you and it certainly decreased your willingness to help around the ranch. You didn't need to feel ganged up on."

From where he was sitting, he could see the informal family portrait taken when he'd been seventeen. His father stood with his arm around his beaming wife and looked happy, while Shane's expression was slightly resentful. He'd always hated it because he was supposed to be on a hunting trip with friends the weekend the photo shoot had been scheduled. The photo seemed to sum up how he'd felt since he was ten.

Mother and son chatted for over an hour after the caterer departed about Elyse's upcoming trip to Boston for her brother Gavin's surprise sixty-fifth birthday party. She and Gavin's wife, Jennifer, were planning a tropical-themed bash because Gavin was also retiring at the end of the month and he and Jennifer were going to Belize to look at vacation properties.

"I need to get going," Elyse said, glancing at her watch. "I promised Jennifer I would call her to firm up the last few details for Gavin's party." She got to her feet and deposited a kiss on Shane's cheek. "Thank you for helping me today."

"It was my pleasure." And in fact, once he got over his initial reluctance, he'd enjoyed spending time with his mom, doing something she took great pride in. "Your party-planning skills are second to none and the centennial is going to be fantastic. Let me know what else I can do to help you."

His mother didn't try to hide her surprise. "You mean that?"

"I do. Send me a list. I'll get it done."

"Thank you," she said, kissing him on the cheek.

After his mom left, Shane remembered something else he'd been putting off. His keys jingled as he trotted down the steps to the driveway. He needed to pick up his stuff from Brandee's. He'd been in such a hurry to leave that he hadn't taken anything with him.

He didn't expect to see her truck in the driveway and it wasn't. It was nearly seven o'clock. The sun was below the horizon and a soft glow from the living room lights filled the front windows. Shane got out of his truck and headed for the front door, remembering the first time he'd stepped onto her porch two weeks ago. So much had happened. So much had gone wrong.

First he tried the doorbell, but when that went unanswered, he tried knocking. Was she avoiding him? Or had she come home, consumed more alcohol and passed out? Shane decided he needed to see for himself that she was okay and used the key she'd given him to unlock the door.

As he stepped across her threshold, he half expected her to come tearing toward him, shrieking at him to get out. Of course, that wasn't her style. Or he hadn't thought it was until he'd witnessed her going after Cecelia, Simone and Naomi today.

He needn't have worried. The house had an unoccupied feel to it.

A quick look around confirmed Brandee hadn't come home. Shane headed to the guest suite and was surprised to find none of his things had been touched. Moving quickly, he packed up his toiletries and clothes. He kept his gaze away from the luxurious shower and the big, comfortable bed. Already a lump had formed in his throat that had no business being there. He swallowed hard and cursed.

What the hell had he expected? That they would live happily-ever-after? Even before he found out she'd been keeping the truth from him about the ranch, that ending hadn't been in the cards. All along Brandee had said she didn't need anyone's help. She'd never wanted a partner or a long-term lover. They might have enjoyed each other's company for a while, but in the end both of them were too independent and afraid of intimacy for it to have worked.

Eager to be gone, Shane strode toward the front door, but as he reached it, a familiar ringtone began playing from the direction of the kitchen. He stopped walking and, with a resigned sigh, turned toward the sound. Brandee had left her smartphone on the large concrete island.

Though he knew he should just leave well enough alone, Shane headed to check out who might be calling. Brandee always made a point of being available to her ranch hands and with her not being home, they would have no way of knowing how to get in contact with her.

Shane leaned over and peered at the screen. Sure enough, it was her ranch foreman. Now Shane had two choices. He could get ahold of Chelsea and see if Brandee was staying there, or he could find out what was up and then call Chelsea.

"Hey, Jimmy," Shane said, deciding to answer the call. "Brandee isn't around at the moment. She left her phone behind. Is there something you need?"

"Is she planning on coming back soon?"

Shane recalled how she'd looked earlier. "I doubt it. She went into town and I think she might be staying the night at Chelsea's. Is there something wrong?"

"Not wrong, but we've got a half-dozen cows showing signs of calving and she said if we needed her to help out tonight to call. But it's okay, we'll make do."

As Jimmy was speaking, Shane's gaze fell on something he hadn't noticed before. A large poster was tacked on the wall near the door to the mudroom. It held pictures of all the teenagers and their dogs surrounding a big, glittery thank-you in the middle. It was a gaudy, glorious mess and Shane knew that Brandee loved it.

He closed his eyes to block out the sight. Brandee didn't have to give her time or energy to a bunch of troubled kids, but she did it because even small events like the one with the rescue dogs had the power to change lives. He'd seen firsthand how her program had impacted each of the teens in some way, and with her camp she was poised to do so much more.

"Why don't I stop down and give you a hand." The last thing he wanted was to spend an endless, freezing night outside, but he knew it was the right thing to do.

"That would be a big help." Jimmy sounded relieved. "But are you sure? Between the cold and the number of cows ready to go, it's going to be a long, miserable night."

"I'm sure. See you in ten."

The way Shane was feeling at the moment, he was going to be miserable regardless. And to his surprise, as he headed back to the guest suite to change into work clothes, his mood felt significantly lighter. Maybe there was something to this helping-others thing after all.

CHAPTER THIRTEEN

BRANDEE CAME AWAKE with a jolt and groped for her cell phone. Jimmy was supposed to check in with her last night and let her know if he needed her help with the calving. Had she slept through his call? That had never happened before.

Yet here she was, six short days after her reckoning with Shane, and already she was disengaging from her ranch. Had she really given up on her dream so easily? She couldn't imagine her father being very proud of her for doing so. And yet what choice did she have? All her capital was tied up in the land and her livestock. With the land returned to Shane, she didn't have a place for her cows and calves. It only made sense to sell them.

When she didn't find her phone on the nightstand, she realized why. This wasn't her room. She'd spent the night at Chelsea's after making a scene at the Texas Cattleman's Club. Brandee buried her face in the pillow and groaned. She hadn't been anywhere near drunk, but her blood had been up and she'd consumed one drink too many.

Thank goodness she'd never have to set foot in the clubhouse again. Of course, that didn't mean she wouldn't be running into members elsewhere. Maybe she could hide out for a month or so while she settled her business with the ranch stock and figured out what to do next.

Should she move away from Royal? The thought triggered gut-wrenching loneliness and crippling anxiety. She couldn't leave behind so many wonderful friends. Two weeks ago, she might have considered herself self-sufficient, but after living with Shane she realized she was way needier than she'd let herself believe.

After sliding out of bed and feeling around the floor, Brandee broke down and turned on the bedside light. Her cell phone wasn't beneath the bed or lost among the sheets. Feeling a stir of panic, she considered all the places she might've left it.

A quick glance at the clock told her it was six o'clock in the morning. Too early for Chelsea to be awake, and Brandee would not borrow her friend's computer to check on her phone's location without permission. She could, however, use Chelsea's landline to call her foreman.

He answered after the third ring. "Hey, boss."

"I can't find my phone. I'm sorry I didn't check in sooner. Is everything okay?"

"It was a pretty crazy night, but me and the boys handled it."

"That's great to hear. I'm sorry I wasn't there to help you out."

"It's okay. Shane said you were staying the night at Chelsea's."

A jolt of adrenaline shot through her at Jimmy's words. "How is it you spoke with Shane?" Annoyance flared. Was he already taking over her ranch?

"He answered your phone when I called."

"Did he say how he'd gotten my phone?" Had she left it in the parking lot of the Texas Cattleman's Club?

"He said you left it at your house." Jimmy's voice held concern. "You okay?"

For a long moment Brandee was so incensed she couldn't speak. What the hell was Shane doing in her house? "I'm fine. I need to get my truck and then I'll be by. Maybe an hour and a half, two hours tops." Cooling her heels for an hour until it was reasonable to wake Chelsea was not going to improve her temper.

"No rush. As I said, we have everything under control."

To keep herself busy, Brandee made coffee and foraged in Chelsea's pantry for breakfast. She wasn't accustomed to sitting still, and this brought home just how hard it was going to be to give up her ranch.

As seven o'clock rolled around, she brought a cup of coffee to Chelsea's bedside and gently woke her friend.

"What time is it?"

"Seven." Brandee winced at Chelsea's groan. "I made coffee," she said in her most beguiling voice.

"How long have you been up?"

"An hour." She bounced a little on the springy mattress.

"And how much coffee have you had?"

She extended the coffee so the aroma could rouse Chelsea. "This is the last cup."

"You drank an entire pot of coffee?"

"I didn't have anything else to do. I left my phone at home and didn't want to use your computer. I think the boys had a rough night and need me back at the ranch."

Chelsea lifted herself into a sitting position and reached for the coffee. "Give me ten minutes to wake up and I'll take you to your truck."

"Thank you." She didn't explain about how Jimmy had spoken with Shane or the anxiety that overwhelmed her at the thought of him giving orders to her hands.

An hour later, Brandee had picked up her truck, driven home, changed clothes and was on the way to the ranch buildings. A familiar vehicle was parked beside the barn where they kept the cows and calves who needed special attention. Brandee pulled up alongside and shut off her engine. It ticked, cooling as she stared toward the barn.

What was Shane doing here?

Brandee slid from the truck and entered the barn. She found Shane standing in front of the large enclosure that housed the breeched calf they'd brought into the world. He stood with his arms on the top rail of the pen, his chin resting on his hands.

"Hey," she said softly, stepping up beside him and matching his posture. "What are you doing here?"

"Jimmy said these two are ready to head to the pasture today."

"So you came to say goodbye?" The question didn't come out light and unconcerned the way she'd intended. Anxiety and melancholy weighed down her voice.

"Something like that."

Since Brandee didn't know what to make of his mood, she held her tongue and waited him out. She had nothing new to say and reprising her apology wouldn't win her any points. The silence stretched. She could ask him again why he'd come out to the ranch or she could demand to know why he'd entered her house without asking.

He probably figured he was entitled to come and go anytime he wanted since the land beneath the house belonged to him. Frustration built up a head of steam and she took a deep breath, preparing to unleash it. But before she could utter a word, Shane pushed away from the fence.

"I'd better go." He looked into her eyes, tugged at the brim of his hat in a mock salute and turned away.

Deflated, Brandee watched him go. She couldn't shake the feeling that she'd missed an opportunity to say or do something that would span the gap between them. Which was ridiculous. Shane hated her. She'd tricked him into giving up all claim to his family's land and he would never forgive her.

Her throat closed around a lump and suddenly she couldn't catch her breath. Tears collected and she wiped at the corners of her eyes before the moisture could spill down her cheeks. All at once she was twelve again and hearing the news that her dad was dead. Faced with an equally uncertain future, she'd gotten on her horse and rode off.

She'd ridden all day, tracing the familiar paths that she'd traveled beside her dad. At first she'd been scared. Where would she go? Who would take her in? Her mother's abandonment had hit her for the first time and she'd cried out all her loneliness and loss until she could barely breathe through the hysterical, hiccupping sobs. Once those had passed, she'd been an empty vessel, scrubbed clean and ready to be filled with determination and stubbornness.

She felt a little like that now. Empty. Ready to be filled with something.

Leaving the cow and calf, Brandee headed for the horse barn and greeted her ranch hands. They looked weary, but smiled when they saw her. Apparently the cows had kept them busy, but the night had passed without serious incident. Next she headed to the ranch office to look for Jimmy. Her foreman was staring blankly at the computer, a full mug of coffee untouched beside the keyboard.

"You should head off," she told him, sitting in the only other chair. "I can handle entering the information."

"Thanks. I'm more beat than I thought."

"I'm sorry I wasn't here," she said again, pricked by guilt.

"It's okay. We had Shane's help and everything worked out fine."

"Shane was here all night?" Brandee's heart jumped.

"He came right after answering your phone. About seven or so."

Shane had been helping out at her ranch for over twelve hours? Why hadn't he said anything just now? Maybe he'd been waiting for her to thank him. If she'd known, she would have. Damn. No wonder he'd left so abruptly. She'd screwed up with him again.

But this she could fix. She just needed to come up with a great way to show her appreciation.

Shane wasn't exactly regretting that he'd promised his mother he'd help with Bullseye's centennial party, but he was starting to dread her texts. This last one had summoned him back to the ranch on some vague request for his opinion.

He parked his truck next to her Lexus and took the porch steps in one bound. Entering the house, he spied her in the living room and began, "Mother, couldn't this have waited..." The rest of what he'd been about to say vanished from his mind as he noticed his mother wasn't alone.

"Oh good." Elyse Delgado got to her feet. "You're home."

Shane's gaze locked on Brandee and his heart stopped as if jabbed by an icicle. "What is she doing here?"

"Shane, that's rude. I raised you better than that." Elyse set her hands on her hips and glared at her son. "She came to see me about this disturbing business about her ranch belonging to our family."

"Let me get this straight," Shane began, leveling his gaze on Brandee. "You called my mother to intervene on your behalf?"

"She did no such thing."

"It was Gabe's idea," Brandee said, a touch defensive. "He said you'd listen to her."

It was all too much. First Gabe, now his mother. Shane crossed to the bar and poured himself a shot of scotch. As soon as he lifted it to his lips, he recognized his mistake and set it back down.

"I don't know what you want," he said, dropping two ice cubes into a fresh glass and adding a splash of vodka.

"I brought this as a thank-you for helping out at the ranch the other night." While he'd had his back turned, she'd approached and set a bottle on the bar beside him.

"I don't want your thanks." Mouth watering, he eyed the rare vintage. "Besides, you've ruined scotch for me." He lifted his glass of vodka and took a sip. It took all his willpower not to wince at the taste.

Her lips curved enticingly. "It's a thirty-five-year-old Glengoyne. Only five hundred were released for sale."

"You can't bribe me to like you."

344   TWO-WEEK TEXAS SEDUCTION

At his aggressive tone, all the light went out of her eyes. Once again she became the pale version of herself, the disheartened woman hunched over an empty glass in the TCC clubhouse.

"Shane Robert Delgado, you come with me this instant." Elyse didn't bother glancing over her shoulder to see if her son followed her toward the French doors leading out to the pool deck. She barely waited until the door had shut behind him before speaking. "How dare you speak to Brandee like that. She's in love with you."

"She tried to cheat us out of our family's land." He tried for righteous anger but couldn't summon the energy. The accusation had lost its impact.

"I don't care. We have more than enough wealth and Bullseye is one of the largest ranches around Royal. Besides, that land was unclaimed for over a hundred years and she paid for it fair and square. If anyone cheated us, it was the person who claimed the land without doing due diligence on the property's heirs."

"So, what do you want me to do? Be friends with her again?"

"I'd like for you to give up feeling sorry for yourself and tell that girl how much she means to you."

"What makes you think she means anything to me?"

"From what I hear, you've been an ornery, unlikable jerk this last week and I think it's because you love that girl and she hurt you."

Shane stood with his hands on his hips, glaring at his mother, while in his chest a storm raged. He did love Brandee, but the emotion he felt wasn't wondrous and happy. It was raw and painful and terrifying.

"Now," his mother continued, her tone calm and practical. "I'm going to go home and you are going to tell that girl that you love her. After which the two of you are going to sit down and figure out a way to get past this whole 'her ranch, our land' thing. Because if you can't, she told me she's going to sell everything and leave Royal. You'll never see her again and I don't think that's what you want."

Shane stared out at the vista behind the ranch house long after the French door closed behind his mother.

When he reentered the house, Brandee was still standing by the bar where he'd left her. "You're still here."

"I came with your mother and she refused to give me a ride back to her house, where my truck is parked." She took a step in his direction and stopped. After surveying his expression for several seconds, her gaze fell to his feet. "Look, I'm sorry about what I did. Whatever you want me to do about the land, I will."

"I don't give a damn about the land and I'm certainly not going to kick you off and take away everything you worked so hard to build." He sucked in a shaky breath.

This was his chance to push aside bitterness and be happy. He'd lost his father before making peace with him and was haunted by that. Losing Brandee would make his life hell.

"What I want more than anything is…" He dug the heels of both hands into his eyes. Deep inside he recognized that everything would be better if he just spoke what was in his heart. Shane let his hands fall to his sides and regarded her with naked longing. "You."

Her head came up. Tears shone in her eyes as she scanned his expression. "Are you sure?" she whispered, covering her mouth and staring at him with a look of heartbreaking hope.

"I am." Shane crossed the distance between them and put his arms around her. For the first time in a week, everything was perfect in his world. "I love you and I can't bear to spend another second apart."

His lips claimed hers, drinking in her half sob and turning it into a happy sigh.

When he finally let her come up for air, she framed his face with her fingers and gazed into his eyes. "Then you're not mad at me anymore?"

"For what? Trying to save your ranch and your dreams?" He shook his head. "I don't think I was ever really angry with you for that. I fell in love with you and when I found the documents I thought you'd been playing me the whole time."

"I should have told you about the blackmail after we made love that first time. I knew then that I was falling for you, but I didn't know how to trust my feelings and then there was that stupid bet." She shook her head.

"You weren't the only one struggling. I lost interest in your land after the tornado tore through Royal. I only agreed to the wager to spend time with you. All along I'd planned to lose."

She stared at him, an incredulous expression spreading across her features. "Then why did you work so hard to win?"

"Are you kidding?" He chuckled. "The bet was for you to fall for me. That was the real prize."

"I love you." Brandee set her cheek against his chest and hugged him tight. "I can't believe I'm saying this, but I'm really glad Maverick blackmailed me. If it hadn't happened, I never would've invited you to move in."

Shane growled. "I'll buy Maverick a drink and then knock his lights out."

"We don't know who he or she is."

"I asked Gabe to investigate. He'll figure out who Maverick is." Shane scooped Brandee off her feet and headed for the master suite. "In the meantime, I'd like to see how you look in my bed."

Brandee laughed and wrapped her arms around his neck. "I'm sure not much different than I looked in mine."

There she was wrong. As he stripped off her lacy top and snug jeans, the shadows he'd often glimpsed in her eyes were gone. All he could see was the clear light of love shining for him. There was no more need for either of them to hide. This was the first step toward a new partnership. In love and in life.

With her glorious blond hair fanned across his pillow and her blue-gray eyes devouring his body while he peeled off his clothes, Shane decided she was the most incredible woman he'd ever known.

He set his knee on the bed and leaned forward to frame her cheek with his fingers. His thumb drifted over her full lower lip. "You're looking particularly gorgeous today."

She placed her hand over his and turned to drop a kiss in his palm. With her free hand, she reached up to draw him down to her. "You're not looking so bad yourself, Delgado."

And when their lips met, both were smiling.

* * * * *

Craving Her Ex-Army Doc

Amy Ruttan

MEDICAL
Pulse-racing passion

Dear Reader,

Thank you for picking up a copy of *Craving Her Ex-Army Doc*.

I've mentioned before that brothers seem to be in my cards. I love writing about brothers and I love my little brother to death—though when we were younger that wasn't always the case. Like my hero Luke setting booby traps for Carson from *His Shock Valentine's Proposal*, I'm afraid I was often duct-taping my brother to various walls.

My mother always warned me my brother would grow up to be bigger than me one day. She was right. He towers over my five-eleven height at six foot four. Thankfully, all transgressions of childhood are in the past and my brother is one of my best friends. Just one word, which doesn't make sense to anyone but the two of us, and we're on the floor laughing.

Carson is Luke's rock, though Luke may not want to admit it. Luke admires his younger brother and maybe… just maybe…envies the love that Carson found with Esme in *His Shock Valentine's Proposal*.

Perhaps love is actually in the cards for lone wolf Luke Ralston, but it's not going to come easy. He's a stubborn man and it's going to take an equally strong and stubborn woman—my lovely heroine Sarah Ledet—to tame him.

I hope you enjoy the second book in my Sealed by a Valentine's Kiss duet.

I love hearing from readers, so please drop by my website, amyruttan.com, or give me a shout on Twitter, @ruttanamy.

With warmest wishes,

Amy Ruttan

For my boys. For the times you have fun together
and the times you drive each other crazy.
Remember this, Aidan, James *will* grow bigger
than you.

Love you both.

PROLOGUE

"GET OUT OF my OR!"

"Not on your life." Luke stood his ground. He wasn't about to be pushed out of the OR by the arrogant upstart trauma surgeon at the hospital. "I got him off the mountain and I'm not going to let him die on my watch. So if you want me out of your OR you're going to have to physically remove me."

Those blue-green eyes behind the surgical mask glittered with barely concealed rage and Luke smiled behind his own mask, knowing he'd pushed the surgeon's buttons. She was some hot-shot surgeon from out east. One who had been teaching a work-shop in Missoula and got called in when Shane was brought in, because Missoula was slammed.

There had been several landslides after a small earthquake rocked the area. All hospitals in a hundred-mile radius were overflowing with the injured. If Luke had the supplies he could've set up a mobile OR in Crater Lake. He'd worked in worse conditions in Afghanistan.

Only, he hadn't practiced surgery since his honorable dis-charge and he certainly wasn't going to start on Shane Draven. He did surgery when needed, but he preferred practicing in the wilderness. So in this situation he'd rather this trauma surgeon work on Shane.

Still, she needed to know he was just as capable as her. He would have done the surgery another way. That was why he was questioning her.

She was cocky and full of herself. She definitely needed to be taken down a peg or two and he was just the guy to do it.

He might not practice as a traditional doctor, but he was just as much a surgeon as this woman. He had spent time on the front line, patching up soldiers in the midst of fire. How many lives had he saved? He wasn't sure, because he didn't keep score. All that mattered was saving lives. That was why he'd joined the army, it was what he'd wanted for so long, but he'd given it up for another.

Don't think about that now.

This surgeon had sized him up the moment he'd rushed in with Shane Draven's stretcher. She thought he was nothing but a first responder or a paramedic. Obviously a surgeon who didn't know any better. Paramedics were on the front line.

Usually he wouldn't question another surgeon in the OR, unless the patient was at serious risk, but the moment he walked into the OR with Shane she'd been treating him like a second-class citizen. Which was why he decided two could play at that game. So he questioned her every move.

She wanted a fight? Oh, he'd give her a fight.

"I will physically remove you," she snapped.

"I'd prefer you focus on my patient, Doctor, rather than argue over my presence here."

Her angry gaze met his. "You're questioning my skill, Mr...."

Luke grinned smugly. "It's Dr. Ralston."

Her eyes widened in obvious surprise. "Doctor? I thought you were a paramedic."

"Looks can be deceiving, I guess, but I am a doctor. Though I'm not insulted you thought I was a paramedic, but I suppose that's the reason why you feel I should be kicked out of your OR."

She cursed under her breath. "Doctor or paramedic, it doesn't matter. I won't have you undermining my authority in my OR."

"This isn't your OR. You're not from around here."

"When I'm operating it's my OR, whether or not I'm from here."

Luke had to admire her spunk. And she was right. Perhaps he'd been undermining her a touch, but this was a man he'd pulled off the mountain and Dr. Eli Draven was this patient's father. He had made it clear that he was going to hold Luke responsible if Shane died, because Luke had allowed Dr. Petersen to place the chest tube.

Luke didn't know what Dr. Draven had against Dr. Petersen and he didn't really care. He'd pulled Shane down off the mountain. He was responsible for Shane's life. Dr. Draven had been throwing his weight around in the Missoula hospital, because the chief of surgery was one of his former students.

Besides, Shane was also the nephew of Silas Draven, who was sending Luke the most work up on the mountain, and Silas Draven was someone he didn't want to mess with. Luke appreciated all the work, but still he felt responsible for taking care of Shane. Luke, his brother, Carson, and Dr. Petersen were all instrumental in getting Shane Draven to Missoula alive.

Luke hadn't left Shane's side since they were airlifted off the mountain and he wasn't going to leave him now.

No man gets left behind. Every life gets saved.

Luke's commanding officer's words rang true to the credo he lived by and it wasn't going to change now. He'd served two tours of duty as an army medic. Even when he couldn't live by that credo, when life couldn't be saved, it still drove him.

Don't think about losing patients now. Not with Shane on the table.

He shook those thoughts away. There was no place for them here.

"I got this man down off the mountain. He's my patient whether this is *your* OR or not."

"If you stay, Doctor, keep your opinions to yourself, then."

She looked away and continued to work on Shane. A true hardened trauma surgeon, as he'd been once.

Damn, she's a spitfire.

He admired that about her and if circumstances had been different, meaning if he had any interest in pursuing a relationship again, he'd go after a strong-willed spitfire woman like her, but she was off-limits.

All women were.

He wanted to say more, but he knew when it was best to keep his mouth shut. As long as Shane's life was saved, and then he could get Eli Draven off his back, but he still watched the surgeon like a hawk.

"Yes, Doctor." And he gave her a little salute.

The surgeon mumbled a few choice words under her breath, but continued working on Shane.

Luke tried not to move toward the side of the table, where the lead surgeon stood, because if he did that then she would have grounds to throw him out of her OR.

He might be a bit of a control freak when it came to his patients, but there was no way he'd push it any further. He wasn't leaving this OR. He wasn't going to leave Shane Draven behind.

He didn't even know her name and he didn't care; she seemed to be competent. That was all that mattered.

When the surgery was over and they were wheeling Shane to the ICU, Luke gave up his perch in the OR. He planned to be on that ICU floor and personally monitoring Shane until he came out of the woods, as it were.

Dr. Ralston is a fine surgeon and a heck of an officer.

Only that wasn't entirely true. Not anymore. He wasn't an officer anymore. He'd given it all up. He didn't renew his commission because his wife was done being an army wife, but then Christine had left him. He did it all for her and for nothing.

Luke shook that thought from his head. Nope. He wasn't going there, because he wasn't going to let that happen again.

No one was going to dictate how his life should be again.

Which was why he wouldn't settle down into a practice with Carson. It had been Christine's wish after he finished his tours of duty. He'd partner with Carson, raise a family with Christine and do what he loved, practicing medicine. He'd been planning to do that. Luke was going to give up the army for his wife to make her happy. At least that had been the plan.

Then it all went to hell in a handbasket.

Christine left him when he finished his second tour, for his best friend, Anthony.

He cursed under his breath as he walked down the hall to the ICU. He was angry at himself for allowing those thoughts to creep into his head again. To let her creep into his thoughts again. It was because he was in a hospital again.

Surrounded by people.

On his mountain it was just the sky, the wind, the trees and the majestic behemoths rising from the earth toward the clouds.

On his mountain he was himself and he had no one to answer to. No one but him controlled his life, his fate, his destiny.

"Hey!"

Luke spun around and saw a woman in surgical scrubs and cap approach him. The physical attraction was immediate. Full red lips, which were slightly pouty. White-blond hair peeked out from under the scrub cap and big blue-green eyes sparkled with annoyance.

Oh. No.

It was the spitfire surgeon. He'd only seen her over the surgical mask. Now seeing that she was a gorgeous woman with a strong personality to boot, well, that was a dangerous combination for Luke.

"Can I help you?" he asked.

She crossed her arms and sized him up. "I'm looking for a Dr. Ralston. Do you happen to know where he is?"

Luke took a step back, in case she started swinging, but then the words sank in and he realized she didn't know who he was. But then, he'd been wearing a surgical mask, cap and gown when he'd been in the OR with Shane. And this surgeon wasn't a local surgeon. She was visiting. She wouldn't recognize one person from another behind a surgical mask, because not being at this hospital every day he certainly didn't.

This could be fun, one part of him thought. While the other part told him to walk away and not entangle himself with her, because he knew she spelled danger.

"Why do you need him?"

She huffed. "If you see him tell him Dr. Ledet is looking for him." She turned to walk away and for a brief moment, one fraction of a second, he saw himself grabbing Dr. Ledet and pulling her into his arms, kissing her. Forcing the image away, he overcame the urge to taste those soft, moist lips, running his hands through her blond hair.

Maybe doing a little bit more than that.

Definitely dangerous.

"Where can he find you?" Luke asked.

She glanced at her watch. "After eight he can't. I'm flying back to New York."

"New York?"

"Yeah, I was here on business and decided to lend a hand for an old teacher. A fat lot of good that did me when I had to deal with an arrogant jerk like Dr. Ralston."

"Well, if I see him before eight I'll tell him."

She didn't thank him, just nodded curtly and walked away.

A New York surgeon, eh? Well, that was too bad, but it was for the best.

He'd never see her again.

It would've never worked anyway and not because of the distance, but because he would never let it.

CHAPTER ONE

Six months later, mid-January,
Crater Lake, Montana

I HATE THE COLD. I hate the cold.

Sarah thought coming from New York she'd be used to the frigid temperatures of northwest Montana. New York State bordered Canada, too; it should be the same, but it wasn't. Not at all. This was a different kind of cold. There was no moisture in the air and as she tried to shake the remnants of bone-chilling frigidity from her brand-new office, she couldn't remember why she'd decided to take this job in Crater Lake, Montana.

Dr. Draven.

Right. Her teacher from medical school. Dr. Eli Draven. She didn't study under him, because she didn't have an interest in becoming a cardio-thoracic surgeon, but she remembered him clearly from her days at Stanford.

He was a good teacher, if not a bit full of himself. He'd taken a shine to her until she'd decided not to pursue cardio; then she was no longer his star, but he still spoke highly of her and when this job was offered to her by Dr. Draven's brother, she couldn't pass up the opportunity, because she was more than ready to get out of New York and out of her father's iron grip.

No matter what she did, nothing was good enough for her parents.

They still saw her as their baby.

And they wouldn't be happy until she was living a pampered life in a Central Park West penthouse, married to an investment banker or a lawyer or even a doctor.

She couldn't be the doctor, however.

That was unacceptable.

Why do you need to work, pumpkin? Your husband, if you marry well, can take care of you.

Her mother's archaic way of thinking made her shake her head. Sarah peeled off the thick parka she'd bought when she moved out to Montana and hung it on the coat rack in her office. There were no cabs in Crater Lake, unless you counted the very unreliable Bob's Taxi, and she didn't.

At least she'd bought a car when she first landed in Missoula and had snow tires put on it. She was well versed in the rugged country living she was immersing herself in, even if she did complain about the cold just a bit.

Why do you want to go work out in the wilderness?

Sarah's sister, who was married to a very prominent surgeon and occupied one of those coveted penthouse suites on Central Park West, couldn't understand what was driving her to do this.

Sometimes Sarah wasn't even sure herself.

Because your dad got you your prestigious appointment in that Manhattan hospital. It wasn't you.

Sarah sighed when she remembered. After a summer of touring around different hospitals in each state, presenting her Attending's research and teaching different surgeons on using the newest model of robotic surgery, she came home to New York to accept one of the most prestigious positions offered to a trauma surgeon at Manhattan Grace, only to find out that the only reason she was chosen to tour the country and work with Dr. Carroll was that her father was friends with Dr. Carroll. They played a few rounds of golf in the Hamptons. Even her brother-in-law pulled strings for her as if she couldn't make it on her own.

It just shook the foundation of everything Sarah had thought she knew.

It had knocked her confidence completely. Perhaps she wasn't the surgeon that she'd thought she was? So she'd turned down the position, much to her father's chagrin.

This was why she distanced herself from people. So many people trying to control the course of her life. She just couldn't trust anyone.

Not even herself.

Do you know how many strings I've had to pull for you over the years? Just so you can play doctor? Come to your senses, Sarah.

Sarah came to her senses all right. She threw the job back in her father's face, sold her apartment on the Upper West Side and took the job offer from Silas Draven to be the general practitioner and general surgeon at his newly opened ski lodge.

The ski lodge was set to open in one month, on Valentine's Day, and Sarah couldn't wait to get started. It would be a slower pace of life, but at least she would be able to help people here. She could be a doctor and not worry that her father was pulling strings to get her whatever she wanted. She was burned-out and really didn't know who she was or what she wanted anymore. She didn't even know if she wanted to be a surgeon and that thought terrified her, because for so long surgery had been her life.

For now a general practitioner sounded good. She could practice medicine and figure out where to go next. It sounded almost too good to be true.

Yeah. She could do this.

She smiled to herself and picked up her diploma from Stanford, in its frame, which was looking so forlorn on her desk. In fact her whole office was a complete disaster, with boxes and supplies scattered everywhere.

This was not an office yet. She couldn't see patients in a place that looked as if a storage unit had exploded. It wasn't very professional.

"Time to make this place my own." She spied the stepladder that had been left by the painters in the corner. She grabbed a hammer and a nail. She'd never hammered anything in her life, but there was always a first time for everything.

"I can do this," she said, as if trying to reassure herself. How hard could it be to hammer a nail into a wall? She had this. Except where she wanted to put the nail in was a little out of her reach for the stepladder. So she climbed to the very top of the ladder and held the wall for a bit of balance. Her perch was precarious, but all she was doing was hammering in one nail and it wasn't that big of a drop down to the carpet.

She lined up the nail and held the hammer, ready to drive the nail home.

"Did you check for a stud?" a male voice asked from behind.

"What...?" Sarah turned, surprised that someone had snuck into her office and she hadn't heard them, but in the process of turning around she forgot what a precarious perch she had on the top of the stepladder and lost her footing.

Sarah closed her eyes and waited for her backside to hit the floor, but instead she found herself landing in two very strong arms and being held against a broad, muscular chest.

"You shouldn't stand on the top of a..." He trailed off.

"Who are you to tell me...?" Sarah opened her eyes and bit back a gasp as she stared up at the most stunningly handsome man she'd ever seen. Brown hair, with just a bit of curl, deep blue eyes and a neat beard, which just added to the ruggedness of his face.

Those blue eyes of his were wide with surprise and then she had the niggling sensation that she'd seen this face before, but couldn't recall when or where.

"What in the name of all that's good and holy were you doing up there with a hammer?" he demanded as he quickly set her down on her feet and took a step back from her as if she were on fire.

"Excuse me?" she asked. Who did this guy think he was?

"I'm telling you that wasn't a smart move climbing up on that ladder. You could've killed yourself if I hadn't showed up."

"Why did you show up? Who are you?"

His blue eyes flashed and he crossed his arms, fixing her with a stare that was meant to frighten her. Well, it didn't scare her.

"I'm here to take you out."

"Out? I don't believe I made any dates with anyone since I arrived in town."

He smirked. "Not on a date, darling. Though if I were to go on a date with someone, you're quite the fetching thing."

"Fetching? Darling?"

He held up his hands. "Look, I was teasing. I'm not interested in dating coworkers, let alone headstrong doctors from out east. I'm to take you out on the skis to show you some of the private residences being built and how to access them."

"Oh." She was slightly disappointed. Not that she had any interest in dating a mountain man, but a fling might've been fun. Especially since this mountain man was deliciously handsome.

Don't think like that. You're here to prove yourself, not date.

Sarah didn't date.

Her parents had tried over and over, setting her up with the *right* sort of man. Well, in their eyes anyway. It was just easier to concentrate on work and not bother with dating, romance or sex.

All the right kind of men Sarah had dated briefly in her early twenties were all wrong. It never felt right. There was never that spark or connection one was supposed to feel when falling in love with someone, but then again, since she'd never experienced it, maybe it was just a myth.

Men seemed to gravitate to her because she was a socialite and came from money. It was all about status for them, and as she was too focused on her career, she never pursued a man on her own and she never made the time to look for a man beyond her parents' circles.

Single life was so much easier.

And lonely.

"Do you know how to ski?" he asked disparagingly, breaking her chain of thoughts.

"No." Then she groaned inwardly at the thought of going back outside in the cold.

"I thought as much," he said condescendingly. "Well, I'll give you a few minutes to suit up so we can head out."

It was the tone that sparked a vivid memory for her suddenly. She could see those dark blue eyes glittering above a surgical mask. Defying her.

Get out of my OR!

Not on your life.

No way. It couldn't be him. It just couldn't be him.

"What's wrong?" he asked. "Don't like the cold?"

"It's not that. I think I know you."

He smiled. "Do you?"

"What's your name?" she asked.

Don't be him. Don't be him.

Then he grinned like the cat who'd got the cream. "Dr. Luke Ralston."

Damn, but then she was ticked. She'd put that memory of her time in Missoula far from her mind, not giving it much of a second thought because, really, what did it matter? She was in New York, let Luke Ralston have Montana.

Besides, Shane Draven had pulled through.

It was all trivial. Except now she was in Montana, working on their patient's uncle's resort and Dr. Luke Ralston was her coworker? This was a totally messed-up situation. Something she was not comfortable with.

"You knew exactly who I was."

Luke shrugged. "Not at first, but when you fell into my arms it all came back to me."

"And you didn't say anything? Like, maybe, 'Hey, we know each other, we've worked together before' or something like that?"

He shrugged again and then hooked his thumbs into the belt loops on the waist of his tight, tight jeans. "What does it matter?"

"It matters a lot. You're a jerk!"

"Why am I a jerk? I mean, I did save you from probably concussing yourself or something."

"You were the guy I talked to in the hallway in Missoula. When I asked who Dr. Ralston was, you said you didn't know where he was. You lied to me."

"I didn't really want to argue with you in the hallway. I was on my way to the ICU to check on my patient. To make sure he pulled through surgery."

"He was my patient."

He grinned, smugly. "I brought him down off that mountain. He was my patient. You were just a locum surgeon. You didn't stay to make sure he made it through the night. You headed back east, to wherever you came from. I knew nothing about you and I didn't trust you. Of course, now you're going to be a regular here in town."

"Had I known there was a Ralston in Crater Lake I would've turned the job down."

Luke chuckled. "You must've taken this job on an impulse, then."

"Why do you say that?"

"If you'd researched Crater Lake you'd realize the family practice in town is run by a Ralston. I wasn't really hiding my identity. Not in my town."

Damn. He was right. She hadn't really looked to see what physicians were in town. She'd taken the job so quickly. She'd just been so eager to get out of New York City and away from her father's control. Crater Lake had sounded like a nice small town, and a job catering to the rich and famous in a resort had sounded perfect. It was a chance to prove herself to those who moved in her parents' circles.

Then maybe she could step out of her father's shadow. She wouldn't be Sarah Ledet, New York heiress and daughter of Vin Ledet, one of the wealthiest men on the eastern seaboard. She'd be Dr. Ledet, physician.

"You're regretting your decision to take this job, aren't you?" Luke asked. "I can see it on your face. You look absolutely horrified."

"Not the job, just who I have to work with."

He grinned and then laughed. "You're still a spitfire."

"Spitfire?"

"It's a compliment."

Sarah tried not to smile. She didn't want to smile. He was the jerk who'd disrupted her OR, given her a hard time and then lied to her. He was the one who'd questioned her surgical procedure and every move she'd made on that patient until she'd snapped. Only his smile had been infectious and she couldn't remember the last time she'd laughed, even though she was ticked off that it was him. The thorn in her side from last summer, standing right there in her office.

She should just throw him out. As she should have done from her OR.

When she glanced back up at him the lighthearted mood had changed. He looked annoyed and uncomfortable.

"What?" she asked.

"Nothing."

"Something changed. Just a moment ago you were complimenting me and joking. Now you look annoyed."

"I'm annoyed we're wasting the light standing around pointing fingers."

"Okay, you're right. I'm sorry."

"Well, I would gear up. I don't have all day to wait around for you." He walked out of her office leaving her standing there absolutely confused.

What had just happened?

Sarah wasn't sure, but she knew it would be best to keep her distance from Luke Ralston, though that was going to be tricky seeing how she was about to be dragged out on the mountain in the bitter cold with a man who was a little bit dangerous.

Not just a little bit dangerous.

A lot.

CHAPTER TWO

DAMN. IT HAD to be the spitfire.

Luke had forgotten all about her when he'd returned to Crater Lake after Shane Draven had pulled through. For a while he'd thought of that trauma surgeon he'd butted heads with in Missoula, but as he'd dealt with the last messy stages of his divorce, he'd put her from his mind.

Dealing with his ex just reminded him of all the reasons why he didn't trust women or romantic entanglements.

It hurt too much, but Christine wasn't the only reason. Hurt went both ways. He liked his life too much and part of that was doing risky things to save lives up on the mountain.

He'd given up his life in the army for a woman he loved and look how that turned out.

To live the life he'd made for himself since leaving the army, he couldn't have love. He wouldn't give up his life for anyone.

He threw himself completely into his work and avoided hanging around the town of Crater Lake as much as possible. It was bad enough being divorced, but having your ex-wife and former best friend, who was now your ex's husband, living and working in the town you grew up in was a little too much for him.

The problem was, his former best friend was the town sheriff. That was why they were staying in Crater Lake, but Luke wouldn't be driven out of town.

He'd grown up here. He was going to stay here.

And an injury to his leg during an avalanche last winter prevented him from returning to active duty, even after giving up his commission.

Besides, he preferred being up on the mountain.

He liked being alone in his cabin. He liked the work; though he missed surgery and envied Carson just a bit for seeing patients every day, there was no way he could've chained himself to a desk, to an office or a hospital. He would suffocate, but he'd been willing to do it for Christine.

Maybe if you hadn't joined the army Christine wouldn't have left. Maybe you could've been happy.

Only his call of duty had been strong. He'd always wanted to serve and further his medical education in the army. And Christine had known that when they'd got together.

Luke cursed under his breath.

No, she would've left. Just as he hadn't wanted to change the course of his career, Christine hadn't wanted to be his wife. Of course now he wasn't a soldier, but by the time his career in the army was over Christine was over him.

No, he wasn't going to think about her. She'd broken his heart and he wouldn't let her or anyone else make him feel that way again.

Why did it have to be her? Why did it have to be the spitfire?

Silas hadn't told him the name of the physician who would be working at the resort. All he'd said was that she was from out east and had asked if Luke could train her on mountain survival and survival medicine.

She's from money, Ralston. I'm sure she's been on skis, but probably not in a way that would satisfy your sensibilities.

Which was why Luke was here. It was just fate was a bit sick and twisted by making that physician Dr. Ledet, the surgeon he'd butted heads with.

As if dealing with her in the summer wasn't enough? Maybe it was karma? He'd teased Carson when Esme Petersen had come to town. Perhaps this was retribution?

The only difference was Carson had found love with Esme and Luke was not looking for that at all.

Carson hadn't been looking, either.

"Is this okay?"

Luke shook that little voice from his head and glanced over at Sarah. She had a good parka on, waterproof mitts, a hat with ear flaps, boots, but nothing on her legs except black stretchy pants that fit her curves like a glove. His blood heated.

Think about something else.

"Where are your snow pants?" Luke asked, tearing his gaze away from her. He didn't want to look at her at the moment. He had to regain control.

"Snow pants?"

"Don't you ski?"

"I told you before, no. I've never skied."

"Doesn't every eastern WASP rich girl ski? Isn't that what the Poconos are for?"

Her stare was icy cold and she put her hands on those curvy hips. Hips he'd thought about touching himself. "Excuse me?"

Luke groaned. He wasn't going to get in an argument with her. "You need snow pants. If you fall out there and your pants get wet there's no way we're turning around so you can change. I'm here to teach you survival skills. If you were out there on your own, there would be no option to change. You'd freeze to death."

Sarah still looked as if she were going to skewer him alive. "Fine. I'll find some snow pants, but, really, stereotyping me, that was so not cool."

"If the shoe fits."

She cocked her eyebrows and smirked. "Oh, really? Didn't we have this argument in the summer? I seem to recall bits and pieces of it…"

He groaned. "Fine. You're right. I did accuse you of stereotyping me. I apologize, but, really, put on some snow pants before we lose the light."

"Fine and, for your information, not all of us 'rich girls' ski. Some of us prefer yachts and sailing." She winked and then disappeared into her office again.

Luke rolled his eyes, but couldn't help but laugh to himself. He still admired her spunk.

When she came out of her office again, she was properly attired.

"Good, now let's get down to the ski shack and get geared up. I'm going to take you up the first of the four main trails at this resort."

Sarah fell into step behind him; the only sound was the swishing of the nylon fabric rubbing together as they walked down the hall and outside. Luke tried not to laugh, because just under that sound was some muttering. And maybe some bad words, but he couldn't quite tell.

"I feel like a marshmallow," she mumbled. "Do I look like one?"

"Yes. You do, but it will keep you warm." He helped open the door to outside. "Ms. Marshmallow."

With a huff Sarah pushed past him out into the snow. "You're a bit of a jerk. Has anyone ever told you that?"

"Several people."

There was a twinkle to her eye and she smiled slightly. "Good."

"Well, now that's all settled. Let's get the skis on and head out." He led the way to the ski shack, which was closed up. It would open on more regular hours when the resort had its official grand opening on Valentine's Day. Right now, Luke had full run of it and of all the equipment.

It was one of the perks he liked about working for Silas Draven. He wasn't a huge fan of skiing, but cross-country skiing on the mountain trails was the only way to access some of the remote residents of Crater Lake. His horse just couldn't handle the deep snow that collected on the side of the mountain in the winter.

And he would never put his horse in the way of a possible avalanche.

He glanced over to the southern peak, to the forest that was thick, before it disappeared into the alpine zone of the mountain. Old Nestor lived up in that dense forest.

Nestor was a hermit. He liked to live off the grid and away from everyone else. Luke admired him and went to check on him often. Nestor was the one who'd taught him many things about surviving on the mountain, since Nestor had been living up on the mountain for as long as Luke could remember and before that.

Only, Nestor was getting old and in the winter the cold bothered him something fierce. So Luke was thankful for access to skis and snowshoes. It made checking on Nestor that much easier.

He unlocked the door and headed over to the rack.

"Oh, cool! Snowshoes," Sarah remarked. "I've always wanted to try them."

"Really?" he asked, surprised.

She nodded. "Anything to make walking on snow easier."

"Snowshoeing is just as much work as skiing. Skis can move you faster."

"Yeah, but cross-country skis don't go uphill. You said you wanted me to learn how to access trails and stuff. Shouldn't I be snowshoeing?"

She's got a point. Skiing will only get you so far.

"You're right," Luke admitted. "Okay. We'll add snowshoes to our pack."

"Pack?"

Luke picked up the large rucksack that he'd stuffed full of emergency and survival gear. The pack was probably half the size of Sarah and when he held it up to her, her eyes widened and her mouth opened for a moment in surprise.

Then she shrugged. "Sure. That's reasonable. Just out of curiosity, though, what's in it?"

"Don't you know?"

She glared at him. "Really?"

"You should know."

"I don't. I've never lived near a mountain. I'm from Manhattan."

Luke shook his head. "Hey, I was trying not to stereotype you."

"I ought to slug you."

He laughed at that. He couldn't help himself; it was easy to tease her. He was enjoying the banter. "I'm sorry. I'll stop."

She crossed her arms. "Fine or I could start talking about mountain men."

"What do you know about mountain men?" he asked.

Sarah shook her head. "Tell me what's in the bag."

Luke knelt down and unzipped it. "This is a standard pack to help you survive in a winter climate on the mountain."

"So I'll only need to carry around this stuff in the winter?"

"No," Luke said. "Some things can be left behind, but if you're working up near the Alpine zone or higher, you'd be surprised how cold it can get even in the heat of summer."

"Okay, so always be prepared for snow?"

He nodded. "Yep. So in this pack you have your essentials like first-aid kit. The only thing I haven't packed in here is a change of clothes for you so I just packed some of my old clothes. If worse comes to worst you can always wear those."

Her cheeks reddened slightly, as if she was blushing, but Luke could've been wrong. It could've been the wind.

She cleared her throat. "Go on."

"Canteen for water."

"What about melting snow?"

Luke cocked an eyebrow. "You're going to need something

to carry it in. I also have a pot, ice pick, rope, matches, GPS, topographical map of the area, one day's worth of rations, sleeping bag and an axe."

"It's like you're camping."

"If you get lost out there, yeah, you'll be 'camping' until help arrives." Then he held out something he was sure she'd never seen before. "This is one of the most important things."

"A compass?"

"Close. It's an altimeter."

"A what?" she asked.

"It's a barometric altimeter. It measures changes in atmosphere. The higher you go, the lower the pressure is. If your GPS or compass isn't working, this can be used along with the map to determine where you are. I'll show you how to use it."

"Good, because seriously my eyes were glazing over there for a second." She laughed nervously and he handed her the altimeter to look at. "Though, really, won't you know if you're at the top of the mountain? How can you get lost if you're up there?"

"You can get lost all right and if you're not used to high altitude you can get acute mountain sickness. Dr. Petersen in town suffered from it last year. Just ask her."

"Dr. Petersen? There's a female doctor in town? I thought the other doctor was your brother."

"Dr. Petersen is a cardio surgeon. She's opened a clinic in partnership with my brother. She sees a lot of heart patients from around this area."

"Huh, I wonder what would make a cardio-thoracic surgeon settle down in a place like this," Sarah wondered out loud. "I mean, the nearest hospital is quite a bit away."

"Why did you?" Luke asked.

The question caught her off guard, because she blushed again and quickly started examining the altimeter.

Did it really matter?

It shouldn't matter to him, but he couldn't help but wonder why. There weren't many single people in Crater Lake. It was small. When they'd first got together, Christine had wanted to stay in Crater Lake, and when he got his posting to Germany she wouldn't go with him. She didn't want to live on a base. She didn't want to be an army wife. So she'd decided to stay and start a family with Anthony.

A family he wanted so desperately.

A family he was never going to have.

Don't think about it.

"Come on, I'll pack the snowshoes, as well. We have some distance to travel and some more stuff I have to show you before it gets too dark, and it gets dark here early." He took the altimeter back from her and packed it in the knapsack.

He didn't have time to focus on the past. To focus on his past hurts or the things he would never have.

He was here to do a job and that was to show Dr. Sarah Ledet how to survive on the mountain. That was all. Once he'd done that, he never had to see her again and he was going to make sure that happened.

Sarah thought her lungs were going to burst. She was sweaty and exhausted. Parts of her that she hadn't even known existed ached and each breath was harder to take.

At least I'm not cold.

She just shook her head and leaned up against a tree as Luke set their skis against a fence line that ran on one side of the trail. He glanced over at her.

"You okay? You look tired."

Of course I'm tired, but she wasn't going to tell him that. All her life she'd been labelled and she'd had enough of it.

"I'm fine. Just catching my breath."

He frowned. "If you get a headache or feel ill, let me know right away. That's a sign of mountain sickness."

"Will do." She didn't feel sick and didn't have a headache. All she was was sweaty and tired. "You said Dr. Petersen had this? How did she get over it?"

"You get off the mountain."

"I live on the mountain."

Luke chuckled. "You don't live that far up the mountain, though."

"I thought it was pretty high up, considering I used to live pretty close to sea level."

"Never thought about it that way." Luke pulled out the snowshoes that had been strapped to the back of the enormous pack Sarah had had on her back, which was now resting under a fir tree on a bed of needles so as not to get wet.

Maybe she was picking up mountain survival a bit.

"You ready for snowshoeing?"

Sarah groaned. "How about we head for home? I'm sure it will be faster downhill on our skis."

Luke chuckled. "We'll head down soon enough. I want to see you practice on these. Just up the trail the snow gets pretty deep. Too deep for skis."

"No one lives up that trail."

"Right, not now, but when this trail is groomed regularly and a lone cross-country skier or snowshoer gets injured or lost up there, you're going to have to know how to get to them."

Sarah sighed, but then took the snowshoes and strapped them on. They were quite easy and didn't look like she'd expected them to. They were made of aluminum and nylon.

"Take a step and tell me what you think," he said as he moved back and then clamped his on.

Sarah began to walk up the trail and it took her a few times to really find her stride, but it wasn't all that bad.

"I think this is easier than the skiing, to be honest." She bounced in her step. "I could get used to these."

"Just be careful," Luke called out over his shoulder.

"Of wha...?" She spoke too soon as she lost her footing and toppled face-first into a large snowdrift. Snow shot up her nose and into her mouth, burning.

I hate winter. I hate winter.

"Are you okay?" Luke was beside her and she could hear the amusement in his voice.

"Fine," she said as she wiped her face. "I really wasn't expecting to do a face-plant with snowshoes on. Skis for sure, but snowshoes. I know I'm klutzy."

"Well, at least this time I didn't have to catch you." He rubbed some of the snow from her face and a rush of butterflies invaded her stomach as she looked up into his eyes. He was smiling at her, but it was tender, as if he really cared that she'd done a horrible face-plant in the snow.

Of course the butterflies could be from that mountain sickness, but somehow she didn't think so.

"Thanks," she said, looking away and glad the snow had made her cheeks red, because if it hadn't he would surely see her blush.

"You should've been wearing your goggles to protect your eyes. Goggles don't belong on your forehead."

"I forgot to put them back on after my break. I was wearing them when we were skiing."

Luke helped her to her feet, his strong arms around her waist as he righted her. She liked the feeling of his arms around her, steadying her. It was comforting.

You don't date. You can't date.

Her mother would set her up on the occasional date, but those were all with men who would take care of her. Who just wanted her to be this pretty, well-dressed society wife. None of them were really interested in her and she'd been burned too many times.

And she never had time to find men on her own, because she was working so darn hard to show her parents that she could have it all, that she didn't need a man to take care of her. That she was old enough to take care of herself.

Men were off-limits.

Of course, her father admitting that he'd had a hand in almost every aspect of her career made her think that all that hard work, all those hours she'd put in weren't worth it. Maybe she should've been out there partying, being seen in all the right places with all the right people, just like her older sister.

Really?

She shook her head. That was all in the past, though. She was in Crater Lake now. In a job of her own choosing and she planned to make the most of it. Even if it meant traipsing around in the snow with the sexiest mountain man she'd ever laid eyes on.

A man that also drove her a bit crazy.

"You ready to try again?" Luke asked.

"Sure. The sooner we get this done, the sooner I can head back to my apartment in the resort and curl up in front of a fire."

"Glad to see you're on board." Luke went over and picked up the knapsack. "You're going to need this."

Sarah moaned as it was placed over her shoulders again. "Thanks. I almost forgot."

"It's your lifeline up here. You can't forget. We'll do a half-mile hike up this trail through the snow, we'll triage a fake patient I have up there and then head back down to the resort. That's after we build a makeshift stretcher."

"You have a patient up there?" Sarah asked. "Who in their right mind would wait out in the cold for hours for you?"

Luke winked. "It's a dummy."

"Clearly."

He rolled his eyes. "It's a simulation. A mannequin. It's not a real person, but it's simulating a very real situation."

Sarah sighed. "Okay. Lead on."

Luke nodded and pulled on his own pack. She watched him for a few moments as he broke a path ahead of her. Even though he was wearing thick snow pants you could still make out the outline of his strong, muscular thighs and his tight butt.

Sarah shook her head. It was apparent she was suffering from altitude sickness, because she was thinking about the strangest things.

Dr. Luke Ralston was off-limits.

He worked for Silas Draven as well, so that meant it was a no go for her. She didn't mix business with pleasure.

So she couldn't think about Luke that way.

She just couldn't.

CHAPTER THREE

IT HAD BEEN three days since she last saw Dr. Luke Ralston and that was a good thing after the torment he'd put her through up on that high mountain trail. He hadn't been kidding about a simulation. When they'd got to the mannequin, it had been half-buried in ice and under a tree trunk. There had been broken skis and fake blood.

Sarah had never picked up an axe before, but she did that day. She had the blister and the splinters to prove it.

Even though she'd wanted to tell Luke his simulation was cracked, she hadn't backed down. She knew that he thought of her as some kind of spoiled rich girl and that was far from the truth. So she'd learned quite quickly how to use an axe. She'd shown him a thing or two.

She'd also learned how to make a makeshift gurney out of broken skis, rope, a tarp and duct tape. After assessing the mannequin's ABCs, they'd got him on their gurney and down off the mountain.

There had been quite a few stares as she'd come down to the lodge with a mannequin on a stretcher splattered with craft-store paint. Still, she'd done it and he'd grudgingly admitted that she'd done a good job and that was the last she'd seen of him.

She thought she was going to be put through some more

training, but so far she hadn't seen him. She should be happy about that and she was, but she wasn't totally. She looked for him everywhere, as if he were going to pop out of the shadows and frighten her. The thought of seeing him actually made her excited, as if she were some young girl with a crush.

There was no denying Luke was handsome. She'd thought that the first moment she saw him. But there was something else about him. A lone wolf quality. He was a man who didn't want or need anyone else. The kind of man who was completely untamed.

He was a challenge, and she'd always liked a challenge.

Focus.

She couldn't think about him that way. Distance. That was what she needed. Right now this time was about her. Career was her life.

If she got together with someone, her parents would never believe she could function on her own. That she was a surgeon.

Even then, she wasn't sure of anything. Everything she'd thought she earned had really come because she was Vin Ledet's daughter. Her father knew people on the admissions board at college. She'd fought so hard for her MCAT scores, achieving one of the highest that year, which should've been enough to get her into medical school, but apparently not enough for her father. Then her residency and her fellowship, her father had had a hand in that. Everything she'd pursued in her medical career her father had had a hand in.

No wonder her belief in herself was fleeting.

Except this place.

She'd earned this on her own by saving Silas Draven's nephew Shane in Missoula.

Silas and her father moved in the same circles and never saw eye to eye.

Sarah knew it wasn't because of who her father was. This job was because of her own merit.

Someone believed in her abilities and she wasn't going to let them down.

She could do this.

This was her focus and she was going to prove to everyone she was up to the task. This clinic was going to be her pride and joy.

Her clinic had opened a bit earlier than she'd planned, but Silas Draven had had a large party of tourists coming in and he'd wanted to make sure that it was up and running. He wanted his resort to be all-inclusive, and didn't want his guests having to go into town and wait at the local clinic.

Even though the resort hadn't officially opened, the large party of skiers was certainly giving her a run for her money. Her clinic had been full the two days she'd been open. It was usually just minor stuff, cuts and sunburns, but she was enjoying the work and, the best part, it was honest work. Though, she missed surgery, the rush of the hospital, but this job she'd got on her own.

Her parents didn't have a hand in it.

Really, Sarah? Sunburns? The only sun you should think about is evening out your tan.

She cursed under her breath, trying to shake away her sister's annoying voice. Her sister had never said those exact words, but she could almost picture her, standing in the waiting room and saying them, because her sister had nagged her about similar things before.

"Patient ten?" Sarah briefly looked up from her chart, to the busy waiting room at her clinic. "Patient number ten?"

A man with a very red face stood up and walked toward her. He nodded and winced. "I am Mr. Fontblanc."

Sarah smiled. "I know, we just use a numbering system here to keep anonymity."

"Ah, oui. Merci beaucoup."

"You can have a seat in exam room one. I'll be with you momentarily."

Mr. Fontblanc nodded again, shuffling off down the hall. She looked at her chart one more time and was about to call the next victim of a really bad sunburn when the door to her clinic burst open. Luke strode into her pristine clinic, dirty and breathless.

"What're you doing?" he asked.

"I'm seeing patients," Sarah said, trying not to look at him. Distance was the key.

"Good, I have a patient for you."

"What? Where?"

"He's in the lobby."

"In the lobby? Why is he in the lobby?"

Luke rolled his eyes and crossed his arms. "Would you stop giving me the third degree and just come to the lobby?"

"I have a patient waiting in my exam room. I can't leave him there."

"Is your patient bleeding profusely with a head injury?"

"That's confidential."

Luke shook his head and pushed past her into the exam room.

"Dr. Ralston!" Sarah tried to stop him, but he was in the exam room. Mr. Fontblanc looked a bit stunned.

"Sorry to keep you waiting…" Luke peered at the man. "Too much sun?"

"*Oui*…uh, yes."

"*Vous êtes Français?*" Luke inquired in perfect French.

"*Oui.*"

Sarah stood back, stunned. She didn't know French at all. Spanish, she knew quite a bit, but French, she was at a loss. Luke seemed to know it. He questioned the man briefly and then pulled out a tube of topical cream from her medicine cupboard, handing it to her patient and then patting him on the back.

The patient still seemed shell-shocked, but overall was happy.

"*Merci.*"

"*Pas de problème,*" Luke said.

The patient left the room and Luke turned back to her. "You ready to go and help the patient in the lobby now?"

"What just happened here?" She watched as Luke began to grab suturing trays, gauze and a bolus for an IV. "What's going on? Why are you stealing my supplies?"

He groaned and grabbed her hand. "Come on. I need another doctor's help with this."

Sarah didn't really have much of a choice as she was dragged from her clinic. The other patients watched her leave, just as confused as she was at the moment.

"If this patient needs another doctor, why didn't you get your brother to help you?" Sarah asked.

"There was no time to take this man to town." Luke pushed the button on the elevator, not looking at her, but watching for the door to light up and open.

"What's wrong with the patient?" she asked.

"Have you ever seen a mauling?"

Sarah gasped. "Did you just say a mauling? By what?"

Luke glanced at her. "A bear."

She shook her head. She'd seen pictures in textbooks when she was a resident. As a trauma surgeon you had to be prepared for everything, but she'd never actually encountered one personally. She was aware of the damage that could be done. Her stomach twisted in a knot at the very idea, but they were in bear country. It was to be expected.

The elevator arrived and they got on. It was a quick ride down to the lobby. When the doors opened everything was in chaos and Sarah could see a trail of blood from the door to a boardroom down a darkened hall.

"I don't get it," Sarah remarked as she fell into step beside Luke.

"What don't you get?" he asked.

"Bears hibernate. It's January."

Luke sighed. "No, not really. It's called torpor. It's like hibernation—they can be woken. This idiot was fool enough to stumble on a bear's den and, instead of leaving the bear well enough alone, he crawled inside to get a picture. Thankfully, people were with him."

"Idiot is right."

He nodded. "If you haven't seen a mauling before, prepare yourself."

She nodded. "I've seen worse stuff in the ER."

"Possible disembowelment and bite marks?"

"Yeah. A car can do damage to a patient, too. I'm ready."

A small smile played on his lips, but just briefly. It was almost as if he was impressed that she didn't shy away or that she wasn't squeamish at the prospect. It scared her. It was something she was completely unfamiliar with. It was something she was a little terrified about herself since moving from Manhattan to a remote town in northwest Montana, but this was her job. She was going to help Luke any way that she could. It was the trauma surgeon in her.

"Did you bring enough supplies down?" she asked.

"We've got enough supplies in here. We have to get him stabilized before the air ambulance gets here."

Sarah nodded. "Okay."

She walked into the room and tried not to gasp. The man was in bad shape. There were deep lacerations to his arm, his legs and torso, but his face was really bad. She could see teeth marks, deep gouging all over; she could see bone on his arm and the bandages on his abdomen were already soaked through, which tipped Sarah off that this guy would need packing if he was going to survive the trip to the nearest hospital. The way his abdomen was distended, she knew from her trained eye he would suffer from compartment syndrome sooner rather than later and that could be fatal if not controlled.

"Buddy, I've brought another doctor here to help me." Luke spoke to the man. "Just take it easy."

The man just moaned.

"I'm surprised he's lucid."

"Me, too," Luke said. "I did give him a shot of morphine in the field when I found him, but he's lost a lot of blood."

Sarah nodded and pulled off her white lab coat. "Gloves?"

Luke gestured in the direction of the sideboard, where a box of rubber gloves was waiting. She slipped on a pair and then grabbed a pack of gauze.

"I need you to hold him down—I'm going to put in a central line," Luke told her.

"You're going to put in a central line here?"

He nodded. "No choice. Look at his arms, and his veins are chunky. The bear did damage. Lots of damage."

"Sure." Sarah leaned over and held the man down. She looked down into his dark eyes, full of confusion and fear. "Don't worry, sir. We're going to get you patched up in no time. Soon you won't be in so much pain. I promise."

"Hold him now for me," Luke said.

"I've got him. Just do it."

Luke inserted the central line quickly and efficiently. She couldn't remember the last time she'd seen someone put in a central line so fast before. She was impressed. The patient barely flinched, but that could be because maybe some of the fight had gone out of him, or it could've been the morphine.

Once he was hooked up to a drip, he passed out and Luke went about stitching what they could to help control the bleeding. Sarah packed his face and set a broken bone in his arm. They didn't say much to each other; there wasn't much to say, really. They were both totally focused on their patient.

The last time they'd worked on a patient together, they were at each other's throats. This was different. It was nice. Comforting almost, as if she'd been doing this with him for a long, long time, and she couldn't remember the last time she'd felt such a familiarity with another surgeon before.

"He has extensive damage to his abdomen. There is nothing I can do here."

"Pack him?" Luke asked.

She nodded. "No choice. If I start poking around to find the source of the bleeders I could do more damage. His body needs to rest before repairs. Does bear saliva have an envenomation? You know, like the wolverine or Komodo dragon?"

"No, but the saliva often carries staph or strep, which can lead to infections and organ shutdown." He frowned and seemed upset for a brief moment. "Either way he'll need a good course of antibiotics, tetanus and rabies. Though rabies from bear bites are rare."

"Why is that?"

"The injury rate from bear attacks in North America is like one person per couple million. Of course, that report by S. Herrero is from 1970. It could be different now."

"Wow."

"The more we encroach on their territory, the worse it gets. I read a lot on animal attacks for obvious reasons."

"Makes sense."

She would have never thought about reading medical papers on animal attacks before coming here. It wasn't something that happened a lot in Manhattan. She'd dealt with dog, cat and human bites in the city.

It was time to broaden her reading if she was going to stay here.

Luke impressed her with his knowledge and that was a hard thing to do. She liked working with him. They could work on the patient seamlessly and still chat easily. She'd never had that kind of rapport with another surgeon before.

It felt so right working with him. It was just sad that this poor man had to suffer and Sarah decided right then and there: she didn't want to mess with a bear in any way, shape or form.

When they had done all they could do, they just monitored him and waited for the air ambulance to come. Nothing but the sound of the portable monitors between them.

"How long do you think it will be before the air ambulance comes?" Sarah asked, breaking the silence.

"Should be here soon, though there was a storm rolling in from the southwest. I hope that didn't hinder the flight in from Missoula."

"If it does?" she asked.

"Great Falls will send one. Missoula is bigger, though."

She nodded and there was a knock at the door. A paramedic stood there. "Someone call an air ambulance?"

They worked with the paramedics to get the patient onto the stretcher and then out into the cold to the waiting ambulance, which would take him down to the airport. The ambulance had landed on Silas Draven's private airstrip.

Once the patient was loaded up the ambulance flicked on its sirens and headed down the long windy road to Crater Lake. Sarah didn't stand outside for too long because it was cold and she didn't have her coat on.

Luke followed her back inside.

"I hope he makes it," Sarah remarked.

"He will. Death is rare. Although compartment syndrome worries me."

"Me, too," Sarah said. "Glad you caught that, as well."

"I've seen compartment syndrome many a time as an army medic. The bowels inflating, then the liver and kidneys begin to shut down. It's a domino effect."

"It is. I thought you would've followed him. Didn't you get him down off the mountain?" she teased, as that had been the reason why he'd stood in her OR last summer questioning her every move.

"I usually would, but he woke a bear up. The bear just didn't go back to sleep. I have to track it and…" He trailed off.

"What?"

"I have to make sure it goes back to its den, but, since the bear has been fully woken up from its torpor, it's going to be looking for food. I don't want to have to destroy it."

She frowned. "Oh. I hope you don't have to do that."

"Me, too. It's not the bear's fault that moron decided it would be a good selfie. Me with a bear."

Sarah chuckled. "A tourist?"

"Close, a surveyor. A new one. The surveyors I train to work up in these mountains know better than that."

"I'm sure they do, but I didn't see his pack."

Luke chuckled. "I think he left it up there on the mountain."

"How are his friends?"

"Shaken up. I should go talk to them."

"Do you want me to?"

"No. It's okay. I can. Thanks for helping me," he said.

"I really didn't have a choice." She smiled at him.

"I'm sorry about that. I overstep my boundaries in emergency situations."

"It's no problem. That's what I'm here for. To help patients."

And then it hit her.

Oh. No.

"Darn it," she cursed out loud. "Darn it."

"What?" he asked.

"My patients in the clinic. How long was I gone for?"

Luke glanced at his wrist. "About forty minutes."

Sarah groaned. "If they complain to Mr. Draven…"

"If they complain I will tell him you helped one of his employees who was dumb enough to stick his face in a bear's den."

"I think Mr. Draven will be more ticked about the patients in my clinic, though."

Luke frowned. "Come on. We'll tell them why."

"Are you serious? We have to protect privacy rights."

"They won't know him. These are tourists. Tourists like bear stories."

Sarah looked at him as if he were crazy. Maybe he was. Maybe he'd spent too many winters up on that mountain and he'd lost his mind. Her patients were going to be mad that she'd left them up there for that long.

Mr. Draven had made it pretty clear that he wanted patients

to be seen within twenty minutes of their arrival and registration at the clinic. Not forty.

"I don't know. I don't think that's a good idea."

Luke rolled his eyes and then took her hand. It shocked her. It was calloused, warm and strong. It sent a tingle of electricity through her and she could feel the heat flooding her cheeks at just the simple act of a touch from him, but then she wasn't used to physical intimacy. It had been so long and her parents weren't exactly huggers. So that simple touch threw her for a loop.

"Come on, we don't have to tell the particulars, but you can bet when I warn that group of European tourists off the mountain trails because of a bear being at large, that will get them talking."

"Or send them packing." Sarah grudgingly let him lead her back to her clinic. "If it were me and I heard that about a bear, I would be packing my bags and leaving the general vicinity. Bears are beautiful animals, but I never want to encounter one in the wild."

He shook his head. "That's because you haven't been properly trained on how to deal with a bear in the wild."

"Please don't show me."

He laughed and pushed the button to the elevator, the doors opening instantly. "If you're living in bear country, Sarah, you really don't have a choice in the matter. Everyone in Crater Lake needs to know what to do in case of a bear. Do you have bear deterrent?"

Sarah shook her head and pinched the bridge of her nose. "Oh, God."

"I take it you don't."

Sarah glanced up at him and could see he was enjoying her torment. "I have a spray can of something in my office, but I didn't buy it. It was just there when I took over."

"I know. I bought it and put it there. Most offices of the permanent staff have a can. It's better to be prepared and, since most of you aren't from Montana, I thought it would be the best."

"You're really enjoying this, aren't you?"

"Enjoying what?" A small smile played across his lips. It was a devious smile, even if it was partially hidden behind his beard. It was the kind that made her a bit weak in the knees and she fought the urge to kiss him. Even though she couldn't remember the last time she'd kissed a man. She resisted the urge to kiss him and gave him a playful shove instead.

"Hey, what was that for?"

"For enjoying my torment and for teasing me." Sarah shook her head. "What am I going to say?"

"Sorry would be a start."

"Not to you. The patients."

"I'll handle it. Besides you don't speak French."

She chuckled. "This is true."

The elevator dinged open and her stomach knotted. She hoped word wouldn't get back to Silas Draven that she'd left a big group of VIP tourists by themselves. She didn't need him to think she couldn't handle her job and she definitely didn't want this to get back to her father.

"Don't be nervous. It will be fine." Luke took her hand and she tried not to gasp at his familiarity. "Come on, you have to face the music."

She took her hand back and marched ahead of him, trying to put some distance between them. "Okay, we can do this."

Facing all those tourists was better than having him touch her. Not exactly better, but safer. Actually she'd rather face a bear over being alone with Luke. Luke was dangerous. He was the kind of dangerous she secretly yearned for. It was electric, intense and was, oh, so wrong.

The patients left in the waiting room were pacing and looked none too pleased when she walked in.

"I'm sorry," she began, but as the words came out the din of French was overwhelming.

Luke stepped into the fray and shouted over the noise. A few choice words and the noise ebbed and the patients sat down again.

"Do you have enough exam rooms for five people?" Luke asked out of the corner of his mouth.

"No, I have two."

Luke made a face. "I guess Mr. Draven didn't really think you'd be this busy on any given day."

"Or maybe he thought two would be enough. I'm sure he didn't expect me to be called away for a mauling."

"I'd call your next patient. I'll help you. We'll get them in and out fast.

"Really? You're going to help me."

"Of course."

Sarah nodded and picked up the discarded patient charts, handing Luke three and keeping two for herself.

"Hey, how come I get the majority?"

"You speak the language." She winked at him and then walked away. Pleased that she was tormenting him just as much as he was her, but most importantly she had to put distance between them.

"Patient eleven?" she called out.

Luke put the last of the files on Sarah's desk. She was typing away on her computer and didn't even bother to look up at him.

"There. All done. Two more sunburns. The French have mountains, don't they? Surely they ski."

"These guests are from an island in the Caribbean called Marie-Galante. It's tropical."

"That doesn't explain sunburns. They should know how to use sunblock."

"Snow sunburns. One of them told me they'd never seen snow before—they didn't think they could get a sunburn in the winter. Actually, I'm glad they spoke French and not Creole."

Luke grinned. "Me, too. I knew a Cajun man once in my unit."

"Right, you were a medic in the army."

"Yeah. Right." Luke should leave, the conversation was turning in a direction he wasn't comfortable with, but he couldn't pry himself away from her and he didn't know why. He was drawn to her. This was why he'd gone out into the woods for a few days.

He'd had to get out of temptation's way.

"Thanks again for helping me," she said. "It's been a while since I've been in a clinic."

"No problem. You helped me with the mauling, but honestly I'm surprised you're in a clinic. I thought you were a surgeon."

"I am a surgeon."

"So why did you leave the OR?"

Sarah's lips pursed together and he was wondering if maybe now he was making her uncomfortable, just as he'd felt moments ago when he'd unthinkingly mentioned his time in the army. Something he was not ready to talk about, because he did miss it and it reminded him of his failed marriage, which was something he wanted to forget.

So what had made Sarah leave surgery?

None of your business.

Only he couldn't help himself. She'd been such a bulldog in the OR last summer. Surgeons with that kind of drive and passion didn't just walk away.

You did.

"I wanted a change of pace," she said.

"A change of pace?"

She shrugged. "Sure, why not? The city was getting to me."

"Somehow I don't believe that."

"You want to talk about truths? Why did you leave the army?"

Luke's spine stiffened. "My tour of duty ended. Well, I better go. Thanks again."

"You're welcome."

He left her office, without so much as a look back. It was for the best. If he looked back, he might stay. The way that she'd looked at him, he knew that she didn't believe him. Heck, he wasn't even sure if he had convinced himself of that fact. This was why Sarah was dangerous. She affected him like no one else had. Not even Christine. Sarah got under his skin. She actually made him yearn for things he used to want. Things that he'd thought were long gone.

He didn't need that.

He didn't want that.

Didn't he?

CHAPTER FOUR

"SHE DID WHAT?"

"She signed out a pair of snowshoes and headed up the lake trail," said the equipment-rental guy. He looked a bit scared, which was good. Luke wanted to strike fear into the guy's heart. Didn't they know there was a bear loose? A bear that had mauled a guy two days ago. A bear that hadn't been tracked down yet.

What was she thinking? Clearly she wasn't. He had to find her before the bear did.

"What trail did she take?"

"The Lakeview trail."

"When did she leave?"

The rental guy looked confused and shrugged. "Like twenty minutes ago?"

"Why did you let her go out?"

The young man just stuttered. "I didn't know I wasn't supposed to. Besides, I just started my shift. She was heading out just as I came in."

Luke cursed under his breath. "Don't let anyone else out. There's a bear on the loose."

"Aren't bears supposed to be hibernating?"

Luke just shook his head and walked away from the rental

guy. He couldn't believe she'd gone out there. Why would she head out on her own?

You haven't seen her for a couple days. Maybe she thinks the bear has gone by now.

It was a foolish assumption. Anyone from around here would know to wait for the all-clear, or at least find out the areas the bear had been seen in.

She's not from around here. It was his fault. He should have explained it to her. Instead he'd kept his distance.

He'd avoided her because she was getting too close for him. Since he'd come home expecting to start a life with his wife and realized his life wasn't going to be how he'd pictured it, he'd been keeping people at a distance.

Less chance of getting hurt that way.

Except, he enjoyed being around Sarah. The back and forth with her was refreshing and it totally caught him off guard. He couldn't be around her, yet here he was, worried about her.

She most likely would be fine on the Lakeview trail as the bear's den was nowhere near that, but, still, she didn't know anything about the mountains.

Luke returned to the rental chalet. "Give me a pair of snow-shoes, please."

Once he had the snowshoes secured to his knapsack, he climbed on his snowmobile and headed up to the Lakeview trail. When he got to the edge of the trail, he parked his snow-mobile, strapped on his snowshoes, pulled on his rucksack and unstrapped the tranquilizer gun.

He could see Sarah's fresh tracks in the snow. She couldn't be too far off. He'd taken her out once; she was good, but she wasn't that good. He was confident that he could catch up with her in no time.

As he headed up the path, he soon saw her. She had stopped not that far into the trail, at a lookout. She was holding her cam-era and was taking pictures.

Luke watched her for a few moments. She had a really fancy

camera. He didn't know much about cameras, but it looked high-tech. Sarah was completely immersed in what she was doing. She was very unaware of everything around her.

Her cheeks were flushed from the cold and the exercise, but she was smiling as she held up her camera and then he couldn't help but smile, too, watching her. It was enchanting.

She's so beautiful.

And he shook his head, because he couldn't think about her like that. She was off-limits to him. It was a beautiful vista; he couldn't really blame her for that. Crater Lake was a beautiful place. This was home.

There had been so many times when he was serving over-seas, in the heat and the desert, trying to patch up wounded soldiers who were flown in from the front lines, that all he'd been able to think about was the mountain with the snow cap. The blue, blue water.

And of Christine. Only she'd never seemed to miss him. Maybe that should have been an indicator that rushing into mar-riage with her hadn't been the best idea. That was her reasoning when he'd come home and found out that she wanted a divorce.

We were too young, Luke. You were going to medical school and you were my first. You were safe. Anthony understands me. We don't have anything in common, Luke. When you were gone he was here. He was always here. I can rely on him...

His smile instantly vanished. Just thinking about Christine and the heartache that she and Anthony caused him ruined the moment.

This was why he couldn't get involved with someone. This was why he was single and kept people at a distance. You couldn't trust people. It was too painful.

"You know, there's a bear on the loose still and you're on a trail that is an avalanche risk."

Sarah lowered her camera and stared at him in shock and there was a touch of annoyance there, as well.

"What're you doing here?" she asked.

"Didn't you hear me? There's a bear out there on the loose."

She paled. "Wait, I thought you caught it."

"Who told you that?"

"The woman at the rental chalet. She said, and I quote, 'I think he caught him or something. Yeah, yeah, he caught it.'"

Luke rolled his eyes. "Well, that explains it. I spoke to a clueless guy. He really doesn't know much."

"Apparently so. I would've never come out here had I known. I really thought the bear issue was a moot point. I figured since I hadn't seen you for a couple days that you'd dealt with it. I thought you'd gone back up into the woods like you do all the time."

"I understand the woods. I'm used to them. I live in the woods."

She cocked an eyebrow. "Really?"

He nodded. "I have a cabin in the woods. It's on the edge of my parents' property. I built it myself."

"Wow, I'm impressed. I mean, I figured you were a bit of a hands-on guy, but I had no idea that you could build a home with your own hands. That's amazing."

"Thanks. Well, when I got back from my tour of duty I had a bit of free time." Then he cursed inwardly, because again just a simple twist in the conversation and he was opening up to her again. How did she manage to do that? He was worried that she would try to turn the conversation back to his time overseas. Something that was off-limits.

"Well, it's quite impressive. Most surgeons I know wouldn't risk damaging their hands by doing something like that."

"I'm not like most surgeons. I'm not traditional in any sense of the word." Besides, he didn't practice much surgery anymore. He missed it, but he loved this more. He loved what he did in Crater Lake.

"That's for sure." She smiled and then looked away, aiming her camera at the mountains.

"Didn't you hear me say there's a bear on the loose?"

"I did, but I just want a couple more shots."

A couple more shots? The woman was infuriating.

"So why are you up here?"

"Taking pictures."

"I thought you didn't like the cold?" Luke asked.

"I don't, but it was a beautiful day."

"So what do you do with the pictures?"

She grinned. "I paint a bit."

She paints?

Now it was his turn to be impressed. He hadn't thought she had any hobbies beyond what he'd seen, and that hadn't been much. He'd thought she was a career-focused surgeon. Usually young surgeons didn't have the time for much else—they were too focused on honing their craft.

It pleasantly surprised him.

"Paint?"

Sarah nodded. "I have hidden depths, too."

Luke laughed. "I guess you do. I build homes and you paint."

"I wouldn't mind seeing it sometime."

His blood heated at her suggestion. The thought of her in his home was definitely a dangerous idea, but not all that unpleasant. Luke cleared his throat. "Maybe sometime, but really we have to get down off the trail. Until I find that bear, I really can't authorize people being out here alone and unarmed."

"I brought that can of deterrent."

He smiled at her briefly. "That won't be enough to dissuade a hungry bear just fresh out of torpor."

Sarah sighed. "You're right."

"Come on, I brought my snowmobile, so at least you don't have to hike the entire way back. Even if it would be good practice for you."

She glared at him as she packed her camera carefully back in its case and into her knapsack. "Ha-ha."

"Glad to see you were taking my advice about the backpack."

"Good advice is good advice. Though I'm a bit worried about avalanches. Do those happen a lot up here?"

Luke nodded. "They do. We can do a little simulation if you'd like?"

Sarah groaned. "Fine, but as long as it's inside."

"I promise. I wouldn't want to risk causing an avalanche out here."

Sarah had been surprised to hear Luke's voice from behind her. She hadn't seen him in a couple of days since the mauling. Every time she seemed to get a little bit closer to him, he turned tail and ran into the woods. Of course, she didn't mind. It was better they had that separation.

She barely knew anything about him and really she shouldn't care all that much, but she wanted to get to know him. Maybe because she was alone here in Crater Lake. She didn't know anyone apart from Luke and a few employees that she greeted in passing at the resort. Then again, when had she really had any friends?

Her whole medical career, heck, her whole life, she hadn't had much time to form any interactions or friendships. And that was the way she wanted it. Her parents had tried to put Sarah into the same activities as her sister. It was just Sarah never really was social. She'd preferred science camp or painting class over tennis camp. She'd been so focused trying to prove to her parents she could do the things she wanted to do, she hadn't made many friends.

Or at least friends who were interested in the same things as she was.

The last date she'd been on the previous year had been so unremarkable. The guy had been handsome, well-to-do, but boring and very full of himself.

Luke was cocky, confident, but there was a difference. He didn't think he was a god. He didn't think he was better than anyone else. He actually tried to help people around him, even if he didn't want people to know that he cared, which she didn't get.

And most of all, he didn't date her because of who her father was.

"You ready?" Luke asked as he straddled the snowmobile.

"I don't have a helmet."

He reached into his knapsack and tossed her one. "There you go. Now get on."

"Do you have furniture in there? Is it like a bottomless bag?"

He chuckled. "Perhaps. You know my motto is be ready for anything."

Sarah laughed and put on her helmet, climbing on the snowmobile behind him. Suddenly she was very nervous about being so close to Luke. Which was ridiculous. They were just coworkers. They weren't even friends.

He's the closest thing you have to a friend.

Which was true and that thought scared her.

"You need to hold on," Luke said over his shoulder.

"Right." Her heart was pounding and she was very aware about how close she was to him. Though she couldn't feel his skin, she was pressed against him enough to feel the hard muscles under all the thick layers of his snowsuit.

At least that was something. There was a wall of protection between the two of them, but for one brief moment she wished there weren't and she couldn't help but wonder what it would be like to be wrapped up in his arms.

Where did that come from?

She shook that thought away, because she couldn't think like that.

Luke was off-limits.

She just held on tight and tried not to think about it. She had to shake the idea of Luke out of her mind. This was her chance to prove to her parents that she didn't need their help to survive. She didn't need anyone's help. She was here because of her own merit. She'd earned the right to be here and she was going to prove to everyone she had the right to be here.

Nothing was going to get in her way.

This was her chance and she had to focus on making this clinic the best. She had to be the best, so there was no time to think about Luke or what might be.

She didn't have time for romance. She couldn't lose her focus and if she got involved with Luke, she probably would. He was so gorgeous, so delicious and so very distracting.

This job was too important to her. Her parents had scoffed when she'd turned down the job her father had got for her and taken this one. They believed she would fail and come back to them with her proverbial tail between her legs.

This job won't wait for you, Sarah. I pulled a lot of strings for you.

She couldn't let them think that way. They might not think she could handle this, but she could.

Luke was not for her, even if she wished she could indulge. She had to be strong around him, keep him at a distance and remember why she was here.

She wasn't here to fall in love. That wasn't in the cards for her.

She was here to be a doctor. She was here to run the most prestigious private clinic in northwest Montana.

This job was her chance, because, even though everything about her medical career had been handed to her, according to her father she was a damn good doctor.

She was a damn good surgeon.

Are you sure about that?

They pulled up to the resort and Luke parked his snowmobile away from the main entrance. When the engine was off, Sarah clambered off the snowmobile, her legs shaking from the ride.

"That was my first and last snowmobile ride, I think," she said, trying to make light of the situation. She handed Luke back the helmet. "Thanks for being prepared."

"No problem. Now, no going back out onto the trails until that bear has been subdued."

"I hope you don't have to kill it."

Luke frowned. "I hope the bear returns to its den, but I doubt it. The game warden is combing the mountains, as well."

"Thanks again for coming to get me. I hope I didn't ruin your day."

"You didn't ruin it, but you put a serious dent in my plans." He winked at her.

"You're an idiot."

Luke was going to say something more, but they were interrupted when a front-desk person came running out of the side door.

"Thank goodness I found you both," she said. "There's an emergency up in Suite 501."

"What's wrong?" Sarah asked.

"A guest has gone into labor."

Luke's eyes widened. "Well, that's something I've never dealt with."

"Really?"

"Not many pregnant soldiers on the front line."

"Well, perhaps I can teach you something." Sarah turned to the front-desk woman. "Get her comfortable, call the air ambulance and tell them we'll be there in ten minutes."

The woman nodded and disappeared back inside.

"You've seriously delivered a baby before?" Luke asked with a hint of admiration in his voice.

"I'm a surgeon and part of the training was a rotation on the obstetrical rounds. I can do this."

"I'm sure you can. Not sure I can."

She grinned. "After today you will. Come on."

Luke nodded and they headed inside.

Sarah didn't want to tell him that she was nervous, too. She hadn't delivered that many babies, but right now she didn't have a choice. She couldn't be nervous. There was a job to do.

There were two lives to save.

CHAPTER FIVE

"Come on, one more push," Sarah urged. "You can do it."

It had been a long time since she'd delivered a baby. She had been nervous for a moment, hoping she'd remember how.

As a trauma surgeon she didn't see many births. When a pregnant woman came into the ER Sarah would look at them briefly before an OB/GYN was called, but the moment she'd checked on the mother at the hotel everything she'd learned had come back to her.

Which was a good thing. This patient needed her.

Luke was behind the mother, holding her up, helping her. The air ambulance had arrived, but by the time they arrived there was no way they could move the mother. The baby was on the way out and moving the mother would put the baby at risk.

"You're doing great," Luke reassured the woman.

Sarah smiled up at him, but he wasn't looking at her. Instead he was focused on helping their patient and it warmed her heart. He could've stood back because he admitted that he didn't know anything about childbirth, but instead he threw himself into the work.

He was gentle. Kind.

For a man that was referred to around the hotel as a lone wolf, keeping people at bay, disappearing into his cabin up in the woods, Luke had a large amount of tenderness to him. It made her chest tighten just a little bit.

There was something about a rough, tough exterior and a gentle hand. It made him endearing.

The mother let out a loud yell and Sarah gently helped the baby girl into the world. Sarah rubbed the baby's back and soon the newborn was crying lustily.

"Good job," Sarah encouraged.

The mom laid back and Luke came over to help her. He was grinning ear to ear as he handed her sterile scissors.

"Good job, Doctor," he whispered in her ear. It sent a tingle down her spine.

She didn't say anything as she cut the umbilical cord and then wrapped the baby up in a blanket and handed her to Luke so he could give her to the mother.

"Congratulations, Mom," Luke said as he carefully transferred the baby to her mother's arms. He glanced down at the tiny girl as he did so, those blue eyes twinkling as he gently cradled her. So little in his big hands. It made Sarah's heart skip a beat.

Having a family had never been on her radar. Maybe because she'd had such a lonely childhood, even with a sister. They were raised by nannies in the old archaic "children should be seen and not heard" style.

How could she even contemplate raising a family when she didn't even know how one was supposed to function?

So she'd never entertained the idea, but in this moment, watching the joy on the mother's face, she yearned for something more.

"She's beautiful," Luke said.

The mother cried tears of joy and exhaustion as she took the small bundle from Luke. It was this moment that Sarah had always enjoyed when she'd been a resident and worked the obstetrical round. The moment of pure joy and elation. The moment when mother and child met. It could warm even the coldest hearts.

And watching Luke hold that small child melted hers completely.

What was it about him?

Most of the time he drove her completely around the bend, but there were times like this, when he was dealing with patients, that made her soften toward him. She wanted to get to know him and she never wanted to get to know anyone. What was it about him?

He's a mystery.

And maybe that was why she was so drawn to him. He was a challenge and she'd never backed down from a challenge before.

You need to back down from this one.

Sarah tore her gaze away from Luke and turned back to the patient. The paramedics stood at the ready. Even though the birth had been simple, mother and baby still had to be taken to the nearest hospital to be checked out.

Once she was finished the paramedics stepped in and started to get ready to transfer the patients. Her job was done. She cleaned up the mess and put it in a trash bag that she would take down to her medical-waste receptacle in her clinic.

Now you're picking up trash? Sarah, you weren't raised to do that.

You can't be an obstetrician. I didn't pay for your medical schooling so you can do obstetrics.

She hated the way her parents' voices were always in her head, trying to control her. For a long time she'd managed to tune them out, right up until she'd discovered what her father had done.

Now they were constantly there, questioning her every move.

Sarah would've liked to have been an OB/GYN surgeon, but her father didn't think it was dignified enough. Of course, he hadn't been too pleased when she gave up training to be a cardio-thoracic surgeon under Dr. Eli Draven, but Sarah preferred general surgery. She preferred trauma surgery.

Most people thought that general and trauma surgery was boring, but it wasn't. It was exciting. She got to work on so much with general surgery, and as a trauma surgeon she saw everything, but still she'd kind of missed her chance on working with mothers and babies.

Even though she'd always stressed that she didn't want to get married, that she wanted to focus on her career, there had always been a part of her that wanted the family she hadn't had as a child.

Sarah had grown up in wealth and privilege. She'd wanted for nothing except love and admiration from her parents. Maybe even to spend some time with them.

Watching this mother dote on her new baby made her wonder if her own mother had ever looked at her that way before, and seeing Luke smile so tenderly at them made her yearn.

In this moment she longed for something more.

She just didn't think that was possible.

Not in the near future anyway. Probably never.

Luke came over and peeled off his gloves and threw them in the bag, interrupting her train of thought.

"Good job, Dr. Ledet."

She chuckled. "I really didn't do much. The mother did all the work."

He smiled at her. "Still, you did a good job nonetheless. I would've been totally lost."

"What about your brother? He's the town doctor, doesn't he deliver babies?"

"He does, but he lives in town. That's at least a twenty-minute drive in this weather. He wouldn't have made it in time."

"No," she agreed. "That baby was coming quickly."

They moved out of the way as the paramedics passed them.

"Thank you, Doctors," the mother said, grinning ear to ear.

"Congratulations," Sarah said. "Everything will be okay."

Sarah watched as they wheeled her patient and the baby out of the suite. It had been so wonderful being a part of that moment, watching a family being formed. Being part of their love. She was sad to watch them go.

She sighed. "Well, that was certainly exciting."

"It was, but I don't understand it."

"What don't you understand?"

"I don't understand why a woman so close to delivering decided to come up here on a ski trip," Luke said as he moved away from her.

"I think it was a family trip. Perhaps she would've been left home alone. I think it was a good thing she was here."

He nodded. "Yeah. You're probably right."

Sarah knotted the trash bag and glanced around the suite. "I feel bad for Housekeeping, but honestly I think that mattress is no good anymore."

"That's the first birth I've attended. I mean, besides my own."

"You've never attended one in medical school?"

He shook his head. "I did most of my training in the army. My residency was in Germany at a hospital there. So not only do I speak fluent French, I speak fluent German, too."

"You're a man of many trades, Dr. Ralston."

"I have a lot of secrets." Then he grinned and winked at her in a way that made her heart skip a beat. She had to get out of the room. She had to put some distance between them.

"I'm sure you do, but I have to take this to the clinic." She held up the garbage bag.

"When are you going to show me your paintings?"

The question caught her off guard. Any time anything had ever gotten too personal between them, he'd disappeared into the woods. So when he asked about her paintings, it shocked her.

No one had ever asked to see her paintings before. And she never told anyone about them. If he hadn't caught her taking photographs, she wouldn't have told him. Most people thought her art and pursuing it was silly.

Again, another dream her parents quashed really fast.

They're called starving artists for a reason, Sarah.

Her mother hadn't wanted her to be an artist, and yet her mother had supported the local arts scene in New York City. Bought paintings, attended galas and gallery openings. Then again, that was what women like her mother did. It was *the* thing to do in her parents' circles.

"You want to see my paintings?"

"Sure. You said you take pictures and then do paintings. I'm interested. I've never met a doctor who painted landscapes or drew or anything for that matter."

Sarah chuckled. "It's good for the hands. Especially surgeon hands. Keeps them strong."

"So, when do I get to see them?"

"I don't know. When do I get to see the house you built?" Then the blood drained away from her face when she realized what she'd just done. This was not keeping him at a distance. This was inviting him in.

"How about tonight?" he asked, surprising her.

"Tonight?"

"You have plans tonight?"

"No."

He nodded then, those blue eyes twinkling with something she wasn't sure of, but it made her heart beat a bit faster.

"Okay, then, so you'll come to my place tonight. I'll see some of your paintings and you can see my handiwork."

"Okay." Sarah looked away and hoped that she wasn't blushing. "I better get this to medical waste."

"I'll pick you up at seven."

She nodded and didn't look back at him. She couldn't, because if she did then he would see how he was affecting her.

Damn him.

And then she cursed herself a bit, wondering what the heck she'd just gotten herself into.

* * *

What have I done?

Luke had repeatedly asked himself that since he'd invited Sarah over to his house. He didn't have anyone at his house. Ever.

Only Carson and that was rare. Usually when Luke got together with Carson he went to Carson's place.

It was larger.

Luke went for the understated. An open-concept cabin. Carson referred to it as a shack, as if Luke were some kind of prospector up in Alaska on a gold claim.

Everything in the cabin he'd made. Well, the furniture anyway. So what if he preferred to live off the grid a bit? He wasn't totally off the grid. He had electricity and running water. No, he didn't have a phone or cable, but he had a radio if he ever got into trouble or if someone wanted to reach him.

There wasn't any cell phone reception where his cabin was and he still hadn't quite figured out why. Probably all the pine trees around it.

Christine had hated this cabin when he'd planned it. Even though it did have creature comforts like a sauna out back and a nice bathroom. Everything was too "rough" for her.

When he picked Sarah up at the hotel, he was actually hoping that she would make up an excuse and cop out, but she didn't. She was waiting for him at the front in her coat with a black portfolio slung over her shoulder.

He had no choice but to live up to his end of the bargain and take her to his home. The truck ride over was tense, because he didn't know what to say to her. All he could think about on the journey was how he was going to get out of this situation. A situation that was his fault. He only had himself to blame.

When he'd told Carson what he'd done, he'd thought his brother had witnessed a miracle healing the way his mouth had dropped open.

"You don't date. You said so yourself and you repeatedly made fun of me when I got together with Esme."

"It's not a date. She's a coworker."

Carson had grinned, smugly. "You keep telling yourself that, my friend. You're not fooling me."

Luke had decided he didn't need Carson's advice, called his brother a few choice names and left. Carson was certainly making him eat crow and maybe he deserved it just a bit, because he'd certainly given Carson a run for his money when Esme had started coming around more often.

Still, that was a completely different situation.

Carson was in love with Esme.

Luke wasn't interested in Sarah. Not in that way.

Liar.

This was a dangerous situation. They were in his cabin, in the woods and they were alone. That wasn't a good combo. His self-control was going to be tested tonight, because any time he was around her it was tested.

All he wanted to do was kiss those pink lips, to run his hands through her blond hair and hold her in his arms, to feel her body pressed against his.

Don't think about her like that. She's not yours. She can't be yours. That's not what you want.

Only the more he tried to convince himself of that the harder it was for him to believe it.

"Wow, so this is it?" Sarah asked as he parked his truck in front of his cabin.

"Yes, this is my shack, as my brother calls it."

"Well, at least it'll be warm. I can see you left the home fires burning."

"Yes, I have electricity, but my house is heated by my wood stove. I live a bit off the grid, as much as I can. I like to rough it."

"Do you grow your own food, too?" She was teasing him.

"No, I don't really have a green thumb. I forage mostly. Our dinner tonight will be moss and various pine needles."

She laughed. "Well, can we go inside? I'd like to see this old shack you built."

"Ha-ha." They climbed out of the truck and he opened the door for her. She stepped in first and stood in the small mudroom of his cabin. She was silent and he found himself starting to sweat, waiting for her approval.

Probably because the last time he'd shown a woman his place it had been Christine and she'd hated it and then it had been only the schematics and blueprints.

You expect me to live here?

You wanted a house when I was done with my tours. I'm building this for us.

Don't think about her.

She wasn't going to intrude into his thoughts. Not tonight.

"Well?" he asked, trying not to seem too anxious. "What do you think?"

"It's beautiful. I'm pretty impressed that you built this place." She took off her coat and hung it on the hooks that he had in the entranceway and then kicked off her boots and stepped on the thick Berber area rug that he had in the living-cum-bedroom area of his home. "The furniture seems to match the house perfectly."

"It should, I made it."

She cocked her eyebrows. "You made the furniture, too?"

He nodded. "Everything. Even the mattress."

Why did I say that?

Pink stained her cheeks when he said mattress, but she wouldn't look in the direction of the king-size bed that he'd built in the far corner. Seeing how he affected her made his own blood heat. Since she'd dropped into his arms in her office a couple weeks back, there had been countless times that he'd pictured her naked in his bed, her legs wrapped around his waist.

What he wouldn't give to peel that pale pink boatneck sweater and those tight blue jeans from her body, to run his hands over her soft skin.

Get a grip on yourself.

He cleared his throat and ran his hand through his hair nervously.

"Yeah, I made the mattress out of feathers I'd collected over time. It used to be a straw tick, but that was quite uncomfortable."

"This isn't *Little House on the Prairie*, Pa."

He laughed with her and it defused the tension. He headed into the kitchen. "Would you like a glass of wine?"

"Did you press the grapes yourself?" she teased, setting her portfolio down on his coffee table.

"No. I do go to the grocery store from time to time. I'm not Davy Crockett."

"Could've fooled me." There was a twinkle in her eyes and she leaned over his counter. "I didn't expect dinner or drinks. I thought you were showing me your handiwork and I was going to show you some of mine."

He shrugged. "I rarely have dinner guests. I'm a bit of a Grinch around these parts."

"So I've heard."

"Who did you hear that from?" he asked.

"I went into town on my first week. Met a woman with these two twins and they mentioned how cantankerous you were. I had to agree with them at the time."

Luke groaned. "The Johnstone twins. Yes, they're not fond of me and I'm not too fond of them."

"Why? They looked like innocent enough children."

Luke snorted. "They delight in spooking my horse."

"You have a horse?"

He nodded. "I board her in a stable close to town in the winter. In the summer I have a pad out back that I keep her in. She can't handle the deep snow up here in the winter. She is getting on in years, sadly."

"You have hidden depths, Dr. Ralston."

You have no idea.

Only he didn't say that out loud. Instead he pulled down two wineglasses from where they were hanging on the wall and set them down before her.

"I'm afraid I only have white, but I think white will do well with the salmon I'm making."

"Salmon?"

"I smoked it myself."

She grinned. "I should've known. White is fine."

He pulled the only bottle he had in his house and uncorked it, pouring it into her glass and then his. He wasn't much of a wine drinker, but Esme really liked wine and so he figured Sarah would, too, but she took a sip and made a face.

"What's wrong?" he asked. "Did it go bad?"

"No, it's fine. It's just… I'm not much of a wine drinker. I like beer instead."

Now it was his turn to be shocked. "Who has hidden depths?"

She laughed. "My mother would be horrified if she knew that I was telling a man this. I was brought up to be prim and proper. I was not brought up to be a roughneck."

"A what?" he asked.

"My mother is from a very proper British family. A roughneck is someone who works offshore in oil or gas. Tough, rugged, dirty. I was meant to be refined and graceful."

"You're a bit of a klutz. I don't think you're all that graceful. I have seen you face-first in a snowdrift."

She laughed again and it warmed his heart to hear it. She had an infectious laugh and he couldn't remember the last time he'd felt so at ease around a woman before. Usually he was hiding behind his wall, but not at this moment. He was exposed and he didn't like that one bit.

What was she doing to him?

Sarah didn't know what she was expecting when Luke brought her out to his cabin. She must've been thinking more of a barren shack. Even though his home was rustic, it wasn't barren. It was cozy. It was homey.

It was the kind of place people from the city rented when they went on ski trips. The only difference was it would probably be larger. It was a little too small for most people, but she kind of liked it.

She was shocked that he made most of the furniture in the home, though she seriously doubted he made the leather L-shaped couch that was in the living room adorned with pillows and a polar fleece throw.

Then her gaze drifted off to the bed in the far corner of the open-concept cabin. It was a large wooden four-poster bed with a thick, down-and-feather-filled mattress. Well, according to him it was.

He made his own mattress?

She shook her head. Stop thinking about the bed.

He was in the kitchen checking on the salmon, his back to her. He'd handed her a beer a few moments ago and then gone about cooking the rest of dinner, leaving her to her own devices and the naughty thoughts that were running through her mind.

She sat down on the couch and tried to ignore the large bed, which felt like an elephant in the room at the moment.

Don't think about it. This is just dinner as friends.

Luke came out of the kitchen, holding a bottle of beer. "Just a little bit longer. Sorry about that."

She shrugged. "I didn't expect dinner tonight. It's a nice surprise."

"After all your hard work today, it was the least I could do."

"I just did my job."

"Yeah and you did a good job." Luke picked up her portfolio. "Do you mind if I look?"

"Go ahead. I am at your mercy." Blood rushed to her cheeks.

Luke grinned at her, that devious grin that made her insides turn to goo. "Well, let's see your artistic abilities."

Sarah's pulse thundered in her ears as he thumbed through

her very small portfolio. It was something she'd never shown anyone before. It was something she'd always felt she couldn't share with someone, but Luke had caught her in the act.

And she couldn't lie to him.

Or she didn't want to lie to him, but now she was regretting it because he wasn't saying much. What if he hated it? What if she sucked at it?

Who cares?

Only she did care. She cared if he hated it. What he thought mattered to her and that scared her.

"These are great. Where was this one done?" He held up a picture of the Black Hills. She'd spent some time around Mount Rushmore when she was a kid. That picture was something that she'd painted from memory, because that trip to Mount Rushmore with her parents was one of her last happy memories. They weren't this socialite family, they were just like everyone else. Except her father had rented a massive cabin on the outskirts of Keystone on this huge ranch that had horses and tennis courts, but still it was a happy time in her life.

"The Black Hills."

Luke glanced at it again. "South Dakota?"

She nodded. "Yes. Keystone, South Dakota."

"Yes, now I see it. I like South Dakota."

"You've been there?"

"Who hasn't? It's like Mecca for American families of our generation. Plus, it's not too far away for a family doctor to take his family for a summer vacation. My father was the only town physician in Crater Lake for a long time, so any vacation had to be taken in a drivable radius to home. Where did your family vacation, other than Mount Rushmore?"

"Jamaica, Brazil... India."

He raised an eyebrow. "Have you been around the world?"

"Pretty much." She took a swig of her beer. "My last job, teaching at different hospitals, took me to a lot of places, too. That's why I was in Missoula that day."

"Teaching?"

She nodded. "I worked with a surgeon who was developing a new technique in robotic trauma surgery. It was a good job."

"Why did you give it up?"

Her stomach twisted as she thought about those last moments. About when she'd found out that the job she'd been working on so hard hadn't really been something she'd earned.

It still made her angry.

"You look tense."

"I don't like to talk about the past too much." She set her beer down on the table. "Maybe I should head back to the hotel. I'm not that hungry."

"You're staying. I'm sorry, I won't pry." He set the portfolio down on the table. "Besides, I think it's done."

She watched as he walked into the kitchen. Why did he have to pry into her history? He didn't share his.

What was she doing here?

You're lonely.

She should just leave. It would be better if she left, only she couldn't.

She was a bit of a masochist.

"Have a seat at the table and I'll bring you dinner."

Sarah picked up her beer and headed over to the dining-room table, sitting down at the end. "Don't tell me you made this too?"

"Yep. I told you. I made most of the furniture here." He came out of the kitchen with two plates and set down in front of her a perfectly cooked filet of salmon, asparagus and new potatoes. It smelled delicious. "For a long time since I returned from the army, I didn't practice medicine and all I wanted to do was build stuff for my home."

"Why?" she asked.

He frowned and she knew she was treading on that dangerous ground. That moment when he would clam up. "I needed time."

"I get that."

He shrugged, but he didn't say anything else and an awkward

silence fell between them. She wished that he would open up and share with her, but then again she wasn't exactly sharing much with him either.

So they were at a standstill.

And maybe that was for the best.

After dinner, she helped him clean up, though he insisted that wasn't necessary. Then they returned to the couch in his living room, where he continued to look at her paintings and drawings. As he was skimming through he found one that absolutely captivated him. It was a self-portrait she'd done and by the date on the bottom it was a few years ago. It took his breath away. The details in the drawing. It was just a pencil sketch, but there was so much life to it.

The kissable lips, heart-shaped face, nose that turned up again, thinly arched brows and beautiful eyes that captured him. In the portrait her hair hung loose over bare shoulders, like wisps. Usually she wore it back in a braid and tonight it was done up in a bun. He resisted the urge to undo that bun and let her hair cascade down all over her shoulders. So he could kiss and hold that woman in the picture. It was as if the drawing showed a hidden part of her.

The true Sarah.

And he longed to know the true Sarah, which scared him.

"Which one are you looking at so intently?"

Luke quickly flicked the page. "Uh, this one. The horse on the plains. It's beautiful."

She smiled. "You can have it if you want."

"Thanks."

The horse one was good. It actually reminded him of his own horse, who he hadn't seen in a couple of days, but he'd rather keep the pencil-drawn self-portrait she'd done.

Why torture yourself?

"You said you have a horse?"

"Yeah. I do."

"What's its name?"

"Her name is Adele."

"That's an interesting choice."

"Well, I didn't really choose it. When I bought her that was her name. I didn't see a point in changing it."

"I love horseback riding." Sarah sighed. "I miss it."

"You know how to horseback ride?"

She nodded. "Regular lessons. One thing I didn't mind my parents pressuring me into."

"Your parents have a large impact on your life?" he asked.

She frowned and then shrugged. "What parents don't?"

"True," Luke agreed, but there was something more to what she'd said about her parents. He wanted to press her further, but decided against it.

He didn't mind this friendly chatter or when they worked so well together when faced with a medical emergency. Anything else was risky and he didn't want her to find a way in. He set down his glass.

"You know, I haven't seen her in a long time. I've been so busy. I should go check on her. Would you like to come?"

Her eyes lit up, as if he were offering her a thousand dollars. "Really?"

He nodded. "Really."

"I would love that."

"Grab your coat." He handed her back the portfolio. "After I check on her I'll take you back to the hotel."

It was a short drive to the stable where he kept Adele. The owner of the stable was used to Luke keeping odd hours and didn't mind that Luke was here to visit his horse at eleven in the evening.

As they got out of the car a brilliant set of northern lights erupted across the sky, because the cloud cover that had been hovering over Crater Lake the past few days had dissipated.

"Oh, my God!" Sarah said, a cloud of breath escaping past her lips. "Look at that."

"Pretty spectacular, isn't it?"

"I've never seen one. Too much light pollution."

"I can imagine that. Cities are so ugly."

She shook her head. "New York isn't ugly. The lights are beautiful. Especially around the holidays like Christmas and Valentine's Day. They light up the Empire State Building and then at Christmas there's this large tree at Rockefeller Square."

Luke wrinkled his nose. "Christmas sounds fine. Valentine's, why even bother? Besides, light pollution has nothing on this. Look straight up."

Sarah leaned back and he watched as her expression turned from amusement to awe. Now that the cloud cover was gone there were millions of stars splattered across the sky. As if Van Gogh's *Starry Night* were painted across the inky black sky.

"Amazing."

He smiled at her as he watched her stare up in amazement at the star-filled sky. He remembered so many times, after working on soldiers for countless hours, walking out of the OR and standing in the dark, staring up at the sky in Afghanistan and wishing for this.

The night sky was different.

And there was no aurora borealis.

Afghanistan's sky was beautiful, silent and cold at night, but nothing beat Montana, the mountains. Nothing beat home.

And in this moment, he wanted to take Sarah in his arms and kiss her. The urge was undeniable and he had to regain control before he did something he would regret.

Who said you'd regret it?

"Come on, I don't want you to catch your death out here. Adele won't like it too much if your teeth are chattering the whole time."

They walked into the stable and as soon as he did Adele stuck her head out of the stall, watching him.

"She knows you're here."

Luke grinned. "I know, but really she's just looking for treats."

"I don't know about that."

Luke's blood heated at her teasing tone, but he didn't acknowledge it; instead he cleared his throat and pulled out Adele's carrot treat.

"Hey, girl," he whispered against her muzzle. "How have they been treating you?"

"I'd love to paint her. She's beautiful."

"Come pet her. She doesn't mind. What she minds is people spooking her."

"Can you blame her?" Sarah asked and then she approached Adele slowly. Adele moved her head slightly, not used to the stranger who was about to touch her.

"It's okay, Adele. This is a friend. Another doctor."

Adele nickered and Sarah was able to stroke her muzzle.

"You're so beautiful, Adele," Sarah whispered.

Luke watched Sarah stroke and touch his horse, and his heart, which he'd thought was safely encased in ice, began to melt for her. She was like no other woman he'd ever met and his blood burned with the need to possess her. To have her for his own.

You can't have her.

"She's beautiful, Luke. So beautiful. I would love to ride her one day, if you'd let me."

Luke cleared his throat. "We'll see. I better get you back to your hotel. It's getting late."

"Sure." Sarah leaned forward and kissed Adele. "Good night, beauty."

And at that moment Luke knew he'd have to put some serious distance between the two of them, or he was liable to carry her off and make love to her.

Right now.

CHAPTER SIX

"YOU'RE A SADIST—you know that, right?"

Luke just grinned at her, as he stood over her in the snow. Gone was the gentle soul of a man she'd seen last night in that horse stable, the gentle giant cradling that fragile infant. That man made her ache with need. She craved him like air, but this guy, torturing her with endless simulations, this guy she wanted to club upside the head.

He'd taken her outside to where the snow plows had been piling the snow from the parking lot. The large snowbank was littered with CPR dummies, half-buried. It was a simulation massacre.

Only he'd dubbed this as avalanche training.

"I thought we were going to do avalanche training inside?"

"How would that work?" he asked.

"We could pretend. Use our imagination."

"We were, until I found this snow pile. It's perfect."

"Great," she mumbled.

"You need to work harder to dig this man out."

Sarah rolled her eyes. "I'm just a hotel doctor. I'm not going to be the first line of defense called for this. You are, your brother probably and every other first responder up here on this mountain."

"You'll be called, too. In situations like this, everyone with medical training will be called into action. That's how it works up in these remote communities. Are you saying that you're not going to come to an avalanche site because you're just a hotel doctor?"

Damn.

He was right. She wouldn't walk away from an emergency situation. She was a doctor and she was trained in trauma, just as he was.

"Fine." She kept digging away at the snow.

"Use your ice axe, too. Chip away at the hard stuff. Just don't hit the patient."

Sarah made a face at him and he just laughed.

"Do you think you can insert a chest tube in below-zero temps?"

"You're not serious, are you?"

"You said you worked in an ER. Haven't you inserted chest tubes before?"

"Of course," Sarah said. "But not in the bitter cold. Usually when I insert a chest tube it's in a trauma pod, sheltered and indoors."

Not negative eighty with a windchill.

"Ah, but sometimes there's no time to get the man down off the mountain and you have to do it in the field." Luke reached into his knapsack and pulled out a chest-tube kit. "Insert a chest tube. The patient's lungs are filling with blood—he needs a chest tube."

Sarah pulled off her mitts and fumbled with the chest-tube tray. She hadn't realized how cold her fingers actually were, but then she remembered that they'd been out here for an hour already while he went through avalanche drills with her.

The mitts were warm, but, after a while digging in the snow, their protective lining couldn't keep out the bitter cold forever. She cursed under her breath, as she prepared the chest tube and inserted it perfectly the first time.

She had always been pretty good at it.

"Good job," Luke remarked. "Now put on your gloves and keep digging."

"I need a break."

"You don't get a break on the mountain."

"This isn't a mountain. It's the snow from the main parking lot and as you can see we're the current entertainment." She pointed to the window where staff and a few guests were watching them cavorting on top of the dirty snowbank, with mannequins strewn everywhere.

"It's mandatory training, but I suppose you can have a break. You were up late last night."

Sarah smiled and tried not to blush as she thought about it. She actually hadn't wanted the night to end, though it had been for the best. If it hadn't ended she might have done something foolish, like kiss him, and maybe that one foolish kiss would have led to something more.

So it was good that the night had ended when it had.

Still, she couldn't remember when she'd had such a good time. "Yes, thanks for the fantastic dinner and the conversation. I enjoyed it."

"Me, too," he said, but then the small smile that he had for her quickly disappeared and he got up, to walk slowly down the side of the snowbank.

For a while after their awkward conversation it was pretty quiet, but then he started asking about her art and her photographs, then the tension melted away. Still, at the mention of last night the atmosphere changed and put distance between them. Maybe he was regretting last night. She certainly hoped not.

He was the closest thing she had to a friend in Crater Lake. Loneliness had never bothered her before, but that was probably because she'd been busier as a surgeon. There were guests at the hotel, but not many as the grand opening was only a couple of weeks away on Valentine's Day and, even then, guests weren't always getting sick.

So far, since her arrival in Crater Lake, she'd treated about eight sunburns, three cases of some gastroenteritis, a bear mauling and a birth of a baby. And because she wasn't as busy as she was in her previous job, she had a lot more free time. A lot more time to remind her that she was alone.

Of course, she didn't really think that if she followed her mother and sister in their footsteps that she would feel any different. Her society friends weren't really friends at all.

None of them had called her since she'd decided to cut ties with New York and move to Montana. Actually, they'd been quite horrified when she'd told them she'd given up the prestigious job and was moving to Crater Lake.

Who cares if your father pulled strings? My father did, too. It doesn't matter.

It matters to me, Nikki. My father doesn't think I can do anything. He's thinks I'm this baby. He thinks I'm helpless. I need to do this on my own.

Thinking about that last conversation with her so-called best friend made her blood pressure rise. It made her angry. It made her remember that she wasn't sure if anything in her life was her own. She wasn't sure if she'd earned anything.

It was humiliating.

Don't think about it. Don't give them the time of day.

"Do you have avalanches here every year?" she asked, hoping that the conversation could turn in another direction and distract her. It would keep her mind off her parents, her so-called friends and Luke.

"Pretty much."

"To this extent?"

Luke shook his head. "No, thankfully we haven't had a major disaster like this in a long, long time, but being in a mountainous region there are always avalanches. Always. That's why we have avalanche zones."

"How do you determine what an avalanche zone is?"

Luke clambered back up the snowbank to stand beside her.

He pointed toward the mountain. "You see that part of the mountain? You see how it's on a forty-five-degree angle? It's considered an avalanche zone. In fact we had a landslide on that slope last year."

"The landslide that almost killed Shane Draven?"

He nodded. "Yes, Dr. Petersen, my brother and I extracted him and got him down."

"All-hands-on-deck type of situation, then?"

He nodded. "You got it."

"So only steep slopes are considered dangerous."

"No, gradual slopes are at risk, too. And shady slopes can pose a threat."

"Why?" she asked. "Wouldn't the snow harden there as opposed to being in the sun?"

"No, the sun actually hardens the snow better. It melts it and then at night ice forms and seals the snowcap better. Shady slopes don't have that chance—it's just powder."

Sarah shuddered. "I hope we never have a bad avalanche, then. I wouldn't know what to do."

"As long as you're aware of the avalanche zones, you'll be fine, but that's why I'm training you. So you know what to do in an emergency. You can get seriously hurt. I broke my leg during an avalanche last winter. Avalanches are a mighty force. You need to learn how to survive." Luke moved behind her and she was very aware that he was close to her. He touched her arms and, even through all those thick layers, it was electric the way he affected her.

"What're you doing?" she asked, her voice hitching because he was touching her.

He leaned over her shoulder, his hot breath fanning the exposed skin of her neck. "I'm teaching you how to survive if you're ever caught in one. This is Special Forces training now."

"Oh," she said. "How can you fight fast-moving snow?"

"Swim." Then he took her arms and moved them gently in a breaststroke. "If you're ever caught in fast-moving snow, drop your gear because it will weigh you down, open your arms wide and swim to the side of the snow pack. Even if you can't make it across, the movement will help keep your head above the snow so you can breathe."

"Swim through snow?" Sarah smiled. "I've never heard of that before. And what happens if I'm covered with snow?"

"Bring your arms and hands to the front of your face and wiggle back and forth. It will create an air pocket and you'll be able to breathe until help arrives."

"Have you ever been trapped in an avalanche?"

"No, never trapped and never been standing at the edge of an active one. The avalanche I was injured in was because I was rescuing someone. I jumped from a helicopter and landed the wrong way, losing my footing. I've never been trapped, thank God, and I hope I never am."

"I hope so, too." Sarah looked up at him, but his face was unreadable because his sunglasses were covering his eyes, protecting them from snow blindness.

"Thanks." He cleared his throat and moved away from her. "We should get back to freeing these victims."

"Good, 'cause I have big plans this afternoon." She was teasing, but his brow furrowed.

"What kind of plans?"

"I'm going to Crater Lake. I haven't been in town since I first arrived. I have the rest of the day off and I thought I would explore."

"I don't go to town this time of year," Luke remarked.

"Why not?"

"Valentine's Day is coming." He shuddered. "The town is going a little bit crazy about it because of the hotel's grand opening that day. There's going to be a big gala or ball or something."

"I know. Silas Draven is insisting all his employees go, but it sounds kind of fun."

Luke grunted.

"You're not a fan of Valentine's Day?"

"Nope. It's pointless."

"Love is pointless?" she asked.

"No, not pointless just…there's no need to celebrate Valentine's Day with such vigor."

"Why do you hate it so much?" she asked.

He just grunted again, but avoided her question and she wondered why Luke thought love was pointless. She didn't know many guys who actually liked Valentine's Day, but Luke was acting a bit like a Grinch about it.

Why should you care?

And really she shouldn't. When did she ever give two hoots about Valentine's Day before? Usually she was in the hospital, doing surgery and stealing candy from the nurses' station as she went from OR to OR.

She'd never had a Valentine before. Still, the idea of a town getting all decked out and celebrating it sounded as if it could be fun.

"I think it will be fun to see what the town is doing," she said, trying to change the subject before Luke shut down on her again and didn't say anything else.

"Well, have fun. I have to take a group of surveyors out on a trail for some training."

"More surveyors?"

Luke nodded as he headed down the snowbank to their next patient. "I guess some more people are trying to cash in on Silas Draven's bright idea to turn Crater Lake into the next Whitefish."

"I thought you worked exclusively for Silas Draven?" she asked.

He grinned. "No, I'm a free agent. Now come on, get down here so we can save this patient and then we can call it quits for the day."

Sarah groaned but climbed down the snow pile toward him, because she was tired of being in the snow. She was cold and, really, what was the point?

Luke was a closed book.

And that was all there was to it.

Luke had lost his mind. Well, he had for a brief moment there when he'd stepped behind Sarah and touched her. He didn't know what he'd been thinking about at that moment. Clearly, he was suffering from the cold.

He'd shown other people how to swim out of fast-moving snow and he did that without touching them. He just told them to open their arms wide and mimic swimming, but with Sarah he'd reached out and guided her arms.

And he had no idea why he'd felt the need to do that.

Probably because he liked to torture himself?

Or maybe it was because he couldn't resist her. When he was around her, he wasn't himself. He didn't guard his walls as carefully as he used to. She made him weak. As if she was his Achilles' heel or something.

Yet, like a masochist he kept going back to her. Kept reaching out to her.

She'll hurt you just like Christine did.

He'd done so much for Christine when they were newly married. She'd known he was going to serve in the army, but she hadn't cared. She hadn't wanted to accompany him to Germany, but their marriage had survived. And it had survived his first tour of duty, too.

It was only when she'd demanded he end his career, that he return home to start a family with his wife, that he'd learned she didn't want him.

She didn't want to be his wife.

She'd rather be Anthony's wife, because he'd always been there for her. Unlike him.

I gave up my commission in the army for you.

It was too late for me then, Luke. It was just too late.

You could've come to Germany with me.

You never asked if I wanted to go to Germany. You just said we were moving there and, no, I didn't want to go live in Germany. I didn't want to stay here in Crater Lake either, but it was better than Germany. Of course, my dreams don't matter to you at all. Why couldn't you just open a practice with your father? What was wrong with that? Why couldn't you bend your plans for me or at least ask me if I shared them?

You want me to practice with my father and Carson. Fine. I will.

It's too late, Luke. You were selfish. My desires and wishes never mattered. I'm sorry, but I can't be with you anymore.

This was why he couldn't be near anyone. Why he thought love was pointless. For him anyway. What was the point of falling in love when it could be taken away in an instant?

Carson found love again.

He shook that thought away. That was a different situation. Carson never married Danielle. Carson was never betrayed as Luke was.

There was no room in his heart anymore. He couldn't let there be.

"So what's wrong with this patient?" Sarah used air quotes.

Luke groaned. "Why are you using air quotes? This is a serious situation."

Sarah laughed behind her hand and he couldn't help but smile. *Darn her.*

Why was it so easy to be around her?

"Okay, so what is wrong with the patient?"

"Do you know how to perform a surgical cricothyrotomy?"

"Yes. I have done one before, but not when the patient is buried in a snowdrift."

"Peel off your mitts, because you're about to do one on this mannequin. It's better to perfect it here in this simulation rather than on someone who is actually buried under snow." He tossed her a cricothyrotomy kit. "I'll time you."

"Do you want me to go through the steps as I'm doing it?" she asked as she pulled off her mitts.

"If you want."

She peeled back the cover on the kit and began to work. "Damn, my fingers are already going numb. This is going to be more difficult than I thought."

"Which is why we're practicing out here."

Sarah nodded. "Cricothyroid membrane detected and trachea grasped. Making incision."

Luke squatted down and watched her. "You're doing good."

She cursed under her breath. "My fingers are already numb."

"I know, but you can do it."

"Okay, making incision."

Luke watched as she made a beautiful incision in the skin. "Now expose the membrane with the handle of the scalpel."

"Got it." She set the scalpel down and finished the rest of the surgical cricothyrotomy. As she was suturing she cursed again. "My fingers are frozen."

"I know, but that's what happens."

Once it was finished, he handed her the mitts, which she hurriedly put on.

"You did a good job." Luke moved away from her quickly. "Well, I have to get ready and take those surveyors up the mountain. I'll see you later."

"Okay. Thanks." She scurried down off the snow pile and headed back inside. He didn't mind that. It was for the best, because she was stirring up things inside him that weren't welcome. Things that he'd thought were buried deep down.

He admired her. He had fun with her and he was highly attracted to her.

He wanted her and that was not good.

That was unacceptable.

CHAPTER SEVEN

AFTER THE TRAINING SESSION, Sarah had a shower and changed her clothes before heading into town. Her hands were still a little bit numb from performing that surgical cricothyrotomy out on the snow pile.

When she got to town she couldn't help but smile to see all the decorations going up. Hearts on the lampposts. Hearts in store windows. It was a small-town feel, like something straight from the movies, and it made her smile, even though she'd never felt so alone.

That was the thing about small towns. Everyone knew everyone. Or at least it seemed that way. Sarah was a stranger. All she knew was Luke and a couple people up at the hotel, but were they really her friends?

None of them were here with her. Really, she had no friends and it had never really bothered her before. She'd spent so many years distancing herself from her parents' world, she'd put up a wall to keep out everyone.

It hadn't bothered her until now. Even then she didn't know what she wanted. She wasn't sure that she could bring down those walls that were safe.

That were comfortable.

Sarah headed into the coffee shop that was on the corner of

the main street. She was still shivering from the cold. When she entered the coffee shop, a few people stopped their conversation and looked in her direction, but only briefly. Being new in town generated some interest, but not enough for someone to come up and talk to her. And Sarah wasn't the kind to go up and start up a conversation with a stranger either.

If they were in a hospital or her clinic, then it would be no problem. She'd be able to talk to them quite easily.

Here, not a chance.

She made her way to the counter and sat down. It was like something out of the fifties. The coffee shop was a mishmash of retro and bohemian, but as long as they served good coffee she didn't care too much.

"What'll you have?" the girl behind the counter asked.

"A large black coffee with a shot of espresso, please."

"Will do." The girl moved away and Sarah undid her jacket and glanced around at all the people chatting. She envied them a bit.

"You're the new doctor in town, aren't you?"

Sarah turned to see a short, blonde woman slip into the seat next to her. It shocked her. In Manhattan this would've never happened. People she encountered in coffee shops there were always in a rush or kept to themselves, just as she did.

"I am," Sarah said. "I'm Dr. Ledet."

"I know." She grinned, her blue eyes twinkling. "I'm Dr. Esme Petersen."

"You're the cardio-thoracic surgeon."

Esme nodded. "I am. Luke mentioned that there was a new doctor up at the hotel. He also mentioned that you briefly worked with Dr. Eli Draven."

"I did. Do you know Dr. Draven?"

Esme nodded. "He trained me."

"I'm impressed. Dr. Draven is a world-class surgeon. Wait, Dr. Petersen, weren't you the one who inserted that chest tube into Shane Draven last summer?"

"I was," Esme said. "How did you know about that?"

"I was the surgeon in Missoula that operated on him."

Esme frowned slightly. "I thought you were from New York?"

"I was training some surgeons on a new technique when I was asked to help with incoming."

"What will you have, Dr. Petersen?" the girl asked as she set down Sarah's coffee in front of her.

"Cappuccino, please, Mary. Thanks."

"Sure thing." Mary walked away again.

"How are you enjoying Crater Lake?" Esme asked.

"It's been great." Sarah took a sip of her coffee. "It's quiet, though."

"Oh, no," Esme said. "You didn't just say that, did you?"

"What?"

"Quiet. I thought you were a trauma surgeon?" Esme said teasingly.

Sarah laughed. "How do you know so much about me?"

"It's a small town and you're new and shiny." Esme winked. "I was new and shiny last summer. I remember clearly."

Mary set down the cappuccino in front of Esme and disappeared again. Sarah could see that a heart was made in the foam.

"Aww, that's sweet," Sarah remarked.

Esme made a face. "I don't like Valentine's Day."

"What? I thought a heart surgeon would love Valentine's Day."

Esme took a swizzle stick and stabbed at the foam heart. "You'd think that, right?"

Sarah laughed. "You're the second person I've met in this town that hates Valentine's Day."

"Really? Who is the other person? Perhaps I should befriend them."

"Dr. Luke Ralston."

Esme laughed. "Luke? Oh, yeah, I forgot. He's such a grouch. I'm surprised he's talking to you, though."

"Why is that?"

"Well, he had a serious hate on for the surgeon who argued with him in Missoula."

Sarah started to laugh. "Yes. We didn't exactly get off on the right foot and I think I've been a thorn in his side."

"That doesn't surprise me. Although, it could work both ways. I think he might be a thorn in your side, too. He is in mine."

"Is he?"

"I'm dating Luke's brother, Carson. So, yeah, he's a bit of a pain in my butt."

"Has he ever dragged you out in the woods and forced you to train for emergency situations in minus-forty weather?" Sarah asked.

"Oh, he made you do that? What a jerk."

They both laughed at that. It was nice to chat with someone. It was nice to talk to someone and feel as if it wasn't superficial. She'd never had an easy chat with another woman before and certainly not another surgeon. She was used to being one of many sharks in a shark pond.

Once the coffee was done, Esme insisted on paying for both and they walked back out into the cold together and stood on the street.

"Thanks for having coffee with me. I was feeling a bit isolated up there," Sarah said.

Esme nodded and wound her knitted infinity scarf around, making a pretty knot in it. "I get it. I was once the new kid in town. Some people around here don't really like change. A few resent the resort community up there and the fact that there are a couple more that will be built, but most are coming around to the idea. It brings more business."

"How do you feel about a fourth doctor in town?" Sarah asked. "Is your practice suffering or is the other Dr. Ralston's?"

"No. It's steady. I get a lot of people from the outlying towns as I'm the closest cardio doctor. Were you worried?"

"Yeah, I didn't want to see an old family practice collapse."

"It won't." Esme reached out and squeezed her arm. "We

should have coffee again or maybe even dinner. Carson's not a bad cook. Maybe we can even convince Luke to come down off that mountain."

Blood heated her cheeks and Sarah shook her head. "I seriously doubt that. He's up there now gallivanting around with surveyors."

Esme smiled. "Well, we'd still like to have you over sometime. Have a good day. Watch out for falling hearts."

"What?"

Esme pointed to the lamppost. "They tend to fall in a strong wind. It happened at Christmas. A Santa landed butt-first on a woman. It wasn't pretty."

Sarah nodded. "Thanks."

Esme walked down Main Street toward the clinic. Sarah glanced up at the glittery, tinsel hearts that were hanging off the lampposts. It made her smile. She jammed her hands in her pockets and headed back to her truck, but as she was walking back to the parking lot there was a rumble. A deep hollow sound followed by a large crack, like thunder, and then a roar like a jet plane was flying overhead. Sarah spun around and watched in horror as a cloud of snow spiraled up into the sky and moved like a wave down the side of the mountain.

It was an avalanche. She could hear screams from other residents of the town as the avalanche wiped away everything in its path.

It was close to home. It was large and it made Sarah's heart stop in her throat.

At least it was on the peak opposite the hotel. The peak was a remote site that could potentially be another hotel.

Then it hit her. That was the Lakeview trail that she'd been on only a couple of days ago. It was the trail that Luke was planning to take a group of surveyors up to.

Luke.

He was up there somewhere on that mountain and could be trapped.

Esme came rushing back up behind her. "Oh, my God. We have to get up that mountain."

"I drove the hotel's truck down."

Esme nodded. "Come help me grab supplies. Carson is already on his way from our place, but we need to get up there and see if anyone's been injured. Do you know where Luke is?"

"He was up there." Sarah pointed at the peak. "He was with surveyors."

Esme cursed under her breath. "I'm sure he's fine. He knows the danger signs. He wouldn't take them somewhere unsafe. Come on."

Sarah nodded, but she felt numb.

As if this weren't happening.

They just did a practice run of an avalanche emergency and now one had actually happened? She'd thought that Crater Lake would be a little bit more laid-back, but a bear mauling, a birth and now an avalanche? This place was just as busy as any city.

And last summer there was a landslide?

She'd thought living in the mountains would be peaceful, but she was beginning to realize just how isolated and dangerous it could be and she prayed that Luke had had the sense to see that taking the surveyors up on the Lakeview trail was dangerous and that he'd got out of the way of the avalanche.

"Luke, you're okay?"

Luke turned around to see his brother approaching the hotel. He was out of breath, as if he'd been running.

"I'm fine," Luke said.

Carson nodded and gave him a hug. "When I heard that crack I feared the worst. I knew you were going out on the trails today."

Luke nodded. "I saw the break in the cap before I set out. So I kept the surveyors at bay. I really thought, though, for a while that it wouldn't go and that they would be ticked off at me for wasting their time."

"Was anyone else on the mountain?" Carson asked.

"No. I shut the trails down to everyone else until that bear was caught. The game warden hadn't given me the okay to re-open them since the bear was subdued. We've had some mild temperatures at night and I knew we were due for an avalanche. I'm glad it was contained somewhat, though I'm still waiting to see how far it reached. There are some remote cabins in the way. I'm hoping it didn't get as far as Nestor's place."

Carson nodded. "Me, too. I'm glad you're okay."

Luke was going to say something further when he saw the resort truck driven by Sarah pull up and in the passenger side he saw Esme.

Great. Just great.

"Who's that with Esme?"

"Dr. Ledet," Luke mumbled.

Carson grinned. "No wonder I haven't seen you for a while. I thought you were spending too much time up at the hotel."

"What's that supposed to mean?" Luke asked, glaring at his brother.

Carson nodded in Sarah's direction. "I've seen her. I'm not blind. Isn't that similar to what you said to me in the summer when Esme came to town?"

"Ha-ha. Your witty humor amuses me."

Carson laughed out loud. "This explains a lot."

"It explains nothing," Luke snapped. "And you better remember that. I do have a large hank of rope in my truck. I still know how to set snares that entangle animals bigger than you."

"Dad said you weren't allowed to snare me anymore, remember?"

"No. I don't." Luke turned his back on his brother, giving Carson the hint he was done with this conversation and not to push him further. He looked back as Carson headed toward the truck to greet Esme and tell her that no one was hurt. Esme looked relieved and Carson kissed her.

Darn him.

Just for a moment Luke was jealous that his brother had that. Then he saw Sarah with a knapsack walking through the snow toward him and he smiled. She had a knapsack with her. She was learning and it made his heart melt, just a bit.

Don't let her in.

"I thought you were in town?" Luke asked gruffly as she set her bag down on the roof of Carson's truck.

"I was and then an avalanche hit. Was anyone hurt?"

"No. You are safe from performing any surgical cricothyrotomies for the moment."

She smiled. "That's great news. It looked so large I thought for sure someone was going to end up injured or worse."

"That actually wasn't too big. That was a medium."

Her eyes widened. "You're joking, right?"

"I don't joke."

"Right. I forgot. You're Mr. Serious all the time."

Luke grinned. "How did you know to bring up Dr. Petersen? I didn't know you knew each other."

"I didn't know her until today. We had coffee together."

Luke's stomach twisted. *Crap.* "What did you two talk about?"

"Wouldn't you like to know?" Her smile stretched from ear to ear.

Oh, Lord.

"Dr. Ralston?"

Luke turned to see one of the rangers coming toward him. "What's wrong, Officer Kyc?"

"The avalanche's zone has extended past Nestor's place. You're the most trained individual to go out and get him. If he was ten years younger and not suffering from cancer he'd be fine up there on his own, but…"

Luke nodded. "I'll get my gear together and go get him."

"Thanks, Dr. Ralston."

"Who's Nestor?" Sarah asked.

"He's a hermit. He likes to keep to himself. He really lives off the grid, taught me everything I know about surviving on the mountain. As much as the army did, but he's getting on in age and I'm not going to leave him up there to die."

"I'll go with you."

"Are you crazy?"

Sarah glared at him. "He might be injured. How are you going to get him down yourself?"

She had a point.

Carson wasn't equipped at the moment to go with him to get Nestor. It would take him over half an hour to get back home and change. There wasn't time. Luke wanted to get to Nestor before nightfall.

"Fine. Hurry up and get changed."

Sarah nodded and headed into the hotel. Luke scrubbed a hand over his face. What was he getting into?

She's just going to help me. Nestor needs help.

That was all there was to it. They were doing their job. That was it. They would go up and get Nestor and bring him back down to the hotel until they could clear a safe path for him to get to and from town. Luke had been giving him heck since the snow started to fly that he should move to town because of his cancer treatments, but Nestor wouldn't leave the mountain.

And really he couldn't blame him.

The mountain might be a harsh, cold and hard mistress, but she stood the test of time. She was more reliable than a heart.

CHAPTER EIGHT

THE SNOWSHOE WALK up to Nestor's cabin was brutal. Sarah knew it was going to be a long haul, but she really didn't have any idea until they were trudging through the snow, roped together for protection. Just in case one of them was swept away.

It terrified her, but she wouldn't back down.

She could do this. She was doing this.

At least Luke didn't treat her as if she were incapable of helping. In fact, he was the first person in a long time who actually appreciated her help. Instead of doing stuff for her, he taught her how. He pushed her to her limits. Made her work and feel things that she'd thought were buried deep inside her.

She hadn't thought that he would let her, to be honest. She knew that he was wary about letting her accompany him, she could see that plainly on his face, but one thing she'd learned about Luke Ralston was he wasn't an idiot.

Sarah knew, just as much as he did, that it would be faster for her to get suited up and assist him than it would for his brother, Carson. She knew that she would be traversing into dangerous territory, but a life was at stake.

She wasn't going to pass up on that. That wasn't the kind of doctor she was.

So without complaint she'd strapped on the heavy rucksack

laden with supplies, strapped on the snowshoes and had let Carson tie a rope between Luke and her. It was a lifeline, just in case she slipped and fell. Or just in case the snowcap decided it would crack again and sweep them away.

When she finally saw the cabin in a small clearing she let out an inward sigh of relief at the sight of it and she quickened her pace to keep up with Luke.

Luke stopped in a small copse of trees and set down his rucksack, but he didn't make a move to untie it.

"Why are we stopping?" Sarah asked, though secretly she was glad. She was in pretty good shape, but she wasn't used to the strenuous pace that Luke had kept, or to how much of a sweat she'd worked up under all her winter gear.

"We need a break. Just five minutes to catch our breath and have some water. You okay with that?"

"Perfectly." Sarah dropped her backpack next to Luke's and pulled out her canteen, taking a big swig of water.

"I'm impressed you brought a backpack," he said.

"Of course. I wouldn't have heard the end of it if I hadn't."

He chuckled. "This is true."

"So, if this Nestor guy is a hermit how do you know him? Don't hermits usually keep to themselves?"

"*Hermit* is probably the wrong word. Nestor just likes to live off the land. He's a pioneer man."

"And how do you know him?"

"He taught me everything I know about survival. I could make up a brilliant story about how he saved my life, or something, but really it was just because my father and he were friends. I always took a real interest in what he had to say. He's like a second father to me. Since my dad moved away and my brother, Carson, started dating Dr. Petersen I've been hanging around Nestor quite a bit." Luke smiled. "He's the only one who ever believed in me when I went to the army."

"Your father didn't approve?"

Luke snorted. "Not really. He wanted me to go to the same

medical school as my brother and then to train in the same hospital. My father wanted Carson and I to be partners, but that's not what I wanted. I never wanted that." Luke frowned. "Anyway, Nestor was the only one who told me to follow my dreams."

Sarah was a bit taken aback. It was the first time Luke had ever really talked, opening up warmly about someone else. She'd thought he kept everyone out. That he was cold and closed-off. But underneath that hard surface there was something more about him.

Something warm and loving.

"Is he the one who taught you how to build a log cabin?"

Luke grinned. "He is. He helped me quite a bit. He would like me to live more off the grid, but I do like some modern conveniences."

"Are you sure about that, Pa?" Sarah teased. "You did make all your furniture."

"Yeah, but I like electricity and running water too much." Luke stood up. "We'd better get going. Night falls fast, and we don't want to be trying to bring Nestor down off the mountain in the dark."

Sarah nodded. "Okay."

They packed their canteens back in their bags and headed out on their journey again. Now she understood why Luke was so concerned about getting up there to see if Nestor was okay. It wasn't just the first responder training in him. Luke *cared* about Nestor.

He was worried, and she couldn't even begin to imagine what he must be feeling.

Can't you?

Then she remembered how panicked she'd been when the avalanche had first hit and she'd thought Luke was up there in its path. That was probably nothing compared to worrying about someone who meant something to you.

Luke means something to you, though, doesn't he?

Sarah shook that thought away. There was no time to think

about things like that. She had to stay focused on the task at hand. She wouldn't be the one to slow Luke down from getting to his friend in an emergency situation.

When they were at the house, they dropped their knapsacks, undid the rope and took off their snowshoes, propping them inside the lean-to.

"If you think I'm rustic, Nestor is worse," Luke said, kicking the snow off his boots. Then he pounded on the door. "Nestor, it's Ralston. There's been an avalanche."

There was no response.

Luke knocked again. "Nestor, open up."

"It's awfully dark in there and there's no smoke coming from the chimney," Sarah said.

Luke grinned. "I'm impressed you noticed that. Most people from the city don't think about a chimney or smoke from a fire. I'm going to check in the back window."

Sarah nodded while Luke put his snowshoes back on and walked to the back of the house. Sarah stood there waiting. The only sound was her breaths. There was no wind howling in the natural wind break where Nestor's cabin was nestled. There were no birds, no rustling of evergreen needles. It was deadly calm, like right before a storm.

It was a nice spot, but as she glanced through the forest she could see a wall of snow from where the avalanche had barely missed his cabin. It was at least six feet high, with broken and snapped trees everywhere.

She shuddered. It was eerie. Something was not right. She didn't know what, but she could feel it in her bones that something was wrong.

"He's gone," Luke said as he came back into the lean-to.

"You mean he's dead?"

"No, I mean there was a note that he got down before the avalanche hit. He left for Missoula two days ago for his chemo treatment."

"For a hermit who lives off the grid on the side of the mountain I'm surprised he's undertaking chemo."

Luke chuckled. "Well, that might be my doing and his son's, too. Greg came up here last summer and gave his father a stern talking-to. He tried to convince him to move to Missoula with him permanently, but he refused. They struck this bargain. Well, the rangers will be glad to hear that he's not in harm's way. Though I wish he'd checked in with them or me at least."

"So we can head back to the hotel?"

He nodded. "Yep. Sorry, I know you're a bit bushed. Though I'm glad you came, and I'm glad you came prepared and were able to keep up with me. I know I move faster on snowshoes than you're used to."

"It's no problem. I had a good teacher."

Luke's easygoing smile disappeared. "Yes...well, I'm glad you came. Had he been injured, two sets of medically trained hands would have been better than one. Especially when both sets are trained in trauma."

She had obviously made him uncomfortable, which had not been her intention. She'd meant every word she'd said about him being a good teacher. A month ago she wouldn't have had a clue what to do.

She shrugged. "It's no big deal. I'm just glad he's not injured and we don't have to drag him back down."

"Me, too. Let's go before it gets too dark."

Sarah nodded and put on her snowshoes and slung on her knapsack. Luke led the way out of the lean-to and retied the rope between them. That was when she noticed that it was getting dark. Fast. The clouds were low, thick and full of snow. She might not be native to Montana, but, after living in New York and now here, she could recognize snow clouds.

"Do you think a storm is coming?" she asked when they were through the trees back out into the clearing, following the same path they'd taken before.

Luke stopped and looked around. "Yeah, I think so, but we'll beat it."

"You sure?"

"Positive, but we…" He trailed off as he looked up the slope. She looked where he was looking and saw a crack, spreading across a huge chunk of snow.

Oh, my God.

The horror dawned on her fast, because they were right in its path.

"Throw your pack and kick off your snowshoes. Now!" Luke shouted.

Sarah's pulse thundered in her ears and she heaved her knapsack as far as she could, before kicking off her snowshoes. She sank into the deep snow as a loud crack thundered across the slope. The rumbling struck dread in her, right down to her very core, as she tried to run back to the cabin. If the cabin was buried, at least it would be some kind of shelter. Nestor had been smart and built it into the slope, but running through the snow toward salvation was like trying to move through deep sand. It was heavy and it felt as if her limbs weighed a hundred pounds.

"Remember to swim, Sarah. Swim!"

Luke was close to her. All Sarah wanted to do was cling to him, but survival instincts kicked in and as that wave of snow hit she used her arms to swim, fighting the current of snow that tried to drive her down the mountain. Her body screamed in agony as she swam, the rope between Luke and her taut. She didn't even know if he was still there.

All she had to do was keep swimming. She had to keep her head above the snow. She had to breathe.

There was a yank on her arm and she was pulled out of the torrent of snow and fell on top of Luke, who was gasping for breath. One arm tightened around her as the snow roared and thundered past them.

She buried her face in his chest and tried not to cry. She just clung to him. He was her lifeline in this moment. When the roar stopped, only then did she lift her head up and see that their path was cut off and the snow swirling around them was a storm just getting started.

She didn't know how long they had been fighting the avalanche. It felt like hours the way her body ached. Snow had crept through every crack of her snowsuit.

"You okay?" Luke asked. There was a deep cut to his forehead, by his hairline. It was bleeding profusely.

"I'm fine," she whispered and then she got off him and stood up, her legs weak and her head spinning. "You're bleeding."

"It's a scalp laceration. I'm okay. We need to get to shelter." Luke got up and winced. "At least we have Nestor's place."

Sarah saw that they had been pushed farther down quite a bit, but at least Nestor's cabin had only been partially buried. The lean-to was uncovered and they had access to the door. It was a way inside.

"Come on," Luke said. "We'll get inside and start a fire. Once the storm dies down, they'll send for help."

Sarah nodded and then she spied the backpacks a few feet down at the edge of the pile. "Look, the backpacks made it."

"Good. The snowshoes didn't. I'll break the path. You follow."

Sarah stayed close behind Luke as he broke a path down to the backpacks. Her legs were like jelly, but the storm was getting worse and they had to seek shelter. Once they retrieved their backpacks they headed up to Nestor's cabin.

Luke managed to force the door and they were out of the wind. It was cold in the cabin, but Sarah didn't care. At least they were safe in here. It was shelter.

"Can you tape some gauze to my lac?" Luke asked.

"You'll need more than a dressing. You'll need stitches."

"I know, but first you'll need some boiling water to clean it out and sterilize and to do that I need to start a fire. It's hard to operate with blood dripping in my eye."

"Sure." Sarah pulled out the first-aid kit and did a quick patchwork on Luke's laceration. Then she helped him bring in a lot of wood. While he started the fire in the fireplace, she grabbed a large pot and filled it with snow from outside the lean-to so they could boil it. Nestor had an old-fashioned water pump, but it was frozen.

It didn't take Luke long to get a fire started, which began to heat up the small cabin in no time. Sarah pulled out their sleeping bags from the bottom of their knapsacks.

"Zip them together," Luke said, wincing slightly.

"What?" she asked.

"Body heat in the night. Nestor only has one small bunk over there. We won't both fit and he's shorter than I am. I know I won't fit on that bunk."

Sarah nodded and zipped the bags together. "I should really take a look at that laceration. Get it cleaned and stitched up. The blood is soaking through the gauze."

Luke agreed, his face pale as he sat down in front of the fire. Sarah found an oil lamp and lit it so she could see a little bit better. She carefully peeled off the bandage and inspected the wound and his head.

"I don't feel a fracture."

"I know," he said. "It's just a laceration. I'm fine."

Sarah glared at him. "Don't play brave with me. It's a deep lac. I'm the one with the needle. I'm sorry I don't have any anesthetic. I do have some morphine for after, though."

He shook his head. "It's okay. I'm not playing brave. I've been stitched up before like this. Just do it."

"Okay. At least it won't need a lot of stitches."

He didn't say much, just looked off into the distance over her shoulder as she got ready to suture. There were a few winces, but mostly he didn't make a peep as she threw four stitches into his forehead, disinfected and then bandaged up the wound. She threw the bloody gauze into the fire and then used the antibacterial foam to clean her hands.

Luke got up and started rummaging around in Nestor's cupboards.

"What're you looking for?" she asked.

"Something to numb the pain," he said.

"I have morphine."

"Ah ha!" Luke pulled out a bottle of amber liquid. "Whiskey. Much better than morphine."

She laughed. "Much better, but won't Nestor be angry that we're rifling through his cupboards?"

"Nah, he'll know this is an emergency. I'll replace everything we have to use."

Sarah began to shiver again. "I think my socks are wet."

"Mine, too. We have to get out of these damp, cold clothes and into the sleeping bag to preserve body heat."

What?

Only she couldn't say that out loud, because her mouth dropped open and she felt a bit dumbstruck at the moment.

Luke moved past her and started to strip off his outer gear and then took off his flannel shirt, exposing his chest and back. Sarah didn't need a fire at that moment, because she realized that he was expecting her to climb naked into a double sleeping bag with him.

"I can't get naked."

He glanced around, hanging up his clothes. The only thing on him was his trousers and she couldn't help but notice how incredibly ripped and tanned Luke was under all those flannel shirts he wore. Her body was very aware that she was going to see all of him in a matter of moments and that he would see her.

She'd never undressed in front of a man before.

The last time she made love to a man, she didn't undress in front of him. It was done in dignity with the lights out and, even then, she really couldn't remember much about that encounter because, like the rest of her past romantic life, it hadn't been overly memorable.

Who says you're going to have sex?

The cabin was heating up and it wasn't just the fire.

"What's wrong? Why can't you get undressed?"

She crossed her arms. "I don't get naked in front of strange men."

"I'm not a stranger. Besides, if you don't you'll most likely get hypothermia. Okay, I'll close my eyes until you get into the sleeping bag. I swear to you, nothing untoward will happen."

"What about the extra clothes in the knapsack?" she asked. "You told me to always pack extra clothes."

"They'll be too cold and we've been exposed outside too long. This is the fastest way to get our temperature back up. Besides, we're doctors. It's not like we haven't seen naked bodies before."

Dammit.

He had a point. The only difference was, she hadn't seen him naked before and vice versa. There was a difference between seeing a patient for an exam and seeing a man you were highly attracted to, naked.

"Okay." She began to peel off her clothes and hung them near the fire so they could dry and just as she did that Luke peeled off his pants and her breath caught in her throat at the sight of his very muscular, well-defined backside.

She tried not to look, because she didn't want him to see the blush that she knew was slowly creeping up her neck into her cheeks.

This was going to be a very long night.

CHAPTER NINE

LUKE WAS TRYING very hard to ignore the fact that in a few moments he was going to be inches away from Sarah and that she was going to be naked. He'd fantasized about having her naked in his bed before, but this was not how he'd pictured it.

When he glanced over at her, her pale cheeks were flaming red and she was looking away. He felt bad for her, so he walked across the room to Nestor's bed and wrapped a blanket around his waist. Then grabbed another quilt and walked back over to her.

"I'm respectable."

She opened her eyes and he held out the blanket. "Where did you get these?"

"Nestor's bed. Besides, the extra blankets will help keep us warm."

She nodded. "Thanks."

He moved away from her and tried not to look at her as he climbed into the sleeping bag. He poured himself a shot of whiskey and swigged it down quickly, trying to numb the pain of his throbbing head and also to try and distract himself from the fact that Sarah was undressing a few feet away from him.

How many times had he thought about this? Too many times.

His pulse was racing, his blood had heated and he was fighting to control his yearning for her.

The only trouble was being in Sarah's presence did that to him.

When he was in her presence he lost all control.

He wished he could just take her in his arms and make love to her like he desperately wanted to.

Don't think about it.

Only he couldn't help it and he stifled a groan.

"You okay?" she asked as she wrapped the blanket around her and then climbed into the sleeping bag beside him.

"My head hurts, just a bit." He didn't want to admit to her that the groan he'd been trying to get under control had nothing to do with the injury to his head.

"Well, that's to be expected. I can get the morphine."

"Stop pushing drugs on me." He winked at her and she laughed, but she still seemed nervous.

She's not the only one.

"Fine. Have another shot of whiskey, then."

"I will," Luke said and he poured her a cup, handing it to her. "First you. It'll warm you up."

"Thanks." She took a sip. "That does help."

He nodded. "I told you it would. You did really good out there today."

"You taught me well." She took another sip of whiskey. "You told me to swim and I did, but that…"

"I know. When that avalanche hit us and I started to swim, it was powerful. More powerful than any current I've swam in, in water. Being in that avalanche was like nothing I've ever felt before. I'm glad we weren't swept away down the side of the mountain. It was a minor one."

"That was minor? I thought you'd experienced an avalanche before?"

"I've seen them, I've helped those injured, but never have I experienced almost being swept away by one."

"At least we weren't trapped." Sarah shivered; he could hear her teeth chattering. So he moved closer, wrapping his arm around her. His blood pounding between his ears, because he was touching her.

You're just keeping her warm. That's all.

Her breath hitched in her throat the moment he pulled her close. Her skin was so soft, the flowery scent of her silken, blond hair surrounding him and he wanted to pull it out of the braid she'd put it in and run his fingers through it.

"No, we weren't trapped. That's a good thing." Only right now in this cabin they were trapped by the storm. Being here with her, with nothing between them, was more dangerous to him than being trapped in that snowstorm.

He was nervous, but he couldn't pull himself away.

You're just warming her, he told himself again.

"That feels good," she whispered.

"What does?" he asked.

"Your arm around me." Then she moved in closer to him and touched his face. Her fingers lightly brushing over his skin, which made him feel as if he were on fire. Her lips so close to his. Then her fingers touched his lips and he closed his eyes, trying to regain control of his senses, but before he could maintain that control, before he could stop what was happening her lips pressed against his in a feather-light kiss. He tried not to cup her face and drag her tight against his body, as he wanted to. He'd forgotten what a woman's kiss felt like.

He'd forgotten what passion tasted like. It had been far too long and he was caught off guard by it. It rocked him to his very core and he didn't want it to end. He wanted more.

Oh, God.

Luke needed to put an end to this before he got carried away and forgot himself. Before he forgot why he distanced himself from women, about why he distanced himself from her.

"Why did you do that?" he asked.

"I wanted to. I've wanted to for some time." Her blue eyes

sparkled in the dim flickering light thrown from the fire. "I want to kiss you again, Luke."

"I don't think that's wise," he said, though his body screamed yes, yes, yes.

"I don't think it's particularly wise either," she whispered, but then her hands ran through his hair and she was kissing him urgently.

He should push her away, but the moment she sighed and melted against him he was a lost man.

He was completely lost to her.

Luke undid the braid in her hair and gently ran his fingers through it. It was as soft as he'd imagined. Like silk. It fanned over her bare shoulder and he couldn't help but brush it away. Ever since he'd first met her, he'd dreamed of touching her skin, her hair, and now he was.

He'd forgotten what it was like.

Christine had hurt him so bad with her betrayal and he'd buried these feelings deep inside. He didn't ever want to feel like that again, but in this moment he was reveling in being with Sarah and he was worried that if he indulged then he wouldn't ever be able to stop.

That he'd want more.

And he couldn't have more.

He wouldn't put his heart at risk again. When Christine left him, he'd promised himself he wouldn't let another woman affect him like that. Love just brought pain.

Who said anything about love?

He moved away. He couldn't do this even though he desperately wanted to.

"What's wrong?" Sarah asked.

"I don't know if we should be doing this."

"Doing what?" she asked.

"Kissing."

"I think we should be." Sarah touched his face again and then kissed him. "I don't think we should stop."

"Sarah, I can't promise you anything."

She smiled at him. "I'm not asking for promises. I just want you. Here and now."

"I want you, too. I can't help myself, but I do."

And it was true. When it came to Sarah, he couldn't help himself.

Sarah wasn't sure what made her reach out and kiss Luke. It wasn't the whiskey, that was for certain. She could hold her drink better than most. No, she was sure it was due to the fact that moments ago she'd almost died.

Working in the ER Sarah had seen countless people face death, sometimes because of the simplest reasons, like a reaction to a medication or food and sometimes because of something more complicated that damaged their body. She'd wrestled with death in the OR, saving patients while she operated on them and, though they could never remember that moment when they came so close to losing the battle because they'd been under general anesthesia, she always wondered what it might be like.

Did they feel anything?

Did they see their life flash before their eyes, even in a dreamless sleep?

Did they understand how close they came and how hard they fought, how hard she fought for them? Overcoming death for her patients was a high. The lives she saved meant more to her than all the money her parents had.

It was why she did what she did.

So when her moment came it was surreal. When the snow came roaring down the hill toward her, there was a clarity.

Live or die.

And she chose life. She fought hard. She swam and when she came through it, it hit her how many chances she'd passed on. Not when it came to her career, but her life. She'd been fighting her whole life to prove to her parents she was her own person, to the point that she didn't know when to stop fighting. Maybe life didn't always have to be such a fight? Maybe she hadn't really been living her life, because she was so busy trying to show everyone that she was capable of doing things on her own that life was passing her by. She wasn't even sure anymore.

When she thought she had been living her own life, she hadn't. Her father had made that painfully clear. She'd spent so long building up walls that now she wanted Luke on the other side with her.

She wanted to live her life. Take chances, take risks, because even though that avalanche had been the most terrifying thing she'd ever experienced, surviving after the fact was equally scary.

Right now, in this moment with Luke, she just wanted to feel. She chose this and she wanted it.

Really she shouldn't but she couldn't fight it anymore. She wanted Luke as she'd never wanted another man before. It was something fierce. Primal, even. It scared her and thrilled her.

She wanted to feel again.

"Sarah, I'll ask again. Are you sure?"

"I'm sure."

Luke rolled over, pressing her against the floor and laying kisses against her lips, her neck and lower. He brushed his knuckles down the side of her face and kissed where her pulse raced under her skin.

"You make me feel," he whispered. Then he leaned down and brushed another kiss against her lips, light and then urgent. His body was pressed against hers. It made her feel right and she loosened the extra blanket he'd given her so they could be skin to skin. She opened her legs to let him settle between her thighs. Sarah arched her hips. She wanted him.

She craved him.

"I have to stop," Luke moaned.

"Why?"

"I don't have protection. One thing I didn't pack for."

Sarah grinned. "It's okay. I'm on birth control and I'm clean."

"So am I. Are you sure you want to, though?"

"Yes. I want to. The question is do you want me?" She bucked her hips and he groaned.

"Oh, I want you."

"How much?"

Luke kissed her again, his tongue pushing past her lips, entwining with hers, showing her just how much he wanted her.

"I want you so much." He ran his hands over her body, his hands hot, branding her skin as he touched her.

"I've tried hard to resist you," Sarah whispered against his neck. "You drive me crazy."

He grinned. "I want you, too, Sarah."

Luke's lips captured hers in a kiss, silencing any more words between them. Sarah pulled him closer and wrapped her legs against his waist. His hands slipped down her sides.

"So beautiful," he murmured.

His hand slid between them and he began to stroke her. Sarah bit her lip to stop from crying out. She wanted so much more. She wanted Luke inside her. She wanted him to take her and make her feel again.

Sarah wanted Luke to remind her of who she was, because she couldn't remember. She just wanted to forget it all and get lost in this one moment with him.

"I love having you under me," Luke whispered against her neck. "I want to be inside you."

"I want you, too."

He pushed her down, covering her body with his and thrusting into her. Sarah cried out then. She couldn't help herself. Being joined with him was overwhelming, but it was what she wanted. It was what she needed.

"You feel so good," he moaned. "Damn."

She moved her hips, urging him to move, but he wouldn't. He just held her still, buried deep inside her.

"You're evil," she gasped.

"I know."

Luke moved slowly at first, taking his time, and it drove her crazy. She wanted him hard and fast. She wanted to feel him moving inside her. She urged him to go faster until he lost all control and was thrusting against her hard and fast. Then she could feel her body succumbing to the sweet release she was searching for. Pleasure overtook her and she cried out again, digging her nails into his back, making him hiss in pain, but it didn't stop him. He kept going until his own release came a moment later.

He rolled away onto his back and she curled up on his chest, just listening to his heart race. It was soothing and reassuring. She'd always liked the sound of the heart. It meant life. Then tears started to roll down her face.

"Sarah, are you okay?"

She sat up, trying to brush the tears away. "I'm fine."

"Do you regret what happened?"

"No," she said quickly. "No. I wanted that to happen. What happened here tonight was a long time coming. It's just…we could've died today."

He smiled softly. "But we didn't."

"I know. You know, it was in that moment on the slope that I couldn't recall if the life I've been living has been my own."

Luke's brow furrowed. "How do you mean?"

"Everything I've accomplished is because my father has had a hand in it."

"What?"

"You want to know why I came here? I came here because my father got my last job for me. Just like every other job. So I came here, without his help. I'm tired of being labelled as his helpless daughter."

Luke nodded. "Stepping out of a parent's shadow can be hard. And you're far from helpless."

Sarah sighed. "I'm not sure if I know myself anymore."

"I understand that."

She frowned. "Do you? You're living out your dream here."

Luke shrugged. "I love the mountains, but it wasn't my dream to be a lone wolf. I was married before."

"You were?"

He nodded. "She left me for my best friend while I was overseas."

"No wonder you have trust issues."

"Yeah. I suppose I do."

Luke turned from her, withdrawing from her once more. But for a moment she had seen a little piece of himself that he kept hidden from the world.

Sarah had been absolutely shocked to learn that he'd been married before. He just didn't seem the type to settle down with a wife, and she couldn't help but wonder what he'd been like before he'd become this walled-off man.

And no wonder, when his wife had left him for his best friend. Two people he'd trusted completely had betrayed him.

It explained so much, but Sarah had a feeling there was more to it than that. There was something else he wasn't saying.

"It's hard to trust when you trust no one."

Luke turned back around. "What?"

"At least you have a family to turn to. I don't. I can't rely on my parents."

"Why?"

"They were never around."

"I'm sorry."

Sarah shrugged. "My mother preferred the company of her friends over her children and my dad was too involved with his businesses. Money drives him."

"Must've been a lonely childhood."

She nodded. The words, though the truth, stung. Her whole life had been lonely up until now. She had just never realized it.

How could she trust a man who guarded his heart so? He'd never open up fully. His ex-wife had hurt him terribly, and in the short time Sarah had known him she'd learned that he didn't give people a second chance.

He was stubborn that way.

Which was a shame.

"It was. I sometimes felt invisible," she said. She hadn't intended to say that thought out loud, but she had.

He moved toward her and touched her face briefly "I get not knowing who you are anymore. I get it, but I want you to know. I see you."

She wanted to believe him. She really did, but she didn't think anyone could see her, especially when she couldn't even see herself. So long she'd been under her family's thumb, she didn't even know it. How could she believe him, when she couldn't even believe in herself?

"You don't believe me," Luke said.

"What?"

"Your expression. I can read you like a book."

She glared at him. "Thanks."

"It's something I've learned to do as an army medic."

"Why did you leave the army?"

His demeanor changed almost instantly. "What?"

"What made you change your mind about the army?"

"I thought I had a wife waiting for me."

"I'm sorry."

Luke shrugged and then unzipped his side of the sleeping bag. "Are you hungry?"

"Sure." She watched him as he dug in his knapsack for his dry pair of pants and slipped them on. "Hey, I thought you said we shouldn't wear our extra clothes?"

He grinned. "That was when we were still damp and cold. I bet you're warm now."

She blushed and then grabbed her knapsack, pulling out the dry set of clothes and pulling on the pants, shirt and socks. There was a definite draught on the floor. She got up and padded toward the window. It was dark, but that was about all she knew. She couldn't see a thing. All she could hear was the howling from the wind.

"Still storming?" Luke asked as he pulled down some cans from Nestor's cupboard and set them down on the counter.

"It looks that way. How long do you think it will last?"

Luke shrugged. "I don't know. Probably not that long. Usually when a bad blizzard is about to whip up, they warn us. The only warning I heard for today was a squall."

"I think that's more than a squall out there."

Luke nodded. "Nestor has beans. I hope you don't mind."

"Yes. I totally mind." She walked over to him. "I don't think those hearts will survive."

"What?" he asked as she rifled through drawers.

"I was in town and they were decorating for Valentine's Day."

Luke snorted. "Of course. They're probably going overboard, too, because of the big party that's going to happen on Valentine's Day at the hotel. Just the idea of the town covered in all that paraphernalia makes me a bit queasy."

"Well, the resident party planners have been working around the clock since I arrived in Crater Lake. I think it's going to be a big party."

Luke snorted again. "Pointless."

"Why?"

"Darn it, do you think Nestor could keep things in a logical spot?" Luke cursed again and bent down to rummage under the counter.

Sarah rolled her eyes. There was no getting through to him. At least not about this or why he left the army. His ex-wife really did a number on him and she felt bad that he'd been hurt. He'd been betrayed by the woman he loved and she'd been betrayed by her parents in a way.

Though really it wasn't the same thing.

They were both damaged souls and she hadn't made any promise to him, just as he had never made any to her. She didn't regret what had happened between them here tonight. She was glad it had happened.

Even if it could never happen again, because she couldn't let it happen again. Luke was her friend and she wouldn't hurt him the way his ex-wife had hurt him and she doubted very much Luke would even let her in if she tried.

His heart was guarded, just as much as she had her own walls of protection up. At least he'd let her in just briefly, even for a moment.

It was better they remained friends. Just friends and coworkers. That was all they could be, but that made her sad and for one brief moment she wished for something more.

CHAPTER TEN

AFTER THEY HAD something to eat they curled up together by the fire to spend the night and even though Luke wanted something to happen again, he wouldn't allow it. If it were warmer in Nestor's cabin he would've had her sleep on Nestor's bunk and he would've stayed on the floor.

Sarah fell asleep almost instantly after they had something to eat, but Luke couldn't sleep. Which ticked him off. If the storm subsided they were going to have to hike out of here. He knew that Nestor had snowshoes and skis in the lean-to, but in order to hike back down to the resort he would need his energy and that required sleep.

Especially after the strenuous activity that they'd engaged in a couple hours ago.

Don't think about it.

He didn't want to let Sarah in and risk his heart. The trouble was, she was already digging her way in there. He couldn't fall in love again. It was too much of a risk.

And living up on a mountain tracking bears and rescuing stranded people isn't?

What if Sarah decided to head back to New York? What if she wanted him to give up his life here and when he couldn't she'd leave him?

He wouldn't be hurt again. He wouldn't put his heart in that kind of danger again. It wasn't worth it. It was pointless.

Luke cursed under his breath and slowly climbed out of the sleeping bag, making sure that he didn't disturb Sarah. He wandered over to the window and peered outside. The snowstorm was beginning to subside. He could see black instead of just a wall of white.

He glanced back over at her, sleeping so peacefully, her blond hair fanned out around her head, and he desperately wanted to go back and join her. If he'd been in a different place.

If he'd never married Christine.

When Christine had left it hurt, but it also relieved him because he was beginning to see that they weren't meant for each other.

It was a clean break.

Still, it hurt. The betrayal stung.

Trust was not something he gave easily or freely.

So yeah, risking his life on the mountain was not playing it safe, but the only one who was affected by the choices he made was him. There was no wife to think about. No kids. He was free.

Really?

He sighed. Yeah, he was free, but the cost of his freedom was loneliness. He hadn't realized how lonely he had been until Sarah ended up in Crater Lake. When he'd started working with her, he'd been dreading it at first, because all he'd remembered was the surgeon from the summer. The one who'd rankled him and had fire in her eyes.

This Sarah was different from that surgeon from the summer.

She still was a spitfire, but something had changed in her.

The fire was diminished. He shouldn't really care why, but he did. And he discovered that he looked forward to all their training sessions. Although, she didn't know that those sessions weren't Silas Draven's idea, but his.

At first he was supposed to show her a bit of emergency first aid and tell her about some of the common injuries that could occur on the mountain, especially injuries that would happen to guests, but, after taking her out that first time and seeing how she threw herself into everything she did, he wanted to show her more.

And he soon found that he liked spending the time with her. Which was bad, because the more time he spent with her, the more his walls came down and he didn't like that.

Those walls were there for a reason. Those walls protected him.

Those walls would protect her.

He didn't want to stop being a first responder. He didn't want to stop doing what he was doing, because it mattered and because of that he wouldn't leave a widow or children behind. A life of solitude was the only answer.

It was the only way. That way no one got hurt.

I need to put some distance between us.

As soon as they were back at the resort, Luke was going to sever ties with Sarah for a while. She'd move on and find someone else. He had no doubt. She was beautiful, kind, funny. Of course, thinking about someone else kissing her made him angry.

She can't be yours.

And he had to keep reminding himself of that fact. The squalling stopped, almost as suddenly as it had started, which was good. He just hoped another system wasn't about to start up again. He didn't want to eat all of Nestor's rations.

Just as he was about to turn away, he saw lights coming up off the trail. Several lights and he realized they were snowmobiles.

"Sarah, wake up!" he shouted.

She bolted upright. "What's wrong?"

"Our rescue team has arrived."

She was confused. "What?"

"The squall ended and there's a pack of snowmobiles headed this way."

She got up and ran over to the window. "Oh, thank goodness. At least we don't have to hike down the mountain tomorrow. I'll start packing up."

Luke nodded and then grabbed his dry flannel shirt, quickly pulling it on as well as his socks and boots. If he didn't know any better, his brother or Esme would be on one of those snowmobiles and he wasn't going to have them catch him half-naked in a cabin with Sarah. He wasn't going to be subjected to their constant questioning for the next few weeks.

As soon as his boots were on there was a knock at the door. "Luke?"

It was Carson. Luke opened the door and his brother let out a sigh of relief and pulled him into a bear hug.

"You're freezing and I just got warm. Get in here."

The rescue team shuffled into the small entrance way of Nestor's cabin. Carson and two other first responders had come up the mountain.

"We were about to call off the search," Carson said. "Then I saw smoke coming from Nestor's cabin. We found out about twenty minutes after you and Sarah left that Nestor was in Missoula with his family getting chemotherapy. And then the avalanche. I'm glad you're okay. I'm glad you're both okay."

"Yeah, we learned he was gone when we got here. We were heading back when the avalanche struck, but we got out of it."

"We swam," Sarah said.

Carson and the first responders looked at her in shock. "You swam? You mean you were hit by the avalanche?"

"Yeah, but it was minor. Then the squall hit, so we got back to Nestor's and broke in. I owe him some provisions and some firewood."

"I don't think he'll mind," Carson said. "We should get back down the mountain before another squall hits. Last check on radar was another one was brewing to the northwest of here."

Luke nodded. "We'll pack our things and get our gear on."

Carson and the other two men stepped outside into the lean-to.

Sarah was shoving the last of her things into her knapsack. The zipped-together bags were undone and the blankets had been folded and put back on Nestor's bed. It was as if what had happened between them had been swept away.

It's for the best.

"I'll be glad to get back to my own bed. Maybe even a hot shower," she remarked as she zipped up her coat.

"Yeah. Me, too." Which was a lie. Even though he knew it was for the best this was happening, deep down he secretly wished he could spend the night with her, but he shook that thought away as he finished packing his things and putting out the fire.

Sarah was already outside, by the time the fire had been extinguished and the oil lamp turned off. The cabin was so dark and lonely. The small window panes illuminated by the headlights from the snowmobiles.

He wished they could stay, just for a bit longer, but this was better.

Luke was getting the distance he needed from her.

And if he did that, he would have a chance for his walls to rebuild.

Yeah. Right.

It was the fastest ride she'd ever been on. One of the responders, named Lee, had said that there was another squall brewing and they were trying to beat it back to the resort.

Sarah didn't care at that moment. All she wanted to do was get back to her bed, electricity and a hot shower. She didn't want to be stuck in another squall, in a shack and eating beans. Although, the company was fine.

She didn't mind that in the least.

Luke was on the snowmobile with his brother and Sarah wished that he were driving one of the machines and that she were riding with him.

Something had changed up there and she didn't know what

it was, other than he was more closed off than before. He barely looked her in the eye and it frightened her.

Who cares? You both were consenting adults and didn't make any promises.

Only, when it was all over with, she found herself craving more. She wanted him again, but that was not possible. If she took up with Luke, her mother would be somewhat happy that she'd found a doctor to settle down with, but then her father would say to her again that she couldn't handle the job in Crater Lake on her own.

You try too hard, pumpkin. You don't need to try so hard.

She hated when her father talked down to her like that. As if she were still four years old. She was the baby and therefore couldn't make it on her own.

As much as she wanted to be with Luke, maybe a little distance was a good thing. Besides, he wasn't telling her something. There was some hurt still buried there. How could she trust him if he couldn't trust her?

He didn't seem to take much stock in love. As was evident by his hatred for Valentine's Day and intimacy.

She didn't understand why he felt this way, other than his failed marriage, but there had to be something more to it than that. How could someone have so much hate for an emotion that also brought joy? Yeah, love did hurt, but in the end wasn't it worth it?

Of course, she wouldn't know anything about love.

She'd never been in it. She'd had crushes or relationships, but love? That was something she'd never experienced. It was scary and messy. She just didn't have time for it.

Why not?

She shook that thought from her head as the snowmobiles slowed down and came to a stop in front of the hotel. Sarah's legs were shaking, but she held her ground and walked toward the entranceway.

There were still people milling around from earlier, but she didn't linger. She just wanted to get back to her room and forget about what had happened between Luke and her.

"Sarah!"

She turned and Luke was headed toward her.

Just say good-night. Turn around and walk away.

Only she couldn't. She was so weak.

"Yeah?" she asked.

"Thank you for stitching up my head."

She nodded. "You should get that checked out later by Carson. Try not to get it wet. You probably know the drill when it comes to stitches."

He smiled. "I do, but thanks."

Turn around. Walk away.

"Will I see you tomorrow?"

You fool.

"Probably not. I have to get back up to Nestor's place and restock some stuff. I actually might rest for a couple of days."

"Of course. Take it easy and thanks for saving my life up there."

"I didn't save your life. You saved your own."

"If you hadn't shown me, I wouldn't have known what to do."

"If I hadn't shown you, you would've never been allowed to come up there with me," Luke said, and she realized his tone had changed. "You shouldn't have been up there with me."

"What are you talking about?" Sarah asked, confused. She'd thought he was happy that she'd gone up the mountain with him. He'd said so. What had changed? Why did he look so guilt-ridden?

Luke grabbed her by the arms, giving her a little shake. "You could've died in that avalanche."

"You could've, too."

He shook his head. "You could've died and it would've been my fault. I couldn't have borne that."

"I wanted to go with you."

Luke pushed her away and cursed under his breath. But she

wasn't going to let him run away so she stood in front of him, blocking his path.

"I wanted to go with you," she stated again. "You said you were glad I was up there. You were glad to have the extra set of medically trained hands. You didn't force me up that mountain. It was my choice. Just like you couldn't have forced me down the mountain. You wanted me up there and I wanted to be there."

"What I wanted doesn't matter. It doesn't matter when it comes to your life. I won't be responsible for that."

And before she could say anything else to him he turned and walked away. She wanted to go after him, but she recognized that look.

He was going to retreat back up into the mountains. When he was ready, she'd see him again, but only when she was ready.

Right now, she wasn't ready to see him for a long time.

CHAPTER ELEVEN

SARAH HADN'T SEEN Luke in the week since they had spent the night together up in the cabin caught between a snowstorm and an avalanche. She'd been expecting it. Any time she got too close to Luke, he hid in the forest for a while.

It was the same with her.

Only she hid in her clinic.

She didn't regret what had happened between them. She'd wanted it. And she'd meant what she'd said about not promising anything to him. It had been only about the moment that night.

Only now she missed him and she wished they'd promised each other that it wouldn't be weird after. That they could still be friends. And she wished he didn't feel so guilty about putting her into a dangerous situation. It had been her choice. He had nothing to feel guilty about, but there had been no telling him that.

She'd gotten so used to him being around, his absence made her heart ache. Loneliness had never bothered her before, until now.

Though she didn't have much time to dwell on it. The hotel was busier than ever. As Valentine's Day and its grand opening approached more and more guests were coming to Crater Lake. Including a lot of wealthy A-listers. The population of Crater

Lake went from just under six hundred people to more than a thousand overnight.

And it wasn't just Silas Draven's hotel that was selling out.

All the guest accommodations in town were full. Even privately owned rental cabins, which had never been rented during the winter season before, were full. Crater Lake was turning into a winter hotspot.

Sarah had been go, go, go since she came down off the mountain. Her clinic was busy with superficial stuff, stomach bugs and someone requesting a bikini wax and Botox, which she didn't do and promptly sent them to the on-site spa. She hadn't a moment to think for herself. So when she finally did get a break she headed to town to grab a cup of coffee and some peace and quiet.

As she walked down the street she spotted Esme in a stationery store and headed in to visit her. Esme was standing beside a large rack of Valentine's Day cards, mumbling to herself and frowning.

"You look like you're going to be sick," Sarah teased, coming up behind her.

"Oh, hey!" Esme laughed then. "I might. Did I mention that I hate Valentine's Day?"

"Yes. You mentioned something about that the first time we met. If you hate it so much, then why are you standing here in a shop that's overflowing with abomination?"

"Because my boyfriend likes Valentine's Day." She wrinkled her nose. "So I thought I would be nice and get him a card that I can shove in his face when he forces me to go to that Valentine's ball gala thing next week and makes me dress up like a princess or something very fluffy."

Sarah chuckled. "Not really romantic to shove something in someone's face and dressing up can be fun."

Esme grinned. "It depends on the dressing up, though."

"I don't know you well enough to talk about that." And they both laughed.

"He knows how much I hate it. He bought tickets just to annoy me." Esme pulled out a card. "This one is perfect. What do you think?"

The card in question had a large chimpanzee on it, making a kiss face. There was also faux fur glued to the outside. It was tacky and hideous, but Esme seemed so pleased with her find.

"That's an interesting choice. What does it say?"

"It says 'It's no monkey business, because I'm bananas for you.'" Esme grinned. "Yes, this is the one."

"That's a terrible card," Sarah said between chuckles. "It makes me cringe. Besides, that's clearly a chimpanzee and not a monkey, so really it's false advertising."

"Which is why it's so perfect. So, how are things with you?" Esme winked and Sarah groaned inwardly. What had she learned? Did Luke say anything and if so what did he say?

Just play it cool. Pretend as if nothing happened.

"I'm good."

"Good, huh? I hear your clinic has been busy."

"It has. More and more guests are arriving every day. A lot of big names."

Esme's expression hardened. "Hollywood A-listers?"

"Yeah, why?"

Esme sighed. "I used to run in that crowd before I came here. It's not my favorite crowd. You know I was engaged to Dr. Draven's son."

"No. I didn't. Wait, you were engaged to Shane Draven? When?"

"A couple of years ago. I ended it and I fell out of grace with that group of people. I don't miss it at all."

Sarah nodded. She didn't miss the glitterati of Manhattan or the so-called friends she'd made in the circles of society her parents traveled in, because once you weren't in that circle anymore you became a ghost. Just a memory that was briefly touched upon during lulls in conversation.

"I couldn't agree more." Sarah picked up a card with a red

heart. One thing she did miss about this time of year was when they would light up the Empire State Building with pink or red, sometimes even a heart.

"Have you seen the other Dr. Ralston lately?" Esme asked.

"Luke?"

"Yeah." There was a twinkle in her eye.

"Why?"

"No reason. I didn't mean to put you on the defensive. Carson told me what happened up there."

Sarah groaned. "Oh, he did?"

"Yeah. I can't even begin to imagine being caught in an avalanche. You were so lucky that you weren't swept away. Why, Glacier National Park had several avalanche-related deaths last year. It's scary. I never really thought about snow as a threat."

"You wouldn't—you come from California."

"I'm actually from Ohio originally. I have a respect for winter, but never seen an avalanche. Heck, until last summer I'd never really seen a landslide and apparently there's a dormant volcano around here."

Sarah laughed. "Guess we really did move to a danger zone."

Esme shrugged. "It's beautiful here, though. I love my life here. I wouldn't change it for anything."

Sarah nodded. "Well, I better head back to the hotel. I only had a small break and I'm sure there's another group of people wanting me to laser off their hair or inject them with silicone or something."

"I hope you're kidding?"

"I wish I was. Why they come to me instead of heading to the spa I can't understand."

She missed being a surgeon. She loved living in Crater Lake and the opportunity to work in Silas Draven's hotel was fantastic, but she missed the ER. For the first time in a long time, she actually missed the hustle and bustle of the ER.

She hadn't thought that she would when she'd first left active trauma surgery, when she'd taken on that job and started touring the country and training doctors. Despite what her father had done, she'd really enjoyed the travel and connections she'd made working with some of the finest surgeons in the world.

Returning back to the ER as a trauma surgeon had seemed like a step back, but now she realized that really this job was a step back. The only thing that really excited her was working with Luke. The bear mauling, the birth, even operating on Shane Draven last summer, all of those instances when she was called in to help in an emergency situation were when she felt like herself.

When she felt free.

And she missed it; she just hadn't realized how much she had until now. She'd leave, but she had a contract to fulfill and she wouldn't back down. She finished things she started. On the other hand she didn't want to leave Crater Lake.

She didn't want to leave Luke.

"Well," Sarah said. "It was nice to see you again, but I have to head back."

Esme nodded and then reached out and squeezed her arm. "It was nice talking with you, too. Will I see you at the Valentine's ball?"

"Yes. I have to go. Silas Draven's orders. I would skip it since I have no one to go with and I'll probably be too busy the next day dealing with hangovers. It would be nice to get the extra sleep."

They both laughed at that. Sarah waved goodbye and headed back in the cold. If she could only remain in Crater Lake, but as an independent doctor, then she wouldn't mind that too much, but how many doctors did a small town need?

If she wanted to return to surgery, she'd have to leave Crater Lake.

It was as simple as that, but she might be persuaded to stay if Luke wanted her to. Even though that was very unlikely.

Luke was not ready for love and she doubted he would ever be.

She couldn't put her career on hold on the off chance Luke

might want her. That was no way to live a life, so, as much as she hated the thought, once her year was up at Crater Lake she was going to find a hospital and go back to her first love of trauma surgery.

Even if it meant breaking her own heart in the process.

Then she thought of that painting he loved. The watercolor she'd done of the horse on the plains. She'd told him to take it, but he hadn't. Maybe she could give that to him as a peace offering.

If they couldn't be anything else, she wanted them to be friends. When she got back to the hotel she grabbed the painting and scrawled *For Adele* on the back before slipping it into an envelope.

Then she headed back to her clinic.

When she arrived she was surprised to find Luke pacing outside her office. The sight of him made her pulse quicken and she could recall every kiss of his lips on her skin, the weight of his body on her and the warmth. It had been over a week since she'd seen him, but looking at him now it felt as if it were just yesterday and that moment in the cabin came flooding back to her.

She both hated and loved the effect he had on her, but she was glad he was here. She'd missed him.

The only telltale sign that time had passed was that he'd had the stitches removed, but the gash had healed nicely, only leaving a small red mark barely visible at his hairline.

"Luke, what a surprise." And she held out the envelope ready to give it to him, but he didn't look at her.

"Where were you?" he snapped.

"In town. It was my morning off."

"I thought you would be here." He was clearly agitated.

"I'm here now. What're you so worked up about?"

Luke didn't say anything; he opened her clinic door, which she'd thought was locked, and dragged her inside, shutting the door behind them and locking it.

"What is up with you?" She tried to touch his laceration. "Do you want me to check your head?"

He grabbed her hand by the wrist and stopped her, shocking her, and then he let go of her hand, but didn't offer up an apology.

"It's not me," he said. "It's Nestor."

"Nestor?" She understood why he was so upset.

He's like a second father to me.

"Where is he? I'll see him right away."

Luke nodded and took her to one of the exam rooms, where Nestor was lying on a bed, pale and barely moving, cocooned in blankets. You could see the effects of chemotherapy. His face was gaunt, yellowish and there wasn't a hair on his face or head.

"What happened?" Sarah asked, setting the envelope down on the counter.

"I found him in a snowbank when I went up to cut some more wood for him. I don't know how long he's been out there. It's hypothermia—I think it's moderate. I knew I had to get him here. I would have administered warm IV fluids, but the cabinet is locked."

Sarah didn't question the fact he'd broken into her clinic and tried to break into her medicine cabinet. He was trying to save his friend's life. There was no time for arguments as she tossed Luke the key from her pocket.

"Not lactated Ringer's. With the chemo I don't know how well his liver is functioning and if he has hypothermia his liver might not be able to metabolize the lactate."

"I know," Luke called over his shoulder.

Sarah pulled out her stethoscope and the moment she touched him, he was cold, but, as she was taught in medical school, the patient was not dead until he was warm and dead. His temperature when she took it was twenty seven. Which was another reason she didn't want lactated Ringer's solution. He was too cold. He was heading toward profound hypothermia.

She tried to listen to the heart, but couldn't hear anything.

"Asystole!" Sarah shouted, then she felt the carotid artery; there was a faint thready pulse. "No, there's a pulse."

The heart was moving, but barely.

Luke came running back with bags of warmed IV fluid. "There's a pulse?"

"It's weak, so no CPR. Let's get the warm bolus into him."

Luke set up the IV and she grabbed warmers. Right now the most important thing was to heat his core; limbs could wait. The best way though to warm up a body that was this cold was cardiopulmonary bypass, but she was not equipped to do that here. Esme might be in town, but Nestor was here and they couldn't move him.

They could lose him if they took him out.

Hopefully the warmed IV would help, but given the state of Nestor's body, which had been ravaged by the chemotherapy, he didn't have much of a shot.

"Come on, Nestor," Luke whispered to the old man. "Come on. You're not going to go out like this. You said you wanted to go out riding a bear like a horse off the side of a cliff. This is not the way to go."

Sarah's heart broke as she watched Luke gingerly touch the old man's face. She knew Nestor was important to Luke, because Nestor had taught him how to survive in the mountains. It pained Sarah to see Luke like this, but there was not a lot she could do here with severe hypothermia.

Watching Luke beg his friend to keep fighting brought tears to her eyes. Here, in this moment, Luke was so raw, so real.

This was the genuine Luke Ralston. Not the lone wolf everyone else saw. This tender, concerned Luke, begging the man he admired so much to hang on, was the man she longed to know.

The man who could feel.

The man who could teach her how to feel.

As she watched the two of them she knew that she didn't have that kind of parent-child relationship with her parents and probably never would.

It made her sad to watch Luke suffer so much. She didn't have the heart to tell him that Nestor might not make it. Though she probably didn't have to tell him that. He probably already knew.

"Did you call the air ambulance?" Sarah asked.

"I did, but we have to warm him up before we can get him out to meet the ambulance."

She nodded, but didn't say anything.

When a patient's core temperatures were below thirty, they required to be rewarmed internally through cardiopulmonary bypass, gastric lavage and other means. Ways that Sarah couldn't provide for him in this private clinic.

Usually people that severe were taken straight to the hospital where aggressive rewarming could start instantly. All they could do with what she had was blankets, heaters and the IV. She took Nestor's temperature again, but it was dropping fast.

She knew what was going to happen next. His heart would stop completely and if they rewarmed him too fast, his heart could collapse, but she couldn't use CPR to keep the brain alive until after he was asystole.

"What's his temperature?"

Sarah sighed. "Twenty-five. Luke, the lowest someone has come back from such a severe hypothermia is thirteen point seven."

"He'll make it."

She listened for cardiac activity, but there was none that she could make out. She felt for the carotid artery and the pulse was gone. He wasn't warm enough to start CPR, but she had no choice.

"Starting CPR. Get the AED."

Luke nodded as she began CPR.

Come on, Nestor. Don't die here. Don't die on me.

Luke got the AED ready and Sarah stopped CPR while Luke shocked Nestor. There was no response. Sarah continued with the CPR and they alternated.

"Nestor, come on," Luke urged.

When she looked at the clock, she could see that they'd been doing CPR for far too long. The ambulance had still not arrived.

"Take his temperature," Sarah said as she continued CPR.

"Dammit, it's fourteen."

Come on, Nestor.

"I can't pronounce him but..."

"Don't say it," Luke begged. "Don't. People survive hypothermia all the time. Cancer kills, but hypothermia can be cured."

Sarah sighed, and continued, but there wasn't much hope. Luke turned his back on the scene. His fists clenched as she worked on. He obviously couldn't stand to watch his friend slip away.

She didn't have any hope...and then Nestor's heart came back under her hand and he groaned, before coughing.

"Oh, my God," she whispered.

Nestor opened one eye, groaned, and passed out again. But the point was, he was alive.

"What?" Luke asked, then leaned over. His eyes widened in shock. "You got him back?"

Sarah had never brought back a person with such severe hypothermia, with a body already so weakened by chemo, from the brink of death. Tears of joy stung her eyes and she laughed out loud because she couldn't contain herself.

Luke smiled at her briefly before turning back to his friend.

She was so relieved. She hadn't wanted to be the one responsible for not saving Nestor's life. She hadn't wanted to hurt Luke like that, and she hadn't wanted him to be reminded of Nestor's death every time he saw her.

She didn't want Luke to remember her like that.

"You brought him back," Luke said, stunned. "I've never seen that."

"I've never done it in this situation before. And especially not outside a hospital."

"I can't believe you did it."

Nestor was still unconscious, but he was stable, and when

she took a temperature again it was rising. He had a good shot at making it now.

The paramedics came then and took over, Sarah gave an update about Nestor's temperature and how long he'd been down. They were going to take Nestor to the hospital and continue to warm him up, but Nestor wasn't out of the woods yet. Chemo took its toll. As did Nestor's age.

She followed the paramedics down out of her clinic and made sure Nestor was in the air ambulance and on his way.

Luke stood beside her, his expression unreadable and his gaze trained on the ambulance as it disappeared from view and on to the nearest hospital. There they could work on him. They walked back up to the clinic to clean up the mess.

Luke cursed under his breath as he picked up Nestor's hat, which had fallen on the floor of the exam room. His eyes were wild, but he wasn't about to cry. It was rage she saw there.

That brief moment of tenderness and joy after she'd saved Nestor's life had faded away. Luke's walls had gone back up again. Like armor.

She wanted to tell him that he didn't need to guard himself in front of her.

He could be himself.

How can he be himself when you can't be yourself?

Sarah touched Luke's arm. "I'm so sorry that happened to him. I wonder what caused him to collapse in the snow."

He shrugged it off. "People don't die from hypothermia and he won't either."

"They do, Luke. You don't know how long he was in the snow for. Or how he even got there. He's alive, but with chemo…his body's been through a trauma."

He scrubbed a hand over his face. "What I meant was that people don't die of hypothermia on my watch. They don't. No man gets left behind. Every life gets saved. Nestor has fought cancer, he can fight this."

"Is that what you would tell yourself in the army?"

His gaze was positively flinty. "What?"

"Why did you leave the army, Luke? It's clear to me you're so passionate about it, why would you leave it?"

Luke snorted and tried to push past her. "I don't have time for this."

"Of course you don't. You never do."

"What's that supposed to mean?"

Sarah shook her head. "It means you'll disappear off into the forest, like you always do, and when you're done sulking you'll come back and pretend like nothing happened. I can't deal with that kind of hot and cold, Luke. I won't deal with that."

"How do you expect me to act, Sarah? A friend of mine almost died. Never leave a man behind, that's the way I've always lived and yet…" He trailed off and then shook his head. "I'm done. I can't deal with this. This is why I keep to myself. This is pointless."

He turned and started to walk away.

"It is. You're a coward, Luke."

He spun around. "I'm the coward? How do you figure that?"

"You're a coward because you won't let anyone in. You won't let anyone help you. I'm sorry you were burned before by people you care about. I'm sorry that you've lost people important to you, but you can't run away from your fears. You have to face them."

"Is that a fact?" He crossed his arms. "And what do you think you're doing here?"

Honestly, she didn't know. She didn't know why she was bothering with him. He clearly didn't want her involved in his life. She should know better.

She was better off alone. Then she only had to answer to herself for her own actions and mistakes. Maybe Luke had it right.

"Working and trying to save lives."

"I mean why are you in Crater Lake? You gave up a prominent job because you were afraid you weren't good enough. You were afraid that everyone would think you were just riding on

Daddy's coattails. You ran away from your talent. You're just as much a coward as I am."

"You're a jerk." She threw the envelope at him. "This was for you, because I thought we were friends. Clearly, I was wrong."

Luke touched his face where the envelope had hit him, snickered and then walked away from her. His words had stung, as if he'd cut her open with a scalpel, but then the truth did hurt. It hurt all the more that it came from him.

Someone she'd thought she could trust enough to tell her darkest fear to. She'd never told anyone else that she'd given up the job because her father had gotten it for her. That was her shame to bear. She'd thought Luke would understand, but she was wrong.

Then again, she was wrong about a lot of other things.

This was no different.

CHAPTER TWELVE

"LUKE, I KNOW you're in there. I can see you."

Luke looked over at the window to see his brother peering through. He'd thought that if he retreated to Nestor's cabin, to clean up a bit and close it up until Nestor could come and claim it, it would help get his mind off the fact that he'd probably broken the heart of the woman he loved.

When he'd said those things to Sarah, the moment they'd slipped from his lips he'd realized what a mistake he'd made. That this time, he'd hurt someone he cared about, but she would move on. Like Christine had and he would be the only one with a broken heart.

It served him right.

Sarah hadn't made any promises the night they made love. That was what he'd thought he wanted; that was what he always wanted. He didn't want any commitments. He didn't want anyone to love, but the problem was she'd gotten underneath his skin.

When she was working so hard to save Nestor's life, when she thought it was completely hopeless, she still fought and she was doing it for him. And she'd brought him back. He knew that. Sarah did the best she could with what she had. She could've turned him away, but she hadn't. She wasn't that kind of person and he admired her for it, but Sarah was not meant to be his.

She deserved so much more. He'd hurt her, dragged her into dangerous situations and he demanded so much of her.

Sarah was better off without him.

He didn't deserve love.

Luke didn't know anything about love. He hadn't been able to keep Christine happy when they were married. He'd chosen his career over her. She hadn't wanted to live in Germany. She hadn't wanted to live in a cabin in the woods, yet he'd been selfish and tried to have it his way.

No wonder Christine had left him.

How could he have love, deserve love, if he couldn't change or bend, too? It was too hard, too painful. The problem was, Sarah had somehow snuck in and captured his heart. He didn't know how, but she had.

Of course, that was all ruined now.

He'd taken that piece of her, the one she'd shared with him, and thrown it back in her face. He'd used it to hurt her. To drive her away. So, no, he didn't deserve love. She'd given him that horse painting, as well. Another piece of her she'd shared with him that he'd tossed back at her like garbage.

He hated himself for it.

He'd made his bed and he was going to lie in it.

Of course, coming back to Nestor's cabin was a huge mistake. Not only because it made him emotional, thinking about the friend he'd almost lost, but also because it reminded him of being in her arms. When she kissed him, when she opened herself up to him. The night they became one. That night he was lost to her because she entrusted him with a piece of her.

Now he'd shattered her heart.

Her words might have stung him, but he'd deserved it because the unseen wound he'd inflicted on her was a thousand times worse.

He'd seen her once in town. He'd wanted to tell her that

Nestor had pulled through, that they had managed to warm him with lavage, but she hadn't looked at him. She hadn't said anything to him. She had been silent, which was odd for her. Since they first met she'd always been frank about what she thought about him.

The cold shoulder had been too much for him to bear. Even though he'd deserved it. So he'd retreated back to the mountains, under the guise that he was cleaning up Nestor's cabin for the family, but really he just wanted to be alone and mend the broken heart he'd caused himself because he let Sarah in and then pushed her away.

You don't know if she loved you back.

Which was true, but it didn't make the pain better and was pointless now, because he'd completely ruined it. Then he glanced at the painting on the mantel where he'd placed it when he came up here. The horse that looked like Adele. Something she'd painted herself; he could see her slender, graceful hand in each delicate brush stroke. Detailed and precise, as a brilliant surgeon should be. It was a piece of her and just knowing that hurt all the more.

"Luke, it's cold out here. Let me in." Carson's shouting from outside interrupted his train of thought.

Luke groaned and got up to open the door. Carson burst past him and stomped his feet at the door.

"What're you doing here, Carson?"

"Looking for you. After Nestor's accident, you disappeared."

Luke shrugged. "I came up here to clean it up. Nestor's son Greg won't be back up here until spring, possibly summer. I wanted to make sure nothing would go bad. I wanted to make sure everything was squared away. Nestor's lucky to be alive. He'll be in the hospital for a while."

Carson nodded. "Right."

"What's that supposed to mean?"

"Exactly what you think it means."

Luke cursed. "I don't have time for this."

"Why? Because you're so busy up here moping?"

Luke glared at Carson, but his little brother was holding his ground and looking quite smug about it.

"What are you grinning about?"

"I'm thinking back to a conversation we had this summer. Do you remember that particular conversation?"

"No."

Which was a lie. Luke vaguely remembered it. He remembered his brother coming to get him in Missoula, struggling with the fact that he was in love with Esme and was scared of getting a broken heart. Scared of possibly walking away from a family practice, because Carson had put it on himself to carry on the family legacy in Crater Lake.

Luke had told him, in a nutshell, to snap out of it and live.

And now the jerk was throwing it back in his face.

Typical.

"I believe you said to me, and I quote, 'Forgive yourself. And for once follow your heart. Do what you want to do. Live.' Wasn't that the line you fed me?"

"It sounds vaguely familiar."

"You're an idiot. You also told me, 'She'll walk away, she's going to walk away and you know who I'm talking about,' and now it applies to you."

"Do you have an eidetic memory or something?"

"No. I just stored those particular lines away for future blackmail and use."

Luke rolled his eyes. "I said those words to you because you deserved Esme. She loved you and you love her."

"Sarah loves you and you're an idiot if you think any different."

Luke shook his head. "You don't know what you're talking about."

"And I'll say it again, you're an idiot."

"I don't deserve love. I blew my first marriage because I was too selfish. And this time around I shut her out because I didn't want to get hurt. It was selfish. I threw it away. For me, love is pointless."

Carson sighed. "Luke, you gave up the army for her. That doesn't sound like someone who is selfish."

"I should've given it up earlier."

"Why? Christine knew your passion for the army before you were married to her. She was just as selfish as you. You gave up the army for her, you tried for her. She ruined it. She found happiness, why can't you? You deserve happiness."

"No. I don't. Maybe it was all me. I can't take the risk again. I don't want to take the risk again. It's better that she leaves. It's better she walks."

Carson took him by the shoulders and shook him. "I love you, but you're an idiot."

"So you've said."

"I'll say it again, like you said it to me. Forgive yourself. Take a chance and live. You love her. You may not admit it, but I can see it as plain as day."

Luke walked away from his brother and sat down on the edge of Nestor's bunk, running his hands through his hair. His hand brushing over the tender scar from the laceration Sarah had stitched up.

That was one of the scariest moments of his life, when he saw that avalanche raging down the side of the mountain toward them and saw the look of horror on her face. All he could do was tell her to do what he'd taught her. In that moment he didn't care much about his life. Only hers, because he couldn't bear it if he lost her.

Yet, he had lost her.

He'd driven her away.

Carson was right. He was an idiot.

"You've realized what a moron you are now." Carson was grinning ear to ear.

"I thought I was an idiot?"

Carson shrugged. "Both, I think."

Luke laughed. "Yeah, you're right."

"I know what happened between you and Christine was bad and the fact that she ran off with Anthony sucks. It does, but you said so yourself, you wanted different things. I think you and Sarah want the same things."

"And what would that be?"

"She's a trauma surgeon and so are you. You're a great first responder, Luke, but you have to get off the mountain and become a surgeon again. Don't you remember what it was like in the OR? I know you loved it. I remember the emails. You were born to be a surgeon. You are a surgeon, you just stopped practicing."

"I don't think she wants to be a surgeon anymore. She left that life behind her."

"She thinks she has. She's a surgeon. Just go live. Do you think that soldier who died would want you mourning his death for the rest of your life? No. Go live your life, Luke."

The words sank in slowly.

He'd been blaming himself so long for his heartache that he didn't realize he'd given up the thing he'd loved the most and that was surgery. He was so busy trying to rescue everyone that he didn't see that he was the one who needed rescuing. He was going to make it up to Sarah. He was going to win her back, even if he didn't know how exactly or if he ever would, but he was going to try.

He couldn't live without her. Of that he was certain.

Luke got up and clapped Carson on the back. "Thanks."

"No problem. I just hope she forgives you." Carson winked. "Now, are you coming down off this mountain? Tomorrow is Valentine's Day. I think that's a perfect time to make up."

"I don't have tickets to that dance," Luke said.

Carson reached in his pocket. "You can have mine. Esme and I aren't going to that dance. I suspect tomorrow we'll have more important things to celebrate."

Luke cocked an eyebrow. "Like what?"

"I'm proposing to Esme tonight. She has no idea."

He grinned. "It's Friday the thirteenth. You know that, right?"

Carson chuckled. "I know, but she really hates Valentine's Day. I mean really hates it. I found a card with a chimp on it."

Luke shook his head. "Would you get out of here? I'll come down off the mountain in time for tomorrow."

"Good." Carson punched him on the shoulder. "Good luck."

"You, too. It's about time you did that, by the way."

"What?"

"Propose to Esme."

Carson snorted. "Look who's talking."

Sarah's heart hurt. It had been a few days since she'd last seen Luke in town briefly. It had looked as if he'd wanted to talk to her, but he'd turned away. He'd looked pale and emotionless. Several times she'd talked herself out of going over to him and comforting him, because really what good would it do?

He would just push her away.

You need to fight harder.

She let out another sigh, because she was all out of fight. How could she fight for the man she was in love with when she couldn't even stand up to her parents? Luke had been right, she should've stayed in that job she'd thought she earned and proven to them she was more than a name.

Even though she'd saved Nestor's life, she'd done so much good here and she wanted more.

She missed the OR.

She missed the chaos of a busy emergency room, the beauty of an OR being prepped by scrub nurses, the feel of the water on her arms as she scrubbed in and the calm she felt as she waited for the patient to go under and the magic of saving a life.

Being around Luke reminded her of that.

How long had she just been walking through the paces of life and not living it?

A long time.

With Luke, she mattered and working with him made her realize she was a damn good surgeon in her own right. As soon as her yearlong contract was up, she was going to find an ER job again. Even if it meant she wasn't running the ER, she still wanted to be where she belonged. She'd known the moment she'd picked up her first scalpel that she didn't belong in her parents' penthouse on the Upper West Side.

Just as she didn't belong in a clinic treating minor injuries.

She belonged down on the front lines and on the surgical floor.

Just as she and Luke belonged together, even if he didn't think they did. She'd never fallen in love before, but, with him, she fell hard and the answer was simple. He brought out the best in her. He made her work harder than she'd ever worked before.

Around him, she felt like herself and she hadn't felt like herself in a very long time. She was so busy distancing herself from her parents, trying to step out of their shadows to prove that she didn't need them, that she didn't realize she'd blocked out everyone.

Including herself.

"Excuse me, are you still open? I know it's four o'clock on Friday and your clinic states you're only open until four, but I'm hoping you can see me."

Sarah looked up from her chart and saw a middle-aged woman, guarding her side, standing in the doorway. She seemed vaguely familiar, but perhaps she'd treated her earlier.

"Of course. Come in."

The woman looked relieved and followed Sarah into an exam room.

"Why don't you have a seat, Ms...?"

"It's Mrs. Vargas, but I can't sit, I'm afraid. I fell while I was skiing and I'm terrified I broke a rib."

Sarah smiled. "It must've been a nasty fall."

"It was. I've never skied before, but my husband insisted we come here for a romantic Valentine's weekend, when really I should be back in Great Falls and working."

"What do you do, Mrs. Vargas?"

"I'm the head of a board of directors for a hospital. We've scouted an area just outside of Crater Lake to build a small hospital that deals mostly with trauma. There's a serious lag around here. Missoula and Great Falls sees most of the trauma, but those locations are too far away to do any help."

"So you're going to build a hospital that only deals with trauma?"

She nodded and then winced. "I'm sorry for boring you, but I thought you might be interested in that seeing how you're a doctor and everything."

"You're not boring me. I totally agree this area is seriously lacking in a trauma center. I can only do so much here."

"Well, I know there's a cardiac surgeon in town and we've offered her use of our operating rooms. It's just a matter of finding a trauma surgeon for next year."

"Well, Mrs. Vargas, you don't have a broken rib."

"Are you sure?"

Sarah nodded. "Positive. If you had a fracture in your ribs you wouldn't be talking to me so easily. You're guarding, but I suspect you've given yourself a nasty bruise. Inhale deeply for me."

Mrs. Vargas did that.

"Did it hurt or was it hard to do?"

"No."

"I'll prescribe you some painkillers, but rest now and put some ice on it."

Mrs. Vargas nodded as she filled out the prescription and handed it to her. Mrs. Vargas stared at it. "Ledet? Are you related to Vin Ledet from New York?"

Sarah groaned inwardly. "Yes. He's my father. Do you know him?"

"No, I just remember someone telling me that Vin Ledet's daughter was a brilliant trauma surgeon. They said you saved their life last summer. Who was it? Oh, yes, Shane Draven. His uncle owns this hotel."

"I really can't say brilliant, but I was that trauma surgeon. I did work on Shane, but he came to me in stable condition thanks to both Dr. Ralstons and Dr. Petersen, who tended to him in the field. I just happened to be a locum surgeon in Missoula, throwing in a hand during a busy stint."

"Well, you're not blowing your own horn. Shane Draven spoke very highly of your skills." Mrs. Vargas pulled out a business card. "If you're interested in returning to an ER and running it as chief of surgery, please do call me."

Chief?

"I think you'd want someone more experienced?"

"The way Shane talks about you I'd say you're experienced enough. I did do a quick background check on you, before realizing you were here. Everyone speaks highly of you as a surgeon."

Sarah blushed. "Thank you, Mrs. Vargas."

"Will I see you tomorrow at the Valentine's Day dance? I would like to introduce you to some members of the board."

"*I* will be at the dance. Silas Draven wants all his staff there, but I don't want to see *you* at that dance. Are we clear?"

Mrs. Vargas winked. "Very well. Please do think about my offer. I would love to have a surgeon of your caliber in charge of this project."

Sarah walked Mrs. Vargas out and when she'd left, Sarah stared at the card for a long time. The offer came because of Shane Draven, not her father. Mrs. Vargas was aware of who her father was, but it was her own merit that preceded her. Not her father pulling strings.

She would take the job to stay in Crater Lake. She loved it here.

She was making friends here.

She was finding her place in this world, when for so long she'd felt as if she was drifting.

Here she wasn't Vin Ledet's daughter. Here she was a surgeon, a doctor. She'd found herself and she'd been foolish not to look sooner. She'd been so busy trying to show her parents who she wasn't that she couldn't show them who she was.

She didn't have to prove anything to them, because there was nothing to prove. Their opinion of her was never going to change and, for the first time in a long time, she was okay with that.

Chief of surgery sounded like a dream job. And she could stay in Crater Lake.

What's keeping you in Crater Lake?

And that realization made her sad.

Luke had made it clear how he felt about love. He thought it was pointless and he'd shut her out. She didn't want to remain in a town where he was.

She loved him too much and it was clear that he didn't return those feelings. So the best thing to do after her contract was up was make a clean break, for both of them.

Even though a clean break was the last thing she wanted, because all she wanted was to be his. To be by his side and in his arms.

She was in love with him and she doubted that feeling would disappear anytime soon, but Luke loved Crater Lake. This was his home. It wasn't her home, even if she wanted it to be. So she'd leave.

Because she loved him so much, she'd leave and let him get on with his life without her. She could find roots in another town, even though she loved Crater Lake.

And she would find another job and of that she had no doubt now.

CHAPTER THIRTEEN

A MONTH AGO you couldn't have paid him enough to be at a gala like this. All the people, the drinking, the noise and decorations were enough to set him on edge. Luke didn't really like being around people who pretended to be nice. Who were putting on a show.

He avoided social situations like this for a reason.

So, no, he wouldn't be at an event like this, not for all the money in the world, but for Sarah he'd walk through fire. For her he'd do anything. She deserved it all and if she let him, if she forgave him, he would spend every waking moment making it up to her.

Since Christine left him he'd always stated his only mistress was the mountain, but the mountain was cold. So cold his heart had been frozen.

Until Sarah came.

Now all he wanted was her and he was going to do everything and anything to get her back.

She was across the room now and he caught glimpses of her through all the people. She was so close, but so far away. To get to her, it would be like walking through fire for him.

He waited until she was alone and not talking with Silas Draven. He didn't want anyone to interrupt this moment.

Carson and Esme had helped him get ready, since the only suit he owned was from when he was eighteen and married to Christine. So that was unacceptable, coupled with the fact it no longer fit him.

So he wore Carson's suit. It was designer and, even though he felt completely awkward in it, Esme had swooned over him. He knew then it was good. That he would fit in for her. He'd even shaved his beard off.

Now he stood on the other side of the gala, remaining in the shadows at the edge of the dance floor watching her. She took his breath away. She was wearing a bloodred, sparkling evening gown that was a halter, so he got to admire her creamy white shoulders, but the seller for him was her white-blond hair was pulled to one side, but down. So it just brushed the top of her shoulder. Just like in that self-portrait she'd done. The one he loved the most.

Of course, when he was presented with the real thing, the drawing paled in comparison. Sarah was beautiful. She was radiant and he noticed other men admiring her, which ticked him off, but no one else approached her. So he didn't have to inflict any bodily harm on would-be suitors.

She looked unhappy standing off to the side and he knew that was his fault. Something he aimed to fix in a moment, because right now he just enjoyed the sight of her. He enjoyed drinking it in. He didn't want to disrupt the magic she was weaving.

He didn't deserve her, but he would work hard to rectify that for the rest of his life. If she would only let him, and he hoped she would. He pulled at his tie and headed toward her.

Luke had faced many dangerous situations in his life. Things that would scare others, but here, in this moment, crossing a dance floor to beg forgiveness and put his fragile heart on the line for the woman he loved was the scariest thing he'd ever done. But for her, he would do anything.

* * *

Sarah didn't want to be at this dance. Mostly because everyone who was at this gala was with someone and she was standing off to the side of the dance floor in her red evening gown, like a wallflower. It was like junior high all over again.

Still, it was a great success. She could see this Valentine's Gala becoming a yearly event for the hotel.

Valentine's never really bothered her, but right now watching all the happy couples dance, kiss and enjoy themselves made her envious.

She should just leave.

Silas Draven had introduced her to all his important guests and then she'd discreetly snuck away, wandering along the edge of the dance floor as the band played endless romantic songs. She was hoping that Esme would be here tonight, so at least maybe she could talk to someone she knew, but Esme hadn't shown up and Sarah hoped that it wasn't because of that goofy chimpanzee card she'd picked out.

The thought of that card made her laugh to herself. A waiter walked by with a tray full of champagne flutes. Sarah took one and as she glanced back across the dance floor her breath caught in her throat at the sight of a man in a well-tailored tuxedo walking across the floor toward her.

And it wasn't just any man. It was Luke and he was clean shaven.

Oh, my God.

Her knees buckled. Those intense blue eyes fixed on her as if he were going to devour her whole and devour her in a good way. A way that made her blood heat with need, with a craving she'd been trying to suppress since he'd walked away from her and broken her heart.

His beard was gone and she could clearly see those delectable lips, which had kissed every inch of her, turning up in a mischievous smile. He stopped in front of her and pulled on the cuff of his jacket, adjusting what looked like cuff links. His brown curls were tamed in a debonair coif, he had a tie on and it didn't look like a clip-on. He rolled his neck and pulled at the tie again. He must be so uncomfortable.

Good.

Even his boots were gone, replaced by dress shoes.

He spun around. "How do I look?"

So good. Only she didn't say that thought out loud.

"Fine."

He cocked any eyebrow. "Just fine?"

No, she wasn't going to be drawn in by his cute banter. She wasn't going to let herself be drawn in by him again. She couldn't.

"I... What're you doing here?"

"I've come to the gala. Am I not dressed appropriately?"

"You're dressed fine. I told you that."

It's more than fine.

In fact she was having a hard time controlling herself from throwing the champagne flute aside, hiking up her long skirt and jumping in his arms, but she controlled herself. She was angry at him.

"Can I have this dance?" He held out his hand, his blue eyes twinkling.

Say no. Say no.

"Okay." She took his hand and he led her out on the dance floor, spinning her around gracefully before pulling her back up against him. "I didn't know you could dance."

"I have hidden depths."

"I'm aware of those hidden depths," she said sarcastically. "I don't know why I'm dancing with you."

"Because you're a forgiving sort of person."

"Am I?"

"I think so."

"I hope you're right. I don't feel so forgiving right now."

"I loved my painting. I put it on the wall," he said changing the subject.

Her heart skipped a beat. "You did?"

Don't fall for it.

Only she couldn't help it when it came to Luke Ralston. She was so weak when it came to him.

He nodded. "Thank you for that. It's beautiful, but that wasn't my favorite the night you showed me your drawings."

"It wasn't?"

"No, it was the self-portrait you'd done." Then he reached out and ran his hands gently through her hair and brushed her shoulder. "It was the pencil drawing with your hair down, your shoulders bare. That's the drawing I loved."

Her pulse thundered in her ears. That was a drawing she'd always hated. One she'd never got right. At least she didn't think so. Maybe because she couldn't truly see herself through her own eyes. She was her own worst judge. But looking into Luke's eyes at this moment, in his arms, she could see what he saw, even if only for a brief moment, and it almost made her cry.

"Why didn't you tell me?"

"I didn't want you to know at the time."

She blushed. "I'm surprised you're here. I thought you didn't like Valentine's Day. It's the one thing you and Esme have in common."

"Me, too, to be honest." He chuckled. "Actually, Esme may be warming up to Valentine's Day, or at least Friday the thirteenth."

"Why?"

"Carson proposed last night and Esme accepted."

Sarah smiled. "Oh, how wonderful. I'm happy for her. I'm surprised they're not here celebrating."

"Well, they wanted me to come here."

She blushed again, her heart racing. "So what're you doing here?"

"I've come to beg for forgiveness."

Her heart skipped a beat. "What?"

"I've been an idiot. I thought love was pointless, but only for me."

"Only for you?"

He nodded. "My first wife left me because I was selfish. I was so focused on what I wanted that I didn't let her have a say. I wanted to be in the army and serve my country as a surgeon, I wanted to train at the army hospital in Germany and nothing was going to stop me. Not even the woman I loved, or thought I loved at the time. Actually, I'm surprised she didn't leave me sooner."

"I understand that kind of drive. You loved serving your country, so why did you leave it?"

"Because I left for her, but by then it was too late. I gave up my commission, but it wasn't enough. So I turned to the mountain. Being alone meant I could live my life the way I wanted. I never wanted to feel that pain or be responsible for inflicting that kind of pain on someone. I thought it was easier to shut people out. To be alone, and then you came along."

Tears stung her eyes. "Oh, Luke. Things aren't so black-and-white."

"I know that now. When you walked into that OR last summer, I knew there was something about you. I knew that you would break through, even if I didn't want to admit it. I love you, Sarah. I'll go wherever you need me to go. If you need to be a surgeon in New York again, I'll go there. I just can't lose you. I need you. I'll change my life, give up everything to be with you."

Her knees went weak and she wasn't sure she'd heard him correctly. No one had ever offered to give up everything to make her happy.

Everyone expected pieces of her, for her to conform, but Luke was offering all of himself to her and she was overwhelmed by it.

She knew there were tears running down her face but there was no stopping them.

"For so long I've been fighting to prove to the world I'm not someone they think I am, I didn't know who I really was, but with you I found who I was again. I shut everyone out. Even me. I shut myself out. I was convinced I didn't need love. That I didn't want love...that I could make it through this life on my own. I was wrong. I love you, Luke. I love you so much it hurts. You see me."

He pulled her tight against him, cupping her face, and then kissed her. His kiss gentle at first, before it deepened. She melted into that kiss, wrapping her arms around his neck, not caring who saw her kissing him. Her whole world had righted itself. She was where she wanted to be. She was who she wanted to be.

She had found out who she was thanks to this man.

When the kiss ended she laid her head against his shoulder, moving with him as they swayed gently on the dance floor. She didn't want to let him go. She'd missed him. She'd missed this Luke Ralston. A man she'd only met in brief glimpses. A man who had been surrounded by high walls.

A man she desperately wanted to love.

"So am I forgiven?" he teased.

"Yes. Though I should've made you work harder."

"Yes. You should've."

"Now you tell me." She glanced up at him and kissed him again. "Thank you for coming here tonight. This is the best apology ever."

"So, where should we move to?" Luke asked. "There's no surgical jobs in Crater Lake sadly."

"There will be next year when my contract is up here at the hotel."

"What?" He was clearly confused. "There's no hospital in Crater Lake. They talked once last year about building one, but nothing ever came of it."

"Not yet. A trauma and surgical center is going up outside of town. A board of directors from a large hospital in Great Falls realized there was a shortfall up in this area for one."

Luke grinned. "You want to stay in Crater Lake?"

"Of course. It's home now. You're my home." And it was true. She'd found a home. She'd found what she was looking for. She'd found herself in him.

Luke kissed her again. "And you're mine. I love you, Sarah."

Sarah kissed him back. "Happy Valentine's Day, Dr. Ralston."

EPILOGUE

Valentine's Day, a year later

SARAH WALKED SWIFTLY through the halls of the new trauma center. Her ER was running smoothly. Her board was in good working order, which made her slightly apprehensive. She'd learned early on as a trauma resident that a smoothly run ER and good board would mean that a huge trauma was due any second to muck it all up.

They'd only been open a month, but already there had been several large traumas, a couple of emergency births and an avalanche. Thankfully no bear mauling.

Sarah shuddered recalling that moment.

The man had pulled through, but required several plastic surgeries.

She'd seen several bears in the summer when Luke was working on building onto his cabin. Their cabin. And a bear had crashed Esme and Carson's wedding that summer, but thankfully none of the encounters had been violent.

Once she'd got the trauma center open, her father had come to tour the facility and he'd donated money to the pro bono fund, which had shocked her, but what was the most shocking moment was when he told her he was proud of her. That she had done well for herself.

And she had.

She was happier than she could ever remember.

Now, if only her boards would stay quiet tonight.

"Dr. Ledet, can you come to OR Four? There's a problem."

Sarah saw a very pregnant Esme running toward her. Esme operated on her cardio patients at the trauma center, but Sarah wondered when she was going to give it up because soon she'd be giving birth.

"You shouldn't be running," Sarah said. "You're due in, like, three weeks. Why are you even working now?"

"It's only an angio," Esme said, as if an angio were nothing. Which was odd for her.

Sarah glanced up at the board and then back to her. "You said there was a problem. If it's only a simple angio, then what's the problem?"

Esme bit her lip. "Oh, I'm not in OR Four. I'm in Three. That board is wrong. I finished my angio, but I was passing OR Four and they were having a problem."

Speak of a quiet board, get swift retribution.

"Okay, let's go." Sarah jogged behind Esme. They put on their surgical caps and then scrubbed. "So what's wrong again?"

"It was a mauling," Esme said. "It's pretty bad."

"Oh, no. Are you serious? Why do tourists insist on disturbing a bear during its hibernation cycle?" She walked into the OR, her hands up and waiting to get gloved when she saw Luke, gowned and standing in the OR alone.

"Bears don't hibernate, Sarah. Have I not taught you anything?"

Sarah glanced back, but Esme had disappeared. "What's going on here? I thought there was a mauling."

"No, no mauling, but I wanted to get you here fast, without arousing your suspicions."

"Well, now I'm suspicious. You're supposed to be in Missoula visiting Nestor. What's going on?"

"Nothing is going on."

"Is Nestor okay?" Sarah asked.

"He's fine. I swear. He hates city living, but you know that."

Sarah sighed in relief. She was glad to hear the older man was okay. She'd grown fond of him and went with Luke to visit him every month.

"So what's going on?" She asked.

"Well, picture this room full of rose petals." Luke grinned. "Only I know it's not."

"Which is good because if it was I would have a panic attack thinking about having to sterilize this OR again top to bottom. Do you know how many patients are allergic to scents?"

Luke crossed his arms. "Really? Don't you have any scope of imagination?"

"No, not on a night when the ER is quiet and my board *was* running smoothly."

Luke moved to stand in front of her. "Well, I was trying to be romantic, but I realize now it's kind of hard to be romantic when we're both wearing surgical masks standing in an OR."

"Yeah, why are we here?"

"Because it was in OR like this that I first met you. You told me to get out of your OR."

"And I'm telling you that now, too." She laughed nervously and then it hit her when she spied Esme in the scrub room, crying. "Oh, my God."

Luke got down on one knee and pulled out a ring. "Don't worry, it's been sterilized. It won't contaminate this surgical field."

"Oh, my God," she said again in disbelief.

"Sarah, I can't live without you. You brought me back from the dead. You taught me to love again, to feel again and I want you to be my wife. Marry me."

She began to cry, soaking the paper surgical mask. "Yes. I'll marry you. Yes!"

Luke slipped the ring on her finger. "Good. Nestor will be thrilled I finally found the nerve to ask you."

Sarah laughed. "Remind me to kiss him next time I see him."

"Kiss him?" Luke asked then ripped off his mask. "Sorry, but you're going to have to sterilize this OR again. I need to kiss my fiancée properly."

Sarah removed her mask and let him kiss her. It wasn't the exact OR where they'd first met, but it was an OR where they worked together constantly, together saving lives, but most of all it was a place where they'd saved each other.

And being in his arms was right where she needed to be.

"There's something else I need to tell you," Sarah said. "It's important."

Luke groaned, but grinned. "You want to move back to New York."

"No. Look, it's…"

A tap on the glass interrupted their conversation and she turned around to see Esme in the scrub room looking quite distressed.

"What's up with her?" Luke asked.

Esme hit the intercom. "Um, I think we need to sterilize that room right now. My water just broke."

Sarah chuckled as Esme was pointing frantically at her belly. "I believe that we're about to be an aunt and uncle. Even though technically I'm not an aunt until we actually get married."

Luke's eyes widened as the reality of what she was telling him sank in. "What?"

"I would go find Carson and bring him here. Esme has gone into labor."

Luke shook his head. "Only her baby would be born on Valentine's Day. I'll get Carson."

"And I'll get Esme comfortable." She kissed him again. "Be careful."

"You, too. I have a feeling she's going to fight back when that pain starts to hit."

Sarah went to Esme and helped her stand, because she was bent over the scrub sink, holding the side as pains rocked through her.

"Sorry, I thought I had more time," Esme panted.

"You can't control it."

Esme cursed under her breath. "It figures, though—my kid had to come on Valentine's Day."

Sarah laughed. "I know, but let's get you to a birthing room and wait for Carson to come."

Sarah walked Esme down the hall and tried not to think about the fact that in nine months she might be walking down this very same hall, with Esme holding her up, and she couldn't help but wonder what Luke was going to think when she told him, because that was something they'd never talked about in their year together.

She'd been going to tell him but then Esme had gone into labor.

Right now their conversation would have to wait, but pretty soon she wouldn't be able to hide it any longer.

"Come on, one more push." Carson was behind Esme, holding her shoulders, and Luke was pacing by the door.

"Stop pacing," Esme shouted over her shoulder. "It's annoying me."

"Sorry," Luke mumbled.

"Come on, Esme. Ignore him and give me one more push."

Esme used some choice curse words that were directed at Carson, but she gave it that one last push and soon Sarah was catching Carson and Esme's baby girl in her hands. The baby didn't even need a back rub; she began to cry lustily.

"It's a girl," Sarah announced. Esme began to cry and Carson kissed her. "Carson, you want to come cut the cord?"

Carson moved toward her and Sarah tied off the cord and

handed Carson the sterile scissors. He cut the cord and then took his daughter gently in his arms, bringing her to Esme, who waited for her with open arms.

"If this doesn't change your mind about Valentine's Day, Esme, I don't know what will," Carson teased as he kissed Esme's sweaty brow again.

Sarah's heart swelled with happiness.

She wasn't used to this kind of love, this kind of family, but she had it all here and as she glanced up at Luke she could see the wonder in his eyes as he looked down at his little niece with love.

A nurse that was on duty took the newborn to weigh her, rub ointment in her eyes and give her a vitamin K shot. Luke did the APGAR on his niece with Carson watching over his daughter and Sarah helped Esme.

Once everything was done, the newest, swaddled, seven-pound-five-ounce member of the Ralston family was handed to Esme again.

"What're you going to name her?" Sarah asked as she gently touched the baby's head.

"Not Valentine," Esme said quickly, glaring at Luke and Carson respectively.

Sarah laughed. "Well, we'll leave you alone for a bit, but really you've come through that beautifully. You can go home in the morning if her vitals remain stable."

Carson nodded. "Thanks, Sarah."

"No problem." She washed her hands and then walked out of one of the two birthing rooms they had in Crater Lake.

"That was amazing," Luke said. "You never cease to amaze me."

"What do you think they'll name her?"

Luke laughed. "My brother's so head over heels for her and the baby, he'll agree to call her anything that Esme wants. And really that's the way it should be."

"Really?" Sarah asked. "So you wouldn't object if I called

our baby something like Asterix or Cantaloupe or some other fashionable name when it comes this fall?"

Luke paused. "What?"

"I was trying to tell you, but Esme interrupted us. I'm pregnant." She waited with bated breath for his reaction, but she didn't have to wait long. Before she had a chance to tease him with other names she was in his arms and he was kissing her.

"Truly?"

She nodded. "Truly. Though I'm terrified I don't have the best example in parents. What if I end up like them?"

"Highly doubtful." He wrapped his arms around her. "You'll be a great mother."

"And you'll be a great father."

"I love you, Sarah." He kissed her again and she melted in his arms. "You're my life, I would do anything for you, but I'm not naming our baby Cantaloupe."

Sarah laughed. "I love you, too."

And as she kissed him again she realized that she'd found her place. She'd found herself and she was right where she needed to be, in Luke's arms.

* * * * *

Mountain Blizzard

Cassie Miles

INTRIGUE

Seek thrills. Solve crimes. Justice served.

Cassie Miles, a *USA TODAY* bestselling author, lives in Colorado. After raising two daughters and cooking tons of macaroni and cheese for her family, Cassie is trying to be more adventurous in her culinary efforts. She's discovered that almost anything tastes better with wine. When she's not plotting Harlequin Intrigue books, Cassie likes to hang out at the Denver Botanical Gardens near her high-rise home.

Books by Cassie Miles

Harlequin Intrigue

Mountain Midwife
Sovereign Sheriff
Baby Battalion
Unforgettable
Midwife Cover
Mommy Midwife
Montana Midwife
Hostage Midwife
Mountain Heiress
Snowed In
Snow Blind
Mountain Retreat
Colorado Wildfire
Mountain Bodyguard
Mountain Shelter
Mountain Blizzard

Visit the Author Profile page at
millsandboon.com.au for
more titles.

For Nafina, who will always be my screen saver and,
as always, to Rick.

CAST OF CHARACTERS

Emily Peterson—The free-spirited poet turned investigative journalist has gotten in over her head.

Sean Timmons—Emily's ex-husband was an undercover FBI agent while they were married. Now he's her bodyguard.

"Bulldog" Barclay—A thug who works for Wynter.

Hazel Hopkins—Emily's great-aunt lives near Aspen and hires Sean to protect her niece.

Greg Levine—The FBI agent based in San Francisco is trying to help. But which side?

Doris Liu—The adoptive mother of Roger Patrone raised the boy in Chinatown.

John Morelli—Working for Wynter, his position is midlevel management, but he's only a thug.

Roger Patrone—Another Wynter employee, he lost his life trying to do the right thing.

Matt and Mason Steele—Brothers who are part of TST Security.

Jerome Strauss—The editor of a blog/newspaper who has gotten involved with the wrong people.

Dylan Timmons—Sean's brother, and a computer genius who helped found TST Security.

James Wynter—The head of a crime syndicate based in San Francisco.

Frankie Wynter—The youngest son of James Wynter is a thug, a spoiled brat and a murderer.

Lianne Zhou—A survivor of human trafficking, she is a powerful figure in Chinatown.

Mikey Zhou—The snakehead smuggler has a soft spot in his heart for his sister, Lianne.

PROLOGUE

San Francisco
Mid-September

THE DOUBLE-DECK LUXURY yacht rolled over a Pacific wave just outside San Francisco Bay as Emily Peterson wobbled down a nearly vertical staircase on her four-inch stilettos. Her short, tight, sparkly disguise gave her a new respect for the gaggle of party girls she'd hidden among to sneak on board. Somehow those ladies managed to walk on these stilts without falling and to keep their nipples covered in spite of ridiculously low-cut dresses.

Her plan for tonight was to locate James Wynter's private computer and load the data onto a flash drive. She'd slipped away from the gala birthday party for one of Wynter Corporation's top executives. The guests had been raucous as they guzzled champagne and admired their view of the Golden Gate Bridge against the night sky. Some had complained about having to surrender their cell phones, and Emily had agreed. It would have been useful to snap photos of high-ranking political types getting cozy with Wynter's thugs.

Belowdecks, she went to the second door on the right. She'd

been told this was James Wynter's office. The polished brass knob turned easily in her hand. No need to pick the lock.

Pulse racing, she entered. The desk lamp was off, but moonlight through the porthole was enough to let her see the open laptop. In a matter of minutes, she could transfer Wynter's data to her flash drive, and she'd finally have the evidence she needed for her human trafficking article.

Before she reached the desk, she heard angry voices in the corridor. She backed away from the desk and ducked into a closet with a louvered door. Desperately, she prayed for them to pass by the office and go to a different room.

No such luck.

The office door crashed open. One of the men fell into the office on his hands and knees while others laughed. Another guy turned on the lamp. Light spread across the desktop and spilled onto the floor.

Her pulse thundered in her ears, but Emily stayed utterly silent. She dared not make a sound. If Wynter's men found her, she was terrified of what they'd do.

Carefully, she stepped out of her red stilettos and went into a crouch. Through the slats in the door, she could see the shoes and legs of four men. The man who had fallen kept apologizing again and again, begging the others to believe him.

She recognized the voice of one of his tormentors: Frankie Wynter, the youngest son of James Wynter. Though she couldn't exactly tell what was going on, she thought Frankie was pushing the man who was so very sorry while the others laughed.

There was a clunk as the man who was being pushed flopped into the swivel chair behind the desk. From this angle, she saw only the back sides of the three men. One of them rocked back on his heel, cracked his knuckles and then lunged forward. She heard the slap, flesh against flesh.

They hit him again. What could she do? How could she stop them? She hated being silent while someone else suffered. Each blow made her cringe. If her ex-husband had been here, he could have made a difference, would have done the right thing. But she was on her own and utterly without backup. Should she speak up? Did she dare?

The beating stopped.

"Shut up," Frankie roared at the man in the chair. "Crying like a little girl, you make me sick."

"Let me talk. Please. I need to see the kids."

"Don't beg."

Emily saw the gleam of silver as Frankie drew his gun. Terror gripped her heart. The other two men flanked him. They murmured something about waiting for his father.

Frankie opened the center drawer on the desk and took out a silencer. "I can do what needs to be done."

"But your father—"

"He's always telling me to step up." He finished attaching the silencer to his handgun. "That's what I'm going to do."

He fired point-blank, then fired again.

When Frankie stepped away, she saw the dead man in the chair. His suit jacket was thrown open. The front of his shirt was slick with blood.

Emily pinched her lips closed to keep from crying out. She should have done something. A man was dead, and she hadn't reached out, hadn't helped him.

"We're already out at sea," Frankie said. "International waters. A good place to dump a body."

"I'll get something to carry him in."

He glanced toward the closet...

CHAPTER ONE

Colorado
Six weeks later

HE'D BEEN DOWN this road before. Though Sean Timmons was pretty sure that he'd never actually been to Hazelwood Ranch, there was something familiar about the long, snow-packed drive bordered on either side by wood fences. He parked his cherry-red Jeep Wrangler between a snow-covered pickup truck and a snowy white lump that was the size of a four-door sedan. Peering through his windshield, he saw a large two-story house with a wraparound porch. It looked like somebody had tried to shovel his or her way out, but the wind and new snow had all but erased the path leading to the front door.

Weather forecasters had been gleefully predicting the first blizzard of the Colorado ski season, and it looked like they were right for a change. Sean was glad he wouldn't have to make the drive back to Denver tonight. He hadn't formally accepted this assignment, but he didn't see why he wouldn't.

Hazel Hopkins from Hazelwood Ranch had called his office at TST Security yesterday and said she needed a bodyguard for at least a week, possibly longer. He wouldn't be protecting Hazel but a "friend" of hers. She was vague about the threat, but he gathered that her "friend" had offended someone with a story she'd written. The situation didn't seem too dangerous. Panic words, such as *narcotics*, *crime lord* and *homicidal ax murderer*, had been absent from her conversation.

Hazel had refused to give her "friend's" name, which wasn't all that unusual. The wealthy folk who lived near Aspen were often cagey about their identities. That was okay with him. The money transfer for Hazel's retainer had cleared, and that was really all Sean needed to know. Still, he'd been curious enough to look up Hazelwood Ranch on the internet, where he'd learned that the ranch was a small operation with only twenty-five to fifty head of cattle. Hazel, the owner, was a small but healthy-looking woman with short silver hair. No clues about the identity of her "friend." If he had to guess, he'd say that the person he'd be guarding was an aging movie star who'd written one of those tell-all books and was now regretting her candor.

Soon enough he'd know the truth. He zipped his parka, slapped on a knit cap and put on heavy-duty gloves. It wasn't far to the front porch, but the snow was already higher than his ankles. Fat, wet flakes swirled around him as he left his Jeep and slogged along the remnants of a pathway to the front door.

On the porch, the Adirondack chairs and a hanging swing were covered with giant scoops of drifted snow. He stomped his boots and punched the bell under the porch lamp. Hazel Hopkins opened the door and ushered him into a warmly lighted foyer with a sweeping wrought-iron staircase and a matching chandelier with lights that glimmered like candles.

"Glad you made it, Sean." Her voice was husky. When he looked down into her lively turquoise eyes, he suspected that a lot of wild living had gone into creating her raspy tone. Though she wore jeans on the bottom, her top was kimono-style with a fire-breathing dragon embroidered on each shoulder. He had the impression that he'd met her before.

She stuck out her tiny hand. "I'm Hazel Hopkins."

Compared with hers, his hand looked as big as a grizzly

bear's paw. Sean was six feet, three inches tall, and this little woman made him feel like a hulking giant.

"Hang your jacket on the rack and take off your wet boots," she said. "You're running late. It's almost dark."

"The snow slowed me down."

"I was worried."

Parallel lines creased her forehead, and he noticed that she glanced surreptitiously toward a shotgun in the corner of the entryway. Gently he asked, "Have there been threats?"

"I had a more practical concern. I was worried that you wouldn't be able to find the ranch and you couldn't reach us by phone. Something's wrong with my landline, and the blizzard is disrupting the cell phone signal."

He sat on a bench by the door to take off his wet boots.

Without pausing for breath, she continued. "You know how they always say that the weather doesn't affect your service on the cell phone or the Wi-Fi? Well, I'm here to tell you that's a lie, a bold-faced lie. Every time we have a serious snowstorm, I have a problem."

The heels on her pixie-size boots clicked on the terra-cotta floor between area rugs as she darted toward him, grabbed his boots and carried them to a drying mat under the coat hooks. She braced her fists on her hips and stared at him. "You're exactly how I remembered."

Aha, they had met before. He stood and adjusted the tail of his beige suede shirt to hide the holster he wore on his hip. "This may sound strange…" he said. "Have I ever been here?"

"I don't think so. But Hazelwood Ranch is the backdrop for many, many photos. The kids came here often."

Her explanation raised more questions. Backdrop for what? What kids? Why would he have seen the photos? "Maybe you could remind me—"

She reached up to pat his cheek. "I'm glad that you're still clean-shaven. I don't like the scruffy beard trend. I'll bet you picked up your grooming habits in the FBI."

"Plus, my mom was a good teacher."

"Not according to the photo on your TST Security website," she said. "Your brother, Dylan, has a ponytail."

"He's kind of a wild card. His specialties are electronics and cybersecurity."

"And your specialty is working with law enforcement and figuring out the crimes. I believe your third partner, Mason Steele, is what you boys call the 'muscle' in the group."

"I guess you checked me out."

"I have, indeed."

He took a long look at her, hoping to jog his brain. His mind was blank. Nothing came through. His gaze focused on her necklace, a long string of etched silver, black onyx and turquoise beads. He knew that necklace…and the matching bracelet coiled around her wrist.

Shaking his head, he inhaled deeply. A particular aroma came to him. The scent of roasted peppers, onions, chili and cinnamon mingled with honey and fresh corn bread. He couldn't explain this odor, but his lungs had been craving it. Nothing else was nearly as sweet or as spicy delicious. Nothing else would satisfy this newly awakened appetite.

His eyelids closed as a high-definition picture appeared in his mind. He saw a woman—young, fresh and beautiful. A blue jersey shift outlined her slender curves, and she'd covered the front with a ruffled white apron. Her long, sleek brown hair cascaded down her back, almost to her waist. She held a wooden spoon toward him, offering a taste of her homemade chili.

He had always wanted more than a taste. He wanted everything with her, the whole enchilada. But he couldn't have her. Their time was over.

He gazed down into her eyes…*her turquoise eyes!*

"You remember," Hazel said, "the wedding."

That Saturday in June, six and a half years ago, was a blur of color and taste and music and silence. His eyelids snapped open. "I recall the divorce a whole lot better."

These were dangerous memories, warning bells. He should run, get the hell out of there. Instead, he followed his nose down a shadowy hallway. Stiff-legged, he marched through the dining room into the bright, warm kitchen where the aroma of chili was thick.

Two pans of golden corn bread rested near the sink on the large center island with a dark marble countertop. She stood at the stove with her back toward him, stirring a heavy cast-iron pot. She wore jeans that outlined her long legs and tight, round bottom. On top, she had on a striped sweater. Over her shoulder, she said, "Hazel, did I hear the doorbell?"

The small, silver-haired woman beside him growled a warning. "You should turn around slowly, dear."

Sean gripped the edge of the marble countertop, unsure of how he was going to feel when he faced her. Every single day since their divorce five years ago—after only a year and a half of marriage—he had imagined her. Sometimes he remembered the sweet warmth of her body beside him in their bed. Other times he saw her from afar and reveled in coming closer and closer. Usually, he imagined her naked with her dark chestnut hair spilling across her olive skin.

Her hair! He stared at her back and shoulders. She'd chopped off her lush, silky hair.

"Emily," he said.

She whirled. Clearly surprised, she wielded her wooden spoon like a knife she might plunge into his chest. "Sean."

Her turquoise eyes were huge, outlined with thick, dark lashes. Her mouth was a thin, tight line. Her dark brows pulled down, and he immediately recognized her expression, a look he'd seen often while they were married. She was furious. What the hell did she have to be angry about? He was the one who had driven through a blizzard.

He stepped away from the counter, not needing the support. The anger surging through his veins gave him the strength of ten. "I don't know what kind of sick game you two ladies are playing, but it's not funny. I'm leaving."

"Good." She stuck out her jaw and took a step toward him. "I don't want you hanging around."

"Then why call me up here? I had a verbal contract, an agreement." TST had a strict no-refund policy, but this was a special circumstance. He'd pay back the retainer from his own pocket. "Forget it. I'll give your money back."

"What money?" Emily's upper lip curled in a sneer that she probably thought was terrifying. Yeah, right, as terrifying as a bunny wiggling its nose.

"You hired me."

"Not me." Emily threw her spoon back into the chili pot. "Aunt Hazel, what have you done?"

The silver-haired woman with dragons on her shoulders had maneuvered her way around so she was standing at the far end of the center island with both of them on the other side. "When you two got married, I always thought you were a perfect match."

"You were the only one," Emily said.

Unfortunately, that was true. Sean and Emily were both born and raised in Colorado, but they had met in San Francisco. She was a student at University of California in Berkeley, majoring in English and appearing at least once a week at local poetry slams. At one of these open-mike events, he saw her.

She'd been dancing around on a small stage wearing a long gypsy skirt. Her wild hair was snatched up on her head with dozens of ribbons. He'd been impressed when she rhymed "appetite" and "morning light" and "coprolite," which was a technical word for fossilized poop. He would have stayed and talked to her, but he'd been undercover, rooting out a drug dealer at the slam venue. Sean had been in the FBI.

When they told people they were getting married, their opposite lifestyles—Bohemian chick versus federal agent—were the first thing people pointed to as a reason it would never work.

The next issue was an age difference. She was nineteen, and he was twenty-seven. Eight years wasn't really all that much, but her youthful immaturity stood in stark contrast to his orderly, responsible lifestyle.

"If you'd asked me at the time," Aunt Hazel said, "I'd have advised you to live together before marriage."

Sean hadn't wanted to take that chance. He had hoped the bonds of marriage would help him control his butterfly. "It was a mistake," he said.

Emily responded with a snort.

"You don't think so?" he asked.

"Are you still here? You were in such a rush to get away from me."

His contrary streak kicked in. He sure as hell wasn't going to let her think that she was chasing him out the door. Very slowly and deliberately, he pulled out a stool and took a seat at the center island opposite the stove top. He turned away from Emily.

"Aunt Hazel," he said, "you still haven't told us why you hired me as a bodyguard."

"You? A bodyguard?" Emily sputtered. "You're not a fed anymore?"

"Do you care?"

"Why should I?"

"What are you doing now?" he asked.

"Writing."

"Poetry?" He scoffed.

She exhaled an eager gasp as she tilted her head and leaned toward him. Her turquoise eyes flashed. Her face, framed by wisps of brown hair, was flushed beneath the natural olive tint. He remembered her spirit and her enthusiasm, and he knew that she wanted to tell him something. The words were poised at the tip of her tongue, straining to jump out.

And he wanted to hear them. He wanted to share with her, to listen to her stories and to feel the waves of excitement that radiated from her. Emily had always thrown herself wholeheartedly into whatever she was attempting to do. It was part of her charm. No doubt she had some project that was insanely ambitious.

With a scowl, she raised her hand, palm out, to hold him away from her. "Just go."

"Such drama," Aunt Hazel said. "The two of you are impossible. It's called communication, and it's not all that difficult. Sean, you're going to sit there and I'm going to tell you what our girl has been up to."

"I don't have to listen to this," Emily said.

"If I'm not explaining properly, feel free to jump in," Hazel said. "First of all, Emily doesn't write poems anymore. After the divorce, she changed her focus to journalism."

"Totally impractical," he muttered. "With all the newspapers going out of business, nobody makes a living as a journalist."

"I do all right."

Her voice was proud, and there was a strut in her step as she strolled from one end of the island to the other. Watching her long, slender legs and the way her hips swayed was a treat. He felt himself being drawn into her orbit. She'd always had the power to mesmerize him.

"Fine," he muttered. "Tell me about your big deal success in journalism."

"Right after the divorce, I got a job writing for the *Daily Californian*, Berkeley's student newspaper. I learned investigative techniques, and I blogged. And I started doing articles for online magazines. I have a regular bimonthly piece in a national publication, and they pay very nicely."

"For articles about eye shadow and shoes?"

"Hard-hitting news." She slammed her fist on the marble island. "I witnessed a murder."

"Which is why I called you," Aunt Hazel said. "Emily's life is in danger."

This was just crazy enough to be possible. "Have you received threats?"

"Death threats," she said.

His feet were rooted to the kitchen floor. He didn't want to stay…but he couldn't leave her here unprotected.

CHAPTER TWO

EMILY COULDN'T LOOK away from him. Fascinated, she watched as a muscle in Sean's jaw twitched, his brow lowered and his eyes turned as black as polished obsidian. He was outrageously masculine.

With a nearly imperceptible shrug, his muscles tensed, but his frame didn't contract. He seemed to get bigger. His fingers coiled into fists, ready to lash out. He was prepared to defend her against anything and everything. His aggressive stance told her that he'd take on an army to keep her from harm.

When she thought about it, his new occupation as a bodyguard made sense. Sean had always been a protector, whether it was keeping a bully away from his sweet-but-nerdy brother or rescuing a stray dog by stopping four lanes of traffic on a busy highway. If Sean had been hiding in that louvered closet instead of her, he would have saved the man she now could identify as Roger Patrone.

Sean reached toward her. She yanked her arm away. She didn't dare allow him to get too close. No matter how much she wanted his embrace, that wasn't going to happen. This man had been the love of her life. Ending their marriage was the most difficult thing she'd ever done, and she couldn't bear going through that soul-wrenching pain again.

"Did you report the murder to the police?" he asked.

"Of course," she said, "and to your former FBI bosses. Specifically, I had several chats with Special Agent Greg Levine. I'm surprised he didn't call and tell you."

"Levine is still stationed in San Francisco," he said. "Is that where the crime took place?"

"Yes."

"In the city?"

"Just beyond the Golden Gate Bridge."

"In open waters," he said. "A good place to dump a body."

It was a bit disturbing that his FBI-trained brain and Freddie Wynter's nefarious instincts drew exactly the same conclusion. *Maybe you need to think like a criminal to catch one.* "As it turned out, the ocean wasn't such a great dump site. The victim washed up on Baker Beach five days later."

"The waiting must have been rough on you," he said. "It's no fun to report a murder when the body goes missing."

Definitely not fun when the investigating officer was buddy-buddy with her ex-husband. She'd asked Greg not to blab to Sean, but she'd expected him to ignore her request. Those guys stuck together. The only time Sean had lied to her when they were married was when he was covering up for a fellow fed.

She wondered if Sean's departure from the FBI had been due to negative circumstances. Had Mr. Perfect screwed up? Gotten himself fired? "Why did you leave the FBI?"

"It was time."

"Cryptic," she snapped.

"It's true."

God forbid he give her a meaningful explanation! Leaving the FBI must have been traumatic for him. Sean was born to be a fed. He could have been a poster boy with his black hair neatly barbered and his chin clean-shaven and his beige chamois suede shirt looking like it had come fresh from the dry cleaner's. He'd been proud to be a special agent. Would he confide in her if they'd fired him? "You can be so damn annoying."

"Is that so?"

"I hate when you put off a perfectly rational query with a macho statement that doesn't really tell me anything, like a man's got to do what a man's got to do."

"I don't expect you to understand."

"Mission accomplished."

Hostility vibrated around him. A red flush climbed his throat. Oh yeah, he was angry. Hot and angry. They could have put him on the porch and melted the blizzard.

"I'll leave," he said.

"Not in this storm," Aunt Hazel said. "The two of you need to calm down. Have some chili. Try to be civil."

Emily stepped away from the stove, folded her arms at her waist and watched with a sidelong gaze as Sean and her aunt dished up bowls of chili and cut off slabs of corn bread. Sean managed to squash his anger and transform into a pleasant dinner guest. She could have matched his politeness with a cold veneer of her own, but she preferred to say nothing.

There had been a time—long ago when she and Sean were first dating—when she was known for her candor. Every word from her lips was truth. She had been 100 percent frank and open.

Those days were gone.

She'd glimpsed the ugliness, heard the cries of the hopeless, learned that life wasn't always good and people weren't always kind. She'd lost her innocence.

And Hazel was correct. She'd gotten herself into trouble from the Wynters. Though she didn't want to be, she was terrified. Almost anything could set off her fear…an unexpected phone call, the slam of a door, a car that followed too closely. She hadn't gotten a good night's sleep since that night in James Wynter's closet.

The only reason she hadn't disintegrated into a quivering mass of nerves was simple: Wynter and his men didn't know her identity. Her FBI contact had told her that they knew there was a witness to the murder, but didn't know who. It was only a matter of time before they found out who she was and came after her. *Tell him. Tell Sean. Let him be your bodyguard.*

Her aunt asked, "Emily, can I get you something to drink?"

Hazel and Sean had already sprinkled grated cheddar on top of their chili bowls and added a spoonful of sour cream. They were headed to the adjoining dining room.

What would it hurt to have dinner with him? The more she looked at him, the more she saw hints of his former self, her husband, the gentleman, the broad-shouldered man who had stolen her heart. She remembered the first time they were introduced when he'd tried to shake hands and she gave him a hug. They'd always been opposites and always attracted.

"I'm not hungry," Emily said.

"There's no reason to be so stubborn," Hazel scolded. "I've hired you a bodyguard. Let the man do his job."

"I don't want a bodyguard."

She glared at Sean, standing so straight and tall like a knight in shining armor. She was drawn to his strength. At the same time, he ticked her off. She wanted to tip him over like an extra-large tin can.

Edging closer to the kitchen windows, she pushed aside the curtain and peered outside. Day had faded into dusk, and the snow was coming down hard and fast. The blizzard wasn't going to let up; he'd be here all night. She'd be spending the night under the same roof with him? *This could be a problem, a big one.*

"I've got a question for you," he said as he strolled past her and set his chili bowl on a woven place mat. "What kind of murder would trigger an FBI investigation?"

"The man who pulled the trigger is Frankie Wynter."

He startled. "The son of James Wynter?"

She'd said too much. The best move now was to retreat. She stretched and yawned. "I'm tired, Aunt Hazel. I think I'll go up to my room."

Without waiting for a response, she pivoted and ran from the kitchen. In the foyer, she paused to put Hazel's rifle in the closet. It was dangerous to leave that thing out. Then she charged up the staircase, taking two steps at a time. In her bedroom, she turned on the lamp and flopped onto her back on the queen-size bed with the handmade crazy quilt.

Memory showed her the picture of Roger Patrone sprawled back in the swivel chair with his necktie askew and his shirt covered in blood. When they came toward the closet, looking for something to wrap around poor Roger, she'd expected to be the next victim. She'd held tightly to the doorknob, hoping they'd think it was locked.

There had been no need to hold the knob. Frankie told them to get the plastic shower curtain from the bathroom. Blood wouldn't seep through. His quick orders had made her think that he might have pulled this stunt before. Other bodies might have gone over the railing of his daddy's double-decker yacht. Other murders might have been committed.

She stood, lurched toward the door, pivoted and went back to the bed. Trapped in her room like a child, she had no escape from memory. Her chest tightened. It felt like a giant fist was squeezing her lungs, and she couldn't get enough oxygen. She sat up straight. She was hot and cold at the same time. Her head was dizzy. Her breath came in frantic gasps.

With a moan, she leaned forward, put her head between her knees and told herself to inhale through her nose and exhale through her mouth. Breathe deeply and slowly. Wasn't work-ing—her throat was too tight. Was she having a panic attack? She didn't know; she'd never had this feeling before.

The door to her bedroom opened. Sean stepped inside as though he didn't need to ask her permission and had every right to be there. She would have yelled at him, but she couldn't catch her breath. Her pulse fluttered madly.

He crossed the carpet and sat beside her on the bed. His arm wrapped around her shoulders. His masculine aroma, a combination of soap, cedar forest and sweat, permeated her senses as she leaned her head against his shoulder.

Her hands clutched in a knot against her breast, but she felt her heart rate beginning to slow down. She was regaining control of herself. Somehow she'd find a way to handle the fear. And she'd set things right.

Gently, he rocked back and forth. "Better?"

"Much." She took a huge gulp of air.

"Do you want to talk about what happened?"

"I already did. I told your buddy, Agent Levine."

"Number one, he's not my buddy. Number two, why didn't he offer to put you in witness protection?"

"I turned it down," she said.

"Emily, do you know how dangerous Frankie Wynter is?"

"I've been researching Wynter Corp for over a year," she said. "Their smuggling operations, gambling and money laundering are nasty crimes, but the real evil comes from human trafficking. Last year, the port authorities seized a boxcar container with over seventy women and children crammed inside. Twelve were dead."

"And Wynter Corp managed to wriggle out from under the charges."

"The paperwork vanished." That was one of the bits of evidence she'd hoped to get from James Wynter's computer. "There was no indication of the sender or the destination where these people were to be delivered. All they could say was that they were promised jobs."

"This kind of investigation is best left to the cops."

She separated from him and rose to her feet. "I know what I'm doing."

"I'm not discounting your ability," he said. "You might be the best investigative reporter of all time, but you don't have the contacts. Not like the FBI. They've got undercover people everywhere. Not to mention their access to advanced weaponry and surveillance equipment."

"I understand all that." He wasn't telling her anything she hadn't already figured out for herself.

"You're a witness to a crime. That's it—that's all she wrote."

She braced herself against the dresser and looked into the large mirror on the wall. Her reflection showed her fear in the tension around her eyes and her blanched complexion. Sean—ever the opposite—seemed calm and balanced.

"Can I tell you the truth?" she asked.

"That would be best."

She made eye contact with his reflection in the mirror. "I didn't actually witness the shooting. I saw Frankie with the gun in his hand. He screwed on a silencer. I heard the gunshot, and I saw the bullet holes…and the blood. But I didn't actually witness Frankie pointing the gun and pulling the trigger."

"Minor point," he said. "A good prosecutor can connect those dots."

"The body that washed ashore five days later was too badly nibbled by fishes for identification." She splayed her fingers on the dresser and stared down at them. "I was kind of hoping he was someone else, someone who jumped off the Golden Gate Bridge, but Agent Levine matched his DNA."

"To what?"

"I'd given a description to a sketch artist and identified the victim from a mug sheet photo. His name was Roger Patrone."

He shrugged. "I don't know him."

"He was thirty-five, only a couple of years older than you, and made his living with a small-time gambling operation in a cheesy strip joint. Convicted of fraud, he served three years."

"You've done your homework."

"Never married, no kids, he was orphaned when he was nine and grew up with a family in Chinatown. He speaks the language, eats the food, knows the customs and has a reputation as a negotiator for Wynter."

"Roger sounds like a useful individual," Sean said. "I'm guessing the old man wasn't too happy about this murder."

"Yeah, well, blood is still thicker than water. The FBI brought Frankie in for questioning, but one of the other guys in Wynter Corp confessed to killing Patrone and claimed self-defense. He took the fall for the boss's son."

Sean left the bed and came up behind her. His chest wasn't actually touching her back, but if she moved one step, she'd be in his arms.

In a measured tone, he said, "You're telling me that Frankie's not in custody."

"No, he's not."

"And he knows there's a witness."

"Yes."

"Did you write about the murder?"

"Agent Levine asked me not to." But she had written many articles about the evil-doing of Wynter Corporation.

"Does Frankie have your name?"

"No," she said. "I write under an alias, three different aliases, in fact. And I have two dummy blogs. Since my communication with these publications is via the internet, nobody even knows what I look like."

"Smart."

"Thank you." Her reflection smiled at his. *So far, so good.* She might make it through the night with no more explanation than that. There was more to tell, but she didn't want to get involved with Sean. Not again.

He continued. "And you're also smart to have left Frankie and the other thugs behind in San Francisco. Hazelwood Ranch seems like a safe place to stay until this all dies down."

Unfortunately, she hadn't come to visit Aunt Hazel for safety reasons. Her gaze flickered across the surface of the mirror. She didn't want to tell him.

He leaned closer, whispered in her ear. "What is it, Emily? What do you want to say?"

The words came tumbling out. "Frankie is here in Colorado. The Wynter family has a gated compound over near Aspen. I didn't come here to give up on my investigation. I need to go deeper."

He grasped her upper arms. "Leave this to the police."

From downstairs, there was a scream.

CHAPTER THREE

"AUNT HAZEL!"

Though Emily's immediate reaction was to run toward the sound of the scream, Sean only allowed her to take two steps before he grabbed her around the middle and yanked her so hard that her feet left the floor. This was why he'd been hired.

He dragged her across the bedroom. There was only one thought in his mind: get her to safety. In the attached bathroom, he set her down beside a claw-foot tub.

"Stay here," he ordered as he drew his gun. "Keep quiet."

"The hell I will."

Though he hated to waste time with explanation, she needed to know what was going on. He spoke in a no-nonsense tone. "If there's been a break-in, they're after you. If you turn yourself in, we have no leverage. For your Aunt Hazel's safety, you need to avoid being taken captive."

"Okay, help her." Her face flushed red with fear and anger. Her eyes were wild. She pushed at his shoulder with both hands. "Hurry!"

Moving fast, he crossed to her closed bedroom door. He wished he was wearing boots instead of just socks. If he had to go outside, his feet would turn to ice. He paused at the door and mentally ran through the layout of the house. From the upstairs landing, he could see the front door. He'd know if some-one had broken in that way.

Sean was confident in his ability to handle one intruder, maybe two. But Frankie Wynter had a lot of thugs at his dis-posal, and they were loyal; one guy was willing to face a murder rap for the boss's son. One—or two or more—of them might be standing outside her bedroom door right now.

But he didn't hear anything. Outside, the snow rattled against the windows. The wind whistled. From downstairs, he heard shuffling noises. A heavy fist rapping at the door? A muffled shout. Sean turned the knob, pulled the door open and braced the gun in his hands, ready to shoot.

There was no one on the upstairs landing.

Emily dashed to his side. "Let me help. Please!"

He'd told her to stay back and she chose to ignore him. Emily was turning into a problem. "Is that tub in the bathroom made of cast iron?"

"It's antique. Now is not the time for a home tour."

"Get inside the tub and stay there." At least, she wouldn't be hit by a stray bullet.

"I'm coming with you."

Was she trying to drive him crazy or was this stubborn, in-furiating behavior just a part of her natural personality? He couldn't exactly remember. He'd had damn good reasons for divorcing this woman. "No time to argue. Just accept the fact that I know what I'm doing."

"I need a gun."

"What you need is to listen to me."

"Please, Sean! You always carry two guns. Give one to me."

He pulled the Glock from his ankle holster and slapped it into her hand. "Do you remember how to use this?"

She recited the rules he'd taught her one golden afternoon six years ago in Big Sur. "Aim and don't close my eyes. No tradi-tional safety on a Glock, so keep my finger off the trigger until I'm ready. Squeeze—don't yank."

"You've got the basics."

He'd treated their lessons like a game and had never insisted that she take his weapon from the combination safe when he was on assignment and she was alone at home. While he was working undercover, he'd worried about her safety, worried that she'd be hurt and it would be his fault. There was a strange irony in the fact that she'd put herself in ten times more danger than he could imagine.

He peered through the open bedroom door onto the upstairs landing where an overhead light shone down on the southwestern decor that dominated the house: a Navajo rug, a rugged side table and a cactus in an earthenware pot. A long hallway led to other bedrooms. The front edge of the landing was a graceful black wrought-iron staircase overlooking the foyer and chandelier by the front door.

Sean peered over the railing.

A menacing silence rose to greet him. He didn't like the way this was going. Emily's aunt wasn't the type of woman who cowered in silence. He gestured for Emily to stay upstairs while he descended.

At the foot of the staircase, he caught a glimpse of flying kimono dragons when Hazel raced across the foyer and skidded to a stop right in front of him.

She glared. "Where the heck is my rifle?"

Looking down from the landing, Emily said, "I moved it to the front closet."

"I had my gun right by the door," she said to Sean. "Emily shouldn't have moved it. Out of sight, out of mind."

The women in this family simply didn't grasp what it took to be cautious and safe. They needed ten bodyguards apiece. He rushed Hazel up the stairs, where she hugged Emily. The two of them commiserated as though the threat were over and done with. Had they forgotten that there might be an intruder?

"Hazel," he barked, "why did you scream?"

"I heard something outside and looked through the window.

A fat lot of good it did, the snow's coming down so hard I couldn't see ten feet. But I caught a glimmer…headlights. I went toward the front door for a better look. At the exact same time, I heard somebody crashing against the back door like they were trying to bust it down. That's when I screamed."

Sean figured that five minutes had passed since they'd heard Hazel's cry for help. "After you screamed, what did you do?"

"I hid."

"Smart," he said. "You didn't reveal your hiding spot until you saw me."

She nodded, and her short silver hair bounced.

"Did you see the intruder? Did he make a noise? Was there more than one?"

"Well, my hearing isn't what it once was, but I'm pretty sure there was only one voice. And I guarantee that nobody made enough noise to tear down the back door."

As Sean herded Emily and her aunt into Emily's bedroom, he tallied up the possible ways to break into the house. In addition to front and back door and many windows, there was likely an entrance to a root cellar or basement. The best way to limit access to the two women was to keep them upstairs. Unfortunately, it also meant they had no escape.

From Emily's bedroom, he peered through the window to the area where the cars were parked. He squinted. "I can see the outline of a truck."

"So?"

"Do you recognize it?" *Is that Frankie Wynter's truck?*

"We're in the mountains, Sean. Every other person drives a truck."

A coating of snow had already covered the truck bed; he couldn't tell if anybody had been riding in back. But the vehicle showed that someone else was on the property, even if there hadn't been other noises from downstairs.

He gave Emily a tight smile. "Stay here with Hazel. Take care of her."

"What are you going to do?"

"I'll check the doors and other points of access."

Her terse nod was a match for his smile. They were both putting on brave faces and tamping down the kind of tension that might cause your hand to tremble or your teeth to chatter. When she rested her hand against his chest, he was reminded of the early days in their marriage when she'd say goodbye before he left on assignment.

"Be careful, Sean."

He tore his gaze away from her turquoise eyes and her rose petal lips. Her trust made him feel strong and brave, even if he wasn't facing a real dragon. He was girding his loins, like a knight protecting his castle. In the old days, they would have kissed.

"I should come with you," Aunt Hazel said. "You need someone to watch your six."

"Stay here," he growled.

Emily hooked her arm around her aunt's waist. "We might as well do what he says. Sean can be a teensy bit rigid when it comes to obeying orders."

"My, my, my." Hazel adjusted the embroidered dragons on her shoulders. "Isn't that just like a fed?"

Hey, lady, you're the one who called me. And he was done playing their games. As far as he was concerned, they'd had their last warning. He refused to stand here and explain again why they shouldn't throw themselves into the line of fire when there was a possible intruder. He made a quick pivot and descended the staircase with the intention of searching the main floor.

The house was large but not so massive that he'd get lost. First, he would determine if an intruder was inside. The front door hadn't been opened. The door to a long, barrack-type wing where ranch hands might sleep during a busy season was locked, and the same was true for the basement door and the back door that opened onto a wide porch. Though it had a dead bolt, the back door lock was flimsy, easily blasted through with a couple of gunshots. As far as he could tell, no weapons had been fired.

When he pushed open the back door, a torrent of glistening snow swept inside. The area near the rear porch was trampled with many prints in the snow. Was it one person or several? He couldn't tell, but Hazel's story was true. She'd heard someone back here.

As he closed the rear door and relocked it, he heard Emily call his name. Her voice was steady, strong and unafraid. Weapon raised, he rushed toward the front of the house. The door was opening. A man in a brown parka with fur around the hood plodded inside.

Though he didn't look like much of a threat, Sean wasn't taking any chances. "Freeze."

"I sure as hell will if I don't close this door."

As the man in the parka turned to shut the front door, Hazel came down the staircase. "It's okay, Sean. This is my neighbor, Willis. He was a deputy sheriff until he retired a couple of years ago."

"I was worried, Hazel." As he shoved off his hood, unzipped the parka and stomped his snowmobile boots, puddles of melted snow appeared on the terra-cotta tile floor. "Couldn't reach you on the phone, so I decided to come over here and check before I went to bed. Hi, Emily."

"Hey, Willis."

"Take off those boots." Hazel pointed to the bench by the door. "Are you hungry? Emily made a big pot of chili."

He sat and grinned at Sean and Emily. His face was ruddy and wet. A few errant flakes of snow still clung to his thick mustache. "And who's this young fella with the Glock?"

"Sean Timmons of TST Security." He shook the older man's meaty hand. "I'm Emily's bodyguard."

Willis was clearly intrigued. Why did Emily need protection? What other kind of security work did Sean do? He pushed the strands of wet gray hair off his forehead and straightened his mustache before he asked, "You hiring?"

"Part time," Sean said. "I can always use a man with experience as a deputy sheriff."

"Seventeen years," Willis said. "And I still work with the volunteer fire brigade and mountain search and rescue."

"Plus you've got your own little neighborhood watch." Sean had the feeling that Hazel got more attention from the retired deputy than the others in this area. "You have a key to the front door."

"That's right."

"Do you mind telling me why you banged on the back door and didn't let yourself in?"

"The back door is always unlocked, and it was a few less steps through the blizzard than the front. When I found it locked, I was pretty damn mad. I yanked at the handle to make sure it wasn't just stuck, and I might have let out a few choice swear words."

"Scared me half to death," Hazel said.

"I heard you scream." Willis looked down at the floor between his boots. He wore two pairs of wool socks. Both had seen better days. "And I felt like a jackass for scaring you."

She patted his cheek, halfway chiding and halfway flirting. "You're lucky I couldn't find my rifle."

While he explained that his keys were in the truck, and he had to tromp back out there to find the right ones, Hazel fussed over him. She was a touchy-feely person who hugged and patted and stroked. Sean noted her behavior and realized how similar it was to methods Emily used to calm him, mesmerize him and convince him to do whatever she wanted.

He glanced toward her. She sat on the fourth step, where she had a clear view of the others in the foyer. Her gaze flicked to the left, but he knew she'd been watching him. A hard woman to figure out. Was she angry or nervous? Independent or lonely?

Earlier tonight, she'd been on the verge of a panic attack.

Her eyes had been wide with fear. Her muscles were so tightly clenched that she couldn't move, couldn't breathe. Scared to death, and he didn't blame her. James Wynter and his associates were undeniably dangerous.

A muscle in his jaw clenched. Why had she chosen to go after these violent criminals? And how did Levine justify leaving this witness unprotected? The FBI had been chasing Wynter for years, way before Sean was stationed in San Francisco. A chance to lock up Frankie Wynter would be a coup.

"Then it's settled," Hazel said. "Willis is sticking around for some chili and a couple of beers. You kids come into the dining room and join us."

"In a minute," Emily promised as she rose to her feet and motioned for Sean to come toward her.

She stayed on the first step, and he stood below her. They were almost eye level.

He asked, "Did you have something you wanted to say?"

"You did good tonight. I know that Hazel and I can be a handful, but you managed us. You were organized, quick. And when we thought we needed you, there you were, charging around the corner and yelling for Willis to freeze. You were…" She exhaled a sigh. "Impressive."

Her compliment made him leery. "It's what I do."

"Not that we actually needed your bodyguard skills." She caught hold of his hand and gave a squeeze. "This was a simple misunderstanding because of the blizzard."

"You have plenty of reason to be worried," he reminded her. "You mentioned the Wynter family compound near Aspen. Tonight it was Willis at the door. Tomorrow it might be Frankie Wynter."

"Don't make this into a worst-case scenario." She continued to hold his hand, and he felt the tension in her grip. "Tonight a neighbor came to pay a visit. That's all. And the blizzard is just snow. It's harmless. Kids play in it. Ever build a snowman?"

"Ever get caught in an avalanche?" He was keeping the tone

light, but there was something important he needed to say. "Seriously, Emily, you need a bodyguard."

"I agree, and the job is yours."

He'd expected an argument but was glad that she'd decided to be rational. He glanced toward the dining room. "I could do with another bowl of chili."

"Me, too."

Before she hopped down the stair step to the floor, she went up on tiptoe and gave him a kiss on the forehead. It was nothing special, the kind of small affection a wife might regularly bestow on her husband. The utter simplicity blew him away.

Before she could turn her back and skip off into the dining room, he caught her hand and gave a tug. She was in his arms. When her body pressed against his, they were joined together the way they were supposed to be.

Then he kissed her.

CHAPTER FOUR

EMILY HADN'T INTENDED to seduce him. That little kiss on his forehead was meant to be friendly. If she'd known she was lighting the fuse to a passionate response, she never would have gotten within ten feet of him. *Not true. I'm lying to myself.* From the moment she'd seen him, sensual memories had been taunting from the back of her mind. It was only a matter of time before that undercurrent would become manifest.

Their marriage was over, but she never had stopped imagining Sean as her lover. Nobody kissed her the way he did. The pressure of his mouth against hers was familiar and perfect. *Will he do that thing with his tongue? The thing where he parts my lips gently, and then he deepens the kiss. His tongue swoops and swirls. And there's a growling noise from the back of his throat, a vibration.*

She'd never been able to fully describe what he did to her and what sensations he unleashed. But he was doing it right now, right in this moment. *Oh yes, kiss me again.*

She almost swooned. *Swoon? No way!* She'd changed. No more the lady poet, she was a hard-bitten journalist, not the type of woman who collapsed in a dead faint after one kiss, definitely not.

But her grip on consciousness was slipping fast. Her knees

began to buckle, and she clung to his shoulders to keep from slipping to the floor. Her hands slid down his chest. Even that move was sexy; through the smooth fabric of his beige chamois shirt, she fondled his hard but supple abs.

This out-of-control but very pleasurable attraction had to stop before she lost her willpower, her rationality...her very mind. Pushing with the flat of her palms against his chest, she forced a distance between them. "We can't do this."

"Sure we can." He slung his arm around her waist. "It's been a while, but I haven't forgotten how."

Tomorrow he'd thank her for not dissolving into a quivering blob of lust. Firmly, she said, "I can see that we're going to need ground rules."

He kissed the top of her head and took a step back. "You cut it."

"What?"

"Your hair, you cut it."

"Too much trouble." She fluffed her chin-length bob. "And getting rid of the Rapunzel curls makes me look more adult."

"Oh yeah, you're really grown up. How old are you now, twenty-one? Twenty-two?"

She didn't laugh at his lame attempt at humor. "I'm almost twenty-six."

Their eight-year age difference had always been an issue. When they first met, she'd just turned nineteen. They were married and divorced before she was twenty-one, and she'd always wondered if their relationship would have lasted longer if she'd been more mature. It was a familiar refrain. *If I knew then what I know now, things would be different.*

More likely, they never would have gotten together in the first place. Older and wiser, she would have taken one look at him and realized that he wasn't the sort of man who should be married.

"I like your new haircut," he said. "And you're right. We need some ground rules."

She gestured toward the dining room. "Should we eat chili while we talk?"

"That depends on how much you want your aunt and former deputy Willis to know."

Of course, he was right. She didn't want to spill potentially dangerous information about Wynter Corp into a casual conversation. Until now the only thing she'd told Aunt Hazel was that she'd witnessed a murder in San Francisco. She hadn't named the killer or the victim and certainly hadn't mentioned that the Wynter family had a place near Aspen.

Regret trickled through her. She probably shouldn't have come here. Though she'd been ultracautious in keeping her identity secret and her connection to Hazel was hard to trace, somebody might find out and come after them. If anything happened to Hazel...

Emily shuddered at the thought. "I don't want my aunt to get stuck in the middle of this."

"Agreed."

"Come with me."

She led him across the foyer to a living room that reflected Hazel's eclectic personality with a combination of classy and rustic. The terra-cotta floor and soft southwestern colors blended with painted barn wood on the walls. The high ceiling was open beam. The rugged, moss rock fireplace reminded Emily that her aunt was an outdoorswoman who herded cattle and tamed wild mustangs. But Hazel also had a small art collection, including two Georgia O'Keeffe watercolor paintings of flowers that hung on either side of the fireplace.

While Emily went behind the wet bar at the far end of the room, Sean studied the watercolor of a glowing pink-and-gold hydrangea. "Is this an original?"

"A gift from the artist," Emily said. "Hazel spent some time with O'Keeffe at Ghost Ranch in New Mexico."

"I keep forgetting how rich your family is. None of you are showy. It's all casual and comfortable and then I realize that you've got valuable artwork on the wall." He made his way across the room to the wet bar. "When I was driving up to this place, I had the feeling I'd seen it before. Did we come here for a visit?"

"I don't think so. Hazel was in Europe for most of the year and a half we were married." She peered through the glass door of the wine cellar refrigerator. "White wine or red?"

"How about beer?"

"You haven't changed." She opened the under-the-counter refrigerator and selected two bottles of craft beers with zombies on the labels. "You'll like this brand. It's dark."

He didn't question her selection, just grabbed the beer, tapped the neck against hers and took a swig. He licked his lips. "Good."

A dab of foam glistened at the corner of his mouth, and she was tempted to wipe the moisture off, better yet, to lick it.

"Ground rules," she said, reminding herself as much as him.

"First, I want to know why I have déjà vu about Hazelwood Ranch. Do you have any photo albums?"

She came out from behind the bar and shot him a glare. "If you don't mind, I'd rather not take a side trip down memory lane. We have more urgent concerns."

"You're the one who introduced family into the picture," he said. "I want to understand a few things about Hazel. How long has she lived here?"

"The ranch doesn't belong to our family. Hazel's late husband was the owner of this and many other properties near Aspen. He renamed this small ranch Hazelwood in honor of her. They always seemed so happy. Never had kids, though. He was older, in his fifties, when they got married."

She scanned the spines of books in a built-in shelf until she found a couple of photo albums. As she took them down and carried them to the coffee table in front of the sofa, she realized that she hadn't downloaded her own photos in months.

Digital albums were nice, but she really preferred the old-fashioned way.

"I knew there'd be pictures," he said.

"Do you remember those journals I used to make? I'd take an old book with an interesting cover and replace the pages with my own sketches and poetry and photos."

"I remember." His voice was as soft as a caress. "The Engagement Journal was the best present you ever gave me."

"What about the watch, the super-expensive, engraved wristwatch?"

"Also treasured."

She went back to the bar, snatched up her beer and returned to sit on the sofa beside him. "I'm an excellent present giver. It's a family trait."

"How are they, the Peterson family?"

"My oldest sister had a baby girl, which means I'm an aunt, and the other two are in grad school. Mom and Dad moved to Arizona, which they love." She took a taste of the zombie beer, which was, as she'd expected, excellent, and gave him a rueful smile. "I don't suppose Aunt Hazel told my mom that she was calling you."

"Your mom hated me."

Emily made a halfhearted attempt to downplay her mother's opinion. "You weren't their favorite."

Her parents had begged her to stay in college and wait to get married until she was older. Emily was her mom's baby, the youngest of four girls, the artistic one. When Emily's divorce came, Mom couldn't wait to say "I told you so."

"Toward the end," he said, "I thought she was beginning to come around."

"It was never about you personally," she said. "I was too young, and you were too old. And Mom didn't really like that you did dangerous undercover work in the FBI."

"And what does she think of your current profession?"

She took a long swallow of the dark beer. "Hates it."

"Does she know about the murder?"

"Oh God, no." She cringed. If her mother suspected that she was actually in danger, she'd have a fit.

Emily opened the older of the two albums. The photographs were arranged in chronological order with Emily and her sisters starting out small and getting bigger as they aged. Nostalgia welled up inside her. The Petersons were a good-looking family, wholesome and happy. In spite of what Sean thought, they weren't really rich. Sure, they had enough money to live well and take vacations and pay for school tuitions. But they weren't big spenders, and their home in an upscale urban neighborhood in Denver wasn't ostentatious.

Like her older sisters, she had tried to be what her parents wanted. They valued education, and when she told them she was considering becoming a teacher, they were thrilled. But Emily went to UC Berkeley and strayed from the path. She was a poet, a performance artist, an activist and a photographer. Her marriage and divorce to Sean had been just one more detour from the straight and narrow.

Aunt Hazel was more indulgent of Emily's free-spirited choices. Hazel approved of Sean. She'd invited him to be a bodyguard. Maybe she knew something Emily hadn't yet learned.

He stopped her hand as she was about to turn a page in the album. He pointed to a wintertime photo of her, wearing a white knit hat with a pom-pom and standing at the gate that separated Hazelwood Ranch from public lands. She couldn't have been more than five or six. Bundled up in her parka and jeans and boots, she appeared to be dancing with both hands in the air.

"This picture," he said. "You put a copy of this in the journal you gave me. I must have looked at it a hundred times. I never really noticed the outline of the hills and the curve in the road, but my subconscious must have absorbed the details. Seeing that photo is like being here."

His déjà vu was explained.

She asked, "What are we going to do to protect Hazel?"

"How does she feel about Willis? Do they have a little something going on?"

She and her aunt hadn't directly talked about who Hazel was dating, but Emily couldn't help noticing that Willis had stopped by for a visit every day. Sometimes twice a day. "Why do you ask?"

"We could hire Willis to be a bodyguard for Hazel. They might enjoy an excuse to spend more time together."

"That's not a bad idea," she said. "His performance tonight—tromping around in the snow looking for a house key—wasn't typical. Usually he's competent."

"I wouldn't want to throw him up against an army of thugs with automatic pistols," he said, "but that shouldn't be necessary. If you settle here and keep a low profile, there's no reason for Wynter to track you down. You're sure he doesn't know you're the witness?"

"I was careful, bought my plane tickets under a fake name, blocked and locked everything on my computer, threw away my phone so I couldn't be tracked."

"How did you learn to do all that?"

"Internet," she said. "I read a couple of how-to articles on disappearing yourself. Plus, I might have picked up a couple of hints when we were married."

"But you didn't like my undercover work." He leaned back against the sofa pillows and sipped his beer. "You said when I took on a new identity, it was a lie."

At the time, she hadn't considered her criticism to be unreasonable. Any new bride would be upset if her husband said he was going to be out of touch for a week or two and couldn't tell her where he was going or what he was doing. She jabbed an accusing finger in his direction. "I had every right to interrogate you, every right to be angry when you wouldn't tell me what was going on."

His dark eyes narrowed, but he didn't look menacing. He was too handsome. "You could have just trusted me."

"Trust you? I hardly knew you."

"You were my wife."

It hadn't taken long for them to jump into old arguments. Was he purposely trying to provoke her? First he mentioned the age thing. Now he was playing the "trust me" card. Damn it, she didn't want to open old wounds. "Could we keep our focus on the present? Please?"

"Fine with me." He stretched out his long legs and rested his stocking feet on the coffee table. "You claim to have covered your tracks when you traveled and when you masked your identity."

"Claimed?" Her anger sparked.

"Can you prove that you're untraceable? Can anybody vouch for you?"

"Certainly not. The point of hiding my identity is to eliminate contacts."

"Just to be sure," he said, "I'll ask Dylan to do a computer search. If anybody can hack your identity or files, he can."

"It's not necessary, but go ahead." She was totally confident in her abilities. "I've always liked your brother. How's he doing?"

"We keep him busy at TST doing computer stuff. You'll be shocked to hear that he's finally found a girlfriend who's as smart as he is. She's a neurosurgeon."

"I'm not surprised." The two brothers made a complementary pairing: Dylan was a genius, and Sean had street smarts.

"I'll use my FBI contacts, namely, Levine, to keep tabs on their investigation." He drained his beer and stood. "That should just about cover it."

"Cover what?"

"Ground rules," Seàn said as he crossed the room toward the wet bar. "You and Hazel will be safe if you stay here and don't communicate with anybody. I'll need to take your cell phone."

"Not necessary," she said. "I'm aware that cell phones can be hacked and tracked. I only use untraceable burner phones."

"What about your computer?"

She swallowed hard. In the back of her mind, she knew her computer could be hacked long distance and used to track her down. There was no way she'd give up her computer. "All my documents are copied onto a flash drive."

"I need to disable the computer. No calling except on burner phones. No texting. No email. No meetings."

Anger and frustration bubbled up inside her. Though she hadn't finished her beer and didn't need a replacement, she followed him to the bar. She climbed up on a stool and peered down at him while he looked into the under-the-counter fridge. When he stood, she glared until he met her gaze.

To his credit, Sean didn't back down, even though she felt like she was shooting lightning bolts through her eye sockets. When she opened her mouth to speak, she was angry enough to breathe fire. "Your ground rules don't work for me."

He opened another zombie beer. "What's the problem?"

"If I can't use the internet, how can I work?"

"Dylan can probably hook up some kind of secure channel to communicate with your employer."

"What if I don't want to stay here?"

"I suppose I could move you to a safe house or hotel." He came around the bar and faced her. "What's really going on?"

"Nothing."

"You always said you hated lying and liars, but you're not leveling with me. If you don't tell me everything, I can't do my job."

The real, honest-to-God problem was simple: she hadn't given up on the Wynter investigation. One of the specific reasons she'd come to Colorado was to dig up evidence against Frankie. She swiveled around on the bar stool so she was facing away from him. "I don't want to bury my head in the sand."

"Explain."

"I want to know why Roger Patrone was murdered. And I want to stop the human trafficking from Asia."

He nodded. "We all want that."

"But I have leads to track down. If I could hook up with people from the Wynter compound and question them, I might get answers. Or I could break in and download the information on their computers. I might find evidence that would be useful to the FBI."

"Seriously?" He was skeptical. "You want to keep digging up dirt, poking the dragon?"

She shot back. "Well, that's what an investigative reporter does."

"This isn't a joke, Emily. You saw what happens to people who cross Frankie Wynter."

"They get shot and dumped."

Wynter's men could toss her body into a mountain cave, and she wouldn't be found for years. When she voiced her plan out loud, it sounded ridiculous. How could she expect to succeed in her investigation when the FBI had failed?

"If you want to take that kind of risk," he said, "that's your choice. But don't put Hazel in danger."

He was right. She shouldn't have come here, and she definitely shouldn't have talked to him. *Trust me? Fat chance.*

Their connection had already begun to unravel, which was probably for the best. He irritated her more than a mohair sweater on a sunny day. Her unwarranted attraction to him was a huge distraction from her work. She should tell him to go. She didn't need a bodyguard.

But Sean was strong and quick, well trained in assault and protection. He knew things about investigating and undercover work that she could only guess about. Her gut instincts told her she really did need him.

"Come with me," she said. "Back to San Francisco."

CHAPTER FIVE

AT FIVE O'CLOCK the next morning, Sean stood at the window in the kitchen and opened the blinds so he could see outside while he was waiting for the coffeemaker to do its thing. He'd turned off the overhead light, and the cool blue shadows in the kitchen melted into the shimmer of moonlight off the unbroken snow. The blizzard had ended.

Soon the phones would be working. Lines of communication would be open. There would be nothing to block Emily's return trip to San Francisco. She'd decided that she needed to go back and dig into her investigation, and it didn't look like she was going to budge.

It was up to him whether he'd go with her as her bodyguard or not. His first reaction was to refuse. She had neither the resources nor the experience to delve into the criminal depths of Wynter Corp, and she was going to get into trouble, possibly lethal trouble. He needed to make her understand her limitations without insulting her skills.

Outside, the bare branches of aspen and fir trees bent and wavered in the wind. So cold. So lonely. A shiver went through him. Their divorce had been five years ago. He should be over it. But no. He missed her every single day. Seeing her again and hearing her voice, even if she was arguing with him most of the time, touched a part of him that he kept buried.

He still cared about Emily. Damn it, he couldn't let her go to California by herself. She needed protection, and nobody could keep her safe the way he could. He would die for her... but he preferred not to.

After she'd made her announcement in the living room, she outlined the plan. "Tomorrow morning, we'll catch a plane and be in San Francisco before late afternoon. There'll be time for you to have a little chat with Agent Levine and the other guys in that office. We'll talk to my contacts on the day after that."

He'd objected, as any sane person would, but she'd already made up her mind. She flounced into the dining room and ate chili with Hazel and Willis. The prime topic of their conversation being big snowstorms and their aftermath. The chat ended with Emily's announcement that she'd be going back to San Francisco as soon as the snow stopped because she had to get back to work.

During the night, he'd gone into her room to try talking sense into her. Before he could speak, she asked if he would accompany her. When he said no, she told him to leave.

Stubborn! How could a woman who looked so soft and gentle be so obstinate? She was like a rosebush with roots planted deep—so strong and deep that she could halt the forward progress of a tank. How could he make her see reason? What sort of story could he tell her?

Finally, the coffeemaker was done. He poured a cup, straight black, for himself and one for her with a dash of milk, no sugar. Up the staircase, he was careful not to spill over the edge of the mugs. Twisting the doorknob on her bedroom took some maneuvering, but he got it open and slipped inside.

For a long moment, he stood there, watching her sleep in the dim light that penetrated around the edges of the blinds. A pale blue comforter was tucked up to her chin. Wisps of dark hair swept across on her forehead. Her eyelashes made thick, dark crescents above her cheekbones, and her lips parted slightly. She was even more beautiful now than when they were married.

She claimed that she'd changed, and he recognized the difference in some ways. She was tougher, more direct. When he thought about her rationale for investigating, he understood that she was asserting herself and building her career. Those practical concerns were in addition to the moral issues, like that need to get justice for the guy who was murdered and to right the wrongs committed by Wynter Corp. He crossed the room, placed the mugs on the bedside table and sat on the edge of her bed.

Slowly, she opened her eyes. "Has it stopped snowing?"

He nodded.

"Have you changed your mind?"

"Have you?"

She wiggled around until she was sitting up, still keeping the comforter wrapped around her like a droopy cocoon. Fumbling in the nearly dark room, she turned on her bedside lamp and reached for the coffee. "I'd like a nip of caffeine before we start arguing again."

"No need to argue. I want to help with your investigation."

"I'd be a fool to turn you down."

Damn right, you would. His qualifications were outstanding. In addition to the FBI training at Quantico, he'd taken several workshops and classes on profiling. When he first signed on, his goal was to join the Behavioral Analysis Unit. But that was not to be. His psych tests showed that his traits were better suited to a different position. He was a natural for undercover work; namely, he had an innate ability to lie convincingly.

"Plus, I'm offering the services of my brother, the computer genius and hacker."

Suspicion flickered in her greenish-blue eyes. "I appreciate the offer, but what's the quid pro quo?"

"Listen to you." He grinned. "Awake for only a couple of minutes and already speaking Latin."

She turned to look at the clock and then groaned. "Five-fifteen in the morning. Why so early?"

"Couldn't sleep."

"So you thought you'd just march in here and make sure I didn't get a full eight hours."

"As if you need that much."

The way he remembered, she seldom got more than five hours. He often woke up to find her in the middle of some project or another. Emily was one of those people who bounced out of bed and was fully functional before she brushed her teeth.

"It's going to be a long day." She drank her coffee and dramatically rolled her eyes. "Plane rides can be so very exhausting."

"Here's the deal," he said. "There aren't any direct flights from Aspen to San Francisco. You'll be routed through Denver first."

Watching him over the rim of her mug, she nodded agreement.

"Since we're already there, let's make a scheduled stop in Denver, spend the night and talk to Dylan. We'll still be investigating. Didn't you say you were looking for documents about imports and exports? He could hack in to Wynter Corp."

"Information obtained through illegal hacking can't be used for evidence."

"But you're not a cop," he said. "You don't have to follow legal protocols."

"True, and a hack could point me in the right direction. Dylan could also check company memos mentioning the murder victim. And, oh my God, accounting records." She came to an abrupt halt, set down her coffee and stared at him. "Why are you making this offer?"

"I want to help you with your new career."

Though he truly wished her well, helping her investigation wasn't the primary reason he'd suggested a stop in Denver. Sean wanted to derail her trip to San Francisco and keep her out of danger. As far as he was concerned, the world had enough in-vestigative journalists. But there was only one Emily Peterson.

Her gaze narrowed. "Are you lying?"

He scoffed. "Why would I lie?"

"Turning my question into a different question isn't an an-swer." A slow smile lifted one corner of her mouth. "It's a tech-nique that liars use."

"Believe whatever you want." He rose from her bed and placed his half-empty coffee mug on the bedside table. "I'm suggesting that you use Dylan because he's skilled, he has high-level contacts and he won't get caught."

She threw off the covers and went up on her knees. An over-large plaid flannel top fell from her shoulders and hung all the way to her knees. The shirt looked familiar. He reached over and stroked the sleeve that she'd rolled up to the elbow. "Is this mine?"

"The top?" Unlike him, she was a terrible liar. "Why would I wear your jammies?"

"Supersoft flannel, gray Stewart plaid from L.L.Bean," he said. "I'm glad you kept it."

"I hardly ever wear flannel. But I was coming to Colorado and figured I might want something warm." She tossed her head, flipping her hair. "I forgot this belonged to you."

Another lie. He wondered if she'd been thinking of him when she packed her suitcase for this trip. Did she miss him? When she wore his clothing to bed, did she imagine his embrace?

He stepped up close to the bed and glided his arms around her, feeling the softness of the flannel plaid and her natural, sweet warmth. She'd been cozy in bed, wrapped in his pajamas that were way too big for her.

She cleared her throat. "What are you doing?"

"I'm holding you so you won't get cold."

He stroked her back, following the curve of her spine and the flare of her hips. With his hands still on the outside of the fabric, he cupped her full, round ass. Her body was incredible.

She hadn't changed in the years they'd been apart. If anything, she was better, more firm and toned. He lifted her toward him, and she collapsed against his chest, gasping as though she'd been holding her breath.

"Ground rules," she choked out. "This is where we really need rules."

He lifted her chin, gazed into her face and waited until she opened her eyes. "You're supposed to be the spontaneous one, Emily. Let yourself go—follow your desires."

"I can't."

The note of desperation in her voice held him back. Though he longed to peel off the flannel top and drag her under the covers, he didn't want to hurt her. If she wanted a more controlled approach, he would comply.

"One kiss," he said, "on the mouth."

"Only one."

"And another on the neck, and another on your breast, and one more on…"

"Forget it! I should know better than to negotiate with you. There will be no kissing." She wriggled to get away from his grasp, but he wasn't letting go. "No touching. No hugging. No physical intimacy at all."

"You promised one," he reminded her.

"Fine."

She squinted her eyes closed and turned her face up to his. Her lips were stiff. And she was probably gritting her teeth. He'd still take the kiss. He knew what was behind her barriers. She still had feelings for him.

His kiss was slow and tender, almost chaste, until he began to nibble and suck on the fullness of her lower lip. His fingers unbuttoned the pajama top, and his hand slid inside. He traced a winding path across her torso with his fingertips, and when he reached the underside of her breast, she moaned.

"Oh, Sean." A shudder went through her. "I can't."

His hand stilled, but his mouth took full advantage of her

parted lips. His tongue plunged into the hot, slick interior of her mouth.

She spoke again. "Don't stop."

She kissed him back. Her hand guided his to her nipples, inviting him to fondle. Her longing was fierce, unstoppable. Her body pressed hard against his.

And then it was over. She fell backward on the bed and buried herself, even her face, under the covers. He loved the way he affected her. As for the way she affected him? He couldn't ignore his palpitating heart and his rock-hard erection. But his attraction was more than that.

"About these ground rules," he said. "Don't tell me there's no physical intimacy allowed. If I'm going to be around you and not allowed to touch, I'll explode."

"You scare me," she said as she crawled out from under the covers. "I don't want to fall in love with you again."

Would it really be so bad? She kept talking about how she had changed, but he was different, too. Not the same undercover agent that he was five years ago, he had learned tolerance, patience and respect.

Much of this shift in attitude came from his developing relationship with his brother; he was learning how to be a team player. Sean still teased—that was a big brother's prerogative—but he also could brush the small irritations away. At TST Security, he didn't insist on being the lead with every single job. He'd be nuts to interfere with Dylan's computer expertise, and their other partner, Mason Steele, was good at stepping in and taking charge.

His relationship with Emily was different. When they had been married, he might have been impatient. The way she kept prodding him about his work had been truly annoying. Why hadn't she been able to understand that undercover work meant he had to be secretive? If he kissed another woman while he was undercover, it didn't mean anything. How could it? In his mind, she was the perfect lover.

"First ground rule." He had to lay out parameters that allowed them to be together without hurting each other. "No falling in love."

"That's a good one," she said. "Write it down."

He sat at the small desk, found a sheet of notebook paper and a pen to jot down the first rule. "What about touching, kissing, licking, nibbling, sucking…" His voice trailed off as he visualized these activities. "I can't even say the words without needing to do it."

"I feel it, too, you know. We've always been amazing in bed, sexually compatible."

"Always."

In unison, they exhaled a regretful sigh.

"How about this?" she said. "No PDA."

Public display of affection? He wrote it down. "I can live with that."

She sat up on the bed and reached for her coffee mug again. After a sip, she proposed, "No physical contact unless I'm the one who initiates it."

He didn't like the way that sounded. "I need to have some kind of voice."

"You mean talking dirty?"

"Not necessarily. I might say something like I want to touch your cheek." Illustrating, he glided his hand along the line of her jaw, and then he leaned closer. "I want to kiss your forehead."

When he kissed her lightly, she pushed his face away. "You can ask, but I have veto power. At any time, I can say no."

"So you have veto power and you can also initiate."

"Yes."

"What does that leave for me?" he asked as he returned to sit at the desk.

She cast him an evil smile. "Begging?"

"I'm not writing that down."

As far as he was concerned, their negotiation was taking a negative turn. The way she described it, she controlled all physical contact. She had all the power. No way would he be reduced to begging. There had to be another way to work it out.

As he doodled with the pen on the paper, he heard the ringtone from the cell phone in his pocket. "Finally we have communication from the outside world."

"Who is it?"

"The caller ID says Zebra929. So it has to be my brother. Dylan likes to play with the codes."

As soon as he answered, his brother said, "This is a secured call, bouncing the signal. It needs to be short."

"Shoot."

"I got a call from FBI Special Agent Levine out of San Francisco. Guess who he's trying to contact?"

"Emily Peterson," Sean said. A chill slithered down his spine. This was bad news.

"Whoa, are you psychic?"

"I'm looking right at her."

"Emily Peterson Timmons?"

Sean heard the amazement in his brother's tone.

"Emily the poet? Emily with the long hair? Your ex-wife?"

"What was the message from Levine?"

"He wanted to warn her. There's a leak in SFPD. Wynter might know her identity."

"Why did Levine call me?"

"He's grasping at straws," Dylan said. "None of her San Francisco contacts know where she went."

"What about her parents?"

"I asked the same question. The Petersons are out of the country."

Actually, that was good news. A threat to Emily could mean other people in her family might become targets for Wynter. Sean asked, "Did Levine mention an aunt in the mountains? A woman named Hazel?"

"Is that the Hazel Hopkins you took a contract with?"

Sean's pulse quickened. Not only had he received phone

calls from Hazel, but he'd looked her up on the internet. It had taken nothing but a phone call for Levine to track him down. If Frankie Wynter figured out that connection, he might hack in to TST Security phones or computers. They could find Hazel. "How secure are our computers?"

"Very safe," Dylan said. "But anything can be hacked."

"Wipe any history concerning Hazel Hopkins."

"Okay. We should wrap up this call."

"Thanks, Zebra. I'll be flying back to Denver today with Emily. We need your skills."

He ended the call and looked toward her. No more fun and games. She was in serious danger.

CHAPTER SIX

EMILY WATCHED SEAN transformed from a sexy ex to the hard-core FBI agent she remembered from their marriage. His devilish grin became tight-lipped. Twin worry lines appeared between his eyebrows. His posture stiffened.

She didn't like the direction his phone call was taking. As soon as he ended the call, she asked, "Why were you talking to your brother about Hazel?"

"If you're in danger, so is your family."

"Not Hazel. Our last names aren't the same. Nobody knows we're related."

"Can you be one hundred percent sure of that?"

"Not really."

When she'd first started writing articles that might be controversial, she disguised her identity behind a couple of pseudonyms. She didn't want to accidentally embarrass her mom and dad or her sister in law school, and she liked being a lone crusader. Anonymous and brave, she dug behind the headlines to expose corruption.

One of her best articles dealt with a cheating handyman who overcharged and didn't do the work. Another exposed a phone scam that entrapped the unwary. This story about Wynter Corp was her first attempt to investigate serious crime.

She should have known better. A personal threat was bad enough, but she'd brought danger to her family. Her spirits crumbled as she sat on the bed listening to Sean's recap of the phone call with his brother. This was her fault, all her fault.

Moments ago, she'd been kissing her gorgeous ex-husband and had been almost happy. Now she felt like weeping or hiding under the covers and never coming out. Why couldn't the blizzard have lasted forever? The snow would have hidden her.

Trying to soothe herself, she rubbed the soft fabric of her sleeve between her thumb and forefinger. Despite what she'd told him, she hadn't worn this top by accident; she knew very well that it belonged to Sean. Cuddling up in his pajamas always gave her a feeling of warmth and safety. Sometimes she closed her eyes and pretended that she could still smell his scent even though the pajamas had been laundered a hundred times.

He sat beside her and took her hand. "Are you okay?"

"Not at all." She heard the vulnerability in her voice and hated it. "You probably want to tell me that I never should have done this article, that I'm a girlie girl and should stick with poetry."

He squeezed her hand. "As I recall, your poetry wasn't all lollipops and sparkles. There was something about a fire giver and vultures that ate his liver."

"Prometheus," she remembered. "He started out trying to do the right thing, just like me. And then he was eternally damned by the gods. Is that my fate?"

"You made some mistakes, had some bad luck."

"I'm being a drama queen." She was well aware of that tendency and tried to tamp the over-the-top histrionics before she threw herself into full-on crazy mode. "Tell me I'm exaggerating."

"It's safe to say you're not really cursed by the gods," he said, "but don't underestimate the seriousness of this threat."

"I won't." Her lower lip trembled. She fought the tears that sloshed behind her eyelids. "Oh God, what should I do?"

"No crying." He held her chin and turned her face so they were eye to eye. "You told me you were an investigative journalist. Well, you need to start acting like somebody who stands behind her words and takes responsibility for her actions."

His dark gaze caught and held her attention. His calm demeanor steadied her. Still, she was confused. "I don't know how."

"You're not Prometheus, and you're not little Miss Sunshine the poetry girl. Think of yourself as a reporter who got into trouble. What should we do next?"

"Make sure my family is safe."

Her parents were currently out of the country, visiting friends in the South of France. She didn't need to worry about Mom and Dad. Her three sisters were back east, and the two who were still in school lived alone. It seemed unlikely that Wynter would hunt them down. Nonetheless, they should be warned. "I should call my sisters."

"I'm going to ask you to wait until we get to Denver," he said. "The signal from your phone might be traced, and Dylan has equipment that's extremely secure."

"What about you?" She pointed to his cell phone. "What about that call?"

"It originated from the TST Security offices behind strong, thick firewalls."

She sat beside him, struggling to think in spite of the static waves that sizzled and shivered inside her head. From outside her bedroom door, she heard her aunt chattering to Willis as they went downstairs. It was early, a little after six o'clock and not yet dawn, but they were both already awake. Did they sleep together last night? Emily smiled to herself. *Ironic!* The senior citizens were getting it on while she and Sean stayed in separate bedrooms.

"I need to talk to Hazel." She looked toward him for guidance. "How much should I tell her?"

"She already knows you've witnessed a murder, so it won't

come as a big shock that she's in danger. Until this is over, I'd advise her to leave Hazelwood, maybe stay in a hotel in Aspen."

"I'm guessing that Willis might have an extra bedroom," she said. "And he would probably be a good protector."

"A former deputy," Sean said. "I'd trust him."

And she didn't think it would take much to convince Hazel to spend more time with Willis. Emily's eccentric aunt had never remarried after her husband had died fifteen years ago, but she had taken several live-in lovers. Willis had always been a friend. Maybe it was time for him to be something more.

She picked up her coffee mug from the bedside table and drained it in a few gulps. Today was going to be intense, and she'd need all the energy she could muster. "After taking care of the family, what do I do?"

"It's up to you."

"The first thing that comes to mind is run and hide." That was exactly what the old Emily would have done. She would have hidden behind her big, strong husband. But that wasn't her style, not anymore. "I want to take responsibility. I'll go after the story."

He shrugged. "San Francisco, here we come."

With Sean at her side, she could handle the threat. She could take down James Wynter and his son. What she couldn't do was…forget. The blood spreading across Roger Patrone's white shirt flashed in her mind. The sounds of a beating and fading cries for help echoed in her ears. She could never erase the memory of murder.

Over coffee in the kitchen, Emily convinced Hazel that there was a real potential for danger and she ought to move in with Willis. It didn't take much persuasion. Hazel agreed almost immediately, and she was happy, as perky as a chipmunk. Her energy and the afterglow of excitement confirmed Emily's suspicion that her aunt and Willis were more than friends.

Hazel dashed upstairs to her bedroom to pack a few essentials, and Willis swaggered around the kitchen, talking to Sean about how he should make sure Hazel was safe and secure. Though Emily had a hard time imagining Willis the kindhearted former deputy facing off with Wynter's thugs, she believed he was competent. Plus, he had the advantage of experience. He knew how to handle the dangers of the mountains and to use the elements to his advantage. His plan was to take Hazel to a ski hut he'd built on the other side of Aspen. The hut was accessible only by snowmobile or cross-country skis.

"What about the blizzard?" she asked.

Willis squinted out the kitchen window at a brilliant splash of sunlight reflecting off a pristine snowbank. "The big storm gave up during the night. We only got twenty or so inches, probably not even enough to close down the airport in Aspen."

She'd lived in San Francisco for so long that she'd forgotten how dramatically Colorado weather could change. Yesterday was a blizzard. Today she could get sunburned from taking a walk outside.

The timer on the oven buzzed. Emily opened the door, and the scent of sweet baked goods rushed toward her. Hazel had popped in a frozen almond-flavored coffee cake to thaw. Not as good as fresh made but decent enough for a rushed breakfast.

Willis went upstairs to help Hazel, and Emily turned toward Sean. "We need plane reservations to Denver," she said. "I'll go ahead and make them."

"You shouldn't." He pointed out the obvious. "Just in case the bad guys have a way to track airline tickets, you ought to avoid using your real name."

"No problem." Her solution was sort of embarrassing, and she really didn't want to tell him. She placed the pan of coffee cake on a trivet on the counter and cut off a slab. With this breakfast in hand, she headed toward the exit from the kitchen. "I'm going to get packed, and then I'll call the airlines."

He blocked the exit. "I hope you aren't thinking about buying plane tickets with a fake ID and credit card. That kind of ploy can get you on the no-fly list."

"It's not exactly fake," she muttered. "Just out of date by about five and a half years."

As realization dawned, his eyes darkened. "The way I remember, you changed your name back to Peterson after the divorce."

"I did."

"Please don't tell me you're using your married name."

"The identity was just sitting there. I doctored an old driver's license and applied for a credit card as Emily Timmons, using my own Social Security number and my address in San Francisco. It works just fine."

"The no-fly list and fraud." Still blocking her way so she couldn't run, he glared at her. A muscle in his jaw twitched. "Anything else you want to tell me?"

"If I confess everything, we'll have nothing to discuss on the flight." She patted his cheek and slipped around him. "You can make the reservations."

"For today, you'll be Mrs. Timmons. And then no more."

"Don't count on it."

"What's that supposed to mean? Are you planning some kind of strange reconciliation that I don't know about?"

"This has nothing to do with you," she said coolly. "But I might need your name for fake identification."

With her almond cake in one hand and coffee in the other, she climbed the staircase and went to her bedroom. She sat at the small desk and activated one of her disposable phones. She couldn't wait until they got to Denver to contact her sisters. If Sean didn't like it, too bad. She really didn't think Wynter would go after them, but they deserved a heads-up. Michelle, who was in law school, asked how she could get in touch with Emily if she heard anything.

"You can't call me back."

"I know," Michelle said. "The phone you're using right now doesn't show up on my caller ID listing."

"Contact me through TST Security in Denver. I hired a bodyguard." Emily hoped to avoid mentioning her ex-husband. "They can get me a message."

"TST Security," Michelle repeated. "I'm looking them up on the internet right now. Found the website. Well, damn it, sis, here's an interesting coincidence. One of the owners of the aforementioned security firm happens to be Sean Timmons."

"I didn't call him."

"Really?" Michelle's tone dripped with sarcasm. "Do you want me to believe that he magically appeared when you were in trouble? Was he wearing a suit of armor and riding a white steed?"

"Aunt Hazel called him." Emily wanted to keep this conversation short. "And I don't have to justify my decisions to you or anybody else in the family."

"But justice will be served," said the future lawyer. "To tell the truth, Emily, I always liked Sean. I'm glad he's watching over you."

Emily avoided mentioning Sean to her other two sisters. Those calls ended quickly, and she jumped in the shower. Though she had time to wash and blow-dry her hair, she decided against it. Going out in the snow meant she'd be wearing a hat and squashing any cute styling.

She lathered up while her mind filled with speculation. No doubt, Michelle would blab to the rest of the family. And the questions would begin. *Would she get back together with him?* That seemed to be the query of the day. A few moments ago, Sean had asked about reconciliation.

Never going to happen. And her sisters should understand. Didn't they remember how devastated she'd been when she'd filed for divorce?

Their attitude about Sean had always been odd. When she first married him, the three sisters talked about how he was

too old for her and his job was too dangerous for a stable relationship. In the divorce, however, the sister witches took Sean's
side. They blamed her for being fickle and undependable when
she should have been supportive. They told her to grow up. She
couldn't always have things her own way.

Maybe true. Maybe she hadn't been the most understanding
wife in the world. But he brought his own problems to the table:
Being inflexible. Not taking her seriously. Concentrating too
much on his work and not enough on his wife.

Wrapped in a towel after her shower, she padded into the
bedroom and pulled out her luggage from under the bed. Since
they were headed back to San Francisco, where she had clothes
and toiletries at her apartment, she packed light. She tucked her
three disposable cell phones in her carry-on. All data had already been downloaded off her de-activated computer.

She hid the flash drive in a specially designed black-and-silver pendant, which she wore on a heavy silver chain. A black
cashmere sweater and designer jeans completed her outfit. Her
practical boots and her parka were in the downstairs closet.

Before she left the bedroom, she checked her reflection in
the mirror. *Not bad.* She didn't look as frazzled as she felt. Her
hair was combed. Her lipstick properly applied. Her cheeks
were flushed with nervous heat, but the high color might be
attributed to too much blush.

Returning to San Francisco was the right thing to do, but she
was sorely tempted to take off for a quickie Bahamas vacation
with Sean. He owed her a trip. On their Paris honeymoon, he
had held her hand in a sidewalk café and promised that every
anniversary he would take her somewhere exciting. Their first
anniversary rolled around and no trip. They couldn't get their
schedules coordinated. And they argued about where to go.
And when she told him to just forget it, he did.

What a brat she'd been! But at the time, she was too furious
to make sense. She'd counted on Sean to be rational. That was
his job. Somehow he should have known that even though she

told him to forget it, he was supposed to lavish her with kisses and gifts until she changed her mind.

Their marriage had crumbled under the weight of hundreds of similar misunderstandings. Underneath it all, she wondered if they might actually be compatible. Certainly, there was nothing wrong with their sexual rapport. But could they talk? Was he too conservative? Were their worldviews similar? Was there any way, after the divorce, that she'd be willing to put her heart on the line and trust him? *I guess I'll find out.* While he was being her bodyguard and they were forced to be together, she had a second chance.

CHAPTER SEVEN

CLEARING THE RUNWAY in Aspen took longer than expected, and their flight as Mr. and Mrs. Timmons didn't land at DIA until after four o'clock in the afternoon. Sean rented a car and drove toward the TST office, where Dylan had promised to meet them.

In the passenger seat, Emily shed her parka and changed from snow boots to a pair of ballet flats. She peeked out the window at the undeveloped fields near the airport. "It's crazy. The snow's already melted."

"Denver only got a couple of inches."

"And the sky is blue, and the sun is shining. Every time I come back to Colorado, I wonder why I ever left."

"You don't have family in Denver, anymore."

"Nope." She gave him a warm smile. "But you do. I'm looking forward to seeing Dylan."

When Emily was being cordial, there was no one more charming. Her voice was as sweet as the sound of a meadowlark. Her intense blue-green eyes sparkled. Every movement she made was sheer grace. It was hard to keep his hands off her.

Sitting close beside her on the plane, inhaling her scent and watching her in glimpses, had affected him. He was going to need more than a flimsy set of relationship "ground rules" to maintain control.

Following the road signs, he merged onto I-70. His real problem would come tonight. Their flight to San Francisco was scheduled for tomorrow morning at about ten o'clock, which meant they'd be sleeping in the same place tonight. After the stop at TST, he intended to take her to his home, where the security was high and he could keep an eye on her. He had an extra bedroom. What he didn't have was willpower. When she was in bed, just down the hall, he would be tempted.

"Sean?"

He realized that she'd been talking while he wasn't listening. "Sorry, what did you say?"

"How did you name your company? I get that TST stands for your initials, Timmons, Timmons and your other partner, Mason Steele. But your logo is a four-leaf clover with three green leaves and one a faded red."

"At one time, there were four of us." Sean had told this story dozens of times, but his chest still tightened. Some scars never heal. This deep sadness would never go away. "We grew up together. Me and Dylan lived down the block from Mason and Matt Steele. Matt was my best friend. We were close in age, went to the same school, played on the same teams and went on double dates. When we were kids we pretended to be crime fighters."

"And when you grew up, you decided to fight crime for real."

"Not at first," he said. "We went to different colleges, followed our own separate ways. Matt joined the marines, and he liked the military life. That was why he couldn't be our best man. He was deployed, working his way up the chain of command."

There must have been a hint of doom in his tone, because Emily went very still. She listened intently.

He cleared his throat and continued. "About five years ago, Matt was killed in Afghanistan. His heroic actions rescued three other platoons, and he received a posthumous Purple Heart."

"I'm so sorry," she whispered.

"His death came right about the time our divorce was final. And I'd finished a sleazy undercover job where a good lawyer got the bad guys off with a slap on the wrist."

Remembering those dark days left a sour taste in his mouth. He'd just about given up. Life was a joke, not worth living. He went on an all-out binge, drugs and alcohol. Thanks to his undercover work, he was familiar with the filthy underbelly of the city, and he went there. He found rock bottom while seeking poisonous thrills that could wipe away his sorrow and regret and the senseless guilt that he was still alive while his friend was not. His judgment was off. He took stupid risks, landing in the hospital more than once. His path was leading straight to hell.

She reached across the console and touched his arm. "If I had known…"

"There was nothing you—or anybody else—could do. I didn't ask for help, didn't want anybody holding my hand."

"How did you get better?"

"I came back to Colorado and got on a physical schedule of weight lifting and running ten miles a day. I visited places where Matt and I used to go." He paused. "This sounds cheesy, but I found peace. I quit mourning Matt's death and celebrated his life."

"Not cheesy at all," she said.

"Weak?"

"That's the last word I'd use to describe you."

"Anyway, I did a lot of wilderness camping. One morning, I crawled out of my tent, stared up into a clear blue sky and decided I wanted a future."

"TST Security?"

"I quit the FBI, contacted my two buds and set up the business. I'd like to think that Matt would approve. We don't take cases that we don't like. And there are times like now when we can actually do some good."

"Is that how you think of my investigation into Wynter

Corp?" She brightened. "As something that could make a difference?"

"I guess I do feel that way."

He hadn't realized until this moment that he wanted Frankie
Wynter to pay the price for murder. Plus, they might take down
members of a powerful crime family, and that felt good.

Exiting the interstate, they were close enough to downtown
Denver for him to point out changes in the city where she'd
lived for so many years. Giant cranes loomed over new sky-
scrapers—tall office buildings and hotels to accommodate the
tourists. New apartment buildings and condos had popped up
on street corners, filling in spaces that seemed too small. Denver was thriving.

Sean applauded the growth. More people meant more business and more opportunity. But he missed the odd, eclectic
neighborhoods that were being swallowed by gentrification.
Like most Denver natives, he was stubbornly protective of his
city.

He parked the rental car in a small six-car lot behind a three-
story brick mansion near downtown. "We're here."

"Your office is in a renovated mansion." She beamed. "I can't
believe you chose such a unique place."

"It's not unusual. This entire block is mansions that have been
redone for businesses. We have the right half of the first floor.
On the left side, there are three little offices—a life coach, a
web designer and a woman who reads horoscopes. We all share
the kitchen and the conference rooms upstairs."

"About the horoscope lady, what kind of conference meetings does she have?"

"Séances."

He opened the back door for her and held it while she entered
an enclosed porch that was attached to the very modern kitchen
with stainless steel appliances and a double-door refrigerator. It
smelled like somebody had just microwaved a bag of popcorn.

"I love it," Emily said. "When you worked for the FBI, you never would have gone for a place like this."

"I've changed."

They went down the hallway to the spacious foyer with a grand staircase of carved oak and high ceilings. To the right, he stopped beside a door with an opaque glass window decorated with old-fashioned lettering for TST Security and their four-leaf clover logo. Using a keypad, Sean plugged in a code to open the door. Before he followed Emily inside, he touched the red leaf that represented Matt, as he always did.

Dylan greeted his former sister-in-law with enthusiasm, throwing his long arms around her for a big hug. He and Sean were the same height, but Dylan seemed taller because he was skinny. During his early years, Dylan was the epitome of a ninety-eight-pound weakling with oversize glasses and a permanent slouch. Sean had taken his little brother under his wing and got him working out. Under his baggy jeans and plaid flannel shirt, Dylan was ripped now.

They had two desks in the huge front office, but that wasn't where Dylan wanted to sit. He dragged her over to a brown leather sofa. On the coffee table in front of the sofa were snacks: popcorn, crackers and bottles of water.

She reached up to tuck a hank of brownish-blond hair behind his ear. "Almost as long as mine. I like the ponytail."

"I remember your super-long hair," he said.

"It was always such a mess."

"Not to me. It was beautiful. But I like this new look."

"Sorry to interrupt," Sean said, "but whenever you're done comparing stylists, there are some very bad men after Emily, and we need to take them out of the picture."

"Impatient," Dylan said as he pushed his horn-rimmed glasses up on his nose. He turned to Emily. "There's no need to be nervous in the TST office. It's one of the most secure spots in Denver. We've got bulletproof glass in the windows, sensors, surveillance cameras all around and sound-disabling technology so nobody can electronically eavesdrop."

"That's very reassuring." She opened a bottle of water and took a sip. "Can you make my computer un-hackable?"

"I can make it real hard to get in." Dylan pushed his glasses up again. "I've got an update."

"Another call from Agent Levine?" Sean guessed as he sat on the opposite end of the sofa from Emily.

"Levine isn't comment-worthy." Dylan plunked himself into a high-back swivel chair on wheels and paddled from a desk to the sofa. "I'm not insulting you, but the feds aren't real efficient."

"No offense taken," Sean said.

"This call was a few hours ago, a man's voice. He claimed to be an old friend from San Francisco. He identified himself as Jack Baxter. Sound familiar?"

"Not a bit," Sean responded. "Emily, do you know the name?"

"I don't think so."

Sitting on the big leather sofa with her hands in her lap and her ankles crossed, she looked nervous and somewhat overwhelmed. Dylan could be a lot to take; he tended to bounce around like an overeager puppy.

Also, Sean reminded himself, she was aware of the threat, the potential for danger. He directed his brother. "We need to focus here. What did Baxter want?"

"Supposedly, he was just thinking of you, his old pal. It seemed too coincidental for you to be contacted by a supposed friend on the same day Levine called." He shot a look at Emily. "He kept asking about you. Suspicious, right?"

Sean remained focused. "Did you track the call?"

"He claimed to be in San Francisco, and his cell phone had the 414 area code. But I triangulated the microwave signal." Dylan paused for effect. "He was calling from DIA."

Emily shot to her feet. "He's here? At the Denver airport?"

Dylan winced. "It gets worse. I ran a reverse lookup on the cell phone. It belongs to John Morelli."

"I know him," she said. "He works for Wynter."

"Bingo," Dylan said. "I've been doing a bit of preliminary hacking on Wynter. And Morelli is vice president in charge of communication."

"That's right," Emily said. "I interviewed him for my first article on Wynter Corp. He's the only person I spoke to in person."

"Which might be why he was sent to Denver to find you," Sean said. "When you met with him, did you use the Timmons alias?"

She shook her head. "Timmons is only for travel and the one credit card. I use another alias for my articles and interviews."

"How did Wynter make the connection between us?"

Dylan rolled toward him on the swivel chair. "Remember how I said the feds were idiots? Well, I think Wynter had their phones tapped. When Levine called here, looking for you, I told him you weren't involved with Emily. But the contact must have sent up a red flag to Wynter."

His deduction made sense. "I want you to dig deeper into Wynter Corp. Check into their bank accounts and expenses."

"Forensic accounting." Dylan nodded. "Will do."

"How much can you find out?" Emily asked. "That information belongs to Wynter Corp. It's protected."

"I've got skills," Dylan said, "and I can hack practically anything. Unlike the feds, I don't have to worry about obtaining the evidence through illegal means because I don't plan to use the data in court. This is purely a fact-finding mission."

She accepted him at his word. "Concentrate on the import-export business. Check inventories against shipping manifests— look for warehouse information."

"I took a peek earlier," Dylan said. "They also handle real estate, restaurants and small businesses."

"For now I'm looking for evidence of smuggling and human

trafficking." She bounced to her feet. "I have information that will give you a starting point."

"Cool," Dylan said. "If you give me the flash drive you've got hidden in your necklace, I'll get started."

"How did you know?" She touched her black-and-silver pendant. "Is it obvious?"

"Only to me," he said as he held out his flat palm.

Although Sean didn't speak up and steal his brother's thunder, he had also figured out where she was hiding her flash drive. *Simple logic.* All day long, she'd been touching her pendant, guarding it. What would she want to protect? Her most precious possession was her work; therefore, he guessed she had her documents on a flash drive. And she'd hidden it in chunky jewelry that wasn't her usual style.

Dylan rolled his chair to a computer station with four display screens and three keyboards. Emily followed behind him, eager to learn the magic techniques that allowed Sean's brother to dance across the World Wide Web like a spider with a ponytail and horn-rimmed glasses.

Long ago Sean had given up trying to understand how Dylan did what he did. The technical aspects of security and investigative work had never interested Sean. He learned more from observing, questioning the people involved and creating a profile of the criminals and the victims. When he'd gone undercover for the FBI, he had to rely on instinct to separate the good guys from the bad. And his gut was good. He was seldom wrong.

He left the sofa and sauntered across the large, open room with high ceilings to the window. It bothered him that John Morelli was in Denver. Dylan's theory of how Wynter got his name had the ring of truth. Tapping the FBI phones was depressingly obvious.

His brother and Emily stared at the screens as though answers would materialize before their eyes. Sean hardly remembered a time when computers weren't a part of life, but he'd never fallen in love with the technology and he hated the way people stumbled around staring at their cell phones. His brother called him a Luddite, and maybe he was. Or maybe he'd made the decision, when they were kids, that computers would be Dylan's thing. Whatever the case, it appeared that Dylan and Emily would be occupied for a while.

Sean announced, "I'm going out to pick up some dinner. Is Chinese okay?"

Barely looking away from the screens, they both murmured agreement.

"Any special requests?"

The response was another mumble.

He went to a file cabinet near the door, unlocked it and took out a Glock 17. He had to pack both of his handguns on the plane and take out the bullets. For the moment, it was quicker to grab the semiautomatic pistol and insert a fresh magazine into the grip. He was almost out the door when Emily ran up behind him and grasped his arm.

"You shouldn't go out there," she said. "Mr. Morelli could be waiting in ambush."

"Mr.?"

"That's what I called him in the interview. He's older, in his forties."

"If he was sneaking around, close enough to show up on Dylan's surveillance, we'd be hearing a buzzer alarm."

She kissed his cheek. "Be careful."

It had been a long time since anybody was worried about his safety. He kind of liked being fussed over.

At the back door, he paused to peer into the trees that bordered the parking lot. There were garages and Dumpsters in the alley behind their office, lots of hiding places if Morelli had staked out the office.

He went down the stairs and got into the rental car to pick up food from Happy Food Chinese restaurant. Then, he backed out into the alley. In less than a mile, he noticed a black sedan following him. Wynter's men had found him. And he'd made it easy. *Damn it, I should have ordered delivery.*

CHAPTER EIGHT

EMILY WATCHED THE numbers unfurling across two screens while Dylan used a third screen to enter the forbidden area of the dark web where you could buy or sell anything. Pornographers, killers, perverts and all types of scum hung out on those mysterious, ugly sites.

She looked away. "What's a nice guy like you doing in a place like that?"

"If you want to get the dirt, you can't keep your hands clean."

Even though her investigation was for a worthy cause, she didn't like spying. Hacking broke one of the ethical rules of journalism that said you needed at least two sources for every statement before you could call it a fact. And they had to be credible sources. Some bloggers just fabricated their stories from lies and rumors. She wasn't like that. Not irresponsible. The thought jolted her. *Wow, have I changed!* When she was married to Sean, he'd complained about her lack of responsibility. Now she was saying the same about other people.

She strolled across the room to a window and looked out at the fading glow of sunset reflected on the marble lions outside the renovated mansion across the street. "We shouldn't have let Sean go without backup."

"He can take care of himself," Dylan said. "He took a gun."

And that worried her, too. If he wasn't expecting trouble, why did he make sure he was armed? "We should go after him."

"Call him." Dylan gestured to the old-fashioned-looking phone on the other desk. "Press the button for extension two. That rings through to his cell phone."

"Are you extension number one?"

"No way." He glanced over his shoulder at her. "That number is, and always will be, Mom."

"Sean told me that your parents are still in Denver."

"And my mother would lo-o-o-ve to see you and Sean get back together. Her dream is grandbabies."

"I heard you're dating someone."

"Her name is Jayne. It's a serious relationship." His eyes lit up. "But we aren't talking about babies."

From the sneaky smile on his face, she could tell that the topic of marriage had come up. Little brother Dylan had found a woman who would put up with his computers. She was happy for him.

As she tapped the extension on the office phone, she hoped that she was worrying about nothing. Sean would pick up and tell her he was fine.

From the other side of the desk, she heard his ringtone. Then she saw his cell phone next to the computer screen. He hadn't taken the phone with him.

"Dylan, we have to go." She hung up the phone. "We have to help Sean."

He lifted his hands off the keys and looked up at her. "Is there something about this Morelli person that I don't know about? Is he particularly dangerous?"

Her impression of the man she'd interviewed was that he was a standard midlevel management guy. He'd worn a nice suit without a necktie. His shoes were polished loafers. His best feature was his thick black hair, which was slicked back with a heavy dose of styling gel. When he spoke he did a lot of hemming and hawing, and she had the sense that he wasn't telling her much more than she could learn from reading about Wynter Corp on the internet.

"Not dangerous," she said. "He was the contrary. Quiet, secretive. Morelli is the kind of guy who fades into the woodwork."

"I'm guessing my brother can handle him."

"I hate to say this." But she remembered those horrible moments on the boat when Patrone was killed. "What if Morelli's not alone?"

That possibility lit a fire under Dylan's tail. He was up and out of his computer chair in a few seconds. He motioned for her to follow, and she ran after him. They raced out the front door and onto the wide veranda to an SUV parked at the curb.

Sean would have known right away that he was being followed if it hadn't been the middle of rush hour with the downtown streets clogged and lane changing nearly impossible. He first caught sight of a black sedan when he was only three blocks away from the office. After he doubled back twice, he was dead certain that the innocent-looking compact sedan, probably a rental from the airport, was on his tail.

Weaving through the other cars on Colfax Avenue, his pursuer had to stay close or risk losing Sean in the stop-and-go traffic. A couple of times, the sedan was directly behind Sean's car. At a stoplight, he studied the rearview mirror, trying to figure out if Morelli was by himself or with a partner.

He appeared to be alone.

Emily had described him as being in his forties. That was the only information Sean had. He should have asked for more details, but he didn't want to alarm her. Leaving the office without a plan had been an unnecessary risk. He knew that. So why had he done it? Was he feeling left out while Dylan did his thing with the computers? Jealous of his little brother?

Envy might account for 5 percent of his decision, but mostly he'd wanted time alone to refresh his mind. Ever since he saw Emily, he'd been tense. And when they kissed…

He checked his side mirror. The black sedan was one car back, still following. Dusk was rapidly approaching. Some vehicles had already turned on their headlights. If he was going to confront the man in the sedan, he should make his move. Darkness would limit his options.

Sean didn't necessarily want to hurt Morelli. He wanted to talk to the guy, to have him send a message back to James Wynter that Sean wasn't somebody to mess around with, and he was protecting Emily. The bad guys needed to realize that she wasn't helpless, and—in his role as her bodyguard—he wouldn't hesitate to kick ass.

He set a simple trap. Accelerating and making a few swerving turns, he sped into a large, mostly empty parking lot at the west end of Cherry Creek Mall. Sean fishtailed behind a building, parked and jumped out of the car before the black sedan came around the corner.

His original plan had been to hide behind his car, but a better possibility appeared. Though the parking lot was bare asphalt right now, there had been snow that morning. The plows had cleared the large lot and left the snow in a waist-high pile near a streetlight. Sean dove behind it.

Holding his gun ready, he watched and waited while the black sedan cautiously inched closer and closer. It circled his car, keeping a distance. The sedan parked behind his car, and a man got out. He braced a semiautomatic pistol with both hands.

"Sean Timmons," he shouted. "Get out of the car. I'm not going to hurt you."

"You got that right." Sean came out from behind the snow barrier. His position was excellent, in back of the driver of the sedan. "Drop the gun and raise your arms."

If it came to a shoot-out, he wouldn't hesitate to drop this guy. But he wouldn't take the first shot. The man set his gun on the asphalt, raised his hands and turned. "We need to talk."

Since they were standing in view of a busy street with rush hour traffic streaming past, Sean lowered his gun as he approached the other man. In spite of the gun, this guy didn't seem real threatening. Dressed in a conservative blue sweater with khaki trousers, he wore his hair slicked back. His pale complexion hinted that he spent most of his time indoors.

Sean asked, "Is your name Morelli?"

"John Morelli."

"Are you a hit man, John?"

"Of course not."

"What do you want to say?"

"It's about your ex-wife." He took a step forward and Sean raised his gun, keeping him back. "If you'll let me talk to her, I can explain everything."

He sounded rational, but Sean wasn't convinced. "You could have called her," he pointed out.

"I tried," Morelli said. "I left messages on her answering machine. She's a hard woman to reach, especially since she gave me a fake name."

That much was true. "How did you find out her real name?"

Morelli didn't answer immediately. He exhibited the classic signs of nerves: furrowed brow, the flicker of an eyelid, the thinning of the lips and the clearing of his throat. All these tics and twitches were extremely subtle. Most people wouldn't notice.

But Sean was a pro when it came to questioning scumbags. He knew that whatever Morelli said next was bound to be a lie.

"It's like this," Morelli said. "I saw her on the street and followed her to her house."

"You stalked her?"

Quickly Morelli said, "No, no, it wasn't creepy. I guessed her neighborhood from something she said at our interview."

"Not buying that story."

"Okay, you got me." He tried a self-deprecating gesture that didn't quite work. "I got her fingerprint at our interview and ran it through identification software."

Sean had enough. "Here's what I think. Your boss, James Wynter, used an illegal wiretap, overheard her name. When he pulled up her photo, you recognized the reporter who interviewed you."

Morelli was breathing harder. A dull red color climbed his throat. "I don't know anything about illegal wiretaps, and I'm insulted that you think I would be that sort of person."

As if being a stalker was more reputable? "This is your last chance to be honest, Morelli. Otherwise, I'll turn you in to the feds. They keep an open file on Wynter, and they'll be interested in you."

"Wait!" He lowered his hands and waved them frantically. "There's no need for law enforcement."

"Don't tell me another lie."

"Truth, only truth, I swear."

Sean tested that promise by asking, "Did Wynter send you to Denver?"

"Yes."

"What were you supposed to do?"

"Find your ex-wife. When he said her name was Emily Peterson, I didn't know who he was talking about. I knew her as Sylvia Plath."

Sean stifled a chuckle. Emily's obviously phony alias referenced a famous poet. "What made you think she might come looking for me? Did you miss the 'ex' in front of husband?"

"After I learned that she'd gone on the run, I checked her background on the internet. Your name popped up, and I knew. The first person the girl would look to for help was her macho, ex-FBI husband who runs a security firm."

His story sounded legit. Or maybe Sean just enjoyed being called macho. He liked that he was the guy to call when danger struck. Or was he being conned?

Morelli was turning out to be a puzzle. He readily admitted that he worked for Wynter and he carried a gun, but he looked like a middle-aged man who had just finished a game of billiards in a sunless pool hall. He was less intimidating than a sock puppet.

Sean made a guess. "You don't get out of the office much, do you?"

"Not for a long time." He gave a self-deprecating smile. "I've had both knees replaced."

Scenes from old gangster movies where some poor shmuck was getting his kneecaps broken with a baseball bat flashed through Sean's mind. But he didn't go there. This was the twenty-first century, and criminals were more corporate...more like the man standing before him.

"There's something bothering me," Sean said. "When you called the TST office, you used your own phone."

"So? I wasn't giving anything away. My number's unlisted."

"An easy hack," Sean said. "I might even be able to do it."

"I should've used a burner." The corners of his mouth pulled down. He seemed honestly surprised and upset. *What is going on with this guy?* If Wynter hadn't sent him to wipe out the witness to his son's crime, why was Morelli here?

Sean said, "What were you supposed to do when you found my ex-wife?"

"To warn her."

"About what?"

"If she prints her article from information I gave her, it's going to have several errors. Wynter Corp is planning a significant move in regard to our real estate holdings."

As he spoke, his face showed signs that he was lying. His lip quivered. He even did the classic signal of looking up and to the right. For a thug, Morelli was a terrible liar.

"Seriously," Sean said. "You want me to believe that you rushed out to Denver, tailed my car through rush-hour traffic and pulled a gun so you could talk real estate?"

"Doesn't make sense, does it?"

"Last chance. Tell me the real reason. What do you want from Emily?"

"I want to find out what she knows."

His statement seemed sincere. "Why would you think Emily has information that you don't?"

"She's been researching Wynter Corp for quite a while, and it's possible she stumbled over some internal operations data that would be embarrassing to Mr. Wynter."

"Lose the corporate baloney. What's the problem?"

"Somebody's stealing from us, and we want to know who."

"Now you're talking." Sean believed him. Wynter wouldn't be happy about somebody dipping into his inventories. "Do you really think Emily might have information you missed? Is she that good an investigator?"

"Her first article on Wynter Corp was right on target."

It occurred to Sean that if he pretended that Emily had valuable information, the hit men wouldn't hurt her. Luckily, he was an excellent liar. "I shouldn't tell you, but she's come up with a working hypothesis. She's figured out what's happening on the inside. If she gets hurt, it all goes public."

"I knew it was an insider." Morelli cleared his throat. "And there's that other matter I need to discuss."

"The murder?"

"She might have imagined seeing something that did not, in fact, happen."

Sean shook his head. "She's sure of what she saw, and she won't be convinced otherwise."

"How much would it take to unconvince her?"

And now Sean had full comprehension. Morelli wasn't here to kill her. He'd come to Denver to seduce her into working for Wynter Corp with cash payoffs and assurances that she was brilliant. Clearly, he didn't know Emily.

It was time to wrap up this encounter. If Sean had still been a fed, he would've taken Morelli into custody and gone through a mountain of paperwork to come up with charges that would be dismissed as soon as Wynter's lawyers got involved. As a bodyguard, he didn't have those responsibilities. His job was to keep Emily safe.

He made a threat assessment. "Are there other Wynter operatives in Denver?"

"No."

But a quick twitch at the corner of his eye told Sean the opposite. "How many?"

For a moment, Morelli sputtered and prevaricated, trying to avoid the truth. Then he admitted, "One other person. He does things differently than I do."

Sean translated. "He's more of a 'shoot-first' type."

"You could say that."

He needed to get Emily out of town before the less subtle hit man caught up with them. He picked up Morelli's pistol, removed the ammo and returned it to him. At the same time, Morelli handed him a business card.

"It's got all my numbers," Morelli said.

"I'll get your message to Emily. If she agrees to talk to you, she'll call. Don't approach her or me again."

They walked away from each other, each returning to his separate rental car. As Sean slid behind the wheel, he wished that he could trust Morelli. It would've been handy to have an inside man at Wynter Corp.

As he drove to the homely, little Chinese restaurant where they always ordered carryout, he checked his rearview mirrors and scanned the traffic. There was no sign of Morelli. He didn't know what the other hit man—the more dangerous thug—would be driving.

At the restaurant, he spotted Dylan and Emily sitting at one of the small tables near the kitchen. He would have been annoyed that she'd left the security of the office and put herself in danger, but this happenstance worked for him.

She stood and faced him. "Next time," she said, "take your damn phone. I was worried."

"Ready to go?" he asked.

Dylan held up a large brown paper bag with streaky grease stains on the side. "It's our usual order."

"Bring it. I get hungry on plane rides."

Emily gaped. "Plane?"

Sean wasn't going to hang around in Denver, waiting for the second hit man to find them. For all he knew, Morelli had already contacted his partner-in-crime. Sean and Emily had to escape. The sooner, the better.

CHAPTER NINE

EMILY HAD NO idea how Sean accomplished so much in so little time. It seemed to be a combination of knowing the right people and calling in favors; she couldn't say for sure. Maybe he was magic. In any case, he'd told her that Denver was too dangerous, and within an hour she was on a private jet, ready to take off for San Francisco.

After she'd been whisked to a small airfield south of town, Sean rushed her into an open hangar and got her on board a Gulfstream G200. Her only other experience with private aircraft was a ski trip on a rickety little Cessna, which was no comparison to this posh eight-passenger jet. Sean left her with instructions not to disembark.

She strolled down the strip of russet-brown carpet that bisected the length of the cabin. Closest to the cockpit were four plush taupe leather chairs facing one another. Behind that was a long sofa below the porthole windows on one side and two more chairs on the other. The galley—a half-size refrigerator, cabinet, sink and microwave—was tucked into the rear.

Her stomach growled, and she made a quick search of the kitchenette. There were three different kinds of water in the fridge and the liquor cabinet was well stocked, but the cupboards were almost bare.

At the front of the cabin, she sank into one of the chairs. The cushioned seat and back cradled her, elevating her to a level of comfort that was practically a massage. Still, she didn't relax. A persistent adrenaline rush stoked her nervous energy.

Bouncing to her feet, she paced the length of the aircraft, all the way to the bathroom behind the galley to the closed door that separated the cockpit from the cabin. Sean had left her suitcase, and she wondered if she should change out of the black sweater she'd been wearing since before dawn this morning. A fresh outfit might give her a new perspective, and she needed something to lighten her spirits and ease her tension.

Not that she was complaining about the way Sean had handled the threat from Morelli. He'd done a good job, but she wished that she'd been there. Somehow it felt like the situation was slipping through her fingers. She was losing control.

Or was she overreacting? The trip to San Francisco had originally been her idea, not his. But she had new information and needed to reconsider. Sean should have consulted with her before charging into the breach and arranging for a private jet. She had opinions. This was her investigation. He wasn't the boss. When push came to shove, he was actually her employee.

A sense of dread rose inside her. She'd felt this way before. Frustrated and voiceless, she was reminded of the final, ugly days of their marriage. Until the bitter end, Sean had tried to make all the decisions. He wanted to be the captain who set their course while she was left to swab the decks and polish the hardware. Her only option had been mutiny.

In the past when she'd tried to stop him, she failed more than she succeeded. He was so implacable. And she didn't want to fight. *Make love, not war.* She'd changed. No longer a nineteen-year-old free spirit who tumbled whichever way the wind was blowing, the new Emily was solid, determined and responsible. As soon as she could get Sean alone, she meant to set the record straight.

Dylan stuck his head through the entry hatch. His long hair

was out of the ponytail and hanging around his face, making him look like a teenager. "I brought you a brand-new, super-secure computer."

He sat and wiggled his butt. "Nice chair."

"Very." She sat opposite.

Obviously he'd been in this jet before. He knew exactly how to pull out a table from the wall. When it stretched out between them, he set a laptop on it, opened the lid and spun it toward her. "As I've said before, about a hundred times, anything can be hacked. This system has extreme firewalls, but when you're not using it, log off with this code."

He typed in numbers and letters that ran together: 14U24Me.

"One for you two for me," she read.

"Easy to remember." He reached into his backpack. "And here's your new cell phone, complete with camera and large screen. It's loaded with everything that was on your old phone, but this baby is also secure. It bounces your signal all around the world."

She stroked the smooth plastic cover. "I've missed having a phone."

"Yeah, well, don't get tempted to play with this. Keep texting to the bare minimum and don't add a bunch of apps. In the interest of security, keep your calls short. And when you aren't using the phone, log off."

"I thought cell phones could be tracked even when they were off."

"Not this one. Not unless somebody hacks my most recent software innovation, and that's not going to happen for a couple of weeks at least." Digging into his pocket, he produced her flash drive. "You can slip this back into your necklace. I've got a copy."

"While we're gone, will you keep hacking Wynter?"

"You bet."

"You might run comparisons between shipping manifests and inventory, plus sales figures."

He pushed the glasses up on his nose. "Morelli seemed convinced that there was theft. That gives me another angle."

In her research, she hadn't uncovered any evidence that someone was stealing from Wynter. But she hadn't been using the sophisticated hacking tools that Dylan so deftly employed. Part of her wanted to have him teach her; the more ethical part of her conscience held her back. Hacking wasn't a fair way to investigate.

Dylan stood. Before leaving, he gave her a brotherly kiss on the cheek. "I know Sean is supposed to be taking care of you. But keep an eye on him, okay? Don't let him do anything crazy dangerous."

"I'll try."

When Dylan left, she was alone in the cabin. Still seated, she peered through a porthole. Through the open door to her hangar, she could see one of the lighted runways, part of another hangar and several small planes tethered to the tarmac. The control tower was a four-story building with a 360-degree view that reminded her of some of the lighthouses up the coast in Oregon. As she watched, a midsize Cessna taxied to the far end of the airstrip, wheeled around and halted. With a burst of speed, the white jet sped forward and gracefully lifted off. Silhouetted against the night sky, the Cessna's lights soared to the right, toward the dark shadow of the mountains west of the city.

Sean came through the hatch and sat in the chair opposite her, where Dylan had been sitting. As easily as Dylan had pulled down the table, Sean removed that barrier between them. He leaned forward with his elbows resting on his knees.

"Are you okay?" he asked.

His gentleness threw her off guard. She noticed that he hadn't shaved, and dark stubble outlined his jaw. By asking how she was, he'd given her an opening to rationally discuss how she should be kept in the loop. Right now she should assert her needs and desires, let him know she was in charge. *Right now! This moment!*

Instead she stared dumbly at his face, distracted by the perfect symmetry of his features. Why did he have to be so gorgeous?

"Emily?" His eyebrows lifted as though her name were a question. "Emily, tell me."

"When did you find time to change?" He'd discarded his turtleneck for a cotton shirt and a light suede bomber jacket. She couldn't say he looked fresh as a daisy. Sean was much too rugged to be compared to a flower.

"Only took a minute," he said. "Are you——"

"You asked if I was okay." She stumbled over the words. "Okay about what?"

"Going to San Francisco," he said. "We're set to leave in ten minutes. A flight plan has been filed, but this is a private jet. You can change your mind and go anywhere."

She wasn't following. "What do you mean?"

"San Francisco is dangerous. There are alternative destinations, like Washington State or heading south to Mexico. We could even go to Hawaii."

Irritated, she pushed herself out of the cozy chair and stalked toward the rear. "I'm not afraid."

"I didn't say you were." He followed her down the aisle.

"But you think I might want to run away." She pivoted to face him. "Maybe I'd like to take a vacation in Hawaii and lie on the beach. Is that what you want? For me to hide in a safe place while Wynter runs his human trafficking ring and his son gets away with murder."

"It's not about what I want."

"I'm glad you understand." But she almost wished he'd be unreasonable. Making her point was easier when he argued against her. His rational approach meant she had to also be thoughtful.

"You don't have to step into the line of fire," he said. "You could keep researching the crimes on computer. Work with Dylan. There's no need for you to confront Wynter in his lair."

"I've considered that." There were threads of evidence that

she needed to be in San Francisco to follow. With Sean to accompany her, she had more access.

"I need an answer on our destination."

"I've got a question for you," she said. "How do you rate a private jet?"

"Don't worry about it."

"I sincerely hope you're not charging my aunt some exorbitant fee."

"This trip is a favor, and it's free," he said. "You'll recognize the pilot from our wedding. David Henley."

She knew the name. "The guy who plays the banjo?"

"Flying planes is his real job."

"Good for him. He couldn't have made much of a living as a banjo picker."

"In addition to this sweet little Gulfstream, he has a Cessna, an old Sabreliner and two helicopters. He freelances for half a dozen or so companies, flying top execs around the country."

The aforementioned David Henley swung through the entry hatch and marched down the aisle toward them. "Emily, my princess. It's been a while."

Though David was an average-looking guy with wavy blond hair, she most certainly remembered him from the wedding. He'd hit on each of her sisters and ended up going home with her former roommate. He tapped Sean on the shoulder. "May I give this princess a hug?"

"Don't ask me," Sean said. "She can speak for herself."

He held his arms wide. "Hug?"

"Don't get too snuggly," she said. "I see that wedding band on your finger."

His arms wrapped around her. "I like to tease the princesses, but that's as far as it goes. My heart belongs to my queen, my wife."

"My former roommate." She remembered the announcement from a few years ago. "Please give Ginger a hug from me."

"She'll be bummed that she didn't have a chance to get together with you."

She preferred this mature version of David to the horny banjo player. "Thanks for the plane ride."

"I'm sorry you're in so much trouble." He held her by the shoulders and looked into her eyes. "Are we going to San Francisco?"

"Yes, so be sure to wear some flowers in your hair."

"Still cute." He turned toward Sean. "I won't be using you as copilot. This flight is a good opportunity to train the new guy I hired. Now, I've got to run some equipment checks before we take off. Ciao, you two."

While David went forward to the cockpit, she asked Sean, "You know how to fly a plane?"

"David's been teaching me. The helo is more fun." He gestured toward the seats across the aisle from the sofa bench. "Get comfortable. I'll see if he's got any food back here."

In the rush to get to the airfield, they'd forgotten the Chinese food. She couldn't honestly say she had regrets. Fast food from Denver didn't compare with San Francisco's Chinatown, but the remembered aroma tantalized her. Her stomach rumbled again. No doubt, Dylan would munch the chicken fried rice, chop suey, broccoli beef and General Tso's for dinner. With an effort, she managed to pull out the table between the two seats.

Sean didn't have much to put on it: Two small bags of chips and two sparkling waters. "This will have to do."

Not enough to appease her hunger, but it was probably good that she wouldn't be settling down and getting comfortable. Other than being starving, things seemed to be going her way. She wanted to go to San Francisco, and that was where they were headed. If she was smart, this would be a good time to stay quiet. But she wanted to lay down the basics of a plan for *her* investigation, with emphasis on *her*.

She cleared her throat. "I want to talk about what we're going to do when we land."

"Right," he agreed. "I need to make hotel reservations."

"We can stay in my apartment."

"You're joking."

"Not really."

He regarded her with a disbelieving gaze. "Morelli came all the way to Denver to find you. I'm guessing that Wynter's men have found your apartment."

"But they think I'm in Denver."

"These aren't the sort of guys to play cat and mouse with. As soon as they figure out where you really are, they'll be knocking at your door or busting a hole with a battering ram."

She deferred to his expertise. "Make the reservations."

"I like the Pendragon Hotel," he said. "It's near the trolley line and close to Chinatown."

"We're not going on a sightseeing trip."

The copilot boarded the jet, bringing cold cuts and bread for sandwiches. *Food!* She almost kissed him.

While she and Sean slapped together sandwiches, they dropped their discussion of anything important. The sight and smell of fresh-sliced ham and turkey and baby Swiss made her giddy. And the copilot hadn't stinted on condiments, providing an array of mustard, mayo, horseradish and extra-virgin olive oil. Her mouth was watering. Tomatoes, cucumbers, baby bib lettuce and coleslaw.

She sliced a tomato thin and placed it carefully on the ciabatta bread between the mustard and the lettuce. "I suppose we should make something for David and the copilot."

"We should." He glanced in her direction. "But you really don't look like you can wait for one more minute."

"I'm ravenous."

"Get started without me. I'll take food to the cockpit."

"Best offer I've had all day."

The sandwich she'd assembled was almost too big for her mouth, but she tore off a chunk and chomped down on it. The explosion of flavor in her mouth was total ecstasy. As the sandwich slid down her throat, she relished texture, the taste and the nourishment. She took another bite and another.

The last food she'd had was that morning in the mountains, and that felt like a lifetime ago. While she continued to eat, her eyelids closed. She groaned with pleasure.

After a few more bites, she opened her eyes to reach for her water and saw Sean standing behind his chair, looking down at her. He grinned and said, "Sounds like you're enjoying the sandwich. Either that or you've decided to join the Mile High Club all by yourself."

She swallowed a gulp of water. "How do you know I'm not already a member?"

"Are you?"

"No way," she said. "I'm pretty sure it takes two."

"I'd be happy to volunteer."

Standing there, he was devilish handsome with his wide shoulders, his tousled hair, his stubble and his hands, his rugged hands. Too easily, she imagined his gentle caress across her shoulders and down her back. His eyes, when they'd made love, turned the color of dark chocolate, and his gaze could make her melt inside.

She shoved those urges aside and returned her attention to the sandwich. She needed refueling. Before she was full, the Gulfstream taxied onto the runway.

"Don't bite my arm off," Sean said as he scooped up the remains of her sandwich. "The food has to move before takeoff. Or you'll be wearing it."

David opened the door from the cockpit. "Fasten your seat belts."

She buckled up, gripped the arms of her seat and braced herself as the whine of the engines accelerated and a tremor went through the jet. Though she'd actually never been afraid of flying or of heights, she suffered an instinctive twinge in her gut and a shimmer of vertigo when a plane took off or when she stood at the edge of a cliff. Again, she closed her eyes.

Her mind ran through various streams of evidence they'd investigate in San Francisco, ranging from a meeting with the feds to a possible reconnaissance on Wynter's luxury double-decker yacht.

In moments, they were airborne.

Her eyelids opened. She looked at Sean and said the first thing on her mind, "Don't let me forget Paco the Pimp."

"I'm hoping that's a nickname for something else."

"He's a real guy. I met him about a year ago when I was doing an article on preteen hookers." She shuddered. "That was a painful experience, one horrifying story after another. I almost decided to quit journalism and go back to soothing poetry or lyric writing. Paco changed my mind."

"By offering you a job?"

"Oh, he did that...several times. Not that either of us took his offers seriously. Anyway, he reminded me of my obligation to shine a light on the ugly truth in the hope that people would pay attention. And the horror would stop...or at least slow down."

He lowered himself into the seat opposite her and pulled out the table. Instead of returning the last few bites of her sandwich, he placed a bottle of red wine and two plastic glasses on the flat surface. "And why do you need to remember Paco?"

"He's got an ear to the street. He hears all the gossip. And I want to find out if he remembered anything from that night." She hesitated. Maybe she was bringing up a volatile topic. She didn't want Sean to be mad at her. "He might have seen something I missed."

He used a corkscrew to open the wine. "Are you talking about the night of the murder?"

Averting her gaze, she looked through the porthole window. The lights of Denver glittered below them. Ahead was the pitch-dark of the Rocky Mountains. She didn't want to answer.

CHAPTER TEN

SEAN WAS FAMILIAR with most of Emily's tactics when it came to arguments. When she didn't answer him back right away, her silence meant she was hiding something. He sank into the plush chair opposite hers. He didn't want to fight. They were on a private jet headed toward one of the most romantic cities in the world, and he hadn't completely ruled out the possibility of inducting her into the Mile High Club.

But he couldn't leave Paco the Pimp hanging. Apparently this Paco had been a passenger on Wynter's deluxe yacht. "You've told me about the night of the murder. You claimed you were at a yacht party. True or false?"

"True."

He poured the wine, a half glass for her and the same for himself. "But you never told me how you got an invite to this insider party. I'm guessing it had something to do with Paco the Pimp. True or false?"

"I don't want to talk about this."

"And I know why," he said. "Your pal Paco was invited to provide a bunch of party girls for the guys on the yacht. And you convinced him to take you along. You went undercover."

"Fine," she snapped. "You're right. I was all dolled up in

a sparkly skintight dress, four-inch heels and gobs of heavy makeup."

"A hooker disguise."

"Sleazy except for my long hair. I had it pinned up on top of my head when I went there. I thought it was sophisticated." She sipped her wine. "Paco said I should wear it down. He thought the men would like it."

Imagining her being ogled in a sexy dress made his blood boil. Of course they liked her long, beautiful hair. "What the hell, Emily? You used to believe that hiding your identity was dishonest and unfair."

"You've got no room to talk," she said. "You used to go undercover all the time."

"And you never approved."

"Maybe not."

"And I was trained for it. I have certain traits and abilities that lend themselves to undercover work, namely, I'm good at deception." He downed his wine in two glugs. "You're not like that. You're a lousy liar."

"I've changed. I know when to keep my mouth shut instead of blurting out the truth. I can be circumspect."

"You can't change your basic nature," he said as he poured more wine. "Undercover work is not your thing."

"I pulled it off on Wynter's yacht."

He glared at her. "Not a shining example of a successful mission."

"I made mistakes," she admitted. "Okay, all right, it was gross. Witnessing the murder was the worst, but being pawed by sleazeballs was bad. One of them grabbed me by my hair and kissed me. Another patted my hair like I was a dog. The very next day, I went to the beauty shop and told them to cut it off."

"You're never going to go undercover again, understand?"

"Don't tell me what I can and can't do."

Through clenched teeth, he said, "I'm sorry."

She looked at him as though he'd sprouted petunias from the top of his head. "Did I hear you correctly?"

"You're right. I can't tell you what to do. However, if you decide to go undercover again, I want to know. Give me a chance to show you how to do it without getting yourself killed."

"My turn to apologize," she said. "You're also right. I had no business waltzing onto that yacht without the proper training. The only reason I got out of there in one piece was dumb luck."

He held up his plastic glass to salute her. The wine he'd already inhaled was taking the sharp edge off, but he was still alert enough to realize that something significant had occurred: they hadn't gotten into a fight.

Both of them had been ticked off. They'd danced around the volcano, but neither had erupted. Instead, they'd talked like adults and settled their differences. Maybe she'd matured. Maybe he'd gotten more sensitive. *Whatever!* He'd gladly settle for this fragile truce instead of gut-wrenching hostility.

He didn't want to discuss their successful handling of the problem for fear that he'd jinx the positive mood. What had they been talking about before takeoff? Oh yeah, the agenda for their time in San Francisco. He wanted to take her to dinner at the Italian restaurant where he proposed.

He gazed toward her. She looked youthful but not too young. Had she changed in the past five years? If he looked closely, he could see fine lines at the corners of her turquoise eyes, and her features seemed sharper, more honed. With her black sweater covering her torso, he could only guess how her body had changed. A vision of her nicely proportioned shoulders, round breasts and slender waist was easy to recall. He hadn't forgotten the constellation of freckles across her back or the tattoo of a cute little rodent above her left breast that she referred to as a "titmouse."

Since he wasn't allowed to touch her without disobeying half a dozen of their weird ground rules, he had to stop thinking like this. Her unapproachable nearness would drive him mad.

Back to business, back to the investigation, he said, "Tomorrow, our first appointment should be a meeting with Levine to see if the FBI has any new info."

"But not at the fed office," she reminded him. "Dylan thinks their phones are bugged."

He considered it unlikely that Levine was working with Wynter, but Sean didn't want to take any chances. "I'd rather not let him know where we're staying. We'll meet him for breakfast."

"After that," she said, "we should go to Chinatown. I had a couple of leads there, and I'd like to talk to Doris Liu again. She's the woman who took in Roger Patrone and raised him."

He'd almost forgotten that Patrone was an orphan who had been taken in by a family in Chinatown. "There must have been something remarkable about Patrone when he was a kid. Most residents in Chinatown aren't welcoming to strangers."

"It's been hard for me to ask around," she said. "Patrone's gambling operation—last I heard it was a stud poker game, Texas Hold'em and two blackjack tables—is in the rear of a strip club in the Tenderloin. Even with the attempts at gentrification, I don't blend in."

The Tenderloin had earned its reputation as a high-crime district. He was deeply grateful that she hadn't tried an undercover stint as a stripper. "I'll go there, no problem."

"And I wouldn't mind sneaking onto Wynter's yacht and looking around."

Breaking and entering didn't appeal to him, but he definitely liked the idea of getting out on the water in the bay. San Francisco had many charms, ranging from unique architecture to culture to amazing restaurants. The best, he thought, were the piers and the ocean...the scent of salt water...the whisper of the surf.

She yawned. "Maybe we should go to the docks. I only tried to get in there once, and it didn't go well. The guys who work with shipping containers ignored me, and the supervisors were overly polite, thinking I was sent by management to check up on them."

"What can we learn there?"

"I'm not sure," she said. "It's another avenue."

They were going to be busy. "Tired?"

"A bit," she said.

"You can take off your seat belt and lie on the sofa. It folds out into a bed."

She peeked out the porthole. "How long before we're in San Francisco?"

"A couple of hours." The flight time on commercial airlines was two and a half hours. The Gulfstream took a little longer.

"I wouldn't mind a catnap," she said.

He moved their wineglasses to cup holders beside the chairs, picked up the nearly empty wine bottle and tucked away the table. Before he transformed the sofa into a bed, he opened a storage compartment and took out a thermal blanket and a pillow. Then he dimmed the lights.

After fluffing the pillow, she stood and fidgeted beside the sofa bed. "I feel selfish, taking the only bed. You're as tired as I am."

"Is that an invitation to join you?"

"No," she said softly. "Sorry, I didn't mean to give you that idea."

Her tone sounded regretful. If he pushed, he might be able to change her mind. But now wasn't the right time. He didn't want to rock the boat while they were in a fairly good place. At least they weren't fighting. It was best not to complicate things with sex. *Great sex*, he reminded himself. They'd always had great sex.

"Not tonight," he said, as much to himself as to her. "Lie down. I'm going up to the cockpit."

"With the other cocks?"

"You might say that." He wouldn't, but she would.

No matter how much she claimed to be a responsible, sober

adult, there was a goofball just below the surface. That was the Emily that drove him crazy, the Emily he loved.

While she slept, Sean spent time with his buddy David and the copilot. He loved the night view from the cockpit with stars scattered across the sky. He felt like they were part of the galaxies.

They talked, and he made coffee to counteract the slight inebriation he'd felt. A professional bodyguard shouldn't be drinking on the job, but he couldn't pretend that this was a standard assignment.

If she'd been anyone else, he would have advised them to leave the investigating to the police. And if they refused, he would have terminated the contract. Not a detective, he was well aware that he didn't have the resources that were available to him when he was in the FBI. On the other hand, he had the hacking skills of his brother and none of those pesky restrictions.

Finally, he was peering through the clouds and wispy curtains of fog to see the lights of San Francisco, and he felt a surge. His pulse sped up. His blood pumped harder. This city was the setting for the best time in his life and the absolute, rock-bottom worst. Emily was intrinsic to both.

He went back to the cabin and found her lying on her side, spooning the pillow. As soon as he touched her shoulder, she wakened.

"I'm up," she said, throwing off the blanket.

"Almost there. You need to put on a seat belt."

"Do I have time to splash water on my face?"

"Okay, if you hurry."

While she darted into the bathroom, he verified their arrangements on his phone. They had a suite reserved at the Pendragon Hotel and there should be a rental car waiting at the private airfield. Sean wanted to believe they'd be safe, at least for tonight, but his gut told him to watch for trouble. He put in a call to Dylan at the TST office.

"We're here," Sean announced, purposely not naming the city in case somebody was listening. "Anything to report?"

"Wynter must be taking advantage of his location near Silicon Valley and hiring top-notch programmers. His security is state-of-the-art, truly hard to hack."

Oddly, Dylan sounded happy. Sean asked, "You like the challenge?"

"Oh yeah. Getting through these firewalls will be an accomplishment."

"I'll leave you to it."

"Hang on a sec. I had a phone call from your new BFF, Morelli. He wanted to make an information exchange."

"What did you tell him?"

"I said you'd call him back."

"Thanks, bro."

He disconnected the call. Morelli's business card with all his numbers was burning a hole in his pocket. Though Sean was tempted to make the call, he'd warned Morelli not to contact him. It might seem weak to call back. But it was possible that Morelli had useful information.

Sean set the scrambler on his phone so he couldn't be traced and punched in the numbers for Morelli's cell phone. As soon as the other man answered, he said, "What do you want?"

"Let me talk to Emily."

"You're wasting my time," Sean said. "Talk."

"Tell her that she's not going to be able to sell her articles to the *BP Reporter* anymore. That's one of the places she published her last article on Wynter."

"Why can't she sell there?"

"A terrible accident happened in their office. The police are saying a leak in the gas main resulted in the fiery explosion that destroyed the building."

"Any deaths or injuries?"

"The editor is in the hospital." Morelli paused for a moment. "It's fortunate that Emily wasn't there."

CHAPTER ELEVEN

ANY COMPLACENCY EMILY had been feeling vanished when Sean told her of the explosion. *BP Reporter* was a giveaway newspaper filled with shopping specials and coupons, and the pay for articles was next to nothing. Most writers saw *BP*, which stood for Blog/Print, as a stepping-stone to actual paying assignments. The editor, Jerome Strauss, wasn't a close friend, but she knew him and she felt guilty about his injuries. She was to blame. There wasn't a doubt in her mind that Wynter was behind the supposed "gas leak" detonation.

Refreshed from her catnap and energized by righteous rage, she found it difficult to wait until they got to the Pendragon Hotel to start her inquiries. They'd gained an hour traveling to the West Coast. It was after two o'clock in the morning when they entered the suite.

She set up her laptop on a desk in the living room and watched while Sean prowled through the suite with his gun held ready. The floor plan for the suite was open space with the kitchen delineated by a counter and the bedroom separated by a half wall and an arch. Sean was thorough, peering into closets and looking under the bed. When he was apparently satisfied that there were no bad guys lurking, he unpacked some strange equipment. One piece looked like an extension rod for selfies.

"What's that?" she asked.

"An all-purpose sweeper to locate bugs, hidden cameras and the like."

Though she appreciated his attention to detail, she didn't understand why it was needed. "How would anybody know we were coming to this hotel and were assigned to this room?"

"I've stayed here before. And I asked for this room. It's on the top floor, the sixth. Since this is the tallest building on the block, it's hard for anybody with a telescope or a sniper rifle to take aim. There's a nice view when the fog lifts."

"It's a nice hotel," she agreed. The exterior was classic San Francisco architecture, and the furnishings were clean lined, Asian inspired. "Why would there be bugs?"

"I want to be sure we're safe." He started waving his long camera thingy, scanning the room for electronic devices. "Get used to this, Emily. From now on, I'm hyperprotective."

Tempted to make a snarky comment about how vigilance sometimes crossed the line into obsessive-compulsive disorder, she kept her lip zipped. He was the expert, and she needed to rely on his judgment. She sauntered across the room to the counter that separated the kitchenette and climbed onto a stool. "I need to start making phone calls. Which phone should I use?"

"It depends on who you're calling."

"How so?"

He explained, "If you're talking to somebody suspicious who might try to track your location, use the secure phone Dylan gave you. If it's somebody you feel safe with, use a burner. We can load up a burner and pitch it."

He seemed to be thinking of all contingencies. "I want to track down Strauss by calling hospitals."

"Burner," he said as he continued to sweep the room.

She called four hospitals before she found the right one. The only information the on-duty nurse would give her was that Strauss was in "fair" condition, but not allowed to have visitors, especially not visitors from the press.

Relieved but not completely satisfied, she wished she had the type of access the FBI and SFPD had. It didn't seem fair. Law enforcement officers wouldn't be barred from the room, but the press—the very people Strauss worked with every day—had to take a step back.

If Strauss was awake, she'd bet he was planning his coverage on the explosion. The story had fallen into his lap. Would he let her be the one to write about it?

She wasn't his favorite reporter. He knew her as Emily, and she submitted only puff pieces, but the explosion might be a way to integrate her real identity with her secret pseudonym. Strauss already did business with her fake persona; the article about Wynter had been published first by an online news journal that paid for her investigative skills. Strauss had permission for a reprint that cost him nothing.

Maybe she could get Sean to use his influence with Agent Levine to sneak her into the hospital room. She went into the bedroom area behind Japanese-style screens to ask.

There were two full-size beds, and he had taken the one nearer to the archway connecting bedroom and living room. He'd pulled back the spread and collapsed onto the sheets. His shoes were off, but he still wore his jeans and T-shirt. In repose, his features relaxed, and he seemed almost innocent. She crept up beside him and turned off the globe-shaped lamp on the bedside table.

Before she could tiptoe out of the room, his hand shot out and grasped her wrist. His movement was unexpected. She gasped loudly and struggled to pull away from him. He held on more tightly. "Turn it back on."

"I wanted to make it dark so you could sleep."

"Can't see an intruder." He hadn't opened his eyes. "Leave the light on."

She flicked the switch, he released his grasp and she scuttled into the front room with her heart beating fast. He'd startled her, and her fear was close to the surface. If he could spook her so easily, how was she going to fall asleep?

If she stayed up, what could she do? It was too early to make phone calls, and she wanted to talk to Dylan before she used the laptop so she wouldn't accidentally trigger any alarms.

A sigh pushed through her lips. Lying down on the bed was probably a good idea. Getting herself cleaned up was next best.

The huge bathroom was mostly white marble with caramel streaks. Fluffy white towels in varying sizes sat on open shelving that went floor to ceiling. She wasn't really a bathtub person, and the glassed-in shower enticed her.

For a full half hour, Emily indulged herself. Steaming hot water from four different jets sluiced over her body. The sandalwood fragrance of the soap permeated her skin, and she washed her hair with floral-scented shampoo while humming the song about San Francisco and flowers in her hair.

She toweled dry, styled her hair with a blow-dryer and slipped into a sleeveless nightshirt that fell to her knees. Before leaving the bathroom, she turned out the light so she wouldn't disturb Sean.

After she pulled down her covers, she glanced over at his sleeping form. Under the sheets, he stretched out the full length of the bed on his back with his arms folded on his chest. His eyes were closed. He'd stripped off his clothes and appeared to be naked, which had always been his preferred way to sleep.

When they were married, she'd always looked forward to those nights when she was already in bed, not quite asleep and waiting for him. He'd enter the room quietly and slip under the covers, and she'd realize that he was completely naked. She remembered the heat radiating from his big, hard, masculine body, and when he'd pulled her into his arms, she was warmed to the marrow of her bones.

The pattern of hair on his chest reminded her of those days, long ago. Her fingers itched to touch him. She sat on the edge of her bed, silently hoping that he'd open his eyes and ask her to come closer.

Their ground rules started with the obvious: no falling in love, followed by no public display of affection. The complicated part was initiating contact. If he went first, he had to ask. But she was free to pounce on him at any time. *What am I waiting for?*

She shifted position, sitting lightly on his bed and watching him for any sign that he was awake. The steady rise and fall of his chest indicated that he hadn't noticed her nearness. Maybe she'd steal a kiss and return to her own bed.

She leaned down closer. Her heart thumped faster. Her entire body trembled with anticipation. Falling in love with her ex-husband was completely out of the question. If anything happened between them, she couldn't expect it to mean anything. *Really? Am I capable of having sex without love?*

A couple of times in the past, she'd engaged in meaningless sex. The result was never good, hardly worth the effort. Maybe that type of sex would be blah with Sean, but she doubted it. He was too skillful, and he knew exactly which buttons to punch with her. The real question was: Did she dare to open herself up to him, knowing that he'd broken her heart and fearing that he might do it again?

A scary possibility, too scary. She was too much of a coward to take the risk. Exhaling a sigh of sad regret, she pulled away from him, turned her head and stood.

"Emily?"

"Yes."

He was out of the bed, standing beside her. She glided into his embrace, and he positioned her against his naked body. They fit together like yin and yang, like spaghetti and meatballs, like Tarzan and Jane. *Take me, Lord of the Jungle!* She was becoming hysterical. If she was going to avoid sex, she'd better stop him now.

His kiss sent her reeling. With very little effort, he'd caught her.

All logic vanished. The pleasure of his touch erased conscious thought. All she wanted was to savor each sensation. He pressed more firmly against her. She couldn't fight him, didn't want to. *If this is what sex without love feels like, sign me up.*

He gathered the hem of her nightshirt in his hands. Looking down, he read the message on the front. "Promote Literacy. Kiss a Poet."

"I'm just doing my bit to promote education."

"Noble," he said.

In a single gesture, he lifted the nightshirt up and over her head. Underneath, she was as nude as he. By the light of the bedside lamp, her gaze slid appreciatively downward, from his shoulders to the dusting of chest hair to his muscular abs and lower. He was even more flawless than she remembered.

"Hey, lady." He lifted her chin. "My eyes are up here."

"And they're very nice eyes, very dark chocolate and hot. At the moment, however—" she gave him a wicked smile "—I'm more interested in a different part of your body."

He scooped her off her feet and dove with her onto the bed. With great energy, he flung off the covers, plumped pillows and settled her in place before he straddled her hips.

For a moment, she lay motionless below him. She just stared at her magnificent ex-husband. Sex always brought out the poet in her. *He was her knight errant, her Lancelot, a conquering hero who would plunder and ravage her.* Which made her... what? Surely not a helpless maiden; she drove her own destiny. And she most certainly would not lie passively while he had all the fun.

Struggling, she sat up enough to grab his arms and pull him toward her. *A futile effort.* He was in control, and he let her know it by pinning her wrists on either side of her head. He was too strong. She couldn't fight him.

"Relax, Emily." His baritone rumbled through her. "Let me take care of you."

She wriggled. "Maybe you could speed it up."

"I've thought about this for a long time." He dropped a kiss on her forehead. "I want it to last for a very long time."

He hovered over her, balancing on his elbows and his knees. In contrast to his flurry of activity, he slowly lowered himself, seeming to float inches above her. Their lips touched. His chest grazed the tips of her breasts.

She arched her back, desperate to join her flesh with his. He wrestled her down, forcing her to experience each feather touch separately. Shivers of pleasure shot through her, setting off a mad, convulsive reaction that rattled from the ends of her hair to the soles of her feet. She threw her head back against the pillow. Her toes curled.

"Now, Sean. I want you, please."

"Good things are…worth the wait."

His seduction was slow and deliberate, driving her crazy. Her lungs throbbed. She breathed hoarsely, panting and gasping as a wave of pleasure rolled over her. Oh God, she'd missed this! The way he handled her, manipulating her so she felt deeply and passionately. Transformed, she was aware of her own sexuality.

"You're a goddess," he whispered.

And she felt like some kind of superior being who was beautiful, brilliant and powerful. If she could be like this in everyday life, Emily would rule the world.

Somehow, magically, they changed positions and she was on top. She kissed his neck, inhaling his musky scent and tasting the salty flavor of his flesh. She bit down. He was yummy, a full meal.

He nudged her away from his throat. "Did you turn into a vampire or are you just giving me a hickey?"

"I'll be a sultry vampire." She raked her fingers through the hair on his chest. "And you can be a wolf man."

"I like it."

"Me, too."

Sex with Sean was a full-contact sport, engaging mind and

body, mostly body, though. He teased and cajoled and fondled and kissed and nibbled.

She'd missed the great sex that only Sean could give her. Not that it was all his doing. She played her part—the role of a goddess—in their crazy, wild affection. And when she reached her earth-shaking climax, she came completely undone, disassembled. It felt like she'd actually left her body and soared to the stratosphere. When she came back to earth, she couldn't wait to do it again.

So they did. Twice more that night.

CHAPTER TWELVE

THE NEXT MORNING, Sean lifted his eyelids and scanned the open-space suite at the Pendragon Hotel. Yesterday might have been the longest day of his life with more ups and downs than a roller coaster, but he wasn't complaining. The day had turned out great. Sex with Emily was even better than he'd remembered. Their chemistry was incredible. No other woman came close.

He gazed at her, sleeping beside him. She was on her stomach, and the sheet had slipped down, revealing a partial view of her smooth, creamy white bottom. He wanted to see more. Carefully, so he wouldn't wake her, he caught the sheet between two fingers and tugged.

Immediately, she reached back to swat his hand away. She peered through a tangle of hair as she rolled to her side and rearranged the sheet to cover her lovely round breasts. *A bit late for modesty*, he thought, but he said nothing. He wanted another bout of sex, and he was fairly sure she was ready for more of the same.

"Time?" she asked.

He stretched his neck so he could see the decorative clock on the bedside table. The combination of chrome circles and squares showed the time in the upper-left corner.

"Eight forty-six." He looked past the archway into the living room, where faint light appeared around the shades. "The sun's up."

"I thought we were going to run out the door early and have breakfast with Levine."

"It'll have to be brunch. Maybe even lunch." He made a grab for her, but she evaded him. "About last night..."

"Enough said." She climbed out of bed with the sheet wrapped around her. "I'm glad we got that out of the way."

She made wonderful sex sound like a distasteful chore. Surely he'd heard her wrong. "Are you talking about us? You and me? About what happened last night?"

"It was just sex."

"Sure, and Everest is just a mountain. The Lamborghini is just a car."

"The tension was building between us, and we had to relieve it. That's what last night was about." With one hand, she clutched the sheet while the other rubbed the sleep out of her eyes. "I promise you—it's never going to happen again."

She pivoted, squared her shoulders and marched into the bathroom while he sat on the bed, gaping as he watched her hasty retreat. *Never going to happen again?* He'd be damned if he believed her. She might as well tell the birds not to sing and the fish not to swim. He could not deny his nature, and his inner voice told him to have sex with her as soon and as often as possible.

His number one job, however, was keeping her safe, and meeting with Special Agent Greg Levine was a good place to start. Sean decided not to make the phone call to set the time and the place until he and Emily were near the restaurant; he didn't want Levine to have time to plan ahead.

After they were dressed, he gave her a glance, pretending not to notice how tiny her waist looked in the belted slacks that hugged her bottom. He stared pointedly at her flat ballet shoes. "Do you have sneakers?"

"They don't exactly go with this outfit." She slipped on the matching gray jacket to the pantsuit. "I want to look professional to meet with Levine, and my suitcase is packed with outdoorsy stuff for Colorado."

"You need to wear running shoes. Obvious reasons."

"Okay." She exhaled a little sigh. "Anything else?"

"A hooded sweatshirt?"

"Don't have one with me. I've got several at my apartment. Can we swing past there?"

She wasn't actually disagreeing with him, but her reluctance to follow his instructions was annoying. "Don't you get it? These guys want to kill you. If they recognize you, you're dead."

Her full lips pinched together. "If we can figure out a way to go to my apartment, I have a couple of already-made disguises to go with my pseudonyms. There's a really good one that makes me look like a guy."

Impossible!

He turned away from her and went to the kitchenette to fill his coffee mug again. "Try to find something that makes you look anonymous. Wynter's men might be following Levine."

When she emerged from the bedroom, she threw her arms wide and announced her presence. "Ta-da! Do I look like a punk kid from the city streets?"

Without makeup, her face looked about fourteen. But her jeans were too well fitted. And her Berkeley sweatshirt looked almost new. "Not a street kid," he said. "You look more like a cheerleader."

"Is that anonymous enough?"

"Still too cute. Men will notice you." He motioned for her to come closer. "Give me the sweatshirt."

In one of the kitchen drawers, he found a pair of heavy scissors, which he used to whack off the arms on the sweatshirt and to make a long slit down from the collar. He turned it inside out and tossed it back to her.

"You ruined my sweatshirt," she said as she pulled it over

her head. Underneath, she wore a blue blouse with long sleeves. "How's this?"

"Better, but I still can't erase your prettiness." He tilted his head to the side for a different perspective. "Maybe we should cut off the jeans."

"I'd rather not. These cost almost two hundred bucks."

He stalked into the bedroom, dug around in his backpack and took out two baseball caps. The one that was worse for wear, he gave to her. "Whenever you go outside, wear this. It won't change your appearance, but it hides your face."

His clothes were more nondescript than hers; people tended not to notice a guy in jeans, T-shirt and plaid flannel overshirt. If he stooped his shoulders a bit to disguise his height, he'd fade into almost any background.

They left the hotel shortly after ten o'clock, late enough that the morning fog had lifted. When he'd been living in San Francisco, he had a hard time adjusting to fog. Sunny days in Denver numbered about 245 a year, and when it was sunny the sky was open and blue. Sean came to think of the morning fog as the day waking slowly, reticent to leave nighttime dreams behind.

This was the city where he first fell in love with Emily, and he saw the buildings, neighborhoods and streets through rose-colored glasses. If last night's sensuality had been allowed to grow and flourish, he would have felt the same today, but she'd squashed his mood.

Behind the wheel of his rental car, he asked, "Is that North Beach café with the great coffee still there?"

"You mean Henny's," she said. "It's there and the coffee is still yummy."

The location wasn't particularly convenient to the FBI offices near Golden Gate Park, but Sean wasn't planning to go easy on his former coworker. The best explanation for how Wynter found out about Emily was that Levine was incompetent enough to get his phone tapped and not know it. At worst, he was working with Wynter.

There was street parking outside Henny's Café, a corner eatery with a fat red hen for a logo. He found a place halfway down the block and parallel parked. He ordered her to stay in the car while he did swift reconnaissance inside the café, which was only half-full and had a good view of the street and an exit into the alley.

Back in the car, he called Levine. The trick to this phone call would be to keep from mentioning Emily or Wynter or the possibility that the FBI phones were tapped.

After the initial hello, Sean said, "Long time no see, buddy. Do you remember that case we worked? With the twins who kept spying on each other?"

"Uh-huh, I remember." Levine sounded confused.

"The big thing in that case has been getting more and more common." Sean's reference was to wiretapping, which had been the key to solving the twin case. "Have you ever had a problem like that?"

"What are you getting at?"

"It's probably nothing. I just hope you aren't infected…" *With a bug on your phone.* "Know what I mean?"

"Damn right I do." His confusion was replaced with anger. As a rule, feds don't like having somebody outside the agency tell them that their phones aren't secure. "What about that other matter? The problem with—"

"The Em agenda," Sean said. "Meet me, within the hour, and we'll talk."

After he rattled off the name of the restaurant and the address, he ended the call and turned to Emily, who had been patiently, quietly waiting.

"He'll be here," he said. "We'll wait in the car until he shows up."

"Did you refer to me as the Em agenda?"

"To avoid saying your name."

"Cool, like a code name." She was off and running, chattering on about how she could be a spy. "Just call me Agent Em."

She needed to understand that they weren't playing a fantasy espionage game. The danger was real. But when Emily followed one of her tangents, she was bright and charming and impossible to resist.

When they were married, it was one of the things he had loved about her. He could sit back and listen to her riff about some oddball topic. She called it free verse; he called it adorable.

"Hold on," he said. "I'm still mad."

"About what?"

"You gave me the brush-off this morning."

"Didn't mean to upset you," she said. "We had an agreement, ground rules. I'm just making sure I don't fall in love with you again."

"There's a difference between sex and love."

"Well, listen to you." Her eyebrows lifted. "Aren't you surprisingly sensitive?"

"I told you I've changed."

"You hardly seem like the same guy who took me to a Forty-Niners game at Levi's Stadium and got in a shouting match that almost came to blows."

"They insulted my Broncos," he said.

"Heaven forbid."

The near fistfight at the football game hadn't been his finest hour, but the undercover work had been eating away at him. He'd needed to let off steam. "I know there were times when I was hard to live with."

"Me, too," she said. "Let's keep it in the past. And never fall in love again."

"As long as we agree that not falling in love doesn't mean we can't have sex."

"That's a deal."

When she held out her hand to shake on the agreement, he yanked her closer and gave her a kiss. He caught her in the middle of a gasp, but her mouth was pliant. Soon she was kissing him back. Emily's recently logical brain might be opposed to sex, but her body hadn't gotten the message. She wanted him as much as he wanted her.

When he turned away and looked out the windshield, he spied Special Agent Greg Levine crossing the street and heading toward Henny's. Walking fast and staring down at the cell phone in his hand, Levine gave off the vibe of a stressed-out businessman and had the wardrobe to match: dark gray suit, blue shirt and necktie tugged loose. His dark blond hair was trimmed in much the same style as Sean's but wasn't as thick. The strands across the front were working hard to cover his forehead.

As Sean escorted Emily up the sidewalk to the café, she asked, "Is there anything I should be careful of saying or not saying? You know, in case Levine isn't on our side."

"Don't mention Hazel. Definitely don't mention that Dylan might hack in to his system." Until they knew otherwise, Sean would treat Levine like an ally instead of an enemy. "First I'm going to pump him to find out how Wynter learned there was a witness. And then how he knew the witness was you."

"I want to ask him what the FBI knows about Patrone's family in Chinatown, the people who took him in when he was a kid."

He nodded. "Anything else?"

"It goes without saying that I want to see if Levine can get me into the hospital to see Strauss."

Inside Henny's, they joined Levine in a cantaloupe-orange leatherette booth at the back. Henny's specialized mostly in breakfast and lunch. The decor was chipper with sunlight filtering through the storefront windows, dozens of cutouts and pictures of chickens and a counter surrounded by swivel stools. A cozy place to wake up, and yet they served alcohol.

Sean did a handshake and half hug with Levine. They'd worked together but never had been close. Since Sean worked undercover, he was seldom in the office; the only agent he cared about was his handler/supervisor, and he knew she'd returned to Quantico. He listened while Levine updated him on other people they knew in common.

The waitress returned to their table with a Bloody Mary for Levine. He must have ordered when he walked in the door. Vodka before noon; not a good sign. Remembering her preference, Sean ordered a cappuccino for Emily. He wanted a double espresso.

"You and Emily," Levine said with a knowing grin. "I always thought you two would get back together."

"We're not together," Emily said. "I hired Sean to act as my bodyguard."

"You're his boss? The one who cracks the whip?" His grin turned into a full-on smirk. "I underestimated you, girl."

"Don't call her girl," Sean said coldly. "And yeah, you didn't give her enough credit. I haven't seen your files, but she's got enough on Wynter for an arrest."

"I'm working on it." Levine swizzled the celery in his glass before he raised it to his lips. "I've got a snitch on the inside."

Sean hadn't expected him to be so forthcoming. As long as Levine was being talkative, he asked, "How did Wynter find out there was a witness to Patrone's murder?"

"The murder was investigated by the SFPD. Patrone was a known associate of Wynter, which put suspicion off Wynter. At first, they investigated Wynter's rivals."

Sean didn't need a history of the crime. "But they came around to the real story. How did that happen?"

Levine couldn't meet his gaze. Dark smudges under his eyes made Sean think he wasn't sleeping well. His chin quivered as he attempted to change the direction of their conversation. "Why do you think my phone is bugged?"

"Simple logic. There's no reason for anybody to connect Emily to me. We haven't seen or talked to each other since the divorce. But you called my office in Denver—"

"I told you," Levine said. "I always thought the two of you would get back together. Hell, you're the reason Emily showed up on our doorstep instead of going to the police. She knew us because of you."

He looked to Emily for confirmation. "Is that true?"

"I thought the FBI would be more careful about keeping my identity secret."

Anger heated Sean's blood. She should have been able to trust the feds, but they'd been sloppy. He glared at Levine. "Did you tell them about Emily?"

"I had to give them something. The cops were off base, asking questions that riled other gangs." His voice held a note of believable desperation. "I said there was a witness and leaked her account of the murder. But I didn't give her name."

Assessing his behavioral cues, Sean deduced that Levine was honestly sorry about the way things had turned out. He'd never meant to put Emily in danger. "I believe you."

"Damn right you do." Levine nodded vigorously. His relief was palpable. "You would have done the same thing."

"I don't think so." Sean didn't allow him to get comfortable. "There are other ways to play a witness, but I'm not here to give you a lesson. You asked why I suspected a wiretap on your phone."

"Right."

"After you called my office, one of Wynter's men made the same contact. How would they know about me if they weren't monitoring your phone?"

Levine took another drink. His Bloody Mary was almost gone, and he ordered another when the waitress brought their coffee drinks. Sean and Emily also ordered breakfast. Levine didn't want food.

While the waitress bustled back to the kitchen, Levine leaned across the table on his elbows and asked, "Did you talk to the guy Wynter sent?"

Sean nodded. "John Morelli."

Levine bolted upright in the booth. It looked like he'd been poked by a cattle prod. "Morelli is my snitch."

CHAPTER THIRTEEN

EMILY TWISTED HER hands together in her lap as though she could somehow physically hold things together. Nothing made sense anymore. Morelli was her contact but also a snitch, and then he'd pulled a gun on Sean, which made him an enemy. The more Levine talked, the more confounded she felt. Had Morelli been lying to Sean when he said he only wanted to talk to her? He'd said she had information about who was stealing from Wynter. It might be important to go through her notes and figure out what he meant.

While Sean and Levine talked about Morelli, trying to figure out if he could be trusted, she pulled her cap lower on her forehead and slouched down in the booth. How was she ever going to make sense of this tangled mess? Maybe Sean had been right when he suggested leaving town and forgetting all about Wynter and human trafficking. She could retract her witness statement and start her life over.

But she couldn't ignore her conscience, and, somewhere in the back of her mind, she imagined the ghost of the murdered man haunting her. She owed it to him to bring his killer to justice.

She spoke up, "It seems like everybody knows I'm the witness. I should just go to the SFPD."

"Makes sense," Sean said. "And that's ultimately what you'll have to do. But right now we're flying under the radar. Let's take advantage of the moment."

"Where do we start?"

"If we figure out why Patrone was murdered, it takes the focus off you."

Similar ideas had been spinning through her mind, but he pulled it together and made perfect sense. Why was Patrone killed? What was the motive?

After the waitress delivered their breakfast, Emily took a bite of her omelet and looked over at Levine. "You might be able to help us."

"What do you need?"

"More background data on Roger Patrone. I know about the gambling operation in the strip club. And I know the woman who took him into her home is Doris Liu." Emily had visited her once and gotten a big, fat, "No comment" in hostile Cantonese. "Patrone must have had other friends and associates outside Wynter's operation."

"He almost married a woman who owns a tourist shop in Chinatown on Grant. Her name is Liane Zhou. Nobody bothers her because her brother, Mikey Zhou, is said to be a snakehead."

Emily shuddered. The snakeheads were notorious gangsters who smuggled people into the country. "Does Mikey Zhou work with Wynter's people?"

"Their businesses overlap."

"If you can call crime a business," she said.

"Hell, yes, it's a business."

"A filthy business."

Her own fears and doubts seemed minor in comparison to these larger crimes. Tearing people away from their homes and forcing them into a life of prostitution or slave labor horrified her. According to her research, parents in poverty-stricken villages sometimes sold their children to the snakeheads, thinking their kids might achieve a better life in a different country.

Others signed up with the snakeheads to escape persecution at home.

"Human smuggling is a complex job," Levine said as he carefully smoothed the thinning hair across his forehead. "They need ledgers and accounting methods to track how many have been taken and how they're transported. Most often, it's in shipping containers. Then they have to determine how many arrived, how they'll be dispersed and the final payout for delivery. But you know that—don't you, Emily? Isn't that why you were on Wynter's yacht in the first place? You intended to steal his computer records and ledgers."

"So what?" She hadn't actually told him about her plan to download Wynter's personal computer, but it wasn't a stretch for him to figure it out.

"Did you get the download you were looking for?"

She'd failed. After Frankie and the boys had cleared out of the office, she had spent the rest of the night running and hiding. But she didn't want to share that information with Levine. There was something about him that she didn't trust. "The only thing that matters is stopping Wynter. How can we disrupt his business?"

"Cut into his profit," Sean said. "But that won't work as long as there's a market for what he's selling."

"It's slavery," she said. "Twenty-first-century slavery. And it's wrong. How can people justify the buying and selling of human beings?"

"Don't be naive," Levine said. "People argue that prostitutes are a necessary vice. And slave labor keeps production costs down. The freaking founding fathers owned slaves. It took a civil war to change our ideas."

She glanced between Levine and Sean. The FBI agent thought she was a wide-eyed innocent who had no clue about the real world. Her ex-husband had told her dozens of times that she was unrealistic and immature. But those complaints were years ago. Sean was different now.

Looking him straight in the eye, she said, "It's our responsibility as decent human beings to expose these crimes and disrupt this network of evil and depravity."

Levine chuckled. "That sounds like a good lead for one of your articles."

"Sounds like the truth," Sean said.

"Do you really think so?" she asked.

"I've always tried to be a responsible man."

A man she could love. She bit her lower lip. *Don't say it, don't.* After the divorce, she'd wondered how two people who were so unlike each other could be attracted. What had she ever seen in him?

This was her answer. At his core, Sean was decent, trustworthy and, yes, responsible. He was a good man.

She straightened her posture and dug into her breakfast. If she was going to save the world, she needed fuel in her system. Listening with half an ear, she heard Sean and Levine discussing lines of communication that wouldn't compromise Sean's location and would make Wynter think his wiretap at the FBI was still operational.

"Then there's Morelli," Sean said. "Can you use your snitch to feed bad information to Wynter?"

"He wasn't always lying to me," Levine said. He fussed with his hair and finished his second Bloody Mary. "I made a couple of arrests based on intel he gave me."

"You can't trust him," Sean said firmly. "Get that through your head. Morelli isn't your pal."

Emily felt Sean's temperature rising. He was getting angry, and she didn't blame him. Levine was beginning to slur, and his eyelids drooped to half-mast.

Before Sean blew his top, she needed information from Levine. "What can you tell me about Jerome Strauss?"

"The editor of *BP*? He's fine, already out of the hospital."

Good news, finally! She waved her hands. "Yay."

"Strauss is one lucky bastard. He'd fallen asleep at the office and just happened to wake up a few minutes before the bomb—which was on a timer—went off. Strauss was in the bathroom when it exploded. The EMTs found him wandering around with no pants."

"So he wasn't badly hurt?"

"If he'd been in the office near the window, he'd be dead. All he had were some bruises and a minor concussion. Lucky, lucky, lucky."

Or not. Emily enjoyed fairy tales about pots of gold at the end of the rainbow and genies in lamps who granted three wishes, but life wasn't like that. There were few real coincidences. Strauss had escaped, and she was glad but...but also suspicious. He might have been complicit in blowing up his own office.

While she and Sean dug into their food, Levine scooted to the edge of the booth. "I should get back to work," he said. "I can't say it's been great to see you."

"Same here," Sean said.

"If I can be of help, let me know." He gave a wave and whipped out the door, obviously glad to be leaving them behind.

She watched him lurch down the street. He stumbled at the curb. "He's about three months away from getting a toupee."

"I didn't remember him as being so nervous." Sean sopped up the last bit of syrup with his pancake. "The FBI in SF has gone downhill since I left."

She nudged his shoulder. "I'll bet you were the best fed since...who's a famous FBI agent?"

"Eliot Ness."

"The best since him," she said. "Tell me, Nessie, what do we do next?"

"I already talked to Dylan this morning," he said, "but I need to call him again and make sure he's hacking in to Wynter's personal computer, the one he had on the yacht. Levine seemed way too interested in whether you'd managed a download."

She was pleased that she'd picked up the same nosy, untrust-

worthy attitude. "Something told me I shouldn't share information with him."

"Good instinct, Emily."

"Thanks."

He didn't allow her time to revel in his compliment. "We
also need to talk to your friend Jerome Strauss. I'm not buying
that coincidental escape from the bomb."

"Me, neither," she said. "But if he knew about the bomb, why
would he stay close enough to be injured?"

"His injury makes a good alibi."

So true. The bomb almost killed him; therefore, he didn't set
the bomb. She wanted to ask him why. What was his motivation
for risking his life? "First we need disguises. Can we please go
by my apartment? I'll only take a minute."

"We had this conversation last night."

"And I agreed that we shouldn't stay there. But a quick visit
won't be a problem."

"Unless Wynter has men stationed on the street outside,
watching to see if you return to your nest."

"They'd never notice me. I have a secret entrance."

Her apartment was on the second floor of a three-story building
that mimicked the style of the Victorian "painted ladies" with
gingerbread trim in bright blue and dark purple and salmon
pink. Following her directions, Sean drove the rental car up
the street outside her home.

"Nice," he said. "You've got to be paying a fortune for this
place."

"Not as much as you'd think," she said. "One of my former
professors at Berkeley owns the property and makes special
deals for people she wants to encourage, artists and writers."

"Wouldn't she rather have you writing poetry?"

"She likes that I do investigative journalism. It's her opinion that more women should be involved in hard-boiled report-
age." She shrugged. "Otherwise, how will idealism survive?"

"Hard-boiled and idealistic? Those two things seem to contradict, but you make them fit together." He glanced over at her. "You're a dewy-eyed innocent...but edgy. That's what makes you so amazing."

Another compliment? He'd already noticed the cleverness of her gut instincts, and now he liked her attitude. He'd called her amazing. "Turn at the corner and circle around the block so we'll be behind my building."

"Your secret entrance isn't something as simple as a back door, is it?"

"Wait and see."

The secret wasn't all that spectacular. It had been discovered by one of the other women who lived in the building, an artist. She'd been trying to evade a guy who'd given her a ride home. He wanted to come up to her place and wouldn't take no for an answer. She said goodbye and disappeared through the secret entrance.

On the block behind Emily's apartment, she told him to park anywhere on the street. She hadn't noticed anybody hanging around, watching her building. But it was better to be cautious.

As soon as she got inside, she intended to grab as many clothes and shoes as she could. Living out of one suitcase that had been packed for snow country didn't work for her.

She led him along a narrow path between a house and another apartment building. The backyards were strips of green dotted with rock gardens, gazebos and pergolas. People who lived here landscaped like crazy, needing to bring nature into their environment.

Her building had three floors going up and a garden level below. A wide center staircase opened onto the first floor. Underneath, behind a decorative iron fence, was a sidewalk that stretched the length of the building. She hopped over the fence, lowered herself to the sidewalk and ducked so she couldn't be seen from the street. There were three doors on each side for the garden-level apartments. She opened an unmarked seventh door in the middle, directly below and hidden by the staircase leading upward.

She and Sean entered a dark room where rakes and paint cans and outdoor supplies were stored. She turned on the bare lightbulb dangling from the ceiling. "In case somebody saw us, you might want to drag something over to block the door."

He did as she said. "And how do we get out?"

"Over here." She'd found a flashlight, which she turned on when she clicked off the bulb. They went from the outdoor storage room to an indoor janitor's closet with a door that opened onto a hallway in the garden level. She turned off the flashlight and put it back.

The sneaking around had pumped up her excitement. She ran lightly down the hall and up two staircases to her floor. Her apartment was on the northeastern end of the building. She wasn't an artist and therefore didn't care if she had the southern or western light.

As she fitted her key in the lock, she realized that she was excited for Sean to see her place. When they were married, they had enjoyed furnishing their home, choosing colors and styles. For her place, she'd chosen an eclectic style with Scandinavian furniture and an antique lamp and a chandelier. Her office was perfectly, almost obsessively, organized.

The moment she opened the door, she knew something was wrong. Her apartment had been tidy before she left for Colorado. Now it was a total disaster.

Ransacked!

The sofa and coffee table were overturned. Pillows were slashed open and the stuffing pulled out. The television screen was cracked. All the shelves had been emptied.

"No," she whispered.

In her office, the chaos was worse. Papers were wadded up and strewn all across the floor and desktop. Every drawer hung open. All her articles were reduced to rubble. *Why?* What were they doing in here? Were they searching?

Barely conscious of where she was going, she stumbled into the bedroom. If they were searching, there was no need for them to go through her clothing. But her closet had been emptied and the contents of her drawers dumped onto the carpet.

Numbly, she stumbled back to the living room. On the floor at her feet was a framed photo that had hung on the wall, a wedding picture of her and Sean. She was so pretty in her long white gown with her hair spilling down her back all the way to her waist. And he was so handsome and strong. She had always thought the photo captured the true sense of romance. Their marriage didn't work, but they had experienced a great love.

The glass on the front of the photo was shattered.

Sean waved to her, signaled her. "Emily, hurry—we need to get out of here."

She heard heavy footsteps climbing the staircase outside her apartment. Her door crashed open, and she gave a yelp.

It was one of the men she'd seen with Frankie on the yacht when the murder was committed. She knew him from mug shots she'd studied when trying to identify Patrone.

"Barclay."

She knew he was a thug, convicted of assault and acquitted of murder. Not a person she'd want to meet in a dark alley.

CHAPTER FOURTEEN

THE MAN WHO stormed into her apartment didn't turn around. He had his back to Sean, and he paused, staring at Emily.

This would have been an excellent occasion to use a stun gun. Sean didn't want to kill the guy, but Barclay—Emily had called him Barclay—had to be stopped.

"How do you know me?" Barclay demanded.

"I'm a reporter. I know lots of stuff." Emily hurled the framed photo at him. "Get away from me."

When Barclay put up an arm to block the frame, Sean saw the gun in his right hand. In a skilled move, he grasped Barclay's gun hand and applied pressure to the wrist, causing him to drop his weapon.

Barclay, who was quite a bit heavier and at least eight inches shorter than Sean, swung wildly with his left hand. Sean ducked the blow but caught Barclay's left arm, spun him around and tossed him onto the floor on his back. He flipped Barclay to his belly and squatted on the man's back.

Sean glanced up at Emily. "I really need to start carrying handcuffs. This is the second time in as many days that a pair of cuffs would have been useful."

Barclay squirmed below him. "Let me up, damn it. You don't know who you're dealing with."

"I know exactly who you are," Emily said. Her face was red with anger. "You were with Frankie when he shot Patrone."

"How the hell would you know about that?"

"I was there."

"No way." Though Sean had immobilized him, Barclay twisted around, struggling to get free. "Nobody was anywhere near. Nobody saw what happened."

She kept her distance but went down on her knees so she could stare into his eyes. "Three of you dragged Patrone into the office. You took turns slapping him around and calling him a coward, a term that more accurately should have been applied to you three bullies. You threw him in the chair behind the desk. Frankie screwed a silencer onto his gun and shot Patrone in the chest, twice."

Barclay mumbled a string of curses. "This is impossible. We were alone. I swore there was no witness."

"You misspoke," she said.

"Don't matter," he growled. "It's your word against ours."

From his years in the FBI, Sean knew Barclay's assessment was true. A hotshot lawyer could turn everything around and make Emily look like a crackpot. Still, he wished she hadn't blurted out the whole story and confirmed that she was a witness. She would have been safer if there had been doubt. "Emily, pick up his gun please."

Barclay twisted his head to look up at her. "You cut your hair. I wouldn't have recognized you."

But now he would. Now he'd tell the others and they'd know exactly what to look for. Sean bent Barclay's right arm at an unnatural angle. "Why are you coming after her? What do you want from her?"

"You're hurting me."

"That's the idea." But he loosened his hold. If he hoped to get any useful information from this moron, he needed to get him talking, answering simple questions. "Have you got a first name?"

"I don't have to tell you."

Sean cranked up the pressure on his arm. "I like to know who I'm talking to."

"They call me Bulldog."

Sean could see the resemblance in the droopy eyes and jowls. "Do you know Morelli?"

"Yeah, I know him."

"Do you have a partner?"

"I work alone."

Bulldog hesitated just long enough for Sean to doubt him. He twisted the arm. "Your partner, is he waiting in the car?"

"I'm alone, damn you."

Sean decided to take advantage of this moment of cooperation. "You were told to be on the lookout for Ms. Peterson, is that right?"

"Yeah, yeah. Let go of my arm."

Sean wanted to know if Bulldog was responding to an alert that might have come from Levine or if he'd seen them sneak through her secret entrance. "Why did you come into the apartment?"

"I saw you."

"Outside?"

"No," Bulldog said. "There are two cameras in here."

Surely someone else was watching, and Bulldog would have reinforcements in a matter of minutes. They needed to get the hell out of there.

Sean should have guessed. Dylan would have figured out the camera surveillance and also would have known how to disarm the electronics. But Dylan wasn't here. Sean needed to step up his game.

"They told you to look for her," Sean said. "When you found her, what were you supposed to do?"

"Not supposed to kill her. Just to grab her, bring her to Morelli or to Wynter."

"What do they want from her?"

"How the hell would I know?"

Sean thought back to his conversation with Morelli, who had also denied that he meant to hurt Emily. Morelli wanted information about a theft. Why did these guys think she knew something about treachery among smugglers?

Using cord from the blinds, he tied Bulldog's wrists and ankles. He could have called the FBI, but he didn't trust Levine. And they couldn't wait around for the cops; Bulldog's backup would get here first. When he pulled Emily out the door, he was surprised to see that she was dragging an extra-large suitcase.

"What's in there?" he asked.

"I'm not sure. I just grabbed clothes and shoes."

Behind the building, she struggled to push the suitcase through the grass. He took it from her and zipped across the backyards to the sidewalk to their rental car.

Using every evasive driving technique he'd been taught and some he'd invented himself, he maneuvered the rental car through the neighborhoods, up and down the hills of San Francisco on their way back to the Pendragon. Sean was good at getting rid of anyone who might be following. Sometimes he pretended he was being tailed just for the practice.

He seemed to be dusting off many of the skills he'd learned at Quantico and in the field. The martial arts techniques he'd used to take down Bulldog came naturally. And he had a natural talent for interrogation.

Still, he didn't have the answer to several questions: Why did Wynter's men think Emily knew who was stealing from them? Were they being robbed? Was it a rival gang?

It was clear to him that he and Emily needed a different approach to their situation. A strong defense was the first priority, protecting her from thugs like Bulldog who wanted to hurt her. But they also ought to develop an offensive effort, tracking down the details of the crime. He couldn't help thinking that Patrone's murder was somehow connected to the smuggling.

"I don't get it," she said. Her rage had begun to abate, but her color was still high and her eyes flashed like angry beacons. "Why did they tear my home apart? What were they looking for?"

"Evidence," he said. "The research and interviews that went into your articles about Wynter must have hit too close to home. Morelli said he wanted information from you."

"What does that have to do with my personal belongings?"

"Flash drives," he said.

"What about them?"

Her outrage about having her apartment wrecked and her things violated seemed to be clouding her brain function. "Think about it," he said. "You'd store evidence on a flash drive, right?"

"And they were searching for those." She did an eye roll that made her look like a teenager. "As if I'm that stupid? I'd never leave valuable info lying around."

She leaned back against the passenger seat and cast a dark, moody gaze through the windshield. He doubted that she even noticed that they were driving along the Embarcadero where they used to go jogging past the Ferry Building clock tower. They'd stop by the fat palm trees out in front and kiss. She'd have her long hair tamed in braids and would be dressed in layers of many colors with tights and socks and shorts and sweats. He'd called her Raggedy Ann.

Long ago, when they'd been falling in love, the scenery had felt more beautiful. The Bay Bridge spanning to Yerba Buena Island seemed majestic. He came to think of that bridge as the gateway separating him from her apartment in Oakland. When he drove across, he'd tried to leave his FBI undercover identity behind.

After swinging through a few more illogical turns, he doubled back toward Ghirardelli Square. "Do you want to stop for chocolate?"

"No," she said glumly. "Wait a minute. Yes, I want to stop." She threw her hands up. "I don't know."

"Still upset," he said. "You were pretty mad back at your apartment."

"I was."

"It showed in the way you threw that picture at Bulldog. For a minute, I thought I'd need to protect him from you."

She chuckled, but her amusement faded fast. Her tone was completely serious as she said, "I need to be able to protect myself."

"I've been thinking the same thing, but I'd rather not give you a firearm."

"Why not?" She immediately took offense. "I know how to handle a gun."

"Too well," he said. "I'd rather not leave a trail of dead bodies in our wake like a Quentin Tarantino film. I think you should have a stun gun."

"Yes, please."

At the hotel, he used the parking structure to hide their vehicle. In their suite, he ran another sweep for bugs and found nothing alarming. He might be overcautious, but it was better to be too safe than to be too sorry.

He sank down on the sofa. "I wish I'd caught the mini-cameras at your apartment. As soon as we walked in the door and saw the place ransacked, I should have known. Electronics are an easier way to do surveillance than a stakeout."

"No harm done." She flopped down beside him, stretched out her legs and propped her heels against the coffee table.

"Now they know what we look like. You heard what Bulldog said. He must have been working off an old photo of you, didn't even know you'd cut your hair."

"And they have a video of you." She smiled up at him. "Not that it matters. They already had photos of you from our wedding pictures."

"You don't keep those lying around, do you?"

"The picture I threw was from our wedding. We were outside my parents' house by the Russian olive tree."

He was surprised that she'd had their photo matted and framed and hanging on the wall. He'd stuffed his copies of their wedding photos into the bottom of a drawer. He didn't want to be reminded of how happy they'd been. "Why did you keep it?"

"Sentimental reasons," she said. "I like to remember the good stuff, like when you kissed me in the middle of the ceremony, even though you weren't supposed to."

"Couldn't help it," he mumbled. "You were too beautiful."

"What woman doesn't want a memento of the sweetest, loveliest day of her life?"

"I guess men see things differently." He slipped his arm around her shoulders and pulled her closer until she was leaning against him.

"How different?"

"If it's over, move on," he said. "Better to forget when you've lost that loving feeling and it's gone, gone, gone. Whoa, whoa, whoa."

Her chin tilted upward. The shimmer in her lovely eyes was just like their wedding when he couldn't hold back. Sean had to kiss her. He had to taste those warm pink lips and feel the silky softness of her hair as the strands sifted through his fingers.

When he brought her back to the Pendragon, he hadn't planned to sweep her off her feet and into the bedroom, but he couldn't help himself. And she didn't appear to be objecting.

After the kiss subsided, her arms twined around his neck. She burrowed against his chest, and she purred like a feminine, feline motorboat. He rose from the sofa, lifting her, and carried her toward the bed with covers still askew after last night's tryst.

The other bed had barely been touched. The geometrically patterned spread in shades of black, white and gray was tucked under the pillows. He placed her on that bed. Her curvy body made an interesting artistic contrast with the sleek design. He could have studied her for hours in many different poses.

But she wouldn't hold still for that. "Don't we have a lot of other things to do?"

He stretched out beside her. "Nothing that can't wait."

"You haven't forgotten the murder, have you? And our investigation?"

The only detective work he wanted to do was finding out whether she preferred kisses on her neck or love bites on her earlobe. He pinned her on the bed with his leg straddling her lower body and his arm reaching across to hold her wrist. Taking his time, he kissed her thoroughly and deeply.

When he gazed once again into her eyes, her pupils were unfocused. The corners of her mouth lifted in a contented smile. But she didn't offer words of encouragement.

"This is not surrender," she said.

"We're not at war. We both want the same thing."

"Later," she whispered. "I promise."

"Don't say ground rules."

He stole a quick kiss and sprang off the bed. It took a ton of willpower to walk away from her when he so desperately wanted to fall at her knees and beg for her attention. But he managed to reach the kitchenette, where he filled a glass with water and helped himself to an apple from the complimentary fruit basket on the counter.

He was ready to get this crime solved. As soon as he did, she'd promised to give him what he wanted. That was an effective motivation.

She appeared in the archway between the living room and bedroom. "We should start in Chinatown. And don't forget that I want to talk to Jerome Strauss."

They could launch themselves onto the city streets, trying not to be spotted by Wynter's men and hoping they'd stumble over the truth. Or they could take a few minutes to reflect and create a plan. He could use the skills he'd learned at Quantico.

"It'll save time," he said, "if we build profiles. That way, we'll know what we're looking for."

"Profiles? Like you used to do in the FBI?"

"That's right."

She'd always hated his work, and he braced for a storm of hostility. Instead of sneering, she beamed. "Let me get my computer. I want to take notes."

Her reaction was uncharacteristic. He'd expected her to object, to tell him that the feds didn't know how to do anything but lie convincingly. Instead, she hopped onto a stool and set up her laptop on the counter separating the kitchenette from the living room.

When she was plugged in and turned on, she looked up at him. "Go ahead," she said brightly. "I'm ready."

Who are you, and what have you done with my cranky, know-it-all ex-wife? The words were on the tip of his tongue, but he knew better than to blurt them out.

She hated the FBI. While they were married, she'd told him dozens of times that he shouldn't be putting himself in danger, shouldn't be assuming undercover identities and lying to people, shouldn't be taking orders from the heartless feds. On one particularly dismal occasion, she'd told him to choose between her and his work. She would have easily won that contest, but he didn't want her to think she could make demands like that.

Her opinion had changed. And he was glad. "We need two profiles," he said, "one for the victim, Roger Patrone, and another for the person or persons who are stealing from Wynter."

"Frankie Wynter killed Patrone," she said. "What will we learn from the victim's profile?"

"We know *who* killed Patrone, but we don't know *why*. Was Frankie acting alone? Following orders from his father? It could be useful to have the victimology."

"One of the last things Patrone said before he was shot was 'I want to see the kids.' Is that important?"

He nodded. "Who are the kids, and why is he looking for them? It's all important."

While she talked, her fingers danced across the keyboard. "You mentioned profiling the person or persons who might be stealing from Wynter. Why?"

"Once we've identified them, we can use that information as leverage with Morelli and Wynter."

"Got it," she said. "Leverage."

He enjoyed the give-and-take between them. "Solving the crime against the criminals gives us something else to pass on to the FBI."

"If this all works out, we could put Wynter out of business and the person or persons who are stealing from him. We could take down two big, bad birds with one investigation." She hesitated. "It's funny, isn't it? When I look at it this way, I'm not really in danger."

"How do you figure?"

"If I tell Wynter's men what they want to know, they'll owe me a favor. At the very least, they'll call off the chase."

Her starry-eyed, poetic attitude had returned full force. Sean knew this version of Emily; he'd married her. He remembered how she'd tell him—with a completely straight face—that all people were essentially good. She was sweet, innocent and completely misguided.

He gently stroked her cheek. "I guess it's safe to say that investigative reporting hasn't tarnished your sunny outlook."

"But it has," she said. "I'm aware of a dark side. Wynter and his crew have committed heinous crimes. They're terrible people."

"Not people you can trust," he pointed out.

"Oh."

"And what do you think these heinous people will do when they find out what you know? They'll have no further use for Emily Peterson."

"And they'll let me go," she said hopefully.

"They'll kill you."

CHAPTER FIFTEEN

PERCHED ON A high stool, Emily folded her arms on the countertop that separated the kitchenette from the living room. She rested her forehead on her arms and stared down her nose at the flecks of silver in the polished black marble surface. She tried to sort through the options. Every logical path led to the same place: her death. There had to be another way. But what? According to Sean, Wynter's men would consider her expendable after she named the person who was stealing from them, which was information she didn't have.

"If I ever figure out who's messing with Wynter," she said, "I can't tell."

"True," Sean said. "But we've got to pretend that you know, starting now."

Crazy complicated! "Why?"

"Information is power. Wynter won't hurt us as long as we have something he wants, either intelligence or, better yet, evidence."

"But I don't," she said.

"It's okay, as long as he doesn't know that you don't know what he wants to know."

Groaning, she lifted her head and rubbed her forehead as though she could erase the confusion. "I don't get it."

"Think of a poker game," he said. "I know you're familiar with five-card stud because I vividly remember the night you hustled me and three other FBI agents."

She remembered, too. "I won fifty-two dollars and forty-five cents."

"Cute," he said.

"I know."

"Anyway, when it comes to Wynter and the info he wants, we're playing a bluff...until we have the whole thing figured out."

"And then what happens?"

"We pull in the feds, and you go into protective custody."

"Or to Paris," she said. That was another solution. *Why not?* They could forget the whole damn thing and soar off into the sunset. "We could have a nice, long trip. Just you and me."

He still hadn't shaved off his stubble, and his black hair was tousled. He looked rather rakish, like a pirate. She wouldn't mind being looted and plundered by Sean. It wouldn't be like they were married or anything...just a fling.

"Havana," he said, "the trade winds, the tropical heat, the waves lapping against the seawall."

"Let's go right now. I could do articles about Cuba and see Hemingway's house. We'd lie in the sun and sip mojitos."

But she knew it wasn't possible to toss aside her responsibilities. She needed to take care of the threat from Wynter before he went after her family. Or her friends, she thought of the explosion at *BP Reporter*. She'd tried to call Jerome Strauss, but he didn't answer and she really couldn't leave a text or a number that could be backtracked to her.

"It might take a long time to neutralize the threat," he said. "What if it's never safe for you in San Francisco?"

"I wouldn't mind traveling the world." Living the life of a Gypsy held a certain romantic appeal. "Or I could settle down and live in the mountains with Aunt Hazel. The great thing about freelance writing is that I can do it anywhere. I might even move back to Denver."

"The city's booming," he said.

"I know. You showed me."

Looking up at him, she saw the invitation in his eyes. If she came to Denver, that would be all right with him. And she wouldn't mind, not a bit. She wanted to spend more time with him. Nothing serious, of course.

"Before I forget..." Sean went to his bag. He tucked away the device he'd used to sweep the room and took out a small, metallic flashlight. "This is for you."

"Not sure why I need a flashlight."

"This baby puts out forty-five million volts."

He held it up to illustrate. With the flashlight beam directed at the ceiling, he hit the button. There was a loud crack and a ferocious buzz. Jagged blue electricity arced between two poles at the end. A stun gun!

Eagerly, she reached for it. "I can't imagine why I haven't gotten one of these before."

"When you're testing, only zap for one second or it'll wear itself out. When you're using it for protection, hold the electric end against the subject for four or five seconds while pushing down on the button. That ought to be enough to slow them down."

"What if I wanted to disable an attacker?" Hopping down from the stool, she held the flashlight like a fencing sword and lunged forward. "How long do I press down to do serious damage?"

"Kind of missing the point," he said. "A stun gun or, in this case, a stun flashlight is supposed to momentarily incapacitate an attacker. Much like pepper spray or Mace."

"Does it hurt the attacker more if I press longer?"

"That's right," he said. "And the place on the body where you hit him makes a difference. The chin or the cheek has more impact."

"Or the groin." That was her target. A five-second zap in the groin might be worse than a bullet.

She released the safety, aimed the flashlight beam at the coffeemaker and hit the button for one second. The loud zap and sizzle were extremely satisfying. She glanced at him over her shoulder. "I'd love to try it out on a real live subject."

"Forget it."

She hadn't really thought he'd let her zap him, and she didn't want to hurt him. She hooked the flashlight onto her belt where she could easily detach it if necessary. "Have you got other weapons for me?"

"A canister of pepper spray."

"I'll take it. Then I can attack two-handed. Zap with the flashlight and spritz with the pepper spray."

"A spritz?" He placed a small container on the counter beside her computer. "Enough with the equipment. We can get started by profiling Patrone."

She climbed back up on the stool. "I've already done research on him."

"You told me," he said. "He was thirty-five, never married, lost both parents when he was nine and was raised by a family in Chinatown. Convicted of fraud, he spent three years in jail, which wasn't enough to make him go straight. He runs a small, illegal gambling operation at a strip club near Chinatown. Do you have a picture of him?"

She plugged a flash drive into her laptop and scanned the files until she located Roger Patrone. The photo she had was his booking picture from when he was recently arrested. A pleasant-looking man with wide-set eyes and a flat nose, he had on a suit with the tie neatly in place. His brown hair was combed. Smiling, he looked like he was posing for a corporate ID photo.

"For a guy who's going to spend the night in the slammer, he doesn't seem too upset," she said. "Does that attitude come from cockiness? Thinking he's smarter than the cops?"

"Maybe," Sean said as he squinted at the picture. "Does he strike you as being narcissistic?"

"Not really. To tell the truth, I feel sorry for him. He's kind of a lonely guy. Doesn't have much social life and never married. Apart from Liane Zhou, I couldn't find a girlfriend. I only talked to one woman at the strip club, and she said he was a nice guy, always willing to help her out. In other words, Patrone was a pushover."

"Characteristic of low self-esteem, he's easily manipulated," Sean said. "But why is he smiling in his booking photo?"

"It's a mask," she said. "When life is too awful to bear, Patrone puts on a mask and pretends that everything is fine."

When she looked over at Sean, he nodded. "Keep going."

"He ignored trouble while it got closer and closer. When he finally took a stand, it got him killed."

"That's a possible scenario," he said. "You're good at reading below the surface."

A thrill went through her. It was comparable to the excitement she experienced when she'd written a fierce and beautiful line of poetry. "Is this profiling?"

"Basically."

"I like it."

"We're using broad strokes," he said. "Our purpose is to create a sketch. Then we'll have an idea of what we should be looking for to fill in the picture."

"Can I try another direction?" she asked.

"Go for it."

"Abandonment issues." She pounced on the words. "His parents left him when he was only nine. And he probably didn't fit in very well with the kids in Chinatown. He didn't know the customs, didn't even speak the language."

"Feelings of abandonment might explain why he joined Wynter. Patrone needed a place to belong, a surrogate family."

"Frankie was like a brother. Patrone trusted him, believed in him," she said. "And Frankie shot him dead."

What had Patrone done to deserve that cruel fate? The Wynter organization was his family, and yet there was something so important that he betrayed them.

Sean echoed her thought. "What motivated Patrone to go against people he considered family?"

"He mentioned seeing the children, which makes me think of human trafficking."

"No doubt," he said. "The theft Morelli mentioned might be about smuggling. Wynter's best profits come from shipping people, mostly women and children, in containers from Asia."

"Someone is stealing these poor souls who have already been stolen." Disgust left a rotten taste in the back of her mouth. "There's got to be a special place in hell for those who traffic in slavery."

"You're passionate about this. I could feel it when I read the series of articles you wrote on the topic."

She was pleased that he'd read the articles, but she wished he hadn't noticed her opinion. "Those were supposed to be straightforward journalism, not opinion pieces."

"You successfully walked that line," he said. "Because I know you, I could hear the rage in your voice that you were trying so hard to suppress. Most people feel the way you do."

"Which is still not an excuse to rant or editorialize," she said. "Anyway, I think we know what was stolen...people."

"Bringing us to our second profile, namely, figuring out who's stealing from Wynter. What are the important points from your research?"

She didn't need to refer to a computer file to remember. "Trafficking is a thirty-two-billion—that's billion with a *b*— dollar business. It's global. Over twelve million people are used in forced labor. Prostitution is over eight times that many. Those are big numbers, right?"

He nodded.

"Less than two thousand cases of human trafficking ended in convictions last year."

She could go on and on, quoting statistics and repeating stories of sorrow and tragedy about twelve-year-old girls turned out on the street to solicit and seven-year-old children working sixteen-hour days in factories.

After a resigned shake of her head, she continued. "Here's the bottom line. Wynter probably imports around a thousand people a year and scoops up three times that many off the streets. His organization has never once been successfully prosecuted for human trafficking. Mostly, this is because the victims are afraid to accuse or testify."

He sat on a stool beside her at the counter. "Much as I hate to be the optimistic one, I'm thinking it's possible that the person who stole from Wynter had a noble motive."

"Free the victims?" She gave a short, humorless laugh. "That's unrealistic, painfully so. The trafficking business runs on fear and brutality. These people are too terrified to escape. They've seen what happens to those who disobey."

When she first dug into the research on Wynter, she'd considered breaking the first rule of journalism about not getting involved with your subject. She'd wanted to sneak down to the piers, wait for a container to arrive and free the people inside. Her fantasy ended there because she didn't know what she'd do with these frightened people. They'd been stolen and dumped in a land where they knew no one and nothing.

"Impossible," she muttered.

"Not really."

"Even with noble motives, it'd be extremely hard to do the right thing."

"Rescuing the victims couldn't be a one-person operation. You'd need transportation, translators, lawyers and more. The FBI would coordinate." He paused to put the pieces together. "I'm sure they aren't involved in anything like this at present. If they had a rescue strategy under way, you can bet that Levine would have bragged to us about it."

Another thought occurred to her. "What if it wasn't a hundred people being stolen from Wynter? What if it was only a handful of kids?"

He jumped on her bandwagon. "A few kids could be separated from the others by an inside man, someone like Patrone."

She built on the theme. "He could have been helping someone else, maybe doing a favor for the woman who raised him. Or it could have been Liane."

She wanted to believe this was what had happened. Patrone had been trying to do a good thing. He didn't die in vain. He was a hero.

"More likely," Sean said, "the human cargo was stolen by a rival gang."

"Who'd dare?" From the little she knew about the gangs in San Francisco, they focused on local crime, small scale. "Wynter is big business, international business."

"So are the snakeheads."

And they were lethal. "Liane's brother is a snakehead."

"Her brother might have used Patrone to get access to the shipments. He could have told them arrival times and locations."

"And Frankie found out."

She shuddered, imagining a terrible scenario with Patrone caught between the brutal thugs who worked for Wynter and the hissing snakeheads.

Which way would he go? Being shot in the chest was a kinder death than what the snakeheads would do to him. She hoped that was a decision she never had to make.

CHAPTER SIXTEEN

WHILE TRACKING DOWN Jerome Strauss, Emily insisted on taking the lead. She was driving when they went down the street where the *BP Reporter*'s offices had been. The storefront windows were blown out, and yellow crime scene tape crossed off the door. The devastation worried her. "If Jerome had been in there, he would have been fried."

In the passenger seat, Sean held up his phone and snapped photos. "I'll send these pictures to Dylan. He might be able to give us a better idea of what kind of bomb was used."

"I'll circle the block again."

She wasn't sure how the attack on Jerome connected to her. He knew her as Emily, a poet who he occasionally published in the *Reporter*. Her journalism was done under a pseudonym. She'd engineered the publication of the Wynter material by Jerome, making sure he got it for free. And they'd discussed the content. But she never claimed authorship.

She thought of Jerome as a friend. Not a close friend or someone she'd trust with deep secrets but somebody she could have a drink with or talk to. She'd hate if anything bad happened to him, and it would be horrible if the bomb had been her fault.

On this leg of their investigation, she and Sean were more prepared for violence. She had her pepper spray spritzer and stun gun. He was packing two handguns, two knives, handcuffs, plastic ties to use as handcuffs, mini-cameras and other electronic devices. Sean was a walking arsenal, not that he looked unusual, not in the least. His equipment fit neatly to his body, like a sexy Mr. Gadget. Under his olive cargo pants and the denim jacket lined with bulletproof material, he wore holsters and sheaths and utility belts.

Her outfit was simple: sneakers and skinny jeans with a loose-fitting blouse under a beige vest with pockets that reminded her of the kind of gear her dad used to wear when he went fishing in the mountains. This vest, however, was constructed of some kind of bulletproof Kevlar. She also wore cat's eye sunglasses and a short, fluffy blond wig to conceal her identity.

Sean's only nod to disguise was slumping and pulling a red John Deere baseball cap low on his forehead. Surprisingly, his change of appearance was effective. The slouchy posture made his toned, muscular body seem loose, sloppy and several inches shorter. He'd assumed this stance immediately; it was a look he'd developed in his years working undercover.

Years ago, she'd hated when he left on one of those assignments. The danger was 24/7. If he made one little slip, he'd be found out. While the life-threatening aspect of his work had been her number one objection, she'd also hated that he was out of communication with her or anybody else. She'd missed him desperately. He'd been her husband, damn it. His place had been at home, standing by her side. To top it off, when he finally came home, he couldn't tell her what he'd done.

Given those circumstances, she was amazed that their marriage had lasted even as long as it did.

At the crest of a steep hill, she cranked the steering wheel and whipped a sharp left turn while Sean crouched in the passenger seat beside her, watching for a tail.

"Are we okay?" she asked.

"I think so. Are you sure you don't want me to drive?"

"I've got this."

Actually, she wasn't so sure that she could find Jerome's apartment. The only time she'd visited him had been at night, and she'd been angry. She wasn't sure of the location. And she didn't have an address because he was subleasing, and there was somebody else's name above his doorbell.

Also, it was entirely possible that he hadn't returned home after leaving the hospital. "I hope he's all right," she said.

"The docs wouldn't have released him if he wasn't."

It was difficult to imagine Jerome in a hospital bed with his thick beard and uncombed red hair that always made her think of a Viking. "I'm guessing that he wasn't a good patient."

"Are we near his apartment?"

"I think so."

Jerome liked to present himself as a starving author with a hip little publication. Not true. He had a beer belly, and his beard hid a double chin. Not only was he well fed but he lived in a pricey section of Russian Hill with a view of Coit Tower from his bedroom. The word *bedroom* echoed in her mind. She never should have gone into his bedroom.

In her one and only visit, she'd been naive, and he'd had way too much to drink. While showing her the view, he lunged at her. She sidestepped and he collapsed across his bed, unconscious. She left angry. Neither of them had spoken of it.

She recognized the tavern on the corner, a cute little place called the Moscow Mule. "Almost there, it's one block down."

As they approached, Sean scanned the street. "I don't see anybody on stakeout, but I'm not making the same mistake twice. Go ahead and park."

In one of the multitude of pockets in his cargo pants, he found a gray plastic rectangular device about the size of a deck of playing cards. He pulled two antennae from the top.

She parallel parked at the curb. "What's that?"

"It's a jammer. It disrupts electronic signals within a hundred yards."

"Inside Jerome's apartment," she said, "hidden cameras and bugs will be disabled."

He handed her a tiny clear plastic earpiece. "It's a two-way communicator. You can hear me and vice versa."

"But won't this little doohickey be disrupted as well?"

"Yeah," he said with a nod, "but I'll only use the jammer for three minutes while I enter Jerome's place. I'll get him out of there, and deactivate the jammer while I bring him down to the car."

Compared to dodging through the broom closet at her place, this was a high-tech operation. She popped the device in her ear. "I'm ready."

He slipped out the door, barely making a sound.

Turning around in the driver's seat, she watched him as he strode toward the walk-up apartment building, staying in shadows. Though Sean was still doing his slouch and his poorly fitted denim jacket gave him extra girth, he looked good from the back with his wide shoulders and long legs. She was glad to be with him, so glad.

As he entered Jerome's building across the street from where she'd parked, she heard his voice through the ear device. "I'm in," he said. "Which floor?"

"Wow, your voice is crystal clear. Can you hear me?"

"I can hear. Which floor?"

"Jerome is three floors up, high enough to have a view, and his apartment is to the right of the staircase. I can't remember the number, but it's toward the front of the house and—"

A burst of static ended her communication. *Jammer on!*

She looked over her shoulder at the apartment building. If it had been after dark instead of midafternoon, Jerome would have turned his lights on. They would have known right away if he was home or not.

Had three minutes passed? She should have set a timer so she'd know when he'd been gone too long. Not that they'd discussed what she should do if Sean didn't return when he said he would. Her fingers coiled around the flashlight/stun gun. If thugs were hiding out in Jerome's apartment, she might actually have a chance to use it.

The static in her ear abruptly ended. She heard Sean's voice, "Jerome's not here. I'm sure it's his place. He's got stacks of *BP Reporter* lying around."

"What a jerk," she muttered. "He promised to distribute these all over town. They're freebies, after all."

"Great apartment, though. Excellent view."

She saw Sean leave the building and jog to the car. He'd barely closed the door when she offered a suggestion. "We should try the tavern down the block. Jerome goes there a lot."

"No need for an earpiece." He held out his hand, and she gave him the plastic listening device. "Let's go to the Mule."

Sean took over the driving duties and chose his parking place so that if they ran out the back door from the Mule, the rental car would be close at hand for a speedy getaway. He wasn't sure what to expect when they entered through the front door. A tavern named Moscow Mule in the Russian Hill district was a little too cutesy for his taste, and he was glad the Mule turned out to be a regular-looking bar, decorated with neon beer signs on the wall and an array of bottles. Stools lined up in a long row in front of the long, dark wood bar. The only Moscow Mule reference came from the rows of traditional copper mugs on shelves.

Jerome Strauss sat at the bar, finishing off a beer and a plate of French fries. He didn't seem to notice them, and Sean led Emily to a table near the back.

She sat and leaned toward him. "I can't believe he didn't recognize me. This blond wig isn't a great disguise."

"Maybe your friend Jerome isn't that bright."

When she chuckled, he noticed Jerome's reaction. His back stiffened, and he tilted his head as though that would sharpen his hearing. Sean wasn't surprised. You can change the tone of your voice, but it's nearly impossible to disguise a laugh.

Whatever the reason, Jerome spun around on his bar stool

and stared at Emily. His big red beard parted in a grin as he picked up his beer and came toward them.

He squinted at her. "Is that you, Emily?"

"Join us," she said.

He wheeled toward Sean. "And who's this dude? Is he supposed to be your bodyguard?"

"That's right," Sean said as he rose to his full height, towering over Jerome. In case the editor wasn't completely intimidated, Sean brushed his hand against his hip to show his holstered gun. "Ms. Peterson asked you to join us."

"Sure." Jerome toppled into a chair at the table.

Emily gave Sean an amused smile. "Would you like to try a Moscow Mule?"

"Not now," he said for Jerome's benefit. "I'm on duty."

"They're really yummy, made with vodka, ginger beer and lime juice and served in one of those cute copper mugs."

Obviously she'd tasted the drink before. It was a somewhat unusual cocktail, probably not available in many places. Sean had to wonder if she'd spent much time with Jerome in this tavern. The newspaper editor had a definite crush on her.

"I like the blond hair," Jerome said.

Sean suspected that he'd like her whether she was blonde, brunette or bald. But they hadn't come here to encourage their friendship. "You don't seem curious, Mr. Strauss, about why Emily is in disguise and why she needs a bodyguard."

"I can guess." When he leaned forward, Sean noticed his eyes were unfocused. Jerome was half in the bag. He whispered, "To protect you from Wynter."

She fluttered her eyelashes. In the fluffy wig, she managed to pull off an attitude of hapless confusion. "Whatever do you mean? I'm a poet. Why would I have anything to do with a murderous thug like Wynter?"

"You can drop the act," Jerome said. "I've known for a long time that you're Terry Greene, the journalist."

She didn't bother to deny it. "How did you guess?"

"I'm an editor, a wordsmith. I noticed similarities in style. Even your poetic voice reminded me of Greene's prose. You have a way of writing that keeps the passion bubbling just under the surface."

"Uh-huh." Disbelief was written all over her face. The fluffy blonde had been replaced by cynical Emily. "Tell me how you really figured it out."

"I wasn't spying on you. It was an accident." He drained the last of his beer. "I noticed some of the Wynter research on your computer, but don't worry."

Jerome waved to the bartender, pointed to his empty bottle and held up three fingers.

"Don't worry about what?" Emily asked.

"I never told those guys, never, ever." The alcohol was catching up with him. Jerome had trouble balancing on his chair and rested his palms on the table as an anchor.

"What guys?" Emily asked. Her disbelief had turned into concern. "Did someone threaten you? Did they blow up your office?"

"Shhhhh." He waited until three beers were delivered and the bartender returned to his other customers. It was too early for the after-work crowd, but there were a half dozen other people at the bar and at tables.

Emily grasped Jerome's hand. "Tell me."

He raised her fingers to his lips and kissed her knuckles. "A guy came to talk to me. Middle-aged, expensive suit, slicked-back hair, he showed me a business card from Wynter Corp, like it was a regular legit business."

"Morelli," she said. "What did he want?"

"He asked for Terry Greene, and I told him that the Wynter article was just a reprint. He'd have to go to her original publisher." Jerome winced. "I knew it was you that he was after, and that's why I blew up my office."

"What!" She spoke so loudly that everybody in the bar

paused to stare. Emily waved to them. "It's okay—nothing to worry about."

"You've got to believe me," Jerome begged. "I'd never tell."

When the murmur of conversation resumed, she glared at him. "You blew up your own office. What the hell were you thinking?"

"I was afraid I might accidentally spill something incriminating, and I didn't want to risk exposing you. Don't you see, Emily? I did it for you."

She surged to her feet and took a long glug of beer. "Please don't do me any more favors."

Sean believed that Jerome was telling the truth, but it wasn't the whole story. Something had scared him enough to make him blow up his office. He was in this bar because he was afraid to go home. And Morelli wasn't all that frightening.

"Who else?" Sean asked. "After Morelli left, who else paid you a visit?"

"I don't know what you're talking about." He lifted the beer bottle to his lips but didn't drink. "I'd never, ever tell. What makes you think there was somebody else?"

His fingers trembled so much he couldn't manage another swig of beer. Though he was half-drunk, Jerome's eyes flickered. He was lying. Sean figured that someone else had been following Morelli, wanting to know what he knew. And the second someone was menacing. "Who was it?"

"Frankie," Emily said. "Was it Frankie Wynter? I feel terrible for putting you in this position. Did he threaten you?"

"I'm the one who should feel bad."

Sean agreed. He figured that Jerome had let vital information slip to the other visitor. It was probably an accident, but Jerome had been terror stricken, numb, and in that state, he'd revealed Emily's true identity. "Was it Frankie? Or someone else?"

"A Chinese guy." Jerome stared down at the tabletop. "A snakehead."

CHAPTER SEVENTEEN

SEAN HAD BEEN hoping to avoid confrontation with the snake-heads. They descended from gangs in Asia that had roots going back hundreds of years. He'd heard that the word *thug* had been invented to describe the snakeheads that, in ancient days, preyed on caravans. Now they specialized in grabbing people from Asian countries and transporting them around the world to North America, Australia and Europe.

After warning Jerome that he was damn right to be scared if he'd crossed the snakehead, Sean told the half-drunk editor that hiding out in the corner bar wasn't going to save him. He needed to go to the police…even if he'd been stupid enough to blow up his own office.

Then Sean swept Emily away from the bar and into their rental car. The answers to their investigation would be found in Chinatown. Sean was certain of it. But he wasn't sure how to proceed.

Taking extra care to avoid being followed, he made a couple of detours to grab something to eat. San Francisco truly was a town for food lovers. The array of fast food included sushi, fresh chowder, meat from a Brazilian steak house and the best hamburgers on earth. He stocked up and then drove back to the hotel.

As soon as she entered their room, Emily yanked the blond

wig off her head and took the carryout bags from him. "I'll set up the food while you do your searching-for-bugs thing."

He placed the jammer on the small round table, pulled up the antennae and turned it on. Sean wasn't taking the smallest chance that they might be overheard. "After we eat, we're going to plan the rest of our time in San Francisco. Then we're out of here."

The corner of her mouth twisted into a scowl. "Do you mind if I ask where?"

"I'm not sure. We're going far, far away from the thugs and Wynter and all the many people who want to kill you."

"I don't understand. I'm such a nice person."

"Speaking of not-so-nice people," he said, "I'd advise you to keep your distance from Jerome. Not only is he crazy enough to set a bomb in his own office but he's a coward."

"What do you mean?"

"I think we have Jerome to thank for making the link between Emily Peterson and your pseudonym."

"But he said…" She paused. "Wasn't he telling the truth?"

"He protested too much about how he'd never tell. I call that a sure sign of a liar."

He swept the room, still finding nothing. Thus far, the hotel had been safe. But how much longer was this luck going to hold? After turning off the jammer, he sat at the table and gazed across at the fine-looking lady who had once been his wife. She liked to set a table, even if they were only eating fast food on paper plates.

Using the chopsticks that came with their order, he picked up a tidbit of sushi. In addition to the California rolls and *sashimi*, he'd ordered fried eel, *unagi*, because it was supposed to increase potency and virility. Not that he believed in that kind of magic…but it couldn't hurt.

"This meal almost makes sense," she said. "We start with the colorful orange-and-green sushi appetizer, then the hamburger and fries main course and finally the doughnuts for dessert."

"Perfect." He wasn't exaggerating. It was an unproven fact that eight out of ten American men would choose burgers and doughnuts for any given meal.

"And what do we do with the lovely hula Hawaiian pizza? And the meat and salad from the steak house?"

"We might not have another chance to eat for the rest of the day. I say we fill up."

She gave an angry huff. "I've told you a million times about how you can't eat once and expect it to last for hours. It's like fuel—you have to keep burning at a steady level."

"Spicy," he said as he assembled a piece of ginger, *wasabi* and *unagi*. "Eat what you want, and we'll take the rest with us."

"Fine." She raised the burger to her mouth. "Tell me about our next plan."

"First we make a phone call to Dylan and find out how much he's learned from hacking. After that, we go to Chinatown."

"After dark?"

He nodded. "At night, we don't stand out as much. Well, I do because I'm tall, but you can blend right in if you keep your head down. While we're there, we need to visit Doris Liu and Liane Zhou, the girlfriend."

"Whose brother is a snakehead," she reminded him. "Do you think Mikey Zhou was the guy who frightened Jerome?"

"It'd be neat and tidy if he was the one," he said.

"Otherwise, we need to start working another angle."

"I don't think so. If this scenario doesn't pan out, we've got to move on. I'd like to resolve the motive for the murder, but it's too dangerous and too complex for us to solve."

"Is it really? Look at how much I got figured out all by my-self."

"That's because you're a skilled and talented investigative journalist."

For a moment, they ate in silence. He enjoyed the stillness of late afternoon when work assignments were winding down and evening plans had not yet gotten under way. The sunlight faded and softened. The streets were calm before rush hour. It was a time for relaxing and reflecting. Though he'd seldom worked at a desk job with nine-to-five hours, his natural rhythm made a shift from work time to evening.

His gaze met hers across the table. She was alert but not too eager. In spite of her mini-lecture about his poor eating habits, she wasn't pushing that agenda. Not like when they were married, and she felt like she had to change him, to whip him into shape.

He didn't miss the nagging, but he wondered why she stopped. It must be that she'd given up on him and decided he wasn't worth all that fuss. He was just a guy she was hanging out with. Technically, he was her employee, not that he planned to charge her or Aunt Hazel for his services. He wouldn't know how to itemize a bill like that. For intimate services, should he charge by the hour or by the client's satisfaction?

"You're smiling," she said. "What are you thinking?"

"I'm imagining you in a waterfall. You're covered in body paint, wild orchids and orange blossoms, and the spray from the waterfall gradually washes you clean."

Her voice was a whisper. "Hey, mister, I'm supposed to be the poetic one."

"We've changed, both of us."

When they'd been married, she never sat still. Nor was she ever silent. He liked this new version of Emily who could be comfortable and relaxed and didn't need to fill the air with chatter.

He wiped his mouth with one of the paper napkins, came around the table and took her hands. "There's one more part to my plan that I didn't mention."

"Let me guess," she said as she stood. "It's the part that takes place in the bedroom."

Hand in hand, they walked into the adjoining room where both beds were messy. He'd hung the "Do Not Disturb" on the door and also requested no maid service at the front desk. He paused at the foot of one of the beds and turned her toward him.

He lifted her chin, gazed into her face. "Nobody ever said it had to be in the bedroom."

"That's a spa shower in the bathroom." A sly smile curled the ends of her mouth. "I haven't figured out how to use all the spray jets."

"We can learn together."

The bathroom also used an Asian-influenced decorating theme with white tile and black accents. On the double-sink counter, there were three delicate orchids in black vases. The tub was simple and small. The shower was Godzilla. A huge space, enclosed in glass with stripes of frosted glass, the shower had an overhead nozzle the size of a dinner plate. Eight jets protruded from the wall at various heights, and there was a handheld sprayer.

He peeled off his Mr. Gadget outfit and dropped the clothes in a pile with his Glock on top for easy access. Earlier, he'd noticed a special feature in the bathroom: dimmer dials for the lights. Playing around with the overhead and four sconces around the mirrors, he set a cool, sexy mood.

"Do you like this?" he asked.

"It's almost as good as candlelight."

She didn't have nearly as many clothes as he did, but it was taking her longer to get out of them. He was happy to help, reaching behind her back to unhook her bra as she wiggled out of her skinny jeans.

He entered the shower. "I'll get the water started."

As she neatly folded her jeans, she said, "Quite a coincidence, Sean. You have a fantasy about waterfalls, and here we are, stepping into a shower."

"Swear to God, I didn't plan this. But it's not altogether a coincidence. The thought of you, wet and naked, is real good motivation to find a shower."

With the overhead rainfall shower drizzling, he opened the

door and took her hand, leading her into the glass enclosure. Her step was delicate, graceful. The dim light shone on her dusky olive skin and created wonderful, secretive shadows on her inner thighs and beneath her breasts.

When she moved under the spray and tilted her head up, he was captivated. She was everything a woman should be. How had he ever let her slip away from him?

With her back pressed into his chest, he encircled her with his arms and held her while her slick, supple body rubbed against him. The intake and exhale of their breathing mingled with the spatter of droplets in a powerful song without words or tune. Swirling clouds of steam filled the shower.

She turned on the jets and edged closer, letting the water pummel her. "That feels great, like a wet massage."

She moved him around, positioning him so he'd be hit at exactly the right place near the base of his spine. He groaned with pleasure.

They took turns soaping each other, paying particular attention to the sensitive areas and rinsing the fragrant sandalwood lather away. She massaged shampoo into her hair.

"Let me," he said, taking over the job. "I remember when we'd wash your long hair. It hung all the way down to your butt."

"A lot of work," she said.

"I like it better this way. No muss, no fuss."

"Like wham, bam, thank you, ma'am."

"Hey, there, if you're implying that I don't want to take my time, you're dead wrong. With all that hair out of the way, I can devote my attention to other parts of you."

He started by nibbling on her throat and worked his way down her body. Though he wasn't usually a fan of electronic aids, he started using the pulsating, handheld sprayer about halfway down.

The way she shimmied and twitched when aroused drove him crazy. Her excitement fed into his, building and building. One thing was clear: he wasn't going to be able to hold back much longer. On the verge of eruption, he had to get her into the bedroom. In the shower, he wasn't able to manage a condom. For half a second, he wondered if using prevention was necessary. Would it be a mistake to have a kid with Emily? He shook his head, sending droplets flying. Now was not the time for such life-changing decisions.

He brought her from the shower to the bed, tangling them both in towels. Condom in place, he entered her. Her body was ready for him, tight and trembling. She was everything to him.

An irresistible surge ripped through him. He felt something more than physical release. More than pleasure, he felt the beginning of something he'd once called love. *Not the same.* He couldn't be in love with her. Those days were over.

He collapsed on the bed beside her. They lay next to each other, staring up at the ceiling, thinking their own private thoughts. Did he love her? He'd give his life for her without a second thought. Was that love? She delighted him in so many ways. *Love?* He was proud of her, of the woman she'd become.

Does it matter? He should let those feelings go. Taking on the biggest gang in the city and the snakeheads, they'd probably be dead before the night was over.

He cleared his throat. "After Chinatown, we've done all the investigating that we can hope to do. Then we leave. We need to put distance between us and the people who want us dead."

"Right."

Reluctantly, he hauled himself up and out of the bed. "I need to make that call to my brother."

Swaddled in the white terrycloth robe provided by the hotel, he went to the desk in the living room and set up his computer equipment to have a face-to-face conversation with Dylan. Through the windows, he noticed that dusk had taken hold and the streetlights were beginning to glow. By the time he was prepared to make contact, Emily had blow-dried her hair and slipped on a nightshirt that left most of her slender, well-toned legs exposed.

She sprawled on the sofa. "Put it on speakerphone."

He took out the earbuds and turned up the volume. Though it was after eight o'clock in Denver, Dylan answered the number that rang through to the office immediately.

"Are you still at work?" Sean asked.

"Of course not. I transferred everything to a laptop, and I'm at my place."

"Turn on your screen and let me see."

"Just a sec."

Sean heard the unmistakable sound of a female voice, and he asked his brother, "Am I interrupting something?"

A slightly breathless female answered, "Hello, Sean. How's San Francisco? It's one of my favorite places. With the cable cars and the fog. Did I mention? This is me, Jayne Shackleford."

She was the neurosurgeon his brother had been dating and was crazy in love with. Sean envied the newness of their relationship. He and Emily would never have that again; they were older and wiser.

"It's a great city." He liked it better when nobody wanted to kill him and Emily. "Put Dylan on."

After a bit of fumbling around, his brother was back on the line. He turned on his screen so Sean could see into his house and also catch a glimpse of Jayne in a pretty black negligee before she flitted from the room.

"Here's the thing," Dylan said. "I've done a massive hack in to Wynter's accounts, both personal and professional. It took some special, super-complicated skills that I'm not going to explain. I'll take pity on your Luddite soul that barely comprehends email."

"Thanks."

"Is that Emily I see behind you?" Dylan leaned close to the screen and waved. "Hi, Emily."

From her position on the sofa, she waved back, "Right back at you, Dylan."

"You did good. You gathered a ton of info with the research

tools at your disposal. But you were missing the key ingredi-ent, namely, James Wynter's personal computer."

"I knew it." She straightened up. "The personal documents are what I was going after on his yacht."

"That's where he kept the real records that didn't synch up with income."

"What does it prove?" Sean asked.

"Somebody's stealing from Wynter," Dylan said. "If I have the codes figured correctly, and I'm sure I do, he lost twelve people last month. They disappeared."

"And there's no way to track them?"

On-screen, Dylan shook his head and rolled his eyes. "What part of disappeared don't you understand? These people—referred to as human cargo—were supposed to arrive at Wynter's warehouse facility. They just didn't show."

Sean took a guess. "Did they come from Asia? Arriving in shipping containers?"

"There was a container. It came up three children short, five-year-olds. All the adult females were accounted for."

And the women would never rat out the kids if they'd some-how found a way to escape. Could those be the children whom Patrone was concerned about?

Sean asked, "What about the other nine?"

"They came on a regular boat. One way Wynter smuggles from Asia is taking his yacht out to sea, picking up the cargo and returning to shore north of San Francisco where he off-loads. Morelli was in charge of the last delivery, which was over six weeks ago."

"When Patrone was killed," Emily said.

"You guessed it," Dylan said. "No human trafficking since then. There's got to be a connection."

"What happened to the nine?" Dylan asked.

"Morelli swore they got onto a truck."

"But they disappeared," Sean said. "You don't happen to know where the yacht off-loads?"

"Medusa Rock, a little town up the coast."

Sean offered his usual brotherly, laconic compliments for a job well done. In contrast, Emily was over the moon, couldn't stop cheering.

"Enough," Dylan told her. "Sean'll get jealous. It's not good to have big brother ticked off."

"He most certainly can be a bear."

Sean growled. "If you two are done, I've got one more question for Dylan. Is Wynter connected with the snakeheads?"

"He's refusing to pay the snakeheads until he gets his hands on the missing twelve. The local gangs are up in arms, inches away from gang warfare."

And Sean and Emily were right in the middle.

CHAPTER EIGHTEEN

EMILY DECIDED AGAINST the blond wig for their trip to Chinatown. Instead she tucked her hair behind her ears and put on a baseball cap. She wore high-top sneakers, jeans and a sweatshirt because it was supposed to be chilly tonight. All her curves were hidden. She looked like a boy, especially when she added the khaki bulletproof vest.

Sean regarded her critically. "Do you have a beret?"

"Not with me. I have a knit cap in cranberry red that I packed for the mountains."

"Put it on," he said.

"Really? But the baseball cap is better. I'm trying to pass for a boy."

He slung an arm around her waist, pulled her close and gave her a kiss. "There's too much of the feminine about you. You look like a girl pretending to be a boy, and that attracts attention."

She dug through her suitcase until she found the cap. It covered her ears, smashed her hair down and had a jaunty tassel on top.

"Better," he said.

"Yeah, great. Now I look like a deranged girl."

"When we're on the street," he said, "keep your head down.

Don't make eye contact. If they don't notice you, they can't recognize you."

He was more intense than earlier today, and that worried her. "Who do you expect to run into?"

"We're walking into the tiger's maw."

"Very poetic."

"I stole it from you," he said, "from a poem you wrote a long time ago. The description applies. Chinatown is home base for the snakeheads and a familiar place for Wynter's men. I bet they even have a favorite restaurant."

"The Empress Pearl."

When she first started her research, she'd gone there several times to watch Wynter's men and try to overhear what they were talking about. She'd often seen Morelli, but when they finally met for his interview, he didn't recognize her, which made her think that Sean was right about being anonymous and, therefore, forgettable.

She asked, "Are we coming back to the hotel?"

"Sadly no, our suitcases are packed."

"I want to make a phone call from here to Morelli. If he tries a trace, it doesn't matter."

Thoughtfully, he rubbed his hand along his still unshaven jawline. "Why talk to him?"

"At one time, we had a rapport, and maybe that counts for something. I have a question I hope he'll answer."

"You're aware, aren't you, that Morelli is the most likely person to be stealing from Wynter? He has inside information, and he signed off on the nine that went missing."

"I think he's being framed," she said.

"We never did a profile on Morelli," he said. "I see him as a corporate climber, a yes-man scrambling to get ahead. He wouldn't take the initiative in stealing from Wynter, but he might support the double-crosser who took off with the nine."

All this crossing and double-crossing still didn't explain why they were coming after her. Like Bulldog said at her apartment,

Wynter wasn't worried about her eyewitness testimony. His expensive attorneys were clever enough to make her look like the crook. If she was about to be framed, she wanted to know why.

She took her last burner phone from her pocket. "I'm making the call."

"And leave the phone behind," he said.

It took a moment to find Morelli's number. He answered quickly, and his voice had a nervous tremor. When she identified herself, he sounded like he was on the verge of tears.

"Emily, I have to meet with you, please. Name the place."

"Actually, John…" She used his given name to put them on a more equal footing. "I was looking for some information. If you help me, I might help you."

"Always the reporter," he said. "Ask me anything."

"According to you and also to Mr. Barclay, aka Bulldog, there's a rumor floating around that I know something about human cargo going missing on shipments from Asia."

"Do you?" He was overeager. If he'd been a puppy, his tail would be wagging to beat the band.

She said, "You first."

"Based on detailed information in your articles about Wynter, I suspected that you had an inside edge. When you talked about our warehouses and distribution, you knew about the supposed warehouse where we stored our human cargo."

"What do you mean 'supposed' warehouse?"

"Don't play dumb with me, Emily. You know it's just a house with mattresses in the basement."

He had it wrong. She had the number of warehouses but not all the addresses. If she'd known where they were keeping the kidnapped people, she would have informed the police.

Morelli continued. "I thought you had inside information, and Bulldog confirmed it."

"Do you always listen to Bulldog?"

"If you didn't want him to talk, you shouldn't have left him tied up in your apartment. It only took ten minutes for some-body to show up and let him go."

"Should we have killed him?"

"Not the point," Morelli said. "He told me that you witnessed the murder from inside the closet in the office."

"That's right." She wasn't sure where this was going but wanted him to keep talking.

"You were in the private office on the yacht...alone with James Wynter's private computer. You were the one who made changes on the deliveries and receipts, trying to cover up the theft."

"I hate to burst your bubble, but everybody on that ship had access."

"Not true. The office was unlocked for a short time only. Only Frankie had a key."

And she'd been unlucky enough to stumble onto the one time when she could get herself in deep trouble. She was done with this conversation. "Here's what I have for you, Morelli. I'm leaving San Francisco and never coming back. I'm gone, so you can quit chasing me. No more threats. Bye-bye."

When she ended the call, she felt an absurd burst of confi-dence. She dropped the cell phone like a rock star with a mi-crophone. *Emily out.*

After dark, Chinatown overflowed with activity. Sean parked downhill a few blocks, avoiding the well-lit entrance through the Dragon's Gate. They hiked toward the glaring lights, the noise of many people talking in many dialects and the explosion of color. Lucky red predominated. Gold lit up the signs, some written in English and others in Chinese characters. Some of the pagoda rooftops were blue, others neon green.

Sean wasn't a fan of this sensory overload. He ducked under a fringed red lantern as he followed Emily toward the shop owned by Liane Zhou. His gut tensed. This wasn't a good place for them, wasn't safe. He wanted to take care of business and get out of town as quick as possible.

Emily stepped into an alcove beside a postcard kiosk and pulled him closer. "It's at the end of this block. I think the name of the shop is Laughing Duck, something like that. There isn't an English translation, but guess what's in the window."

"Laughing ducks."

"I think you should do the talking. I've already met Liane, and she was tight-lipped with me. You might encourage her to open up."

The only thing he wanted to ask Liane was if her snakehead brother intended to kill them. If so, Sean meant to retreat. "What did you talk to her about before?"

"I didn't know about the missing human cargo, so I concentrated on Patrone. At that time, he was only missing, and I didn't tell her about the murder."

"And what did she say?" he asked.

"Not much." She scowled. "She might open up if you spoke Chinese. Do you know the language?"

"A little." He'd picked up a few phrases when he was working undercover. Needless to say, the people who taught him weren't Sunday school teachers. In addition to "hello" and "goodbye," he knew dozens of obscene ways to say "jerk," "dumb-ass" and "you suck."

"Liane is easy to recognize. She's five-nine and obviously likes being taller than the people who work for her because she wears high heels."

Glumly, he stared through the window into the fish market next door. A pyramid arrangement went from crabs to eels to prawns to a slithering array of fish. He hunched his shoulders and marched past the ferocious stink that spilled from the shop to the sidewalk. They entered the Laughing Duck, a colorful storefront for tourists with lots of smiling Buddhas, fans painted with cherry blossoms, parasols, pouches and statuettes for every sign of the Chinese zodiac. Since his zodiac animal was the pig, he pretty much disregarded that superstition. Emily was a sheep.

A young woman met them at the front with a wide smile. "Can I help you find anything?"

"Liane Zhou," he said as he entered the shop.

The narrow storefront was misleading. Inside, the shop extended a long way back and displayed more items. He knew from experience that Liane very likely sold illegal knockoffs of purses and shoes and other merchandise that was not meant to be seen by the general public.

Most of these shops had a dark, narrow staircase at the rear that led to second and third floor housing. An entire family, including mom, dad, kids and grandmas, might live in a two-bedroom flat. All sorts of business were conducted from these shady little cubbyholes, ranging from legitimate cleaning and repair services to selling drugs.

Emily's description of Liane was accurate. The tall, slender woman stood behind the glass-top counter near a cash register. She wore a bright blue jacket with a Mandarin collar over silky black pants and stiletto heels. Her sleek black hair was pulled up in a ponytail and fell past her shoulders. Her lips pursed. Her eyes were shuttered.

Hanging on the wall behind her were several very well-made replicas of ancient Chinese swords and shields. He knew enough of history to recognize that the Zhou dynasty was one of the most powerful, long-lived and militaristic. Liane was the daughter of warriors, a warrior herself.

It seemed real unlikely that she'd open up to him...or to anybody else. He decided to start off with a bombshell and see if he could provoke a reaction.

He met her gaze. Sean had been told, more than once, that his eyes were as black as ebony. Hers were darker. In a voice so quiet that not even Emily would overhear, he asked, "Do you want revenge for the murder of Roger Patrone?"

She blinked once. "Yes."

CHAPTER NINETEEN

A FIERCE HATRED was etched into the beautiful features of Liane Zhou. Looking at her across the counter, Sean was convinced that the lady not only wanted revenge but was willing to rip the replica antique Chinese swords off the wall and do the killing herself.

Instinctively, he lifted his hand to his neck, protecting his throat from a fatal slash. He nodded toward the rear of the shop. "We should go somewhere quiet to talk."

Without hesitation, she shouted in Chinese to the young woman running the shop, and then she strode toward the back. When Liane Zhou made up her mind, she took action. It was an admirable trait...and a little bit scary.

Emily had fallen into line, walking behind him, and he wondered if Liane had noticed her. Behind the hanging curtain that separated the front from the back of the shop, Liane rested her hand on the newel post at the foot of a poorly lit staircase and looked directly at Emily. "Good evening, Terry Greene."

"Good evening to you," Emily said. "That's not my real name, you know."

"You are Emily Peterson. You were married to this man."

"I'm sorry I lied to you," Emily said as she pulled the cranberry knit cap off her head. "I thought an investigative reporter needed to go undercover and use an alias. I was wrong."

"How so?"

"There's never a valid reason to lie."

Liane Zhou turned her attention toward him. Her gaze went slowly from head to toe. "You," she said. "You are very...big."

Unsure that was a compliment, he said, "Thank you."

Liane took them to the second floor and unlocked the door to her private sitting room. Compared with the musty clutter in the rest of the building, her rooms were comfortable, warm and spotlessly clean.

When Liane clapped her hands, a heavily made-up woman who was skinny enough to be a fashion model appeared in an archway. Liane gave the order in Chinese, and the wannabe model scurried off.

Liane said, "We will have tea and discuss my revenge."

They sat opposite each other. Liane perched on a rattan throne while the two of them crowded onto a love seat. On the slatted coffee table between them were two magazines and a purple orchid.

Sean said, "You knew Roger Patrone for a long time."

"We arrived in Chinatown at the same time. Roger's parents sold him to Doris Liu."

Sean had never heard this version of the story. He knew the parents were out of the picture, but he didn't know why. They sold him? Sean mentally underlined abandonment issues in their profile analysis of Patrone.

"He was a boy with special talent," Sean said, taking care not to phrase conversation in questions. He wanted Liane to see him as an equal.

"He was smart." Her voice resonated on a wistful note. "But not always wise."

"A typical male," Emily muttered. "Why did Doris want him so much that she'd pay for him?"

"His English was very good. Written and spoken. And he

picked up Chinese quickly, many dialects. He took care of her correspondence."

"It's a little odd," Emily said, "to trust a nine-year-old with that kind of sensitive work."

"Doris preferred using a child. She wanted him to depend on her for his food and shelter. She owned him, and he had no choice but to obey."

"How much?" Emily asked. "I'm curious."

"A thousand dollars. Doris didn't pay. Her boyfriend bought Patrone as a gift. How could that ugly old hag have a man?" She scowled. "Must be witchcraft, *wugu* magic."

The wannabe model brought their tea on a dark blue tray with a mosaic design in gold and silver. She gave a slight bow and left the apartment.

Though they appeared to be alone, Sean didn't trust Liane. Until he felt safer with her, he'd keep the conversation in the past, going over information that wasn't secret and held no current threat. "You didn't live with Doris Liu."

"Only when I chose to," she said. "My parents would never sell me. They were brave and good. In China, we were poor. Life was difficult. But they would not abandon me. They were killed by snakeheads who stole me and my brother."

"I'm sorry," Emily said.

"As am I."

Sean wished he could warn Emily not to blurt the truth. If she confirmed that she'd seen Frankie kill Patrone, there would be little reason for Liane to talk with them.

He sipped his tea and complimented her on the taste and the scent. "You mentioned your brother, Mikey Zhou."

"Do you know him?"

Why would he? Again Sean struggled to remain impassive. "I'm aware of him, but we've never met."

"Agent Levine said you were a good friend. Yet he has not introduced you."

Shocked and amazed, Sean swallowed his tea in a gulp.

Levine had told them he had a snitch, and he'd identified that snitch as Morelli. Mikey Zhou, too? Sean's estimation of Special Agent Levine rose significantly. No wonder the guy had been slugging back vodka at breakfast. Levine was playing a dangerous game.

While he sat silently, too surprised to speak, Emily filled the empty air space.

"Greg Levine is an old friend," she said. "He came to our wedding, and we went our separate ways. You know how it is. And then Sean moved back to Colorado after the divorce."

"You made a mistake," Liane said. "You should never have let Sean go."

"Right," Emily said. "Because he's so...big."

Liane inclined her head and leaned forward. "Is it true?"

Emily looked confused. "Is what?"

"Did you witness the murder?"

Sean jumped back into the conversation with both feet. "Your brother is a snakehead. But you said the snakeheads killed your parents and abducted both of you."

"The last wish of my father was for Mikey to protect me. He did what he had to do." She exhaled a weary breath. "I was twelve, and my brother was eight. When the snakeheads took us, I knew my fate. As a virgin, I would fetch a good price for my first time. They would make me a sex worker."

Emily reached across the table and took her hand. "How did Mikey stop them?"

"He sacrificed himself. A handsome child, he could have been adopted. He might have worked as a servant. But he refused. Instead he disfigured himself. He made a long scar across his face. He was damaged goods."

"Did they hurt him?" Emily asked.

"He was beaten but not defeated. He did their bidding with the understanding that I would come to no harm. Mikey labored until he collapsed. He took on every challenge. Ultimately, the snakeheads came to respect him."

"And what happened to you?"

"The expected," she said darkly. "My flower was sold for many thousands but not enough to set me and my brother free. I wore pretty things and worked as a party girl until I was treated badly, ruined. Luckily, I had a head for numbers and learned to help Doris and others in Chinatown with accounts and contracts."

"You and Patrone worked together," Sean said.

"Patrone, my dearest friend, translated and negotiated deals with smugglers, local gangs, Wynter Corp and snakeheads. He helped me save until I could open Laughing Duck."

While he was learning to profile, Sean had heard a lot of traumatic life stories. Few were as twisted as the childhood of Liane and Mikey…and Patrone, for that matter. No wonder Mikey Zhou had become a snakehead. And Patrone had been murdered. No doubt, Liane had secrets and crimes of her own.

"I have told my story," she said. "Now Emily must tell me. Who killed my dearest friend?"

Emily glanced at Sean. When he gave her the nod, she cleared her throat and said, "I saw Frankie Wynter and two others drag Patrone into an office on the yacht. Frankie shot him. They threw his body overboard."

Liane bolted to her feet. Her slender fingers clenched into fists at her side, and she spewed an impressive stream of Cantonese curses that Sean recognized from his undercover days.

"I promise," he said as he stood. "We'll bring Frankie Wynter to justice."

"Your justice is not punishment enough. He must die."

Sean was going to pretend that he never heard her threaten Frankie's life. The world would be a better place without the little jerk, but it wasn't his decision. And he wouldn't encourage Liane to take the law into her own hands.

"You're right, Liane." Emily also stood. "It's not fair, and it's not enough pain. But we want to get the person who is truly responsible."

"What do you mean?"

"Frankie pulled the trigger, but he isn't very clever and certainly not much of a leader. He was probably following orders from someone higher up."

"True." Liane spat the word. "Morelli?"

"Or James Wynter himself."

"Wait!" Sean said. "We've got to investigate. We need proof that it's Morelli or Wynter or somebody else."

He glanced from one woman to the other. They couldn't have been more different. Emily had had a charmed childhood and grew up to be a poet and journalist who loved the truth. Liane had suffered; she had to fight to survive. And yet each woman burned with a similar flame. Both were outraged by the murder of Roger Patrone.

"One week," Liane said. "Then I will take my revenge against Frankie Wynter."

Sean couldn't let that happen. He feared that Liane's attack against Wynter would end in gang warfare with the snakeheads.

"We need more information," he said. "What do you know about the human cargo that's gone missing from Wynter's shipments?"

"I help these people," she said simply. "So does Mikey. If you want to speak to him, he is at the club where Patrone worked."

"How do you help them?" Sean asked.

She pivoted and stalked down a narrow hallway. Carefully, she opened the door. Light from the hall spilled across the bed where three beautiful children were sound asleep.

Liane tucked the covers snugly around them and kissed each forehead.

CHAPTER TWENTY

ON THE SIDEWALK outside the strip club where Patrone had run an illegal poker game in the back room, Emily stared at the vertical banner that read, "Girls, Nude, Girls." The evening fog had rolled in, and the neon outlines of shapely women seemed to undulate beside the banner. A barker called out a rapid chatter about how beautiful and how naked these "girls" would be.

"Not exactly subtle," she said as she nudged Sean. "At least it's honest."

"That depends on your definition of beauty. And I'd guess that some of these ladies left girlhood behind many years ago."

"How did you get to be an expert?"

"When I was undercover, I spent a lot of time in dives like this, the places where dreams come to die." He gave her arm a squeeze. "You always wanted to know what I did on my assignments. You pushed, but I couldn't say a damn word. The information I uncovered was FBI classified. And I felt filthy after spending a day at one of these places."

She knew his undercover work had been stressful. One of the reasons she'd pushed was so he could unburden himself. "If you'd explained to me, I would have understood. It had to be hard spending your day with addicts, strippers, pimps and criminals."

"They weren't the worst," he said. "I was. I lied to them. I knew better and didn't try to help."

"I never thought of your work that way."

"But you understand." He gazed down at her, and the glow from the pink neon reflected in his eyes. "You told Liane that you were wrong to lie when you were investigating."

"Maybe we're not so different." Why was she having this relationship epiphany on a sidewalk outside a strip club? "Let's get in there, talk to Mikey and go on our way."

He nodded. "There's not much more we can learn. I'll report to the FBI, sit back and let them do their duty."

She watched the patrons, who shuffled through the door with their heads down, looking neither to the right nor to the left. With her dopey cranberry hat pulled over her ears, she fit right in with this slightly weird, mostly anonymous herd...except for her gender. The few women on this street looked like hookers.

Inside the strip club, she pulled her arms close to her sides and jammed her hands into her pockets. The dim lighting masked the filth. The only other time she'd been here was in daylight, and she'd been appalled by the grime and grit that had accumulated in layers, creating a harsh, dull patina. Years of cigarette smoke and spilled liquor created a stench that mingled with a disgusting human odor. The music for the nude—except for G-string and pasties—girls on the runway blared through tinny speakers. Emily didn't want to think about the germs clinging to the four brass stripper poles.

Long ago, this district, the Tenderloin, had been home to speakeasies, burlesque houses and music clubs. Unlike most of the rest of the city, the Tenderloin had resisted gentrification and remained foul and sleazy.

Fear poked around the edges of her consciousness. Nothing good could happen in a place like this. She moved her stun gun from a clip on her belt to her front pocket so it would be more accessible. And she stuck to Sean like a nervous barnacle as she tried to think of something less squalid than her immediate surroundings.

Liane's life story had touched her. The woman had gone through so much tragedy, from witnessing the murder of her parents to the loss of her "dearest friend." Though she hadn't admitted that Patrone was her lover, it was obvious that she cared deeply about him. And he must have felt the same way about her. He had stolen the three children for her.

After Liane kissed the children, she explained. Patrone had been part of the crew unloading the shipping container. He'd arrived before anyone else because he was supposed to conclude negotiation with the snakeheads. When Patrone saw the kids, his heart had gone out to them. He'd unloaded them from the container and moved them to the trunk of his car. The poor little five-year-olds had been starving and dehydrated, barely able to move. Patrone had taken them to Liane.

This wasn't the first time she'd rescued stolen children and their mothers, protecting them from a life of servitude to women like Doris Liu. Liane fed them and nursed them. The plight of these kids wakened instincts she never thought she had. Though she was unable to bear children, she felt deep maternal stirrings.

Emily hoped that these three children would be Liane's happy ending. According to Emily's calculations, the children arrived shortly before Patrone was murdered. Only six weeks, but Liane loved them as though she'd raised them from birth.

Emily was content to let the story end there. She tugged Sean's sleeve and whispered, "We should go."

"After we check out the poker game," he said. "If Mikey isn't there, we're gone."

"Did Liane call him?"

"She said he'd know we were coming."

Behind a beaded curtain and a closed door, they were escorted into the poker game by the bartender, whom Sean had bribed with a couple of one-hundred-dollar bills. Emily didn't know Chinese, but she could tell from the bartender's tone as he introduced them that she and Sean were being described as rich and stupid, exactly the people you'd want to play poker with.

There were four tables: three for stud poker and one for Texas Hold'em. Emily narrowed her eyes to peer through the thick miasma of cigar and cigarette smoke. Almost every chair at the tables was filled. Most of the patrons were Asian, and there was only one other woman.

Sean guided her to a table and sat her down. He spoke to the others in Chinese, and they laughed. He whispered in her ear, "I said you were my little sister. They should be nice to you, but not too nice because you like to win."

"Are you leaving me here alone?"

"I'll be close. Don't eat or drink anything."

"Don't worry."

When she felt him move away from her, it took an effort for her to stay in the chair and not chase after him. The dealer looked at her and said something in Chinese. She nodded. Since she knew how the game was played, she could follow the moves of the other players without getting into trouble.

The player sitting directly to her right was an older man with thinning hair and boozy blue eyes. He spoke English and directed one condescending remark after another to her. If she hadn't been so scared, she would have told him off.

Her plan was to be as anonymous as possible. Then she was dealt a beautiful hand: a full house with kings high. Her self-preservation instinct told her to fold the hand and not attract attention to herself. But she really did like to win. She bid carefully, taking advantage of how the others at the table paid her very little regard.

While she was raking in her winnings, she looked around for Sean and spotted him by the far wall, talking to an Asian man with a shaved head. He gave her a little wave, and she felt reassured. He was keeping an eye on her.

She quickly folded the next two hands and then tried a bluff that succeeded. *Really?* Was she really holding her own with these guys? The condescending man on her right gave his seat to another, and she turned to nod. His thick black hair grew in a long Mohawk and hung down his back in a braid. His arms and what she could see of his chest were covered in tattoos. The scar that slashed across his face told her this was Mikey Zhou.

He leaned closer to her. His left hand grazed her right side, and she felt the blade he was holding. "Fold this hand and come with me."

"Yes," she said under her breath. Frantic, she scanned the room. Where had Sean disappeared to? How could he leave her here unprotected?

Though terrified, she managed to keep focus on the game. Lost it but played okay. She rose from the table, picked up her chips and allowed Mikey to escort her toward a dark door at the back of the room. His grip on her arm was tight.

He whispered, "Don't be scared."

Though she wanted to snap a response, her throat was swollen shut by fear. She could barely breathe. The fact that she was moving surprised her because her entire body was numb. She was only aware of one thing: the stun gun in her pocket. Somehow she got her fingers wrapped around it. She got the gun out of her pocket without Mikey noticing.

When he shoved her into a small room filled with boxes and lit by a single overhead bulb, she whirled. Lunging forward, she pressed the gun against his belly. She heard the electricity and felt the vibration.

Mikey shuddered. His eyes bulged, and he went down on his hands and knees.

Before she could move in to zap him again, another man appeared from the shadows and grabbed her arms from behind. He knocked the gun from her hand.

She kept struggling, but couldn't break free. When she tried to kick backward with her legs, he swept her feet out from under her, and she was on her knees with her arms twisted back painfully. She tried to inhale enough air to scream. Could she summon help? Who would come to her aid? Nobody in this club was going to cross Mikey Zhou.

He stood before her and leaned down. His long braid fell over his shoulder. Roughly, he yanked her chin upward so she had to look into his dark eyes. Even with the tattoos and the scar, she saw a resemblance to Liane in the firm set of the jaw.

"Emily," he said. "Special Agent Levine said you would cause trouble."

"Let me go," she said. "I'll leave and you'll never see me again, I promise."

"I will not harm you."

He said something in Chinese to the man who was holding her arms, and he released her. She sat back on her heels. What was going to happen to her? *And where is Sean?*

If Mikey didn't intend to hurt her, why did he grab her? She wasn't out of danger, not by a long shot. "What do you want from me?"

"Wynter has an arrangement with snakeheads. It has been thus for many years. There is disruption. Why?"

"Do you want me to find out?"

Mikey rubbed at the spot where she'd zapped him. "The disruption must end."

Slowly she got to her feet. Common sense told her that only a fool picked a fight with the snakeheads, but she didn't want to lie. The whole reason she was in trouble could be traced to her lies when she'd used an alias and posed as a hooker.

If she told Mikey that she'd help him by finding out who was messing up the smooth-running business of human trafficking, that wouldn't be the truth. She hated that the snakeheads were buying and stealing helpless people from Asia, and she also hated that Wynter Corp distributed the human cargo. Couldn't Mikey see that? After what happened to him and Liane, couldn't he understand?

She inhaled a deep breath, preparing to make her statement. These might be the last words she ever spoke. She wanted to choose them carefully.

The door whipped open, and Sean entered the room. As soon as she recognized him, he was at her side, holding her protectively.

"Are you all right?" he asked her. "Did he hurt you?"

Mikey laughed as he returned her stun gun. "Other way around."

She looked up at Sean. "He wants me to help him. I can't do that. I'm against human trafficking, and if it's interrupted, I'm glad."

"I want peace," Mikey said. "I do not hurt my own people. Explain to her, Sean."

"That might take a while."

She didn't understand what they were talking about, but it was obvious that they'd had prior contact. Did Sean know that Mikey was going to grab her and scare her out of her mind?

Mikey said, "You go now."

Sean whisked her toward the exit door from the small room. When he opened it, she saw the foggy night blowing down an alley.

"Hold on," she said, jamming her heels down. "I need to cash in my chips."

"Not tonight."

As if she'd ever return to this place? Reality hit her over the head, and she realized that she was lucky to be walking out this door with no major physical injuries.

She went along with Sean as he propelled her around the corner and down two streets to where he'd parked. A misty rain was falling, and she was wet by the time they got to the rental car. As soon as they were inside the car, he started the engine.

"We need to hurry," he said.

"Why?"

"There's another shipment coming in tonight."

She snapped on her seat belt. She had to do whatever she could, anything that would help.

CHAPTER TWENTY-ONE

MIKEY THE SNAKEHEAD would not be getting any pats on the back from Sean. After Emily told him how Mikey had mishandled her, Sean was glad she'd zapped him with her stun gun.

"He wasn't supposed to scare you," he said.

"Well, he wasn't Mr. Friendly. When he got close to me, I felt the knife in his hand."

"His comb." Mikey's long braid didn't just happen. He worked on that hair. "A metal comb."

"How was I supposed to know?" she grumbled. "All he had to do was tell me you were waiting for me. And his friend grabbed me. He twisted my arm and forced me down on my knees."

"After you zapped Mikey with a stun gun?"

"Okay, maybe I was aggressive."

"You shot forty-five million volts through him."

She huffed and frowned. "What did he mean about wanting peace?"

"I'll explain."

The fog parted as he drove toward the private marina where the Wynter yacht was moored. It was after midnight. The city wasn't silent but had quieted. Misty rain shrouded the streets.

Though Mikey was a member of the notoriously cruel and

violent snakeheads, Sean was inclined to believe him. In his experience, the guys who were the most dangerous were also the most honest, flip sides of the same coin. Besides, Mikey had nothing to gain from lying to Sean.

"Mikey says he's not involved in the actual business of human trafficking. His hands aren't clean, far from it. His job is to take care of snakehead business in San Francisco, buying and selling and extracting payments. His sister's dearest friend, Patrone, helped him negotiate."

"And that's why he knows Levine," she said.

"Right. Mikey's not a snitch. He's more like a local enforcer. He knows that if the snakeheads and Wynter keep losing money, there's going to be a war."

"And we're supposed to stop it?" The tone of her voice underlined her disbelief. "I didn't sign up for this job."

It wasn't fair to drag her any deeper into this quagmire. Until now, she'd been ready to go. Mikey must have scared her, made her realize that she was in actual danger. "You're right."

"Am I?"

"I can turn this car around, hop onto I-80, and we'll be back in Colorado in two days. You'd be safer with your aunt. Better yet, TST Security has a couple of safe house arrangements."

She sat quietly, considering his offer. With a quick swipe, she pulled off the knitted cap, fluffed her hair and tucked it behind her ears. She'd been through a lot in the past few days, and Sean wouldn't blame her if she opted to turn her back on this insanity.

In a small voice, she said, "I started investigating Wynter Corp six months ago, and I've learned a lot. I want to see this through. I want justice for Patrone. And I want the bad guys punished."

Damn, he was proud of her. She'd grown into a fine woman, a fine human being. He was glad she'd chosen to stay involved. If they dragged the FBI into the picture too soon, the investigation could turn messy. Liane might lose the kids and Mikey could be in trouble. If Sean handled the things, the case would be gift wrapped and tied up with a pretty red bow.

At the marina, he parked behind a chain-link fence, grabbed a pair of binoculars and went toward the gate. Security cameras were everywhere. "We can't get much closer. Do you remember where Wynter's yacht was moored?"

"I remember every detail of that night. My red dress and the shoes I could hardly walk in. I remember the other girls, several blondes, a couple of brunettes and some Asian. And I remember Paco the Pimp. He was incredibly helpful. Sure, he charged me a hefty bribe, but he was efficient and kind. Do you think we should talk to him?"

"Save Paco for another story," he said. "Do you remember where you boarded the yacht?"

"Near the end of the pier." When she squinted through the fog, he handed over the binoculars. She fiddled with the adjustments and then lowered the glasses. "I don't see it."

"I was hoping we could catch them before they took off," he said, "but it was a long shot."

"The cargo might be arriving via container ship. We'd have to go to the docks in Oakland to check it out."

A chilly breeze swept across the bay and coiled the fog around them. He wrapped his arm around her shoulder, welcoming the gentle pressure of her body as she leaned against him. She turned, her arm circled his torso and she looked up at him.

Her cheeks were ruddy from the cold. Her eyes sparkled. Before he could stop himself, he said, "I love you."

Her lips parted to respond, but he didn't want words. He kissed her thoroughly, savoring the heat from her mouth and the warmth of her body. She felt good in his embrace, even with several layers of clothes between them.

Saying "I love you" might have been one of the biggest mistakes in his life. He might have sent her reeling backward, frantically trying to get away from his cloying touch. But he wasn't going to take back his statement. He loved her, and that was all there was to it. He'd never really stopped loving her from the first day he saw her.

When he ended the kiss, he didn't give her a chance to speak. "We need to hustle."

"Where are we going?"

"Medusa Rock."

In the car, he immediately called his brother to get the coordinates for the place where Wynter off-loaded cargo. As usual, Dylan was awake. Sean was fairly sure that his genius brother never slept. They discussed a few other electronic devices before Sean ended the call and silence flooded into the car.

After a few miles, she pointed to the device fastened to the dashboard. "Is this the GPS location?"

"That's right."

"Medusa Rock," she said. "Do you think there are a lot of snakes?"

"I don't know. It's a good distance up the coast."

Again, silence.

With a burst of energy, she turned toward him. "We had ground rules, Sean. There's no way you can tell me you love me, no way at all. We had our chance, we had a marriage. When it fell apart, my heart shattered into a million little pieces. I can't go through that again."

"I apologize," he said. "I couldn't stop myself."

"I never thought I'd say this." When she paused, he heard a hiccup that sounded as though she was crying. "You're going to have to practice more self-control."

"Never would have believed it." He tried to put a good face on a bad move. "This time I'm the one who can't keep himself in check. I couldn't stop myself from blurting. What's the deal? Am I turning into a chick?"

"Not possible." She reached across the console and patted his upper thigh. "You're too...big."

* * *

When he told her he loved her, she thought she'd explode. The longing she'd been holding inside threatened to erupt in a sky-high burst of lava. And then, to make it worse, he kissed her with one of those perfect, wonderful kisses.

They had both changed massively since the divorce, but she still wasn't ready to risk her heart in another try with Sean. Maybe she'd never be ready. Maybe they were the sort of couple who was meant to meet up every ten years, have great sex and go on their merry way.

While he drove, she kept track of their route on the GPS map. Soon this would be over, and she'd be able to use her phone again. Right now she really wanted to know about the possibility of snakes at Medusa Rock. According to the map, this place was a speck about a hundred miles north along the Pacific Coast Highway from San Francisco.

At their current speed, which was faster than she liked, they'd be there in about an hour. There was almost zero traffic on this road. In daylight when the fog burned off, the view along this highway was spectacular.

"There's a blanket in the backseat," he said. "It might be good for you to get some sleep. If we catch Wynter's men in the act, we'll need to follow them. And probably will switch off driving."

She didn't need much convincing. The spike of adrenaline from her encounter with Mikey had faded, leaving her drained of energy. She snuggled under the blanket. An hour of sleep was better than none.

It seemed like she'd barely closed her eyes when the car jolted to a stop. She sat up in the seat, blinking madly. She grasped Sean's arm. "Are we safe?"

"You're always safe with me." His voice was low and calm with just a touch of humor to let her know he was joking…kind of joking. "We're here."

"I see it." Medusa Rock sat about a hundred yards offshore.

Shaped like a skull, it had shrubs and trees across the top that might have resembled snaky hair. "Looks more like Chia pet to me."

The heavy fog from San Francisco had faded to little more than a mist. The car was parked up on a hill overlooking a small marina where Wynter's party boat was moored. Sean placed the high-power binoculars in her hand, and she held them to her eyes. The running lights on the yacht were off, but there was still enough light to see four men leaning over the railing at the bow and smoking.

"How long have we been here?" she asked.

"Just a few minutes."

"They're waiting for something."

"If they take delivery from another boat," he said, "there's nothing more we can do. But if it's a truck, we'll follow."

She sat up a bit straighter in the passenger seat and fine-tuned the binoculars. The resolution with these glasses was incredible. She could make out faces and features. "Guess who's here."

"I'm pretty sure it's not big daddy James," he said. "Frankie boy?"

"The next best thing." She made a woofing noise. "It's Barclay the Bulldog, the guy who wrecked my apartment."

"It's good to know he doesn't specialize in ransacking."

"The Bulldog is an all-purpose thug." She chuckled as she continued to watch the yacht. "If they drive, we'll be able to see where they make the drop-off."

"We'll coordinate with Levine," he said. "It's not really fair. We do all the work, and that jerk gets all the glory."

"Not necessarily," she said.

She passed the binoculars to him. A fifth man had joined the other four on deck. She'd recognized him right away from his nervous gestures. It was Special Agent Greg Levine.

CHAPTER TWENTY-TWO

OUTRAGED, SEAN STARED down the hill at the fancy yacht with four thugs and a rat aboard. Levine was a double-crossing bastard who might precipitate a gang war that would tear San Francisco apart. Why hadn't Sean seen the problem before? It should have been obvious to him when he heard that Levine was using both Morelli and Mikey. *Quite a juggling act!* Levine wasn't a charmer and had nothing to offer. Neither of those men had a reason to work with him.

"Maybe," Emily said, "this is a sting."

Sean calmed enough to consider that scenario. On a scale of one to ten, he'd give it a three. Levine wasn't clever enough to set up a sting like this. And Sean hadn't noticed FBI backup in the area. Still, he conceded, "It's possible."

"But not likely," she said.

"Not at all."

They watched for another half hour. The night was beginning to thin as the time neared four o'clock, less than two hours before sunrise. Would Levine dare to drive into San Francisco during morning rush hour? Either he was massively stupid or had balls the size of watermelons.

A midsize orange shipping truck with a green "Trail Blazer" logo rumbled down to the pier. The driver jumped out and trotted around to the back. As soon as he rolled up the rear door, the armed men on the boat herded a ragged group of people who had been belowdecks, waiting in the dark. Sean counted seventeen. Only two men; the rest were women and children. He was glad to see that they also loaded bottles of water and boxes he hoped were food.

"Now what?" she asked.

"We follow," Sean said. "As soon as we figure out his plan, we'll call for backup."

"Why wait?"

"I don't want to waste this opportunity." He was thinking like a cop, not a bodyguard, which probably wasn't a good thing. Undercover cops took risks, while bodyguards played it safe. He promised himself to back down before it got dangerous. "Their destination might lead to another illegal operation."

"Like a sweatshop," she said. "We might be able to track the distribution network for the sex workers."

The orange truck pulled away from the pier with Levine behind the wheel and two armed men in the cab beside him. Staying a careful distance behind so they wouldn't be noticed, Sean followed in the rental car.

The roads leading away from Medusa Rock were pretty much empty before dawn. As soon as possible, Sean turned off the headlights, figuring that their nondescript sedan would be almost invisible in the predawn light.

The orange truck wasn't headed toward San Francisco. Levine was taking them east. *Where the hell is he going?*

With his assistance, Emily set up a conference call with his brother, who was—surprise, surprise—asleep. It was worth waking him up. If anybody could figure out how to track a moving vehicle, it was Dylan.

"Big orange truck?" His yawn resonated through the phone. "What do you want me to do with it?"

"We're trying to track it," Sean said. "When the sun comes

up, in a couple of minutes, the driver of the truck might notice that we're tailing him. I want to drop back...way back."

"That sounds right," Dylan said. "What should I do? Turn you invisible?"

"Wake up, baby brother. I need you to be sharp now—right now."

"I have an idea," Emily said. "Satellite surveillance."

"It's hard to pull off," Dylan said. "If there are any clouds, it blocks the view."

"You could use a drone," she suggested.

"The only drones in the area are probably operated out of Fort Bragg, and I'm not going to hack in to the Department of Defense computers. Stuff like that could get me sent away for a long time."

"There must be something," she said.

"An idea," Dylan said. "Sean, do you have any of those tracking devices I put together a while back?"

"I have the big ones and the teeny-tiny ones."

"Slap a couple of each on the truck when he stops for gas. Turn them on right now, and I'll see if I can activate from here."

While they continued to follow, Sean told Emily where he kept the tracking devices in his luggage. Following his instructions, she checked batteries and made sure they were all working. She activated each.

"Good," Dylan said. "I've got four signals."

Emily chuckled. "You're amazing, Dylan. You can track us all the way from Denver?"

"And I kind of wish I could see what was going on. In the next generation of trackers, I'm adding cameras."

"Where are we?"

"On the road to Sacramento," Dylan said. "According to my maps, there aren't any major intersections on your route."

"But he might be stopping here," Sean said as he dropped back, slowing the rental car and allowing the truck to get almost out of sight. He stretched the tense muscles in his shoulders. He didn't like keeping surveillance in crowded traffic, but these empty roads were equally difficult.

After rummaging around in his backpack, Emily found energy bars and a bottle of water. Both food and drink were welcome. He hadn't slept last night, and the sun was rising.

The orange truck rumbled through Sacramento, still heading east.

Dylan called them back with an alert. "Make sure your car has enough gas. It looks like the route he's taking is Highway 50, otherwise known as the loneliest road in America."

"That's right," Emily said. "I'm reading the road signs. It's Highway 50, and it goes to Ely, Nevada."

"The road's quiet," Sean said, "but not that lonely."

He'd actually driven Highway 50 on one of his trips between San Francisco and his parents' house in Denver. On the stretch across Nevada, there were maybe fifteen towns, some with populations under one hundred.

The good thing about the desolate road was that it wouldn't be difficult to keep track of the orange truck. The negative was that there was nowhere to hide. If he didn't stick the trackers onto the truck soon, he'd never be able to sneak up and do it.

Finally, just outside Ely, the truck made a rest stop. If Levine and the other guards had been decent human beings, they would have made sure the people in the back of the truck were okay. That didn't appear to be part of their plan.

Sean drove up a gravel road behind the gas station and parked on a hillside behind a thicket of juniper and scrub oak. With the tracking devices in his pocket, he started down the hill. Emily caught his arm.

"One kiss," she said.

They made it a quick one.

Emily paced behind the car, stretching her legs after too many hours sitting. She needed to take her turn behind the wheel. Sean was exhausted, and she wanted to help.

Looking for a vantage point, she moved along the edge where the hill dropped off. Behind a clump of sagebrush, she crouched down and lifted the binoculars to watch Sean. He'd found a hiding place behind the gas station, not far from the orange truck.

Her heart beat faster as she realized he was in danger. He had to stay safe, had to stay in one piece. She couldn't bear to lose him again. But that was exactly what was going to happen.

She saw him dart forward and place the tracking devices, and then she lowered the binoculars. Their investigation was wrapping up. Soon, it would be over, and Sean would leave her. If they couldn't be in love, they couldn't be together. He'd be gone.

Behind her right shoulder, she heard the sound of a footstep. Someone was approaching the rental car and being none too subtle about it. She couldn't see him but as soon as she heard him wheezing from the hike up the hill, she knew it was Bulldog.

He whispered her name. "Emily. Are you here, Emily?"

What kind of game is he playing? She still had her stun gun in her pocket and wouldn't hesitate to zap him. But that meant getting close, and she preferred to keep her distance.

Again he called to her. "Come out, Emily. I have a surprise for you."

She ducked down, making sure he couldn't see her.

"Forget you," he said. "I'm outta here."

She heard him walking away and knew he'd take the gravel road rather than scrambling up and down the hillside. She scooted around the shrubs and sagebrush to get a peek at Bulldog and see what he was doing. He jogged down the hill toward the truck. Before reaching the gas station, he paused and looked back toward the rental car.

Incongruously, he held a cell phone in his hand. With his chubby fingers, he punched in a number. The answering ring came from the rental car. That innocent sound was the trigger.

The car exploded in a fierce red-hot ball of fire.

The impact knocked her backward and she sat down hard.

Her ears were ringing, and she fell back, lying flat on the dusty earth, staring up at a hazy sky streaked with black smoke from the explosion and licked with flames. The earth below her seemed to tremble with the force of a second explosion. Vaguely she thought it must be the gas tank.

Sprawled out on the ground, she was comfortable in spite of the heat from the flames and the stench of the smoke. Moving to another place might be wise. There was a lot of dry foliage. If it all caught fire, there would be a major blaze. Her grip on consciousness diminished. A soft, peaceful blackness filled her mind.

Sean was with her. He scooped her up and carried her down the hill to the gas station. The orange truck was gone.

In the gas station office, he sat her in a chair and leaned close. "Emily, can you hear me?"

"A little."

"Do you hurt anywhere?"

She stretched and wiggled her arms and legs. Nothing was broken, but she was as stiff and sore as though she'd run a marathon. "I do hurt a little."

"Where?"

"All over." Though wobbly in the knees, she rose to her feet. She grabbed the lapels of his jacket and stared into his face. "I. Love. You."

She wasn't supposed to say that, but she meant it. If he said it back, they'd be on the same page. It would mean they should be married, again. *Say it, Sean.*

"Emily." He kissed the tip of her nose. "You need to sit down."

He guided her back into the chair, brought her cold water and a damp washrag from the restroom. Her hearing was starting to return as she watched the volunteer fire brigade charge past the gas station windows and attack the blaze.

"It was Bulldog," she said to Sean. "He set off a bomb."

"I know."

"How did he know I was with the car?"

He shrugged. "He must have spotted you through binoculars. I was worried that they'd notice us following."

"Did you take care of the plants?"

"Mission accomplished." He ran his thumb across her lips. "You're going to be okay. I want you to stay here. I'll come back for you."

Not a chance. "This is my investigation. You're not going to leave me behind."

He didn't argue with her. As she drank her water and nibbled a sandwich the gas station owner had given her, she was aware of Sean striding around, yakking into his cell phone and making plans. If he had figured out some way to follow Levine, she was coming with him, and she told him so after he loaded her into the back of the local sheriff's car, and they went for a short ride. Had she really said, "I love you"?

As they sat in a pleasant lounge in the Ely airport, Emily's mind began to clear. She was picking up every third or fourth word as Sean buzzed around the room, talking on two phones at once. She figured, from what Sean was saying, that Dylan was able to track the orange truck. Levine wasn't getting away; he was driving into a trap.

The local sheriff and some of his deputies were in the lounge with her. Law enforcement was involved, and she was glad. She and Sean had taken enough risks. *Like saying I love you?* It was time for somebody else to step up.

Sean sat beside her. "It's almost over."

With all the excitement and confusion swirling around them, she had only one cogent thought. She loved him.

"I can't take it back," she said. "I can't lie."

"You love me," he said.

Not to be outdone, she said, "And you love me right back."

He gently kissed her, and she drifted off into a lovely semi-conscious state. Still clinging to her bliss, she boarded a private plane flown by none other than their buddy David Henley. This

Cessna wasn't as big or as fancy as the Gulfstream they'd taken to San Francisco, but she liked the ride.

"Sean, where are we going?"

"Aspen."

"Of course."

It made total sense. They'd gone from intense danger in San Francisco—crooked FBI agents, the crime boss's thugs and Chinese snakeheads—to the peaceful, snow-laced Rocky Mountains. She smiled. "I think we should live in Colorado."

"As you wish," he said.

"I also think I'm awake," she said. "Can you give me an explanation?"

"Dylan's tracker worked. Levine and the two idiots drove the truck on Highway 50. The feds and law enforcement are keeping tabs on them. I thought we could join in the chase at Aspen."

"Why Aspen?"

"The timing seemed right," he said. "Ely is about eight hours from Aspen."

It occurred to her that the orange truck could keep rolling all the way across the country, leading a parade of FBI agents and police officers to the Atlantic shoreline.

But that was not to be.

By the time they landed in Aspen, Sean received word that the orange truck had stopped at a ranch in a secluded clearing. The FBI was already closing in.

He turned to her. "Do you want to stay here? I could arrange for your aunt to pick you up."

"I'm coming with you. I won't let you face danger all by yourself…"

"Half the law enforcement in the western United States will be there to protect me."

"But you need me, and I need you."

"I love you, Emily."

"And I'm a reporter." She gave him a hug. "I'm not going to miss out on this exclusive story."

Sean and Emily arrived at the scene in time to see the people in the orange truck go free, as well as dozens of other women and children who had been assembling electronics at this secluded mountain sweatshop.

Greg Levine was arrested, along with the rest of the men working at the ranch and their leader. The big boss was none other than Frankie Wynter himself.

Three weeks later, when Emily's four-part article was published, she was able to say that Frankie had been charged with the murder of Roger Patrone. Though she knew Patrone was killed because he had saved three children and thwarted Frankie's operation, she managed to write her story without mentioning the kids. Liane Zhou deserved her family.

And so did Emily. Resettling in Denver was easy. She fit very nicely into Sean's house.

On the wall by the fireplace, there were two wedding photos: one from the original wedding and another from the mountain ceremony at Hazelwood.

* * * * *

Keep reading for an excerpt of
Alejandro's Revenge
by Anne Mather.
Find it in the
Vintage Classics: Volume One anthology,
out now!

CHAPTER ONE

THE CAR RADIO was droning on and on about the temperature in Miami, the highs and lows, the relative humidity. But actually Abby was finding it anything but relative. And heat, or the lack of it, was a subjective thing anyway.

When she'd stepped out of the shadows of the airport buildings half an hour ago she'd been dazzled by the sunlight. Perspiration had soon been trickling down her spine and between her breasts. Now, in the air-conditioned luxury of the limousine, she was practically freezing, and all she really wanted to do was reach her destination and lie down until the throbbing in her head subsided.

But that wasn't going to happen. Not any time soon anyway. The arrival of the limousine, which surely couldn't be Edward's property, seemed to prove that. Instead of Lauren being there to meet her she'd been faced with a blank-faced chauffeur who, apart from the necessary introductions, seemed unable—or unwilling—to indulge in polite conversation.

At first she hadn't been concerned. The roads leading away from the airport had been jammed with traffic, and when her swarthy driver had turned off the main thoroughfare to thread his way through a maze of streets only a native of Miami would recognise she'd assumed he was taking a short cut to the hospital.

Which just went to show that you shouldn't take anything for granted, she thought uneasily. Although they'd rejoined the freeway, she was fairly sure they were heading away from the city and South Dade Memorial Hospital where her brother was lying, injured, waiting for her to rush to his bedside. What little she recalled of her first and only other visit to the area was convincing her that they were heading into Coral Gables. And the only people she knew who lived in Coral Gables were Lauren's parents.

And Alejandro Varga, her treacherous memory reminded her unkindly, but she ignored it.

Still, if they were going to the Esquivals' home then she would just have to put up with it. And at least they'd be able to tell her how serious Edward's injuries were. Perhaps Lauren was staying with them while her husband was in hospital. She hadn't thought to ask any questions when Edward had called her.

Concentrating her attention on her surroundings, she looked through tinted windows at a scene straight out of a travel ad. The broad tree-lined avenue they were driving along ran parallel with the glistening waters of Biscayne Bay, and yachts and other pleasure craft were taking advantage of the late afternoon sunshine. This area, south of Miami, was known for the beauty of its scenery, for the lushness of its vegetation. Palmetto palms and other exotic trees were commonplace here, and the richness and colour of plants and flowering shrubs gave the place a decidedly tropical feel.

Coral Gables, she knew, possessed some of the oldest buildings in Miami, and the architecture showed an innately Spanish influence. There were squares and plazas, pools and tumbling fountains. It was also one of the wealthiest parts of the country: Edward's in-laws had taken some pains to impress that upon her, too.

Thinking about Lauren's parents brought her mind back to the reason she was here, and she wished one of them could have come to meet her if their daughter couldn't. They must have known she'd be worried about her brother. Had something happened? Had something gone wrong? Was that why they were bringing her here?

Perhaps he was dead!

The horrifying thought came out of nowhere. It couldn't be true, she told herself fiercely. Dear God, she'd only spoken to him two days ago, and, although he hadn't spared her the details of the car smash that had resulted in him being hospitalised, at no time had he given her the impression that his condition was critical. He'd been upset, yes; resentful, even. But she'd understood that that was because he still felt like a stranger, hospitalised in a strange country.

Though that was a little ridiculous, too. Technically, Edward was a US citizen. He'd lived in Florida for over three years, and for the last two of those years he'd been married to Lauren Esquival. Well, she'd changed her name to Lauren Leighton when she'd married Edward, of course, Abby corrected herself. Even if it had always been hard to attribute such an Anglo-Saxon surname to her essentially Hispanic sister-in-law.

Abby heaved a sigh.

Something told her this was not going to be an uneventful visit. And, remembering Ross's reaction when she'd told him what she planned to do, going home was not going to be without incident either. Her fiancé—it was still hard to think of him in those terms—had never been one to pull his punches. In his opinion it was high time Edward grew up and started taking responsibility for his own actions, instead of calling on his sister every time he had a problem.

Which wasn't entirely fair, thought Abby a little defensively. All right, when he was younger Edward had been something of a tearaway, and he had relied on his sister to get him out of many of the scrapes he'd got himself into. Nothing too serious, of course. Lots of youths his age had spent money they didn't have. He wasn't a criminal. Nevertheless Abby had spent a goodly portion of her teens and early twenties paying his debts.

Then, when he was nineteen, he'd had what to him had seemed the brilliant idea of going to work in the United States. He'd been studying for a catering diploma at the time, and although Abby had had her doubts when he'd started the course he'd definitely shown an aptitude for the work.

Or perhaps his diligence had been due in part to his infatuation with one of his fellow students, Abby reflected a little cynically now. Whatever, when Selina Steward had taken off for Florida Edward had wasted no time in getting the necessary paperwork and following her.

Abby had been twenty-four then and, although she'd never have admitted as much to Edward, she'd been desolated by his departure. For so long he'd been an integral part of her life. She'd shunned any lasting relationships to be the mother he hardly remembered, and when he'd left she'd had only her career as a teacher to console her.

Still, she'd survived, she conceded ruefully. And she'd been glad when Edward had adapted well to his new surroundings. She'd even convinced herself that it would work out when he'd phoned to say he was going to marry the daughter of the man who owned the Coconut Grove restaurant where he worked. The fact that he and Lauren had only known one another for a matter of months wasn't important, he'd insisted. And, what was more, Abby had to come over for the wedding...

But she was digressing. The wedding and its painful aftermath were long over, and she had to focus on why she was here now. But even the sight of acres of manicured turf—courtesy, so the sign read, of the Alhambra Country Club—and the sunlit plaza that adjoined it couldn't compensate for the feelings of anxiety that were growing inside her. If only she knew what was going on. If only she knew how Edward was, *where* he was...

He had to be all right, she told herself fiercely. She'd never forgive herself if anything had happened to him. All right, as Ross had so painstakingly pointed out, she couldn't hold herself responsible for Edward's decision to move to Florida, and at twenty-two he was surely old enough to look after himself. But Edward would always be her little brother, and Abby supposed it was her own thwarted maternal instinct that made her so protective of him still.

But that was something else she didn't want to get into now. Looking down, she massaged her finger where Ross's diamond sparkled with a cold light. They'd been engaged since Christmas, after knowing one another since before Edward had left for the States. But it was only in recent months that they'd become close.

And now Edward was causing a rift between them. Ross considered her decision to come rushing out here at her brother's behest nothing short of foolhardy. They were planning to get married in six months, for heaven's sake, he'd protested. Wasting money on airfares to Florida, when she had no real proof that her brother was in any danger, was downright stupid.

Well, Ross hadn't exactly said she was stupid. He was far too prudent for that. But he had maintained that after they were married things would be different. She would have to stop behaving as if Edward still needed her to hold his hand.

Abby grimaced. When they were married. Somehow the words had even less conviction here than they'd had back in London. It wasn't that she didn't care for Ross, she told herself. She did. Perhaps she'd just been single too long. Why did she find it so hard to contemplate putting her future in any man's hands?

Or had Alejandro Varga...?

But once again she steered her thoughts away from that disastrous memory. Like her mother's desertion, and her father's subsequent death from alcohol poisoning, it was all water under the bridge now. It had no bearing on the present. She was here to support Edward and nothing else.

Unless Alejandro visited his cousin while she was here.

But that wouldn't happen, she assured herself. His association with Lauren's parents had seemed tenuous at best. As far as she remembered Alejandro was a distant cousin of Mrs Esquival, and his presence in their home had been because of the wedding. Besides, he had a wife. And somehow Abby didn't think he'd want to introduce them.

Her throat tightened in spite of herself, and she was glad that the sudden slowing of the car brought her quickly back to the present. For a few moments she'd been lost in thought, but now she saw that they had entered the residential district where she knew the Esquivals had their estate.

It wasn't an estate such as was meant by the word back in England, of course. The Esquivals' property comprised a rather large villa set in cultivated grounds. There was no parkland surrounding it, no gatehouse. Just a high stone wall protecting it from public view.

The names of the various streets they passed were appealing, and Abby forced herself to look for South Cutler Road, where Lauren's parents lived. Fortunately it was nowhere near Old Okra Road, where Alejandro had his house. She'd have been far more apprehensive if it was.

Abby was just admiring the Renaissance façade of the newly refurbished Gables Hotel when the chauffeur turned his head and spoke to her over his shoulder. 'I guess this is your first visit to Florida, ma'am,' he said, albeit with a heavy Spanish accent, and Abby was so taken aback that for a moment she could only stare at him.

'I—my second,' she got out at last, trying not to feel aggrieved that he'd waited so long before speaking to her. Also, being addressed as 'ma'am' took some getting used to, as well. She touched her hair defensively. Did she really look that old?

'So you've been to the Esquivals' house before?' he went on, and she swallowed.

'Is that where we're going?' she asked, gathering her composure with an effort. 'What about my brother? Do you know how he is?'

'No one told me anything about that, ma'am,' responded the chauffeur annoyingly. 'But as he's staying with the Esquivals right now I guess you'll soon find out.'

Abby's jaw dropped. 'He's staying with the Esquivals?' she echoed disbelievingly. 'But—I understood he was in hospital.'

'Guess he's recovered,' the man remarked laconically. 'Like I say, you'll soon see him for yourself.'

Abby realised she must look as stunned as she felt, and hastily pulled herself together. But all Ross's misgivings were coming home to roost. She should have insisted on speaking to Edward's doctor before she left England. She just hoped her brother hadn't brought her here on a wild-goose chase.

Any further speculation was balked by the realisation that the chauffeur had halted the impressive limousine outside tall electrically operated gates. He barely had time to roll down his window and identify himself to the security cameras before the heavy gates started to open, and they drove up the curving driveway to the Esquivals' sprawling residence.

Not surprisingly now, Abby was anxious, and she found herself moving to the edge of her seat. It was as if she hoped she could precipitate her arrival. For the moment all she could think about was seeing her brother again, and she barely looked the beautiful Spanish-style house with its ornamental and trailing vines.

The car braked before double-panelled doors, and mediately they opened to allow a uniformed maid the shallow steps to meet them. Small and for ance, she seemed unusually eager to please of the limousine, inviting Abby to step o

'Thanks.'

Abby did so, brushing down the s'

khaki pants. In fact, she was sure she must look distinctly travel-worn, and she wished she'd thought about taking a change of clothes onto the plane.

The khaki pants and cream shirt would have to do, though she thought about taking her jacket out of her haversack. But now that she was out in the sunlight again the heat was almost palpable. She certainly didn't need a jacket. And it was only March.

'Welcome to Miami, *señora*,' the maid greeted her politely as the chauffeur got out to heft Abby's suitcase from the boot. Then, with a distinctly flirtatious air, she added, *'Hola, Carlos. Como esta?'* How are you?

As Abby digested the fact that she now knew the chauffeur's name, he responded to the maid's greeting with rather less enthusiasm. *'Bien, gracias,'* he said, which Abby knew was usually followed by *Y usted?* but wasn't in this case. Then, to Abby, 'I'll leave this here, ma'am.' He put down the heavy case. 'And I hope all goes well with your brother.'

'Oh—thank you.' Abby blinked, wondering if the house was off-limits to the other staff. But when he got back into the limousine and drove away she revised her opinion. She had probably taken him away from his usual work.

To her chagrin, the maid took charge of her case. Lifting the strap, she tugged it on its wheels up the steps, waiting rather impatiently now for Abby to join her.

'Come,' she said, leading the way into the wide entrance hall. It was cooler inside, and a huge urn of flowers spilled scarlet blossoms over the marble surface of a stone table.

Air-conditioning cooled the heat that had beaded on Abby's head, and she ran a nervous hand over her hair, feeling the strands clinging to her cheeks. She probably looked as and harassed as she felt.

ng about her, she had to admit she'd forgotten exactly ful the Esquivals' home was. Cool and spacious, it ll that was good about Spanish architecture. Long windows looked out onto an inner courtyard and hanging baskets edged an arching colonnade.

'Mees Leighton—Abigail!' The voice that accosted her was soft and feminine, and Abby turned to find Lauren's mother emerging from the salon that adjoined the reception hall. Small and plump, but exquisitely dressed, Dolores Esquival matched her surroundings, her sleek chignon of dark hair putting Abby's explosion of crinkled red curls to shame. 'Welcome to Florida,' she added, her high heels tapping across the polished floor as she came to meet her guest. Air kisses whispered at either side of Abby's head as she continued, 'I hope you had a good journey, *cara*.'

'I—yes. Thank you.' Abby felt a little bemused as she returned the greeting. Lauren's mother was behaving as if she was here for a holiday instead of flying out to be at her brother's bedside. 'It's very—kind of you to ask.'

'Not so, *querida*.' Was Abby mistaken or did Dolores's mouth tighten a little. 'We are very happy to have you here.'

'Yes, but—'

Ignoring her now, Lauren's mother switched her attention to the maid, who was hovering in the background, directing her to take their guest's suitcase upstairs. At least that was what Abby thought she was doing. Her imperious signal towards the curving staircase seemed to indicate it was.

'Oh, but—' Abby began, eager to explain that she had no intention of presuming on the Esquivals' hospitality, but Lauren's mother turned to her again.

'This way,' she said, apparently deaf to Abby's protests. 'I am sure you are eager to see your brother,' she added, heading into the salon. 'Everyone is through here.'

Afterwards, when she was unwillingly installed in the first-floor suite she had occupied on her first visit to Florida, Abby marvelled that she had had no suspicion that Alejandro might be there.

Yet how could she have? she asked herself defensively. She'd believed that he was just a distant relative, invited to the wedding because family politics dictated as much. She'd had no idea that he was such a close friend of the Esquivals, nor that Lauren seemed to regard him with a distinctly possessive affection.

Still, when she'd followed Dolores into the enormous salon that seemed to stretch right across the back of the house, she'd had eyes only for her brother. Besides, she'd still been slightly dazzled by the change from sun to shadow. With spots of brilliance dancing before her pupils, she'd been in no condition to instantly register all the people in the room.

Edward was there, she'd seen with some relief, apparently confined to the cushioned divan where he was reclining. With one leg encased in plaster from hip to knee, he had apparently been incapable of coming to greet her. She had hesitated only a moment before hurrying to his side.

'Oh, Eddie,' she exclaimed huskily, suddenly inexplicably near to tears. 'What on earth have you been doing to yourself?'

She bent to kiss his cheek and Edward captured one of her hands and held onto it. 'Hey, Abbs,' he greeted her urgently. Then, in an undertone, 'Thank God you've come!'

Abby's eyes widened at his unexpected words. But before she could say or do anything rash, another hand touched her sleeve.

'Abigail,' declared a vaguely familiar voice. 'How—good it is to see you again.'

Abby turned, straightening, to find Luis Esquival standing right behind her. Lauren's father was only slightly taller than his wife, with a broad dark-skinned face and luxuriant moustaches. He extended his hand towards her. 'Did you have a pleasant journey?'

Abby was confused, as much by her brother's words as by the fairly obvious conclusion that there was nothing seriously wrong with him. He had let her believe that he'd be in hospital for some time, whereas now it appeared that apart from a probable fracture he was okay. Heavens, she thought ruefully, Ross was going to love this.

But Lauren's father was waiting for an answer and, summoning her composure, she managed a polite smile. 'It was—tiring,' she admitted. Plane journeys were not her thing, and she'd had the doubtful privilege of being seated next to the toilets. 'Thank you.'

She glanced round then, expecting to see Lauren, but her sister-in-law wasn't in the room. Instead she saw an elderly woman seated by an arrangement of potted palms, and behind her, standing in the shadows near the ornate brick fireplace, was a tall man dressed all in black.

It was strange, but even then she had no inkling that she might know him. So far as she was concerned the only other person she was eager to speak to was Lauren herself. She wanted to find out what was behind Edward's desperate words. She wanted to know why he'd felt the need to send for her.

But once again Luis Esquival demanded her attention. 'We were most surprised when Edward told us you intended paying us a visit,' he said silkily. 'As you can see, your brother is recovering very well.'

Abby was nonplussed. Her eyes sought Edward's, but he was suddenly intensely interested in the cast on his leg. Below the hem of his navy shorts the plaster looked extremely white against his bare skin, and as she watched he shifted a little uneasily in his seat.

'I—I thought—' she was beginning, when the man beside the fireplace suddenly moved into the shaft of sunlight slicing through the half-drawn blinds.

'I am sure—Abigail—was concerned when she heard about her brother's accident,' he drawled in the low, seductively sensual tone that Abby remembered not just in her mind but in her bones. And as she swung round, hardly daring to believe he'd have the nerve to come here and face her, Alejandro Varga acknowledged her dismay with an ironic little smile. 'Abigail.' He inclined his head towards her with all his old arrogance. 'What an unexpected pleasure!'